HOUSTON

HOUSTON

★

DOUG BOWMAN

FORGE

A TOM DOHERTY ASSOCIATES BOOK
NEW YORK

HOUSTON

Copyright © 1998 by Doug Bowman

This book is printed on acid-free paper.

A Forge Book
Published by Tom Doherty Associates, Inc.
175 Fifth Avenue
New York, NY 10010

Forge® is a registered trademark of Tom Doherty Associates, Inc.

Library of Congress Cataloging-in-Publication Data

Bowman, Doug.
        Houston / Doug Bowman.—1st ed.
            p.   cm.
        "A Tom Doherty Associates book."
        ISBN 0-312-86246-6 (acid-free paper)
        I. Title.
    PS3552.O875712H68   1998   97-29859
    813'.54—dc21   CIP

First Edition: March 1998

Printed in the United States of America

0 9 8 7 6 5 4 3 2 1

To my sisters: Edna, Nell, Dot, and Jean. And to my tireless literary agent, Robbie Robison, who took me on in 1992 when I was about ready to give up.

HOUSTON

I

The traveler, dressed in blue denim and riding a big strawberry roan, halted at the spring. He looked around cautiously for a few moments, then stepped down from the saddle, intent upon watering himself and his horse.

"Stand right where you are, fellow!" a deep voice commanded from behind the green willow saplings. "You're covered with three shotguns!"

The traveler stood still for a moment, then slowly raised his hands above his head.

"Drop that gun belt slow and easy," the voice continued, "then take off that coat. Shirt and pants, too."

The man complied, then stood in his underwear awaiting the next order.

"Take that rifle out of the scabbard and lay it on the ground, along with your saddlebags and bedroll. Then take off the saddle and bridle, and give that horse a whack across the rump."

A short while later, the horse, minus its saddle, galloped off into the woods.

"Now," the voice commanded, even louder now, "start walkin' and don't look back."

Looking toward the saplings, the traveler finally spoke: "I suppose you could say that I'm a tenderfoot. Do you mind if I put my boots back on?"

"Guess you can. You've got a long walk ahead of you. Put 'em on, and be quick about it."

With his boots on, the traveler spoke to the willows again. "Which direction?"

"East," was the response. "And if you look back, you're dead."

Wearing nothing but his underwear, boots and Stetson, the traveler moved away from the spring in short order. He did not look back.

A considerable length of time elapsed before Tom Baker stepped from the willows to review his booty. He decided quickly that he had made a fair haul. The purse he found in the inside coat pocket contained two hundred dollars. He threw the coat aside and picked up the pants. He tinkered with a fob for a moment, then pulled the chain, extracting an expensive-looking watch from a small pocket just below the belt loops. He searched the pockets thoroughly, but found nothing else of value. He discarded the pants.

When he found that the saddlebags contained only a few hard biscuits, and the bundle tied behind the cantle consisted of nothing more than a bedroll and a change of clothing, he discarded them also. He picked up the gun belt and the Henry rifle and trotted back to the willows, where he mounted his swift bay and headed west.

Though mounted on a speedster, Baker rode along at an easy trot. He never pushed the animal unless crowded. A man had to take care of his horse.

Tom Baker had been a thief all of his life, but only recently had he turned to such serious crimes as the robbery he had pulled off just now. His third within the past six months.

A native Texan, and the only offspring of a poor dirt farmer and his sickly wife, Baker was now twenty-four years old, stood a little less than six feet tall, and weighed about one-ninety. He had brown hair and eyes, and a ruddy complexion. Quite ordinary in appearance.

He had never worked at any one job for more than a few weeks at a time, and had done most of his eating at his mother's house. The frail woman had died the year before, and since then Baker had been living on whatever he could steal. He was a fair hand with guns, long or short, and had often imagined himself the leader of a band of tough outlaws. A dozen men. That's how many it would take to pull off some of the jobs he had in mind. And the newspaper writers would no doubt begin to call the outfit "Baker's Dozen" right from the start. He smiled at the thought, and chuckled softly.

He patted the two hundred dollars in his pocket. Easy money. The whole job had taken less than two hours. A hundred dollars an hour. He patted the money again. He had spotted the well-dressed traveler in the town of Leatherwood that morning, and had noticed his purse when he paid for his breakfast. After determining the man's direction of travel, it had been a simple matter to outdistance him and lie in wait at the spring. The man would surely stop to water his horse.

Nor could the traveler ever identify him, for the man had not seen Baker's face. In fact, the man had seen nothing. Baker would sell the traveler's Peacemaker, rifle and watch to someone at least fifty miles away, and never hear a word about the robbery. He would hole up at his dead mother's cabin for a while, then begin to scout around for something bigger. Something really big. Big enough to require the help of a dozen men.

As he rode into the yard and stepped from the saddle, he laughed aloud and began talking to himself. "I'll have to remember that shotgun trick, 'cause that joker sure bought it. Big as he was, he wasn't wantin' no truck with three shotguns. I could have claimed to have twenty and he'd have believed it, 'cause he sure couldn't see nothin'. Yessir, I'll be usin' that shotgun trick again."

He loosed his horse in the flimsy corral, then returned to the cabin, where he hung the traveler's rifle and gun belt on the bedroom wall. Then he took a seat in a kitchen chair, where he sat for a while admiring the watch he had stolen. Its case was made of solid silver, he decided, with lots of fancy tooling, and the large Roman numerals on its face appeared to contain a sprinkling of gold. Baker began to talk to himself again. "Purtiest watch I ever saw," he said softly. "Prob'ly made over in Europe somewhere. I'll bet they don't give these things away, and I won't be givin' it away either. No, sir, whoever gits it is gonna pay a right smart for it." He finally laid the watch on the small table beside his bed, then set about building a fire in the stove.

Half an hour later, he sat at the table eating warmed-over rabbit stew. The fact that the stew was thin and watery bothered him not, for very soon he would be eating considerably higher on the hog. He had cash money now, and would have even more after he turned over the guns and the watch. He would ride down to Menardville tomorrow and see what the market would bear. Selling the guns would be easy, but he might have to ride all the way to Fort McKavett to dispose of the watch. Any officer at the fort would be proud to show off such a fancy timepiece, and they all had money.

Baker loitered away the remainder of the day around the cabin, then went to bed at dusk without ever lighting a lamp. He slept soundly throughout the night, for he was a man without conscience.

He was on his feet at daybreak, eager to begin his busy day. He buckled on his gun belt, then stopped in the kitchen to eat a few bites of the leftover stew. He ate sparingly, for he intended to order up a large T-bone steak when he reached

Menardville. He dumped the remainder of the stew in the yard, then filled the pot with water. No more rabbit stew for him this week.

He took a few steps toward the barn, then changed his mind. He must make a trip to the outhouse first. He changed directions in midstride, taking the trail that led to the dilapidated, one-hole affair. The door squeaked on rusty hinges as he opened it and stepped inside. He hung his gun belt on a large nail that he had long ago driven into the wall for that purpose, then dropped his pants and began to make himself comfortable.

He had scarcely taken his seat when the door squeaked again, and he found himself staring into the business end of a .41-caliber, double-barreled derringer. Behind the deadly little weapon stood the traveler Baker had robbed at the spring. The man held the gun about twenty inches from Baker's nose. "Good morning," he said, smiling.

All color drained from Baker's face instantly. "Whatcha think you're doin', fellow? Whatcha—"

Baker never finished the question, for the traveler had squeezed the trigger. "Just wanted to hear that voice one more time," he said, as Baker's eyes turned to glass and his lifeless body slumped against the wall, "to make sure I had the right man." The traveler retrieved his purse from Baker's pocket and saw that his money was still intact. He stepped outside, and when he removed his hand, the rusty hinges squeaked again as the door closed on its own. Then he dropped the little Remington into his pocket, just standing there for a moment.

Baker's career as a holdup man had been short-lived, for yesterday, he had waylaid the wrong man. Of all the men in Texas that he could have chosen to rob, he had picked Camp Houston, a man who was feared, or at least respected, by every gunman in the West.

Houston had originally come from Arkansas, and had been in Texas off and on for the past ten years. He had been involved in three cattle drives from Texas to Kansas, and had walked the streets of Abilene, Ellsworth and Dodge City. He had been as far north as Montana Territory, and west to California, and had forgotten none of the things he had learned during his travels.

He had been raised on a farm a few miles west of Little Rock, the only child born to John and Rebecca Houston. He had been given the somewhat unusual first name "Campbell" because it had been his mother's maiden name. The name was shortened to "Camp" before the boy was knee-high.

Aside from the horses and cattle that were produced on the John Houston farm, hogs and chickens were sometimes butchered and, along with garden truck, peddled on the streets of Little Rock. Consequently, during his growing years young Camp learned not only how to farm and raise livestock, but how to market his merchandise as well.

Camp's had been a happy childhood, and he had already been about grown when his parents had their final argument. His mother moved out of the house the year he was fifteen, and remarried a year later. His father remarried a few months after Camp's seventeenth birthday. That was the day the youngster decided to leave Arkansas for good. He had no ill feeling toward his father's new wife; he simply believed that at six foot three and a hundred ninety-five pounds, he was big enough to be on his own. The very next day, carrying a thousand-dollar stake provided by his father, he loaded a pack mule, then caught up the best saddle horse on the premises. He shook his father's hand, then hugged his new stepmother, who was only six years older than he. Then he picked up the mule's lead rope and threw a leg over the big bay saddler. A few minutes later, he was out of sight. That had been ten years ago, and Camp had not been back to Arkansas since.

He found work on a ranch near Waco right away, and stayed there all summer. When the winter layoffs began, he was the first man to go. He had saved his money, however, and could very easily survive the winter without a job. Which is exactly what he did.

He took a job on a ranch near El Paso the following spring, worked till after the fall roundup, then drew his pay and headed north. It became his custom over the next few years to work hard and save his money through the spring and summer months, then loaf and travel all winter. It was a simple, uncomplicated life to which Camp Houston adapted quite easily, for he loved traveling and learning new things.

His life suddenly took a different turn shortly after his twenty-second birthday. That was the year he killed his first man. The shooting took place in the town of Brownsville, when a local gunslinger named Lew Thompson accused Houston of attempting to romance a saloon woman that Thompson considered his own. Houston's claim that he had never even met the woman went unheard as Thompson slapped him across the mouth and challenged him to a gunfight in the street.

One thing Camp Houston had never been short on was guts. He accepted the challenge immediately. He had practiced with his Colt for years, and was an expert marksman. And though he had never fired a shot at another human, he felt that he was fast enough to defend himself against any man. He was confident as he stepped out on the street to face the gunman.

There was no waiting around and no arguing. Nor did Houston wait for the gunslinger to call the draw. He simply drew his Colt and shot Thompson between the eyes. Thompson got off a shot as he fell, which went through his own foot.

The Cameron County sheriff arrested Houston within the hour, and kept him in jail overnight. He released Camp next morning, however, because one citizen after another, and sometimes several men at a time, came to his office complaining that young Houston was guilty of nothing more than executing his God-given right to defend himself; that he had been slapped and falsely accused, then challenged to a gun-fight. The saloon woman herself had provided the clinching testimony, saying that she had indeed never met Houston.

"Half the people in town are raising hell about me locking you up," the sheriff said as he unlocked the cell door. "Guess you ain't gonna be needing that lawyer you mentioned, 'cause there ain't gonna be no charges." He walked the few steps up the hall to his office, and Camp followed.

"Here's your hardware," the lawman said, handing over Houston's gun belt. "If I were you I'd damn sure strap it on, 'cause I've got a feeling you're gonna be needing it pretty often. Lew Thompson was known as a fast gun, and his rep-utation's on your back now." As Camp buckled on the gun belt, the sheriff stood by rolling a cigarette. He gave it a final twist, then touched it with a burning match. He blew a cloud of smoke, then began to nod very slowly. He pointed to the Colt on Camp's hip. "They'll be coming," he said. "You mark my words: they'll be coming."

The sheriff's prediction had been correct: they came. For the next three years they came on a regular basis, some a few years older than he, most younger. Would-be gunslingers had sought a reputation elsewhere of late, however. It had been two years now since anybody had insisted on testing Camp's hand, most likely because the word had gotten around that there were no survivors.

Now, standing outside Tom Baker's outhouse, Camp Houston opened the door again and took the dead man's Colt. Then he moved cautiously toward the cabin. After deciding that no one else was on the premises, he walked to the bed-room, where he immediately spotted his guns hanging on the wall. He dropped Baker's gun on the bed, checked the loads in his own Peacemaker, then strapped the gun belt around his middle.

He took his Henry off the wall and checked to see that it was still loaded. When he spotted his watch lying on the bed-side table, he picked it up and checked the time. Eight o'clock.

He returned it to his watch pocket and reattached the chain to his belt loop. He had bought the watch from a Mexican last year. Though the fancy workmanship was enough to make an unknowing person think it cost a lot of money, it was actually quite inexpensive. It had been made in Mexico, and sold new for about five dollars. Camp had bought it for a dollar, and it had proved to be a good conversation piece and a dependable timepiece as well.

He stepped into the yard, then walked to the barn. He opened the corral gate, freeing Baker's horse, then walked at a fast clip to the other side of the hill, where his own saddler was tied to a sapling. He shoved his rifle in the boot, then mounted and headed back to the spring at a canter. The big roan covered the distance in less than two hours.

As the animal drank from the spring's runoff, Camp sat in the saddle rethinking yesterday's event and shaking his head. The holdup man had not been very smart. When ordered to leave the spring in his underwear, Camp had walked no more than three hundred yards, then watched from concealment as the robber searched and discarded Houston's belongings and then rode away on a good-looking bay.

When Camp walked back to the spring and saw that the robber had taken only the money, the watch and the guns, he put on his clothes, picked up the bridle and began to track his horse. He had walked only about a mile when he came on the animal in a small meadow, munching grass. Catching the roan was easy, for he would stand if a man talked to him softly and approached slowly.

Mounting bareback, Houston rode back to the spring. He saddled the roan, retied his bundle behind the cantle, then remounted.

Having tender feet had not been Camp's only reason for asking the thief for permission to put on his boots, for high inside the leg of the left boot, in a special pocket sewn by an Austin bootmaker, rode the little Remington derringer. Camp had removed the weapon from his boot as soon as he reached the woods, and carried it in his hand. All the while, he was hoping that the robber did not decide to follow him, for the accurate shooting range of the little double-barrel was woefully short.

As he took up the trail, Camp could plainly see the bay's tracks, for the ground was soft here close to the spring. He rechecked the loads in the derringer, and shoved it into his pocket. Ever mindful of the fact that he could very easily be riding into an ambush, he continued west at a slow walk, one eye tracking the horse, the other on the terrain ahead.

He lost the trail more than once during the afternoon. At those times, he simply made a guess as to which way the rider would go. Each guess turned out to be correct, for he was soon reading the tracks again.

The day was almost over when he topped the hill above the run-down homestead. He dismounted and tied the roan, then crept as close to the cabin as he dared. He watched the place from behind a clump of bushes till full dark, but saw nothing resembling a human. Nevertheless, he believed that his man was in that cabin, and, even though the light of day was fading fast, he thought he recognized the bay in the corral.

He retraced his footsteps to the top of the hill, then led the roan partway down the other side. He picketed the animal on the best grass he could find in the dark, then made himself a bed under a bush. He would be back on the other side of the hill at first light, hoping the element of surprise might allow him to get the drop on the thief.

He was hidden in Baker's barn at dawn, with his eyes glued to the cabin door. The excellent condition of the bay told Camp that the animal had been eating grain on a regular basis, probably twice a day. In the West, even the lowest class of man was likely to take good care of his horse, for the animal was his only means of transportation. The man in the cabin would be no exception. When he awoke this morning, he would come to feed the bay. And Camp Houston would be waiting.

Half an hour later, Baker walked from the cabin, a gun belt buckled around his waist. Houston stood watching as the man walked a few steps toward the barn, then spun on his heel and headed for the outhouse. Camp was pleased, for he believed that the man would be completely unprepared for company. As soon as the man was inside and the door closed, Houston made his move. A few moments later, he jerked the door open, the little Remington in his fist.

Now, after watering the roan and slaking his own thirst, Houston remounted, and cast his eyes to the southwest. Those eyes were gray, and his hair was light brown. His complexion was dark, somewhat like well-oiled leather. He was a big man, standing six-foot-four in his socks, and his weight varied between two-twenty and two hundred thirty pounds. Square-jawed and thick-chested, he was broad at the shoulder and narrow at the hip, and a physical specimen that few women could resist giving a second look. He was at least as powerful as he looked, and more than a little handy with all kinds of weapons. Many men who had seen him draw claimed that he was the fastest gun Texas had ever known.

Houston was aware of the fact that many men would scorn the act of shooting a man off a toilet seat. He himself believed that it mattered little what a man was doing when he died. Camp had already made up his mind to kill the robber, so the man would have been just as dead even if he'd been someplace other than the outhouse. If the thief had had a gun in his hand, he would have died at precisely the same time. The no-good bastard had called the tune . . . and had paid the fiddler.

Houston rode away from the spring at a fast pace, for he was very hungry. He intended to order up a large T-bone steak when he reached Menardville.

2

★

Sixty-year-old George Angleton was the owner of the Rocking A, a five-section ranch in eastern Menard County. He had started the ranch a few years earlier when he inherited the land, along with eighty head of longhorns, from his father-in-law. Though small, by Texas standards, the ranch was situated in prime cattle country. Perennial grasses were abundant, with plenty of shade and a water supply that included the San Saba River. Indeed, everything a longhorn needed in order to thrive was usually right under its nose.

Though otherwise in seemingly good health, Angleton sometimes suffered from a back ailment that hindered his actions considerably and on more than one occasion had confined him to bed. He never knew what originally brought on the condition, or why he could sometimes go for months without suffering. At times, he could stack hay with the best of them. Then sometimes all he could do was sit on the porch and watch, for working or riding a horse was out of the question.

He knew little about the cattle business when he inherited the ranch, for he had been a carpenter. He hired two men almost as old as he was to manage the cattle, then proceeded to put his own vocation to good use. Within the first year, he built a two-story house, a large barn, two corrals and, though small, the most elegant bunkhouse in the county.

Angleton and his wife, Bama, had raised three daughters. All had married and left Texas at the first opportunity. The youngest had left for Louisiana the same year her parents moved to the ranch. Bama Angleton had been overjoyed with the move, for she was a lifelong student of nature. The new way of life also meant that her husband would sleep in his own bed at night, instead of sometimes being off working on a building project a hundred miles from home.

She wasted no time putting in a large garden, and filled enough jars during the summer to make sure that everyone on the premises had green vegetables throughout the winter. Five years younger than her husband, the small, gray-haired lady was full of life, and loved by all who knew her.

The Rocking A cattle had been allowed to reproduce unmolested for more than four years now, and the herd was not so small these days. In fact, Angleton had contributed five hundred head to a community trail drive to Kansas the year before. John Calloway, a drover from San Antonio who was reputed to be among the best, had bossed the drive.

Calloway had delivered two thousand head of longhorns to a buyer in Dodge City, and was paid for the herd in cash. He paid off each of his trail hands in the same fashion. Then, being a serious man, and somewhat religious, he found himself a room at a boardinghouse, declining all invitations to join in the partying and hell-raising that had come to be expected of cowboys whose pockets jingled with newly acquired coin.

Next morning at sunup, accompanied by Bill Fisher and Joe Plenty, Calloway headed for Texas. Once there, he would deliver the money to the three men who owned the herd, each rancher's percentage of the poke being dictated by the number of cattle he had contributed to make up the drive.

John Calloway never reached Texas. The second day out, he and his two companions made camp at a small stream two hours before sunset. They had scarcely brought their coffee to a boil when five men rode into their camp. None of the campers was alarmed, however, for the riders were all well known to them: the very same men who had helped deliver the herd to Dodge City.

It was over in less than a minute. The riders dismounted; then, at some kind of prearranged signal, every man drew his gun and started shooting. Each of the campers was shot more than once, for the idea, of course, was to leave no witnesses. A few minutes later, after taking the money for the herd and robbing the pockets of the drovers, the renegades remounted and left the area.

All of these details were known because, although he had been shot four times and left for dead, and later lost both an arm and a leg to a surgeon's saw, Joe Plenty had survived. More dead than alive, he had been found by some trail hands two days after the carnage occurred. With the cook playing the role of nursemaid, Plenty was hauled back to Dodge City in the chuck wagon and turned over to a young doctor.

Minus the limbs that had been shattered by gunfire, Plenty was quickly on the mend. He was back in Austin three months later, telling the story to all who would listen, including a few seemingly disinterested lawmen.

Camp Houston listened to the story attentively and absorbed every detail, for John Calloway had been a personal friend. Houston also had a soft spot in his heart for George Angleton. Holding down the job of ranch foreman, Camp had once lived on the Rocking A, and had come to love George and Bama Angleton like family.

He had visited the couple two weeks earlier, and stayed on the ranch for three days. That was when he informed them that he had waited as long as he intended to for action by

U.S. marshals, that he himself was about to take up the trail of the men who had slaughtered and robbed the trail hands.

Angleton sat staring between his knees for a while, then nodded. "I guess you'll be needing some traveling money, then."

"No, no," Camp said quickly. "At least, not yet." He was on his feet now, looking toward the corral. He shook the skinny, gray-haired man's rough hand, then hugged the lady of the house.

"You need something, Camp, you just holler," Bama said, squeezing his arm as tightly as she could. "We've got a little money. We can help."

Ten minutes later, the Angletons stood on the porch waving as Houston rode down the hill. He stood in his stirrups with his hat in his hand for a moment, then he was out of sight.

He was in Austin four days later, where he spent several hours talking with Joe Plenty. The gaunt, hollow-eyed skeleton of a man presented a pitiful picture. His voice was clear and easily understood, however, and he seemed to be in complete control of his mind. He described the incident thoroughly, and supplied the name and description of every man involved.

"I was looking right at Walt Turner," Plenty said with a growl, his hatred for the man obvious. "Looking right at the sonofabitch when he started pumping lead into us. Then all of them were shooting; must have fired at least twenty rounds. We didn't have no chance to fight back, 'cause they caught us off guard. We didn't have no reason to expect trouble from them. Hell, we knew every one of them; been working with them for months. Looked to me like Walt Turner was the head honcho. At least he was the first one to draw a gun. His first shot hit me in the chest. Went clear through me without hitting any vital organs, is what the doc said. Otherwise, I guess I wouldn't be here, huh?"

"Guess not," Houston agreed.

When Camp asked if there was something that he could do to make life a little more enjoyable for the man, Plenty shook his head. "Don't need anything," he said. "Mama keeps me fed good, and I quit smoking cigarettes on the very first day that I didn't have two hands to roll one."

When he left Austin, Camp not only had the names and descriptions of all five of the killers, he had some information that might prove to be much more valuable: somewhere in San Antonio, where the trail drive had originated, there was a picture.

"Bill Fisher was the one who found the photographer," Plenty had said. "Hired him to take a picture of the whole crew. Bill wanted it to put in a scrapbook. We all got together and posed for it, looking silly with our guns out and all. Even Mr. Calloway was there, but he didn't take his gun out, like the rest of us. The photographer told Bill he could pick up the picture at the end of the week, but Bill said he wasn't going to be there, that he'd come by for it after the drive was over. Of course, Bill never made it back."

"Do you think the photographer would still have the picture?" Camp asked, getting to his feet.

"Don't see why not," Plenty answered. "I can't think of anybody else that would buy it, and besides, I think fellows like him keep copies of all their work."

"Do you remember exactly where his business is located in San Antonio?"

Plenty shook his head. "Never did know. He came to the livery stable to take the picture, wanted the stable and the corral to be showing in the background. Don't reckon I ever heard his name called, so I wouldn't know it either."

Camp stood thinking for a while. "Several livery stables in San Antonio," he said finally. "Do you remember which one it was?"

"Sure don't, 'cause I don't know the town. Never been there but that one time. I do know that the stable's on the west side, though. We stayed at a little hotel close by, and rode out of town early next morning."

Now, in the town of Menardville, Camp sat at a table for a long time after finishing his meal. Drinking one cup of coffee after another, he was busy reliving the events of the past two weeks and making plans for the immediate future. His decision to get on the trail of the killers and stay there till he had located every last man was final: cut and dried.

Sid Blankenship, the local liveryman, after hearing of Camp's decision to take up the hunt, had offered the loan of a packhorse and anything else that was needed. Today, Houston would inform Blankenship that he was accepting the offer, after which he would take a room at the Menardville Hotel. Then, after resting himself and his roan for two days, he would head southeast. If the picture of the trail hands was in San Antonio, he intended to find it.

3

Two days later, astride the big roan and leading a ten-year-old black gelding, Houston rode out of Menardville. The pack animal carried everything Camp would need for the trail, including two small sacks of grain for the horses and a one-man sleeping tent that he would probably never use. Today he was headed for San Antonio, which was, unless a man pushed his animals, a four-day ride. Being a man who seldom rode his horse more than thirty miles in one day, Houston would be taking his time. There was no hurry; the killers would keep.

He crossed the San Saba at a rocky ford where the water was less than a foot deep. Then, heading the roan in a south-easterly direction, he spent the day riding steadily, never once pushing the animal past a walking gait.

An hour before sunset, and a few miles after crossing the Mason County line, he halted at the Llano River. He stripped the saddle from the roan, and the pack from the black, then watered and picketed both animals. Neither would receive a portion of grain tonight, for green grass was plentiful. The grain would be saved for hard times, when no grass of any kind was available.

He found deadwood easily enough, and soon had a fire going. He moved out from under the big oak tree, and pitched his bedroll where there was nothing but clear sky overhead. He had long ago learned about camping under trees. Birds roosted in trees and shit all over everything underneath.

When his coffeepot came to a boil, he removed it from the fire and placed his skillet on the bed of gray coals. He dropped several slices of German sausage into it, then added two biscuits. As the bread and meat slowly heated, he sat peeling two of the hard-boiled eggs he had bought from the hotel cook. He was soon enjoying a good meal, after which he extinguished the fire and crawled into his bedroll. He lay there in the darkness for a long time, thinking.

He had not the slightest intention of giving up the hunt until he had found all five of the killers. Nor did he intend to bring the law into the picture. The law had already had more than enough time to make some headway. Even now they were claiming a jurisdiction problem, saying they had been unable to establish whether the crime had been committed in Kansas or in Indian Territory. "The lawmen are lying through their teeth," Joe Plenty had said. "I told every damn one of them exactly where it took place. Told them every creek, bush and rock in the vicinity. They know damn well it happened in Kansas. They just don't give a shit. You can just forget the U.S. marshals and the Kansas lawmen, too. Ain't none of them gonna do a damn thing. Just plain scared, is what they are."

Though Camp agreed with Joe Plenty to a certain extent, he also knew that the description did not fit all lawmen. He personally knew one sheriff who was not afraid of the devil himself. The man hounded criminals day and night, and had more than a few times laid his life on the line against the rowdy element.

Camp believed that it was men such as that particular

sheriff, whose jurisdiction was limited to one county, who should be U.S. marshals, with unlimited jurisdiction. Appointments to those positions were usually political, however, and rarely based on merit.

Though he had no desire to be a lawman, and had declined several opportunities to wear a badge in the past, Camp would be on the trail of the killers just as soon as he could find a starting place, and follow it to the last man. Nor would he turn any of them over to the law. Awaiting them all was the same fate that had befallen the unsuspecting trail hands in a Kansas gully.

Three days later, Houston rode into San Antonio from the west. He stopped at the first livery stable he came to and questioned the owner, who introduced himself as Ralph Hicks. Camp had not expected it to be so easy. "Yeah," Hicks said, getting to his feet and nodding several times. "I remember 'em takin' that picture. Must've been somewhere around June of last year, 'cause I remember it was hotter'n hell."

Camp seated himself in the chair he was offered, then continued. "The reason I'm asking questions, Mr. Hicks, is that I'm looking for the man who took that picture. I was hoping you could help me."

Hicks was a beefy, red-faced man, who appeared to be about fifty years old. He wiped sweat from his brow with his sleeve, then spat a mouthful of tobacco juice through the open doorway. "Could be," he said, wiping his mouth on the same sleeve. "His name is O'Malley or O'Bannon or sump'm like that. Hell, he wouldn't let me forget him. He was down here earlier this year tryin' to get me to pay for that picture. I told him I didn't order no damn picture, that he'd hafta take the matter up with the trail hands." He dropped his eyes to the floor and began to speak more softly. "I hear that some of them didn't make it back from the drive."

"You heard right, Mr. Hicks." Camp told the liveryman the whole story.

"You don't mean to tell me!" Hicks said, his voice now reverberating around the small office. "You're tellin' me that the same men who helped Calloway take the herd to the rails were the ones who killed and robbed him on the way back?"

"Exactly."

"Well, I'll be damned! Hell, I knew one of 'em, old Red Bentley, from down around Corpus Christi. Sure wouldna never thought he'd be in on sump'm like that, though."

"Neither did the trail hands," Camp said, shaking his head. He paused for a few moments, then continued. "A man named Joe Plenty was the only survivor, and I've had a long talk with him. He named Red Bentley as one of the men who did the shooting. I have the name and description of every man involved, Mr. Hicks, but I'd sure like to get my hands on that picture."

"You aim to go huntin' 'em up?"

Houston nodded.

"Well, I see that little fellow who took the picture around town pretty often." The liveryman walked to the front of the building, and Camp followed. Hicks pointed north. "He operates out of a little hole in the wall beside Berry's Restaurant, three blocks from here."

Camp nodded. "I appreciate the information, sir." He walked to the hitching rail and untied his horses, then led them forward, handing the reins to Hicks. "I'll be leaving them with you for a while, if you don't mind."

"Mind?" the hostler asked, smiling. "It's the way I make my living, young fellow." He led the animals down the wide hall toward the stables.

Houston began to walk north at a fast clip, his saddlebags across his shoulder. He found the "hole in the wall" easily enough, and quickly decided that the liveryman had aptly described the photographer's headquarters. The building was about ten feet wide, and probably no more than twice as deep. A weathered sign over the front door read simply, PHOTOGRAPHY, then went on to inform one and all that Abner Overton was the proprietor.

A bell attached to the top of the door announced Camp's arrival when he stepped inside. Then, climbing over or around one obstacle after another, a small man made his way to the front of the cluttered building. He stepped behind the counter. "Hello," he said in a high-pitched voice. "My name is Ab Overton. May I help you?"

"I hope so," Camp said, introducing himself and offering a handshake. Overton grasped the hand and pumped it a few times as Houston continued to talk. "I'm here to talk about a job you did nearly a year ago. Do you remember taking a picture of some trail hands down at Ralph Hicks's livery stable?"

"Of course, I remember it. I never took but one picture down there. A man named Bill Fisher talked me into doing it, but he didn't tell me till later that he wasn't going to be around to pay for it. Finally told me that he was going on a trail drive, that he'd pick it up when he got back. Well, I'm still waiting."

"Do you still have the picture?"

"Of course. I never discard my work. I tried to sell it to the newspapers back when they were all printing stories about the trail drives, but none of the editors was interested." He paused for a moment, then asked, "Just what is your interest in the picture, Mr. Houston?"

"John Calloway was the trail boss, and he was my friend. He's dead now, and I'd like to have a picture of him. Bill Fisher won't ever be coming back to pay you anyway, for he's dead, too. They died together, killed and robbed by outlaws."

In an honest show of emotion, all color drained from the little man's face, and he looked as if he might cry. "Oh, my Lord," he said, his voice sounding almost feminine. "Couldn't the outlaws have robbed them without killing them?"

Houston shook his head emphatically. "No. Not men like John Calloway."

Overton said nothing else, just went about the room looking on shelves and pulling out drawers. After several minutes, he laid the picture on the counter.

Camp spotted John Calloway immediately, and the man

beside him bore a striking resemblance to what was left of Joe Plenty. The picture was of very good quality, and Houston stared at it for a long time. Every feature was so clear that it seemed as if his old friend should be able to speak.

"I'll say one thing for you," Camp said, reaching into his pocket. "You certainly know how to take a picture." He had his purse in his hand now. "I'll be happy to pay whatever you think it's worth."

Overton dropped his eyes to the counter. "Don't know," he said slowly. "Don't guess I ought to charge anything, since the trail hands had such bad luck. Seems sort of like taking money from the dead."

Houston spoke quickly: "Those men being dead has nothing to do with the fact that you should be paid for your work, Mr. Overton. Besides, it's my money you'll be taking; I'm alive."

The little man smiled. "Guess you've got something there," he said. "I believe I told Mr. Fisher that it would cost a dollar. Does that sound reasonable?"

"Absolutely." Camp laid the money on the counter, then turned to leave. "It was nice meeting you," he said, "and I'm sure glad you hung on to this picture." He shoved it into his saddlebag, then added, "If I ever need your services in the future, I know where to find you." Then he was out on the street.

A few minutes later, he rented a second-story hotel room one block west of the livery stable. He paid for the room, then, without climbing the stairs, walked back to the street. It was almost suppertime, and he was very hungry. He chose a small restaurant two doors west of the hotel.

A tall, gray-haired man stood behind the counter. He greeted Camp with a toothy smile, and told him to choose any table he wanted. Houston was soon sitting near the back wall, close to the kitchen. Once seated, he became even hungrier, for the establishment was very clean, and he could smell the strong aroma of something baking.

A young waitress, who was obviously of Mexican descent, was soon at his table. "Thank you for coming to the Beacon, sir," she said in perfect English. "May I bring you something to eat?"

"I'll have one of your best beefsteaks," he said, "and everything that goes along with it. And I'd like some of whatever that is I smell baking."

She chuckled softly, and continued to offer a beautiful smile that seemed genuine. "It's fresh bread, sir, and I think you're just in time." She tucked the bill of fare under her arm, then headed for the kitchen.

Half an hour later, he was enjoying a meal he would not soon forget: steak, potatoes, greens, beans, and a large slab of peach pie. The buttered, freshly baked bread was hot and delicious, and if he had ever drunk a better-tasting cup of coffee, he could not remember where or when. He took more time than usual with his meal, and sipped more coffee afterward. Then, leaving a dime on the table to show that he appreciated good service, he paid for his food and left the building.

He bought a newspaper on the street, then walked to the livery stable. He informed Ralph Hicks that he had been successful in his meeting with the photographer, and thanked the hostler again for his information. Then he retrieved a change of clothing from his pack, along with his razor and his shaving mug. A few minutes later, he was back at the hotel.

Once in his room, he tested the mattress immediately. The bed was soft, yet firm. Like everything else in the room, it was clean, and it had two feather pillows. There was a medium-sized table against the wall, on which rested a large pitcher of water. A washbasin was also there, along with soap and a washcloth.

There was a foot-square mirror on the wall behind the table. It had obviously been placed there by a woman, or at least a short man, because Camp had to stoop until his body was in an uncomfortable position in order to see his image. He smiled, then took off his shirt. He placed both pillows in a chair, then pulled it up to the table and took a seat. Now he was looking into the mirror dead center.

He shaved his face and washed his body as best he could, then sat down on the bed and began to study the picture. The trail hands had posed around a few bales of hay, with the corral and several horses in the background. John Calloway sat on one of the bales, a serious expression on his face. Behind and on either side of him stood the remaining trail hands. All wore silly grins, and each man had a gun in his hand.

Camp had written Joe Plenty's descriptions of the men in a small notebook. Now, holding the photograph in one hand and the notebook in the other, he had no problem putting a name on every man pictured. He sat for a long time, committing each man's face and description to memory. Finally, he slipped the picture back into his saddlebag, convinced that he would recognize any of the men on sight:

Walt Turner, who was thought by Joe Plenty to be the leader of the pack, was about thirty years old. A six-footer who weighed about one-ninety, he had coal-black hair and dark eyes. He had near-perfect teeth, and smiled often. Plenty believed that Turner came from Fort Worth, for during their months on the trail together, the man had mentioned that particular town more than any other when talking about bygone days.

Red Bentley was considerably smaller. He stood no more than five-seven, and weighed about one-forty. As his nickname implied, his hair was fiery red, and his face was covered with freckles. He openly boasted about rustling cattle in the past, and always carried a roll of money. Plenty had once heard one of the other hands use the nickname "Lightning" when referring to Bentley. Did the man's use of that particular word mean that Bentley was exceptionally fast with a sixgun? Plenty believed that it did. So did Camp Houston, and he had made a mental note of it.

Bill Wiggins had originally come from Brackettville, and very often said as much: "I'm Bill Wiggins, from down Brackettville way," he would inform any man whom he was meeting for the first time. Tall, skinny and bowlegged, Wiggins wore sideburns that reached below his ears and blond, stringy hair that he allowed to grow to his shoulders. Though Plenty said that the man was in his late twenties, he knew little else about him. Wiggins was the quiet type, he said, and appeared to spend much of his time daydreaming.

Sam Lott was a twenty-one-year-old braggart from Waco. Plenty said that Calloway had finally begun to put Lott on early guard duty every night because the serious-minded trail boss had grown tired of listening to the young man's high-pitched voice. If allowed to remain in camp after supper, Lott thought nothing of keeping the other men awake with his boasting.

He was quick to say that he himself might very well be the fastest gun alive, that he had never seen a man who could match his draw. A six-footer who weighed about one-sixty, Lott was a blue-eyed blond. He seldom if ever shaved his face, for his beard amounted to little more than a sparse crop of white fuzz. The young outlaw would surely die with a gun in his hand, Joe Plenty had said, for he was anything but smart.

Among the five outlaws, both Camp Houston and Joe Plenty thought Jack Little was the poorest excuse for a human being. The man had been on three trail drives with John Calloway. He had always received top dollar for his work and, on occasion, what some of the hands thought was preferential treatment.

"You oughta seen the sonofabitch buddying up and trying to kiss Mr. Calloway's ass," Plenty had said. "Always pretending to be his friend. They usually ate their meals together, and slept side by side under the chuck wagon at night. I know for a fact that they once shared the same room in Dodge City. I tell you, it gripes my ass just to think about it. We all trusted that sonofabitch, then here he comes pumping lead into us. I saw it with my own eyes, just before I passed out."

Jack Little was a twenty-five-year-old native of Corsicana.

He was obviously a good cowhand, for John Calloway, a man widely known for his keen knowledge of the cattle business, had hired him on at least three occasions.

At six foot three and two hundred twenty pounds, Little was by far the largest of the five. He had brown hair and gray eyes, with the right eye having a permanent squint. Though slightly stoop-shouldered, he was nevertheless a very strong man, and known to be handy with his fists. Plenty did not know how good a gun hand Little was, but said that he always carried a Peacemaker in a low-hanging, cutaway holster.

Camp slipped the notebook into his saddlebag beside the picture, then dozed off. He slept for more than three hours, and awakened to a dark room. He was on his feet quickly, and touched a burning match to the wick of the coal-oil lamp.

He dressed in clean clothing and buckled on his gun belt, then headed for the stairway. Moments later, he was out on the street.

He was hungry again. As much as he had enjoyed his meal earlier in the afternoon, one glance at the Beacon told him that the restaurant was closed. Camp smiled, and nodded. The owner was probably smart, he was thinking: the man obviously stayed open throughout the daylight hours, fed all the people who were serious about eating a quiet meal, then closed early enough to avoid all the nighttime drinkers and hell-raisers.

He walked past the Beacon, and continued west. A few doors down, and on the same side of the street, he came to a large, well-lighted building. The signs over the door and on the windows gave no hint as to the name of the establishment, but stated that food, drink and the game of billiards could be found inside. Camp counted a total of nine saddled horses at the two hitching rails.

He stepped inside and stood against the wall for a few moments, looking over the layout. A three-sided bar stood in the middle of the room. The kitchen and eating area were on the west side, with the billiard tables on the opposite. The poker tables were all located along the rear wall, past what appeared to be a small, hardwood dance floor. At the moment, no cardplayers were present.

Nor was there any action at the billiard tables. From where Camp was standing he had a good view of everything in the building and, try as he might, he could not see half enough men to ride off all of those horses out front. There were only three men sitting at the bar. Camp walked forward and spoke to the fat bartender. "Kitchen still open?"

The man nodded and finished off his drink, then wiped his mouth and pointed. "Just knock on the wall over there, then have a seat. She'll be with you pretty quick."

Camp did as he had been told, and a middle-aged woman was at his table immediately. "I was jist about ta call it a day," she said tiredly. "Shore hope ya want sump'm simple."

"How simple?" Camp inquired.

"Well, sump'm it don't take all night ta fix." She pulled a strand of gray hair out of her eyes and tucked it behind her ear, then continued. "Tell ya what I could do. I could warm ya up some stew purty quick, 'cause I've prob'ly still got some red coals in th' fahrbox." When Camp was slow to speak, the lady continued. "I made it outta fresh beef, an' it was mighty good at dinner." She looked Houston in the eye for a moment, then added, "Ya git a good-sized bowl fer a dime, fifteen cents if ya want biscuits an' coffee."

Camp nodded, then offered a big smile. "Sounds like just what I need," he said. "Bring me the whole works."

As he sat enjoying his meal, it soon became obvious that the men who owned those horses outside were definitely in the vicinity. Camp watched as a man came through the back door and spoke to one of the men sitting at the bar. Then the drinker gave up his stool to the newcomer, and himself walked through the back door. Camp sat smiling as he realized that he might well be dining in the biggest whorehouse in Texas.

After he had eaten and paid for his meal, Houston walked to the bar and ordered whiskey. Never once making eye contact, the bartender poured the drink. "Dime," he said, holding out his hand. Camp ignored the hand, and laid the money on the bar. The man scooped up the coin, then turned his back and walked away.

When Camp turned his head toward the far end of the bar, he could see that the drinkers were staring at him. When he returned their inquisitive looks with a steely stare of his own, all three men quickly averted their eyes. A moment later, Houston upended his drink and set the empty glass on the bar. Then, without a word, he walked through the front door and headed for his hotel room. He wanted to get an early start next morning, but first he must decide where he was going.

Long after he had blown out the lamp, he lay on his bed, thinking. He finally decided that, since it was closer to his present whereabouts than any of the other towns he would eventually have to visit, he would begin his search in Brackettville. Plenty had said that Bill Wiggins seemed proud, maybe even boastful, of the fact that he had been born and raised there.

Camp knew that most wandering men occasionally return to the place of their beginnings, however short the visit might be. He was hoping the pattern might hold true in the case of Wiggins. Plenty had said that the man was a daydreamer. Had one of his dreams been to come back to Brackettville with a pokeful of money? Was he at this very moment living in a fancy home while passing himself off as a successful investor?

After thinking for a while longer, Camp discarded the latter possibility. Though one share of the proceeds from the robbery might well be enough to build a fancy home, it was hardly the kind of money necessary to secure an impressive position on the social ladder of even a small town.

Nope, the take had simply not been big enough for five men to live the good life forever. John Calloway had been carrying thirty-five thousand dollars, which, split evenly, would have put only seven thousand dollars into the pockets of each of the robbers.

Camp Houston doubted, however, that there had been an even split. Outlaws were usually not very bright, and any man in the bunch who was actually capable of putting together a workable scheme could easily convince the others that he should be the leader of the pack, and that his extraordinary brilliance entitled him to a lion's share of the booty. A lopsided split usually followed all robberies that were committed by more than one man, with Boss Thief often claiming as much as half the take.

As did Joe Plenty, Houston believed that Walt Turner had bossed the robbery in Kansas, and probably kept the larger portion of the money for himself. If that was the case, and if Turner's underlings had been living high on the hog for the past year, they should all be running short of money just about now. Especially since they had received less than an equal share.

Lying on his bed in the dark, Houston nodded at his thoughts. One thing he knew for sure was that when a man's funds began to run low, he changed his habits. He ate, drank and slept in places that he might have shunned when his bankroll was adequate. Camp believed that a man who was down and out could be much harder to find than one whose poke was full.

A man who was well-off got noticed, for he usually dressed well, ate in expensive restaurants and stayed at the better hotels, places whose business it was to know who their customers were. A man whose poke was empty, however, would likely drop his bedroll behind any old bush, and avoid crowds altogether. Then when he did come to town, which he would eventually have to do if he hoped to better his circumstances, he would inevitably head for the seamy side, where seedy characters mostly looked at each other through unseeing eyes. There he could move about freely, and often be remembered by nobody.

Nodding again, Camp pulled a blanket over himself and turned on his left side, his normal go-to-sleep position. In the morning, he would get on Bill Wiggins's trail, and he would assume that the man was broke, or nearly so. He fluffed up his pillow, then closed his eyes. He was asleep quickly.

It was past ten o'clock when he rode out of San Anto-
nio next morning. He was getting a late start because he had
waited for some of the stores to open. He had first retrieved
his animals from the livery stable, then ridden to the Shebang.
There he bought two half-gallon glass jars, complete with lids
and sealing rubbers. He also bought a smoked ham and a bag
of crackers.

Then he rode to the establishment in which he had eaten
supper the night before. He ignored the fat bartender as he
walked past the bar. When he knocked on the kitchen wall,
the lady opened the door quickly. She looked him up and
down, then smiled. "Lord, whatcha gonna do with them?"
she asked, her eyes taking in the jars he held in his hands.

"I was hoping you would put something to eat in 'em," he
said, his smile as big as her own. "Do you have enough leftover stew and beans to fill 'em?"

She chuckled softly, and reached for the jars. "Guess by gosh I do. Been wonderin' what th' heck I wuz gonna do with it all." She turned toward the kitchen, then spoke over her shoulder: "I'll put th' lids an' rubbers on th' jars, then brang 'em out here fer you ta seal. I ain't near strong enough in my hands to do it, nowadays."

Ten minutes later, she brought the jars to his table. One was almost full of beef stew, and the other was filled with warmed-over red beans. Camp gave each of the lids a hard twist. The jars were now sealed, and would not leak.

He ordered a ham-and-egg breakfast, then asked the lady to bake him an extra pan of biscuits and put them in a bag. "I'll be on the trail for a while," he said, "and I like my biscuits."

She nodded. "Won't take long. Th' oven's already hot."

Half an hour later, he was headed west at a fast trot. The roan could hold this pace all day long, and Sid Blankenship had said that the same was true for the packhorse. Camp expected to be halfway across Medina County by nightfall.

He reached Hondo Creek an hour before sunset. *Hondo* was a Spanish word meaning "deep," and the creek had been aptly named. He quickly decided to camp on the east bank, for he could see no place where fording was possible. He would seek out shallow water in the morning, for he had no intention of swimming the animals across and wetting everything they carried.

He dropped his pack and his saddle beside a willow, then watered and picketed the horses. Grass was at least adequate along the creek, so he would save the grain for another day.

He raked a pile of leaves and twigs together, then broke up a dead limb across his knee. He needed only a small fire for boiling his coffee and heating his stew; then he would rake several handfuls of dirt over the coals.

After a pleasing supper of hot stew and biscuits, he put out the fire and crawled into his bedroll. He lay staring at the stars for a long time, thinking about the ranch he intended to build on Calf Creek, a few miles north of the Mason County line. He had bought three sections of land there four years earlier, and if all went well, he would make the last payment to John Butterworth next January.

Once he had a clear deed, he would build a home and some outbuildings, then stretch his credit to stock the property with cattle. He would start with longhorns because they were cheap, but he fully intended to buy some Hereford bulls at the first opportunity. He would allow the bulls to run free with the cows, and keep none of the half-breed male offspring. After a few years, the longhorn strain would be gone, and he would have a herd of Herefords.

The ecology of the Calf Creek property was ideal for the raising of livestock. The vegetation consisted of open grasslands and oak savannahs. Woodlands occurred along the water courses, and shrubs were restricted to very shallow soils and steep slopes. The property also had a history of its own:

On November 21, 1831, James Bowie, Rezin P. Bowie, David Buchanan, Cephas D. Hamm, Matthew Doyle, Jesse Wallace, Thomas McCaslin, Robert Armstrong, James Coryell and two servants, Charles and Gonzales, fought a twenty-four-hour battle with more than a hundred fifty Caddo and Lipan Indians.

Though the Bowie party suffered no casualties, they killed eighty warriors before the Indians withdrew. James Bowie, who would later die at the Alamo, erected a marker of sorts, proclaiming Calf Creek the location of the battle.

Camp would build his home very near the conjunction of McCulloch, Menard, and Mason Counties, where Calf Creek emptied into the San Saba River. Moving about in the area should be a little safer now that the shooting had ceased in what had come to be known as the "Mason County War." Newspaper writers had very quickly begun to use the term "Hoo Doo War" when writing about the deadly hostilities.

During and for several years after the Reconstruction period, lawlessness in general, and cattle rustling in particular, were prevalent along the entire Texas frontier. State lawmen were of little help, for being a very corrupt organization, they themselves were part of the problem. The problem reached major proportions in Mason County in 1875.

Rustling had been going on for years when the newly elected sheriff, John Clark, intercepted a large herd of cattle being driven to Llano. When ownership of the cattle could not be determined, Clark arrested nine men and took them to the Mason County jail. All were soon out on bail provided by local citizens.

The men were ordered to remain in the town of Mason until their hearing took place. When Sheriff Clark learned that they were not in town, as their bonds stipulated, he rearrested the five men that he could find, and placed them in jail.

Several nights later, a group of unknown men held the sheriff, deputy sheriff, and a Texas Ranger named Dan Roberts at bay while making off with all five of the prisoners. Three of the alleged rustlers were killed, one was brought back to the jail, and the fifth was never heard from again.

During the next few months, several arrests were made on charges of cattle rustling, and a group of unknown assailants killed one man even while he was in the custody of a deputy sheriff.

Men from other counties soon became involved in the fighting, and during the summer of 1875 the killings increased dramatically. First, a rancher was shot from ambush. Then a deputy sheriff was killed, followed closely by two men from out of the county. Another stockman and a gambler were killed soon after.

The newly reorganized Texas Rangers, under the leadership of Major John B. Jones, were ordered to send a force to Mason County. A small contingent, which included Major Jones, arrived at the Hedwig's Hill community, in the southern part of the county, during the afternoon of September 28, 1875.

Then, hearing rumors of trouble in the Loyal Valley community, Jones turned south and headed there, instead of continuing on to Mason, as had been the original plan. Next morning, a county official was shot and killed from ambush while walking down the street in Mason.

The male population of the county was by now split into three groups. One group remained neutral and tried to keep the peace, while the other two fought at every opportunity. The line between the two feuding groups had never become clear. Nor had the reason for all the bloodshed.

Supposedly, Sheriff Clark was the leader of one of the factions, but the leader of the other was never identified. Many names appeared, but nothing was ever proved.

Sheriff Clark and nine of his "faction" were charged with minor offenses stemming from the initial arrest. All but Clark were found innocent in October, 1876. The sheriff posted bail, and was never heard from again.

The following winter, a stockman was killed at his home in Llano County. Then, in what was hopefully the last act of the Hoo Doo War, the Mason County Courthouse was torched on January 21, 1877. It was believed by all and stated by many that the building had been burned to destroy all evidence that was to be used against those involved.

Most of the county's residents believed that by now, the leaders of both factions either were dead or had left the area. At any rate, the killing stopped just as suddenly as it had begun. And though many names were mentioned, no charges were ever filed concerning the courthouse fire.

Camp Houston had not fired a shot during the Mason County War, for he had spent the entire period working as foreman of John Butterworth's Lazy B Ranch, in Mills County. He had nevertheless been acquainted with some of the men who had died in the senseless feud, and believed that he knew who had killed them. Even so, his lips were sealed, for it had long been his policy to stay clear of other men's squabbles.

The night air finally turned cool, and after turning over in his bed for the tenth time, Camp dozed off and slept like a log.

He awoke with the sun shining in his eyes next morning, and lay still for a few minutes trying to remember how long it had been since he had slept so soundly. He had not even gotten up during the night to relieve himself, as was usually the case. He smiled, and reached for his boots.

He was soon on his feet gathering dead grass to start his morning fire. Both of his horses began to whinny when they saw him moving about. The breakfast of oats they were hinting at would not be forthcoming this morning, for they had grazed most of the night. Good grass would become more difficult to find as he moved farther west, however; then the animals would have to be grained at least once a day.

When his coffeepot came to a boil, he pulled it off the fire. With his folding knife, he cut several slices of the smoked ham into his frying pan, added some of the biscuits, then placed the pan on the hot coals. He poured himself a steaming cup of coffee and added a spoonful of sugar. A few minutes later, he was enjoying a tasty breakfast.

An hour later, he was riding north along the creek, looking for a place that was shallow enough to ford. After traveling for half a mile, he gave up and reversed his direction. A mile to the south he found a natural ford with a rocky bottom, where the water ran less than two feet deep. His animals took to the water eagerly, and he stopped midstream and allowed them to drink their fill.

He crossed the Sabinal River shortly after noon, and arrived at the Frio an hour before sunset. Flowing directly out of the mountains and through Frio Canyon, the Frio River was cold and clear, and usually ran shallow enough to be forded at almost any location.

Hondo Creek last night had been the exception, for it had long been Houston's policy to cross a stream before bedding down. A hard rain anywhere upstream could drastically change the character of a creek or river within a matter of hours, making it difficult or impossible to cross for several days. He watered his horses, then waded them to the far side. He would make camp on the west bank.

He had eaten a supper of beans and biscuits and was sipping a cup of coffee when a covered wagon drawn by two horses crossed the river and stopped a few yards from his camp. A couple who appeared to be in their thirties sat on the seat, and Camp could see at least two youngsters poking their heads around the canvas. He waved at the newcomers, and his greeting was returned.

He dashed his coffee grounds over his shoulder, then walked to the wagon. "Deadwood's mighty scarce in this area," he said, speaking to both the man and his wife. "My fire's still burning, and you're welcome to use it. I'll move my gear a little farther down the river."

"Well, now," the man said, stepping down and offering a handshake, "I'd say 'at's mighty white uv ya. Been wonderin' how'n th' heck I wuz gonna git Maggie a fahr started, now here ya come offerin' us yore'n. Yessir, 'at's white uv ya . . . mighty white."

Camp grasped the man's hand. "My name's Camp Houston," he said, "and I'm just passing through. I've already eaten my supper, and like I said, you folks are welcome to my campfire."

"My name's Ed Crane," the man said, pumping Camp's hand. He pointed to the wagon. "Th' lady on th' seat there's my wife Maggie, and them two young uns ya see peepin' aroun' th' canvas is our ten-year-old twins, Mark an' Sarah."

Camp waved to the woman and the kids, then turned to walk away.

"Ya don't hafta move none o' yer stuff," Crane called to him. "We c'n use 'at fahr with ya settin' right whur ya been settin'."

Houston turned halfway around. "No, Mr. Crane. You folks just take over my campsite and get yourselves a good night's sleep. I'll be moving." Within a matter of minutes, he had moved his belongings fifty yards downriver. Half an hour later, he was sound asleep.

He rode west at sunup, after washing a breakfast of cold ham and biscuits down with water from his canteen. Though he usually began his day by drinking at least two cups of steaming coffee, this morning would be the exception, for there had been no wood available for a fire. Maybe later in the day he would come across some fuel; then he would dig out the coffeepot.

He supposed that the Crane family would also have to eat a cold breakfast, for they had no wood in the wagon, and the area around the campsite had been picked clean. It would probably be some time yet before the Cranes concerned themselves with that problem, however, for although Houston had made no particular effort to prepare for his departure quietly, no member of the family had stirred.

The two humps beneath the wagon probably represented father and son, Camp was thinking, with mother and daughter sleeping in the wagon. Just before riding out of sight, he took one last look. The humps were deathly still. He smiled, and nodded. The folks had obviously been tuckered out completely, and would sleep until the heat of the day awakened them.

He held his animals to a fast walk. He expected to ford the Nueces River by noon, then camp on the west bank of the West Nueces before nightfall. He would wake up in Kinney County in the morning, and should be in Brackettville by midday.

Several times during the morning he dismounted to pick up deadwood, adding it to the packhorse's burden. When he reached the west bank of the Nueces, he first fed each of the horses a hefty portion of oats. Then he finally had his morning coffee and a hot meal as well. He ate the last of his beef stew, then, after washing out the empty jar with sand and water from the river, returned it to his pack. He had every intention of acquiring a refill in the very near future. If not another jar of beef stew, he'd find something else that he liked.

5

★

It was an hour past noon when Houston arrived in Brackettville next day. The weather was hot and dry, and little clouds of dust sprang from the hooves of his animals as they walked down the wide street. He was headed for the livery stable, which he could already see three blocks ahead. The few men he passed paid him no mind. Most were soldiers, no doubt stationed at nearby Fort Clark.

Fort Clark was the sole reason for Brackettville's being, for the settlement had originally been established in 1852 as nothing more than a supply village for the cavalry units stationed there. And though the town had by now become a trade center for surrounding ranches and irrigated farms, the prosperity of many local merchants was still largely dependent upon the military, especially the men who owned the hotels, restaurants and saloons.

Most civilians slept and ate their meals at home, and a respectable number of men did their drinking there. Consequently, there was a never-ending campaign among the town's watering holes to separate the soldiers from their pay, and a few of the saloons even allowed those in good standing to drink on credit.

Over the years, the drinking establishments had several times been placed off limits to all military personnel, usually to punish the soldiers for one infraction or another, but a few times to teach Brackettville's businessmen a lesson. The lesson was learned quickly, and each occasion sent the saloon owners to Fort Clark, begging the camp commander to lift the restrictions. Then, when the commander complied and the soldiers were once again in town with their money, they were welcomed enthusiastically, and could get away with anything short of murder in almost any saloon in town.

Camp continued down the street till he reached the livery stable. The stable and corral stood at the end of the street, with ample room for two-way traffic on either side. There was an open-air blacksmith shop beneath the wooden awning, and two wagons and a buggy bearing FOR SALE signs were parked nearby. Houston dismounted and led his horses to the watering trough.

A tall, hatless man with gray hair stood in the wide doorway. "Saw you coming more than a mile away," he said, beginning to walk toward the trough. "Seems to me that it's just too damn hot for traveling." He nodded in the direction of the horses. "You gonna leave them for a while?"

Camp nodded, and handed over the reins. "They're probably at least as tired as I am," he said, "and you're right about the weather being hot." He unsheathed his rifle, then extracted his razor and a change of clean clothing from his pack. "Don't know how long I'll be in town," he said, "but I'll trust you to take care of my animals till I need them."

"I'll treat them like they were my own," the man said. He offered a handshake, adding, "My name's Rufus Bunt."

Houston accepted the hand. "I'm Camp Houston," he said.

Camp felt Bunt's firm grip turn to mush, and the man extracted his hand quickly. "I . . . I guess I don't have to tell you this," he said softly, "but that name is well known around this town—around this whole area, for that matter."

Camp nodded curtly, then changed the subject. "Any particular hotel in town that you'd recommend?"

"Don't guess so," the hostler said. He pointed up the street. "Three hotels in town, and you just rode past all of them. I'd say they're all about the same, but the Frey has the most business. That's where most of the soldiers and the cowboys hang out. The hotel bar downstairs is crowded every night of the week. Plenty of gambling and easy women, if a man's hunting that sort of thing."

Camp smiled faintly. "I'll be at the Frey," he said. He patted the roan on the rump, then walked down the street.

A middle-aged man wearing a straw hat sat behind the counter at the hotel, and offered Camp his choice of an upstairs room or one on the first floor. "I'd rather sleep upstairs," Houston said, signing his name to the register.

The clerk stared at the signature much longer than was necessary, and Camp knew that once again his name had been recognized. He had considered using a name other than his own for his manhunt, but had decided against it. Now he was not so sure that had been wise. Maybe he should reconsider picking a name out of the air for hotel registers.

"Thank you for choosing the Frey, Mr. Houston," the clerk said. He dropped the key to room number twenty in Camp's hand, adding, "I certainly hope you have a nice stay, and if there is anything I can do to make it more enjoyable, just let me know."

Houston dropped the key into his vest pocket. "I'm sure everything will be all right," he said. "I don't know how long I'll be in town, but I'll settle with you before I leave."

"Yes," the clerk said nervously. He nodded several times. "Yes, of course. There was never any doubt in my mind."

Camp picked up his gear and headed up the stairway, then

paused momentarily to look over his shoulder. The clerk had already stepped away from the counter, no doubt eager to head for the barroom with the news that Camp Houston was in town. Camp shook his head, and continued up the stairway.

He unlocked the door to number twenty, then stepped inside. He stood still for a few moments, pleased with what he saw. Though the Frey Hotel was hardly impressive from the outside, the room he had rented was exceptionally nice, and much larger than he had expected.

The window had curtains, and there was a colorful spread on the bed. There was a chest of drawers in one corner, and a large table in another. A smaller table with two chairs was closer to the center of the room, and held a coal-oil lamp and a pitcher of water. A pan of water, a bar of soap, a washcloth and two towels rested on the corner table, and a medium-sized mirror hung on the wall. There was even a small recess in the wall that could have been called a closet, with an overhead rod for hanging clothing.

Camp laid his gear on the corner table, then sat down on the bed. The mattress was springy, yet firm. He fluffed up one of the pillows, and smiled. The hotel clerk had given him a quality room all right, well worth the dollar-twenty-a-night price tag.

He stripped and washed himself, then lathered and shaved his face. He pushed his rifle as far under the bed as he could reach, then dressed in clean clothing. A few minutes later, he walked down the stairway and into the restaurant. He took a seat at a table on the far side of the building, with his back against the wall.

The restaurant and the barroom were separated by nothing more than a thin wall, with batwing doors that even a short man could see over. And as he took his seat, Camp could see the heads of several men peering over the doors, no doubt wanting to see if Camp Houston was as big as his reputation. When Camp smiled and waved to them, every head disappeared quickly.

Houston ordered a plate of chicken and dumplings from the Mexican waiter, then sat sipping coffee as he waited for his meal. He cast his eyes toward the barroom occasionally, but saw no one else peering over the doors. He had already decided that, as soon as he finished off his meal, he would belly up to the bar and give them all a good look. He blew air into his cup, then took another sip.

Half an hour later, he pushed his way through the batwing doors and moved quickly to one side, waiting for his eyes to adjust to the dimmer lighting. Standing just inside the doorway, he was the center of attention. None of the men wanted to be singled out, however, and all found something else to look at each time Camp attempted to make direct eye contact. The room was eerily quiet.

Houston himself broke the spell. "Howdy!" he said loudly, his deep bass voice bouncing off the back wall. A few men mumbled a soft greeting, then quietly resumed their previous conversations. There was an empty stool at the corner of the bar, against the wall, and Camp walked there now. He leaned across the bar on his elbows, then spoke to the young bartender. "Have you got any Bourbon County whiskey?"

The bartender, who appeared to be still in his teens, laughed bravely. "Not so you could tell it," he said. "Ain't never been no Kentucky whiskey in this place that I know of." He laughed again. "Only thing I can offer you is some stuff that was cooked up in San Antonio about three months ago. Can't guarantee it to be good, but I can sure guarantee it to make you drunk."

Houston chuckled softly, then nodded. "Give me a bottle and a glass."

The young man complied, then held out his hand. "Sixty-five cents," he said. Once he had been paid, he skedaddled to the other end of the bar.

Camp poured whiskey in his glass, then offered a drink to the man on the next stool. "Don't mind if I do," the man said, reaching for the bottle. He poured his glass full, drank half of it, then filled it again. Then the pitifully thin man, who appeared to be at least sixty years old, looked at Houston through bloodshot eyes. "That bartender knows what he's talking about," he said. "This stuff'll turn your head around." He gulped another mouthful.

"I can certainly believe that," Camp said, retrieving his bottle and placing it near his left elbow, well out of the old man's reach.

The old-timer sipped at his drink noisily, then began to speak again. "Ain't never set next to nobody like you before," he said. "Ain't never even talked to nobody famous."

Houston wet his lips with whiskey, and said nothing.

"No, sir," the old man continued, "it ain't every day that a man like Camp Houston shows up around here. It's my guess that you're hunting somebody, otherwise you wouldn't be caught dead in a godforsaken place like Brackettville."

Looking over his shoulder, Camp spotted an empty table behind him. He spoke to the old man: "Why don't we move to that corner table, old-timer? If this bottle runs out, we'll get a new one."

The old man led the way, surprising Houston with his steadiness. They seated themselves, and Camp poured whiskey in both glasses. "Looks like you already know my name," he said, "but I don't recall hearing yours."

"The name's Jack Fondon," the old man said. He licked his lips and took another drink.

Camp scratched at the label on the whiskey bottle with a thumbnail. "You say you think I came to town hunting somebody," he said. "What if I did?"

"Hell, I don't know," Fondon answered. "I was just thinking, kinda wondering who it might be. Reckon I know about everybody who lives here, and a whole lot of people who don't."

Houston got to the point. "Do you know a man named Bill Wiggins?"

"Used to," Fondon said, a smile playing around the corners of his mouth. "Don't no more."

"What does that mean?"

"It means that he ain't around no more; been dead since last winter. A man from Waco gunned him down right out there at the hotel's hitching rail, two days before Christmas. Wiggins took two shots in the gut and one in the mouth, and died without ever speaking."

Camp sat thinking for quite some time, continuing to scratch at the label. "The man who shot Wiggins," he said finally, "was his name Sam Lott?"

"Sure was," Fondon said quickly. "How'd you guess?"

"It wasn't entirely a guess."

The old-timer poured more whiskey in his glass. "Lott claimed Wiggins drew on him," he continued, "but I never believed it. Wiggins wasn't no fast gun, and he knew that better'n anybody else. He never would have tried to pull on no damn gunslinger. Of course, his gun was lying there in the dirt, but I damn sure don't believe he was the one dropped it. The town marshal said it appeared to him like nothing more than a shootout between two enemies, and since there weren't no witnesses to the actual shooting, he had no choice but to take Lott's word for what happened. He ordered Lott to get his ass out of town and stay out. The county buried Wiggins next morning, 'cause his wife said she sure didn't have no money.

"Now, Lott claimed that Wiggins had been in debt to him for a long time, and when he came to town to collect, Wiggins went for his gun. Now, he might have owed Lott money, maybe a bunch of money, but he damn sure didn't go for no gun." The old man helped himself to another drink of Camp's whiskey, adding, "I'd bet a hundred million dollars on that."

Camp pushed back his chair and got to his feet. "Where's the marshal's office? What's his name?"

"His office is one block east, on the opposite side of the

street, and his name is Seth Ringling. He's one of the nicest young fellows you'll ever meet, but he don't put up with no shit out of nobody. He's damn sure man enough to back up whatever he says, too."

Camp pushed the bottle across the table. "Here," he said. "Drink up and enjoy yourself." A few seconds later, he stepped out on the street and headed east.

After introducing himself he was soon shaking hands with Marshal Seth Ringling, a very muscular man who appeared to be in his late twenties. The lawman offered a firm grip, speaking as he pumped his visitor's hand. "Camp Houston, huh?" he asked, then pointed to a chair.

Camp nodded, and seated himself.

"No use in me pretending that I haven't heard your name before," the marshal said. "In fact, I doubt that a week ever goes by when I don't hear it." He took a seat behind his desk. "Is there something I can do for you?"

"I don't really know. I came to town looking for Bill Wiggins, but I hear a man from Waco already found him."

Ringling nodded. "A fellow named Sam Lott shot him dead in front of the Frey Hotel last Christmas. Claimed Wiggins drew on him."

"Did you believe Lott's story?"

The marshal shuffled some papers around, then sat thinking for a while. "What I believe or don't believe is not worth a hill of beans," he said finally. "What I can prove is the only thing that counts, and in this case, I can't prove anything. What I found when I arrived on the scene was the same thing I've seen at every other shootout I've ever investigated: a dead man with a cold Peacemaker lying at his feet, and a live man holding another Peacemaker with a hot barrel and three spent shells."

Ringling got to his feet and began to pace about the room. "Hell, no, I didn't believe Sam Lott's story, but my hands were tied. He claimed he shot Wiggins in self-defense, and no jury in Texas would have convicted him. I believed then and now that he was guilty of murder, but there were no witnesses, and his word was law." He walked to the opposite side of the room, then returned, stopping in front of Houston. "You say you came to town looking for Wiggins. Was he a friend of yours?"

"Not by any stretch of the imagination," Camp said, getting to his feet. He told the marshal about John Calloway's trail drive, and the cold-blooded murder of the drovers in a Kansas gully. "I was looking for Bill Wiggins because I intended to kill the sonofabitch."

Ringling shook his head very slowly. "Since Sam Lott and Wiggins were both in on the robbery, maybe the gunplay here in town really was over money," he said.

Camp stood quietly for a while. "That's altogether possible," he said finally, "but it's my guess that Wiggins was killed because the others were afraid he might decide to do some talking. They probably gave Sam Lott the job because he had the fastest gun and the weakest mind. A fellow who knows him very well told me that Lott barely has sense enough to come in out of the rain."

"I talked with him a few minutes the day of the shooting," Ringling said. "He seemed to me like a backwoods kid that just never did quite grow up." The lawman stood in the doorway looking down the street for a moment, then spoke over his shoulder: "I suppose you'll be calling on Mr. Sam Lott before long, huh?"

"Guess I'll take a trip to Corpus Christi first," Camp said, moving closer to the door. "Fact is, I intend to get a good night's sleep and head out in the morning." He stepped out on the small porch. "Good-bye, Marshal. I'm glad to have met you."

"Same here," Ringling said. "Damn shame I can't go with you."

Houston spent the next hour sitting on a barstool in a rundown saloon two doors east of the marshal's office. When Camp ordered a beer, the bartender served, collected, then moved away, obviously evading any questions Houston might want to ask.

Two beers later, Camp suddenly decided that he had drunk enough for one day. Besides, he was tired of trying to understand the muted conversation around him. The room had grown strangely quiet when he entered; then the incessant mumbling had begun. That he himself was the topic, he had no doubt. He slid off his stool and nodded to the bartender, then headed for the front door.

He ate a light supper in the hotel restaurant, then climbed the stairway to his room. He undressed, put his Peacemaker under the extra pillow, then stretched out. The wide, comfortable bed put him to sleep in short order.

6

Camp was at the livery stable shortly after daybreak. The hostler was already up, standing in the doorway sipping from a steaming coffee cup. "Good morning," Houston said, pointing toward the corral. "I've come for my horses."

"Figured as much," Bunt said. He took a coil of rope from a wooden peg, then headed down the hall. "Pot of hot coffee on the stove there in the office," he said loudly just before he disappeared around the corner. "Drink all you want."

"No, thanks," Camp said to himself, for the liveryman was already out of sight. Unlike most western men, Houston liked a little sugar in his coffee, and it never failed to interfere with his appetite if he loaded up early in the morning. He would have breakfast at the hotel restaurant a few minutes from now, and he would drink his coffee then. He pulled up a nail keg, then sat down to await the delivery of his horses.

When the hostler returned, he was leading both animals.

"Fed 'em more'n an hour ago," he said. "They ought to both be raring to go."

"Just like me," Camp said. He saddled the roan and shoved his rifle into the boot. Then the liveryman helped him balance and fasten his packs to the black's packsaddle. He rolled up the soiled clothing he had taken off yesterday, and placed it in one of the packs. Mother Nature would take care of his laundry while he slept tonight.

Camp had used to hunt up a washerwoman every time he accumulated a sack of dirty clothing. He still did that occasionally, but not when he was traveling. He had hit upon a way of washing his own clothing several years earlier, and nowadays he used it with regularity when he was on the trail, especially in hot weather.

He almost always camped beside a stream with a strong current, and it was a simple matter to stake his clothing out in swift, shallow water before going to bed. In the morning, all he had to do was wring the water out of the garments and hang them on his packhorse. The sun would dry them quickly after he began his day's traveling, then he would roll them up and place them in his pack. They were always clean, and smelled good.

Houston said good-bye to the liveryman, then mounted the roan and yanked on the black's lead rope. A few minutes later, he tied both animals to the hotel's hitching rail. The restaurant had its own separate entrance, and Camp pushed the door open and stepped inside. He had no problem getting the cook's attention, for there were only three customers in the restaurant at this early hour.

The middle-aged cook smiled and nodded when Camp handed him the jars and requested that they be filled with something edible. "Got half a pot o' chili and a couple pounds o' roast beef that I'm dyin' to get rid of," he said, chuckling. "How does that sound to you?"

"It sounds just right," Camp said. "I'll have a platter of flapjacks and eggs for my breakfast. Then if you'll bake a pan of biscuits and bag them for traveling, you'll be making me happy all around."

The cook chuckled again. "Your breakfast'll be ready in a jiffy," he said. "The rest of your order'll take a little longer." He headed for the kitchen.

Less than an hour later, Camp was riding east on the same road that had brought him to Brackettville, with his horses no doubt stepping in their own tracks occasionally. His hat was pulled low over his eyes, for the rising sun he was facing seemed both hotter and brighter than usual, and appeared to be exactly at ground level.

He held his animals to a fast walk hour after hour, expecting to make the West Nueces River by midafternoon. Once there, he would lie down under a willow and spend the remainder of the day enjoying the cool breezes that blew across the water. He also knew that his horses would appreciate the location, for there was green grass in abundance.

All morning long he kept an eye out for anything that would burn, for he knew that a search for fuel anywhere near the river would be fruitless. Not only had all of the deadwood been used, but low-hanging limbs from many of the trees had also been burned. And just as if there would be no tomorrow, campers had even chopped off as many of the living trees' roots as they could find running along on top of the ground. Most of the trees had survived, but some had not.

By the time Houston reached the West Nueces, he had as much bark, dry grass and deadwood on the packhorse as he was likely to need, since a small blaze would be sufficient to reheat his precooked food and boil his coffee.

He watered his animals, then forded the shallow river, selecting the same campsite that he had used on his way to Brackettville. He rubbed his horses with handfuls of grass till their backs were dry, then released them on long picket ropes. He would move the animals to new grass about sunset, for they would eat everything they could reach by then.

He built his fire underneath the willow, then dug his coffeepot and an iron skillet out of his pack. He was very hungry, and had been thinking about food for the past two hours. He filled the coffeepot with water from the river, then dumped in a handful of grounds. Then he twisted the lid off one of the jars and poured the skillet half full. A short time later, he seated himself on his bedroll and began to wolf down the hotel cook's chili right from the skillet.

He had eaten only a few bites when he suddenly stopped chewing and set the skillet down. He spat the contents of his mouth into a bush, and very quickly made a beeline for his canteen. He drank several swallows, then sat for a long time sloshing water around in his mouth.

He remembered hearing the cook say he was "dyin' to get rid of the chili." Small wonder. Camp had always liked food with a peppery taste, but the concoction he had tried to eat just now was nothing short of ridiculous. Nor did he believe that any other man really preferred his food fiery enough to peel the inside of his mouth.

Though Camp had once seen a man eat a large pod of red chili without the benefit of additional food or water, Houston knew that the man was weak in the head, and trying to impress a group of other men. Camp considered the act silly, and had no doubt that it might be harmful to the man's health.

He was still staring into the skillet when he heard a splashing sound. He raised his eyes to see a rider fording the river from the west. Camp was on his feet quickly, for both man and animal looked familiar. The rider halted his horse in midstream, pointing and laughing. "Tell me that my eyes don't deceive me," he shouted loudly. "Tell me that I'm looking at a fellow named Camp Houston."

Camp complied. "All right," he said. "You're looking at a fellow named Camp Houston." He doffed his hat, and motioned the rider into camp. "Come on over, Runt. The coffee's still hot."

The two men were soon shaking hands and patting each other's back. Camp took the extra cup from his pack and filled it with coffee. "Drink this," he said. "It won't cool you off, but it might taste good."

As the man accepted the coffee and began to sip, Houston continued to talk. "Damn, Runt," he said, shaking his head. "I wouldn't have thought of you for the world. How long has it been since I've seen you? Three years? Four?"

"Be five years this coming winter. Don't reckon I've seen you since you went to work for George Angleton, on the Rocking A." He refilled his cup, then placed the coffeepot back on the dying campfire.

The man had been christened Hiram Fowler shortly after birth, but few men knew him by that name. He had stood six foot six and weighed two hundred fifty pounds on his eighteenth birthday, and had acquired the nickname "Runt" along about that time. He had grown no taller since his late teens, but was probably twenty or thirty pounds heavier nowadays.

And although Fowler possessed all of the necessary capabilities, a brawler he was not. He was simply an oversized, good-natured man who was liked by all who knew him, and though it was obvious that he held a physical advantage over most people, and could quite easily kill a man with his bare hands, he had never been known to lift a finger in anger.

Though he could not move about as quickly as the skinny fellows, especially in hot weather, Fowler was a dependable cowhand, and always knew what needed doing without being told. He had no ambition whatsoever, always content as long as he had enough to eat and a roof over his head. Exactly the type of man most ranch owners liked to have around.

Houston and Fowler had been friends for many years. They had made cattle drives up both the Chisholm and the Western Trails together, and walked the streets of Abilene and Dodge City side by side.

Fowler had thick, brown hair that looked as if it belonged on a brush, and he kept it cut short year-round. His eyes were also brown most of the time. At other times they took on a metallic hue, more like copper. Despite having two rows of

perfect teeth, his face was nevertheless homely, with a potato
nose and large ears that stood out from his head. The young
women he loved to look at always avoided him, and the only
way he could get any attention from them was to pay for it.

Other than a younger brother, who had left for California
several years before, Fowler had no family. He had never
known for sure who his father was. His mother had been a saloon whore who dropped out of sight more than twenty years
earlier, and it was doubtful that she herself knew who had fa-
thered her sons. Newt Fowler, a man who claimed to be their
uncle, had raised the boys on his ranch near Laredo.

The boys had asked few questions about their parents as
they were growing up, for Uncle Newt was always quick to
tell them to get their minds on whatever jobs they had been assigned. Consequently, Runt had been almost grown when one
of his relatives told him that Uncle Newt was not his uncle at
all, that the man was most likely his father.

By that time each of the brothers weighed more than two
hundred pounds, and were no longer afraid of Newt Fowler.
When they cornered him about the extent of their blood relationship, the man insisted that he was their mother's brother,
then refused to discuss the matter further. Neither of the
young men believed what he was being told, and both left
home shortly thereafter.

Both Runt and his brother Milton were good ranch hands,
and quickly found jobs on separate neighboring ranches. They
kept in close contact for a year or so; then Milt came by with
the news that he was headed for California. Twelve years had
passed since then, and Runt had heard nothing from his
brother.

Houston nodded toward the grassy slope. "Stake your
horse out there with mine, Runt. You're not going anywhere
else today."

"Nope. Not after running into you, I ain't." He dropped
his saddle and bedroll beside the willow, then led his horse
away.

Camp laid on another stick of wood and blew on the coals till he had a flame, then headed for the river to get water for a fresh pot of coffee. When he returned, Fowler was busy spreading his bedroll a few feet from the willow. "Never did like to sleep right under a tree," the big man said. "You never know what the hell you'll have on you when you wake up."

Houston nodded, and put the coffeepot on the fire. Then he seated himself and motioned toward the skillet. "Plenty of chili there," he said, a mischievous smile playing around the corners of his mouth. "I've already eaten all I wanted."

Without a word, Fowler set the container on the fire and began to stir the chili with the spoon. A few moments later, he crumbled two biscuits into the skillet and devoured its entire contents before coming up for air.

Camp had watched closely. The laugh he had expected to get at Runt's expense would seem out of place now, for the man was still holding on to the skillet and licking his lips. Houston shook his head and reached for the jar, which was still more than half full. "More chili in here," he said, handing it over. "Eat it all, if you can, so I can wash out the jar."

Fowler emptied the jar into the skillet, heated the chili, and ate it all. Then he walked to the river, where, using one handful of sand after another, he scrubbed both jar and frying pan until there was no trace of grease in either.

Camp sat quietly rethinking his opinion about men and pepper. Maybe some men really did like the taste of red chilies. After all, he had just watched Runt eat almost half a gallon of fire, and the man had never even stopped licking his lips. Camp shook his head again, and forced himself to think about something else.

"Where have you been, Camp?" Fowler asked when he returned to the fire. "And where are you going?"

"I'm looking for some men, Runt." Camp related the story of the murdered drovers, and Fowler listened attentively.

"Hell, I knew Bill Wiggins," he said, "knew him for at least ten years. I heard about him getting killed in a gunfight, but nobody seemed to know what brought on the shooting. Guess you'll be going after that fellow in Waco now, huh?"

"I'll get around to him. At the moment, I'm headed for Corpus Christi." Camp filled both cups with coffee, then continued. "I'll ask you the same question, Runt. Where have you been, and where are you going?"

"Been down in Maverick County to get some money that was owed me. Guess I'll go on up to Mason or Menard County and see what I can find. I hear all the shooting's stopped around Mason, that the so-called Mason County War's over."

"I believe so, Runt, at least for now."

Fowler smoothed out his bedroll, then stretched out. "You still got that land on Calf Creek, Camp? Did you ever do anything with it?"

"Yes and no."

"Yes, you've still got it, and no, you haven't done anything with it?"

"Right."

Fowler raised himself up on an elbow. "A hell of a lot of good it's doing you just lying there. I know that Calf Creek area like the back of my hand, Camp, and it's some of the best ranching property in Texas. You need to build something on it."

"I know, Runt, but every time I get ready to start on it, something else always comes up. I'll eventually get around to it. I intend to build a log house right there on the hill where I showed you, and leave those two big oaks standing in the front yard."

"I remember exactly where it is," Fowler said, sitting upright now. "One of the prettiest places I ever saw."

Darkness had settled in now, and both men were quiet for a long time. Finally, Houston's eyelids grew heavy. He was just dozing off when Fowler's deep voice startled him. "Want me to build that house for you, Camp?"

Houston did not answer right away, for he was busy thinking. He had no doubt that Fowler could handle the job. He remembered a log barn that Runt had built for John Butterworth several years earlier. The barn was not only a solid building, it looked better than the house Butterworth lived in. "Did I hear you right, Runt?" Camp asked finally.

"Sure. I can build the house while you're running around the country. It'll give me somewhere to be, and something to do."

"I'll give it some thought, Runt. One thing I have to figure out is how much I can pay you."

"That ain't no problem," Fowler said quickly. "You don't have to pay me anything till I finish the job, then just pay me whatever you can. I ain't gonna hurt none. I've got enough money to tide me over till next spring. The first thing I'll do is build myself a small shelter close to the homesite, something tight enough to winter in. Then I won't have to be in any hurry on the house, just take my time and do it right. I'll build a barn and some corrals, too."

"Let me think myself to sleep on it, Runt," Camp said after a time. "You'd sure be needing a lot of things that cost money."

"Yeah? Like what?"

"Like a team and a wagon," Camp began. "Like tools, chains, lumber to seal the inside and build the floors, and either tin or shingles to build a damn roof. Not to mention several kegs of nails and a stove to cook your grub on."

"Well, yeah," Fowler mumbled. "Stuff like that, sure."

Once again Camp told his friend that he would think on the idea, that they would discuss it further in the morning. Houston was still thinking on it when he went to sleep two hours later, but he had reached a decision: he would soon be the proud owner of a fine homestead on Calf Creek, and Runt Fowler would be his builder.

They ate a breakfast of smoked ham and biscuits next morning. Then Camp spent the next half hour drawing pictures and directions in the sand with a stick. Fowler studied the drawings intently, nodding all the while. "I know exactly what you want, Camp. You told me the day you showed me the property."

"Sorry, Runt." He slapped Fowler on the back and threw away the stick. "I didn't mean to keep harping on it. I just wanted to be sure you understand the layout I want. If you build something in the wrong place, you're stuck with it."

Camp dug around in his pack for a while, spent a few moments writing, then handed Fowler a bank draft for two hundred dollars. "Take this by the bank in Mason," he said, "and Roy Holder'll give you the cash. Then go on to Menardville and talk to Sid Blankenship, at the livery stable. Tell him I said to let you have a good team and wagon, that I'll settle with him when I see him. Do as much of your trading right there in Menardville as you can, 'cause the community needs the money. Any merchant in town'll bend over backward to help you, and there's not a shyster in the bunch. I suppose about all the teenage boys around there are out of work. Hire one of them when you need some help."

Fowler looked at the draft, nodded and put it in his vest pocket. "Guess by God it's time I was heading for Calf Creek, huh?" He dashed his coffee grounds into the bushes, and headed for his big piebald.

A short time later, the men shook hands and Fowler rode north. Houston stood watching till Runt disappeared from sight, then stepped up into his own saddle and turned the roan's head southeast.

7

★

The town of Corpus Christi was situated on the Gulf of Mexico, and Camp expected the ride to take at least a week. He allowed the roan to choose its own pace. He crossed the Nueces River at noon, halting only long enough to eat some ham and biscuits and feed his animals. Then he continued in a southeasterly direction. He skirted the town of Uvalde just before sunset, and made camp on the west bank of the Frio.

He found good grass for his horses easily enough, and although there was plenty of deadwood lying around, he built no fire. He washed the cold beef and biscuits down with water from his canteen, then spread his bedroll. By the time full darkness came on he had surrendered to his drowsiness and the blood-sucking mosquitoes that would feed on him all night.

He continued to spend most of every day in the saddle, and almost always held his animals to a walking gait. This was certainly not the time of year to be in a hurry, for the weather was very hot, and horses had been known to fall dead from heat stroke with no warning.

He arrived in Corpus Christi at four o'clock in the afternoon, eight days after leaving Brackettville. He had been enjoying the cool breeze from the gulf for the past several miles, and it had dried not only the shirt he wore, but the backs of his horses as well.

As he rode down the street toward the livery stable, he was quickly reminded that he was in a tourist town, for few of the men he encountered were dressed in western garb. Instead, they wore every color of shirt that could be imagined, and some even wore light-colored hats that appeared to be made from leaves. Camp smiled, and rode on.

At the livery, he draped his saddlebags across his shoulder and dismounted. He unsheathed his rifle, then handed the reins to a middle-aged man. He did not introduce himself, nor did he ask the hostler's name. "Need to rest my horses for a couple days," he said. "Traveling in this heat's taking its toll on 'em."

"Yep," the liveryman said, flashing a standard commercial smile. "It's showing on 'em, all right." He handed the roan's reins to a teenaged boy, saying, "You heard the man, Trent. Put 'em in them two new stalls and rub 'em down. Then grain 'em good and give 'em two blocks of hay apiece. Leave the doors open, now, so they can get fresh water out there in the corral."

Knowing that every word spoken by the hostler had been designed not to instruct the kid but to impress the customer, Camp stifled a chuckle. The youngster appeared to be at least sixteen years old, and had no doubt grown up around the stable; hardly the type who would have to be told how to take care of a horse. Nevertheless, the hostler was not quite done yet. He offered Camp the same toothy smile, then shouted down the hall toward the stables. "Rub them horses till they're good and dry, now, Trent!"

Then the liveryman spoke to Camp again: "He'll leave your packsaddle back yonder, but he'll bring all your packs up here." He pointed over his shoulder to a windowless room at the front of the building. "I keep all that kind of stuff in the office, under lock and key."

Houston nodded. "That's nice to know," he said. "I need to get my razor and some clean clothing out of one of those packs, anyway."

A few minutes later, Camp walked up the street toward the nearest hotel, his saddlebags across his shoulder, his rifle and clothing in his hands. The hostler had asked him to pay in advance for the lodging of his horses. The exorbitant fee only served to once again remind him that he was in a tourist town: back in Menard County, the same money he had just paid for a two-night stay would have bought enough oats to feed his horses for a month.

He walked west till he reached the corner of the next block, then stopped at the Lighthouse Hotel. The desk clerk greeted him with the same commercial smile as the hostler, and charged him two prices for the key to an upstairs room. Houston climbed the stairway, found his room and turned the key in the lock.

Standing just inside the doorway, he began to feel a little better about the price he had paid, for the room was spacious and very well appointed, almost elegant. A chest of drawers, two chairs, a large table, and even the bedstead appeared to be made of mahogany, and a full-length mirror was attached to the closet door.

The usual coal-oil lamp and a pitcher of water rested on the table, along with a washcloth, soap and towel. Closer to the closet, and about a foot from the wall, was an oversized washtub that was half full of water.

A sign on the wall informed Houston that, should he so desire, hot bathwater could be had. All he had to do was make that desire known to the management and pay a "small" fee.

Camp smiled, and dunked his hand in the tub, deciding that splashing around in the cool water for a few minutes was exactly what he needed.

An hour later, he stepped out on the street. He had shaved, bathed and changed into clean clothing, and most of the weariness had left his body. He walked about the town for a while, occasionally being jostled by someone attempting to hurry along the crowded street.

He was paying close attention to the number of horses hitched in front of the various buildings. He was searching for a crowded saloon, for according to Joe Plenty, Red Bentley spent a large portion of his time in such places. Besides, Camp was not quite ready for supper. He would have a much stronger appetite after having a drink or two.

He finally chose a place called Mookie's, which sported a sign boasting that drinking, gambling and dancing took place inside. The two hitching rails held as many horses as they could accommodate, as did two rails across the street where businesses had closed for the day.

He pushed his way through the large building's batwing doors, then stepped aside quickly, leaning against the wall. Once his eyes had adjusted to the dim lighting, he immediately recognized the bartender as Casey Holbrook, a man he had known for many years.

Holbrook was a jack-of-all-trades, and every time Camp had ever seen him, the man had been working at a different type of job. A dark-haired six-footer, in his early thirties, Holbrook knew how to do any number of things, and do them well. He had shifted from one profession to another all of his adult life, and moved from place to place anytime he felt the urge, usually with the changing of the seasons.

He had even worked on the Lazy B for a while, where Houston had been his foreman. And although he had been a good cowhand, he had a strong aversion to sixteen-hour days in the saddle, and had quit just before the fall roundup began.

After a while, the bartender's face broke into a broad

smile, and he motioned Houston over. Knowing that he had also been recognized, Camp stepped forward and pushed his right hand across the bar. "Good to see you, Casey," he said, pumping the man's hand. "Whoever said it was a small world sure knew what the hell he was talking about."

Holbrook released the hand, then grabbed Houston's shoulder, giving it a little shake. "I don't think I've ever been so surprised to see a man, Camp." All the while, he had been reaching under the counter with his left hand. "I keep the good stuff under here," he said, chuckling. "Have a seat."

Houston seated himself, and Casey poured him a stiff drink, refusing payment. "Didn't think I'd ever see you again, Camp," he said. "Not unless I went back up around Butterworth's place, and I ain't likely to do that."

Houston sampled the whiskey, then wiped his lips with the heel of his hand. "Well, I don't know, Casey," he said. "Sometimes I think a man's likely to end up most anywhere in the world except where he thought he'd be."

"You just said a mouthful, Camp." Holbrook stood thoughtful for a while, as if trying to make a difficult decision. Finally, he poured a glass half full of whiskey, clinked it against the one held by Houston and proposed a toast: "To old times."

"To old times," Camp repeated, and touched his glass to his lips.

Neither man spoke for a while. When Holbrook finished his drink, he set the glass down noisily. "Excuse me for a minute," he said. He untied his apron and rolled it up, then moved away. He unlatched a small gate at the end of the bar, then headed for a separate room that was probably the office.

Camp sat at the bar alone for what seemed like a long time. He had finished his drink and was thinking about finding another saloon when Holbrook appeared beside him. "I took the rest of the night off," he said. "Let's go somewhere else."

Houston was off the barstool quickly. "Lead the way," he

said. "Are they gonna have something to eat where we're going?"

Holbrook stood quietly for a few seconds, then smiled. "Hadn't thought about you being hungry," he said. "How about the Fisherman's Wharf? They've got the best seafood of any restaurant in Corpus."

Camp pointed toward the front door. "Lead the way," he repeated.

They walked north till they reached the blue waters of the gulf, then turned east. After passing boathouses, bait houses and a few small dwellings, Holbrook pointed out the Fisherman's Wharf, located in a small cove. Most of the building hung out over the water, supported by pilings of heavy timber, and as the name implied, a wharf made of thick planks led to its front door.

They stepped onto the wharf and headed for the restaurant. The sound of their bootheels striking the hardwood boards brought a smile to Camp's face. He began to make a conscious effort to walk more quietly, but was unsuccessful.

A beautiful, dark-haired hostess, who was obviously of Mexican descent, greeted them at the door. A blond-haired waiter, who appeared to be still in his teens, escorted them to a table, then headed elsewhere. Still another waiter, a gray-haired man who was probably past fifty, brought a pitcher of coffee. He filled two cups with the steaming liquid, left each man a copy of the bill of fare, and then he too disappeared.

When yet another waiter appeared, pad and pencil in hand, Houston waved him away. He spoke to Holbrook softly: "I'm not used to this much attention, Casey. I don't need all this shit."

Holbrook laughed aloud. "It's designed to make a man think he's somebody special," he said, "so he won't hit the ceiling when he sees the bill. I don't ever worry about the bills, 'cause I don't have to pay 'em. I treat people here several times a month, and just charge it to the saloon." He patted Camp's hand and laughed again, adding, "So, my good man, just make your wishes known. Even though Mookie Mitchell don't know you, your supper's on him tonight."

Holbrook crooked his finger at the waiter, then spoke to Camp again. "Order anything you want," he said, "but the seafood platter's the best thing in the house: shrimp, clams, flounder, stuffed crab and a big bowl of oyster gumbo on the side."

Houston nodded. "I'll take your word for it," he said. "Order for both of us."

The meal was just as good as Holbrook had promised, and they sat at the table long after the food disappeared. Even as they ate, they had discussed Houston's mission. "Red Bentley ain't a hard man to find," Holbrook said. "You can usually hear him bragging long before you see him. He hangs out in Rockport, about twenty miles up the coast. He bought Kate King out about a year ago, so he's got his own saloon now. He probably stays pretty close to home nowadays. You see, Rockport's a small town, and Bentley likes being a big duck in a little puddle.

"I guess the story is as old as time, and you've certainly known men like Bentley before. The sonofabitch is pissed off at the rest of the world because he himself is such a damn runt. I've heard some pretty knowledgeable men say that he's fast with a six-gun, though, so I guess he is. He killed a man named Dave Hunter last winter, but one man who saw it said that Hunter was so drunk he couldn't find his ass with both hands. I believe every word of that, Camp, because I know Red Bentley."

Holbrook had just snuffed out a cigarette, and was busy rolling another. "By the way," he added, as he licked the paper and gave it a final twist, "Bentley's given name is Calvin, and that's what he likes to be called. I've heard it said that he once threatened to shoot somebody for calling him Red."

Camp leaned closer, for the restaurant was noisy. "Did you say Calvin?"

"Yep. And he gets madder'n hell if anybody mentions his red head."

Houston nodded. He would remember the things he was hearing. "What's the name of Bentley's saloon?" he asked.

"Used to be called Kate King's Korner, and the place is so well known that I can't imagine Bentley changing the name. You can't miss it if you go looking. When you ride into town from the west you'll be on First Street, and the saloon's right there on the left-hand corner."

Camp sat for a while digesting the information, then spoke softly: "Who's the town marshal in Rockport?"

"I don't believe they have one right now. Whittaker resigned several months ago, and I don't think anybody else has shown any interest. The marshaling job don't pay enough for an honest man to live on, and it's dangerous as hell besides.

"Clyde Cash is sheriff of Aransas County, but he don't give a shit what goes on in Rockport, even though it's the county seat. They say that he's afraid of his shadow, and even more afraid of Red Bentley." He held up the empty coffeepot for a few moments to get the waiter's attention, then continued talking. "Clyde Cash ain't gonna give you any shit, no matter what you do to Bentley. And Bentley ain't gonna be a problem for you either. Hell, he's never been up against anybody with know-how. He's made his whole reputation shooting drunks and inexperienced men who scarcely knew one end of a six-shooter from the other. He runs off at the mouth constantly, and I've heard it with my own two ears. He brags about how good he is to anybody who'll listen, and I think that he really believes it. Overconfidence is a dangerous thing, Camp, and if the truth was known, it's probably what gets most of the animals in the woods killed.

"I'd even bet that a rabbit gets a little braver every time he gets away from a small dog. And after he does that a few times, the next thing he'll do is sit around in the tall weeds somewhere and convince himself that he can outrun a damn hound. Then it ain't very long till he don't have any problems of any kind."

Houston chuckled. "You sure have a way of putting things, Casey, but I doubt that anybody's ever gonna mistake your meaning."

"I hope not," Holbrook said, getting to his feet.

At the door, both men flirted with the hostess, then stepped outside. Although the night was as black as pitch, several lighted lanterns hung from posts along the wharf, lighting it all the way to the street. They returned to the saloon by the same route they had come. They continued to talk as they walked, sometimes having to raise their voices in order to be heard above the din of barking dogs.

When they reached Mookie's Saloon, Camp stopped at the front door. "I guess I'll get on back to the hotel, Casey. I don't want to drink any more, and I need a good night's sleep. I'll be heading for Rockport in the morning."

"You gonna come back to Corpus when you get done up there?"

Camp nodded. "Yep, I'll have to. I'm gonna leave my packhorse here at the livery stable, so I'll have one less thing to worry about. I don't expect to be gone long."

Holbrook put a hand on Houston's shoulder and squeezed. "You take care, old buddy, and be sure you don't let that bastard get the drop on you." He stepped inside the saloon, continuing to speak over the top of the batwing doors. "I hope you'll let me know something as soon as you get back."

"Count on it," Camp said, then disappeared down the shadowy street.

The sun was straight overhead when Houston rode into Rockport next day. He saw very quickly that Bentley's ego had overruled his business sense, for he had indeed changed the name of the saloon. According to the sign out front, Kate King's Korner was no more, and the place was now Cal Bentley's Saloon and Recreation Hall.

Camp tied the roan at a hitching rail across the street, then seated himself on a sidewalk bench in front of a hardware store. He leaned his shoulders against the wall and relaxed, for he was in no hurry. He was in town on business, and it would be handled in a businesslike manner.

From where he sat he could see up and down both sides of the street, and had a good view of Bentley's saloon. He had spoken to no one, nor did he intend to until it became necessary. He planned to sit tight for a while, hoping that he might spot his quarry going in or coming out of the saloon.

An hour later, however, he changed his mind, for he was very uncomfortable. The noonday sun shone directly on the bench, and his shirt was already wet with sweat when he got to his feet. He led the roan across the street and tied it at the saloon's hitching rail, then stepped up onto the plank sidewalk.

He leaned against the saloon for a while, trying to decide on some way to flush Bentley out. He had about decided to take the bull by the horns and go in after the man when he heard a clattering sound behind him. He turned to see a middle-aged man who was obviously headed for the saloon, his peg leg striking the planks noisily as he hurried along.

As the man drew abreast, Camp spoke to him softly: "I was wondering if you'd do me a favor, mister. I—"

"Whatcha want done?" the man interrupted.

Camp withdrew a dollar from his pocket. "Well, I need you to carry a message to Calvin Bentley, and I'm willing to pay for it."

The man accepted the money and shoved it into his vest pocket, then raised his eyebrows questioningly, waiting for further instructions.

"Just tell him that I want to see him out here at the hitching rail," Camp said.

The man nodded, and walked through the swinging doors.

He was back in less than two minutes, shaking his head nervously. "He says to tell you that if you want to see him you'll have to come to his office, like everybody else does."

Houston stood quietly for a few moments, thinking. He believed that if he challenged Bentley publicly, the man would come through the front door immediately. And he believed that Bentley would come alone, for his ego would forbid his asking for help, thereby admitting that he was afraid to face another gunman.

Houston moved away from the building, readjusted his gun belt, and spoke to the man again: "Make sure all of Bentley's friends hear you when you give him the second part of the message: Tell him that I stayed out here because I don't want to make a mess in there. Tell him that I'm here to kill him."

The man nodded, and disappeared inside the building.

Camp pushed his hat to the back of his head and stood waiting, his body bent slightly forward and his feet spread apart. When the noise inside the saloon ceased abruptly, he knew that the message had been delivered.

A few moments later, the batwing doors flew open and Bentley, red-faced and thoroughly antagonized, was suddenly on the sidewalk. He looked Houston in the eye, and spoke loudly: "You the one out here shootin' his mouth off? Who in th' hell—"

"The name is Camp Houston," Camp interrupted.

All color suddenly drained from Bentley's face. He had heard the name many times, and was well aware of the reputation associated with it. "Camp . . . Hou—" Just as if he had come down with lockjaw, he stopped talking for a moment. Then he held his left hand out, palm forward, and began to stammer again: "Now, they ain't no use'n . . . ain't no use'n me an' you—"

Houston cut him off again: "I'm here about John Calloway, Bentley. He was a good man, and he was my friend."

"I . . . uh . . . I didn't—"

"You shot him down like a rabid dog, you sonofabitch." Camp shifted his feet again, and pointed to the Colt hanging low on Bentley's hip. "Make your play, fellow! It's the only chance you've got!"

Bentley hesitated for only a moment, then made his play. And even as he took a shot in the mouth he got off one of his own, with the slug knocking splinters off a board between Camp's feet. The man had been fast, all right, quite possibly the fastest gun Camp had ever faced.

Two men stepped to the sidewalk to inspect the body, and several more stood just inside the saloon, staring over the batwing doors.

Houston still held his Colt in his right hand. He untied his horse with his left, and stepped into the saddle. Then he spoke loudly, almost shouting. "Listen up, men, and listen good!" When he had the attention of all, he related the story of the hapless drovers. When they heard that there was a survivor who pointed the finger directly at Red Bentley, and even called him by name, the men began to nod back and forth, talking excitedly among themselves.

Camp turned his horse's head, and continued to speak: "If it turns out that the U.S. marshal wants to pursue this matter, he can find me if he comes looking. My name is Camp Houston." Then, still clutching his Peacemaker, he kicked the roan to a canter. He did not reholster the weapon until he was out of sight.

Houston was back in Corpus Christi an hour before sunset. He dismounted at the livery stable, and handed the lathered roan's reins to the hostler. "Take good care of him. He's had a hard day."

"Always do," the man said, taking the reins. "By the way," he added, loosening the saddle girth, "my name's Hullet." When Houston said nothing, the liveryman continued, "I don't reckon I heard your name."

"The name's Camp Houston."

"Oh," Hullet said. He turned to lead the big horse away, adding, "I was wrong about not hearing it. I've been hearing it for years."

Houston entered Mookie's Saloon a few minutes later, and Holbrook was on duty. He sat on a stool behind the bar doing absolutely nothing, for this was the slack period of the day. Only three drinkers were in the building, all of them seated at the far end of the bar.

Casey was on his feet quickly, reaching for a bottle. Houston took a seat on a barstool, and Holbrook poured a glass half full of whiskey. "You already been to Rockport and back?" he asked.

Camp nodded, and wet his lips with whiskey.

Holbrook smiled, and lowered his voice. "Did you take care of that piece of business?"

Camp nodded again, and took a big swallow from his glass. The whiskey went down easily, for it was a premium brand. Casey had poured the drink from the special bottle, which he had quickly returned to its hiding place under the counter.

"Did that piece of business put up a fight?"

Camp nodded again.

Holbrook leaned forward, both elbows resting on the bar. "By God, you're a talkative cuss tonight, Camp. Don't know when I've had anybody feed me so much information."

Houston chuckled, and took another drink. "There ain't really a whole lot to say, Casey. I called the man, and he accepted the challenge. That's about all there was to it."

Holbrook laughed loudly, but continued to talk softly. "All there was to it? Humph. Must have been a little more than that to it, 'cause here you sit drinking the best whiskey in town. I'd bet a damn dollar that he ain't up there in Rockport doing the same thing."

Camp looked Holbrook in the eye for a moment, then shook his head slowly. "No, Casey. He won't be needing a drink tonight."

They were quiet for a while as Camp finished off his drink. He set the empty glass on the bar noiselessly, then slid off the barstool. "I'm gonna eat supper and call it a night early, Casey," he said, pushing his right hand across the bar for a parting handshake. "It's been a pleasure running into you again, and I appreciate the hospitality. Guess my place on Calf Creek'll be up and running by this time next year. If you're ever out that way, stop by and stay as long as you like."

Holbrook squeezed the hand, pumping it a few times. "I know the place," he said. "I don't expect to be out there, 'cause life's treating me pretty good here on the coast. Of course, like you said last night, a man never knows which road he might be taking in the future. I'll remember the invitation."

Next morning at nine o'clock, Houston rode out of town. And although his destination was otherwise, he would first have to ride west for several miles. Then, as soon as he had left the big water behind, he would turn the roan's head due north. The trip ahead would be a long one, for he had decided to pay a visit to Jack Little, in Corsicana. He expected to be in the saddle for twelve or fourteen days, for the distance was more than four hundred miles.

Houston had eaten breakfast in the hotel restaurant. Then the cook, after having filled Camp's jars with precooked beans, wrapped up a dozen biscuits and a cake of leftover corn bread. As Camp began his journey, everything he was likely to need was on the packsaddle, including two fifty-pound sacks of grain for the horses.

He traveled steadily all day, and, an hour before sunset, forded Medio Creek. He halted on the north bank, and, after feeding each of his animals a portion of oats, picketed them on long ropes. Finding deadwood was no problem, and he soon had a fire going. Half an hour later, he was eating warmed-over beans and corn bread, washing it down with sugared coffee.

Darkness did not actually come this night, for when the sun disappeared over the western horizon, it was replaced by a full moon. Lying on his bedroll, Camp could even see his horses grazing in the small meadow more than fifty yards away.

He had not even unrolled a blanket, for it was simply too hot for covering. He had taken off his boots, but did not undress, for his clothing offered a certain amount of protection against the mosquitoes. As he lay slapping at his neck, he decided that he would make camp a hundred yards from water tomorrow night, hoping that fewer of the pests would find him.

Sleep was slow to come, for Camp had many things on his mind: Runt Fowler should be settled in on Calf Creek by now, he was thinking. The man had had enough time to build livable quarters for himself, and would probably be starting on Houston's log house anytime now.

That the house would be something he could be proud of, Camp had no doubt, for Runt Fowler was not to be taken lightly. He was not only an honest man but a master builder, and would never take on a project unless he was confident of the outcome. Houston smiled at his thoughts. He was thinking that he might have the pleasure of selecting furnishings for his new home by Christmastime.

And once he had his own home and a herd established on Calf Creek, he would travel to Little Rock to visit his father. And this time, Camp really meant to do it. He had thought about making the trip many times in the past, but always decided that he would do it next year. Next year had always turned into next year, however, and now more than ten years had passed.

Camp would have been hard pressed to explain why he had written only two letters to John Houston, and both of those during the first year after leaving home. It had certainly not been due to ill feelings, or that Camp did not love and respect his father. The elder Houston had always treated his son well, and the two had parted on good terms.

John Houston had even given his son a thousand dollars on the day of his departure, no doubt suspecting that the young man might have difficulty making it on his own.

Camp had indeed made it on his own, however, and even after ten years, the thousand-dollar stake was lying in the bank in Mason gathering interest. Of course, he would soon be using both the interest and the principal to furnish his home and stock his ranch. Then he would travel to Little

Rock. Maybe his father would even return with him to Texas, and spend some time on Calf Creek.

He was still tossing and turning an hour later, his mind now on the business at hand. He knew that Waco was closer to his present position than was Corsicana, but he had a burning desire to face Jack Little as soon as possible. Though all of the killers were equally guilty, Little's betrayal of John Calloway rankled Camp more than the actions of all the others combined.

The others had been hired simply because they happened to be available when Calloway needed men. Little, however, had probably been hired because he was a friend, with the fact that he was a good cowhand being secondary. At any rate, he had been the first man hired. According to Joe Plenty, John Calloway had hunted the man up with a job offer several weeks before the drive began.

Camp had to grit his teeth each time he thought about Jack Little. Calloway had given the man work on three separate occasions, and had obviously paid him well. They had worked, eaten and slept together for months on end, and even shared a hotel room in Dodge City.

The very thought that Little had turned traitor and pumped lead into his longtime friend for no reason other than money stuck in Camp's craw like glue. He spat toward the bushes, as if ridding his mouth of a bad taste, then turned over again. A few minutes later, he finally went to sleep.

He reached the town of Giddings five days later, and put his animals up at the livery stable. Then he rented a hotel room, for he intended to rest himself and his horses for a while. For three days now Camp had been traveling only in the early morning and late afternoon, but the hot weather had nevertheless taken its toll on both man and animals.

"No use in the world in a man having to travel in this kind of heat," the hostler had said, when Camp turned over his horses. "Friend of mine dropped dead from a heat stroke a year ago this month, just fell out of his saddle right out there in the middle of the street. After I saw I couldn't do him no good, I caught up his horse, but two hours later, the horse was dead, too."

Camp nodded, and said nothing. With his saddlebags over his shoulder and his Henry cradled in the crook of his arm, he soon stood in the lobby of the town's only hotel, located half a block from the livery stable. A bald-headed man with a white goatee sat behind the counter. "If ya want a room, ya better git it now," he said, pointing up the stairway with his thumb. "Ain't got but one left. Th' price is a dollar a night."

"I'll take it," Camp said. He produced the money as the clerk handed him a key. Houston reached for the hotel register and signed "W.C. Fanning," a surname that he had recently read on the label of a pickle jar.

Inside the room, he pushed his rifle under the bed, then washed his face and hands. He had deliberately left his razor and his clean clothing in his pack at the livery stable. He did not intend to shave his face in the near future, and changing clothing in this kind of weather was unlikely to make a man smell better for more than a few minutes. Even as he splashed water on his face, Camp could feel beads of sweat rolling down his back.

He raised both of the windows and tied back the curtains, hoping to create a crosscurrent of air that would eventually cool the room. Then he locked the door and headed for the stairway. He knew that he was unlikely to find a place that was cool enough to be comfortable, but believed that a cold beer would make the heat seem more bearable. A moment later, he stepped out onto the street.

Now Camp sat in a small saloon, three doors down from the hotel. The table he had chosen was at the front of the building, near a double window, and he had a good view of the sidewalk, the street beyond and the passersby who used both. He was in the act of pouring his third glass of beer from the pitcher he had bought when the skinny bartender, who had no other customers at the moment, approached his table. "Would your name happen to be Camp Houston?" he asked, his green eyes darting around the room nervously.

Houston shook his head. "The name is W.C. Fanning," he said. "Been traveling north for about a week now, but I decided to stop in your town and try to cool off some. I was concerned that the heat might kill my horses, and it certainly wasn't getting any easier on me."

The bartender continued to stand beside the table, absentmindedly twisting the corner of his apron. "They're saying this heat wave is gonna be over by the end of the week," he said, making no attempt to explain exactly who "they" were. He pulled out a chair and took a seat at a nearby table. "Have you ever seen Camp Houston?" he asked.

Camp did not offer a direct answer to the question. He took the last sip of beer from his glass, then wiped the foam from his lips with the heel of his hand. "I've been told before that I look like Camp Houston," he said, pouring more beer from the pitcher.

The bartender began to drum his fingers on the table. "Whoever told you that was sure telling the truth, 'cause it's a fact." He leaned forward, appearing to study Camp's face more closely. "I saw Camp Houston up in Waco a few years back," he continued, "just a few minutes after he shot Dick Manville. Now, I didn't see him up real close, mind you, 'cause the sheriff and several other men were standing around talking to him. Houston did look my way a few times, though, and judging from what I saw that day, I'd call you a dead ringer."

Camp sipped at his beer again. "A dead ringer, huh?"

"You sure look more like him than anybody I've ever seen. Truth of the matter is, there ain't many folks around who are as big as Camp Houston—just a few men like you, and maybe Jack Little."

Jack Little! The name hit Houston like a sledge. His hand

froze in midair for a moment, then set the glass on the table noiselessly. "Who's Jack Little?" he asked, in the most nonchalant tone he could muster.

The answer came quickly: "Little owns that feed store at the edge of town. Not only that, but it's my understanding that he's doing a land-office business with his freight wagons. He's got several of 'em, and most of the time they're on the road day and night. Reckon he must have some kind of franchise deal with the H&TC Railroad, 'cause his wagons are the only ones allowed to pick up freight at the depot. I mean, just about every train that comes through here drops off something on that platform. Then about once a week they sidetrack a boxcar. Jack Little's wagons haul the freight on to wherever it's supposed to end up.

"Little moved to Giddings sometime last fall. Don't think he ever told anybody where he came from, but he must have brought some money with him, 'cause he went into business right away. He's done right well, too. He's got a lot of people working for him, but he don't seem to be afraid of getting his own hands dirty. Even now, he usually drives one of the wagons himself; makes more money that way, I guess."

"I guess," Camp repeated. He asked no more questions concerning Jack Little, for he had learned as much as he needed to know.

Nevertheless, the bartender continued to talk. "They say that the best way in the world for a man to get his ass whipped is to go sassing Jack Little. I don't know all that for sure, now, but I've certainly seen the scars on his knuckles. I've also been told that Little is the main reason every gunslinger in Texas gives this town a wide berth. He's mighty fast, according to all the talk going around."

Camp continued to sit quietly, and placed his hands in his lap so that the scars on his own knuckles could not be seen. A short while later, the bartender, no doubt tired of talking to an unresponsive listener, got to his feet and returned to his stool behind the bar.

Houston was on his feet quickly, headed for the front door. "Gonna hunt up something to eat," he said to the bartender. "The beer made me hungry."

Established on the H&TC Railroad when track was laid from Brenham to Austin in 1871, the town of Giddings was chiefly settled by Wendish immigrants who moved to the railroad from the original community, six miles to the south. Because of its proximity to the railroad, and the fact that it was surrounded by prime farming and ranching country, the small town prospered right from the start, and was soon named the seat of Lee County.

Now, after walking up one side of the street and down the other, Camp stood leaning against a building, admiring the scenery. Evidence that the town had been put together by master German builders, who were obsessed with practicality, could be seen in any direction: a six-horse team and wagon could be turned around in the middle of the street, and every building in town looked as if it belonged exactly where it had been erected, and nowhere else.

Even from where he stood, Camp could see Jack Little's feed store, but he would go no closer. Neither would he approach the railroad depot, which was also within eyeshot. Since the bartender had said that Little often drove one of his freight wagons himself, Houston would bide his time. He felt that if he did not rush things, he would eventually be able to face his man in open country, well away from the town limits of Giddings.

Camp was even hungrier now that he had walked around for a while. He chose a small place that he had walked past earlier, which had painted-over windows and signs advertising hot food. Standing in front of the restaurant, he took a last look up and down both sides of the street, then entered.

He selected a table at the rear of the building, where he could sit with his back to the wall. He had no idea how successful he had been in his effort to convince the bartender that his name was W.C. Fanning, but he was taking no chances.

The skinny man had talked as if he were at least an admirer of Jack Little, and getting word to him that there was a man in town who bore a strong resemblance to Camp Houston would be a simple matter.

He sat for a while reading the bill of fare, then laid it down and got to his feet. At that very moment, a dark-haired waitress arrived at his table. She smiled, and spoke softly: "I'm sorry to have kept you waiting, sir. May I bring you something to eat?"

He nodded. "Bring me some German sausage and sauerkraut to this table," he said. "I've got a short errand to run, but I'll be back by the time you are."

He walked through the front door and headed down the street with long, quick strides. When he reached the saloon, he pushed his way through the doors and stepped inside. The drinkers who had been present earlier were gone now, and the bartender was alone in the building.

Houston leaned over the bar and spoke to the skinny man: "Do I still look like Camp Houston to you?"

"Well, now," the bartender began nervously, "you sorta . . . you kinda—"

"You were right the first time," Camp interrupted, "but so far, you and I are the only two people in this town who know it. I'm asking you to keep this information under your hat."

"Oh, you can count on me doing that," the man said, his lower lip quivering slightly. "You can sure count on me."

Camp nodded, turned to leave, then stopped in his tracks. Deciding that he had not been firm enough with the man, he returned to the bar. "Look," he began. "Lots of people have promised me things in the past that didn't necessarily turn out that way. I'm gonna take your word that you'll keep quiet about this, but if you don't, I think you should know that I'll be back. If you tell one single person that I'm in this town, you're gonna answer to me." He stared into the man's eyes for a while, then added, "And it won't be pleasant."

"No, sir, Mr. Houston," the barkeep said shakily. "Not a word to anybody."

Camp was soon back in the restaurant, arriving at his table just as his food was being served. He smiled at the waitress and pulled out a chair, his eyes sizing up the platter of steaming food. "Looks good," he said.

"Bread pudding with raisins for dessert," she said gushingly. "I believe the cook's taking it out of the oven just about now." Before he could speak again, she was gone to the kitchen. She returned with his pudding a few minutes later, and Camp never saw her again.

The sun was disappearing in the west when he left the restaurant. He stood on the corner for a few moments, looking up the street to the depot. No boxcar stood on the sidetrack, nor was there any freight on the platform. According to the bartender, that situation might very well change with the arrival of the next train, however. If the picture did change, Camp would certainly know about it, for he almost had a bird's-eye view of both the sidetrack and the platform from the window of his hotel room.

He bought a newspaper at the drugstore, then decided to get off the street, for he wanted to be seen by as few people as possible. He headed for his hotel room and the coal-oil lamp, for darkness was coming on fast. Tonight would not be the first time he had used the *Fort Worth Democrat* to read himself to sleep.

He was soon lying on his bed enjoying the cool of the evening. The windows he had opened earlier in the day had created a draft, and the temperature in the room was now pleasant enough. So pleasant, in fact, that he went to sleep with the lamp burning. He was still reading the front page when his eyes closed and the newspaper fell to the floor.

A loud, clanging noise woke him, and he immediately recognized the sound. He shielded his eyes from the lamplight with one hand, and reached for his pants with the other. He looked at his watch, and was not surprised to learn that it was three o'clock in the morning. He had slept for more than seven hours.

He sat on his bed for a few moments listening to the sound that had awakened him: a train was at the depot, pulling forward, then backing up, jerking and clanging the boxcars against each other. Knowing that a freight car was being uncoupled on the sidetrack, Camp slipped on his pants, then blew out the lamp.

As the clanging noise continued, he walked to the window and stood looking toward the depot. By the light of the flickering lanterns they carried, he could make out the forms of several men walking up and down the track. Through the open window he could very clearly hear them shouting back and forth, and even understood some of their words.

Feeling his way around the dark room till he found a chair, he pulled it over to the window and sat watching. He knew that he would be able to see better in just a short while, for daylight came early in the summertime. A number of the townspeople had already touched fire to the wicks of their lamps, for now Camp could see lighted windows where darkened buildings had stood only moments before. He had obviously not been the only one awakened by the train.

He was still sitting by the window when the black of night turned to gray, and he began to make out a certain amount of movement on the street. He saw no mounted men, however, just a few people moving hurriedly from one building to another. Then, as dawn chased away the last remnants of darkness, he pulled the flimsy curtain between himself and the window and continued his vigil.

Just as the first rays of sunshine hit the street, Camp heard the sound he had been waiting for. Even as he sat listening, two wagons rolled into view from the east. The heavy freighters, with their oversized wheels, were coupled together and pulled by six large mules. The vehicles rolled right under

Camp's window, and he could easily see the double-barreled shotgun behind the seat of the lead wagon.

He also got a look at the driver. Though the hat pulled low over his eyes hid much of his face, the man was the right size, with the same stooped shoulders that Camp had been told about. And though a teamster wearing a sidearm was a rarity, the man driving the mules under the window wore a Peacemaker on his right hip.

Camp had seen enough, and had no doubt that the man on the wagon was his quarry. He seated himself on the bed and slipped on his boots, for he had been sitting at the window barefoot. Then he gathered up his things and was out of the room quickly. A few minutes later, he was at the livery stable.

"I need to use the roan for a while," he said to the hostler. "I'll just leave the packhorse here for the time being."

The liveryman nodded, took a coiled rope from a peg on the wall and headed toward the corral. When he returned a few minutes later, he was leading the roan. He handed the reins to Houston. "Want me to saddle him for you?"

"No," Camp said. He saddled the animal, shoved his Henry in the boot, then mounted. With his saddlebags still lying across his shoulder, he rode through the doorway and up the wide street. There was a small restaurant on the corner, just before the street reached the railroad. He tied the roan at the hitching rail, then stepped inside.

Seating himself at a table by the window, where he could easily see the freight car on the sidetrack, he ordered breakfast from a middle-aged woman. While he was waiting for his order, he took the picture of the drovers from his saddlebag and slipped it into the pocket of his vest. Then he sat sipping the coffee the lady had brought, his eyes on the action at the depot.

The sliding doors on each side of the boxcar were open now, and several men were moving about. And though it appeared that at least one of the freighters was on each side of the car, the dual hookup that had passed under Camp's window was on the near side. After being driven as close as was practical to the boxcar, the sideboards on one side of each wagon had been removed, and the grunting men were now busy sliding heavy crates down a wooden ramp and onto the lead wagon. The mules would no doubt be driven a few steps forward when it was loaded, then the process would be repeated with the second vehicle.

Camp had finished eating his steak and eggs and was drinking his third cup of coffee when he saw the workers put the sideboards back on the wagons. Then the big man climbed to the seat and turned the mules around, heading them right back through town. Houston held his seat as the wagons passed. This time his view was much better, and there was no doubt about it: the man on the driver's seat was none other than Jack Little.

Camp left the restaurant and stood beside the hitching rail for a while, then mounted and headed east, riding down the street very slowly. He halted at the edge of town and sat watching, waiting to see which way the wagons headed. At the fork in the road, two hundred yards east of town, Little took a left-hand turn in the direction of Caldwell, in Burleson County. Camp waited till the wagons had disappeared around the bend, then he guided his horse onto the dusty road.

Though he did not intend to let Jack Little reach the town of Caldwell, Camp would have been more than happy to hold off on a showdown till after the man crossed the county line. The Burleson County sheriff, a man named Henry Pugh, had been a friend of Camp's for many years. In fact, on Houston's very first cattle drive, when he had helped push two thousand steers up the Chisholm Trail to Abilene, Pugh had been the trail boss. The two men had gotten along very well, and though they seldom saw each other nowadays, the friendship was still intact.

Although he had no way of knowing if Henry Pugh had personally known John Calloway, Camp thought it was highly possible, since both men had for many years been in the same line of work. However, even if Pugh had not known Calloway, Houston believed that the sheriff would empathize with the pitiful plight of a fellow drover. Camp shook his head. No, sir, he was not the least bit concerned about leaving Jack Little's remains in Sheriff Henry Pugh's county.

Camp continued his pursuit from a distance of several hundred yards, always making sure that he could not be seen. Then, after he had followed the wagon across Yegua Creek and moved into Burleson County, he turned off the road and kicked the roan to a canter.

He made a wide half circle to the southeast, then north. When he returned to the Caldwell road, he was a few minutes ahead of the wagon. Afraid that his horse might whinny and give away his presence, he dismounted and tied the animal a hundred yards from the road. Then, remembering that Little had been sitting on the left end of the wagon seat, Camp crossed to the north side of the road.

He took up a position at the base of a small hill, behind a clump of tall bushes. His wait was not a long one. No more than ten minutes passed before he began to hear the rattling of chains and the sound of the oversized wheels crushing the dry, hard earth. Then the mules were upon him, trotting down the hill to stay ahead of the wagons that literally pushed them along, in spite of the fact that Little was busy yanking on the brake.

Then, just as the animals leaned into the harness to begin the hard pull up the incline, Houston stepped into the road. He raised his left hand high into the air, signaling the driver to stop. His right hand held a Colt .45 that was pointed at the man's head. The mules halted in their tracks. "Tie up the reins and get down, Little!" Camp said loudly, motioning with his gun barrel to emphasize his words. "You've got some business with me!"

Little sat with his mouth half open as his face literally changed colors. Even his right eye—the one with the permanent squint—was wide open now. "I . . . I think I know who you are," he said through quivering lips, "and I sure ain't got no squabble with you."

"Get down!" Houston ordered, even louder now.

Little complied. He wrapped the reins around the brake, then jumped to the ground, facing his antagonist.

Camp did not keep him waiting. "John Calloway was a friend of mine, Little. I suppose that should tell you why I'm here." He stood quietly for a few moments, then added, "I'd also like to have a talk with your old buddies Walt Turner and Sam Lott. Now, where would I be likely to find them?"

As Camp had expected, the man did not answer the question. Little continued to fidget nervously, then began to stammer, "Well, I don't guess I . . . what I mean is . . . I've got money now. Why, I can give you—"

"I'm sure that you do have money now," Camp interrupted, "but I wouldn't be interested." He slowly holstered his Peacemaker, spread his legs apart and leaned his body slightly forward. "I'm here to collect more than money, fellow. Go for your gun, you no-good bastard!"

Little shook his head. "I . . . I know exactly who you are now," he said. "You're Camp Houston, that's who you are, and I ain't about to draw against you." Then, as if to make sure there was no misunderstanding, he clasped his hands together behind his back.

Houston continued to stare into Little's eyes, surprised at the man's actions. "You pretended to be John Calloway's friend for years," he said, "then by God you shot him in the back for nothing more than the money he was carrying. I'm giving you the chance that you never gave him, Little: I'm gonna count to three, then I'm gonna start shooting."

Little continued to stand with his hands behind his back even as the count began. True to his word, when Camp reached the count of three, he drew his Colt and put two slugs in Little's chest. Only then did the man unclasp his hands. He grunted loudly, then fell on his face at the side of the road.

When Houston was convinced that Jack Little had taken his last breath, he moved the wagons off the road, then unhitched and unharnessed the mules and turned them loose. Then he walked to his saddler, mounted, and took a shortcut to the Giddings livery stable to pick up his packhorse.

9

Five days later, Camp crossed the Brazos River on the long, swinging bridge that separated Waco east from west. He knew the town well, for his very first job after coming to Texas had been on the Flying W, a nearby ranch owned by a man named Albert Wells.

He turned south after crossing the bridge. Riding down the street toward the livery stable, he scanned along the sidewalk for a familiar face, but saw none. He even had to look around him occasionally to pinpoint his exact location, for though all of the prominent landmarks remained the same, Waco had changed much in recent years.

The fact that the Chisholm Trail ran right through town had brought prosperity to most of Waco's merchants. Many had put new faces on their establishments, while others had erected new buildings altogether. The majority of the merchants who had rebuilt had relocated, giving the street an entirely different look from the one Camp remembered.

The Bryan Hotel still looked the same, however, as did the Texas Saloon. He rode past both buildings on his way to the livery stable, which was located at the end of the street. At the stable, a teenaged boy relieved him of his horses, promising to treat them as if they were his own.

After renting a room at the hotel, Houston walked to the adjacent barbershop, where he bought a shave and a bath. Then, after changing into clean clothing, he was on his way to the Texas Saloon, for he remembered that the establishment used to serve what was widely referred to as the best Mexican food in Texas.

In bygone years the Texas had employed Mexican cooks in its kitchen, and their south-of-the-border concoctions had been one of the saloon's main drawing cards. Knowing that good businessmen were reluctant to change a winning combination, in this case good food, good whiskey and pretty women, Camp thought it highly unlikely that owner Al Foster had allowed the quality of the food to deteriorate.

A few minutes later, he pushed through the saloon's batwing doors and headed for the dining room, which was nothing more than a roped-off area adjoining the kitchen on one side and the dance floor on the other. A smiling, flirting, dark-haired waitress was there quickly. She first served him a cup of steaming coffee, then took his order for an enchilada dinner.

"Your food will be at least half an hour in coming, sir," she said, moving his silverware around while deliberately leaning across the table to offer him a good look at her ample bosom. "If you need more coffee in the meantime, just lift your empty cup and wave it around a little." She laughed, then was gone to the kitchen.

He sat looking around the large room while waiting for his food. There had been few changes over the years, and Camp well remembered his visits to the saloon when he was a young greenhorn. It was on one of those visits that he had experienced his first intimate contact with a woman, with the encounter taking place in a fifty-cent bedroom at the top of yonder stairway.

He had spent many a Saturday night dancing on that hardwood floor, and had probably eaten off the same table at which he was now sitting. And there was the same fifty-foot bar, with stations for three bartenders. On weekends there was a man at each of the stations, for the Texas was by far the busiest saloon in McLennan County.

An hour later, after having enjoyed his dinner, Camp walked to the bar and seated himself on a stool. "I'll have whiskey and water," he said to the tall, skinny bartender, who appeared to be in an unsound state of health. His complexion was a sickly-looking sallow and the skin on his face hung loosely, suggesting that he had once been a much heavier man. His short, coal-black hair grew almost down to his eyebrows, not unlike some of the animals Houston had once seen in a zoo.

Limping noticeably as he moved about, the man set two glasses on the bar, one of them half full of water. Then he reached into a cabinet under the counter for a bottle of whiskey, setting it on the bar noisily. "I usually let a man pour his own, if he ain't too drunk," he said. "That way, nobody ever accuses me of slighting 'em."

Camp nodded, and poured himself a drink of what, according to the label, was an acceptable brand of whiskey. He smiled at the thought, however, for he knew that labels meant very little in most saloons: a saloon owner or a bartender could simply take a bottle bearing a respectable label and fill it with rotgut. Then it would take its place on the shelf beside the good stuff, and any man ordering a drink from that particular bottle would be charged a premium price.

Bartenders seldom poured from such bottles if a man was ordering his first drink of the day. Once he had consumed several drinks, however, the man who could tell the difference between rotgut and premium whiskey was rare. And even if a bartender did get a complaint, he could always shrug, turn his palms upward and play dumb. The trick was to pour the fraudulent bottles a little less than full, so the customer would expect the seal to be broken.

Camp took a sip from his glass, and quickly decided that the whiskey was genuine. He had expected no less, for even though Al Foster was a high-stakes gambler, he had the reputation of being a square shooter. And during all of the years he had known the man, Houston had never heard anybody say otherwise.

The bartender stood quietly for a few moments, then poured himself a drink. He inhaled the whiskey in one quick gulp, then dropped the empty glass into a pan of water. He continued to eye Houston for a while, then spoke: "Didn't you used to work out at the Flying W?"

Camp nodded. "Worked out there for several months in '68," he said. "Been living farther west since then."

"Well, I thought I'd seen you before. Then I remembered that you used to come into my place with the Flying W hands. You probably don't recognize me, but I owned the Longhorn Saloon back then. A man cut a tree down on my right leg three years ago, and I lost the business while I was laid up. Lost everything I owned, in fact."

"I'm sorry to hear that," Camp said. He continued to look the bartender over, glancing elsewhere occasionally to keep from staring. Then the man's identity hit him, and he spoke quickly: "Are you Flint Hastings?"

The man wiped at a wet spot on the bar and began to nod, smiling broadly. "One and the same, my boy. I didn't expect you to know me; hell, I've lost a hundred pounds since you saw me. I stayed in bed for nearly a year. Then when I did get up I wasn't worth a damn. No, sir, you ain't the only one that don't recognize me nowadays. I can't even recognize myself. My poor little wife's been having to shave my face every morning for the past two years. I quit using mirrors a long time ago. Got tired of looking at a damn corpse."

Not wishing to dwell on the bartender's health problems,

Camp poured himself another drink, then changed the subject. "How's Albert Wells doing these days, Flint?"

Hastings chuckled softly. "Albert Wells is doing the same thing he's always done, getting richer by the day." He poured himself another drink, then continued, "I know I don't have to tell you what a good layout that ranch is. Wells bought several sections that bordered him on the west, and the Flying W reaches all the way to the Bosque River now. He's got thousands of longhorns, perennial grasses, and he'll never have to worry about water again. I know for a fact that he's sent three herds north to the rails this year, and I hear that the Kansas buyers paid his asking price for all of 'em. I'm talking about the first two herds, of course, 'cause the third one ain't got there yet. It just left here ten days ago."

Houston sipped at his drink. "I sure don't envy those drovers," he said. "This is the hottest time of the year, and half of the grass is already dead. I wonder why Albert waited so late to send up this last herd."

"I don't think he planned it that way. From what I hear, Wells wasn't gonna send this bunch up till next spring, but one of the buyers got real anxious, wanted two thousand head of longhorns right now. Fellow told me that the buyer offered Wells a bonus big enough to cover the entire expense of getting the herd up there, including the salaries of the drovers. Now, you and I both know that Albert Wells ain't gonna pass up a deal like that."

Camp shook his head. "Can't think of anybody who would." He emptied his glass, then refilled it. "Don't guess there's a soul left out at the Flying W that I'd know," he said. "After all, it's been ten years since I was there."

"Not much chance," Hastings said. "It's a whole new bunch out there now, all of 'em what you and I would call youngsters. Even the foreman's a loudmouthed, blond-haired kid with a squeaky voice. Ain't got a bit of hair on his face, and he sounds like he might not have none on his balls."

Camp was suddenly very interested. "What's the foreman's name?" he asked.

"You wouldn't know him. Kid named Sam Lott. Grew up right here in Waco."

Houston sat quietly for a while. He sipped at his drink nonchalantly, showing no sign that he had heard the young foreman's name before. "Like I was saying," he began, raising his voice for emphasis, "I sure don't envy those drovers. During these first few weeks it's gonna be the hottest drive any of 'em ever made, then they'll probably freeze their asses off coming home. I've been on those Kansas plains in the fall of the year, and that wind can make a man wish he'd never seen a damn longhorn. It's liable to blow hard and cold for weeks, twenty-four hours a day, then dump a foot or two of snow on you before you can find a hole to crawl into."

"Know what you mean," Hastings said. "I've done some traveling myself, and I've certainly felt that November wind whipping across the wide-open plains. The drovers are gonna feel it too, 'cause there ain't no way in hell that they can get back here before Thanksgiving Day."

Camp nodded, and finished off his drink. "Thanksgiving Day sounds about right to me," he said. Houston had heard enough. He had no business in this town at the present, and knew that he would be heading for Calf Creek at sunup. Then, come the last week of November, he would be visiting Waco again. He slid off the stool, paid for his drinks and waved good-bye to the bartender.

As Camp reached the front door, Hastings called after him: "You never did say what your name was!"

"The name is Bo Granger," Houston said over his shoulder. He stepped onto the sidewalk and headed for his hotel room. He would get a good night's sleep, then head for Menardville.

10

★

The ride to Calf Creek took six days, and Camp arrived at midafternoon. He topped the hill above his homesite and sat his saddle for several minutes. He could hear the sound of hammers, but saw no workmen. Nevertheless, he was pleasantly amazed at the scene below: the outer walls of his home, built of foot-thick logs, appeared to have been completed.

Sporting a shiny tin roof, the building had been placed exactly where Camp suggested, with the two large oaks in the front yard, and the spring only a few steps from the back door. A pole corral with a shed and tack room at one end had been constructed farther down the hill. And even from where he was sitting, Camp could see that a ditch had been dug to reroute the spring's runoff through the corral, so the horses could water themselves.

A rock chimney had been built on the north side of the house, and a joint of stovepipe that was no doubt connected to the kitchen stove protruded from the roof closer to the middle of the building. A stack of what appeared to be planed lumber had been placed on the south side, and even as Camp watched, a man he had never seen before approached the stack and sighted down the edge of a board to determine its quality. He repeated the process with several of the boards, then, apparently satisfied that they were straight enough, put them all on his shoulder and disappeared around the corner of the house.

Camp knew that he was listening to the sound of more than one hammer, and that the action was taking place on the opposite side of the house. He guided the roan down the hill and stopped in the front yard. Runt Fowler and two young men were in the process of flooring a porch that ran the length of the building. Since Camp had approached from the south, and all three of the workers were on their knees facing north, none of them saw him ride into the yard. Nor did they hear him, for they were making too much noise with their hammers. He sat watching for a while, more than a little pleased with what he was seeing.

When Fowler finally turned around to get another handful of nails, he spotted Houston. "Well, I'll be damned!" he said loudly, getting to his feet. "I've been thinking about you just about all day, Camp. I sure didn't expect you back this soon, though."

"Neither did I," Camp said, dismounting. He tied the roan to a post. "I ran into a little problem, and thought I might as well do my waiting at home. I'll be going out again in the fall." He walked backward for several yards to get a better look at the place, then smiled and shook his head as he returned to the doorsteps. "It looks mighty good, Runt, but I sure didn't expect you to be this far along with it."

Fowler smiled broadly. "I've had a lot more help than what you see," he said. He pointed to his helpers, who appeared to be in their late teens. "These are the Wooten brothers, Willie and Randy, and they've been with me right from the start. I guess you know Cornell Wooten, don't you?"

"Sure do. Good man."

Fowler pointed to the boys again. "Well, these two are Cornell's sons. Cornell himself helped us for the first three weeks, him and his oldest son, too. They both had to leave on account of an earlier commitment, but they damn sure knew what they were doing." He made a sweep with his arm to indicate the entire layout. "It don't take five good men forever to get something done."

"I believe you, Runt." Camp stepped onto the finished portion of the porch, and shook hands with each of the young men.

"I've sure heard a lot about you, Mr. Houston," the boy named Randy said. "Been hearing about you since I was little."

Camp gave the youngster a serious look. "You probably shouldn't believe everything you hear," he said.

"Most times I don't," the boy said. "But it ain't all just something I heard. I read a whole lot of it in the newspaper."

Camp bit his lip. "Well, they don't always get their stories straight either," he said. He placed his hand on the boy's shoulder and looked him squarely in the eye. "No matter what you hear or what you read, Randy, don't try to be like me." He stepped off the porch and untied his horses, then led them to the corral.

He unburdened the animals and loosed them into the corral, then stowed his saddle, the packsaddle and the grain bag in the tack room. He spent a few minutes in the shed inspecting the oversized wagon, which appeared to be almost new, then walked to the corral to look over the draft horses, for which he no doubt owed Sid Blankenship a bundle. Solid blacks with blaze faces, the two animals stood in the opposite corner of the corral, as if separating themselves from the saddle horses by choice. After seeing that Camp did not have a rope in his hand, they moved in his direction and stood staring.

Camp stood at the gate for several minutes, taking in the size of the horses. Runt had certainly chosen a team that was big enough to get the job done. Any job. Their feet were as large as dishpans, and Camp decided that each of the animals would weigh at least fourteen hundred pounds. And they would, of course, eat accordingly, he was thinking as he headed for the house.

"We started spreading our bedrolls in the house last week," Fowler said as Camp took a seat on the edge of the porch. "Soon as we got the roof on, we moved in."

Houston nodded. "Like I said before, Runt, I'm surprised and pleased. I'll be spreading my own bedroll inside the house about sundown." He sat looking down the hill for a few moments, then continued, "I like this homesite even better now that I see something on it. You did everything just the way I envisioned it, Runt, and I won't be forgetting it."

Fowler chuckled softly. "I hope not," he said. "Hell, I expect you to be a rich man one of these days."

Camp changed the subject. "I noticed the stovepipe, so I guess you've already got a cookstove in the house."

Fowler nodded. "Sure do. Got it from old lady Sommerville up in Brady." He smiled broadly. "She sold it to me too cheap, but she set her own price and I sure as hell wasn't gonna argue with her. She said she'd let me have it for two dollars 'cause it used to be a bunkhouse stove, and it was real old. Hell, Camp, an old stove is just as good as a new one, if it ain't got no cracks in it. I looked it over, then me and Randy put 'er in the wagon right quick. It had been in the barn for a long time and had a little rust on it, but I got that off real easy. It even has a hot water tank, and the oven works perfect. I baked corn bread in it just last night."

Camp smiled. "Maybe I should let you do all of my shopping, Runt." He got to his feet and stepped inside the building. Fowler walked beside him, talking all the while. "That's three bedrooms back there," he said, pointing to the east side of the house. "We ain't floored 'em yet, 'cause we didn't think there was any hurry. We'll do that tomorrow, 'cause I expect you'll be wanting to put a bed in at least one of 'em."

Camp nodded, and continued to inspect the building.

Planed, tongue-and-groove lumber had been used to floor the living room, and the boards fitted together so tightly that the floor appeared to have been made from a single piece of wood. And the story was the same in the kitchen. Back in the living room, Houston ran his hands over both the inside and the outside of the fireplace. He took a long look up the chimney, then spoke: "You've done a good job on everything, Runt. Have you checked this chimney to make sure it'll draw?"

Fowler shook his head. "I haven't built a fire in it, but it'll draw all right. Hell, I built it just like I built a dozen others, so it can't do anything but draw."

Camp smiled. "I'm inclined to take your word for it, Runt." They returned to the front of the house and took a seat on the doorstep. "I guess you wrote down how much money I owe," Camp said, "and who I owe it to."

"I didn't write anything down," Fowler said, "didn't have anything to write. I only did business with two men, and both of them said they'd settle with you later. I bought the team and wagon from Blankenship, and all of the tools and building material from Spike Nettleton's hardware store. He said he'd give you a discount on everything, but even at that, I'll bet the price of that damn tin is gonna be outta sight."

"I expected no less," Camp said. "But it won't leak, and it'll last a mighty long time. A whole bunch of men who ought to know what they're talking about have told me that a tin roof is the best way to go nowadays."

"I would agree with that," Fowler said. He fished around in his pocket for a moment, then offered Camp a small roll of bills. "Since you're home now, I guess you ought to be keeping track of your own money. Roy Holder cashed the check you gave me, and I spent a little of it for food. Most of what I spent, though, went for wages. Cornell and his boys didn't charge me but a dollar a day apiece, so I've still got nearly a hundred dollars here."

Camp shook his head. "Keep the money, Runt," he said. "You've still got a lot of building to do, and you need those boys to help you. Besides, I'm gonna be mighty busy for the next few weeks, and I won't be spending much time around here. I will take the wagon to town with me tomorrow, though. I'll be bringing back a load of stuff for the house, so make a list of the things you need." He got to his feet and stepped into the yard, adding, "Just go ahead and put a floor and a ceiling in that southeast bedroom. I'll probably be gone for several days, but I'll have a bed with me when I get back."

As the workmen resumed their hammering, Camp walked past the corral and down the hill to the east bank of Calf Creek. He stopped at a fallen log and sat thinking, his chin in his hands and his elbows on his knees. He remembered that he had been sitting on this same log with a fishing pole in his hand the day he decided to discuss buying the property with John Butterworth.

The rancher had not only been willing to sell, but had even seemed eager, and made Camp an offer that he could not resist. Camp would pay the final seventy-five-dollar payment within the next week or two, then he would own the three-square-mile area free and clear. The property was all located in McCulloch County, but bordered both Mason and Menard Counties on the south.

Butterworth also owned three sections of land directly across the county line, and had offered to sell it to Camp on the same easy-payment plan. Now, Camp smiled and nodded at the thought, for within the past few minutes, he had decided to take the rancher up on his offer. Then he would own six square miles in three counties, all of it prime grazing land.

The sun was dropping over the western horizon when Houston left the creek. He walked up the hill slowly, stopping at the tack room to get his bedroll. When he reached the house, all three of the workmen were sitting on the porch eating from clay bowls. "Some pretty good soup in there,

Camp," Fowler said. "I just put a little of everything I had in the pot, then baked some corn bread to go with it."

Camp nodded, and headed for the kitchen. Moments later, he rejoined the men on the porch, a bowl of soup in one hand and a steaming cup of coffee in the other. He took a seat on the top doorstep. "I'll try to find a decent buy on a table and some chairs while I'm in town," he said to no one in particular.

"You can buy some chairs if you want to," Fowler said around a mouthful of food, "but I don't think you oughta rush into buying a table. The way I've got it figured, we're gonna have enough of that tongue-and-groove lumber left over to build one. A damn sight better table than you could buy, too."

Camp chuckled, and mimicked a British accent: "Very well, sir, I shall heed your words." He got to his feet and dashed his coffee grounds into the yard. "I'm still gonna look around some while I'm in Menardville. Even if the wagon's loaded, I can tie a few chairs on it somewhere." He walked across the porch and paused at the door. "I don't know about you fellows, but this day's over for me. I'm gonna spread my bedroll in there by the fireplace." Five minutes later, he was sleeping soundly.

At sunup, he ate a breakfast of smoked ham, flapjacks and maple syrup, then headed for the corral. He harnessed and hitched up the team, then took the wagon road to Mason, a journey that would take most of the day. As he drove around the bend, he could hear that the hammering had already started again. The sound was like music to his ears.

Less than an hour of daylight remained when he arrived in Mason. He parked the wagon outside the livery stable and turned the team over to the hostler, a man named Hamm Harrison. Although probably past sixty years of age, Harrison was apparently in good health, and had been the town's liveryman for many years. He was well known and respected throughout the county.

"Ain't seen you in a coon's age, Camp," he said, accepting

the team's reins. "I think I remember hearing somebody say you went hunting. Any luck?"

"Not much," Houston said, with a tone of finality meant to discourage further questions. He held the hostler in high regard, but the old man was a talker, and Camp did not intend to furnish him with the details of his manhunt. He pointed to the corral, and changed the subject. "Didn't I just see Will McDavid's chestnut out there?" he asked.

"Yep. Will wants me to try to sell the animal for him. From the way he talked, I'd say he needs the money pretty bad."

Camp headed for the corral and stood leaning on the top pole. Tossing its head about friskily, the chestnut walked directly toward Houston till it was halfway across the corral. Then, just as if making its own attempt to attract a prospective buyer, the beautiful animal stopped in its tracks and made a quarter turn, offering a broadside picture. Houston spoke to the hostler, who had followed him to the corral: "Best-looking quarter horse I've seen in a long time," he said.

Harrison nodded. "About as good as they get, I reckon. I doubt that Will really wants to get shed of the horse, but like I said, I believe he needs the money."

Camp, who was something close to an expert on horse-flesh, crawled between the poles and walked into the corral for a closer look. The animal stood its ground and made no attempt to evade Houston's probing hands as he began his head-to-hoof inspection.

As a man who had grown up around fine horses, Camp had long been aware of the peculiarities possessed by outstanding quarter horses: the head is neat, but distinctly shorter than that of the Thoroughbred, and the muzzle is small. The knees must be big, broad and flat. Like the other joints, they should be hard, with no sign of puffiness. The belly is longer than the back, and should contribute to the chunky impression and the compact symmetry of the outline.

The cannons are short. The hocks are set low to the

ground and have a high degree of flexion. The horses normally stand sixty to sixty-three inches in height, and their heavy, muscular quarters, which give them a chunky appearance overall, are characteristic of the breed.

After running his hands over the gentle animal and inspecting every single detail, Camp decided that he might very well be looking at the best of the best. Indeed, the chestnut seemed to have it all. Camp Houston not only knew how an outstanding quarter horse should look, but knew the history of the breed.

He knew that the quarter horse was the oldest all-American breed. First bred in Virginia in the seventeenth century, they were used for many purposes, including work on the farm, rounding up cattle, hauling goods and lumber, drawing carriages and riding. They were also frugal horses, demanding less food than most breeds. Versatile though they were, the most prized characteristic of these early horses was their ability to sprint over short distances from an explosive standing start.

The sports-loving English settlers raced their horses over quarter-mile stretches laid out most anywhere they had room, usually within easy walking distance of towns or villages. For this reason the new breed became know as the "quarter horse" or "quarter-miler."

The power and muscular conformation of the quarter horse were ideally suited to this type of racing. By the year 1656, quarter horse racing was well established in Virginia, and the breed was widely recognized as the supreme short-distance racer.

Later, when the Thoroughbred was introduced to the United States, oval tracks were constructed and the sport of long-distance racing began to thrive. As a result, the popularity of the quarter-mile sprints quickly declined, and within a short time these races were abandoned altogether in the eastern states.

The quarter horse then shifted to the West, where it quickly adapted to the job of herding cattle. It moved at such high speed that it was said to be able to "turn on a dime from an all-out gallop, and toss you back nine cents change." Indeed, the breed early on exhibited a high degree of "cow sense," and within a few years every rancher in the West was firmly convinced that its speed, balance and agility, as well as an uncanny instinct for the job, made the quarter horse the best cow pony in the world.

Houston took one last look at the chestnut's teeth, and decided that the animal was six years old. He spoke to the hostler again: "Did Will put a price on this horse, Hamm?"

"Yep. Said he wants a hundred and forty dollars. I told him I didn't believe he was gonna get that much."

"Neither do I," Camp said. He gave the horse a pat on the rump, then walked to to the wagon and retrieved his rifle. "I'll be staying in town overnight, Hamm. Got some business to take care of in the morning."

"Well, I'll be around here all day tomorrow, so you can get your team anytime you take a notion." He turned to lead the team down the hallway, then stopped. "I couldn't help but notice how close you looked that quarter horse over," he said, smiling broadly. "You want to make an offer on him, just in case Will decides to take a little less than he's asking?"

Camp stood thinking for a while. "I'd pay ninety dollars for the horse real quick," he said finally. "Might pay a hundred after I rode him." He turned to leave, continuing to speak over his shoulder: "Just tell Will that I don't mean to insult him, but if he wants to let the animal go for a hundred dollars, I'll be at my place on Calf Creek."

"I'll tell him," Harrison said, chuckling loudly at something that Houston did not understand. "Probably be several days before I see him, though."

Camp nodded, then headed up the street, his rifle cradled in the crook of his left arm. He ate a supper of stuffed pork chops at a small restaurant, then rented a room at the town's only hotel. A few minutes later, he locked the door, blew out the lamp and crawled into bed. He was asleep quickly.

He was back on the street at sunup, and walked to the edge of town, where he had breakfast at Ma Franklin's boardinghouse. He had eaten in the establishment many times before, and knew that the food was some of the best the area had to offer. The lady had a vested interest and did her own cooking; therefore, the food was consistently of the highest quality. Although well past the age of sixty, she was spry and apparently in good health, and ran the business year-round with the help of only one hired hand, a middle-aged Mexican woman.

One of the few three-story buildings in the area, the house had been built in the late 1840s by James and Edward Franklin as a place to raise their families. And though they collectively produced five children, both men had died at a relatively young age. Edward had been killed by Indians, and James had been kicked in the head by a mule.

The Franklin brothers' offspring, all of them boys, had now scattered to the four winds, leaving Edith, widow of James, sole owner of the property. Now referred to as "Ma" by everyone in the community, the lady had several years earlier turned the huge residence into a boardinghouse, and business had been good right from the start.

As Houston walked down the hall and into the dining room, he could see that the lady was already busy clearing dishes from the long table. "Am I too late for breakfast?" he asked.

"Nope." She smiled, and pointed to a chair at the end of the table. "Good to see you, Camp. Take a seat right there."

"I could have been here a long time ago," he said, "but I had no idea that you served breakfast so early."

"I have to feed my boarders at daybreak," she said. She placed a steaming cup of coffee before him, jokingly adding, "Some men have to work for a living, you know."

He faked a dejected look. "I suppose that means you think I don't work, huh?"

She did not answer the question. "I've got ham and sausage cooked already," she said, beginning to walk toward the kitchen. "I can fry eggs and heat up some biscuits pretty quick."

He continued to sip at the coffee while he waited. A look at his watch told him that it was a quarter past seven, and he decided that he was right on time. As soon as he ate breakfast, he would head for the livery stable and hitch up his team. By then it would be close to half past eight, at which time the bank would open.

An hour later, he tied the team at the bank's hitching rail. Being a few minutes early, he stepped onto the sidewalk and took a seat on the narrow wooden bench that the bank provided for its customers. He was still sitting there when Roy Holder, the bank's vice president, walked down the street and put a key in the lock. "Good morning, Mr. Houston," he said as he pushed the front door inward. "Been waiting long?"

"Just a few minutes," Camp said, getting to his feet. "I need to withdraw some money, then I've got some more business I'd like to talk over with you."

The frail, middle-aged man's smile seemed almost as wide as his shoulders. "Well, you've certainly come to the right place," he said, "and I'll help you any way I can. Please step inside."

Later in the morning, Houston drove the team west toward Menardville, knowing that it would be well past dark when he arrived there. He had had a long talk with Roy Holder, and the banker had readily agreed to advance him the money to stock his property with longhorns. "I wouldn't feel very comfortable financing more than two hundred fifty head, however," Holder had stated plainly. "Not if you only have three sections of land."

Houston had expected to hear those very words. "I understand," he said. "But I expect to own six sections by this time next week."

"Very well," Holder said quickly. "In that case, I see no reason not to go with five hundred head."

Camp was on his feet now, offering a parting handshake. "I guess that about covers it, then. I'll get back with you after I make a deal with John Butterworth." A few minutes later, he drove the team out of town. He traveled continuously till midafternoon, with the wagon jostling over the rough road so badly that it eventually gave him a slight backache. When he halted for an hour at Big Rock Spring, it was more to rest his back than to let his animals blow.

He sat on a rock beside the spring, thinking of the well-stocked ranch that he would soon own. In fact, he had thought of little else throughout the day. He had little doubt that he could deal with Butterworth, for at one time the man had even tried to talk him into taking the three sections off his hands.

All of which was easily understandable, for Butterworth's Lazy B Ranch was in Mills County, with all of San Saba County and more than half of McCulloch County separating it from the three sections in question. Indeed, the rancher had never intended to actually use the property. He had simply taken advantage of a bargain, and bought the land as an investment.

Camp's ranch would be mortgaged to the hilt, of course, as would every cow that fed on its perennial grasses. And even though he intended to make the last payment on his original three sections within the next few days, the deal could still fall through unless he could convince John Butterworth to hand over a clear deed to the additional property, with nothing more than Camp's promise to pay for it. And a clear deed was a must, for expecting Holder's bank to stock the six sections without holding a first mortgage on every head of cattle and every acre of land was out of the question.

An hour later, Camp climbed back to the wagon seat and returned to the rough, rocky road. He had business to attend to in Menardville, part of which was paying Sid Blankenship for the team and wagon. He whipped the horses to a fast trot, hoping to arrive there before the liveryman's bedtime.

II

Ten days later, Houston was at the Lazy B Ranch, in Mills County. It was midafternoon when he rode the roan through the gate, past the big red barn that Runt Fowler had built, and into the ranch house yard. He sat his saddle quietly for a while, looking toward the bunkhouse. When he detected no sign of life there, he rode to the porch and helloed the house.

Seconds later, Nellie Butterworth opened the door and stepped onto the porch. Though past the age of sixty, she was nevertheless a striking woman. Standing almost six feet tall, she was probably just as slender now as she had been when she married John Butterworth, forty-two years ago. With copper-colored eyes that sometimes appeared to be too big for her face, she had been a brunette in her youth. Now, only a trace of that color could be seen atop her milky-white head.

She stood just outside the front door for a few moments, shading her eyes from the sun with her hand. She smiled, then hurried down the steps and into the yard. "Campbell Houston!" she said excitedly. "Of all the people I didn't expect to see today, I guess you'd be at the top of the list. What in the world brings you to Mills County?"

He threw his right leg over the horse's neck and slid to the ground, taking the lady's small hands in his own. "You mean to tell me that you don't know?" he asked, releasing her hands. Not waiting for an answer, he led the roan to the hitching rail just outside the yard, then climbed the steps to the porch, accepting the cane-bottom, ladder-back chair the lady offered. "I still owe you and your old man some money," he said, seating himself. "Remember?"

She smiled again and shook her head. "I can honestly say that I didn't, Camp. Not till you mentioned it. I don't concern myself with things like that anymore, and I don't believe John spends much time thinking about money. Not the way he used to, back when he had to keep track of every penny."

Camp nodded. "I'm truly glad that John doesn't have to worry nowadays," he said, "and this place couldn't have happened to a better man. I've ridden over every mile of it, and I know that it's one of the finest ranches in the state. I also know that he started it with nothing but a keen mind and a lot of determination. I think he told me himself that he was broke when he first came to Texas."

"Well, not exactly broke," she said, laughing aloud. "We had forty-two dollars. Forty-two dollars, two skinny horses and a wagon, a turning plow and a fifteen-year-old milch cow. But just as soon as John saw this place, he said to dig in, and that's what we both did: dug in." She folded her hands in her lap and sat quietly for a while, then added, "Life has been mighty good to us, and I can't think of another thing that we need. We've raised two fine daughters who both married well, and I reckon the good Lord must have taken a liking to my dear husband right from the start. John didn't have the slightest idea what he was doing when he first started out, no more'n I did, but he's made more right decisions over the past forty years than any man on Earth is entitled to. Every move he's made has turned out well, and he gives thanks to the Almighty every day. You see, John knows just as well as I do that he didn't make all those good decisions alone."

Camp sat quietly for a while, digesting her words of wisdom. He held both the lady and her husband in high regard, and knew that John Butterworth possessed the same degree of humility as did his wife. "You're a smart woman, Nellie," he said finally, "and you married a very smart man. When I get my own place up and running, I'd be happy to accept any advice I can get from either of you."

"Oh, I'm sure John'll help you any way he can," she said, getting to her feet. "He decided several years ago that he liked you, and he talks about you often. He liked it when you were his foreman, and he hated it when you quit. I've heard him say so plenty of times." She stood in the doorway for a moment, then added, "He left for San Saba early this morning to take care of some business and pick up a few things for the cook. He took the buggy and a fast-stepping mare, so he should be back anytime now." She pointed toward the corral. "You just take care of your horse, then come on back. I've got some cool cider in the cellar."

He nodded, and stepped into the yard. At the barn, he unsaddled the roan and led him down the hallway. Camp shook his head and smiled as the big animal jerked on the reins and headed straight for the last stable on the right, the same one that had been home to him during the time his master had been employed at the Lazy B. No doubt about it, the horse knew exactly where he was. He began to neigh immediately, and did not stop till Camp poured a bucketful of oats in the trough.

A short while later, Houston stood leaning against a corral post, reminiscing and looking things over. Other than the fact that a new corral had been built and the bunkhouse painted, the place looked the same as when it had been home to him. He had spent some happy times on these premises, and no man had ever treated him better than had John Butterworth. Camp had been paid well, and his only reason for leaving was that he intended to start a ranch of his own somewhere. When he explained that to Butterworth, the man was eager to help, and offered him a once-in-a-lifetime deal on the property in McCulloch County.

Camp was still standing at the corral when he saw Butterworth's buggy come around the bend. After passing under the Lazy B's welcome sign, the rancher stopped the buggy and jumped to the ground, swinging the gate open wide. Then, of her own accord, the mare pulled the vehicle through the opening and forward just far enough to allow the gate to be closed. Then she halted again, and waited patiently till her master had reclaimed his seat.

Always quick to appreciate a good horse, Camp smiled as he watched. The mare had probably done the same thing a hundred times before, he was thinking. She had been trained to do exactly what she did, and she would never forget.

As the buggy closed the distance, Houston headed for the cookshack, for he expected that to be the rancher's first stop.

Butterworth began to talk before the vehicle even came to a halt. "Think of the devil, and there he is!" he said loudly. He dropped to the ground, beaming. "I've been thinking about you off and on for most of the day, Camp. Don't ask me why, 'cause I don't know." He pumped Houston's arm and patted his shoulder. "Things been going all right?"

"At least as well as I could expect." Camp tied the mare's reins to the hitching rail. "I can tell at a glance that you're doing all right, John. I believe you look healthier right now than you did the first time I ever saw you. Have you got some kind of secret that I ought to know?"

"Nope, don't reckon there's any secret to it. What I do, anybody can do. You see, I always take some time out to talk to the Lord, and it sure ain't time lost. Now, I don't take up His time asking Him for a whole lot of stuff for myself. He already knows what I need and don't need. I don't recall ever asking Him for anything more than good health for Nellie and me, but He sure must've heard my prayers, 'cause neither of us has ever been sick with anything worse than a bad cold."

Though John Butterworth stood less than six feet tall, he was nevertheless a large man, with long arms, thick chest and broad shoulders. Today he had his shirtsleeves rolled up against the hot weather, and even though he was well into his sixties, his bulging biceps and muscular forearms were conspicuously noticeable.

Looking at the rancher nowadays it was easy to see how he had attracted such a beautiful woman as Nellie when he was younger, for even now, he was a handsome man. He had dark, intelligent eyes, and his complexion was the color of well-tanned leather. And though its color had turned to salt and pepper, he still possessed most of his hair. He had a disarming smile, which he used now. "If you'll help me unload this buggy, we'll put up this mare and go to the house. I've got something good to drink in the cellar."

Camp nodded, and picked up a fifty-pound can of lard. "Nellie already offered me some cider."

"Humph!" the rancher said, hefting a bushel bag of dried beans to his shoulder. "I had something a little different in mind."

When they had transferred the supplies from the buggy to the cookshack, the rancher made the introductions between Camp and the cook, a man named Hubie Biddle. When Biddle appeared to be bored by the entire proceedings, mumbling and staring over Houston's shoulder while offering a limp handshake, Camp's reaction was quick. "Pardon me all to hell, fellow!" he said loudly. He jerked his hand away. "I just decided that I'm about as interested in this damned meeting as you seem to be." He headed for the yard, and did not look back.

Butterworth was there immediately. "I hope you won't feel too hard at Hubie, Camp. That's just his way."

"Well, I don't care much for his way."

The rancher laughed. "I can see that," he said, "and I'd even make a bet that Hubie knows it now. Let's stable this mare, then go get us a bottle of wine."

Nellie met them at the porch, carrying a tray containing a pile of cookies and two glasses of cider. "These cookies'll hold the two of you over till supper," she said, "and the cider ought to cool you off some."

The rancher winked at Camp, and accepted the tray. He patted his wife's hand. "Why, thank you, my dear," he said softly. "This is mighty thoughtful of you, and I'm sure the cider is just what we need."

No sooner had Nellie returned to her household duties than Butterworth slid off the corner of the porch and headed for the cellar, a deep excavation beneath the house that could be entered from the outside as well as the inside of the living quarters. Houston heard the rusty hinges squeak each time the rancher opened and closed the cellar door.

A few moments later, Butterworth rounded the corner and handed him a gallon jug. "I believe this is a little older than that cider," he said. He wrapped his hands around the corner post and pulled himself to the porch. Smiling from ear to ear, he dashed the cider into the yard and reclaimed his seat. Then he removed the cork from the jug and poured both glasses full of dark red wine, handing the first one to Houston. "I think you're gonna like this a little better," he said.

As both men sat sipping, Butterworth proceeded to extol the so-called benefits of wine consumption. "Drinking wine is probably one of the healthiest things a fellow can do," he began. "I even heard a doctor say one time that a man would live a lot longer if he drank some good wine every day." He held his glass up in front of his eyes, squinting at its contents. "And this is good wine, Camp, about as good as wine ever gets." He closed one eye and peered into the glass again. "At least it ought to be—it's been down there in the cellar for about two years, maybe three."

Camp tilted his glass again, then wiped his mouth with the

heel of his hand. "I don't know that I've ever tasted better, John. Did you make it yourself?"

"No, no. A Bohemian family up in the northern part of the county makes it. I just did a little trading with them; wound up with twenty gallons."

Camp nodded, then chuckled. "Well, I suppose that ought to be enough wine to keep you healthy for a long time," he said.

They spent the remainder of the afternoon on the porch, sipping and talking. When the ranch hands rode in and paraded to the bunkhouse, Camp saw no one that he knew, and with his introduction to Hubie Biddle still fresh in his mind, he made no effort to meet any of them.

He spent an enjoyable night with the Butterworths, and when he left the Lazy B Ranch next morning, he was a happy man. After eating a supper fit for royalty, he had paid the rancher the final installment on the three sections of land north of the county line, and expressed his desire to own the three additional sections to the south. His only problem, he told Butterworth, who was listening attentively, was that he needed a clear deed to all six sections, so he could mortgage the property to the bank. Otherwise, obtaining financing for the five hundred head of breeding stock that he had in mind was out of the question.

Butterworth slid his chair away from the table noisily. "Roy Holder?" he asked loudly. "That sorry sonofabitch?" He turned to Nellie and begged her forgiveness for using such language, then continued, "I know that no-good bastard well, Camp. So does every other man in this country who's been around for a while, and we all know him for the horse's ass that he is. The sonofabitch'll cheat you out of your underwear even while you're looking at him." He walked to the washstand and drank water from a gourd dipper. "The next time you see Roy Holder," he continued, "you tell him to kiss your ass." He dropped the dipper back into the bucket and returned to the table. "You just go on to bed and get yourself a good night's sleep while I think on it. I'm sure I can figure you out a better deal than you're ever gonna get from Roy Holder."

Butterworth had announced his decision at the breakfast table this morning, offering Camp another once-in-a-lifetime deal: "I'm gonna give you a clear deed to the whole six sections, Camp, but I can't bring myself to stand by and watch you mortgage it all to Holder's bank. I've figured out a way to stock the place that I think will be beneficial to you and me both. You see, I've got more breeders than I actually need. In fact, my north range is in danger of becoming overstocked unless I get some of that old stuff off of it within the next few months."

He dumped several spoonfuls of jelly onto his plate, then sat thoughtfully while he buttered himself a biscuit. "What we'll do is drive five hundred head of my older cows down to your place. Then at roundup time, you can touch every third calf with my iron, and put your own brand on the rest. Won't be too long till you have a herd of young stuff of your own, and you'll be indebted to no man. As for the property in Mason and Menard Counties, just pay for it any way you can, at the same price you paid before." He took a sip of his coffee, then laughed. "I guess the best part of the deal, as far as you're concerned, is this: if I happen to die before you get the money to pay me, you won't have to pay anybody, 'cause you'll already have a clear deed." He smiled, and patted his wife's arm. "Of course, you could give the money to Nellie here, and I'm sure she wouldn't go putting a time limit on you."

The lady shook her head, and said nothing.

Camp had been staring into his plate. He pushed his chair away from the table and got to his feet. "I don't think I know the right words to tell you how much I appreciate this, John," he said, attempting to swallow the lump that had suddenly appeared in his throat. "But I will tell you that I'll hold up my end of the bargain, and you can rest assured that I'll pay Nellie for the land in case you're not around."

Continuing to stand beside the table, he thanked the lady for her hospitality, then shook the rancher's hand. "I'll be getting on back to Calf Creek now," he said. "I've got a lot of things that need doing before we move the cows down there."

As Camp saddled the roan at the corral, Butterworth stood by talking. "You don't have to break your back getting that place ready, Camp; you've got plenty of time. We'll wait till after the first of the year to move the cows, maybe late March or early April. The next time I'm in San Saba I'll have my lawyer spell out our arrangement on paper. I'll get your copy down to you before long."

Camp tightened the cinch another notch, then climbed into the saddle. "Like I said before, John, I appreciate what you're doing, and I won't be forgetting it."

Butterworth shook his head. "Don't give it another thought," he said, waving his hand back and forth as if to dismiss Camp's words of gratitude. "You just go on and take care of yourself." He took a few steps toward the house, then stopped and turned halfway around, adding, "Don't go hiring up no bunch of men to make the drive, now. When the time comes, my riders will deliver five hundred cows to you. Five hundred cows and twenty bulls." Then he headed for the house, and never looked back.

Heading the roan in a southwesterly direction, Houston kicked the animal to a canter, a gait that he would hold for most of the day. He would travel steadily till he reached his new home, for he was completely unprepared for a night on the trail.

12

★

It was close to midnight when he rode into his own yard. He helloed the house loudly, and Fowler answered quickly. "Just wanted you to know that it was me moving around out here," Camp said. "Go back to sleep." He rode to the shed and sat his saddle for a few moments, staring into the corral. Though the moon was only in its first quarter, and provided no more than a faint glow of light, it was enough for Camp to recognize the chestnut quarter horse that he had seen in the corral at Hamm Harrison's livery stable.

Once he had unsaddled and fed the roan, he spoke to the chestnut. The horse answered with a soft nicker, then walked to the middle of the corral and snorted loudly. Standing just outside the enclosure, Houston leaned against a fence post.

Pleased with what he was seeing, he came to a quick conclusion: Harrison had no doubt passed Camp's bid of a hundred dollars on to Will McDavid, who had accepted the offer and delivered the horse himself. Camp knew of no other explanation for the animal being in his corral. McDavid would hardly be making a social call, for he and Houston had never been more than casual acquaintances. Camp smiled, and headed for the house. He would put the chestnut under a saddle in the morning and find out if he had gotten his money's worth—if the animal was actually worth the one hundred dollars that he now owed to Will McDavid.

At the house, he moved around in the dark quietly till he found his bed, then stretched out. Although he was very tired, sleep did not come right away. He lay for a long time thinking about the deal he had made for the cattle, and how his former employer had bent over backward to help him establish a herd of his own.

And it should take no more than two years for him to get that herd. Some of Butterworth's cows would no doubt already have calves following them when they arrived next spring, and most of the others would be pregnant, for they all ran with the bulls year-round. Two calf crops was all Camp would need to stock his place, then he would return the old cows to Butterworth. The rancher could either make room for them on the Lazy B or send them to the rails in Kansas.

Then Houston's thoughts returned to his newly acquired quarter horse. Tomorrow he would put the animal through its paces. He had no doubt that the chestnut would be fast, maybe even faster than a Thoroughbred, for the first few hundred yards. Of course, a quarter horse could not be expected to stay with a Thoroughbred over a great distance. The swift sprinters were bred for short races, while the Thoroughbreds were both bred and trained for the long haul.

Quarter horses were even excluded from the Kentucky Derby, a Thoroughbred race that had been organized in Louisville in 1875. The race had been run on the first Saturday in May for the past four years, and Camp had read somewhere that this year's winner was a horse named Day Star. In fact, he had read several pieces of published literature concerning the Derby. Most stated that the decision to make the race exclusive to Thoroughbreds had been reached early on. No other breed could be expected to hold up under such a hard run, for the fathers of the Derby had set the distance of the race at one and one-half miles.*

Camp fluffed up his pillow and turned over in bed. He was thinking of the Kentucky Derby and what a grueling test of endurance the race must be. He doubted that he himself had ever owned a horse that could run all-out for a mile and a half. Nor would he ever attempt to push an animal that far at top speed. Not unless it was a matter of life and death.

He tossed and turned for a while longer, then managed to clear his mind. When he finally dozed off, he slept soundly.

The sun was two hours high when he rolled out of bed next morning. Sensing that he was alone in the house, he headed for the kitchen, where he filled a tin cup from a coffeepot that had been pushed to the back of the stove. When he stepped out on the porch, he could see Fowler moving around down at the shed. Camp took a seat on the doorstep and began to sip his coffee.

Fowler spotted Houston quickly enough, and came lumbering up the slope. "I thought about checking to see if you were still alive," he said, "but then I decided that you probably rode all the way from the Lazy B without any rest."

"You decided right," Camp said, taking a sip from his cup, then dashing the remaining coffee grounds into the yard.

Fowler took a seat on the doorstep beside Camp, then pointed down the hill. "I've been up since daybreak," he said. "Took that horse for a three-mile run right after sunup." He nodded toward the corral. "Guess you saw my new horse last night, huh?"

Camp sat thinking for a moment, and did not answer the question.

*Distance changed to a mile and a quarter in 1896.

"Quarter horse," Runt continued, "and he can take you for the ride of your life. Yessir, fellow gets on him, he damn sure better hang on to his hat."

Houston nodded, and continued to listen.

"I bought the horse from Will McDavid yesterday morning," Runt was saying. "Will actually came up here looking for you, but of course you weren't home. Then when I noticed that quarter horse he was leading, I made up my mind right away that I was gonna have that animal, and damn the price. Will just started hemming and hawing around when I first let him know that I was interested, but I wound up getting the horse anyway." Then Fowler filled Camp in on the story:

He had been stacking firewood on the corner of the porch and just happened to be looking down the hill when he noticed a large black dog trotting around the bend. The animal was soon followed by a man riding a tall, gray Appaloosa and leading a muscular chestnut whose weight Runt guessed to be somewhere around a thousand pounds.

As man and animals continued up the hill, Fowler eventually recognized the rider as Will McDavid, and walked into the yard to meet him. "Get down and rest yourself, Will," he said, taking hold of the Appaloosa's bridle. "I can stir up the fire and put on the coffeepot in short order."

McDavid shook his head. "I don't have time," he said, and did not dismount. "I just rode up to see Camp. Is he around?"

"Nope. He's up at the Lazy B Ranch, in Mills County."

McDavid nodded. "I know where it is. John Butterworth's been a friend of mine for years." He drew in and exhaled a deep breath, then turned the Appaloosa's head in the direction from whence he had come. "No telling when he'll be back, so I guess I'll be getting on home. I just rode up 'cause Hamm Harrison said that Camp told him—"

"How come you're leading such a good-looking quarter horse around?" Runt interrupted. "You want to sell him?"

"Well, that's what—"

"How much you want for him?" Fowler interrupted again.

"Well, I was asking a hundred forty dollars, but—"

"Hundred forty?" Runt asked loudly. "Hundred forty dollars? You've got it, mister. Just turn him into the corral down there, then write me a bill of sale. I've got the money on me." McDavid did as he had been told, and rode off the hill a few minutes later with Fowler's money in his pocket.

Houston continued to sit on the doorstep. "Did Will ever say why he wanted to see me?"

"Nope. I asked him if he wanted to leave a message for you, and he said no, said it wasn't necessary."

Camp nodded, and headed for the kitchen to refill his cup. He smiled as he poured the coffee, and made himself a promise that he would never reveal the whole story behind Fowler's quarter horse deal. Runt would never know that Will McDavid had actually ridden to Calf Creek to deliver the animal to Camp for a hundred dollars.

Fowler was obviously pleased with his purchase, and Camp could certainly find no fault with McDavid for accepting more money than he had expected to get. Houston shrugged, and shoveled a spoonful of sugar into his coffee. Things usually happened for the best, he was thinking. He didn't really need another horse anyway, for his current saddler was still relatively young. And though not a good cow pony, the roan was an exceptional animal for traveling, always eager to hit the road.

And the packhorse that Sid Blankenship had lent him was still in the corral. Camp had mentioned it the day he paid the liveryman for the team and wagon, and offered to return the animal immediately. Blankenship had said that was completely unnecessary, and suggested that Houston keep the horse at his own place until he was sure that he would not need it again. Moreover, when he learned that Camp would be going hunting again in a few weeks, the liveryman offered him money to help with his traveling expenses. Houston declined.

Camp took a sip of his coffee to test its sweetness, then returned to the porch. "I saw that quarter horse down at Hamm Harrison's stable a while back," he said to Fowler, who was still seated on the doorstep, "and I looked him over good. I'd say you're gonna be plenty satisfied."

The big man's homely face brightened, and he smiled broadly. "I already am satisfied," he said. "Smoothest horse I've ever been on. He don't even bounce you around when he's trotting. Want me to saddle him up so you can see what I'm talking about?"

Camp shook his head. "Maybe some other time." He finished his coffee and set the cup aside, then changed the subject. "I guess you'll be busy enough right here for the rest of the year, Runt. What do you intend to be doing next spring?"

Fowler peeled a splinter off the wooden handrail, using it to pick his teeth. "Hell, I don't know," he said. "I never plan that far ahead. Why do you ask?"

Camp sat staring down the hillside. "Because yesterday I made a deal for five hundred head of cows and twenty bulls. They'll be delivered to me right here in March or April."

"Five hundred head?" Fowler was on his feet now, shaking his head. "Seems to me like that's driving it up mighty tight, Camp. I mean, three sections is enough land that a man can shit anywhere he wants to, but it ain't all that much when you start talking about running five hundred head of cattle. On top of that, every damn one of the cows is gonna have a calf following her around before long. You'll either have to sell your calves or get rid of your breeders after the first year, 'cause you'll be outta room."

Camp chuckled. "I'll get rid of the breeders, Runt, but I won't have to do it the first year. While I was dealing yesterday, I acquired three more sections south of the county line." He explained the details of the arrangement he had made with John Butterworth.

Fowler guffawed, then began to speak slowly, still chuckling intermittently. "Now, let me be sure I understand this," he said. "Butterworth is gonna sell you three sections of land on credit, with no collateral whatsoever, then he's gonna furnish you with five hundred head of breeders and twenty bulls. And all he expects out of it is a third of the calf crop. Have I got that right?"

Houston nodded.

Fowler laughed again. "I won't ask you what you've got on that man, Camp, but it sure must be something bad. Either that or you're a better bargainer than anybody else I know."

"I didn't do any bargaining at all," Camp said, getting to his feet. "It was all John's idea. The man's well-off, Runt, and he's getting on in years. He knows he can't take it with him, and I guess he just took a liking to me. That must be the case, 'cause he's done about everything an older fellow can do to help a younger man get a place of his own." He headed for the kitchen. "Nope," he said over his shoulder, "I didn't make a single suggestion. John thought up the whole deal himself." He walked to the stove and added wood to the firebox, then began to prepare himself a bacon-and-egg breakfast.

A few minutes later, Fowler poured himself a cup of coffee and took a seat at the table. Camp dumped half a dozen scrambled eggs into a bowl. "You want to help me eat these?"

"Nope. Ate about a pound of that smoked ham over there when I first got up." He blew into his cup, then took a sip of coffee. "I wanted to talk to you about the barn. Guess I'll be starting on it within the next day or two."

Camp folded his hands on the table. "All right, let's talk."

"Well, I first intended to put it down there about where the shed is now, but I'm beginning to think a whole lot less of that idea. Maybe we should put the barn and the corral both on that slope across the road. Just those few showers we had last week washed most of that horse manure right down the hill and into the creek. Now, I don't know that it's gonna hurt the creek any, but right there in that deep pool below the big tree is where we all bathe ourselves. I don't care to do my bathing in a creek full of horse shit, so I think we oughta move the whole shebang across the road." He pointed to the east side of the house, then down the hill. "When the heavy rains come this winter, all the fertilizer'll wash right down into that field yonder. It'll just be lying there waiting when we get ready to plant a garden next spring."

Houston had unfolded his hands, and was busy eating now. He washed down a mouthful of food, then chuckled. "You've convinced me, Runt. Build the barn wherever you think is best. And I guess we should have a bigger corral, 'cause we're eventually gonna need more horseflesh."

"Done thought of that, too," Fowler said, getting to his feet and dropping his empty cup into the dishpan. "Gonna make it a lot bigger. Fact is, I'm gonna start marking off the whole layout right now. Later on, I'll dig a ditch to send the spring's runoff through the new corral." He headed for the door. "You want to come along?"

Camp shook his head. "Nope. You just go ahead and do things your own way. I've got some business in Menardville, and I want to visit a few people. I'll be gone for two or three days, maybe longer." Half an hour later, he saddled the roan and rode off the hill.

13

★

Houston arrived at the Rocking A Ranch two hours before sunset. Even as he rode up the hill, he could see that Bama
Angleton was on her knees beside the porch tending her rose-
bushes. Hearing the horse's footfalls and the creak of saddle
leather, she quickly became aware of Camp's presence. She
placed one hand on the doorstep and pulled herself to her feet
as he rode into the yard. "Camp Houston!" she said loudly,
laying the trimming shears aside. "I do declare."

He dismounted and tied the roan. "It's good to see you,
Bama."

Her big smile and dancing eyes made it obvious that she
was delighted with his visit. She crossed the yard to meet him,
placing both of her hands in his. "You're one of our very favorite people, Camp. Thank you for coming. George and I
have both been concerned, and we sit right here on this porch
talking about you almost every night."

He released her hands and hugged her tightly. "No reason for you to worry about me, Bama. I'm not gonna fall in a hole. I know this country too well."

She nodded, and began to lead the way toward the house. "Yeah," she said, "I guess you do. But we've both been worried ever since you went after those men, afraid that maybe things wouldn't . . . uh . . . turn out right."

"Well, you can stop worrying. I'm doing great, and I never felt better." Camp seated himself in one of the porch chairs as Bama disappeared inside the house.

When she returned, she handed him a large glass of lemonade. "George is in Menardville today," she said. "Left about an hour after sunup." She pulled up a chair and took a sip from her own glass. "He probably couldn't make it back today even if he wanted to," she added, giving Camp a knowing wink. "Of course, I don't think he wants to. I believe he likes things just fine right there at the great Menardville Hotel."

Camp sipped at his drink, deciding that he would say nothing on the matter. Not in a million years. He changed the subject. "I bought some more property up on Calf Creek, Bama; got six sections now."

"I'm so proud for you, Camp. You got the place stocked already?"

He shook his head. "Won't have my cattle till next spring. Runt Fowler's already built the house, though, and he's working on a barn right now."

"Then I suppose you'll have a good house and barn both," she said. "George knows him well, and he's told me more than once that Mr. Fowler's mighty handy with hammer and saw. Sounds like you've got the right man up there."

He nodded. "I believe so. I've certainly been pleased with everything he's done so far." He drained his glass, and set it on a nearby table. "I was actually headed to Menardville myself," he said, "but I decided that I couldn't get there before midnight. I hate traveling in the dark, so I rode by here to see if you'd let me sleep in the bunkhouse tonight."

She shook her head emphatically. "No, sir, Camp Houston. There'll be none of that sleeping in the bunkhouse. Nobody's slept in that back bedroom for years, and it's a good bed. It's yours for the night, or for however long you want it."

Camp chuckled, and got to his feet. "Well, I guess by gosh I know when I'm well off, so I'm not gonna argue with you." He stepped into the yard and headed for the barn. When he had watered and curried the roan, he stabled the animal and poured a bucketful of oats in the trough. He would leave the horse in the stable overnight. The Rocking A corral was larger than most, and, being close to an expert at dodging a rope, the roan was not always easy to catch. Camp tossed a forkful of hay into the stable, then hooked the latch. When he opened the door with the bridle in his hand in the morning, the horse would have nowhere to run.

He spent the next hour sitting on the porch alone. The familiar sounds that he could hear from the kitchen told him that he would soon be eating a good supper. He had eaten numerous meals in this house in the past, and enjoyed all of them more than anything he had ever been served in a restaurant.

He was still sitting in his chair when the ranch hands began to ride in from several different directions. When they had taken care of their horses, some of them walked to the cookshack, while others headed for the bunkhouse. And though all of them looked the house over, and surely noticed him sitting on the porch, Camp offered no greeting, for he saw no one that he knew. He sat quietly watching the men till they entered the other buildings.

Then he was on his feet, playing a game that he had played many times before: he was trying to identify the aroma that was coming from the kitchen, so that he would know what was on the table long before he was called to supper. He sniffed a while longer, then nodded as he became convinced that he had identified the smell. He took a seat on the doorstep, looking forward to eating the meal of beefsteak, corn bread and fried Irish potatoes.

The lady called him to supper a few minutes later, and Camp was more than ready. He walked first to the back porch to wash his hands, then on through the kitchen to the dining room. He seated himself at the end of the table and eyed the food hungrily: pork chops, thick gravy, candied sweet potatoes, cabbage, black-eyed peas, hot buttered biscuits, and a pie made from dried apples.

He was quick to notice that none of the things he had expected to see was on the table, and decided that maybe his sense of smell was not so keen after all. He would remember that, for he might someday be in a situation where following his nose could get him in trouble.

He sat with his hands in his lap while the lady continued to move around the table. Finally, she poured two cups of coffee, then pulled out a chair for herself. She thanked the Lord for providing the food and asked Him to bless it, then spoke to her visitor. "I want you to eat everything in sight, Camp. Looks to me like you've fell off a lot since the last time you were here."

Camp was busy loading up his plate. "You're probably right," he said. "Of course, I've been traveling for most of that time, and good food is not always easy to come by." He smiled, then began to cut into a pork chop. "I've never yet known of anybody getting fat on the trail," he added.

Night came on before the meal was over, and they finished eating by the light of a coal-oil lamp. Then they sat on the porch in the darkness, listening to the entertaining sounds of countless nocturnal insects and animals that would never be seen in the light of day.

When the mosquitoes finally chased them inside an hour later, Camp headed for the bedroom he was shown. Even after he blew out the lamp and stretched out on the bed, he could still hear Bama moving around in the kitchen. He smiled at the sound. The saintly lady was no doubt cleaning up her kitchen, getting ready to prepare him another big meal in the morning. He turned over once, then went to sleep.

It seemed that he had just closed his eyes when he heard her knock on the bedroom door. "It's daylight already," she said softly. "Breakfast'll be ready by the time you are."

He dressed himself quickly, then left the house through the rear door. After a trip to the outhouse, he stopped on the back porch and washed his face and hands in the ever-present pan of water, then used the towel that hung from a nail driven into a post. He combed his hair with his fingers, then walked to the dining room, where he took a seat in the same chair he had occupied for supper.

The beefsteak he thought he had smelled cooking the night before was now on a platter beside his plate, which held a stack of flapjacks and several scrambled eggs. Another platter in the center of the table held a sliced cantaloupe, and a smaller dish contained garden-fresh tomatoes. He sat quietly as Bama talked to the Lord about the food, then seated herself at his elbow. He buttered his flapjacks, then poured on a river of syrup, saying, "If I ever marry, I sure hope I get a woman who can cook like you, Bama."

She chuckled softly. "I don't reckon they're terribly hard to find, Camp. Not if a handsome man like you lets them know he's looking. As soon as the word got out, I'd say that a lot of them would be going out of their way to strike up a conversation with you. Young girls are usually just waiting for a man like you to come along, and most of them know how to cook. The ones who don't can learn."

He washed a mouthful of food down with coffee. "I can't be thinking about a wife right now. I've got too many things to do." He sat quietly for a few moments, then added, "As for getting the word out, I wouldn't have the slightest idea of how to go about that." He laughed aloud. "Should I just put an ad in the newspaper?"

"You don't have to put an ad anywhere," she answered quickly. "You see, a young girl wants whatever she thinks all the other girls want. All you have to do is escort one or two of them around town a little, then stand back and take your pick when the rest come running."

He pushed his chair away from the table and got to his feet, shaking his head and laughing. "I never heard it put quite like that, Bama, but I suppose you should know. Maybe I'll try it sometime."

He walked to the bedroom and buckled on his gun belt, then returned to the dining room, hat in hand. "Thanks for putting me up, Bama, and I appreciate all the trouble you went to."

"No trouble at all," she said, "and I enjoyed your company." She followed him to the door.

He stepped onto the porch, then put on his hat. "I'm headed for Menardville, so I might meet George on the road. Is there anything in particular that you want me to tell him?"

"There sure is," she said, chuckling loudly. "Tell him that I've done run off with a younger man."

A few minutes later, he put the roan to a trot down River Road. Both the road and the San Saba River ran west from the Rocking A Ranch to Menardville in almost a straight line. Camp always enjoyed the ride, especially during the early morning. The air was always cool, and the sparkling dew on the wildflowers created a scene that was pleasing to the eye.

Grass was plentiful on both sides of the river, and wild game was so abundant that even a greenhorn would have no problem filling his bag. Though Camp had ridden no farther than a mile this morning, he had already seen a large number of animals, including three deer that had trotted across the road in front of him, well within rifle range. Indeed, Camp knew of no location that offered better hunting.

And though there had been reports of antelope sightings in Menard County over the years, Houston was more than a little skeptical. He knew that the speedy animals would not long remain in a brushy area, but would seek out more level country where they could depend on their keen vision and fleetness of foot to defeat predators.

He could not recall the name of any man claiming to have seen an antelope, but had heard the tale many times. He shook his head at the thought. He himself had not only been scouting and hunting in the area for several years, but he also knew something about the habits and preferences of the animals in question. To any group of men he heard discussing the claim, he was always quick to offer his own firm opinion: there were no antelope in Menard County.

Camp stopped once to relieve himself, then continued at a steady trot. The road crossed the river at John's Ford, and he arrived there three hours later. Looking toward the west bank, he could see that George Angleton was also there, about to ford the river on his way home. Camp moved to the side of the road and sat waiting. The rancher's horses waded the shallow water, then leaned into their collars, straining to pull an overloaded wagon to the top of the sloping east bank.

When Houston kneed the roan into the road, Angleton yanked on the reins, bringing the team to a halt. "Who in the world is that I see?" the rancher said loudly, wrapping the reins around the brake and stepping to the ground. "I sure can't think of anybody I'd rather see this morning. How've you been, Camp?"

Houston was on the ground now, extending his right hand. "Things just keep getting better as I go along, George. I can't think of a single thing that I'd have the gall to complain about."

Angleton grasped the hand and pumped the arm for a long time. "Me either," he said. "I ain't gonna be doing no complaining this year." He finally released the hand. "What're you doing traveling on River Road? Did you go by my house?"

Camp nodded. "Slept there last night," he said. "Ate up most of your grub."

The rancher's skinny body began to shake, and he made a sound that was somewhere between a giggle and a snort. "Well, by gosh I'm happy to hear that," he said. "Bama's always liked you, so I bet she fed you good."

"She did that, all right. She also asked me to tell you that she's done run off with a younger man."

Angleton guffawed and slapped his leg. "Funny woman, Camp. Funny, funny."

Camp led the rancher's team to the side of the road, then pointed to the wagon, which was loaded with gunny sacks stacked high above its sideboards. "I never knew you to load a wagon that heavy, George. Must be gold in those sacks."

"Aw, I knew it would be a big drag on the team, but I've been taking it easy on them. I just got a bargain on some shelled corn that I couldn't pass up. It ain't every day that you find it for twenty cents a bushel."

Camp nodded, satisfied with the answer. "I don't suppose you could even grow it that cheap," he said.

"That's the truth," Angleton agreed. "The corn's been in Bill Williams's barn for three years, and he finally had to damn near give it away in order to move it out. He's got a big crop in the fields right now, and it's almost harvest time."

"Sounds like Williams might be needing another barn," Camp said, chuckling. "Maybe I should inform Runt Fowler of that fact when he gets done at my place."

They stood at the roadside talking for more than an hour. Then Camp shook the rancher's hand and bade him good-bye.

He trotted his animal for the remainder of the morning, and at one o'clock in the afternoon rode into Menardville. At the livery stable, he dismounted and handed the reins to his longtime friend, Sid Blankenship. "I'll be staying in town tonight," he said. "Might be around for two or three days."

Blankenship led the roan forward and loosened the cinch. He was a dark-haired, barrel-chested six-footer who was about forty years old, and had been the town's busiest blacksmith as well as its most popular liveryman for at least a dozen years. "Glad to hear that you're gonna be around a while," he said. "All of us people who worry about you don't get to see you very often." He stripped the saddle from the roan and placed it on a nearby sawhorse. "Maybe we can have a drink together after I close up here. You gonna be at the hotel?"

Camp nodded. "Come on up," he said. "I'll probably be in the hotel bar about dark." He walked through the wide door-way and up the street, stopping at Riley's Restaurant. He had eaten in the establishment many times, and was not only ac-quainted with both the owner and his wife, he also knew everyone else who worked there. Or thought he did.

As he seated himself at a table against the wall, he noticed that everything in the building had been rearranged since the last time he was here. And though he could see several em-ployees moving around, he recognized none of them. No doubt about it, he was thinking, all the signs suggested that the restaurant was under new management.

His suspicion was confirmed when a young woman ap-peared at his table, pad and pencil in hand. Her pink lips parted on perfect white teeth as she went into her well-rehearsed spiel: "Hi, and welcome to Riley's," she began stiffly. "My name is Ellen Bice, and I'll be your waitress. My uncle, Henry Trout, is the new owner, but he has elected not to change the name of the restaurant. Nor will the motto change. We remain committed to serving the same good food at the same reasonable prices." She paused for a breath of air, then asked, "May I have your order, sir?"

Camp took his time about answering. That the young lady was new at this line of work was obvious, and he was think-ing that he might very well be her first customer—ever. He had been impressed with her lovely voice, however, a little lower in pitch than that of most girls, but nevertheless totally feminine. Even so, he knew that the long-winded spiel that someone had written for her should be discarded, for people in this town already knew all there was to know about Riley's Restaurant. When they walked through the door they would be expecting food, not conversation.

He had noticed right away that the girl wore no wedding band. "I'll have a T-bone steak," he said, smiling flirtatiously, "and a platter of fried potatoes."

She smiled and fluttered her long eyelashes, then headed for the kitchen. Camp followed her with his eyes till she disappeared behind the batwing doors. She was a well-proportioned brunette with sky-blue eyes, and appeared to be eighteen or twenty years old. The fact that she was not a local girl was obvious, for her accent suggested that she had come from someplace north of Texas.

The girl was still on Houston's mind when he paid for his food and stepped out onto the street an hour later. When she delivered his food to the table he had introduced himself by name, and, to satisfy his curiosity, asked her from whence she had come. "I grew up in Lincoln, Nebraska," she said, "and I came here two weeks ago to live with Uncle Henry and Aunt Mary." She smiled and headed elsewhere, and Camp did not see her again. He did leave a twenty-cent gratuity on his table, however, making sure that Ellen Bice would not forget him or his name.

He walked west till he reached the Menardville Hotel, where he rented a room on the second floor.

Just before sunset, Camp seated himself on a stool at the hotel bar. "Nice to see you again, Wes," he said, offering a handshake to the middle-aged bartender, who was a former heavyweight prizefighter named Wesley Hawks. "I'll have a beer."

Hawks grasped the hand. "Good to see you, too, Camp. I just opened a new keg, and the first mug's always free." He delivered the beer, then added, "I sure ain't seen much of you lately. Where've you been keeping yourself?"

Camp had been about to take a sip of his beer. He stopped his arm and held the mug in midair till after he answered the question. "Oh, I've been in town several times within the past few months," he said. "I guess the reason you didn't see me is because the urge to have a drink didn't hit me. I slept right here at the hotel, though."

Hawks nodded. "I don't ever really know who's in town. About the only people I see are the ones who come in the bar.

Hell, I come to work at ten o'clock in the morning, and everybody's done gone to bed by the time I get off at night." He poured himself a drink of whiskey, which he drank in one gulp, then dropped the empty glass in a pan of water. "Things have been slow in this place all year, and I ain't had no trouble that I couldn't talk my way out of." He laid his hands on the bar as if to invite Houston's inspection. "First time my damn knuckles have had a chance to completely heal in several years."

Camp shifted his eyes from one of the man's scarred hands to the other, then took a sip of his beer and nodded. "Your knuckles look good to me, Wes," he said with a chuckle. "I'd almost bet that they'd hold up for at least another hundred rounds."

"A hundred rounds, my ass." Hawks said as he refilled Camp's mug. "Don't wish nothing like that on me, 'cause I'm getting too old for that shit."

Camp continued to sit at the bar till Sid Blankenship arrived a short while later. The liveryman bought a bottle of whiskey, then he and Camp moved to a table in the far corner of the room. Blankenship poured drinks for both, then held his own glass aloft, proposing a toast. "Here's to your success next time you go hunting."

They touched glasses, and Camp nodded. "It'll be a while yet," he said, "but I appreciate the thought." He wet his lips with the whiskey. "Meanwhile, if you need that packhorse, just holler. I can get him back to you in one day."

Blankenship set his glass on the table noisily. "There you go again, Camp. How many times do I have to tell you that I don't need that horse? I don't need him today, tomorrow or next week."

Camp was quiet for a while, then said, "I just thought maybe somebody might be wanting to rent a horse, that not having him might be costing you money."

"No. Of course, everything does actually boil down to a matter of supply and demand, but my supply is always considerably bigger than the demand. Besides, the way I happened to come by that horse, I don't have but ten dollars in him."

Camp raised his eyebrows. "Ten dollars? Surely you don't mean that. He's a damn good horse, Sid."

Blankenship smiled. "Of course he is," he said, then laughed aloud. "But I'm a horse trader, remember?"

Camp sat thinking for a few moments. "Maybe I should hire you to do my horse buying," he said finally. "I expect to be needing several cow ponies next year." He told Blankenship about the additional property he had acquired, and that he would stock the place with longhorns in the spring.

The liveryman listened attentively, nodding all the while. "Just let me know how many head you want," he said, "so I can put out the word. Probably won't take long."

They were quietly sipping their drinks when Wesley Hawks approached their table a short time later. "I forgot to mention it earlier, Camp," he said, pulling up a chair, "but there's a fellow been hanging around town asking about you. Did he find you?"

Houston shook his head and set his glass on the table. "I don't believe he did, Wes. What does he look like, and where is he now?"

"I don't have any idea where he is," the bartender said, seating himself at the table, "but he's been in here three or four times during the past few days, buying drinks for some of the customers and asking questions about you. I guess I can give you a pretty good description, though: he's a skinny fellow with coal-black hair, probably not more'n twenty years old. Not very tall, either. I guess if you took him out of them high-heel boots and that high-crown Stetson, he wouldn't measure no more'n five-seven. Five-eight at the most. Probably weighs about a hundred forty pounds, if you count that Peacemaker on his left leg. Wears it hanging halfway to his knee in a tied-down holster, like he might need to get at it in a hurry sometime."

As Houston sat listening and thinking, his facial expression slowly turned to granite. He had been through it all before, and had no doubt as to why the young man had decided to seek him out. He spoke to the bartender: "Of course, he didn't say anything about why he wants to see me. Right?"

"Right. I don't reckon he ever told anybody whether he was friend or foe, but I guess we all just figured that he was probably a friend. Don't reckon he made no threats, or nothing like that."

Blankenship, who had been silently listening to the exchange, spoke now. "A fellow fitting that description was in my place two days ago, but he didn't ask me any questions. Bought a feed of oats for his bay, then had me trim the animal's hooves and nail on four new shoes. Flashed a good-size roll of money when he paid his bill, then mounted and headed east. I haven't seen him before or since."

Camp turned to the liveryman. "Any markings on that horse, Sid?"

Blankenship shook his head. "Just a bay," he said. "Bay all over. No stockings, no blaze. I'd say the horse weighs about nine-fifty."

Camp pushed his glass aside. The last thing he wanted right now was another drink of whiskey. He motioned toward the few drinkers who were scattered about the barroom, then spoke to Hawks. "Is there anybody in here right now who talked with the man, Wes?"

"Don't think so," Hawks said, looking over his shoulder. Then he turned his body halfway around, so that he could see every man in the building. "Nope. I sure didn't see any of this bunch talking with him." He was getting to his feet now, about to return to his position behind the bar. "I just thought it was a little bit strange, this fellow going around asking questions about Camp Houston, then refusing to give out his own name when somebody gets curious. One of the men asked him who he was, but he said it didn't matter, said he didn't need no name." Continuing to shake his head, Hawks returned his chair to the adjoining table, then walked away.

Houston and Blankenship sat quietly for a while. They well understood the implications of what they had been hearing, and each man waited for the other to speak first. Blankenship finally broke the silence. "You're gonna be a sitting duck in that hotel room, Camp. I think you ought to spend the night at my house."

Camp sat quietly for a moment, then asked, "You got room?"

The man nodded. "Sure do. My cellar is actually a fortress, and it's got a good bed. My wife and kids slept down there during the Hoo Doo War, when a lot of crazy bastards were sneaking around taking potshots at people."

"All right," Houston said, "I'll be sleeping in your cellar." He sat staring at the wall for a while. "I've been wondering about something else, Sid," he said finally. "Did that fellow have a bedroll behind his saddle?"

"Yep. Had a tarp, too, and both of his saddlebags were stuffed. I don't believe he was out riding just for the hell of it, old buddy; the shoes on his horse weren't much thicker'n a dime. He's been on the move, all right."

Blankenship returned the half-full bottle to the bartender and Hawks gave him back half of his money, allowing him to pay for only as many ounces of the whiskey as they had drunk.

Camp joined the liveryman at the front door, and the two walked out into the night together. Avoiding the street, they walked down a little-used trail till they reached the livery stable, then turned south. The road leading up the steep hill to Blankenship's house was no more than three hundred yards long, and ended in his front yard.

Both smooth and wide, the well-drained stretch of road had been built by the same contractor who built the house. Camp had heard Blankenship discuss that very thing in the past. "I could have built the house and the road myself," the man had once said to Houston, "but it might have taken me two or three years. Hell, I needed a place to roost right then, 'cause my wife had done started having babies. I was tied up ten or twelve hours a day down at the stable, so I just hired the Wicker brothers to do my building. I never have been sorry, either. They not only know exactly what they're doing, they've got the right equipment to get it done."

When they reached the house, Blankenship unlocked the door and touched the wick of a coal-oil lamp with a burning match. Then he lighted a second lamp and handed it to Camp, pointing wordlessly to the staircase that led to the cellar.

Camp accepted the lamp and crossed the room. Knowing that Blankenship's wife and children were by now sound asleep, he descended the stairway as light-footedly as possible, surprised that none of the steps creaked in protest to his two hundred thirty pounds. Sid had been right about the building contractors, he was thinking. Anything they built was likely to stand for several generations, according to Runt Fowler, who readily admitted that most of what he knew about building he had learned by studying the methods of the Wicker brothers. They were the master builders of west Texas, he declared, and their services did not come cheap.

A short time later, Camp blew out the lamp and stretched out, his Peacemaker close at hand. Sid had not overstated the quality of the bed, he decided. Springy yet firm, the wide mattress was actually longer than his body, which was seldom the case. He tossed and turned as he relived the night's events, recalling the words spoken by Wesley Hawks as he described the young man who had been asking questions.

Houston racked his brain for a long time, but could think of no left-handed acquaintance who fit the description. The man was obviously seeking a showdown, he decided; another youngster hoping to gain a reputation by outdrawing and gunning down Camp Houston. The same thing had happened so many times that Camp was no longer unnerved by it. He shrugged, and fluffed up his pillow. After a while he managed to push all thoughts of the inquisitive stranger out of his mind, and began to think about how well things had gone for him lately. His eyes eventually closed of their own accord, and he slept soundly.

It was long after sunup when he was awakened by Blankenship calling from the top of the stairway. "You're gonna have to come on up here if you're going with me, Camp. I've got to get down to the stable."

Houston got to his feet and dressed himself quickly. At the top of the stairs, he spoke to his host: "I'll visit your out-house, then meet you in the front yard. And you can tell your wife to forget about feeding me. I'll eat breakfast at Riley's."

A few minutes later, they walked down the hill together. They parted company at the stable, then Camp walked up the street toward Riley's, his eyes constantly darting from one place to another, sweeping the entire area for anything that did not look right. When he reached the restaurant he stepped inside quickly, staking out a table along the rear wall.

Accepting the cup of coffee delivered by a Mexican waiter, he ordered a ham-and-egg breakfast, then sat sipping the steaming liquid as he awaited the preparation of his food. The first of his two reasons for choosing Riley's was the restaurant's reputation for serving the best victuals in town. The second reason was nowhere to be seen. He shrugged, and continued to sip his coffee, supposing that Ellen Bice only worked during the afternoon and early evening.

He sat thinking for a while, and decided that he would pay a visit to the town marshal, even though his heart would not be in it. It was not that Marshal Paley and he had ever been on opposite sides of any particular issue, but for some reason that had never been discussed, each of the men simply acted as if the other did not exist.

Joe Paley had been Menardville's chief lawman for more than three years now. He had been appointed town marshal at the height of the Hoo Doo War, simply because he was the only man who applied for the position when the former marshal gave it up voluntarily. Marshal Manley Kincaid had re-signed shortly after all of the unexplained shooting and killing started, proclaiming the job too dangerous for a family man.

Since becoming town marshal, Joe Paley had not spoken to Camp except on the few occasions when they had almost run over each other on the street. Even then he had always looked over Houston's shoulder while mumbling something inaudible. Of course, Camp was not the only person Paley ignored; the man never spoke to anybody unless it was absolutely necessary.

Though his dark-complected face was far from homely, the marshal wore a perpetual scowl, and from all appearances had few close friends. Several men with Menard County interests had even privately questioned Paley's activities during the Hoo Doo War, though it seemed that those expressing doubt of his honesty usually spoke in low tones.

Occasionally, however, some brave soul would speak openly and loudly about the fact that, while practically everyone else in the county had lost property to roving bands of thieves, nothing the marshal owned had ever been stolen. And though senseless vandalism had occurred on almost a daily basis throughout Mason and Menard Counties, Joe Paley's property had not even suffered as much as a torched haystack. The same thoughts had crossed Houston's mind more than once, but had immediately been discarded. He had long ago made a firm decision not to spend one second of his life worrying about something over which he had no control. As was usually the case, it would all come out in the wash. If Joe Paley was a dishonest lawman, his day of reckoning would come.

Houston took his time with his breakfast, and sipped several cups of coffee afterward. When he finally left the restaurant, he very casually walked up one side of the street and down the other, then headed for the marshal's office.

15

★

The marshal's office and the jail were located in the county courthouse, two hundred yards west of the town's main commercial area. The large building also provided office space for the circuit judge, county prosecutor, tax collector and at least two criminal defense lawyers. Paley's office faced the street on the east side of the building, and had a small porch with two rocking chairs.

The front door of the office was open wide, and even as Houston walked into the yard he could see the man sitting at his desk, his attention on some kind of printed material that he held in his hands. Camp stopped at the porch and knocked on a post. "Have you got a minute, Marshal?"

Paley continued to concentrate on whatever he was reading for a moment, then raised his eyes. "Guess so," he said gruffly. "The door's open."

Houston walked into the office and stood before the over-sized desk, for he had not been invited to sit down. The marshal laid his magazine aside, and spoke again. "You got a problem of some kind?"

Camp crossed his arms and stood staring at the man for a while. Though Paley was not a tall man, five-ten at the most, he was solidly built, and appeared to be in good physical condition. Though not yet out of his thirties, it was obvious when he was hatless, as he was now, that his thinning dark hair was rapidly turning to gray. His walrus mustache also contained more salt than pepper.

After receiving no answer to his question, he began to shift about nervously under Camp's constant stare. Finally, he tried again, speaking in a much softer tone. "Is there something I can help you with?"

Camp continued to stand, looking Paley in the eye. "There's a man traveling around asking questions about me. He's been here in Menardville several times, and I seriously doubt that he's looking for me because he wants to shake my hand. I was just wondering if you've seen him, or know who he is."

Paley shook his head. "I doubt that it's anybody I'd know, and I haven't seen any strangers recently. Of course, I haven't been on the street lately, don't ever go down there unless somebody sends for me. I don't know if it's because the merchants don't like lawmen in general, or me in particular, but judging from their attitude, I'd say that most of them like it better when I don't come around."

"I don't know about that," Houston said. He took a few steps toward the door, then stopped, adding, "I came by because I thought you ought to be told about this fellow, not because I expected you to do something about him. If he's really hunting me, he'll find me." He stepped into the yard and headed toward town.

Paley, who was standing on the porch now, called after him, "If you happen to run into that fellow anywhere within the town limits, just be sure that you're not the first one to start shooting!"

Houston stopped in his tracks. He stood still for several seconds, then turned quickly and spoke loudly. "Are you suggesting that I give some sonofabitch a free shot at me, Marshal?"

"Well, not . . . I mean . . . just don't . . ."

Camp turned his back to the stammering lawman and walked away.

He drank another cup of coffee at Riley's, then continued on down the hill. Long before he reached the livery, he could see a bay saddler standing in the stable's wide doorway. Sid Blankenship was holding the animal's bridle while carrying on an animated conversation with a man much shorter than he. Believing that he was now looking at the man who had been asking the questions, Camp stepped between two buildings and stood watching.

Though he had a clear view of the stable, he could not get a good look at the shorter man, for he was standing on the far side of the bay. Nevertheless, enough of the man's head towered above the horse for Camp to see that it was crammed as deeply as possible into a high-crown Stetson.

The two men continued to talk for several minutes, and Camp got the idea that maybe Blankenship was using some kind of stalling tactic, keeping the man in the doorway as long as possible in case Houston should happen by. The liveryman finally led the bay into the stable, and the shorter man followed, offering Camp a broad view of his back. The gun belt around the man's waist was easy to see, and the Peacemaker hanging low on his left leg told Houston all he needed to know.

He waited till both men had disappeared down the stable's dark hall, then went into action. Moving as fast as he could without running, he turned north through an alley and continued in that direction till he reached the woods. Then he turned east again, and did not stop till he was slightly behind and north of the stable. He watched from behind a clump of bushes till he was convinced that both men were still inside the building, then crossed the road quickly and quietly.

Now against the north wall of the stable, he began to make his way noiselessly toward the front of the building, where he would simply wait. He had no intention of going inside, for once he stepped in front of that wide-open doorway he would be a perfect target, while the man inside would be almost totally concealed by the dim lighting. Moments later, he stood at the front corner of the building, waiting.

He was still standing in the same position several minutes later when a wagon rattled down the road, headed into town. A farmer and his wife were sitting on the seat, and two small boys rode behind them, their bare feet dangling from the rear of the wagon. The farmer nodded as his vehicle passed within a few feet of the stable. Camp ignored the greeting, for every single one of his senses was attuned to the business at hand.

Standing against the wall, he could hear a conversation going on inside the stable, but could understand none of the words. Blankenship's deep voice was easy to identify, however, and Camp could tell that it was getting closer to the front of the building. Then he began to hear a different voice, even closer now.

Continuing to talk as he walked, the young man was suddenly through the doorway and into the yard. He took a few steps in the direction of town, then turned halfway around to offer a few parting words to Blankenship. "I guess I'll be back about—"

His voice cracked and he froze in his tracks as he saw that Houston, his legs spread apart and his body leaning forward in a slight crouch, was now standing where the liveryman had stood only a moment before. Camp spoke quickly: "I hear that you've been looking for Camp Houston. You've found him."

The man did not speak. He stared sideways at Camp for only a moment, then made a decision that bordered on stupidity: even as he attempted to complete his turn, with his body essentially off balance, he made his play. And though his gun was in his fist very quickly, he died before he could line it up, taking a shot in the mouth from Camp's Peacemaker. A second shot hit him in the throat and knocked him over a wooden sawhorse, where he collapsed and lay still.

Houston stood in the doorway for several moments, his eyes on the fallen man. Though Camp had been through it all before, he had nevertheless been somewhat surprised at the way the showdown came about. He had expected the man to go for his gun, but not before he had completed his turn, planted his feet, and regained his balance. He had obviously convinced himself that he was the fastest draw around, and that he could do it from any position.

Camp stood reliving the past few seconds in his mind. The young gunman had been fast, all right, but he had clearly put himself at a disadvantage by moving too soon. Indeed, the lifeless bundle that now lay on the ground beside the sawhorse had only a few moments ago been nothing short of a quick-draw artist, but he had also been a young man, and young men made mistakes.

Camp holstered his weapon, then walked forward. He turned the body over and decided quickly that he had never seen the gunman before. When he went through the man's pockets he found forty dollars, a watch, a sack of Durham, several matches and a letter addressed to Ben Gillam, in Corpus Christi, Texas.

Camp stood holding the letter for a moment, having no doubt that he was now looking at the remains of one Ben Gillam. Finally, he extracted the single sheet of paper from the envelope. The message consisted of only two lines, but the words jumped out at him instantly: *"STOP CAMP HOUSTON!"* it commanded, then went on to suggest that the Menardville area would likely be the most fertile hunting ground. And though there was no signature, the writer had initialed it. The *W.T.* at the bottom of the page told Camp the name of the sender. He folded the letter and slipped it into his pocket, already anticipating the day when he would wave it in front of Walt Turner's nose.

Blankenship was beside him now. "We're about to have company," he said, pointing up the hill, "and I believe Marshal Paley's leading the pack."

Knowing that the sound of gunfire never failed to bring people out, Camp had expected no less. Looking up the street, he could see several men headed toward the stable. He could even hear them now, speculating back and forth on the reason for the gunshots. As Blankenship had said, the marshal was the point man.

Paley arrived in the stable yard first, and bent over to inspect the body. Wesley Hawks took a quick look, then walked on past the lawman and spoke to Houston: "That's the man who's been asking all the questions, Camp. I see he found you."

Houston nodded curtly, and said nothing.

The young gunman's Peacemaker still lay in the dirt, where he had dropped it when he took the first shot. Paley now walked to the opposite side of the sawhorse and picked up the weapon, sniffing its barrel. "Everybody said they heard two shots, mister!" he said to Camp sarcastically, much louder than was necessary. He held the gun in his right hand and pointed to it with his left. "This gun ain't been fired since no telling when!"

"That very well may be one of the reasons I'm still standing!" Camp said just as loudly, making a conscious effort to match Paley's tone. "You're exactly right, Marshal, the gun hasn't been fired this morning." He pointed to the corpse, speaking even louder now. "But it damn sure ain't his fault!"

Sid Blankenship, who had so far stood in the background and remained quiet, stepped forward now. "It was clearly a case of self-defense, Joe." Though the liveryman's comment had been directed to the marshal, his deep voice carried to every man in the crowd. "He's been hunting Camp for more than a week," Blankenship continued, "and just happened to find him here at my stable. I stood right over there in that doorway and watched it all." He motioned toward the body. "That man tried his damnedest to kill Camp Houston."

Paley sniffed the barrel again, then shoved the Colt behind his waistband. He spoke to the liveryman: "Did you hear every word of it, Sid? Did you hear him threaten Houston? Exactly what did he say?"

Blankenship stared at Paley for a while. "The man didn't say a goddam word," he said finally. "The second he laid eyes on Camp, he just went for his gun." He pointed to the body again, adding, "As you can see, it cost him dearly."

Paley shrugged, then dropped his hands to his sides. The sullen expression on his face made it obvious that he was less than pleased with the liveryman's testimony, but he also knew that there was nothing he could do to change it. He was well aware of the fact that Blankenship's popularity exceeded his own by a wide margin, and that the men of Menardville would accept any statement the stable owner made as gospel. The lawman fidgeted for a moment, exhaled loudly, then turned to Camp. "Did you know the man, Houston?"

"His name was Ben Gillam," Camp said softly. "He lived down at Corpus."

Paley nodded. "Well, you're gonna have to pay for his burial," he said, his own voice softer now. "The town of Menardville sure ain't gonna do it."

Camp's reaction was immediate. "I don't think so, Marshal. I'll let him buy his own funeral. He's got the money right there in his pocket."

"In his pocket? How do you know what he's got?"

Houston ignored the marshal's question, and spoke to Wesley Hawks. "I'd take it as a favor if you'd get hold of the undertaker and tell him to take care of this, Wes. Tell him the dead man's name and where he came from, and that he's got forty dollars in his pocket to pay for his burial."

Hawks nodded. "I'm on my way," he said, then headed up the hill.

Camp stood watching the departing bartender for a few moments, then turned to Blankenship, speaking loudly enough to be heard by every man in the crowd. "I'd appreciate it if you'd catch up my roan, Sid. I've got a home to go to nowadays."

Five minutes later, the liveryman led the big horse through the doorway, the saddle already in place. Without another word to anyone, Houston tightened the cinch, mounted and guided the roan to the road. Then he turned east and kicked the animal to a canter. He was out of sight in less than a minute.

16

It was long after dark when Camp rode into his yard and helloed the house. He sat his saddle patiently till Fowler had acknowledged his greeting, then rode to the shed and fed his horse by the light of a full moon. A few minutes later, he entered the house and poked around in the dark till he found his bed. He was asleep quickly.

At the breakfast table, he showed Fowler the letter that he had taken from Ben Gillam's body, and announced that he himself was about to take a trip to Fort Worth.

"I don't know of anything else you can do, Camp," Fowler said. He handed the letter back. "Hell, this thing makes it pretty plain what Walt Turner's up to. If the sonofabitch sent one man after you, how do we know that there ain't a whole bunch of them out there dogging your trail?"

Camp shook his head. "No way of knowing for sure. It would be my guess, though, that he would only send one man at a time. I believe he'll wait till he finds out what kind of luck

Gillam had before he dispatches another gunman. What I'm hoping to do is reach Walt Turner before the news of Gillam's demise does."

He ate a large breakfast, then wrapped up some leftover ham and biscuits for later. He put his bedroll, razor and a change of clothing together, then headed for the corral. No need to worry about cooking and eating utensils; they were still in his pack from the last trip, along with his coffeepot and a good supply of coffee and sugar.

He had already saddled the roan and had just caught up the packhorse when Fowler walked under the shed, carrying a sack in his hand that he laid on a stack of lumber. "I came down to help you fasten the packsaddle on that horse and balance the load," the big man said, taking the harness from a peg on the wall.

Camp backed the horse under the shed. "I appreciate it, Runt. It's a lot easier to do with a man on each side."

Fowler threw the contraption across the horse's back. "At least your old buddy, Sid Blankenship, lent you a good pack-saddle," he said.

Camp reached for a strap to buckle. "There's none better. Not at any price."

The packsaddle was a Grimsley, which, to men who were knowledgeable about such things, was enough said. Made by the T. Grimsley Company of St. Louis, Missouri, it was open at the top, with a light, compact, strong tree, whose rawhide covering was put on green and drawn tight by the contraction of drying. It had a leather breast strap, breeching and lash strap, with a broad hair girth.

Several different types of packsaddles were in use, many of which were mere instruments of torture on the backs of the pack animals, lacerating them cruelly and causing them con-tinuous pain. Not so with the Grimsley, which could easily be fitted to the back of an animal of any size. At the outset, these packsaddles had been designed with the comfort of the beast of burden receiving top priority. Indeed, both mules and horses that were equipped with Grimsleys had been known to carry heavy burdens all the way across the country, all of them arriving in California with backs that were unblemished. Without exception, Houston considered the Grimsley the best packsaddle ever devised by anyone.

Just as Camp thought he had the pack loaded, Fowler presented him with the sack he had brought from the house. "Some sweet potatoes in here," he said. "You can bake one of them in the hot ashes of your campfire every night. They're good, and they're good for you, and you don't have no pots or dishes to wash. I'll guarantee you, Camp, that a big bowl of beans and a big sweet potato will stick to a fellow's ribs just as long as beefsteak."

"You might be right," Camp said, accepting the sack. "I've eaten them before, and I'll eat these. I like the taste, and they're sure easy to fix."

He put the potatoes in the pack, then stood looking at the site that Fowler had chosen for the new barn and corral. He fished around in his pocket for a while, then handed the man a hundred dollars. "Get hold of Cornell Wooten," he said. "Hire him and all three of his sons to help you with that barn, if you can. It's too damn much work for one man."

Fowler folded the money and shoved it into his pocket. "I could have done all of it by myself eventually, Camp, but I can sure use the help. With two men cutting and hauling logs, and three men peeling them, notching them and putting them were they belong, that barn's gonna start taking shape in a hurry. A damn sight quicker'n you'd think."

Camp shook his head. "Not quicker than I would think, Runt. I've seen you in action before." He mounted the roan and took up the slack in the packhorse's lead rope. "You take care, now, and don't strain yourself. Let your hired hands do some of the work." He checked his pockets to make sure he had his watch and his pocket compass, then rode off the hill.

When he reached the valley floor, he turned in his saddle and lifted his hat to Fowler, who was now standing at the top of the hill waving. Then he kicked the roan to a fast trot and headed for the town of Brady. There he would buy some bologna, cheese, crackers and several tins of sardines, then head for Comanche, a town that was almost exactly halfway between his home and Fort Worth.

With the exception of a short stop in Brady, he traveled steadily. He even rode a few hours after nightfall on the first day, for the full moon provided as much light as he needed. He finally made a dry camp and slept six hours, but was in the saddle again well before sunup.

At midafternoon of the second day, he halted at the big Colorado. And though the sun was still three hours high, he forded the river and selected a campsite, for he knew that both he and his animals needed a good night's rest. Though that in itself was a good enough excuse, his main reasons for deciding on an early camp had been that, even from the opposite side of the river, he could see that the grass was good on the north bank, and deadwood was plentiful. Of course, such an ideal campsite had not gone unnoticed by other travelers.

Two covered wagons were parked a hundred yards to the west, and their teams grazed in a small meadow nearby. Two additional horses that Houston took to be saddlers were also picketed on the lush, green grass. Closer to the wagons, several people sat around on the ground, probably all members of the same large family, Camp was thinking.

Between the wagons and the riverbank was a campfire that was far too big for cooking purposes, with flames sometimes shooting several feet into the air. A woman whose head and face were mostly hidden by a large bonnet stirred the fire occasionally, obviously waiting for it to burn down some before she began to prepare supper for her family.

Houston unburdened, watered and picketed his animals, then began to gather fuel for his own fire. When he had placed several small sticks of deadwood on a pile of dead grass, leaves and bark, he touched it all with a burning match, then walked to the river and returned with his coffeepot full of water. He threw in a handful of grounds, then set the pot on the fire. A few minutes later, he poured himself a cup of strong coffee.

He had finished eating his supper of bologna, cheese and crackers and was sitting on his bedroll sipping a second cup of coffee when he had a visitor: a skinny young man who was almost as tall as Houston himself approached the campfire, his right hand extended. "Howdy," he said, his wide smile revealing two rows of perfect teeth. "I just saw you over here by yourself, and thought maybe you might like some company. My name's Bo Patton, and I'm from Ringgold, Georgia. I've been on the move ever since I left there, nearly two months ago."

Houston was on his feet now. He introduced himself as he pumped the man's hand, returning its firm grip. He turned to his pack and dug out an extra cup. "The coffee's still hot," he said, pointing, "and there's plenty of cold stuff here to eat. Just help yourself, if you're hungry."

The young man did not hesitate. "I am a little bit hungry," he said. He filled his cup, then took a seat on the ground. As he tore into the bologna and cheese, and began to stuff crackers into his mouth by the handful, it became obvious that he had been more than a little bit hungry. Camp dug into his pack again and added two tins of sardines to the offering. "Eat all you want," he said. "I'm not short on anything."

Camp sat sipping his coffee and watching as the young man continued to eat everything in sight. Sometimes, when he turned his head a certain way, Bo Patton appeared to be a little older than he probably was. Even so, he couldn't be more than eighteen years old, Houston decided; and his long blond hair, dimpled chin and beardless, freckled face made him look even younger.

Camp believed that the young man stood at least six foot two in his socks, and very well might shoot up a few more inches before he stopped growing. He had big hands, long arms and legs, and his shoulders were unusually broad. All of which suggested that, when he finally stopped growing and filled out his frame, he would be a hard man to push off whatever ground he decided to stand.

Camp motioned toward the wagons with his thumb, and spoke to Patton, who was still busy eating. "Is that your family you're traveling with?"

"No, no," the young man said around a mouthful of food. "That's the Joneses over there. I just met up with them a few days ago, and I've been traveling with them. I've been eating supper with them every night, too. Now, there ain't none of them mentioned it to me, but I believe they might be running a little short. Anyway, they eat the same thing every day: corn pone and fried potatoes, and the portions are kinda small, like maybe they ain't got very much." He swallowed the last of his food and sat quietly for a moment. Then his cheeks suddenly turned red, and he began to speak softly and self-consciously: "I guess I ought to just tell you the truth: the only reason I walked over here was because I was hoping you'd offer me something to eat."

Houston nodded. He had suspected as much. "How old are you, Bob?" he asked.

"Twenty-one." Patton pulled the coffeepot off the fire and refilled his cup, then turned to face Camp. "That ain't the truth either," he said, his face flushing again. "I've been telling that lie for so long that I've just about started believing it myself, but it ain't done me a damn bit of good. I ain't but seventeen years old; be eighteen next March."

Camp nodded again. "Where are you headed, and what are you gonna do?"

"Don't know for sure. Mr. Jones said that when he finds some work, I might be able to get a job helping him." He picked his teeth with a splinter for a moment, then looked at Camp sheepishly, adding, "He said I could marry one of his daughters if I wanted to, but I told him I didn't know so much about that."

Houston was smiling now. "What do you know how to do?" he asked.

"I grew up farming, but I hated every minute of it. I'd sure be willing to do it now, though. As broke as I am, I'd take on any kind of job that's honest."

During the next hour, Camp learned a great deal more about the young man, who actually seemed eager to talk about his past. Houston put on a fresh pot of coffee, then leaned back on his elbows, ever the willing listener. Sensing that he had Camp's undivided attention, the youngster also relaxed, and began to speak freely:

Patton had never known his father, who had died on a Tennessee battlefield during the Civil War. After his mother's death, when the boy was ten years old, he had been shifted back and forth between two of his maternal uncles. It had been one of the uncles who had bestowed the nickname Bo on young Julian Patton, and the boy had rarely been addressed by his given name since.

When young Patton reached the age of sixteen, he said good-bye to both of his uncles and took a job on a nearby cotton farm. The living conditions on the new job were a big improvement over anything he had experienced before, especially the food. And though the wage was pitifully small, he nevertheless managed to save enough money to buy a reasonably good saddle and the ten-year-old bay that was at this moment picketed in the meadow beside the wagon teams.

Several weeks ago, after months of reading magazine articles extolling the innumerable virtues of living in the West, assuring the reader that year-round jobs on Texas ranches could be had for the asking, Bo Patton made his move: with one blanket, two changes of clothing and nine dollars in his pocket, he saddled the bay and headed west. Now, after seven weeks of traveling and job hunting, he sat at Houston's campfire.

"What little money I had's been gone for nearly a month

now," Patton said, as he filled both coffee cups and handed one to Camp. He blew air into his cup and sipped at the coffee, then sat staring across the river for a long time, as if in deep thought. "It ought to be against the law for them damn magazines to put out a bunch of lies," he said finally. "Just about every one you pick up back home's got at least one story about how easy it is to get a job on a Texas ranch. I've been asking for work at one ranch after another, but most of them are laying men off, not hiring. All the rest said they only hire men with experience, and I don't know much about cows. My horse don't either."

Camp had listened to Patton's story with interest, and by sunset had taken a liking to the young man. "I suppose there's room for one more down at my place," he said. "One of my friends is in the process of finishing the house, putting up some outbuildings and shaping up the place in general. Since you have nothing else to do, maybe you could help him out."

Patton nodded, and his whole face seemed to break into a smile. "Never have built anything on my own," he said, "but I sure know how to do what I'm told."

Camp chuckled. "Well, my friend's a good builder and a good man; he'll show you what needs doing."

"You got a ranch?"

"I've got thirty-eight hundred acres and a house on Calf Creek, and—"

"Thirty-eight hundred acres?" the boy interrupted. Clearly impressed, he began to shake his head. "Thirty-eight hundred acres!" he repeated loudly.

Camp was quiet for a while, then spoke softly: "I know that sounds like a lot of land to you, and back where you came from it would be. But in Texas, a six-section ranch is considered small. Very small. I don't have any cattle yet, but I expect to stock the place with longhorns next spring. If you happen to be on hand then, you'll get a chance to learn all you need to know about cattle." Houston yawned and stretched his arms over his head, suggesting that the conversation was about over. "The ranch is producing nothing right now, Bo, so I can't pay you much. But if you stay on through the winter, you'll have a few dollars in your pocket, plenty to eat and a warm place to sleep. Then, after I bring in the cattle next spring, you'll be paid full wages."

Patton did not have to think about the proposition for long. "All of that sounds mighty good to me," he said quickly, "and I'd sure be beholden to you."

Camp pointed across the river. "If you'll get an early start in the morning and stay with that road yonder, you'll be in the town of Brady before nightfall." He handed the youngster five dollars. "This'll be enough money to put you up at the hotel and feed you, and to pay for stabling your horse.

"When you leave Brady the day after tomorrow, you'll be headed due south. The road's pretty good, and it passes almost within a stone's throw of my place. You'll know when you reach Calf Creek, 'cause your horse'll either have to wade it or turn around. That's where you leave the main road and turn west. The new log house at the top of the hill is mine, and the man you need to see is Mr. Fowler. If for some reason he happens not to be there at the time, just make yourself at home. He'll be back."

Patton had listened to his instructions closely, nodding occasionally. He put the money in his pocket. "I guess all that means that you ain't gonna be around, huh?"

Camp nodded. "I've got business in Fort Worth, and I have no way of knowing when I'll be home. You'll be in good hands down there, though. Just watch what Mr. Fowler does and listen to what he says. You'll learn plenty."

When Camp yawned again, the young man got the message. "I guess I'll go on over and crawl into my bedroll, Mr. Houston." He got to his feet and offered a parting handshake. "I intend to be on that road before sunup, and like I said, I'm mighty beholden to you."

Camp shook the boy's hand. "Just take care of yourself, and eat a big beefsteak before you leave Brady. It'll stick with you a lot longer than flapjacks."

"Yessir," Patton said, then walked toward the wagons.

As the young man's image faded into the darkness, Houston kicked dirt over the campfire and dragged his bedroll between two bushes. Then he pulled off his boots and stretched out, his Peacemaker close to hand. A few minutes later, he was sleeping soundly.

He awoke once during the night to relieve himself, but soon dozed off again. When he next opened his eyes it was after daybreak, and the eastern horizon had already turned pink. What had awakened him had been a loud splashing sound close by. When he sat up and looked across the river, he could see a rider headed down the road in a southwesterly direction. He was pleased. Bo Patton had just forded the river, and was on his way to Calf Creek.

Houston rekindled the fire, and a short while later sat eating another meal of bologna, cheese, sardines and crackers, and washing it all down with several cups of freshly made coffee.

When Camp had first awakened, the Joneses had been busy harnessing and hitching their teams to the wagons. Now, with that chore completed, the vehicles rolled right in front of him before fording the river and taking the road to Brady. And though three people rode in each of the wagons, and all of them took a good look at Houston, no one offered so much as a nod, or otherwise acknowledged his existence.

Camp was somewhat amused. He believed that the slight had been deliberate, and the direct result of his having hired Bo Patton. The old man had no doubt viewed the youngster as a prospective son-in-law who might eventually gain employment and help him feed the pack, while the girls had had ample time to fall in love. The three young ladies, each of whom appeared to be in her teens, had all given Camp a malevolent stare as they passed.

He watched till the wagons disappeared down the road, then dashed his coffee grounds into the fire and got to his feet. He washed his coffeepot in the river, then rolled up his bedroll and put his pack together. He retrieved his horses from the meadow, and a short time later mounted and headed northeast.

Even though the bright sunlight in his eyes hampered his vision, it was a good day for traveling. And because he wanted to put as much of the crooked road behind him as he could during the cool of the morning, he pushed his horses to a mile-eating canter. Unless they began to show signs of overheating, he would maintain the same pace for much of the day. He expected to arrive in Comanche before nightfall, where good accommodations for both man and animals could be obtained at reasonable prices.

17

★

The town of Comanche had been established as a trade center for surrounding ranches in 1858. And although severe Indian raids inhibited its growth right from the start, the town's well-armed residents and the cattlemen of the area eventually decided to band together for their mutual defense. Within a matter of weeks they had collectively produced a body count that was totally unacceptable to the marauding Indians. Their depredations then came to a sudden halt, and it soon became obvious that they were no longer in the area. Nobody seemed to know where they had gone, but most believed they had headed for Mexico, hoping to find more plunder and less resistance.

With the threat of renegade Indians now a thing of the past, the area began to prosper, and when Comanche County was partitioned in 1859, the town of the same name became its seat. And though no population boom followed, the town held its own, and even attracted a few additional residents each year.

While most of the new faces belonged to people who would be productive citizens and good neighbors, the area also proved to be a magnet for a different element: as had been the case with many other Texas towns, Comanche had suffered an invasion of cutthroats and gunslingers early on, and gunfights, at one time or another, had taken place in practically every location in town, often in broad daylight.

And although more than a dozen men had died in shootouts during the early years of Comanche County, no one had ever been brought to account. Even during the Reconstruction period, the Union soldiers had rarely interfered with the combatants, seeming to find the idea of Texas killing Texans highly acceptable.

Years later, when Texas Rangers served notice on the rowdy element that their shenanigans would no longer be tolerated, the town took on a different look almost overnight. Most of the thieves and hustlers quickly found reasons to be somewhere else, while the few who remained curtailed their criminal activities and became almost law-abiding.

These days, the streets of Comanche were as safe as those of any other Texas town, and kept so by a thirty-year-old former trail boss named Bill Pennington, who had been town marshal for the past five years. Most outlaws made a special effort to bypass his town, for it was widely known that he was extremely fast with a six-gun and had the guts of a wolverine. He had little tolerance for thieves, and none whatsoever for ruffians who would run roughshod over those least able to defend themselves. Both facts could easily be confirmed by a short walk through the local cemetery: Bill Pennington had provided occupants for at least five of those graves at the top of the hill, one of them so fresh that the grass had not yet grown over it.

Camp Houston rode into Comanche from the west, when

the sun was still two hours high. He halted at the edge of town to take in the familiar view for a few moments, then kneed the roan down the street, his eyes scanning everything in sight. With the exception of several new buildings on the north side of the street, he could see few changes since his last visit, more than four years earlier.

One of the changes he could see, however, even from a distance, was that the town marshal now had his own office and jail, right in the middle of town. Long before Camp reached the building he could see a familiar figure sitting on the small porch beside the office door. Moments later, he brought his animals to a halt at the hitching rail. "Hello, Bill," he said loudly.

The marshal, who had been paying attention to something across the street, turned his head instantly, seeming to recognize the voice. He was on his feet in a second, his face breaking into a broad smile. "Well, I'll be damned, Camp," he said, walking into the street and offering a handshake. "Ain't been more'n three days since I heard a bunch of fellows talking about you, and here you come riding in outta nowhere."

Camp dismounted and shook the marshal's hand. "I'm on my way up to Fort Worth, and decided to stop off here for the night." He tied the roan to the hitching rail, then added, "Cooking on a campfire and sleeping on the ground gets a whole lot less agreeable as I get older."

Pennington laughed. "It never was agreeable to me, even though I just about lived outdoors for several years. I've been sleeping in a good bed ever since I got this job, so I guess the ground would feel even harder nowadays."

The marshal motioned toward his office, and led the way. "I've got just about anything you'd like to drink," he said over his shoulder. "I bought a little of it myself, but I took most of it away from drunks bent on raising hell." He opened a wall cabinet to reveal a shelf lined with bottles. "Name your poison," he said.

Camp shrugged. "I'll drink whatever you're having."

Moments later, Pennington was busy pouring. "I got this bottle without even having to argue about it," he said as he filled two tin cups with expensive rum. "The fellow I took it from didn't even remember having it when I turned him out of jail next morning." After reading a question in Houston's eyes, the lawman added quickly, "That's not exactly like it sounds, now. I don't mean that I steal their whiskey. You see, even though they almost always aggravate the hell out of me and give me a hard time, I don't fine them one cent for getting drunk unless they tear up something. They actually come out ahead, Camp. Where else could they get a night's lodging and a hot breakfast for the price of a bottle of whiskey?"

Camp smiled, took a sip from the cup and did not answer the question.

They had first met in Kansas almost ten years earlier. Pennington had been a trail boss from the San Antonio area at the time, and Houston was a green cowhand who had just completed his first cattle drive up the trail to Abilene. And though a wide gulf separated their respective ranks as far as the other drovers and cowboys were concerned, the two had nevertheless struck up a lasting friendship, no doubt due to the similarity of their ages and backgrounds.

Because of a holdup in getting bank drafts converted to gold or acceptable currency, both men had remained in Abilene for several days. They walked the streets together at all hours of the day and night, taking in one bawdy house or saloon after another. Then, almost a week later, when the bank solved its problem and began to trade bags of cash for bank drafts, both Pennington and Houston were paid in full, and each went his own way.

Although they had never worked together, they had remained friends, and for the next several years had run into each other frequently. Then Pennington had taken his current job, which had brought his traveling to a halt. Today was only the second time Camp had seen him in five years.

Now the marshal sat with one elbow on his desk, his chin

resting in the palm of his hand. "How long has it been since you've been in this town, Camp? For the life of me, I can't remember."

"Four years." Camp finished off his drink and handed the lawman the empty cup. "The fellow you took that bottle away from had good taste, Bill. I believe I could stand a refill."

Pennington poured both cups half full, then returned the bottle to the cabinet, saying, "I don't suppose a week ever goes by that I don't think of you." He reseated himself behind his desk, and chuckled. "The number of men on Earth that I truly like is pretty small, Camp. You're one of the chosen few." He sipped his drink, then wiped his mouth on his sleeve. "You say you're headed for Fort Worth, so I guess you're traveling on business, huh?"

"I've got business there, all right. At least, I think I do." Camp set his cup on the desk and got to his feet. He walked back and forth across the room while he told Pennington the whole story, raising his voice occasionally to emphasize a point.

When Camp finally stopped talking and reseated himself, the marshal set his own cup down and exhaled loudly, as if he had listened to the story without breathing. "I knew about the bushwhacking in Kansas," he said, "and I knew John Calloway. We weren't big buddies or anything like that, but I talked with him once in Abilene, then a few times in Dodge City. I guess one of the reasons I remembered him was because he never would have a drink with the rest of us. More than once I saw him belly up to the bar and buy whiskey for everybody else, but he sure wouldn't drink it himself."

"I never knew John to take a drink, Bill, and I knew him well." Camp sat quietly for a few moments, then handed Pennington the letter he had taken from Ben Gillam's pocket. "Read this, then tell me if you think Walt Turner wrote it."

The marshal walked to the window and stood reading. "Hell, yes!" he said, almost shouting. He handed the letter back. "Hell, yes, Walt Turner wrote it. Who else wants you dead bad enough to hire some punk to kill you?" He stood looking through the window for a few moments, then continued. "You've been killing off his partners, Camp. Just a little common sense is enough to tell him that his own number's gonna be coming up. I'll tell you something else: I'd bet a bundle that Sam Lott's real reason for killing Bill Wiggins down in Brackettville was to avoid giving him his share of the booty. I'd bet that Turner ordered Lott to eliminate Wiggins, so the two of them could keep his share for themselves." He turned to face Camp again. "And I'd also bet that the damn split between Lott and Turner was far from even."

"That's the way I've got it figured, Bill, and I think you're right about Turner. I believe he knows that I'm coming."

"Hell, yes, he knows, and you're gonna get your ass killed if you go riding into his den." He walked around the room once, then stood in the doorway for a while. When he turned back to face Houston, he spoke more softly. "Put your horses up at the livery, Camp, then get yourself a room at the hotel. I'll turn the office over to my deputy as soon as he comes in, then join you at the hotel. We need to talk about this some more. I might be able to get Walt Turner to ride right down that street out there, if I go about it right."

Camp was smiling now. "The hell you say!" he said loudly, then immediately softened his voice. "You think he'd come alone?"

"No," the marshal said firmly. "But I don't think he'd bring a pack of wolves, either. Might bring along a bodyguard or two, but—" Pennington shrugged, rolled his eyes toward the ceiling and left the sentence unfinished.

Camp had heard enough. "I'll go to the hotel and register right now," he said, "then come by here and tell you the room number. After I put up my horses and eat supper at the hotel restaurant, I'll go to my room and wait for you." He took a few steps toward the door, then stopped and turned halfway around. "Bring the rest of that fellow's rum, if you think of it." Then he was gone.

The marshal wrapped the bottle in a newspaper and laid it on his desk. He would eat his own supper at the boarding-house, then join Houston at the hotel.

Bill Pennington had been born and raised on a dairy farm in Ohio, and had come to Texas the year he turned seventeen. He found work on a ranch in the San Antonio area right away, and immediately set about learning the complexities of pro-ducing longhorns. The knowledge he had gained while tend-ing dairy cattle back home had helped him immensely on the new job, for to a certain extent, a cow was a cow. He learned fast and continually, and at the age of twenty bossed his first trail drive to Kansas.

Dark-complected, with brown hair and eyes, Pennington was neither big nor tall. He stood about five-ten, and weighed no more than one-seventy. He had broad, drooping shoulders and unusually long arms that reached almost to his knees. As he walked the streets of Comanche he appeared to be ready for anything, with his ham-sized hand hanging flush with the holstered Peacemaker that was a constant on his right leg. And although his methods of keeping the peace were scorned by some, most of them female do-gooders, even they felt a sense of security with his presence, for none doubted that, should the occasion arise, he would be quick to use the gun they preached against to defend them.

Camp Houston had chosen a room on the top floor of the three-story hotel. He raised a window on each side of the room and had just taken a seat on the bed when he heard a faint knock. He walked the necessary steps, then drew his Colt and eased the door open.

Marshal Pennington stepped inside quickly, his eyes on the gun Camp held in his fist. "Turner's not here yet," he said, chuckling.

Houston holstered the weapon. "It's just a habit that I picked up several years ago, and I'm not likely to drop it. I be-

lieve that many a man has gone to an early grave because he
opened a door empty-handed when somebody knocked. I'll
do all I can to keep it from happening to me. I can't believe
that you don't take the same precaution, Bill."

"Of course I do," Pennington said, seating himself in the
room's only chair. "I can't remember the last time I opened a
door without being loaded for bear." He unwrapped the bottle and discarded the newspaper, then poured rum into two
cups, handing one to Houston.

Camp reseated himself on the bed. "You said you might be
able to get Turner down here," he said. "How are you gonna
do that, and how come you're willing to get involved?"

The marshal answered quickly. "I'm willing because I had
a strong liking for John Calloway, and deep down, I'm still a
trail boss at heart. Another reason is that I don't like Walt
Turner. I never was around him much, but it sure wasn't his
fault. The sonofabitch hit me up for a job on at least three occasions, but I never would hire him. I just didn't like the looks
of him, Camp; didn't like the way he shifted his eyes around
all the time, talking out of one corner of his mouth.

"As to getting him down here, I don't know that I can do
it, but if I handle it right, I think he'll come running. You see,
Turner's an insurance salesman nowadays, and I've even heard
it said that he owns a piece of the company. Now, if you were
in his shoes, and the town fathers of Comanche sent you word
that they wanted your company to insure everything the town
owned, including all of the buildings and their contents, and
preferred that you write up the policy personally, what would
you do?"

Camp chuckled loudly. "I'd come running," he said.

"And that's exactly what I expect Walt Turner to do." The
lawman was on his feet now. "Of course, it'll be several days
before we'll know whether he bought it or not." He took a sip
of his rum, then set the cup on the table. "I can't go out on a
limb with this now. I'll have to do something to cover my
tracks. I'm not gonna ask the town council to get involved,

but the head councilman owes me a few favors, and I intend to collect one of them tonight. We won't send Turner a written invitation, or do anything else that might point to any particular man down here. What I've been thinking about doing is sending a rider who has no name to tell Turner that the Comanche town council wants to buy a policy from him personally, and that he should get here pronto."

Camp was on his feet. "That'll work," he said. He finished off his drink, but held on to the empty cup. "You've already got it figured out, Bill; why the hell do you need the head councilman?"

"Because he does the thinking for the whole damn board. None of the others is gonna question a single thing he says."

Camp nodded. "I see."

Pennington walked to the door and stood with his hand on the knob. "This is the last time I'll visit you here," he said. "I'll get a rider off early in the morning, and it's possible that we'll see the result in about four days."

They shook hands, then the marshal was gone down the hall. Camp closed the door and locked it, then poured a pan of water from the pitcher. He would wash himself and shave his face, then go to bed early.

18

★

Camp was sitting at the marshal's desk at nine o'clock next morning, sipping his third cup of coffee of the day. "Our rider left for Fort Worth three hours ago," Pennington said. "He'll use a name other than his own, and claim to have been dispatched by the town council. He says that, even though he'll stop somewhere and sleep a few hours tonight, he'll be in Fort Worth by late afternoon tomorrow."

Houston nodded, and drained his cup. "You don't think he'll have any trouble finding Turner?"

"Nope, he knows exactly where to go. Even if he don't find him right off, he knows how to ask around. A man ain't all that hard to find, Camp, especially one as well known as a successful insurance salesman would have to be." He pulled the coffeepot off the stove and refilled their cups. "I think Walt Turner will have the message by sundown tomorrow, then he'll spend the night trying to figure out a way to fatten his commission on the big policy he's about to write."

"I guess you've got it figured out, Bill," Camp said, getting to his feet. "I think you figured it right, too." He set his empty cup on a small table beside the desk, then stood quietly for a while, looking through the window thoughtfully. "There's no way in the world that Turner could get here before Monday afternoon," he said finally. "This four-day wait's gonna seem like four months."

Pennington nodded, then began to chuckle. "Of course, you could speed things up by walking over to the saloon and getting yourself a couple more bottles of that rum. Drink enough of that, and four days'll seem like four hours."

"Not a chance, old buddy." Camp walked to the door. "At least I'm gonna have time to get my horses shod. The liveryman looked their hooves over real good when I turned them over to him yesterday. He even picked up my saddler's forefoot and had a look, but he didn't mention the job that both of us knew needed doing. I'll go down there right now and tell him to trim their hooves and nail on some new shoes."

"Russ is good, Camp, but he's not pushy. If you want something done, you'll have to tell him."

Houston opened the door and stepped onto the porch, then spoke over his shoulder. "Tomorrow being Saturday, I guess the town'll be full of people, huh?"

"Always is," Pennington answered. "If you walk around among 'em for a while you might run into somebody you know."

"I guess it's possible," Camp said. "I've always heard that it's a small world." He stepped off the porch and headed for the livery.

Holmes's livery stable, which also served as a blacksmith shop, was located at the east end of Main Street, and was the largest building in town. Russel Holmes, the stable's owner and operator, had brought his young family and all of his tools to Comanche in two covered wagons twelve years before. He bought four lots, hired a helper and immediately set about building the large barn and adjoining corral. He, his young wife and two small children lived in the wagons till the barn was completed, then lived in the barn till he could build a house a quarter mile from town. Nowadays, the muscular thirty-five-year-old Holmes was known and respected throughout the county, and his establishment did more business than both of the town's other stables combined.

When Houston reached the barn, the liveryman was standing in the doorway, wiping his brow. He smiled, and laid the towel aside. "You gonna be leaving us already?" he asked.

Camp shook his head. "Not for a few days yet. I came down to ask you to shoe my horses."

"Be glad to," Holmes said. "I noticed 'em yesterday. The packhorse's hooves need trimming pretty bad."

"They've covered a lot of miles this summer," Camp said. "I hope to leave 'em in the corral this winter; I've got a lot of things to do besides travel."

The liveryman reached for a leather apron that hung from a hook on the wall, and tied it around his waist. "Guess I'd better hop to it," he said. "The later it gets, the hotter it gets." Obviously a man who put business ahead of small talk, he grabbed a rope and headed for the corral, leaving Camp standing alone in the doorway.

Houston walked the streets for the next hour, occasionally stopping in front of a store to gaze at the merchandise in its window: boots, hats, coats, rings, watches and a wide assortment of other things, all showcased for the prospective buyer's inspection. And although he walked past numerous buildings, and peered into dozens of windows, the one thing that caught and held his attention was a large apple pie, sliced into wedges and displayed in the window of a small restaurant. He stepped inside, and found that he was the establishment's only customer.

A dark-haired woman about his own age stood behind the counter. "Thank you for coming in, sir," she said sweetly, her smile revealing two rows of perfect teeth. "May I help you?"

Camp had so far made no move toward a chair. Standing

just inside the door, he pointed to the window. "I think I'd like a slice or two of that pie."

"Certainly, sir." She pointed over her shoulder toward the kitchen. "I've got two more exactly like it that I just took out of the oven. In fact, I believe they're still warm."

"That'll be fine," he said, then seated himself at the nearest table.

A short while later, the lady delivered a platter containing two large slices of apple pie. "Will you be having coffee, sir?"

"Yes," he said. He glanced at her ringless left hand, then added, "Just call me Camp, if you will."

"All right," she said, then headed for the kitchen. Moments later, she set a mug of steaming coffee in front of him, saying, "My name is Bess Bullard, but most of the local people just call me Idaho." Then she was gone through the batwing doors again, no doubt to continue her preparation of the noonday special.

What Camp had in front of him amounted to half of a large pie, for the lady had simply quartered it and served him two slices. He picked up his fork and dug in, although he doubted that he would clean the platter. That doubt disappeared very quickly, however, for the pie was delicious. Though it contained enough sugar to make it sweet, it also had a tart aftertaste that was very pleasing, somewhat like green apples. Stopping only occasionally to take a sip of coffee, he continued to eat until the pie was gone.

A few minutes later, he stood at the counter waiting to pay. "Just leave the money on the counter," the lady called through the open window separating the kitchen from the dining area. "The pie and the coffee'll be fifteen cents."

Camp counted out twenty cents, then left the building. The fact that she had not come to the counter to accept his money had disappointed him, for she was a beautiful woman, and he wanted to know her better. He continued to think on the matter for a moment, then headed for the marshal's office.

Bill Pennington could answer any questions Camp had about Bess Bullard. He would go talk to Bill.

"Bess Bullard, huh?" the marshal asked, when Camp mentioned the dark-haired beauty. "Is that the name she's using this week?" Pennington began to chuckle loudly. "Did she also tell you that she grew up a poor little orphan, that she had to beg on the street and eat out of garbage cans?"

Houston shook his head, and said nothing.

The lawman moved away from his desk and opened the door. He stood in the doorway looking down the street toward the little restaurant for a while, then turned. "Let me tell you a few things about that woman: she's a good cook, and a lot of us like to eat at her restaurant. She's a good-looking bitch that a lot more of us would like to take to bed. But she's bad news, Camp. Avoid her like the plague.

"She's been here about three years, and nobody knows what her real name is. She's even changed it two or three times since she's been here. About two years ago a fellow passing through Comanche said he knew her up in Idaho Territory, and all of us started calling her Idaho after that. Now, that fellow claimed to know her well, but of course he didn't know what her true name is. He said he first met her in a gold camp on the Clearwater River, where she was living under the name of Ruth Meadows. What she did on the Clearwater was the same thing she's doing now, cooking and selling good food to hardworking men. Of course, she eventually sold her restaurant and started marrying lovesick miners.

"That fellow swore that she'd killed at least one husband, and most likely two. At any rate, she married two miners within a period of six months, and neither man lived over it. Both died under mysterious circumstances. According to him, every man in the camp had a suspicious feeling, but none acted on it, for they were simply too busy to take the time off to investigate. He said that gold seekers go at it like ants and won't let up for anything, 'cause most of them are convinced that the next big strike lies only one more shovelful of dirt away.

"Now, if she didn't get around to handing you that orphan bullshit, I guess it means that she has a different story in mind for you. You see, she'll tell one man that she was a poor little orphan who had to eat garbage, then the next fellow gets told that she was the daughter of a wealthy New Orleans banker, and that she got cheated out of her rightful inheritance by greedy relatives. Then occasionally some lucky diner gets to hear the story about—"

"Hell, Bill," Camp interrupted, laughing loudly, "you've made your point. You can let up now. I've already decided to do my eating somewhere else."

Pennington returned to his desk and seated himself. "I don't see any reason why you shouldn't eat up there. Hell, she's the best cook in this town, and I eat there myself when her special of the day happens to be something I like. I just told you all of this because you asked, and because I want to make sure you don't fall for whatever line of shit she decides to feed you."

"Well, you can relax now. Anything she says to me will go in one ear and out the other." He stepped out the door and onto the porch, continuing to talk through the open doorway: "I'm gonna buy something to read, then go back to the hotel. Might even take a nap if I get sleepy." He walked across the street and bought a three-day-old copy of the *Fort Worth Democrat,* then headed for his room. He stretched out on his bed with the newspaper, and fell asleep before he had finished reading the front page.

19

★

Houston did not visit Idaho's restaurant again. He also avoided the marshal's office for the next few days. He took several two-hour walks during the weekend, and spent many of the daytime hours reading a book about cattle breeding. He spent the early part of each evening in the hotel saloon, having a few drinks and trading stories with a bartender who liked to talk about fishing.

He was sitting on the side of his bed at daybreak Monday morning, alternately staring through the window and reading the last chapter of his book, waiting for the town to come to life. When the sun finally topped the horizon and he began to see people moving about on the street, he closed the book and laid it on the table for the next man to read. Half an hour later, he was having breakfast in the hotel dining room. He ate his food slowly and sipped two cups of coffee afterward, for he doubted that the marshal was in his office yet.

When he finally stepped out on the street he saw that there

had been no reason for his waiting around, for he could already see Pennington sitting in the doorway of his office. He pointed his boots in that direction, and began to step lively.

"Our rider woke me up about an hour before daylight," Pennington said, not waiting for Houston to come to a complete stop.

Camp leaned against a post. "Well, what's the verdict?"

"Turner bought it. Said he'd head for Comanche Sunday morning, which was, of course, yesterday. If he goes about traveling anything like I do, I'd say he'll be here this afternoon or early in the morning."

"He'll be here today," Camp said. "A man'll hurry his horse along quite a bit to avoid having to spend an extra night on the trail." He stepped onto the porch and took the seat beside Pennington. "Did your man figure out anything else about Turner, like whether or not he intends to bring a small army along?"

"He didn't have any way of knowing. He said Turner was alone when he talked with him, and he saw no sign that anybody else was hanging around. Sounds to me like Turner don't have room for anybody else. My man says his office is just a hole in the wall with a desk and two chairs."

Camp sat staring down the street at nothing in particular. "Are you saying you think he might come down here alone, Bill?"

"No," the lawman said quickly. "But like I said at the start, I don't think he'll bring a bunch. One man, maybe two, but they'll be the sorriest sonsofbitches Fort Worth has to offer, conscienceless bastards who'd cut their own mothers' throats for a few dollars."

"You're probably right, Bill." Camp pointed to the dusty street. "Do you think Turner'll ride right into town?"

Pennington shook his head. "I don't think you should let him. Hell, he'll be hunting some of the members of the town council, and they've never even heard of him. I never could find the head councilman, so he don't know anything about it either." He pointed down the street with his thumb. "I believe you ought to intercept Turner at the livery stable."

Camp was thoughtful for a moment. "That was my first thought," he said, "but I had no idea how Russel Holmes would feel about it."

"I'll talk to Russ," Pennington said, getting to his feet. "Fact is, I'll do it right now." He stepped off the porch, then spoke over his shoulder: "You just sit where you are. I won't be long." Then he walked toward the stable.

Houston sat on the porch for what seemed like a long time. The town was wide awake now, with people of all ages, shapes and sizes scurrying from one place to another. Dozens of men rode up and down the street in wagons or on horseback, and Camp could see more women on the sidewalks than was usual for such a small town.

Of the many men who passed directly in front of the marshal's office, all were quick to notice the stranger sitting on the porch. Houston nodded a greeting to those with friendly faces, and attempted to outstare the others. He was still playing the game when Marshal Pennington returned from the stable, more than half an hour later.

"Russ don't give a damn what you do," Pennington said, ignoring the step and taking hold of a post to pull himself to the porch. "I told him about Turner and his bunch slaughtering the drovers up in Kansas, and that one of his hired gunmen had already tried to kill you. Holmes says he can't find any fault with what you're doing. All he asks is that you be careful not to shoot any of his livestock."

Houston nodded. "That goes without saying." He got to his feet and looked at his watch. "It's already past ten o'clock, Bill. I think I'll saddle up and ride a couple miles east of town. I'll hunt myself a good, comfortable seat at the top of the hill and stay there, 'cause I'll be able to see nearly halfway to Fort Worth."

"That's a good idea," Pennington said. "You'll see him an hour or two before he gets to town, so that'll give you plenty of time to beat it back here and get me. I intend to be in the barn with you."

Camp had already taken one step toward the stable. He hesitated now. "The fight's mine, Bill. I appreciate everything you've done, but there's no reason for you to be involved in the showdown."

"Well, now," Pennington said, stepping to the edge of the porch. "You may be right, and you may be wrong." He stood with his thumbs hooked behind his belt. "If Turner comes alone, you're right. If he brings some help, you're wrong. I won't hold still for you facing more than one man at a time, Camp. As soon as you spot Turner, I want you to ride like hell to this office and tell me. We'll walk down to the stable together, because I intend to at least be a bystander." He stood quietly for a moment, then added, "Will you do that?"

"Yes, Bill," Camp said, heading for the stable. "I'll do that."

Less than an hour later, Houston was at the top of the hill, sitting in the shade of a large mesquite tree. He had picketed his horse on the west side of the hill, a hundred yards below the skyline. His view of the road to Fort Worth, while not entirely unobstructed, was at least as good as he had expected. There were several long stretches where no growth at all occurred, and probably an equal number of shorter ones where he could not see the road at all for a quarter mile or more.

He was paying all of his attention to the bare stretches in the distance now, however, for if anyone had been traveling in one of the obstructed areas when he first sat down, they had already had more than enough time to come back into view. He doffed his hat and leaned against the rough bark of the mesquite tree, his eyes glued to an open quarter-mile section of road far ahead. He took a sip of water from his canteen and relaxed, convinced that he could see a man on horseback from a distance of at least five miles.

Two hours later, he was feeling uncomfortably warm in the heat of the early afternoon. The sun had already moved to the opposite side of the hill, and the sparse leaves of the mesquite now provided no shade whatsoever. Looking north, then south, he could see no place where he might escape the hot sun and still maintain a good view of the road.

He had just taken another sip from his canteen when he spotted two specks in the road several miles to the northeast. He wiped the sweat from his eyes and continued to stare. Were the specks moving? He could not tell. After a while he picked out a third speck that he believed to be stationary, a little closer and well off the road, most likely a large bush or small tree. Then he sat watching, minute after minute, as the distance between the specks diminished. When the two specks were finally even with the third, Camp had his answer: he was no doubt looking at two mounted men. He picked up his canteen and his hat, and crawled to the other side of the hill. Moments later, he pointed the roan toward town and kicked the big beast to a hard run.

Marshal Pennington was standing in the doorway of his office when Camp slid the roan to a halt and dismounted. Houston tied the animal to the hitching rail, then held up two fingers. "Two riders coming," he said. "I'd guess them to be no more than five miles away."

Pennington nodded. "Just about what I expected," he said. Then the two men obviously had the same thought at the same time, for each of them stepped inside the office and began to move his gun up and down in its holster, making sure it was riding loosely. Neither man spoke again. They simply nodded to each other, then headed for the street.

They were at the livery in less than three minutes. Holmes greeted them at the front of the building, and Pennington spoke to him: "Two men coming from the east, Russ, and there's liable to be some trouble. I'd appreciate it if you'd go up to the restaurant and have a cup of coffee." Holmes nodded, and said nothing. He headed up the street at a fast clip.

The barn had large doors on opposite sides, and a hall that was wide enough for two wagons to pass each other. The door on the west side, facing the town, stayed open most of the time, but today both were open, flooding the building with light.

Houston took up a position inside the doorway of a stable on the north side, while the marshal stood behind a large stack of baled hay across the hall. "People coming in from the east usually use the back door if it happens to be open," Pennington said. He pointed to the hitching rails behind the building. "I expect them to tie up out there, then walk right in here and say hello."

Each man's position offered a good view of the road to the east, and both stood watching quietly. Ten minutes later, the riders came into view. When they were within two hundred yards of the barn, they brought their horses to a halt and held a short conversation, gesticulating back and forth with their hands. Then they kneed their animals and came on at a fast walk. Houston caught Pennington's eye, and both men nodded curtly.

Both of the riders rode black horses, and neither led a pack animal. And just as the marshal had predicted, they dismounted at the hitching rail on the east side of the building.

Pennington turned his head toward Houston, a slight smile on his face. He nodded again, then winked, for he now recognized both riders.

Hooty Folsom was the man's name who now stood beside Walt Turner at the hitching rail. A dark-haired six-footer who weighed about one-eighty, he was a gunman of some renown, but his reputation as a cattle thief and bushwhacking murderer was more widely known. He had twice been tried for murder in Tarrant County, but had walked out of the courtroom a free man each time. He had gained a self-defense ruling for killing a seventy-year-old man, and an outright acquittal on a charge that he had raped and murdered a young woman from Fort Worth.

Every time he had a few drinks he was likely to stand at the bar boasting to any man who would listen, bragging about his fast gun and all of the shootouts he had survived. Not all of his braggadocio was fiction, however, for although he only did so when he was thoroughly convinced that he had the upper hand, he had indeed initiated a few gunfights. Even now a Colt Peacemaker hung on his right leg, halfway between his hip and his knee.

The fact that Walt Turner appeared to be unarmed surprised neither of the men waiting in the barn. He considered himself a big businessman nowadays, and businessmen did not wear guns; they hired their shooting done. Besides, he had a meeting scheduled with the town council, and the chances of any council buying an insurance policy from a man wearing a gun in a quick-draw holster were somewhere in the neighborhood of zero.

The riders tied their horses and walked to the barn. They stopped just inside the doorway and looked around for an attendant, then walked on down the hall. "Is anybody home?" Turner called loudly.

Houston and Pennington stepped into the hall simultaneously. "Of course we're home," the lawman said.

Both Turner and Folsom froze in their tracks. Pennington stepped closer, then pointed to the gun on Folsom's hip. "I'm kinda surprised that you'd wear that thing into my town, Hooty. You see, it just might give me the wrong impression."

"Naw, I didn't mean nothing at all, Marshal, I—"

"Let me introduce you to my friend here," Pennington interrupted. "His name is Camp Houston, and he's got a little business to conduct with Walt Turner." His eyes were locked onto those of Folsom. "Is that all right with you, Hooty, or did you sign on to stick with Turner through hell and high water?"

Folsom shook his head several times. "I . . . I'm just along for the ride. I don't aim to do nothing at all to put myself in your cross hairs, Marshal, and I damn sure don't want no truck with Camp Houston."

"Unbuckle the gun belt, Folsom," Pennington ordered. "Let it fall to the ground, then move away from it." Folsom complied quickly, then took a seat on a bale of hay several feet from his weapon. The marshal was smiling when he turned to Houston and waved his arm in a sweeping motion, no doubt mimicking some entertainer that he had seen somewhere. "The stage is all yours, Camp."

Houston had been watching Turner like a hawk. He took two steps toward the man. "I've been wanting to meet you for a long time, Turner, but I don't suppose I'll be buying a policy from you today. What I had in mind was you and me discussing a trail boss named John Calloway and two of his hired hands named Bill Fisher and Joe Plenty. You remember them, don't you, Walt?"

Turner stared over Camp's shoulder, and did not answer.

"Oh, come on now, Walt," Camp continued. "Jog your memory a little bit. You remember yourself and four other nogood sonsofbitches riding into their camp in a Kansas gully, don't you? Don't you remember the five of you pumping all three of them full of lead, then stealing the money Calloway got for the herd? I'll bet you even remember that you yourself were the first man to draw a gun, and that your first shot went through Joe Plenty's chest.

"Well, Joe Plenty didn't die, Turner, although he lost an arm and a leg. He's very much alive nowadays, and he put the finger on the whole damn bunch. He knew all of you well, 'cause you were the sonsofbitches who helped drive the herd to Dodge City. The fact that the drovers knew all of you didn't bother you one bit, though, because you didn't intend for any of them to be alive to identify you."

Camp reached into his vest pocket. "I have a picture here of the entire crew, Turner." He held it high so the man could easily see it. "Remember the day all of you posed for the picture in San Antonio? Well, this is it, old buddy." He pointed to the picture. "Five of these people are dead now. Of course, you know about Calloway and Fisher, because you killed them. But three members of your bunch are no longer with us, either. You remember Bill Wiggins, Jack Little, and Red Bentley, don't you?"

He took the envelope from his pocket, extracted the single page and waved it in front of the man's face. "Remember this?" he asked. "I took it off the body of a man you sent to kill me. You remember your old friend Ben Gillam, don't you?" Turner continued to stare over Camp's shoulder silently.

Houston folded the letter and returned it to his pocket, then spoke to the man again. "Get your gun out of your saddlebag and strap it on, Turner."

Turner spoke now. "I never carry a gun."

Houston stared at the man contemptuously for a long time. "You don't carry a gun? You spend half of your life using a gun to rob, bushwhack and shoot people in the back, then all at once you don't carry a gun?" Houston was talking louder now. He raised the volume of his voice still another notch, and pointed. "Pick up Folsom's gun and strap it on. Right now!"

Turner shook his head very slowly. "No," he said. "I've given up guns completely, and I refuse to be pushed into a gunfight."

Though Houston was seething inside, he fought to maintain an outward calm. "Just like your bushwhacking partner, Jack Little," he said, looking Turner in the eye. "That murdering sonofabitch wouldn't fight either, but it didn't save his ass." He turned to face the marshal. "Walk over there and search him, Bill. See how many hidden guns and knives he's got on him." Pennington nodded, and moved to comply. "Look in his boots, too," Houston added.

Pennington stepped behind the man and searched him thoroughly, then moved away. "No weapon," he said.

Camp spoke to Turner again: "How many men did you send after me besides Ben Gillam, fellow?"

He received no answer.

Houston unbuckled his own gun belt and handed it to the marshal. He glared at Turner fiercely for several seconds, then spoke again: "You've been doing your damnedest to have me killed, old buddy. Here's your chance to do the job yourself." He began to walk toward the man. "Put up your hands, Turner. This is a fight to the death."

Turner stepped out to meet Houston and they collided noisily, each man blocking and swinging violently. And although Turner put up a defense that under most circumstances would have served him well, it was woefully inadequate protection against Houston's battering fists. The struggle lasted less than five seconds, for Houston landed a smashing blow to the jaw that turned Turner's eyes to glass. The man collapsed instantly, and now lay in the dusty hallway.

Camp hesitated for only a moment, then he was astride the unconscious man, his knees pinning Turner's arms to the ground. Then, seemingly of their own accord, Houston's big hands locked themselves around Turner's throat in a death squeeze, and held on until all signs of life had vanished.

Camp stood up for a moment, then knelt again, turning the man's head from side to side. After confirming that his fists had left no visible marks on Turner's face, he turned to Hooty Folsom. "Let me tell you how we're gonna handle this, Mr. Folsom: we're gonna tie Turner's body on his own horse, and you're gonna take it back to Fort Worth. Now, whatever story you put out when you get back up there is gonna reach my ears, and it damn sure better be the kind of story I want to hear." He pointed to the corpse. "Walt Turner took a fall from his horse and broke his neck, and when I start inquiring about a week from now, I'd better hear that you saw it happen. Have you got that, Folsom?"

The man nodded several times.

Houston gave Folsom a hard look that he believed the

man would remember. "All right," he said finally. "Go get Turner's horse."

They lashed the body to the saddle, then Folsom took the road to Fort Worth. One hour later, astride his roan and leading his pack animal, Camp Houston took the same road, although he was headed in the opposite direction.

20

Houston was back on his own property on Wednesday afternoon. He brought the roan to a halt a hundred yards above the house, and sat looking down the hill at the men building the barn. Cornell Wooten and both of his youngest sons were sitting on top of the building hammering, while Bo Patton was busy helping Fowler sink corral posts in the ground. Houston sat watching for at least half an hour. Things were shaping up nicely, and he was convinced that within a few short years he would own one of the better spreads in the area.

He had decided to call his place the Three County Ranch, for the simple reason that it was partially located in three different counties. He would register his 3C brand within the next few days, then hire Sid Blankenship to make up several branding irons.

He watched his young hired hand pound the earth with a post hole digger for a few minutes longer, then rode down the hill to the barn. He dismounted and spoke to Patton. "I see you found the place all right."

The youngster laid the digger aside. "I came straight to it, 'cause you gave me good directions. I appreciate you putting me on, Mr. Houston, and I'm glad you're home now." He walked to a water bucket and drank from a gourd dipper.

Camp waved to the Wootens, who were busy fitting another log into place. "It looks mighty good, Cornell," he called to the father, "and I certainly appreciate you fellows coming over to help." The Wootens acknowledged the greeting by waving their arms and nodding, then continued with their work.

Runt Fowler was beside Houston now. "I was expecting you back just about now," the big man said. "Did you find your man all right? Did you settle up with him once and for all?"

Camp nodded to both questions, then turned to lead his animals to the corral. Fowler walked along beside him. The big man stripped the saddle from the back of the roan, placing it on a sawhorse in the shed. Then he began to unburden the packhorse. "I'm kinda surprised that you don't use a mule for packing, Camp." He stowed the packsaddle in the far corner of the shed, then added, "A mule's the best damn watchdog in the world. Anytime a man wants to know what the hell's going on around him, all he has to do is look at that mule."

Houston knew from experience that fowler spoke the truth. Although mules had a reputation for stubbornness, and often refused to be hurried, they were far more sensitive to their surroundings than were horses. A horse could see fairly well, hear even better, and possessed a sense of smell approaching that of a dog. All of his senses paled, however, when compared with those of his floppy-eared cousin. The mule was one of the most observant creatures on Earth, day after day after day. Nothing escaped the attention of a mule.

"You're right, Runt," Camp said, "and I used to use one.

The benefit of using a mule is that they can stand more heat, they eat and drink less, and they're usually cheaper to buy. The bad side is that, if a man happens to be in a hurry, they can be a mighty big hindrance." He patted the packhorse on the rump. "Of course, this horse here belongs to Sid Blankenship. All things considered, though, if I had to buy a pack animal today, you can rest assured that I would choose a mule."

Fowler grunted, then returned to his work on the new corral. When Houston walked inside the house, he was pleased to see several thick mats scattered around the floor of the main living room. At least the workers were not sleeping on the ground.

He dropped his pack off in his bedroom, then walked to the kitchen. When he touched an oversized iron pot on the stove and found that it was still lukewarm, he lifted the lid, then stirred the contents with a wooden ladle. At least two gallons of stew, he decided, and whoever cooked it had been more than generous with the beef. He used the same ladle to fill a large bowl, then grabbed a piece of leftover corn bread and headed for the porch.

He was sitting on the doorstep eating when all five of the workers approached. "I decided we'd done enough for today," Fowler said. "All of us have been at it since before sunup."

Houston swallowed a mouthful of stew, then shook his head. "There's no reason for you to kill yourself or anybody else, Runt. The world won't end if it takes a little longer than we expected to build that barn. I think you should cut down to eight hours a day, ten at the most."

"That ain't an easy thing to do, Camp," Fowler said. "There are fifteen, maybe sixteen hours of daylight at this time of the year. It's hard to knock off early, then sit there on the porch for six or seven hours looking at all the things you need to be doing."

Camp chuckled. "I see your point, Runt. Just don't push yourself and your help too hard." He wiped his mouth with the heel of his hand, then set the bowl aside. "Whoever made that stew did it right," he said. "That stuff's plenty good."

Fowler pointed to Patton. "Your young hired hand from Georgia is the man responsible for the stew, Camp, both the fetching and the cooking. He shot the deer just before dark yesterday, then had the stew done before nine this morning. He tells me that all of his family and kinfolk cook venison the same way."

Camp turned to Patton, who appeared to be embarrassed. "I believe that's the best stew I ever ate, Bo. Hell, I thought I was eating beef." He chuckled softly. "You sure you didn't line up your sights on somebody's calf?"

Patton smiled, and shook his head. "Young buck," he said.

Houston spent the remainder of the day simply walking around and looking, impressed with all the progress that had been made on the house, barn and corral, and making a mental note of the things yet to be done. He could see with one eye, however, that the workers would soon be running short of building material. He mentioned that fact to Fowler just before sunset.

"We're gonna be needing some half-inch boards to deck that barn," Fowler began, "and we ain't got near enough tin to roof it. We'll be needing some more nails, and I broke a handsaw yesterday. And I reckon we need—"

"Just make a list, Runt," Camp interrupted. "I'll hitch up the team at daybreak and head for Menardville." He motioned toward Patton. "I'll take him with me and introduce him to the people we do business with, especially Spike Nettleton at the hardware store. Then, whenever you need something from town, you can send Bo after it. He'll be able to get it whether he has the cash money or not."

"Makes sense," Fowler said. He got to his feet, adding, "I'll make the list while I've still got some daylight left." Then he was gone inside the house.

Patton, eager to be off to see new places, woke Camp before daybreak, as he had been instructed. Houston was in the kitchen three minutes later, for all he had to do was follow the beam of light to the burning lamp. Bo had already built a fire in the stove, and had a pot of coffee boiling. He offered to fry some eggs and heat some smoked ham. "None for me," Camp said. "I just get sick of eggs sometimes, especially during hot weather. I'd rather have a bowl of that stew, if there's some of it left."

"Plenty," Patton said, pulling the pot over the stove's firebox.

They were off the hill before sunup, with Patton driving the team. Camp had put all of the tinned food from his pack into the wagon, so they were carrying at least as much as they would need to eat before reaching Menardville. He had busied himself with that, and pretended to be busy with several other things, while Patton hitched up the team.

Camp had kept a close eye on the harnessing and hitching process, wanting to find out if the youngster knew what he was doing. He did. Houston leaned against a front wheel watching as Patton backed a harnessed animal up to the wagon, omitted a corresponding number of links in each of the trace chains, hooked them to the whiffletree, then hooked the whiffletree to one end of the doubletree. He repeated the process with the second animal, then walked in front of the team and hooked up the tongue and connecting reins. "I guess we're ready," he said.

Camp nodded, and climbed to the seat. "You drive."

Workhorses were seldom eager to run, and almost never did so of their own accord. Houston's team, however, on this particular morning, refused to travel at a walking gait. Each time Patton pulled the animals down they would walk for only a short distance. Two minutes later, they'd be moving at a fast trot.

The team had just begun to move out again when Camp spoke to Patton: "Let 'em choose their own pace, Bo. I don't know what the hell their problem is, unless they're just in a hurry to get home. They were both raised right over here where we're going, but I wouldn't think they know it."

"I'll bet by gosh they do," Patton said quickly. "And mules know it better than horses. I remember an old stripe-legged mare mule we used to have. Her name was Ida, and you couldn't ride her away from where she was raised no matter how much you whipped her. You could make her pull a wagon away, but you weren't gonna ride her nowhere. She'd just go around in circles. Around and around."

Camp chuckled. "I know a little bit about stubborn mules, Bo. When he makes up his mind not to do something, he'll dig his heels in mighty deep. I once saw a farmer shoot one dead in its tracks when it refused to pull a plow."

Patton sat thoughtfully for a few moments, as if trying to remember something from the past. "I don't reckon I ever saw one actually balk in the field," he said finally, "but I've sure felt like shooting one a time or two. I guess they have days when they don't feel like working, just like people do, but it still makes you madder'n hell when they won't mind a word you say."

They rode quietly now, each man taking in the passing scenery. "This sure is pretty country," Patton said after a while. "Ain't nothing like it in Georgia."

Camp smiled, and said nothing. He himself had spoken almost the same words on his first visit to the region several years before. He had decided early on that he would eventually put down roots in the three-county area, for, although he had done his share of looking, he had found no place that was more suitable for ranching. The weather was usually agreeable to humans and animals alike; the summers were warm, but the temperature seldom reached a hundred degrees. Both spring and fall were mild, and the winters were comfortable, with no more than a few days of below-freezing temperatures. It snowed only once every few years, then only a few inches that would be gone a day later. The scenery of the area was easy on the eyes at any time of the year, but spring offered an added bonus with its profusion of wildflowers, especially the colorful bluebonnets that covered the hills and meadows and lined both sides of the road.

Autumn brought the brilliant colors of fall foliage: the crimson leaves of the sumac and red oak; the gold of the cottonwood, sycamore and wild chinaberry; and, lining many of the crystal-clear streams, the golden needles of the bald cypress. And if a man was lucky, he might occasionally come upon an isolated group of maple trees, their tops ablaze with their distinctively radiant red.

And there was absolutely no excuse for any man with a rifle going hungry in this country, for game was abundant. Five deer had already crossed the road in front of the wagon this morning, and so many rabbits that Camp had not even bothered to count them. Indeed, any man who could force himself to stand still in the woods could get meat for his pot quite easily.

A good example was the buck Patton had shot two days before. Bo said that he had been sitting on a log for no more than ten minutes when he scored. He shot the animal less than two hundred yards from the house, and said that even as he fired, he could hear the other men talking on the porch. The deer had no doubt heard the conversation also, but had not been alarmed.

Though they stopped to make coffee and eat their tinned goods at midday, they held to a steady pace during the afternoon, and arrived in Menardville two hours before sunset. Camp delivered Fowler's list to the hardware store immediately, then made the introductions between Spike Nettleton and Bo Patton. They left the wagon parked directly in front of the warehouse at the back of the store, so the man could load the material as he selected it.

Then, with Patton leading the team, they walked down the street toward the livery stable. They met several of Camp's acquaintances moving in the opposite direction, and he waved or nodded a greeting to all of them. They came abreast of Riley's Restaurant just as Ellen Bice was arriving for work. She had been about to open the door, but took a step backward when she saw Houston. "Hi," she said, waving to him and moving away from the door. "We haven't seen you lately. Have you found a better restaurant?"

Camp stopped for a moment. "I haven't been looking for a better restaurant," he said. He looked her up and down admiringly, then added, "And staying away hasn't been easy." He pointed down the hill. "We're headed to the stable to put up the team, then we'll eat supper with you."

The girl disappeared inside the restaurant, and the men continued on down the hill. "I think she's pretty," Patton said. "What do you think?"

"The same thing you do," Camp said. He paused for a few seconds, then added jokingly, "I'm liable to get around to marrying her one of these days."

"Oh," Patton said, then dropped the subject.

They turned the team over to Sid Blankenship, who went about caring for the tired animals immediately. Meanwhile, Camp seated himself on a bale of hay near the front of the building, and spoke to Patton: "I need to talk with Sid for a few minutes when he gets done there, Bo. Why don't you go back up to the restaurant and wait for me? Order up anything you like, and tell the waitress that I'll be eating whatever's on special."

"I'll do that," Patton said. He moved off at a fast clip, and did not look back.

Houston walked deeper into the building, stopping at the stables. Blankenship had already grained the horses, and was busy tearing apart a fresh bale of hay. "I'm certainly relieved to see you again," he said to Camp. "Just a little common sense told me that you'd gone hunting Walt Turner. Did you have any luck?"

Houston nodded. "I found him."

Blankenship grasped a currycomb and began to drag it

along a horse's back. "I suppose the fact that you're standing there tells the rest of the story," he said.

Houston made no other comment concerning Walt Turner. As the liveryman curried both horses, animals that he himself had bred and raised, Camp stood by watching quietly. When he finally spoke, it was to ask a question. "Has most of the talk about that thing with Ben Gillam died down, Sid?"

"When Joe Paley lets it," Blankenship answered quickly. "Nobody in this town gives a shit about Ben Gillam, and they all know that you did exactly what you had to do. Paley won't let it go at that, though. He's always running his mouth about how you're trying to turn the town of Menardville into a shooting range."

Camp made a motion to leave. "I don't know what Paley's problem is," he said, "but if he keeps trying to poison me, I'll probably discuss it with him eventually." He took a few steps, then stopped. "I'm going up to Riley's and eat supper, then get a room at the hotel. I'll be in the hotel bar later tonight, and I'll have a bottle of decent whiskey on the table."

"That last remark settles it," the liveryman said, laughing. "I'll be there."

Camp joined Patton at the restaurant, and both men ate a supper of baked beef ribs covered with some kind of spicy sauce. "One of the best-tasting things I've ever eaten," Houston said to Ellen Bice as she retrieved his empty platter. "I'll be back at this same table for breakfast."

"Thank you," she said. "I won't be here, but I'm sure my uncle appreciates your business."

Camp glanced at her with raised eyebrows, then began to stare at the table, a childish look of dejection on his face. "All right, then," he said jokingly. "I refuse to eat breakfast if you're not gonna be here."

She finished clearing the table, then smiled flirtatiously. "You'll survive," she said. She disappeared into the kitchen, and did not return.

Camp rented a separate hotel room for Bo Patton, for he

was not sure that he himself would be sleeping alone. He had been without a woman much longer than usual, and intended to at least look over the possibilities in the hotel saloon. He remembered that the last time he was in town he had decided to do the same thing, but the only two sporting women he encountered during the night were old enough to be his mother, and both were disgustingly drunk.

Sid Blankenship arrived at the saloon shortly after dark, and just as Camp had promised, he had a bottle of the good stuff on the table. Houston motioned to the bartender for another glass. Hawks was there quickly, shaking hands with the liveryman. "Good to see you, Sid," he said, pouring whiskey from Camp's bottle. "Thank you for stopping in." He pushed the glass across the table to Blankenship, then returned to his position behind the bar.

They had been sitting at the table drinking for more than an hour when Patton excused himself and headed for the outhouse. Blankenship took this opportunity to pass on some additional information to Houston. He leaned across the table and spoke softly: "If I were you I wouldn't trust Joe Paley any farther than I could throw him, Camp."

Houston smiled. "I don't," he said.

"Well, what I told you earlier ain't the only things he's said. He said that one of these days you were gonna make the mistake of crossing him, then he'd show the whole town just how overrated your shooting arm is. Now, I didn't hear him say that, but Mark Harvey swears that he did. You and I both know that Mark don't shoot no shit."

Camp nodded. He knew Mark Harvey well, and knew him to be an honorable man whose spoken word would be doubted by few. Houston sat thoughtfully for some time. "I know Mark," he said finally, "but he'd be the last man I'd expect to hear repeating something that was obviously told to him in confidence. I wonder why he decided to go spreading it around."

"He didn't do it voluntarily," Blankenship said, then

hoisted his whiskey glass. He wiped his mouth with his hand, then added, "I fished it all out of him after I saw him and Paley having a long talk. They stood at the hitching rail in front of the dry goods store for damn near an hour. Now, there ain't no way in hell that they've got that much in common, Camp. Neither can Paley talk that long without shooting off his mouth. Next time I saw Mark I just asked him what the hell the marshal was talking about, and he told me."

Camp accepted everything he had just heard as gospel. "Well, that's something I'll be keeping in mind," he said.

They spent another hour in the saloon, then called it a night. Blankenship went home, while Houston and Patton returned to the hotel. Camp said good night to his young hired hand, then once again went to bed alone. The pickings in the saloon had been dreadfully slim, and besides, hearing all the things that Paley had been saying had dulled Houston's desire for female companionship. He tossed and turned a few times, then he was sound asleep.

They had breakfast in Riley's Restaurant at sunup, then walked to the livery stable. Half an hour later, they hitched the team to the loaded wagon in front of Nettleton's warehouse, then headed for Calf Creek. The animals showed no inclination to trot this morning, for the wagon weighed three times as much as it had when empty.

21

November brought unusually high winds and below-freezing temperatures to the Calf Creek area. Most of the hardwood trees gave up their leaves very quickly, and the perennial grasses turned a golden brown, cured on the stem by a week of heavy frosts. Then, just as suddenly, the weather turned mild again, and the days and nights were almost like summer.

On the twentieth day of the month, Houston decided it was time for another trip to Waco. He left his bed early next morning, and was at the new corral at sunup. Runt Fowler followed, and caught up the packhorse while Camp saddled the roan. Then, working together, they lashed the packsaddle to the back of the black.

"Shouldn't take no more'n five days for you to get to Waco," Fowler said as he added a sack of grain to the animal's burden.

"More like four," Camp said, "unless I get delayed." He

mounted and pulled on the packhorse's lead rope. "Take care of yourself, Runt. Teach Bo as much as you can, and don't look for me back here till you see me coming." Then he was off the hill. He would be traveling in a northeasterly direction beside the San Saba River, and expected to be in the town of the same name by noon the next day.

He traveled about thirty miles the first day, and made camp at the point where Brady Creek emptied into the river. He dropped off his saddle and packsaddle at the spot where he intended to build his campfire, then picketed the horses in the nearby meadow. There was plenty of grass, and though it was no longer green, the animals took to it eagerly.

He found deadwood easily enough, and was soon eating warmed-over food and sipping strong coffee. At sunset, he kicked dirt over the fire and pulled his bedroll away from the smoking remains. He was no longer averse to sleeping near the water, for the recent freezing weather had played havoc with the pesky gnats and blood-sucking mosquitoes. Of course, both would be back tenfold in the spring, when the eggs left behind by this year's crop began to hatch.

As darkness closed in, he gathered up twigs, small pieces of bark and several handfuls of dry grass and placed it all under his pack. He had learned tricks like this the hard way, by waking up to find his kindling so wet with dew that it was difficult or impossible to start his morning fire.

A few minutes later, he stretched out on his bedroll, and, after tossing and turning for close to an hour, finally went to sleep.

He rode into Waco three days later in a steady drizzle. The rain had started to fall shortly after daybreak, and continued all day. The upper portion of his body was dry because he was wearing his slicker, but both legs were wet and he had water in one of his boots. He headed straight for the livery stable.

The middle-aged hostler accepted the horses eagerly, and thanked Houston at least twice for bringing them by. Maybe there were more stables in Waco than there used to be, Camp

was thinking. Maybe the man had lots of competition. "I
wonder if I could use your office for a few minutes," Camp
said, taking clean, dry clothing out of his pack.

The hostler understood Houston's predicament very well.
"Why, o' course, young fellow," he said, pointing to the small
room. "You just help yourself there. I'll be busy with these
horses for a while."

"Thank you," Camp said, and headed for the office. He
changed his clothing and was back in the stable before the
hostler was. He took a seat on an upended nail keg and
waited. He felt like a different man now that his legs and feet
were dry. He had also slipped on a new waistcoat that he was
wearing for the first time. He had bought it the month before
for no other reason than that it had a small pocket on each
side. Of course, he also liked the fact that it was made from
light material that could be worn comfortably at any time of
the year. And since there were no sleeves, he had free movement of his arms, and the garment stopped well short of his
gun belt.

"You figure to be staying in town for a while?" the hostler
asked when he had taken care of the horses.

"I don't have any way of knowing, sir," Camp answered,
"but just as soon as I can take care of my business, I'll be
gone. Should I give you some money for my horses now, or
pay when I leave?"

"You pay when you leave," the man said. "I'm just glad I
could be of service."

Camp nodded. "Good day to you," he said. He walked
out the door to find that it had stopped raining, and the sky
was growing lighter in the east. He stepped around a mud-
hole, then made a beeline for the Bryan Hotel.

A young man who appeared to be in his late teens greeted
Camp at the desk. "May I help you, sir?"

"You got a vacancy on the top floor?"

"Yes, sir, eighty-five cents a night. Dollar and a dime, if
you want a bath."

Camp smiled. "I've been riding in the rain all day, so I feel like I've already had a bath. Maybe tomorrow, if I'm still around." He laid a dollar on the counter.

"No, no," the youngster said, pushing the money away. "Just sign the register. You don't pay till you get ready to leave."

Houston wrote the name "Bo Granger" in the book, and the kid handed him a key. "Room two-twelve," he said.

Moments later, Camp stepped inside the room and locked the door. He laid his pack on the bed, then walked to the window and raised the shade. He not only had a good view of the street below, but could even see people moving around on the opposite side of the river. The sky was much lighter now, and it appeared that the rain was gone for the day. He stood at the window for a while, then returned to the bed and took his shaving soap and razor out of his pack. He was soon busy scraping off a four-day growth of beard.

A few minutes later, he was standing in the doorway of the hotel, looking up and down the street. He was trying to decide where he was going to eat supper, for he could see at least three restaurants. He glanced at his watch to learn that it was already four o'clock, time for him to put on the feed bag if he intended to beat the suppertime rush. He headed for the Texas Saloon, for he well remembered the good Mexican food he had eaten there so many times.

He stepped inside the establishment a few minutes later, and moved away from the door quickly. He stood with his back to the wall till his eyes adjusted to the dim lighting, then headed for the dining room, which amounted to nothing more than a roped-off area separating the diners from the drinkers. He immediately recognized the bartender as Flint Hastings, the same man who had been behind the bar the last time he had been in Waco.

Houston ignored the bartender and the few drinkers at the bar, and walked to a table along the rear wall. A young Mexican waiter stood at the table waiting for him, bill of fare in hand. "I'll just have the regular enchilada dinner," Camp said. He pulled out a chair and seated himself, then added, "I'd also like a bowl of those peppery Mexican beans."

Still clutching the bill of fare, the waiter nodded and headed for the kitchen. The young man had had no reason to speak. Camp believed that he could surely speak English, however, for very few of the Texas Saloon's patrons were of Mexican descent. The majority of the Mexicans did their drinking along the river several hundred yards to the south, in rickety clapboard buildings owned by other Mexicans.

Twenty minutes later, the waiter was back at the table with Camp's supper. "I hope you enjoy your food, sir," he said in perfect English. "If you need something else, just hold up your hand."

Houston nodded, and dug in. The food was just as good as he had remembered, and he emptied both the plate and the bowl in short order. He was in no hurry to leave the table, however, so he took much longer than was necessary to drink the remainder of his coffee. He could see that he had not been the only one with the idea of beating the rush hour, for several men had come in while he was eating. Four tables were already occupied on the opposite side of the room, and even now, three men who were dressed like lawyers were moving into the dining area.

Camp paid for his food and left the building, for the last thing he wanted at the moment was a conversation with this particular bartender. He walked to the corner and turned north, continuing up the hill until he reached the McLennan County Courthouse. The sheriff's office was on the ground floor, and Sheriff Dave Dubar had just locked the door and stepped onto the sidewalk when Houston arrived. The lawman stopped in his tracks and stood beaming. "Well, I'll be damned!" he said loudly. He stepped forward with his right hand extended. "Camp Houston! Seems like a hundred years since I've seen you."

Camp pumped the hand a few times. "It hasn't been quite

that long, Dave, but I'll admit that I do think of you once in a while."

"Same here," the sheriff said. "You just visiting, or here on business?"

"I'm on business, Sheriff, and that's what I want to talk to you about." He motioned to the office. "Can we go back in?"

"Absolutely." The lawman unlocked the door, and Camp followed him inside. "Sounds kinda funny hearing you call me Sheriff," Dubar said. "Hell, we go back to the days when both of us were punching cows or busting broncs for thirty a month. Just call me Dave, if you will. Especially when we're alone like this."

Camp nodded, and accepted the chair he was offered. It was true that the men had known each other for a long time. Houston had been eighteen years old when they first met, and Dubar about twenty-five. They had both been ranch hands at the time, and although they worked and lived on different ranches, they had nevertheless become close friends, and saw each other often.

Dubar had taken a job as deputy sheriff the same year Houston left the area, and ascended to his present position in 1872, when Sheriff Hampton Pitts died after a fall from a horse. Dubar had been McLennan County's top law officer ever since, and was liked and respected by most.

Camp got right to the point. "Did you ever know a man named John Calloway, Dave?"

"Heard of him, didn't know him. I do know that he's dead now."

"That's right," Camp said, "and one of the sonsofbitches who bushwhacked, robbed and killed him lives right here under your nose." He pointed to the chair behind the lawman's desk. "Just take your seat and listen while I tell you a few things about a bastard named Sam Lott."

Dubar hung his high-crown Stetson on the wall, revealing a healthy crop of dark, curly hair. He pulled out his chair and seated himself. "All right," he said.

Talking nonstop for the next fifteen minutes, Houston laid out the entire story. He exaggerated nothing; the only thing he failed to mention was the exact manner in which Walt Turner had died. He ended the long-winded narrative by adding, "I know you weren't acquainted with John Calloway, Dave, but if you could see what's left of Joe Plenty, and talk with him a few minutes, you'd want to burn Sam Lott at the goddamn stake."

Dubar had listened attentively, and had not interrupted once. He got to his feet and began to walk around the room. "I had already heard part of the story, Camp. Of course, I hadn't heard the part about you going around the country eliminating the participants." He stopped for a drink of water, then dropped the dipper into the bucket noisily. "I've known Sam Lott for most of his life," he continued, "and I've known that he wasn't worth killing for almost that long. I've heard it said that some folks suspect him of being one of the bunch who robbed and killed the drovers, but a man's liable to hear damn near anything. Sure as hell ain't nobody charged him with it. Anyway, there ain't a thing in the world I could do about it even if I wanted to. I'm just a Texas sheriff, and I reckon the crime took place in Kansas."

Camp nodded. "According to Joe Plenty it did, and I believe every word he says. He's been up that trail time after time, and he knows the country. If he says it happened in Kansas, by God it happened in Kansas." He got to his feet and helped himself to a drink of water, then continued. "One more thing, Dave, just so you don't read me wrong. I'm not asking you to do anything about Sam Lott. I'm just asking you not to get in my way." He stared through the window for a moment, then spoke loudly: "I intend to kill the sonofabitch!"

Dubar was quiet for a while, then began to chuckle, sounding much like he often had in the old days. "To tell you the truth, I've got more important things to do than worry about whatever kind of trouble Sam Lott might have gotten himself into." He reseated himself and continued, "The town marshal's name is John Bisco, and he's the exact same type of low-down sonofabitch that Lott is. Bisco ain't gonna give you no shit about killing Lott, though. He hates Same Lott's guts."

The sheriff had been busy building a cigarette. He returned the makings to his vest pocket, then struck a match on the sole of his boot. He took a long puff and inhaled deeply, then got to his feet again, blowing a cloud of smoke toward the ceiling.

Dubar was not a big man, weighing in the neighborhood of a hundred fifty pounds. He stood about five-nine, but his stooped shoulders sometimes made him appear to be even shorter. And this was one of those times. As Dubar stood looking through the closed window, puffing on the cigarette, Camp noticed that the lawman's shoulders drooped considerably more than in bygone days. Maybe the problem, whatever it happened to be, was getting worse. The sheriff turned back to his desk and snuffed the cigarette out in an ashtray. "I don't know whether Lott's got back from Dodge City yet or not," he said. "He took a herd up the trail for Albert Wells about three months ago."

"More than four months ago," Camp corrected.

Dubar took his seat again, then smiled. "Whatever you say," he said. He stared at his desk thoughtfully for a full minute, then spoke again: "It ain't gonna do for you to go walking around asking questions, Camp. I can personally guarantee you that Sam Lott ain't a damn bit above putting a dozen gunslingers on you. And neither he nor the bunch he runs around with would be very particular about whether or not they were looking you in the eye when they pulled the trigger. They'd just as soon shoot you from the back as from the front, and creeping on you in the dead of night wouldn't be out of character for a damn one of them."

Camp took a seat on the edge of the sheriff's desk, leaving one foot on the floor. "I've been thinking about that, Dave. I can't just hole up at the hotel, but I'd probably be foolish to think that somebody won't recognize me if I keep walking around. If word gets out that I'm in town, I don't think it'll take Sam Lott long to figure out why."

"Of course, you're assuming that he knows he's your quarry."

Camp nodded. "Yes," he said, "I'm assuming. But it didn't take a whole lot of imagination."

Dubar was on his feet once again, busy with another cigarette. He dumped a small pile of tobacco in a paper and smoothed it out evenly with a forefinger, then licked the edge of the paper and twisted it a few times. After he lighted up again, he continued to talk: "I can find out the things you need to know, but you're gonna have to keep your ass outta sight while I'm doing it."

Houston nodded. "I can handle that."

Dubar pointed to the window. "As you can see, this day is just about over. If you'll stay here till it gets dark, then ease on back to the hotel, I'll either come by or send somebody to talk with you before the night's over. What's your room number?"

"Two-twelve."

Camp was back in his room in less than an hour, lying on his bed and reading by the light of a coal-oil lamp. He had bought the magazine at the drugstore across the street from the sheriff's office, and had stopped nowhere else. He had walked through the dark alleys on his way back to the hotel, and had met no one.

He read a short article about Arizona Territory, then tackled a longer story about the California goldfields. Two hours later, he was still reading the writer's directions on how to strike it rich when the magazine slid from his fingers and fell to the floor. He was sound asleep.

Houston heard the three faint knocks on the door, but the sound failed to bring him out of a hard sleep. As the knocks continued, he began to dream that he himself was knocking on somebody's door, and that what he was hearing was his own knuckles rapping against the wood. When he got no answer, he began to knock harder, till the sound became loud enough to wake the dead. And wake the dead it did, for Camp was suddenly on his feet.

His head cleared instantly, and he knew right away that someone had been knocking on his door. "Hold on," he called softly. "Be there in a minute." He stepped across the room quickly, holding his six-gun behind him as he unlocked the door with his left hand.

A small, dark-haired woman stood in the hall. Her face was heavily painted, and she appeared to be about twenty-one years old. "The sheriff sends you a message," she said, almost whispering. "He wants to meet you for breakfast in the morning at seven o'clock." She pointed south. "He'll be at Kate's Restaurant, right next door to the hotel."

Camp nodded. "Thank you."

Though she had delivered her message, the young woman was in no hurry to leave. She peered into the room, licking her lips and fluttering her eyelashes seductively, then spoke again: "Do you always spend your nights alone?"

He took his time about answering. Although it was not going to be easy, he knew that he must send the woman on her way. She was a pretty thing, all right, but he had seen it all before. He had known more than one man who had hunted for a doctor only a few days after an encounter with a hotel woman. And some of those women were even prettier than the young thing who stood at his door now. He finally answered her question, using the tried-and-true method of discouraging aggressive women. "No," he said, "I don't always spend my nights alone. I usually sleep with my wife."

"Oh," she said. She spun on her heel and headed for the stairway.

Houston closed and locked the door, then undressed. Believing that his earlier nap would make going back to sleep difficult, he left the lamp burning and picked up his magazine. He stretched out on the bed and once again began to read about some of the get-rich-quick schemes for finding gold in

California, most of them written by men whose knowledge of the West had been gained by traveling all the way to western Pennsylvania.

He read for an hour, then blew out the lamp. He tossed and turned for another hour, then went to sleep.

He walked into Kate's Restaurant at ten minutes to seven next morning. Sheriff Dubar was already there, sitting at a table in the far corner. Looking neither left nor right, Camp pulled his hat low over his eyes and made a beeline for the table.

"I see you got my message," Dubar said, pushing out a chair with his boot.

Houston nodded, and seated himself.

The waiter was there immediately. He delivered two cups of hot coffee, then both men ordered ham and eggs. When they were alone again, the lawman got down to business. "Your boy's out at the Flying W," he said. "Got home two days ago. I guess he's resting up from his trip to Dodge City and back."

Camp blew air into the steaming cup, then took a sip. "I appreciate you getting the information, Dave. About all I can do now is wait till he comes to town."

Dubar shook his head. "I don't figure that'll be long," he said. "He likes to drink and raise hell on Saturday night, and today is Saturday. He'll be in town after the sun goes down, you can just about count on that."

Camp was thoughtful for a while. "Where does he do his drinking?" he asked finally.

"He makes 'em all. He'll be in every saloon in this town before midnight, some of 'em more'n—" Dubar left the sentence hanging, for the waiter was back at the table. He delivered their food and refilled their coffee cups, then disappeared. The sheriff sat quietly for a while, then began again. "I think you should try to catch him at the Texas, Camp, for several reasons: number one, it's his favorite hangout, so he's gonna be there eventually. Number two, I believe that Marshal Bisco is a silent partner in the ownership of the saloon, and like I told you before, he hates Lott's guts. Number three, Al Foster, who claims to be the sole owner of the establishment, hates the man at least as much as Bisco does. In truth, each of them probably hates Lott about as much as the other does.

"Neither of them has ever attempted to put a stop to Sam Lott's overbearing behavior because they're afraid of him. Of course, Foster's an old man, but the marshal's just plain yellow. You just go ahead and do whatever you think you ought to, Camp. I can tell you right now that John Bisco ain't gonna try to arrest you if you shoot Sam Lott, and Al Foster'll probably hunt up some kind of damn medal to hang around your neck."

Both men had finished eating. Camp held up his hand, and the waiter was there quickly. He refilled both coffee cups, then departed. Dubar sipped at the liquid, then spoke again: "One thing's got me puzzled a little bit, Camp. If Lott is such a damn big thief, and if he helped kill those drovers for only a small share of the money they were carrying, why is it that he just now returned from Dodge City carrying all the money Albert Wells had coming? Hell, he could have disappeared with every dollar he got for the whole damn herd, and he wouldn't have had to share it with anybody."

Camp had been listening closely, nodding occasionally. "I've thought about the same thing," he said. "I don't have a good, solid answer, but I do have an idea: what if Lott has something bigger in mind? What if he plans to someday skip the country, change his name and set himself up on his own ranch in grand style? All that would take a lot of money, Dave, much more than was in the poke that he just brought home to the Flying W. You see, there were only two thousand head in the herd he just delivered, so I believe that Sam Lott is setting Albert Wells up for the kill. You and I both know that the Flying W will send two big herds to Kansas next spring, with a total of at least seven thousand head. I daresay that Sam Lott plans on being the man who collects the money for both herds in Dodge City. I also daresay that Albert Wells will never see a dollar of it."

Dubar chuckled, then beat on the table with his fist. "By God that's it, Camp," he said. "I hadn't thought of it that way, but by God that's it. He's just setting the old man up. It was a long time ago, but you've worked out there, so you know that Wells will believe just about anything somebody tells him. Now, he's bound to have heard somebody say that Lott might have been in on that thing with the drovers, but Lott probably told him he wasn't guilty, and the old man took him at his word. Lott must have been mighty convincing, too, 'cause Wells put him in charge of the whole shebang." He hit the table with his fist again. "You've got it figured exactly right, my friend. Lott plans on bossing seven thousand, maybe eight thousand head of cattle up the trail next spring, and when the buyers take 'em off his hands and cough up the money, he intends to be long gone."

Camp nodded. "If he's a thinking thief, I'd say that's what he's got planned."

The sheriff was on his feet now. "I hate to ask you to stay in that hotel room," he said, "but I certainly believe that's the best thing for you to do. When your man hits town I'll know it, and I'll send somebody to tell you. I guess the reason I won't be coming to tell you myself is obvious. I'll also make sure that I'm not in the Texas Saloon when you call Sam Lott's number. It just wouldn't look right."

Camp continued to sit at the table. "Just go ahead, Dave, and I'll wait here for a few minutes. There's no reason for us to even be seen talking to each other. You have to live in this town, but I don't. Fact is, if I'm still in good heath after this thing with Lott is over, I expect to be out of town within three minutes, five at the most." He pointed to the front door. "Go on, now. I'll pay for your breakfast."

The sheriff nodded, and walked toward the front of the building. Camp sat at the table till he heard the front door slam, then got to his feet. He left a coin on the table for the waiter, then headed for the counter with his purse in his hand.

He spent the next several hours in his room, then ate an early dinner in the same restaurant, speaking to no one except a waiter. Then he returned to the hotel. The young desk clerk had been nowhere around earlier, but was now sitting behind the counter. He offered Camp the standard commercial smile. "Will you be staying another night, sir?"

"Not exactly," Houston said. He fished money from his pocket and laid it on the counter. "I expect to be gone before nightfall, but I don't know what time I'll be leaving. Just take enough money for both nights, then it won't matter."

The boy took one dollar and gave Camp fifteen cents change. "I'll just charge you for last night," he said. "You ain't supposed to pay for something you ain't gonna use. If it turns out that you're still here when the sun goes down, then you'll owe me another eighty-five cents."

Houston nodded, then climbed the stairs and stretched out on his bed, intent upon taking a nap. Though it had been said of Camp that he had nerves of steel, he nevertheless felt a fluttering in his stomach, and going to sleep proved to be impossible. He reached for his magazine and began to thumb through it, smiling occasionally at the latest offerings from the political cartoonists. He was still reading when he heard an indefinite sound outside his door. "Who's there?" he asked, swinging his feet to the floor.

He got no answer, but this time there was a definite knock. With his gun in his hand as usual, he opened the door slowly. The same woman who had visited him last night stood in the hall. Her appearance was much more pleasing to his conservative eye on this visit, however, for today she wore no paint whatsoever. Knowing that she was undoubtedly here to deliver another message, he looked at her with raised eyebrows, then stood waiting.

"The sheriff sent you this," she said. She handed him a folded piece of brown paper, then disappeared down the hall.

He relocked the door and took a seat on the bed, then

read the message. With no salutation at the top and no signature at the bottom, the note contained just six words: *"The rabbit is in the box."*

Camp slipped the note into his pocket, then got to his feet. He pulled the shade down on both windows, then spent the next ten minutes practicing his fast draw. His speed was incredible, his actions nothing more than a blur as he slapped his leg and brought the Colt into firing position. He went through the motion more than twenty times, then added a sixth shell to the cylinder and shoved the weapon back in its holster. Then he draped his saddlebag over his shoulder and headed for the stairway.

When he reached the lobby, he spoke to the clerk. "I'm leaving now," he said, continuing to walk toward the street. "You can rent that room to whoever wants it now." He was out the door quickly and headed for the livery stable, moving as fast as he could without running.

The hostler was sitting in front of his office, leaning against the wall with only two of his chair's legs touching the ground. He jumped to his feet quickly. "Looks like you might be about to leave us," he said.

Camp nodded. "Yes," he said. "I'd like my horses just as soon as you can get them out here."

The man said nothing else, just grabbed a rope and headed for the corral at a fast walk. He had both animals up front in less than five minutes, then proceeded to help Camp saddle the roan and lash the packsaddle on the black. Houston paid his bill, mounted the roan and yanked on the packhorse's lead rope. "I appreciate your business," the hostler called as Camp rode through the wide doorway. "If you ever come this way again, you know where I'm at."

Three minutes later, Houston tied his animals to one of the Texas Saloon's three hitching rails. He stood beside the roan for a few moments, taking stock of his surroundings and trying to picture exactly what he would be facing once he was inside the building. He counted five saddled horses at the rails, and noted that only one of the animals, an oversized bay, wore the Flying W brand.

Did this mean that Lott, like a few other foremen Camp had known, had sought out various chores for the ranch hands to perform, while he himself spent the day and night in town drinking? Camp suspected that it did. Four of the five horses now standing at the hitching rails were from other ranches, and he doubted that any of their owners would risk life and limb to side with Sam Lott. There was only one way to find out, he decided. Having no clear idea of what he was walking into, he stepped to the sidewalk and pushed his way through the batwing doors, depending entirely on his quick reflexes to see him through.

Visibility was always better inside the Texas than in most saloons, and today the bartender had all of the shades up and the windows open, letting in even more light than usual. Houston needed no time to adjust his eyes. He recognized his quarry immediately, for the man towered above the two shorter men who stood beside him at the bar. Camp moved quickly to reduce the distance separating him from the three men, who were laughing and talking among themselves and paying little attention to anyone else. Houston stopped thirty feet away, spread his legs slightly and went into a crouch. "Everybody except Sam Lott move away from the bar!" he commanded loudly, almost shouting.

Both of the men standing beside Lott turned to face Camp, but neither moved away from the bar as ordered. Lott looked half around and half over their heads, and caught Houston's eye. "Well," he said sneeringly, tucking a wayward strand of dirty blond hair behind his ear. "I do believe I have company." He emitted a nasal chuckle, then spoke again: "To who and what do I owe this honor?"

Houston's steel-gray eyes bore into those of the skinny foreman. He spoke loudly enough for every man in the room to hear. "I'm here on behalf of John Calloway, Bill Fisher and Joe Plenty, Lott! My name is Camp Houston!"

The two men standing beside Lott moved away from the bar like they had been shot out of a cannon, for they had both heard the name before.

The sneer disappeared from Lott's face quickly. He stepped away from the bar and began to point with his left hand, attempting to divert Camp's attention to something across the room. All the while, his right hand was easing downward. He died in his tracks, for Houston had failed to buy the well-worn ruse. Lott had managed to get his gun in his hand, but had not lived to fire it. He had taken a .45-caliber slug between his eyes just as he cleared his holster. He dropped the weapon to the floor, then fell on top of it. He never moved again.

Houston still held his gun in his hand as he stepped sideways and laid twenty dollars on the bar. "Give this to the undertaker," he said to the bartender. "And tell Al Foster that I'm sorry about the mess I made in here." He walked backward till he reached the front of the building, then holstered the Colt and stepped through the doorway. He mounted quickly and pointed the roan south. He was not headed for Calf Creek just yet. He was on his way to Austin to talk with a friend named Joe Plenty.

22

★

The residents of the 3C began to eat fresh meat three times a day during the month of December. Bo Patton usually took a rifle or a shotgun into the woods every day, and he seldom returned empty-handed. And the meat would not spoil now. Hanging inside a small enclosure on one end of the back porch, it would be kept fresh by the near-freezing temperatures and the cold wind. And in this area, the wind usually blew day and night during the last few weeks of the year.

"I hate hunting in the wind," Fowler had said to Patton a few days earlier, while watching the young man dress out a doe. "The wind is all I can hear, and if it's cold, it always gives me an earache."

"Not me," Patton said, wielding the skinning knife expertly. "I just put cotton in my ears or tie something around my head, and use that wind to help me find game. If you walk slow enough and quiet enough for long enough, and keep that wind blowing right in your face, you're gonna eat meat for

supper. Ain't no animal in the woods gonna know that you're
around if you move about quietly, and keep him upwind."

"Well, it's kinda obvious that you know what you're talking about," Runt said, pointing to the carcass. "There hangs
the proof." He accepted the deer liver Patton handed him,
then headed for the kitchen. It was his turn to cook supper.

Most of the construction at the 3C had been completed,
and the Wootens had long since vacated the premises. Fowler
had several additional things in mind for the house, however,
among them adding another fireplace and chimney. He was
constantly touching up one thing or another, or searching out
something that had been overlooked in the rush. Only yesterday he had torn down the makeshift outhouse, and replaced
it with a sturdy one that would never leak. He also intended
to build a small bunkhouse soon, for Bo Patton had repeated
Camp's jocular remark that he might marry Ellen Bice.

On the twenty-first day of the month, Houston rode off
the hill at daybreak. He had business in both Mason and
Menardville, and intended to spend one night in each town.
He led the packhorse, but not because he needed it. He was returning the animal to Sid Blankenship.

He traveled at a steady pace, and reached Mason in
midafternoon. He turned his horses over to Hamm Harrison
at the livery stable, then headed for the bank, which was his
only reason for being in town. Roy Holder, whose office door
was open, spotted Houston as he entered the building, and
was quickly in the lobby pumping Camp's hand. "I've been
expecting you," he said. "I figured it was about time you got
serious about stocking that ranch, and like always, we'd be delighted to be of assistance." He motioned toward his office.
"Yes, sir, that's exactly what we're here for."

Camp shook his head. "I'm not in the mood to take on a
large debt right now, Mr. Holder. I've been doing a lot of
building at my place, and I'm just here to withdraw some
money to pay the people that I already owe."

Undaunted, Holder pointed to his office again. "I understand," he said. "But we need to work out some of the details, so—"

"No," Camp interrupted. "The only thing I'm gonna talk about today is the two hundred dollars I came here to withdraw."

"Very well, sir," the banker said, still smiling broadly. "Just step right over to the window, and Mr. Bradley will take care of it."

Camp was back on the street three minutes later. He walked through town at a fast pace, and did not stop till he reached Ma Franklin's boardinghouse. When he announced his presence with a loud knock at the door, he received an answer from somewhere down the hall: "Just go on into the dining room, Camp. I'll be in there pretty soon."

He recognized the voice, and stepped into the building. "Thank you, Ma," he called. A moment later, he seated himself at the end of the long table.

The lady was there soon after, and walked straight to the stove. She stoked the fire and pulled the coffeepot over the firebox, then walked to the table. "I guess you can drink warmed-over coffee, can't you?"

He nodded. "I do it pretty often, Ma."

She took a seat beside him and offered her usual smile. "Well, if it seems too bitter, just remember that it's not costing you anything." They were both quiet for a few moments, then she spoke again: "I've heard that you've turned that hill above Calf Creek into a show place. Have you stocked it with cattle? Have you got married yet?"

"Whoa, Ma," Camp said, laughing loudly. "Let's talk about these things one at a time. I don't know who you've been talking to, but I certainly don't have a show place. What I've got on Calf Creek is exactly what you'd find on any other ranch: a house and the necessary outbuildings. I must admit that Runt Fowler did an outstanding job on the layout, but it's hardly a show place. As far as stocking the ranch is concerned, I'll be doing that next spring, about April, I suppose.

As for that last question, I'll answer it by asking you one: Married? Me married? Who in the world would want to marry me, Ma?"

She sat staring at him for a while. "Well, I'll be damned," she said finally. She walked to the stove and poured two cups of coffee. "Who'd want to marry you?" She handed him one of the steaming cups, then reclaimed her seat and answered the question herself. "Just about any young girl would want to marry you, Camp Houston. That is, any girl who knows which side her bread's buttered on." She sat thoughtful for a moment, then added, "But I'm sure you know a lot of things about Camp Houston that I don't. Maybe I should be asking you just why it is that none of the girls wants to marry you."

He laughed, then shook his head. "I just said that to be having something to say, Ma. I didn't mean it the way it sounded. But in all honesty, I sure don't recall ever seeing a bunch of pretty young things tripping over themselves trying to get my attention."

"I certainly know at least one of the reasons for that," she said quickly. "It's the expression you carry on your face. I mean, most of the time you look like your mind's a thousand miles away." She sipped at her coffee, then continued. "You just take stock of yourself and think about what I'm telling you, 'cause I know exactly how a female thinks: she might be dying to speak to you, but she won't do it, not with you looking like your mind is in a different world.

"You're one of the best-looking men around, Camp, and if you change your ways a little bit, you'll have more female friends than you can shake a stick at. Whenever you see a woman that you'd like to know better, you've got to give her an encouraging look. Just slow down, look her right in the eye and give her that big old handsome smile of yours. Let her know you're interested, and she'll make the rest of it easier for you. If you want to court her, say so. If you want her to go somewhere with you, ask her. Hell, she won't bite you."

Camp leaned back in his chair. His body shook a little, for

he was laughing inside. "You sound just like Bama Angleton," he said.

"That don't bother me none. Bama Angleton is a smart woman, and I'd almost bet that she told you the same thing I'm telling you."

He sat staring at the table with tight lips for a moment. Then his face slowly broke into a smile. "Well, it was pretty close."

He talked with the lady for another hour. Then, when she informed him that she had work to do, he sought conversation elsewhere. He spent the remainder of the afternoon on the front porch talking with two of her regular boarders, then joined them at the supper table and ate two helpings of everything in sight. A short time later, he was shown to the only unoccupied room on the premises, where he slept in a better bed than he could have found at any hotel in three counties.

He was back at the livery stable early next morning, and rode out of town at sunup. He kicked the roan to a fast trot immediately. The trip to Menardville was a full day's ride, and he had no intention of spending the night on the road. He traveled steadily throughout the morning, and reached Big Rock Spring an hour past noon. The spring was roughly the halfway point between Menardville and Mason, and a common stopover for traffic headed in either direction.

A covered wagon was parked beside the spring's runoff, and a young couple and two children sat beside a campfire eating. Houston waved to them, then dismounted. The man, who appeared to be about Camp's own age, returned the greeting. "We've got more hot coffee here than we're gonna use," he said. "You're welcome to drink it if you want to. All we'll do is just pour it out."

Camp nodded. "That's the best offer I've had today," he said. "After I take care of my horses I'll be right over." He watered the animals and poured grain in their nose bags, then dug his cup out of his pack. A few moments later, he approached the dying campfire. "I appreciate this," he said, offering his cup. "It sure beats washing my biscuits down with water."

The man poured the cup full and handed it back. "I guess you had coffee of your own on that packhorse," he said, "but the hard part is finding wood to heat it. We always carry kindling in the wagon, 'cause campers have already gathered up most of the stuff along the road that'll burn. They ain't overlooked nothing within a quarter mile of this spring."

"I never even think about building a fire here when I'm traveling on horseback," Houston said. "This road is pretty heavily traveled, and almost everybody stops because of the spring. I'd bet that there's been a shortage of deadwood here since the Civil War."

The man looked Houston over closely. Then his face suddenly took on a serious look. He got to his feet quickly and refilled Camp's cup, then dashed the remainder of the coffee into the fire. "All right, Tom and Jane," he said to the children, "get yourselves into the wagon. We've gotta get moving." The children moved instantly, as did both parents. The man removed the nose bags from his horses and watered them again. Then he helped his wife to the seat and climbed up beside her. Without another word or so much as a glance in Camp's direction, he backed his team away from the ditch and headed down the road toward Mason.

Leaning against the big rock from whence the spring's name derived, sipping the coffee and eating ham and biscuits provided by Ma Franklin, Houston stood watching the wagon, still thinking about the man's odd behavior. Though the man seemed friendly enough at first, he had grown quiet seemingly in midsentence, and his wife had never spoken at all. Houston stood shaking his head as the full realization hit him: his own reputation as a gunman had spread far and wide, and the family's quick departure simply meant that he had been recognized.

He swallowed the last of his food, then washed his cup in the spring's runoff. A few minutes later, he was headed for

Menardville. Trying to make up for lost time, he traveled at a canter for several miles, then slowed to a trot.

He arrived in Menardville shortly after dark, and was pleased to find that Sid Blankenship was still at his bellows. By the feeble light of a coal-oil lantern, the muscular blacksmith was busy pounding on a long piece of metal with a heavy hammer. He laid the work aside when he saw Houston. "Hello, Camp," he said, wiping his hands and offering a handshake. "It's good to see you."

They shook hands, then Blankenship pointed to his unfinished work. "I've been hoping to get that damn rim fixed for old man Bouton before I call it a night, but I ain't gonna make it." He motioned toward the rimless wagon wheel leaning in the corner. "He'll be wanting that thing about sunup, but he'll just have to wait a while."

Haley Bouton was a grouchy, white-haired farmer who was past seventy years old, and very well known in the vicinity. "The old man'll wait, all right," Houston said, chuckling, "but only because he has no other choice. He'll probably give you a piece of his mind while he's doing it, too."

"Of course he will. He bitches about everything I do for him. He keeps coming back, though, so I guess I can't complain."

Houston stood quietly for a moment, then pointed over his shoulder. "I brought the horse and the packsaddle back to you, Sid. I don't suppose I'll be needing them anymore."

Blankenship nodded. "Are you saying that Calloway's bushwhackers are in the ground?"

"All of them."

"Well, I'll be damned," the liveryman said. "That news'll be easy to live with." He walked to the hitching rail and untied the black, then led the animal inside the barn. He began to unlash the packsaddle. "I knew you'd get 'em, Camp. I knew it right from the first day you told me that you were going hunting. It's just a good thing that we've got somebody like you around to help rid the country of such riffraff."

Houston changed the subject. "I'll be in the hotel bar later on, if you want to join me for a drink."

Blankenship shook his head. "Not tonight. I appreciate the offer, but I'd better get on home. That oldest girl of mine ain't feeling too good lately, been sick for nearly a week."

"I'm sorry to hear that," Camp said. "Maybe she'll be feeling better tomorrow." He turned to leave. "I guess I'll have to settle for a little conversation with Wesley Hawks, then." He took a few steps toward the doorway, then stopped suddenly. "Oh," he said, "I almost forgot." He fished a piece of paper out of his pocket and handed it over. "I need some Three C branding irons made up. Can you do it?"

Blankenship stood looking at the "3C" Houston had written on the paper. "I sure don't see anything complicated about it," he said. "How many do you want, and when are you gonna need 'em?"

"Just make up six or eight. No hurry about it. I'm not gonna have anything to brand for a long time yet."

Blankenship nodded. "That'll give me something to work on when business is slow. They'll be ready before you need 'em."

Camp lifted his hand in a saluting gesture. "I'll see you sometime tomorrow," he said. Then he was gone up the hill. He stopped at a hole-in-the-wall restaurant and ate a bowl of stew, then registered at the Menardville Hotel half an hour later. Having left his saddlebags at the livery stable, he was empty-handed, and had no reason to head for his room just yet. When he walked into the saloon he saw right away that he was the only customer in the house. He seated himself at the bar, directly in front of the idle bartender. "How's business, Wes?" he asked jokingly.

Hawks placed a glass on the bar and reached for a bottle of good whiskey. "It's just like it's been for the past two weeks," he answered. "It'll pick up Friday, on account of that being Christmas Eve, but it'll just be good for that one day. New Year's Eve'll be along a week later, and you won't even be able to get in the place then. But on the first day of January, she'll die a natural death."

Camp took a sip of whiskey. "A natural death, huh?"

"Absolutely. The hotel carries the saloon in the off-season. This bar don't even do enough business to pay its own way in the wintertime. The people who own it are the same ones who own the hotel, and they just keep it open for the convenience of the guests." He laughed. "From where I stand, it all looks like a losing proposition. I doubt that the hotel has more than five or six rooms rented right now. Maybe seven, if you're gonna be staying overnight."

Houston pushed his glass forward for a refill. "Seven," he said.

By the time Camp left the saloon he had decided that Hawks's complaint about business being slow was valid, for the bartender had had only one other customer during Houston's two-hour stay: a man who bought a bottle of whiskey and walked right back out the door. All of which was no skin off Hawks's nose, Camp was thinking. The man obviously received the same monthly salary no matter how much whiskey he did or did not sell.

In his hotel room, he slid under the covers as quickly as possible, for the night was cold. Once his body was warm, he began to think about the approaching holidays: Saturday would be Christmas Day, and a week later, most people would party in the new year. Christmas. Although he could not get as excited about it as he had when he was a child, he nevertheless still appreciated its meaning.

And tomorrow, he would buy gifts for a few friends. Sid Blankenship already had everything a man was likely to need, so Camp would buy him a bottle of premium whiskey to sip at his pleasure. And he had already spotted knives at Spike Nettleton's hardware store that he would buy for Fowler and Patton: a three-bladed folding knife for Fowler, and a fine hunting knife for Bo Patton. He smiled at the thought, then went to sleep.

He was up early next morning, and walked to the same small restaurant that had fed him a good bowl of stew the night before. He had a breakfast of flapjacks and sausage, then decided to head for the livery stable, where he had left his shaving soap and razor in his saddlebag. He would shave his face in Sid's office, for he was taking no chances that he might accidentally run into Ellen Bice while wearing a two-day growth of beard.

Menard County Sheriff Walter McMichen was just passing the restaurant as Camp walked out the door, and the two almost collided. "Excuse me, Sheriff," Camp said quickly. "I guess I need to watch where I'm going."

"No harm done," the lawman said.

Sheriff McMichen was at least sixty years old, and had openly stated on more than one occasion that he was too old for the job. The county voters had disagreed, and reelected him for another term just the year before. Most of those same voters had now begun to believe that McMichen had known what he was talking about, however, for immediately after the election he began to spend at least ninety percent of his time at his farm, rarely coming to town unless sent for. Today was the first time Camp had seen the man in at least a year.

"I haven't seen you in a while, Sheriff," Camp said, extending his right hand. "You're looking good."

McMichen grasped the hand and pumped it several times. "I don't get around much these days, Mr. Houston. I've sure been hearing a lot of things about you, though. You just keep up the good work." He walked around Camp and continued on up the hill. Houston stood watching till the man turned the corner, then he himself headed down the hill to the stable.

When Spike Nettleton opened his hardware store an hour later, Houston was there with money in his hand. "I want to settle up whatever I owe on that last load of building material," Camp said. "Then I want to buy two of those knives at the end of the counter."

A few minutes later, he left the store with the knives in the saddlebag that he now carried over his shoulder. He walked around town for a while, trying to decide what to do next. He knew that he could make it home before dark if he left now. He also knew that he wanted to see Ellen Bice, and that she only worked at the restaurant during the afternoon and early evening.

He was walking down the hill casually, looking at the merchandise in the window of one store after another, when he suddenly realized that he was abreast of Riley's Restaurant. Maybe he would have a cup of coffee, he thought as he opened the door and stepped inside. Ellen Bice stood behind the counter. When she spotted Houston, her beautiful face broke into the most honest-looking smile he had seen in months. "Hello, Camp," she called sweetly. "Do you want to come and sit at the counter?"

Did he want to sit at the counter? Of course he did. The closer the better. And she had called him by his first name. "Give her that big old handsome smile of yours," Ma Franklin had instructed. He spread his lips and offered the broadest smile he could muster. "Well," he said, beginning to walk across the room. "There stands the prettiest girl in this town." He stood at the counter for a moment watching her blush, then seated himself on a stool. "It's good to see you again, Ellen, and I mean it when I say that you look prettier every time I see you."

She blushed again, and fluttered her eyelashes. "Thank you, Camp. I must say that this is sure something different, coming from you. I really didn't think you'd ever paid much attention to me."

He was getting braver by the moment. "Why, I paid all of my attention to you. Fell in love the first time I ever saw you." He took a sip of the coffee she had set on the counter, then added jokingly, "Made up my mind right on the spot that I was gonna take you to Calf Creek with me one of these days."

She giggled softly, and slapped his arm playfully. "I wonder how many other girls you've said that to."

His facial expression suddenly turned serious. "I've never said that to anybody else, Ellen." Then, almost as if taking an oath, he added, "And that's the truth."

Her own smile faded quickly. "I believe you," she said.

He was not about to stop now. He pointed over his shoulder. "It's entirely too cold to enjoy it anytime soon, but I was wondering if you'd want to take a buggy ride with me when the weather warms up."

She answered quickly. "I'd like that, Camp. Sunday would be the best day for me, because I don't have to work then." She picked up a bill of fare and stood looking across the room, for five people were now busy seating themselves in the dining area. She leaned close to his ear and spoke almost at a whisper: "I'm going to be real busy for the next few hours, and I won't have time to talk. I'll be looking forward to the buggy ride, though." Then she was gone to check on the diners.

He walked out of the restaurant with a feeling of accomplishment. Ma Franklin had known what she was talking about, all right. By doing exactly as Ma had told him, he had broken the ice with the girl from Nebraska. He bought the bottle of whiskey that was to be Blankenship's Christmas gift, then headed down the hill to the livery stable as fast as he could walk. Twenty minutes later, he mounted the roan and took the road to Calf Creek.

23

One afternoon in the last week of March, John Butterworth's buggy rolled into Houston's yard. The rancher jumped to the ground spryly as Runt Fowler hurried from the house to meet him. "Hello, Runt," Butterworth said, his right hand extended. "I'm sure Camp told me that you were down here, but it must have slipped my mind. It's mighty good to see you again."

Fowler grasped the hand. "I'm glad to see you, too, Mr. Butterworth." He motioned toward the barn. "Camp's down there fooling with some new horses he bought from Blankenship, and I doubt that he even knows you're on the premises." He cupped his hands around his mouth and called Houston's name at the top of his lungs.

Camp stepped from a stable, and recognized his visitor immediately. He was in the yard moments later, shaking the rancher's hand. "I've been thinking about you all day, John," he said. "I've even thought about riding up to your place."

"No need for that. My men are busy cutting out five hundred head of old stuff right now, so your breeders'll be here in about ten days. Four of the riders'll stay around to help you for a week or two, or however long it takes for the cows to settle down."

"That's mighty good to hear, John. I guess they'll start dropping calves anytime now, and I've already had some branding irons made up."

"A lot of 'em have done dropped. I'd say that about twenty percent of 'em have got calves following 'em already."

"I like the sound of that, too," Camp said. He pointed up the hill. "Come on up to the house. I don't have any wine to offer you, but I can have a pot of coffee ready in a hurry."

The rancher stepped to his buggy and reached under the seat. "I brought my own wine," he said, coming away with a gallon jug in each hand.

The three men were soon sitting at the kitchen table, sipping the rancher's wine from tin cups. Butterworth handed Houston an official-looking piece of paper. "I registered the whole six sections in your name," he said. "Then I got to thinking that maybe I'd better come down here and show you where the corners are. Ain't no way in the hell you'd ever find 'em all by yourself."

Camp accepted the document, then laughed. "I don't know exactly where any of the corners are," he said. "Thank you for coming."

At that moment, Bo Patton walked into the house, a double-barreled shotgun under his arm. "I've got that big old tom turkey outside," he said as he laid the gun on two wooden pegs that had been driven into the wall for that purpose. "I've been calling him for a month, and he's been answering for a month, but he never would come into shotgun range." He smiled victoriously. "I reckon my calls must have sounded more like a real hen today, 'cause he came running like the woods were on fire." He chuckled aloud. "Damn near ran down my gun barrel."

Camp introduced Patton to Butterworth, and when the handshaking was over, spoke to the youngster: "What do you plan to do with the turkey, Bo?"

"Weather's too warm to keep him overnight. I'm gonna pluck him and singe him, then put him in the oven to bake." He walked to the stove. "I'll start a fire so the oven'll be hot by the time I need it."

"Never mind, Bo," Houston said, getting to his feet. "Just go ahead and work on your turkey. I'll build the fire." Patton nodded, and headed for the backyard.

During the next two days, Butterworth pointed out all four corners of the six-section ranch to Houston, Fowler and Patton. They, in turn, would acquaint the Lazy B riders with the boundaries. As each corner was pointed out, Fowler and Patton cleared all of the vegetation away from the immediate area and drove an iron stake in the ground. A piece of red cloth was then tied around the top of the stake.

The rancher spent one more night on the ranch after his mission had been accomplished, then announced at the breakfast table that he was about to head for the Lazy B.

"I wish you'd stay around a little longer, John," Camp said, making an all-out effort to saw through a chunk of tough venison with a dull knife. "The cows'll probably be here in less than a week."

"Nope, gotta be getting on home." He took a sip of coffee, then frowned as he set his cup on the table noisily. "Besides," he added jokingly, "we've drunk up all of the wine."

Camp lifted his cup. "I can't do anything about that," he said. "All I've got is bitter coffee."

An hour later, after having said his good-byes and shaking hands all around, the rancher climbed to the seat of his buggy. He waved good-bye once more, then slapped the mare's hip with the reins. He was off the hill quickly, and just before he disappeared around the curve, Camp saw him move one of the empty wine jugs to the back of the buggy, as if their rattling against each other had already begun to get on his nerves.

Camp stood in the yard with a lump in his throat long after the buggy was out of sight. He had a special feeling for the driver of that vehicle, for no man had ever treated him so kindly. John Butterworth had bent over backward to help him get started with a place of his own. And though Houston could think of nothing that he himself had ever done to deserve such treatment, he was determined to turn the 3C into a profitable concern. He would bring in some Hereford bulls at the beginning of the third year and begin to upgrade his herd. And the old man would be proud. Camp swallowed hard, then headed for the barn. He wanted to be alone for a while.

He stood outside the corral for a while, looking over the four black horses he had bought the week before. Though he had ridden them before buying and decided that they were sound animals, he had had no way of determining their knowledge of cattle. They would surely be tested when the breeders arrived the following week.

Blankenship himself had known little about the animals. "I got 'em from old man Whitten down in Kimble County," he said, "and he assured me that they're all excellent cow horses. If it turns out that that ain't the case, bring 'em back. I'd nearly bet that they're gonna be all right, though. The old man never has lied to me yet, and he certainly wouldn't have a reason to start now. He knew that I was getting the horses for you, and he knows that you know all of the differences between a cow pony and a jackass." He lifted a front foot of one of the animals and inspected the frog. "Why would he lie when he knows that he's gonna get the horses right back if they don't please you?"

Camp laughed. "All right, Sid, you've got me convinced. I have no doubt that the horses'll work out fine, and I especially like the price. Where else could I have bought cutting horses for forty dollars apiece?"

Blankenship shot him a knowing look. "Aw, I reckon that's about the going rate, Camp. The bottom's out of horse-flesh right now."

Houston nodded. "Good. I might be needing a couple more head before long."

Now, Camp stepped into his own corral and angled toward the larger of the black horses, speaking in low tones as he walked. All of the other animals shied away, but the one he had chosen stood waiting, stiff-legged. Camp rubbed the horse's neck and shoulder for a while, then, taking a firm hold on its lower lip, led the animal to the barn.

A few minutes later, he rode the black through the gate and headed down the hill. He took the Brady road and let the animal run at an easy canter for a couple miles, then turned up the slope and into the woods. Riding through or sometimes around the scrub thickets and underbrush, he began to think about just how fast a fire could devastate the area if somebody got careless.

Of course, it could happen without somebody getting careless. Mother Nature had her own ways of renewing the land, the most obvious of which was to burn everything in sight and start over. And she had her own ways of starting fires. Camp knew that his property would be in better shape right now if a raging fire had swept it a couple years ago. Had that happened, much of the area that was now covered with underbrush would instead be producing graze for animals.

But it was too late to be thinking about that now. With the cattle on the way, the last thing he needed was a fire. He would caution all of the riders to be extra careful with their campfires and cigarettes, for the vegetation was almost as dry as powder, and a careless spark could get out of hand in an instant.

Camp rode the black for another three hours, by which time he had decided that the animal possessed all of the qualities required of a good cow pony: he was quick, surefooted, well balanced, and could turn on a dime. On the way home, Camp ran him all-out for more than a mile, and he was not breathing hard. Good lungs, Camp thought. Which meant that the horse could cut calves out of a herd all morning without a break. "If," Camp said to himself, "he actually knows what a damn calf is." He kicked the animal to a canter and headed home.

He fed and curried the black, then walked to the shed and seated himself on the wagon tongue. He was thinking of Ellen Bice and the buggy rides they had taken together. He had called on her twice driving a rented rig, and expected to do the same again two days from now. Tomorrow was Saturday. He would ride the black cutting horse to Menardville and spend the night at the hotel, then pick her up early Sunday morning and spend the day in the country.

On each of their previous rides, one in January and the other in February, they had spent the entire day traveling up and down the San Saba River, eating dinner from a lunch basket, and talking about Nebraska. On the second occasion, Camp had suggested riding south to the Leon River, but the girl had correctly decided that they would probably not be able to make it back to Menardville before dark. Which, of course, would not have bothered Houston in the least, except for the fact that she had asked him a direct question: Could they make it to the Leon and back before darkness overtook them? He reluctantly admitted that they could not.

He had held her hand for most of the day on both buggy rides. He had never kissed her, but she had almost kissed him once. Or he believed that she had at least been thinking about it: they had been sitting on a blanket on the bank of the river. He had been telling her stories about his childhood, and about how he used to walk up and down the streets of Little Rock peddling garden produce.

She learned that he had been almost grown before he outgrew his dislike for shoes, and that when people in Little Rock sometimes asked why he walked around barefoot, he would tell them that he was from a poor family and could not afford to buy shoes. Then the people almost always bought something from him. Of course, he was not from a poor family, and he had several pairs of shoes in his closet. The real reason he was barefoot was because he hated shoes.

She had been giving him her undivided attention as he talked, and every word brought her face a little closer to his. Her lips were almost touching his cheek when she suddenly jerked her head away. She sat blushing once she realized what she had been about to do, and was probably even more embarrassed because she knew that he had read her actions. She began to fiddle around with the picnic basket and soon laid out their dinner. Camp never mentioned the fact that he knew she had almost kissed him.

He sat on the wagon tongue reminiscing, trying to recall every conversation that had ever passed between them. He usually tried to keep her talking as long as she would, for her soft voice was much like music to his ears. Besides, she was the only person he had ever spent much time around who spoke the English language the same way it was printed in the books he read.

When Camp got to his feet, the blaze-faced black was standing with his head hanging over the top pole of the corral, looking like he was ready to go for another run. "Early in the morning," Camp said, as if the animal could understand. Houston would saddle the black in the morning and be on his way to Menardville at sunup. He must catch up on all of his running around, for by this time next week he would be married to five hundred twenty-five head of longhorns.

He walked into the house to find Fowler standing by the stove stirring the iron pot, and Patton sitting at the table sipping coffee. "Saw you giving one of the blacks a workout," Runt said. "What do you think?"

Camp nodded. "He's a solid animal, Runt. He's quick on his feet, he can spin like a top, and he can run like hell. Got good wind, too." He chuckled. "Now that I've said all of that, I guess we'll have to wait till next week to find out whether he's worth a shit or not."

Fowler laughed, then changed the subject. "We're gonna have some good stew here in a little bit. It's got two fox squirrels and a rabbit in it: a big cane cutter."

Houston filled a coffee cup and took a seat. "Bo, I'm gonna take the blaze-faced black with me tomorrow, but I want you to give all three of the others a good workout every day between now and the time the cows get here."

Patton nodded. "I'll put 'em through their paces," he said. "My pa used to say that if you leave a horse in the corral long enough, he'll finally get the idea that all he has to do to earn a bucket of oats is stand around switching his tail."

Camp got to his feet and dropped his empty cup in the dishpan. "Your pa was right," he said, then left the room.

He was off the hill shortly after breakfast. The cold air was invigorating, and the black wanted to run. Camp allowed the animal to set its own pace, which turned out to be a steady canter. And although the wind finally set Houston's nose and ears to stinging, he continued to let the horse run. Anyway, the colder his face became, the better the morning sun felt on his back.

After about three miles, the animal slowed to a trot, then to a walk, which was pleasing to Camp. He had been riding with the reins wrapped around the horn and both of his hands in the pockets of his heavy coat. He was using the top button of the garment for a change, with the collar turned up around his ears.

As he rode along he was thinking that tomorrow morning would probably be just as cold. If so, he would wait till about midday to call on Ellen Bice. Or, if the afternoon turned out to be too cold for a buggy ride, he would simply visit her at home, for both her uncle and her aunt had treated him with the utmost courtesy.

Indeed, Mary Trout never passed up a chance to praise Ellen's cooking ability whenever Camp was present, and seemed to be overjoyed that her niece might be involved in a budding romance with a local rancher. "Don't reckon she's ever been serious about a man before," the lady had once said to Camp, ignoring the fact that her words might be embarrassing to the girl, who was well within earshot. "She's gonna be twenty years old next May, too." Ellen had given her aunt a polite look of tolerance, then climbed into the buggy.

Houston led the black into Blankenship's stable two hours before sunset. The liveryman accepted the reins with humor. "It hasn't been long since you were bitching about the horses I sold you, then here you come riding one of 'em."

Camp smiled. "Dammit, Sid, I didn't bitch about the horses. I just mentioned the fact that I didn't know anything about 'em." He pointed to the black. "Now, that horse rides good and he handles good, but I'm still not sure that he knows a cow from a damn jackrabbit."

The liveryman led the horse forward a few steps and unbuckled the cinch. "He knows." He laid the saddle and blanket on a wooden rack, then led the animal toward a stable, leaving Camp standing alone. Houston walked into the office and seated himself in a ladder-back chair. Blankenship was there a few minutes later, and took a seat on his desk. "You just come from Calf Creek?" he asked.

Camp nodded.

"Well, I don't guess you've heard the rumor, then."

"I don't hear anything on Calf Creek, Sid. You know that."

The liveryman got to his feet and stood looking through the window for a few moments. "I don't know exactly how much truth there is to it," he said to the windowpane, "but the word is out that the town council is fed up with Joe Paley." He turned to face Houston, adding, "The latest scuttlebutt is that they're gonna fire him at their next meeting."

Camp sat thoughtful for a while. "What's Paley done that pissed 'em all off?" he asked finally. "Who's gonna be their new town marshal?"

"I think it's just his overall attitude that's about to do him in," Blankenship began. "It could be that the council members are just tired of watching his lordship strut around town barking at people. He's overbearing as hell when he runs across somebody that he knows'll put up with it, Camp."

When Blankenship failed to answer the second part of the question, Houston repeated it. "Who's gonna be their new marshal?"

The liveryman reseated himself on his desk, then laughed aloud. "I don't guess they really know yet, but I've heard it said that, before they consider anybody else, they're gonna offer the job to a man named Camp Houston."

Camp was on his feet instantly. "Bullshit!" he said loudly. "That's completely out of the question." He stood quietly for a few moments, then began again: "I want to nip this shit in the bud, Sid. I don't want to have to hurt Ned's feelings, so I'd appreciate it if you'd get word to him that I don't have the slightest interest in being Menardville's town marshal, and that I positively will not accept the job if he offers it. Besides, I don't even live in this county. Part of my ranch runs over into it, but my house is in McCulloch County."

"I'll tell him," Blankenship said, continuing to smile. "But he sure thinks you'd make a good marshal."

"It don't make a shit what he thinks, Sid. It's what I think that counts, and I think the whole idea is ridiculous." He walked around the room for a while, then added, "Even if I wanted the damn job I couldn't accept it. I'm just now getting my place in good shape, and I've got five hundred head of longhorns coming next week."

"I'll tell him," Blankenship repeated, still smiling.

"I appreciate it," Camp said. He walked to the door, then turned. "I'm going up to the restaurant and get something to eat. I'm hungry enough to eat a skunk."

24

The supper crowd was already gathering in the restaurant, and Houston seated himself at one of the few vacant tables. With a coffeepot in her hand, Ellen Bice was there quickly, looking even prettier than he remembered. When she was working, she usually wore her dark hair in a ball at the back of her head, held there by several large combs. Today it hung loose on her back and shoulders, and supplied a perfect background for her sparkling, sky-blue eyes. She smiled as she filled his cup. "I was hoping you'd come today," she said softly.

"I wouldn't have missed it for the world, been planning it for nearly a month."

Her smile widened. "Thank you." She waved her arm toward the diners. "As you can see, this is the rush hour, so I won't have any time for conversation." She laid the bill of fare on the table. "If you'll decide what you want for supper as quickly as you can, I'll be able to get on with my work."

He ignored the bill of fare, and sat looking into her eyes. "I think you're smart enough to look at me and tell what I need. I'll eat whatever you bring me." He folded his arms and continued to gaze into her eyes, adding jokingly, "Anyway, after I take you to Calf Creek you're gonna be planning all of my meals."

She stuck out her tongue playfully, then headed for the kitchen.

Half an hour later, he sat eating a juicy, tender beefsteak that weighed at least a pound. There was also a bowl of brown beans and a separate platter containing fried potatoes, pickled beets and buttered biscuits. And off to the side, in a smaller dish, a large wedge of apple pie awaited his attention. He had definitely made the right decision, he was thinking: Ellen Bice had known exactly what he needed.

When he had finished his meal and walked to the counter to pay, Mary Trout was there to accept his money. "Ellen is real busy right now," he said to the lady. "Will you give her a message for me?" Not waiting for an answer, he continued, "Tell her that I'll be over in the morning, that if it's not too cold, I'll be in the buggy."

She nodded. "Early in the morning?"

"About ten."

"I'll tell her." She leaned across the counter, speaking more softly now. "Ellen sure looks forward to your visits, Mr. Houston, and there's never a day goes by that she doesn't bring up your name."

"That's nice to hear," he said. "Good night."

He paid for two consecutive nights' lodging at the hotel, then walked into the saloon to find that the bartender was the only man in the room. Wesley Hawks sat on a stool behind the bar, reading a magazine. Camp offered the man what had become his usual greeting when entering the empty saloon: "How's business?"

Hawks laid the reading material aside. "I wish to hell you'd think of something new to say, Camp. Seems like everybody who walks through that door spits out that same tired joke."

"Well, pardon me all to hell, old buddy. I had no idea that it bothered you."

"Bother me? You know me better'n that, Camp. I was just kidding with you. I don't let anything bother me. I learned a long time ago that there wasn't a single thing in this world that I could change, so I just take it all however it comes. You gonna have a drink?"

"I'll just have a beer, Wes, something that won't cloud up my mind too much."

Hawks soon set a foamy mug in front of Houston, then slid his own stool down the opposite side of the bar. He poured himself a stiff drink of whiskey, then took a seat on the stool. "I hear the town council's gonna can Joe Paley's ass," he said, then took a sip from the glass.

Camp wiped the foam from his lips with his hand. "I heard the same thing," he said. "But I've learned to take most of the things I hear with a grain of salt."

"Me, too, but I think you can sort of count on that happening. Ned Riddle is the head councilman, and he's done said that Paley's got to go." He took another sip, then continued, "Of course, I didn't hear that from Riddle's own mouth, now. I got it secondhand, but the man who told me ain't one to go around spreading a buncha shit."

Camp finished off his beer. "Well, we'll see," he said, pushing his mug forward for a refill.

Two hours later, he climbed the stairs to his room. He crawled into bed and pulled up the covers quickly, for the night was cold. He lay wide awake for a while, thinking. He was hoping for some still air in the morning. The sun would surely shine, for that was almost a given at this time of the year. The wind was what made the difference. If it blew again tomorrow, he would sit by the fire with Ellen Bice. If not, he would show up in the buggy about ten.

Miss Ellen Bice. Since he had come to know her, it sounded like the prettiest name he had ever heard. And the girl herself was no less. She was a true beauty who was a joy to be around, and Camp got a warm feeling every time he thought of her. "There's never a day goes by that she doesn't bring up your name," her aunt Mary had said. Camp smiled into the darkness. He fluffed up his pillow and was soon sleeping soundly.

He left his bed at sunup, and was on the street a short while later. The morning air was still, and from all appearances, a beautiful day lay ahead. He stood around on the corner for a while, then stepped inside the small restaurant next door to the hotel, whose breakfast specialty was pork sausage, gravy and buttermilk biscuits. Once inside, he saw very quickly that he was not the only man who liked the simple things in life, and he had to stand in line for half an hour before he could even get a stool at the counter. Once he managed to get a seat, however, his food was not long in coming.

Once he was done eating, he was up from the stool and out of the building. He had plenty of time to kill and would normally have done it at that counter, but he did not possess the necessary gall to sit nursing a cup of coffee while hungry men stood in line waiting for a seat. Back on the street and looking down the hill to Blankenship's office, he could see smoke coming from the flue. Knowing that Sid always had a coffeepot on in the morning, he headed for the livery stable.

The liveryman sat in his office with a coffee cup in his hand. He got to his feet and filled another cup for Camp, then reseated himself. "I've been sitting right here for the past hour trying to come alive," he said. "I believe this is about my fourth cup of this damn stuff." He set the cup on the small table. "I think after you drink a certain amount of coffee, something happens to you, Camp. I mean, you finally get to where it won't even wake you up."

"I imagine that might be the case with most anything if a

man overdoes it, Sid. I've even heard that a drunkard finally reaches a stage where whiskey don't make him drunk anymore."

"Maybe so," Blankenship said. Then he began to laugh. "Hell, you can get drunk on coffee, Camp. I know that for a fact, 'cause I'm drunk on it right now."

They sat talking for more than an hour. Then, when told that he could use a rig free of charge if he roped and hitched up the animal himself, Camp grabbed a rope and headed for the corral. A short time later, he backed a harnessed mare between the shafts and hitched her to the buggy. Blankenship sat on an upended nail keg, watching. "That cargo you're gonna be hauling this morning is the best-looking thing in this town," he said to Camp. "But I suppose you knew that without being told."

Houston was bent over hooking up a trace chain. He straightened his body and made a show of trying to readjust his back with his hand. "I must admit that I had already noticed that, Sid." He climbed to the buggy seat. "I expect to be back before sunset, so I guess you'll still be here."

The liveryman made no effort to rise. "I don't know of anyplace I'd be going," he said. "I don't feel worth a damn today, Camp; felt bad when I woke up this morning." He pointed down the hall. "I've got to shoe that gray mule sometime this afternoon whether I get to feeling better or not, though. Man's coming by to get him before dark."

Houston nodded, then slapped the mare with the reins and headed up the street. He waved or nodded a greeting to the few acquaintances he passed, and soon left the town behind. Ten minutes later, he reached his destination. The Trouts lived in a small, two-story home a mile west of town and two hundred yards off the main road. The front porch was no more than six feet long, and most of the townfolk probably considered the place to be quite ordinary.

But there was nothing ordinary about it as far as Houston was concerned. He thought it was one of the prettiest places in the county, and kept so by a middle-aged couple who spent at least twelve hours a day, six days a week, at their restaurant. The white house with green trim always had the appearance of being painted yesterday, as did all three of the outbuildings.

And, of course, there was the matter of the lawn, which was two hundred yards long and a hundred yards wide. The grass was always well trimmed during the growing season, and several flower beds dotted the landscape. He doubted that the Trouts had ever employed a yard man, for Camp had often seen both the man and his wife working there on Sunday afternoons.

Henry Trout had spent several years in the United States Navy, which was where he had learned to cook. Upon his return to civilian life he had continued to earn his living as a chef, and had worked in a dozen different restaurants over the years. Then, when Riley's came on the market at a price they could afford, the couple jumped at the chance.

The navy had taught Henry Trout about as much as any man needed to know about food, Houston was thinking as he sat at the end of the long drive admiring the whitewashed trees in the yard. Maybe Trout had acquired his penchant for neatness there, too.

Camp trotted the mare down the drive, circled the tall mesquite and stopped in front of the doorway. The girl was already on the porch, smiling as always. "I saw you coming down the road, and wondered why you stopped."

He jumped to the ground. "I was just sitting there admiring this pretty place, and wondering how they're gonna keep it looking like this after I take you to Calf Creek."

She ignored his words, and reached for the door. "I'll be right back." Moments later, she placed a blanket and a picnic basket in the buggy, then held out her hand. He assisted her to the seat, then walked around the vehicle and joined her. "Where are we going today?" she asked, after they reached the main road.

"Same old place, I guess. The road along the San Saba's the only pretty place that's close enough to visit and still get back before dark." He placed his hand on hers, and could not resist adding, "I don't mind that at all, though, little one. One of these days we won't have to worry about the sun going down. We'll be spending all of our nights together after I take you to Calf Creek."

The girl looked straight ahead and said nothing for several minutes, causing Camp to rethink what he had just said. In fact, he had said almost the same thing to her several times in the past, and had always gotten about the same reaction. It was time for him to think of something different to say, he decided. "I'm sorry, Ellen," he said. "It finally dawned on me that you probably don't see any humor in what I've been saying about me taking you to Calf Creek. I won't say it anymore."

She squeezed his hand and smiled. "Thank you."

Though Camp always spoke in a jocular manner, and made sure that he had a smile on his face when he mentioned taking her to Calf Creek, he had never been joking. He had decided months ago that he would eventually ask her to be his wife. And he believed that she would agree if he gave her enough time and did not scare her off beforehand. Ma Franklin had told him exactly how it was with women. He would try to remember all of the things the lady had said, and be more careful of what came out of his own mouth from now on.

They spread the blanket on the riverbank in the early afternoon, where they ate a dinner of fried chicken and potato salad. "Did you cook this stuff yourself?" he asked, gnawing on a drumstick.

She smiled, then nodded. "Right after I got up and saw that we had a pretty day."

They sat on the blanket for the remainder of the afternoon, holding hands and talking. Houston tried to kiss her on the mouth once, but she moved her head quickly, and his lips barely touched her cheek. "I don't want to get into that," she said, sounding almost apologetic, "because I don't do anything halfway. I know what you want, and I know that I have it, but I'm not ready yet. I've got to have more time."

He continued to hold her hand, and apologized for the second time today.

The sun was still two hours high when he delivered Ellen Bice to her home. He had thoroughly enjoyed the day, despite his slight disagreement with the girl on how much kissing was too much. She had given him another peck on the cheek just before they reached her home, although she was careful to do it before they came in sight of the house.

As Houston turned off the main road he could see that both Henry Trout and his wife were busy working in the yard. He waved to them and continued on down the long drive. When the buggy reached the front door of the house, the mare stopped of her own accord. Then she turned her head and stood looking back at her passengers. Camp chuckled. "Smart mare," he said. The girl smiled at the incident also, but said nothing.

Camp wrapped the reins around the brake and jumped to the ground. He helped her from the buggy, then continued to stand with his hands encircling her small waist. "I'm down now," she said finally, smiling broadly and stepping backward out of his reach.

"I'm sorry," he said for the third time today, "but you just felt so nice and soft that I couldn't let go."

They stood holding hands for a few moments. "Good-bye for now," she said. She kissed his hand lightly, then stepped inside the house and closed the door.

He climbed into the buggy and slapped the mare's hip with the reins. He waved to the Trouts once again as he passed, then turned onto the main road.

25

He had traveled no more than halfway through town before he decided that things were not right. He had seen hardly anyone on the street, and as soon as he came within sight of the stable he could see that a crowd of men had gathered there. He urged the mare down the hill at a fast trot. He tied up at the hitching rail, and spoke to Corey Harned, a man he had known for many years. "What's going on here, Corey?"

"It's Sid," Harned answered, sounding as if he had a frog in his throat. "He's dead, Camp." The man's voice cracked and he swallowed hard several times. Corey Harned had been one of Blankenship's longtime friends, and was himself a respected blacksmith. Both Harned and his eldest son had in the past worked for Blankenship on a part-time basis, and Corey had on one occasion drawn a steady paycheck at the stable for three years running.

A brown-haired, muscular man of medium height and appearing to be about thirty-five years old, Harned had come to Menardville from somewhere in Florida several years earlier, traveling with a pregnant wife and a young son. He had quickly convinced Sid that he needed another man around the place and that he, Corey Harned, was that man. He had gone on Blankenship's payroll immediately, and had stayed there for the next three years. The man was good at what he did, and Camp had several times stood around watching him shoe horses, including Camp's own. Now Corey Harned was standing in front of him telling him that Sid Blankenship was dead.

Houston stood in his tracks for a while, dumbfounded. "Dead?" he asked finally. "Sid? Hell, I just talked with him six hours ago. He said he wasn't feeling good today, but I sure didn't think—"

"He didn't just up and die, Camp," Harned interrupted. "He was killed. That gray mule kicked him right square between the eyes. It was all just as plain as the nose on your face: that mule tied to the post, and him standing right there beside Sid's body. Already had three new shoes on, and the other one was lying in the dirt beside Sid's hammer. If Sid coulda just managed to nail the shoe on that last hind leg he'd have been done, and he'd still be alive.

"As I said before, there ain't no question about what happened. The calks on that shoe left imprints on his forehead just as plain as day." He shook his head a few times, then continued, "What I'm having trouble understanding is Sid being careless enough to let it happen. I've known him for a long time, Camp, and I've never known him to give any animal a chance to do that. Especially one as unpredictable as a damn mule."

"Who found the body?" Houston asked.

"Me," Harned said. "Me and my boy, Zac. We came down here to talk about some work, see if he was gonna be needing us again this spring. When I called his name and he didn't answer, we walked on down the hall and there he was, lying there with his eyes wide open."

"Is his body at home now?"

Harned nodded, and pointed to a wooden door leaning against the wall. "Four of us put him on that door right there and carried him up the hill. His wife wanted him put on his own bed, so that's where he is now. Dr. Henson has already been up there to look him over, and he said the same thing the rest of us did: that mule kicked him dead center."

Camp motioned toward the barn. "Is the mule still in there?"

"No. The old man that owned him took him outta here at a run, probably afraid somebody'd shoot him. Wouldn't nobody have bothered that mule, of course. That mule don't know that he's hurt a soul."

Camp was busy untying the mare. "No," he said. "The mule's not at fault." He parked the buggy underneath the shed, then unharnessed the mare and led her to water. Then, when he had dried and curried her coat, he left her in her usual stable with a bucket of oats and two blocks of hay. Moments later, he was walking up the hill to have a talk with Sid Blankenship's widow.

When the tiny, dark-haired woman met him at the door, she was sobbing uncontrollably, and almost fell into his arms. He hugged her shoulders, patted her back and let her cry. "It's awful, Camp," she said finally. "It's just awful."

"I know, Stella," he said softly. "I know." He continued to pat the top of her head, which was well below his own shoulder. "You've always been a strong woman, and you've got to be even stronger now. There's nothing in the world that you can do to change it, so you've got to learn to live with it. You've got children to raise."

"Oh, I know it. I know it."

He led her to the kitchen table and helped her into a chair. "Thank you, Camp," she said, "and thank you for coming." She wiped her eyes on a towel. "I . . . I'll be all right now."

He touched her shoulder. "Stay right here, Stella. I'll be

right back." He headed for the bedroom to view the body. It was not so much that he distrusted anyone; he merely wanted to satisfy himself that the cause of death had been correctly diagnosed.

Although the sun still shone brightly outside, the shades had been drawn on the bedroom windows. A coal-oil lamp on a bedside table provided as much light as Camp needed, however. He stood close to the bed, gazing solemnly at the face of his departed friend. Someone had washed the blood from his head and face, and a coin now lay on each eyelid. When Houston looked closely at the dead man's forehead, he could plainly see the imprints left by the calks on the animal's metal shoe. There was no doubt about it: the gray mule had ended the liveryman's life with one instinctive kick.

Houston returned to the table and took a seat beside the widow. There were other people about the house, for he could hear them talking, but none entered the kitchen. Maybe they sensed that the woman wanted to be alone with a close friend. Except for an occasional sniffle, she was quiet now, and though swollen, her eyes were dry. He reached across the table and covered one of her small hands with his own. "Is there anything I can do, Stella? Anything at all?"

Her answer was slow in coming. She got to her feet unsteadily, stoked the fire in the stove and pulled the coffeepot over the firebox. Then she placed two empty cups on the table and reseated herself. "I can't think of anything anybody can do, Camp. Other than the fact that we're gonna be by ourselves, I guess we'll make out all right. Sidney was always a good hand at putting most of his money by, so I don't reckon any of us'll go hungry."

"How about the livery stable?"

"Oh, I'll keep that," she answered quickly. "Selling that stable would be the last thing in the world Sidney would have wanted me to do. Besides, it provides us with a good, steady income. Corey Harned says he'll run the place for me, and you know yourself that he's a good man. I never mentioned it to my husband, of course, but I've heard that some people thought Corey might actually be a better blacksmith than Sidney."

"I don't know about that, but I've watched Corey work, and it's obvious that he knows what he's doing. He's well liked, so I believe that he can at least hang on to Sid's regular customers. I also believe that he's an honest man, so you'll get every dollar that's coming to you."

She nodded, and said nothing.

He got to his feet and poured their cups full of coffee, then reclaimed his chair. "Have you decided where you're gonna bury Sid?"

"Me and him talked about that very thing last winter," she said. "We both decided that we wanted to be buried over there on the hill above the old Spanish fort, so that's where we'll be taking Sidney tomorrow. I've done sent word to the undertaker, so he'll take care of getting the grave dug and everything. One thing Sidney didn't want is a lot of preaching. He just wanted some of his friends to speak a few words, whatever comes to their minds." She smiled weakly now. "He said the last thing he wants to hear before they cover him up with dirt is somebody singing his favorite song, "Home Sweet Home."* Do you know anybody who can carry a tune? Somebody who might know the right words?"

"Offhand, I can't say that I do. There are no professional singers around here, and talking somebody into singing a solo in public would be more than a little bit difficult. It might be a lot easier if we just ask all of his friends to sing the song together at graveside. I think about everybody knows most of the words."

She was thoughtful for a while. "Yes," she said finally, "I reckon that would be better. Hearing the voices that he rec-

---

*Written by John Howard Payne in 1823, it was one of the most popular songs in the West for the next hundred years.

ognizes would mean more to him anyhow. Somebody's gonna have to lead 'em in the singing, though."

The funeral procession formed at the livery stable at one o'clock the following afternoon. Because the deceased had not been a churchgoer, and had requested that no preaching take place at his funeral, the religious element was largely missing. And since a majority of his friends were male, so was the segment of the population who would be following the body up the hill to its final resting place. Although he made no effort to count them, Houston estimated the number of men in the crowd to be about forty. The widow and her two daughters were the only females present.

Stella Blankenship had politely refused the undertaker's offer of a hearse. Her husband would want to ride up the hill in one of his own wagons, she said, and that wagon should be drawn by one of his own teams. Town Councilman Ned Riddle, who had largely taken charge of the funeral arrangements, saw that the lady's wishes were carried out: the pine coffin now lay in one of Sid's new wagons, with two of his black horses in the traces.

The widow and her daughters sat on the seat of the wagon, which would be the only vehicle involved. Everyone else in the procession would be afoot, including both of the dead man's young sons. No man in the crowd wore a sidearm, though Camp's little Remington that sometimes rode in his boot was now tucked away in his inside coat pocket. For a man with his reputation and potential enemies to walk around completely unarmed would have been pure folly, even in a funeral procession.

At a word from Riddle, who would lead the team, the procession began its slow trek up the hill. Camp Houston, accompanied by three other men, led the way, followed by the wagon, then the remainder of the mourners.

At the top of the hill, two men standing beside mounds of fresh dirt marked the location of the open grave. Camp saw one of the men hide the picks and shovels behind a nearby bush as the procession drew near. Riddle parked the wagon a good forty feet away, for the last thing he wanted to see was the family of the deceased gazing down into that hole.

Several wooden benches had been set up, and four men now placed the coffin between the benches and the grave. The Blankenship family was then seated on the bench nearest the coffin. A few of the others seated themselves, but most remained standing.

Ned Riddle did not tarry. "We've all come together to say good-bye to a dear friend," he began, "and to offer our deepest regrets to his family. Sidney Blankenship was an asset to this community, a good-hearted soul who always had his hand out to help his fellow man." He hesitated for a moment, then added sheepishly, "In fact, I owed him eight dollars myself, a debt that I shoulda and coulda paid a long time ago. Of course, he won't need no money where he's at now, but I'll be handing it over to his widow before this day's out." He pointed to the coffin. "Right there lies the remains of one of the best men ever born." He motioned toward the crowd. "I'm sure there's somebody else here who can say it a lot better than I can, so I'll get out of the way."

No man moved or spoke. After enduring several moments of silence, Houston, who sat on the end of the family's bench, got to his feet, hat in hand. "I guess Ned has already described my own feelings for Sid Blankenship," he said. "I'd just like to add that Sid was one of the best men I've ever known, every day of the week, and I feel honored that he called me his friend." Camp returned to his seat, and the crowd was silent again.

After a few moments, Riddle was back on his feet. "The deceased himself chose the song he wanted to hear at his funeral. My own voice ain't much, so I'm asking all of you to join in and help me. I reckon you all know the words." Then he began to sing, waving his arm in an attempt to lead the others. No one else joined in the singing. Riddle rushed on alone, however, arriving at the last line of the song in less than a minute: "Be it ever so humble, there's no place like home." Then he raised both of his arms and shouted loudly, "I declare this funeral over and done! Let's all move back down the hill now. There are men here to inter the coffin after we're gone!"

The crowd dispersed. The wagon disappeared down the hill quickly as Corey Harned drove Stella Blankenship and her children home at a fast trot.

When Harned returned to the livery stable with the empty wagon, Houston was standing out front. "I wish you'd catch up my roan before you bother with the team, Corey," Camp said. "Even if I leave now, it'll be nearly midnight when I get home."

Harned nodded. "Won't be but a few minutes," he said. He tied the team to the hitching rail, then headed for the corral with a rope in his hand. Three minutes later, he was busy helping Houston saddle the roan.

Camp stopped at Riley's a few minutes later, and ordered a bowl of beef stew. Ellen Bice's face was a little longer than usual, probably because she knew that he was mourning the loss of a friend. "I'm real sorry about Mr. Blankenship," she said. "I know that the two of you were real close."

"It was an accident," he said, "and worrying about it is useless." He changed the subject. "I'm gonna empty this bowl as fast as I can, then head home. I've got a herd of cattle coming any day now, and I need to be there."

She laid her hand on his. "I understand, Camp, but please don't stay away any longer than you have to." Then she was gone to the kitchen. He paid his way out of the place a few minutes later, then mounted and headed for Calf Creek.

26

Two miles north of 3C headquarters, there was a plateau that was at least a mile long and half as wide. The area was treeless and almost brushless, and was probably the best graze on the premises. It was here that the cattle would first be driven. They would be allowed to graze on the plateau for the remainder of their first day on the 3C, then bedded down and guarded throughout the night. Next morning, the calves would be branded, then the herd would be allowed to scatter at will. The cows still belonged to John Butterworth, and would continue to wear the Lazy B brand.

On Wednesday morning, Houston and Fowler hauled two wagonloads of wood to the plateau, and off-loaded it in two separate piles. Mostly oak, it would burn slowly and create hot branding fires. Houston dropped off four branding irons at each woodpile. "I expected to hear something from Bo before now," he said. "You think he found that perch we told him about?"

"Oh, yeah," Runt answered. "If he don't find it right off he'll know it, and keep looking around till he does. He may be young, but that Georgia boy don't think near as slow as he talks."

Camp chuckled. "I know that for sure," he said.

At sunup that morning, Patton had been dispatched to a particular ridge four miles northeast of the ranch house. The ridge was the highest elevation within a twenty-mile radius, and would offer the youngster an unobstructed view for at least five miles in the direction of Mills County. When he spotted the cattle, Bo's instructions were to ride to the plateau to inform Houston and Fowler, each of whom had a saddled cow pony tied at the edge of the woods.

At the plateau, Camp sat on the tailgate of the wagon, his long legs resting on the ground. He took a sip of water from his canteen, then wiped his lips with his sleeve. "I'm just wondering if the drovers ran into some kind of problem, Runt. The cows ought to be here by now." When Fowler said nothing, Houston added, "I can't imagine an easier cattle drive. The only body of water they have to cross is Brady Creek, and I've never seen it much more than knee-deep."

"Quit worrying, Camp," fowler said, taking several swallows from his own canteen, then throwing it into the wagon with a loud thump. "The cows are coming."

Fowler had hardly finished speaking when Bo Patton rode out of the woods from the east. He sat his saddle a half mile away waving his hat, which was the agreed-upon signal. "See?" Fowler asked, pointing. "He's spotted the cows."

A few minutes later, Fowler untied their saddle horses at the south edge of the clearing, and Camp tied the wagon team to the same tree. Then both men mounted and headed east, joining Patton at the lower edge of the plateau.

They met the herd an hour later, and sat on a small rise waiting for the point man to reach them. The rider trotted up the slope on a small bay, and stopped almost within touching distance. A small man with sandy hair and a copper-colored beard, he spat a mouthful of tobacco juice, then spoke: "You Camp Houston?"

Camp nodded. "Sure am. What we—"

"Which way?" the man interrupted.

When Houston pointed west, the man motioned for him to get out of the way, then waved the drovers on up the slope. As the herd continued to move up the rise at a steady gait, the point man moved his bay alongside Houston's stirrup. "Didn't mean no disrespect back there. I just wanted to keep these critters moving. It's too damn hard to get 'em lined out again if we let 'em stop and start milling around."

"I understand perfectly," Camp said with a toothy smile. "I've been right where you are more than once." He offered a handshake. "I appreciate you fellows bringing 'em down."

"I'm Dub Hamilton," the drover said, pumping the hand, "and I'm in charge of the drive. I reckon I went to work at the Lazy B just a few days after you quit the job of ranch foreman. Everybody there spoke mighty highly of you."

"Well, that's nice to hear," Camp said, then introduced Runt Fowler and Bo Patton. Even as the men shook hands they continued to walk their horses west, and the cattle followed.

After meeting and sizing up Dub Hamilton, Camp had instructed Fowler and Patton to stay clear of the herd and offer no assistance whatsoever. Nor had he himself approached the cattle. Three hours later, however, when they came to the plateau, Houston made his wishes known. He met Hamilton in front of the herd and rode beside him stirrup to stirrup, pointing north all the while. "Lead 'em on down to the lower end of this plateau," he said, "then circle 'em back uphill and bring 'em to a halt. We'll let 'em graze the rest of the afternoon, then bed 'em down right here. We'll brand the calves tomorrow, then let 'em all scatter and hunt up some water."

Hamilton nodded obediently, and turned his horse downhill.

Then Camp rode at a canter to the top of the clearing,

where Fowler and Patton stood beside the wagon. "What do you think of Hamilton?" Runt asked as Camp dismounted.

"Aw, he's probably all right," Camp said as he tied his horse to a wagon wheel. "He might be a little bit touchy, but I don't guess it's carved in granite that we have to like him. He's already done everything that we needed him for, so as far as we're concerned, he can just head on back home now."

"You tell it while I pat my foot," Fowler said gruffly. "I can tell by his actions that I don't like him, and I ain't likely to the next time I see him."

"Mr. Butterworth said that four men are gonna stay here to help us," Patton said, "and that ain't but half of this bunch. I've already counted eight men, so I guess four of 'em'll be going back home right off. I believe Mr. Hamilton'll be among that four. Might leave this afternoon, if we're lucky."

Patton's prediction proved to be accurate. The herd had no more than been circled back into itself and the cattle begun to graze when Hamilton approached Houston's wagon. "The boss told me to leave four men with you," he said, "so I'll be leaving the Brown brothers, Weed Ellum, and Sim Waltrip. I reckon feeding them's gonna be your problem, so I'll take the cook and the pack animals on back to the Lazy B with me." Although it was considered a breach of western etiquette for a mounted man to attempt to carry on a conversation with a man on the ground, and even worse to offer a handshake to any man who was not also mounted, Hamilton continued to sit his saddle as he extended his right hand. "We'll be leaving now," he said.

Camp walked the few steps and took Hamilton's hand. "Tell John that we're all thinking of him," he said. "Tell him I'll be up to see him some time this summer."

Hamilton nodded, then whirled his bay and went down the hill at a canter. The three men who would accompany him back to the Lazy B waited at the edge of the clearing. All four disappeared toward the northeast a few minutes later, the lead ropes seeming to stretch the necks of the lagging pack mules.

Camp motioned down the hill to the mounted men. "Know any of 'em, Runt?"

Fowler squinted into the late afternoon sun, then shaded his eyes with his hand. "That short one might be Low Boy Brown. Looks like him from here, anyway. And that fellow talking to him right now might be his younger brother, Harmon. Everybody calls Harmon High Boy, 'cause he's at least a foot taller than Low Boy."

Houston chuckled. "High Boy and Low Boy, huh?"

"Yep," Fowler said, untying his horse. "High Boy's about six-two, and Low Boy ain't but five feet. Why there's so much difference in the size of 'em is anybody's guess. Just looking at 'em you'd have to say that they had the same daddy, 'cause they look as much alike as two peas in a pod." He mounted, and turned his horse down the hill. "Big pea and little pea," he added.

Houston and Patton mounted and followed Fowler down the hill, and within minutes, Fowler and Low Boy Brown had introduced every member of both groups. Runt had been correct in his identification of the Brown brothers, both of them lean, wiry, dark-complected men with black beards.

Weed Ellum was the tallest of the bunch, and had no doubt come by his nickname because of the fact that he was so skinny. Camp estimated that the man would weigh about a hundred forty pounds with his boots on. He had blue eyes, a ruddy complexion and blond hair that curled around his ears. He appeared to be about thirty years old, and had the firmest handshake of any man in the group.

A man of medium height and weight, Sim Waltrip was the least talkative of the drovers. His gray hair, badly in need of a trim, hung around his neck and ears loosely, and he appeared to be well past the age when most men hung up their spurs and sought a different line of work. However, the fact that looks can be deceiving was once again brought home to Houston as Waltrip dropped Camp's hand in the middle of a handshake and galloped up the hill like a man half his age. A cow had bolted from the herd and headed for the woods at the top of the plateau. Waltrip beat her to the timber, and lashed her back into the herd with his rope. Houston had sat watching. *Nope, Sim Waltrip's not quite done yet,* he was thinking.

Hamilton had left the bedrolls belonging to Waltrip, Ellum and the Brown brothers, along with a large tarpaulin, in a pile at the eastern edge of the clearing. Pointing in that direction, Houston spoke to Patton: "Take the wagon and move those bedrolls up the hill, Bo. Drop 'em off right there by the woodpiles, where the branding fires are gonna be. Then I suppose you ought to build a campfire and get supper started. This is gonna be a hungry bunch."

Half an hour later, Patton had a campfire going in the levelest place he could find. The two big boxes that Fowler had loaded onto the wagon that morning were now resting on the tailgate, along with two coffeepots. Several jugs of water were also in the wagon. Fowler had brought twelve tin cups, the same number of tin plates, and enough spoons for a small army, for he had had no way of knowing how many men would have to be fed.

There was a big iron pot half full of presoaked beans, and a hindquarter of venison wrapped in oilcloth. One of the boxes contained two cakes of corn bread and twenty biscuits, along with salt, pepper and sugar for coffee. As he peered into the boxes, taking stock of the things on hand, Patton quickly decided that he himself had little to do. He would simply add water to the pot and put the beans on to boil, fry up a dozen slices of venison and make two pots of coffee, then get the hell out of the way. He stoked the fire again, then reached for a jug of water.

Houston and Fowler had both joined the drovers in chasing cows back into the herd. Surprisingly, not a single one of the bulls had attempted to quit the bunch, and even as Camp watched, one of them had found a willing cow and was busy earning his keep. The cow now being bred had a calf beside her that was no more than two months old.

"We call her Old Broke Horn," Weed Ellum said to Camp, pointing. "Mr. Butterworth says she's eleven years old, and has calved like clockwork every eleven months since she was a yearling."

Houston smiled. "Good," he said. "She's exactly the kind of cow I need."

The riders continued to circle the cattle, never crowding them, giving them plenty of room to graze like there was no tomorrow. Finally, with full bellies and the sun about to set, they began to lie down: first one, then two, then ten, then a hundred head. When only one old bull was left standing, Fowler chuckled and pointed. "Makes me want to go up there and kick his legs out from under him."

"He's the boss," Waltrip said. "That sonofabitch would charge you like a tiger if you went up there messing with him or any of his girlfriends. Especially if you happened to be afoot."

Because the moon was already up when the sun went down, there never was a period of total darkness on the plateau, and none of the cows could hope to sneak away from the herd without an alert cow pony being right on her tail. Eventually, the cattle seemed to reach that same conclusion, and simply lay around chewing their cuds.

Two hours after sunset, Patton began to feed the riders two at a time, while the other four continued to hold a circle around the herd. Though the cattle were all lying down now, Houston was taking no chances. "These old cows have been through it all before," he said to Weed Ellum. "They know exactly what's gonna happen in the morning, and they're probably lying there right now trying to figure out some way to hide their calves in the brush."

"Hell, yes, they are," Ellum agreed. "I've seen it a hundred times: about the time you get to thinking you've got 'em under control"—he snapped his fingers—"they're gone." He motioned toward the still herd. "If that bunch right there all of a sudden took it in their little minds to head for the brush, it would happen so damn quick that anybody who ain't seen it wouldn't believe it. Within one minute we wouldn't have the slightest damned idea which way any of them went."

"Well, the fact that they're all old cows makes 'em less likely to run," Houston said. "They don't have as much get-up-and-go as they once did."

When all of the riders had been fed, Camp announced that Fowler and he would take the first watch. "You fellows go ahead and hit your bedrolls," he said to the Lazy B men. "You've all been putting in some long days, and Runt and I haven't been straining ourselves lately. The two of us'll stay with the cows till after midnight, then I'll wake Ellum and Waltrip. Then about three o'clock in the morning they can wake the Brown brothers and let them finish out the night." He stepped into a stirrup and threw his leg over the saddle. "Is that agreeable to everybody?" Several of the men mumbled assents, then headed for their bedrolls.

Houston and Fowler then rode down the hill and began to circle the herd in opposite directions. Though the campfire was allowed to die, two lanterns burned all night. "We ought to keep some kinda light going," Waltrip had said early in the evening. "Cattle associate lanterns with humans. As long as they can see the light from that lantern they know that humans are on guard, and that no predator is gonna come anywhere near the herd."

Houston had never before given any thought to what the man was saying, but it certainly made sense. Besides, Waltrip had been herding cattle longer than most of the others had been alive, and Camp was not about to take the man's advice lightly. He ordered Patton to place one burning lantern next to the wagon and another at the bottom of the hill, on the opposite side of the herd.

The night passed without incident, and Patton rekindled the fire at daybreak. He made two pots of coffee, then put the leftover beans and venison on the fire. Then he called to the sleeping drovers, all of whom rolled out of their blankets and walked to the woods to relieve themselves, then congregated around the fire.

"Ain't got much to offer for breakfast, men," Patton said as he poured each man's coffee cup full. "Just more of what we had for supper. Soon as we get done with the branding, I'll fix a good dinner back at the house." He pointed to the cattle. "Mr. Waltrip says there ain't more'n about fifty of them calves, and that we'll have 'em marked, branded, cut and sent running long before dinnertime."

No man complained as each of the riders picked up a tin plate and lined up for the leftovers. "Hell, this stuff tastes better than what I've been getting at home," one man said after a while.

Camp had been busy building a branding fire. When it was roaring, he joined the men at the campfire. "As soon as that burns down a little, we'll start heating the irons," he said. "I had intended to use two fires, but we don't have as many calves as I expected. With one man holding 'em down and another man branding, cutting and marking them, we should run through this little bunch in two hours or less. We'll need two men roping, and the other two will be responsible for holding the herd together while the branding's taking place." He turned to Patton. "Bo, you'll be the man who keeps the irons hot. I mean red-hot." Patton nodded, and headed for the branding fire.

As Camp filled his coffee cup, Low Boy Brown walked to the fire and stood beside him. "Ain't none of my business to be trying to line things out here," he said, "but I believe it would all move along faster if you let me and my brother do the roping. Of course, Runt is the biggest one here, so he oughta do the holding and let Sim do the branding and castrating. Sim's mighty good at that. That'll leave you and Weed to make sure the herd don't leave the county while we're busy with the calves."

Camp took a sip of coffee, then chuckled. "Hell, Low Boy, I believe you've already got things lined out. Just go over there and tell everybody what they're supposed to be doing. Then as soon as the irons get hot we'll get on with it. You and Harmon just drag 'em up to the fire. Fowler's plenty big enough to hold 'em."

The branding got under way a few minutes later, and was over in less than two hours. Fifty-seven calves now wore the 3C brand, thirty-two of them heifers. Camp stood watching as the drovers headed the herd toward Calf Creek, then allowed them to scatter at will. Thirty-two heifers! he was thinking. Nothing to boast about, but it was a start. They would all calve next year, and their offspring would do the same the next. And the cycle would continue indefinitely. Indeed, a million head of cattle would eventually walk the earth whose bloodlines could be traced right back to the thirty-two head of heifers they had just branded. As the last of the calves disappeared into the underbrush, Houston stood shaking his head at the wonderment of it all.

Patton poured a jug of water on the fire, and a short while later, with the remainder of the wood and all of their bedrolls loaded onto the wagon, they were ready to head for the ranch house. Fowler untied the team, then motioned Patton up to the driver's seat. "I guess we'd better get on home and eat that good meal you promised us, Bo." The youngster climbed to the seat and clucked to the team, and all of the mounted men followed the wagon.

27

Butterworth's riders stayed on the 3C for nine days. On the tenth morning, with a bedroll tied behind each saddle, they rode into the yard to say good-bye to the ranch's three residents. "You've all treated us quite nicely," Waltrip was saying. "If any of you ever come up to the Lazy B, we'll try to return the favor."

"Oh, I'll be up there eventually," Fowler said, "If for no other reason than to see if that barn I built is still standing."

Waltrip sat thoughtful for a while. "Didn't know you built it," he said finally, "but it's sure as hell standing. Best barn in Mills County."

Fowler nodded, and accepted the compliment with a smile.

Bo Patton spoke to no one in particular: "I never have seen a ranch anywhere near as big as the Lazy B. Maybe Camp'll let me ride along with him next time he comes up there."

Although he had heard the youngster's words, Camp stood

by noncommittally. Then he addressed the riders as a group: "I appreciate it all, fellows. Tell John that I'll see him later in the year."

"Will do," Weed Ellum said. He pointed toward the shed, adding, "We left that heavy tarp in your wagon. It's cumbersome as hell without a packhorse, and don't none of us feel like fooling with it. You'll have a need for it sooner or later."

"I'm sure I will," Houston said. He tilted his head skyward, inspecting the clouds. "I don't think it's gonna rain in the near future, so you won't need the tarp when you make camp tonight."

Ellum glanced toward the Brown brothers, and all three began to chuckle. "Make camp?" he asked. "Hell, we ain't gonna be making camp. Today is Friday, and there ain't no way in the world that we're gonna show up at the Lazy B on a weekend. We'll just ride up to Brady and have us a blowout tonight and tomorrow night, then start moping on back home Sunday morning." When all three of his companions nodded their assents, Ellum yanked on his horse's reins. "Hallelujah!" he shouted loudly, and led the way down the hill.

"I like all of them men," Patton said, as the riders disappeared up the road toward Brady. "I reckon they know just about everything there is to know about cattle, and I learned something from every single one of 'em."

Houston nodded. "They know what they're doing," he said. "Otherwise, they wouldn't be working for John Butterworth." He headed for the corral, and motioned for Patton to follow. "Runt's gonna be busy stretching string and driving stakes today, Bo. He's decided to get started on that bunkhouse he's been talking about for months." He pointed to the horses. "Put your saddle on one of them, then fill our canteens with fresh water. Better wrap us up a bite to eat, too. You and I are gonna be riding boundaries today."

With biscuits, venison and a full canteen of water in each of their saddlebags, they mounted two of the black cutting horses a short time later. As Blankenship had predicted, all four of the animals had turned out to be good cow ponies. Camp pointed up the hill to the north. "You know where all of the boundaries are, Bo. Ride north to the northeast corner, then west to the northwest corner, then turn south. You should meet me sometime around noon, 'cause I'll be circling in the opposite direction."

Patton nodded. He kneed his horse, and the animal jumped instantly. "One more thing!" Houston called after him. Patton brought the black to an abrupt halt, and sat listening to his boss. "If you have to chase any cows back onto the 3C," Camp continued, "hit 'em hard enough to hurt 'em. If you lash 'em as hard as you can with the end of that rope, they'll remember it."

Patton turned his horse's head north again. "I'll whip 'em good," he said, "but I sure don't think they'll remember it." He headed north at a canter.

Houston turned his own mount south. "I don't either," he said softly.

He rode south into Mason County till he reached the southeast corner of his property, then turned west. Two hours later, he was at the southwest corner, in Menard County. He took a sip of water from his canteen, then headed north at a slow walk. He had been riding for almost four hours, and had not seen a single cow. All of which could be a good sign, he was thinking. It could mean that the cattle had found suitable graze in the vicinity of Calf Creek, and were content to remain somewhere near the center of the ranch.

He met Patton an hour later. "Have you seen any cattle, Bo?"

"Not a cow," the lanky youngster answered, dismounting. "It's like they all just flew away." He unwrapped his biscuits and venison, and took a seat on a log.

Camp joined him, and also began to eat. "If the cows have bunched up around the creek, which I believe is the case, I'm gonna be real pleased, Bo. Of course, when they eat everything in sight they'll scatter to hell and gone, but they'll be more familiar with the ranch by then. So will we, for that matter."

Patton washed down a mouthful of food. "I stopped once in a while just trying to hear a cow, but I never heard a sound."

"Like I said, I believe they've settled in close to the creek for the time being. The grass is good, and they don't have to hunt water. We'll finish eating, then cut right through the middle of the ranch. If they're on the creek, we'll see 'em."

As they made their way home, they found the cattle easily. Sitting their saddles on a hilltop above the creek, they could see at least a hundred head, some grazing alone, but most in bunches of ten or twenty. "Let's turn south and ride around them," Camp said. "We certainly don't want to upset this good thing we've got going."

Early Saturday morning, Houston saddled the roan and rode off the hill on his way to Menardville. As he had done several times before, he would spend the night at the hotel, then call on Ellen Bice the next day. Though the day was starting out unseasonably warm, and he rode in his shirtsleeves, his fleece-lined coat was tied behind the cantle, for he knew that the area's weather could change drastically from one day to the next.

He allowed the roan to set the pace, and as usual, the animal chose the canter. Always the canter, and the horse would hold the same gait until he began to tire, which was usually about halfway between Calf Creek and Menardville.

He arrived at the livery stable at midafternoon, and Corey Harned was standing out front. Camp dismounted, and immediately noticed the double-barreled, ten-gauge shotgun leaning against the wall just inside the doorway. He pointed to the weapon. "What are you gonna do with that cannon, Corey? Are you expecting somebody to try to rob you?"

Harned pointed up the street. "There's a shitstorm going on uptown, Camp, and I'm just making sure that I don't get caught off-guard. Got me two barrels of double-aught buck there."

Houston handed over his horse's reins. "You say there's a problem uptown?"

Harned dropped the reins to the ground. "You damn well said it. Joe Paley's already killed Ned Riddle, and shot Sheriff McMichen in the leg. I'll tell you right now, he sure as hell better not come down here—"

"Whoa, Corey," Camp interrupted. "Why don't you start all over and tell me what's going on?"

The liveryman related the story as Houston leaned against the wall, listening. The town council had voted to relieve Paley of his duties as town marshal, and, as head councilman, it had been Riddle's job to inform Paley of the decision. Riddle had fired the man late yesterday afternoon, and demanded his badge right on the spot.

Paley had spent the rest of the day hunting up one councilman after another. Cursing and calling them names, he informed every member that, regardless of their votes to the contrary, he was still the marshal of this town. He was the only lawman Menardville needed, he said, and he fully intended to serve out the remainder of his term.

"I reckon Paley must have just seethed on it all night," Harned added, "because about eight o'clock this morning, he put a bullet right between Ned Riddle's eyes."

Camp was still leaning against the wall. "Do you know where Ned was when Paley shot him?"

"Right on the damn street, is what I heard. I ain't been up there myself, but I've been told that he was walking up the hill toward his office, and that Paley just stepped right up to him and blasted him in the face."

Camp stood thoughtful for a while. "Do you know where Paley is now?" he asked finally.

"Locked himself in his office . . . I mean, what used to be

his office. I reckon he's still there. One of the councilmen sent
a rider after the sheriff, but hell, Paley ain't scared of him.
McMichen walked up there to try to talk Paley into coming
out, but Paley put a bullet through his leg and sent him hop-
ping back down the hill. McMichen's deputy ain't around to
take a hand, 'cause him and two more men that the sheriff
deputized are on their way to the Huntsville penitentiary to
deliver a prisoner." Harned exhaled loudly. "I tell you, there
ain't no telling what the hell's gonna happen next."

"Where's the sheriff now, Corey?"

"Up there at Riley's, I guess. At least that's where he was
a few minutes ago. I heard that his wound ain't bad at all,
that the bullet went clean through his leg without hitting anything that's gonna cripple him." He began to laugh loudly.
"I'll betcha one damn thing. I'll betcha there ain't nobody
having to hold him down to keep him from rushing back up
that hill."

Houston smiled, and said nothing.

Twenty minutes later, he stepped into Riley's Restaurant to
discover that the place was filled almost to capacity. Though
he was well acquainted with most of the men in the room, he
spoke to no one as he made his way to a table along the rear
wall, where, with a white bandage around his left thigh, Sheriff McMichen was seated with two men Houston had never
seen before.

The sheriff used his good leg to push out a chair as Camp
drew near. "Mr. Houston!" he said loudly. "Have a seat, and
tell me what you think we ought to do."

Camp remained standing. "About what?" he asked.

"Well, uh . . . I just thought you might have some ideas
about how to get Paley out of that office. I'm gonna charge
him with murder and attempted murder."

"Do you know of any reason he'd have for killing Ned
Riddle, Sheriff? I mean, other than the fact that Riddle fired
him?"

McMichen shook his head. "Hell, no," he said. "That's it

in a nutshell. Paley thinks he's God's gift to the rest of us poor souls. He's been strutting up and down the street like the cock of the walk for so long that he just couldn't handle it when the council voted him out. That man don't give a damn about nobody, Mr. Houston." He pointed to his bandaged leg. "Hell, you see what he done to me just 'cause I went up there and tried to talk some sense into him."

Houston nodded. "I see."

It was then that he spotted Ellen Bice. Standing next to the kitchen's batwing doors, she was looking directly at him and smiling. He walked to meet her. "I finally got my cattle moved onto the 3C," he said. "Then I just had to see you."

Her hair was down on her shoulders again today, and she had never looked prettier to him. "Thank you," she said. "I'll be up early in the morning."

He pointed across the room. "Will you bring me a cup of coffee and a plate of something good? I'll be sitting over there with the sheriff."

She nodded, and headed for the kitchen.

When he returned to McMichen's table, the lawman introduced his friends, each of whom appeared to be past the age of sixty. Camp shook hands with Bill Hardwick and Manley Jefferson, then accepted the chair and seated himself. "What's wrong with just waiting Paley out, Sheriff? I mean, how long do you think he can stay locked up in that office?"

"Could be a good while. I know he keeps that two-gallon bucket full of water all the time. He's probably got a buncha tinned meat, too."

Hardwick nodded, and wiped his gray beard out of his mouth. "Even if he ain't got nothing to eat he could hold out for a long time. A man can live several weeks without food if he's got plenty of water. Now, if he's got two gallons of that, he ain't likely to come out of there anytime soon."

Houston sat listening as the others talked among themselves. Only when Ellen placed a platter of stuffed pork chops and fried potatoes before him did he speak again. "I'll bet that's just as good as it looks," he said, then dug in.

"I guess a bunch of us could just storm that office and take Paley out of there," Manley Jefferson said. "Probably a dozen men right here in this room who'd be for that."

Houston sat looking around the room for a while, then shook his head. "I don't think you'll find many men in here who are willing to do any storming with you, Mr. Jefferson. They've all seen what happened to Ned Riddle and the sheriff, and they also know that there's no cover whatsoever on the front side of that building. There's not a tree or even a stump within thirty yards of the front door. It would be like shooting fish in a barrel to Paley, and I don't suppose there's anybody left who doubts that he'll shoot."

Jefferson pushed back his chair. "One way to find out," he said. "Let me just talk to a few of—"

"Forget it, Manley," Hardwick interrupted. "This man here's exactly right: that storming idea ain't gonna do nothing but get a bunch of men killed." Jefferson stood quietly for a few moments, then reseated himself.

Hardwick placed his elbows on the table and leaned forward. "That front door ain't the only way into that office, Mr. Houston. You see, I worked on one of the crews that put up that building, twenty years ago. We built the jail, too. There are five of them offices under the same roof, with connecting doors between them." He leaned closer and spoke more softly. "In other words, if you get inside one of 'em, you've got access to all of 'em. The tax assessor's office is on the west side, with three rooms between it and the marshal's office. I remember for sure that we didn't put no locks on them doors, and I don't guess anybody else ever did. Wouldn't have been no reason for it, 'cause there ain't nobody s'posed to have nothing to hide."

Having cleaned his plate, Houston sat for a while without speaking. He was quietly trying to figure out what might be going on in Joe Paley's mind. The man had to know that he would have to come out of the office sooner or later, and that he would eventually have to face a jury. He had killed an un-armed man who was well liked in the community, and put a bullet through the county sheriff's thigh. Had Paley intended to kill McMichen rather than wound him? Houston believed that he had, otherwise he would have shot lower.

Although the conversation at the table continued, Camp scarcely heard a word. He was concentrating on the long building at the top of the hill, for he had decided to try to get Joe Paley out of it. "Any windows between those rooms, Mr. Hardwick?" he asked.

"No. We just put two windows in each office, both of 'em on the front side."

When Camp was quiet for a while, the sheriff spoke: "Are you thinking about trying to get at Paley, Mr. Houston?"

Camp nodded.

"Here," McMichen said, fishing around in his pocket. "Let me give you this, so you'll have some authority." He laid a deputy sheriff's badge in Houston's hand. "I hereby appoint you a deputy sheriff of Menard County, Texas." He looked to-ward Hardwick and Jefferson. "You men heard me deputize Mr. Houston, now, so you're both witnesses to the fact."

The men nodded. "That we are," Hardwick said.

Houston put the badge in his pocket. "Have you got any prisoners in your jail, Sheriff?"

"Nope. Last one I had is on his way to the Huntsville pen right now."

Houston drummed his fingers on the table for a moment. "Give me the key to that big cell right down the hall from your desk," he said.

McMichen handed him a roll of keys. "It's that square-ended one right—"

"Take it off of the ring, Sheriff," Camp interrupted. "I don't want anything on me that might rattle." He pocketed the single key a moment later, then spoke again: "I'll take it as a favor if all three of you men'll sit right here till you hear from me again. And don't say a word about this to anybody."

"We'll be here," the sheriff said as both of the others nodded.

Camp walked through the front door and turned left. He circled the restaurant on its south side, and headed north. After traveling about two hundred yards, he turned west and walked at a fast clip till he reached the top of the hill. Then he turned south through the woods that grew right up to the rear of the building, with the tops of some of the trees hanging over its roof.

He moved from tree to tree cautiously till he eventually worked his way to the west end of the building. He peered around the southwest corner and saw no one. Nor could he see anyone on the street in the direction of town. He added a sixth shell to the cylinder of his Colt, then shoved the weapon back into its holster. Then he stood looking down the front side of the building to the marshal's office, knowing that Joe Paley could not see him without first stepping outside.

Houston saw little danger to himself in what he was doing, for he had no intention of letting Paley see him. He had climbed the hill counting entirely on the off chance that a door or window had been left unlocked on one of the offices. He pinned the deputy's badge to his shirt, then leaned against the end of the building and took off his boots. Then he stepped onto the porch in his stocking feet, dreading the creak of a board that did not come.

He peeked into a window of the tax assessor's office and saw nothing but a counter and the wall beyond. Paying close attention to its construction, he could see that the window had no locking device, so he believed that he could raise it. How much noise that would make remained to be seen. One long step carried him past the window and to the door. When he tested the knob it turned easily, and the door was suddenly ajar. Whether it had been left unlocked out of carelessness or habit was anybody's guess.

He paused for a few moments, then pushed it open noise-lessly and stepped inside. He noticed immediately that the door connecting this office to the adjoining one was in the middle of the east wall. He could see that it had no locking de-vice, or even a knob. Much like the doors of some saloons, it simply hung there on hinges, and could be opened from either side with a slight push.

He had no more than crossed the room to the connecting door when he heard someone moving in the adjacent office, making no effort whatsoever to muffle the sound of their foot-falls. Houston read the situation instantly: obviously, it had fi-nally dawned on Joe Paley that he might be vulnerable from this end of the building, and he was on his way to check it out.

Knowing that the ex-marshal was about to walk through the doorway, Houston drew his gun and moved to the north side of the door, the side the hinges were on. Camp could hear the man walking around in the adjoining room, no doubt checking the front door and the windows.

Moments later, when Paley pushed his way into the tax as-sessor's office, the door he stood holding open was at the same time hiding Houston. Then, gun in hand, Paley removed his hand from the swinging door and walked across the room, paying all of his attention to the front door. Houston stepped in behind him. "Drop the gun, Paley!" he said loudly. "Don't even think about putting up a fight!"

Paley stood motionless and held on to his gun, no doubt weighing his chances. "Houston?" he asked finally.

"That's right," Houston said. "For the time being I'm Deputy Sheriff Camp Houston, and you're under arrest. Drop the gun! Drop it now!" Though he was slow about it, Paley finally complied with the order. "Move over there and face the wall," Camp commanded. "Put both hands high above your head, palms flat against the wall."

Camp searched the man thoroughly, including his boots, but found no other weapon. He picked up the ex-marshal's

Peacemaker from the floor. "Clasp your hands behind you, Paley," he said with authority. "Then we're gonna walk over to the sheriff's office real slowly. We'll be stopping at that first cell behind the sheriff's desk."

A few moments later, Houston locked Paley in a cell that the ex-marshal knew very well, for he himself had caged dozens of men there in the past. "I suppose somebody'll see about getting you some food and water pretty soon," Camp said, pocketing the heavy key.

"How come you don't do it?" Paley asked sneeringly. "You're the one locking me up."

Houston spoke over his shoulder: "I'm not gonna have time, Paley. I'm on my way right now to resign this deputy sheriff's job." He was quickly out the front door. He retrieved his footwear, then walked down the hill.

When he entered Riley's Restaurant a few minutes later, he saw all of the same faces. Indeed, it appeared that nobody had even moved during his absence. He walked straight to McMichen's table and laid the badge and the key before the aging man. "I'm resigning the deputy's job, Sheriff. Joe Paley's locked in that first cell behind your desk. Maybe you ought to see that he gets something to eat."

With one hand on the table and the other on the back of his chair, the sheriff pushed himself to his good leg. "You hear that, everybody?" he asked loudly. "Listen up, everybody! Camp Houston just yanked Joe Paley out of that office and locked him up in jail, where he belongs!"

The applause was both loud and immediate. "Camp Houston for marshal!" one man yelled. "Camp Houston for sheriff!" shouted another.

Houston began to wave his hands from side to side to discourage the adulation, frowning and shaking his head in an effort to convince them all that he was not the least bit interested in either job. He spun on his heel and headed for the front of the building, only to have Ellen Bice step between him and the door. She had a serious look on her face that he had not seen before. "Do you still want to take me to Calf Creek?" she asked softly.

He stood speechless for a moment as he realized what the beautiful Ellen Bice was saying. "You . . . I . . ." he stammered, then started over: "I've always been serious about that, Ellen. I've always—"

"I'll be waiting at home in the morning," she interrupted. "My bags are already packed." Then she headed for the kitchen.

He stepped through the door and stood in the gathering darkness for a few moments thinking, finding it hard to believe that he was about to get what he wanted most. The lovely Ellen Bice was about to become the mistress of the 3C Ranch. He would rent a team and wagon as soon as the livery stable opened in the morning, and pick her up early. Hell, he knew a preacher who lived right beside the Calf Creek road. He chuckled aloud, shot his fist into the air and headed for the hotel saloon to break the news to Wesley Hawks. This called for a cup of good rum. Two . . . three cups of good rum.

THE

Mark Wine ... ls, including
the bestsell

'The mea ... brilliantly
recrea ... iginal.'

'[Written ... w literary
flouri ... spans'

'Impressive ... inegardner's

'This new ... nuity ...
Winega ... ecessor.'

The Times

'Winegardner ... has done an excellent job ... The politicking, the
election, the roles of showbiz and the unions are all skillfully and
convincingly handled' *Daily Telegraph*

THE GODFATHER'S REVENGE

MARK WINEGARDNER

WILLIAM HEINEMANN : LONDON

Published by William Heinemann, 2006

2 4 6 8 10 9 7 5 3 1

Copyright © The Estate of Mario Puzo, 2006

Mark Winegardner has asserted his right under the Copyright, Designs
and Patents Act 1988 to be identified as the author of this work

First published in 2006 by G.P. Putnam's Sons, part of the Penguin Group (USA)
Inc., New York

William Heinemann
Random House, 20 Vauxhall Bridge Road,
London SW1V 2SA

www.randomhouse.co.uk

Addresses for companies within The Random House Group Limited can be found
at: www.randomhouse.co.uk

The Random House Group Limited Reg. No. 954009

A CIP catalogue record for this book
is available from the British Library

ISBN: 043401561X
ISBN 13: 9780434015610

The Random House Group Limited makes every effort to ensure that the papers
used in its books are made from trees that have been legally sourced from well-man-
aged and credibly certified forests. Our paper procurement policy can be found at:
www.randomhouse.co.uk/paper.htm

Printed and bound in Australia by
Griffin Press

Ancora una volta,
alla mia famiglia

Men must either be flattered or crushed, for they will revenge themselves for slight wrongs, while grave ones they cannot. The injury, therefore, that you do a man should be such that you need not fear for revenge.

— MACHIAVELLI, *The Prince*

PROLOGUE

D ressed in a tuxedo and his ratty old fishing hat, Fredo Corleone, who was dead, stood before his brother Michael in the middle of the dark cobblestone street in Hell's Kitchen where they'd lived as children, a fishing rod in one hand and a naked woman on his arm. It was twilight. Fredo seemed poised between laughter and tears, which was heartbreakingly familiar. At the end of the block, the Eleventh Avenue freight train, which had long since been rerouted and dismantled, rumbled toward them but was still out of sight.

"I forgive you," Fredo said.

Blood began to pour from a wound in the back of his head.

Michael Corleone did not know what he was seeing, but he knew it wasn't a dream. He certainly did not believe in ghosts.

"That's impossible," Michael said.

Fredo laughed. "True," he admitted. "Only God can do that, right?"

Michael, on the stoop to their apartment building, felt nailed to the spot. There was no one else around. The woman was curvy and milky white, raven-haired, a little bit sheepish about being out in public like this but also brave, the kind of woman who didn't care too much about what other people thought.

"God," Michael said. "Right."

"You want to fish?" Fredo extended the rod, grinning. "Or do you want to fuck around?"

The woman stepped forward. As she moved through the mottled light, she changed into a rotting corpse, then back into Michael's very ideal of beauty.

"Let me know, huh?" Fredo said. "Contrary to what you may think, I can set things up. I know you're lonely. I know you're all alone. If not this, then something. I want to help you, Mike. I want you to be happy."

"Happy?" Michael said. "Don't you think that's a little childish, Fredo?"

Michael immediately regretted saying this, but Fredo didn't seem to take offense.

The woman kissed Fredo, and he kissed her back. At the end of his fishing pole, there suddenly appeared a tuna almost as big as Fredo himself. The tuna thrashed, then began to bleed, too, as if it had been both speared and clubbed. The naked woman looked at the fish and started crying.

"I keep getting confused," Fredo said to Michael. "Why did I have to die?"

Michael sighed. Same old Fredo, even dead, in need of explanations for things he should have understood by instinct.

"I understand revenge and all that, but what happened to me compared to what I did—it don't exactly balance out. It makes no sense. This ain't exactly your eye-for-an-eye justice, Mike."

Michael shook his head sadly. "Fredo," he whispered.

"I'm not saying I didn't fuck up, because I did." Fredo was still bleeding, but slower now. "Those fellas I gave that information to, Roth and Ola and them? I told 'em things not knowing how they'd use it, but, to be honest with you, what'd I tell 'em that amounted to anything? When you'd be at home? Christ. There was only one road into and out of your place in Tahoe. A goddamned *babbuino* could have figured out when you were home. So when they tried to kill you, how was it *my* fault? As for the other things I told them that might've helped bring about peace, I understand it was wrong to go against the Family on that. But it's also true everything that happened would've happened anyhow. With or without me. Right? You know I'm right. None of it hurt the organization, made it any less strong than it was. On top of which, everybody outside the Family who knew about what I did? Dead. You had 'em taken care of, every last one. The only living people who know about it are you, Hagen, and Neri—and you're always talking about how you'd trust them two with your life. So they're no problem, right?"

"There's Nick Geraci." Awake, Michael wouldn't have said the vanished traitor's name aloud.

Fredo slapped the palm of his hand against his forehead. Blood sprayed everywhere. "Right! I think of him as dead, but you're right."

"I will avenge your death. You have my word."

"That's comical." He pointed to his wounded head. "Al pulled the trigger. You gave the order. You gave the order to kill Nick, too. You tried to sacrifice him, like in chess, like losing a knight or a bishop to cover up what's really going on. Except in chess, the bishop don't have no chance of swimming away from the discard pile and back on the board, changing its colors, and coming after you. So, sure, kill him. What choice do you have?"

The bleeding from Fredo's wound seemed finally to have stopped. He was drenched in blood. He whispered something to the naked woman, and she nodded but kept crying.

"At the time you did this," Fredo said to Michael, "neither one of us knew that Nick was behind it. You were certain you'd killed off everybody who knew what I'd done. What I want to know," he said, "is who you thought would've held it against you if you hadn't've killed me? Who'd've thought you were weak for showing me some mercy? *Name one person.*"

"Fredo, I—"

"I'm not angry, Mike. Far from it. What happened to me was my destiny and all that stuff Pop liked to talk about. On the other hand—and forgive me for saying this—it's hard to imagine that Pop, under the same circumstances, would've had me *killed*, y'know? Look. What I'm trying to do is understand what's in your head. I know what's in your heart, OK? Your heart's obvious. But what goes on in your head, I gotta say, it's a mystery to me."

Hagen, Michael thought.

With a pang of clarity, he realized that Tom Hagen, his *consigliere*, had been the reason he'd done it. That's who'd have held it against him. Hagen, who both was and wasn't his brother, who was but wasn't exactly family. Who wasn't even *Italian* and therefore, strictly speaking, shouldn't know *anything*. And he knew *everything*. Tom Hagen was the link to Vito, the old man. It was Tom who kept the lines of communication open during the years Michael was in youthful revolt against his father and everything his father stood for. Hagen's job was to give Michael advice when asked, to resolve certain situations when dispatched, and he did so with great skill and greater obedience. Yet until now it had never clicked that it was Hagen's disapproval Michael most dreaded, Hagen's intelligence Michael most needed to one-up, Hagen's deceptive toughness Michael most needed to surpass, even if doing so meant going against his own nature. His own blood. After Michael and Fredo's last embrace, what had Fredo done? He'd put on his lucky fishing hat and gone to teach Michael's son Anthony to fish. And what had Michael done? He'd gone straight to his office: to do business, yes, but also to bust Tom's balls about his loyalty, which was never in question, and his mistress, which meant nothing, just to put him on the defensive. Why? So that Tom couldn't question him in the matter of Hyman Roth? No. It was about that long look toward Fredo and Anthony that Tom had taken as he'd walked into the room. About Michael's fear that Tom would disapprove.

This insight flowed through Michael Corleone like a deep breath. Yet he couldn't quite speak the answer to his bloodied brother's question.

"No, you tell *me*, Fredo. Since it's so obvious. What *is* in my heart?"

"Oh, boy," Fredo said. The naked woman shrank away from Fredo, ducked her head, and turned around a little, now clearly embarrassed. "That's your problem in a nutshell, Mike, ain't it? You don't know your own heart."

Michael folded his arms. He wanted to embrace his brother and tell him he was right about everything. But he couldn't bring himself to do it. "Are you finished, Fredo? Because I have business I need to take care of."

Michael struggled to remember specifically what the business was. Someone else's problems, no doubt. The particulars of his day's work now seemed strewn about in his head and just out of reach. The rump of that raven-haired woman suddenly struck Michael Corleone as the most beautiful sight he had ever seen. He imagined himself running his tongue along the curve of her wide and perfect hips. He shivered. He forced himself to avert his eyes. At the end of the block, the old train roared by, boxcars filled with the nameless dead.

"I have a warning for you!" Fredo shouted over the train. "But what's the point? You wouldn't listen to me, would you? Coming from me, you'd think it was a joke. You'd think it was bullshit. You'd never give it a second goddamned thought. You never give *me* a second goddamned thought, I bet."

Fredo was mistaken: Michael thought about him all the time. He'd been wrong about Fredo. Michael had made betrayers out of other allies. Sally Tessio, Nick Geraci, on and on. Fredo wasn't the only one, and he was probably the least valuable one, but it was Fredo who haunted Michael most.

"You were dead to me when you were still alive, Fredo," Michael was horrified to hear himself say. "You think being dead changes anything? Nothing has changed. Go away, Fredo."

Michael didn't mean a word of it.

He wanted to hear the warning, truly he did. Not that it stood to be a surprise. There was the matter of the Bocchicchios, that nearly extinct revenge-mad clan, who supposedly did not blame the Corleones for the death of Carmine Marino, a Bocchicchio cousin. There was the matter of

Nick Geraci, the former Corleone *capo,* who had conspired with the late
Dons of the Cleveland and Chicago outfits to trick Michael into killing his
friend Hyman Roth and—just for spite—Fredo, too, who had eluded
Michael's vengeance and was still out there, somewhere. There was the
president of the United States, who owed his election to Michael Corleone and yet gave every sign of turning on him.

On and on; of such threats there was no end. Michael had a gift for anticipating trouble. What mattered to Michael wasn't the news Fredo had,
because he was confident it would not be news. What felt important was
that Fredo had come to deliver it.

The train was gone now and, somehow, so were the tuna, the fishing rod,
and the luscious naked woman who was sometimes a corpse. Fredo turned
and started walking away, a pink mist of blood obscuring the wound at the
back of his head.

What was happening to Michael now might be perfectly logical. Some
kind of hallucination, brought on by a diabetic reaction. He might even
die. More likely, someone would find him, help him, give him an orange
or a pill or a shot.

He called out to Fredo to wait.

Fredo stopped and turned to face him. "What do you want?"

Michael was on a gurney now, stable, heading for the emergency room.
Al Neri—who shot Fredo with two slugs from a .38, at Michael's behest and
without the slightest resistance from Fredo himself—hovered nearby,
yelling about sugar to people Michael could sense but not quite see. There
was a woman here, too, coming into view, in Michael's own robe: Marguerite Duvall, the actress. Rita. She was sobbing. Her dyed red hair looked
like a madwoman's. The robe gapped to reveal a dark nipple almost as big
around as her small breast. Rita had been with Fredo, years ago, back when
she was just a dancer in Vegas, back before Johnny Fontane had helped
make her a star, back before she had that brief affair with Jimmy Shea.
Fredo had even gotten her pregnant. Michael knew about that, and Rita
no doubt knew that he knew, and they never talked about it. Michael

wasn't lonely. There were friends and family he'd drawn near him, right in this building. And there was this woman, Rita. Michael tried to reach out to her. She smiled at him through her tears and muttered something in French. Then Al Neri told her to stand back, taking her by the arm and tugging her away from Michael.

"What do you want?" Fredo repeated. "I'm losing my patience here, kid."

Kid. Fredo never called him that. Sonny called him that.

Michael closed his eyes and willed himself to use reason.

A needle jabbed his arm, and Michael opened his eyes. The gurney was moving, and its wheels were squeaking, shrieking, and Rita's hand was on his arm and then batted away, and he somehow saw both the ceiling of his apartment rushing by and also Fredo on that dark street in his tuxedo, dabbing at his wound with a blood-drenched pocket square.

"You deaf?" Fredo said. "Answer me."

Michael felt as if he were living two lives at once, both equally real.

"I want you to wait, Fredo," he murmured. "That's what I want. I want you to stay."

"*Madonn'.*" Fredo backed away, angry now. "No, Mike. I mean, what do you *want?*"

"Nothing I can have."

Fredo laughed, mirthlessly. "And you call *me* dead," he said. "You got a lot to learn, kid. Give Rita and the baby a kiss for me." Fredo turned his back. In his bloody tuxedo and Mary Janes, he walked toward where the train had passed. Michael was falling through space now, in what must have been the elevator.

Rita and the baby? Rita didn't *have* a baby.

Michael turned his head, trying to get a last glimpse of his brother. Fredo was still walking away. From this angle, at this increasing distance, it looked to Michael as if most of his brother's head had been shot off. And then Fredo was gone.

BOOK I

CHAPTER 1

Three black Chevy Biscaynes—each carrying two armed men, squinting into the harsh sunlight, clench-jawed—rocketed single file toward New Orleans on U.S. Highway 61, that queen of American long roads. Highway 61 ran the length of the country, right through its engorged and corn-fed heart. Its terminus lay dead ahead. Alongside this highway, men of God have both sinned against us and died for our sins. At its crossroads, genius has been bought for the bargain price of a human soul. On nearby backstreets and dusty roads, the misfit children of shopkeepers, of ex-slaves, of unappreciated schoolteachers, have seen fit to assume aliases. Buddy, Fats, Jelly Roll, T.S., and Satchmo. Bix, Pretty Boy, Tennessee, Kingfish, and Lightnin'. Muddy, Dizzy, and Bo; Son, Sonny, and Sonny Boy. B.B., Longhair, Yogi, Gorgeous, and Dylan. Thus disguised, they left home on this very highway and unleashed America's strange, true voice on an unsuspecting world. At least one lowly truck driver traveled this road to his improbable destiny as king, at least one prostitute to hers as queen. Both died young, as the royals along Highway 61 reliably do—the king on his gilded throne and the queen on the road itself, her blood soaking into the blacktop. Along this highway, a nation's idea of itself died and was born again. And again. Over and over.

It was 1963. A Sunday, unseasonably hot for January. The men in the three black Biscaynes drove with the windows down and did not appear to be sweating or nervous. The New Orleans skyline loomed. The speed limit changed, and the drivers slowed down.

Ahead, on the left, a few miles shy of the end of the highway, was the Pelican Motor Lodge, where Carlo Tramonti kept his office. No out-of-towner would have guessed that the nondescript cinder-block restaurant next door, Nicastro's (closed Sundays), served the best Italian food in the city. The best that money could buy.

The best food, period, was available every Sunday, a few blocks away, at Tramonti's plantation-style home, where Nicastro's gifted young proprietor/chef—along with nearly every other man related by marriage or blood to Carlo Tramonti—was on this day sipping red wine and taking his leisure under a massive live oak that obscured any view of the house from the street. The house was white, lovely, in scale with the rest of the neighborhood. The backyard overlooked a swampy, magnolia-lush corner of one of the finest country clubs in New Orleans. Tramonti was the first Italian the club admitted; he'd been sponsored by the governor himself.

Children of all ages swarmed the yard.

A game of *bocce* had sprung up and become an excuse for good-natured taunting among the men. As usual, Agostino Tramonti—the smartest and shortest of Carlo's five younger brothers—came in for the worst of it. He had a talent for sports and games but took them too seriously.

From inside the house came the sharply barked Italian commands of Gaetana Tramonti, wafting into the midday haze along with the aroma of baking chicken, roasting sausages, and various simple sauces her chef son-in-law could imitate but never perfect. Gaetana was a stout Neapolitan matriarch, Carlo's wife of forty-one years. An army of bickering daughters and daughters-in-law did her bidding, exasperated in a way everyone here understood as love.

Carlo Tramonti strolled among his guests with a walking stick, kissing his grandchildren and tousling their hair, listening to the problems of his nephews and cousins. He looked like a Mediterranean shipping magnate, from his sun-bleached, perfectly trimmed white hair and double-breasted navy blazer right down to his sockless, loafered feet. He was five-eleven, the tallest man here. He wore enormous black sunglasses. His aristocratic air had come gradually. He'd started out as a shrimp-boat hand and part-time bookie and risen though the ranks. In those days, the city's underworld was run by two warring factions, families who'd come from the same little town on the west coast of Sicily and whose grievances went back for centuries. Tramonti had negotiated peace and united the survivors of that negotiation into the clan he'd run for almost thirty years. No Family ever enjoyed better political protection or such a complete monopoly over its territory. No Family was ever less violent. The fear the Tramonti clan inspired was akin to the fear that the devout have of their God: a subservience to power and a form of love. To most people in New Orleans and throughout Louisiana, the Tramontis were the big black king snake that lived quietly under the house, dining on water moccasins, pygmy rattlesnakes, and disease-laden rats.

Carlo finally joined the *bocce* game. There was a gracefulness to his every fluid motion. His presence calmed his brother down. Augie Tramonti was a foot-shorter version of Carlo—same haircut, same tan, same custom-made clothes from the same tailor—except that he walked on the balls of his feet, bouncing, a man with too much to prove.

The pasta course was set out on long tables on the wraparound porch. The women called out to the men and the children to come eat.

It would of course be difficult to exaggerate the significance in most Italian homes of good food and big family meals, especially in New Orleans—the oldest Italian community in the New World, where the vigilante murder of innocent Sicilian immigrants was once ordered by the city's mayor and publicly condoned by the president of the United States, and yet where that Italian creation, the muffaletta, was the city's true Communion host.

The Tramontis were a family, a New Orleans family, and meals like this kept them that way. No outsider could hope to understand how much the bounty now set before the Tramonti clan was both taken for granted and cherished. Carlo Tramonti made his usual toast, just a warm and simple "*La famiglia*."

His family echoed him and drank.

The Tramontis set down their glasses. "*Mangiamo!*" Gaetano called out.

As she did, the men from the black cars appeared on the lawn, guns drawn.

Women and children screamed.

Carlo Tramonti got to his feet. He made no attempt to flee. Absurdly, he grabbed a steak knife and held it aloft. These men could not be cops. Tramonti owned the cops. Several shades of color had drained from his face. He looked down at his plate, at his wife's spaghetti puttanesca. He could not have expected anything like this would happen to him, in front of his family, on a Sunday afternoon, as he was about to eat.

"INS!" the lead agent shouted. "Immigration!"

Carlo Tramonti cocked his head, obviously confused. He'd been in New Orleans for almost sixty years, about as long as jazz and—certainly in the eyes of his family, at least—just as American. Even the Tramonti grandchildren must have imagined that the badges were fake.

Augie Tramonti—who, after the recent death of a trusted old uncle, had been promoted from head of the Family's drug-trafficking operation to *consigliere*—asked if he could look at the badges. The agents politely complied. He bit his lip, looked at his brother, and shrugged. Who'd ever seen an immigration agent's badge?

If they really *were* from the INS, it did explain quite a bit. They weren't cops or even FBI, and they probably weren't there to kill him. It explained how they got past the associates Tramonti had stationed out front. It explained why they stormed the place, rather than the more subtle approach the CIA would probably have used on him.

Carlo Tramonti slowly set his steak knife down.

In fact, he had never quite managed to become an American citizen. By the time he was old enough to apply for citizenship himself, he was up to his sleepy-lidded eyeballs in various rackets that might have made the process difficult. But those same involvements had given him the means to avoid the issue altogether. Four years earlier, Carlo Tramonti had even testified before a subcommittee of the United States Senate—taking the Fifth Amendment sixty-one times—without the question of his citizenship ever coming to light.

The lead agent first asked him if he was *Señor Carlos Tramonti, from Santa Rosa, Colombia.* Tramonti stared at him.

Another agent said *"La Ballena."* Spanish for "the Whale." Other agents chuckled.

Nicastro, the chef, perhaps from years of hearing customers mispronounce Italian words, and surely also from the stress of the situation, blurted a correction: *"La Balena."*

Other members of the Tramonti clan glared at him. No one called Carlo Tramonti by that nickname, not to his face.

Carlo looked only at Gaetana, at the other end of the table, standing now, hair damp with sweat, tears streaming down her round cheeks.

"I'd like to have my lawyer present," Carlo Tramonti said.

"That won't be necessary," said the head agent.

Tramonti shrugged. Who can say what's necessary?

"We just have a few questions for you," the agent continued. "A minor matter. We'll be finished in no time."

"A minor matter can wait," Carlo Tramonti said, "until Monday."

"I'm afraid not." The agent asked Tramonti to go get his passport and come with them.

"It's at my office."

One of the other agents produced a pair of handcuffs.

"There's no need for that," Carlo Tramonti said.

The agents handcuffed him anyway. "Procedure," they insisted. They cuffed his ankles, too.

In Italian, Carlo Tramonti asked Gaetana to go get him some cash.

The agent in charge smirked. "No need for that, either."

"My toothbrush, then," Carlo said to his wife, still in Italian.

"No," the agent said.

The agent's colleagues seemed to enjoy marching Carlo Tramonti from the table, past a din of protest from his alarmed family, past the terrified faces of his grandchildren.

Carlo looked back over his shoulder at Gaetana and told her to, please, eat without him.

"We'll be back in time for dessert," Augie said, scrambling to his feet and following.

Augie told the agents that he'd meet them at the office. He nodded to another brother, one who ran several of their legitimate businesses—warehouses, parking lots, dog tracks, strip clubs—and who'd know the right lawyers to call.

Gaetana ordered her family to eat, as sternly as she would on any given Sunday.

"Your *procedures*?" Carlo Tramonti hissed as he was shoved into the backseat of one of the black Biscaynes. "Spite and humiliation, these are *procedures*?"

"I'm afraid," the head agent said, "that in cases like yours, that's an affirmative."

THE PELICAN MOTOR LODGE WAS A CLEAN, WHITE CEMENT rectangle of rooms surrounding a landscaped courtyard and a drained kidney-shaped swimming pool. The pool had a stockade fence around it. Tramonti kept his offices in a suite of four gutted, remodeled rooms in the far back corner, largely obscured by an artfully trimmed thicket of nandina.

The agents frog-marched Tramonti into the suite's reception area, where, weekdays, his sister-in-law Filomena answered the phone and screened visitors.

Carlo Tramonti's name did not appear on the thick door to his office. Instead, painted right onto it in large, flowing gold script, was an epigram: *Three may keep a secret if two of them are dead.* The lettering had been a birthday gift from his brother Joe—a painter of local renown, whose canvases (jazz scenes, Negro funerals, gators) sold briskly in the French Quarter and who was represented by a gallery there (which Joe also owned). He was also the man in charge of the Family's jukebox and vending-machine interests.

Inside, the paneled office walls sported several framed newspapers, yellowing and biased accounts of that *infamia*, the mob that had claimed the life of Tramonti's grandfather, among many others. The rest of the walls were all but covered with more than a hundred carefully arranged family photographs. The mahogany desk gleamed. The carpeting smelled new. Tramonti replaced it every year. There were no ashtrays here and, famously, no trash can. Carlo Tramonti supposedly found it distracting to conduct business in any room that was not perfectly neat, a compulsion that extended to trash cans, even empty ones.

The agent in charge of this charade asked Tramonti for his passport.

Tramonti sat down heavily in his leather desk chair. "I wish to have my lawyer present."

In the reception area, Augie Tramonti arrived, out of breath. Agents grabbed him by the shoulder and restrained him just outside the open door. Before he'd gone on to bigger things, Augie "the Midget" Tramonti, small as he was, had enjoyed a long, sadistic run as an enforcer. If dead men could tell tales, many would say they'd seen Augie look at them with the same cold contempt he now showed these agents.

"My brother's not going to talk to you people without a lawyer." Augie's voice was raised but even. "So forget it. And he don't like that, the smoking there. The lawyer's coming." When Augie Tramonti mentioned the lawyer's name—a distinguished one in Louisiana for more than a century—it seemed to mean nothing to the agents, who continued to smoke.

The agent in charge took out a letter from Attorney General Daniel Brendan Shea and read it aloud. It accused Tramonti of being a citizen of Colombia, not Italy, as his work visa claimed. As evidence, the letter cited several trips to Cuba for which Tramonti was alleged to have used his Colombian passport. It cited the fact that Tramonti apparently had no Italian birth certificate (he was hardly the only person born in the Sicilian countryside in the nineteenth century who did not). It cited his lack of an Italian passport (it had expired under the reign of the hated Mussolini; Augie used his connections in Colombia to get a passport there for his brother). It alleged that Tramonti had used a "pattern of bribes and coercion" to keep his work visa current. "Because of this pattern of falsification," the letter went on, it was "incumbent" on the INS to deport Tramonti to his "native Colombia." Carlo Tramonti had never set foot in Colombia, but of course everyone here knew that. The cost of "said transportation" would be recovered by placing a tax lien on Tramonti's home.

The agent in charge nodded. His associates started pulling out file and desk drawers, dumping their contents onto the carpeted floor. Carlo Tramonti reddened but did not speak.

"You need a warrant!" Augie called.

"We need you to kindly shut up," the agent said, "sir. And, no, for an illegal foreign national, we don't need a warrant. In matters of national security such as this, our only directive is to protect the American people."

Carlo Tramonti closed his eyes and rocked slightly back and forth.

"We *are* the American people!" Augie Tramonti shouted. "You're just the fucking government."

Carlo Tramonti groaned, and then he bent over and vomited.

The chains prevented him from spreading his legs far enough apart, and the vomit—red wine; coffee; peppers and eggs—spewed onto his shoes and into the cuffs of his trousers.

"Found it," an agent announced. Top desk drawer. The most obvious place, and the last place the agents chose to look. Another agent rushed outside to vomit in the shrubbery.

The agent in charge took the Colombian passport from his colleague, stepped around the pool of Tramonti's reddish vomit, pointed toward the door, and said something in Spanish.

Tramonti cocked his head.

"My brother," Augie said, "don't always hear everything so good sometimes."

The agent repeated himself. "Your brother doesn't appear to speak Spanish, either."

"What Spanish?" Augie said. "Spanish how?"

"I was just reading his door," the agent said. "'Three can keep a secret if two are dead'—sounds like a sign my kids would hang on their tree house, right next to NO GIRLS ALLOWED."

Carlo sat up straight but did not answer. He shot a look at his brother. Augie was the kind of man who would take pleasure in humbling this nothing, this federal nobody, by answering the question. For a moment, though, he held his tongue.

"Oh, I get it," the agent said. "It's some kind of knife-wielding-Guido manifesto."

"For your *information*," said Augie Tramonti, "the fella who said that there was none other than Mr. Benjamin Franklin. OK? Who I'm not surprised if you never heard of, since he's one of the ones who signed the Constitution of Independence, which, with all due respect, it seems like you gentlemen aren't familiar with, huh?"

"Benjamin Franklin signed the *Declaration* of Independence, not the Constitution."

Augie Tramonti shook his head in disagreement, Carlo in disapproval. "He signed 'em both," Augie said. "Guarantee, hey? Grade school, you should have learned that, which is . . . how is it people say it? Shocking but not surprising."

"Enough." Carlo rose unsteadily to his feet. One of the agents blew cigarette smoke in his face. Carlo swallowed hard and withstood it.

The agents pushed Augie aside and led Carlo out into the fresh air, back to their plain black cars.

"I am being kidnapped," Carlo Tramonti said. It was a clear accusation, evenly leveled.

The agents ignored him and kept moving.

"This is America!" Carlo Tramonti hissed.

"Correct," said the agent in charge. He slammed the door.

"This is not how people are treated in America!"

"From here on out," said the agent in charge, "for people like you, it sure as heck is."

As the three black cars drove away, Augie Tramonti, standing alongside Highway 61, pointed and stomped and screamed Sicilian curses.

AT THE NEW ORLEANS AIRPORT, THE ATTORNEY GENERAL OF the United States waited on the tarmac in a black limousine. An aide brought him word that the Whale was on his way. Outside, other aides were putting the finishing touches on a makeshift podium—Justice Department seal, American flags, sound check. They informed the network television crews it wouldn't be long now. Daniel Brendan Shea looked amply ready for his close-up. He was an almost pretty man, black Irish with sharp cheekbones, long white teeth, and the kind of disproportionately large head the cameras love. In person, Danny Shea looked less like his brother than he did a Hollywood actor cast as President James Kavanaugh Shea, a taller man, whose handsome features were more recognizably human.

Sirens drew closer. A jet airplane was parked nearby, engines running and crew on board.

The A.G. stepped out of his limo and stood, alone, squinting and shading his eyes, facing the direction of the sirens. The cameramen and reporters shouted at him, but he either did not hear or pretended not to. As the three Chevy Biscaynes came speeding into view, escorted now by what looked like an endless string of state and local police cars, Danny Shea turned his face into the wind, folded his arms, and shook his head in a way that suggested hard-won victory. If this was only a pose, it was nonetheless an excellent one.

What *was* Danny Shea thinking? He had to have known that this would never hold up in court. That this was just for show.

Was the motivation revenge? Four years ago, he'd sat behind his then boss, Senator Theodore Preston Davies of New York, and been captured on TV getting increasingly angry as Carlo Tramonti took the Fifth Amendment again and again, reading it off a printed card his lawyer gave him. The more agitated Shea got, the more times he whispered in his boss's ear, the more Tramonti seemed to be enjoying himself. It's possible that this deportation was Danny Shea's way of wiping the smug grin off Carlo Tramonti's face—particularly since other aspects of his initiative against the so-called Mafia would give it the appearance of a vendetta. There was, for example, the suspicious death of one of Shea's young attorneys, William Van Arsdale (whose people were the Van Arsdale Citrus Van Arsdales), who was killed the year before in a hit-and-run in D.C. His mistress had been guilty of adultery, she admitted, but not murder. The jury unanimously disagreed. No hard evidence ever came to light that Billy's widow, Francesca, the daughter of the late Santino Corleone, somehow had the mistress framed. But recently declassified documents did show that the A.G. had dedicated this entire operation to the memory of William Van Arsdale. The rationale for this has never been definitively proven, which of course only made it a more delicious morsel for conspiracy theorists.

Historians, however, favor the theory that Danny Shea was trying to atone for the sins of his father, the late M. Corbett Shea, former ambassador to Canada. Danny must have known that Tramonti had made his first few millions off slot machines that came his way via Vito Corleone, just as Mickey Shea made his first millions off bootleg liquor hauled to New York in Vito Corleone's olive oil trucks. Danny's chilly, unyielding father had been brought low by a stroke not long after the election, but he'd lived long enough to catch televised glimpses of his sons running the free world as they saw fit, distancing themselves from the old man's prejudices and un-holy alliances.

Was it possible that Danny Shea didn't quite know his father's history? That he had no idea how his brother really got elected? Was it possible that the A.G.'s motive was to serve the public good and nothing but the pub-lic good? Possible. Some people believe in simple, noncontradictory mo-tives, and in America people are at least nominally entitled to their beliefs. The American soul has been bought and paid for at the crossroads of Fact and Belief.

As the convoy passed Danny Shea, cameras recorded his thumbs-up to the INS agents. But nothing in his body language or facial expression be-trayed what was on his mind.

The cars stopped. The INS agents got Tramonti out and ushered him in a camera-friendly way toward the plane. It was impossible to walk in chains on TV and not look guilty. What the cameras captured was a wild-haired old man, staggering across the tarmac in stained trousers, raving like a debased evil genius. Tramonti was actually shouting about the princi-ples on which America was built, but the airplane's engines drowned him out. On camera, he might as well have been yelling, *I'll get you for this, Superman!*

Two uniformed MPs appeared in the doorway of the plane and took Tra-monti inside, where—other than the pilot and copilot and the MPs—it turned out he would be the only one on board.

The plane took off.

Several members of the press corps broke into applause.

The attorney general lowered his head, turned, and strode to the podium.

"Today," he said, "the United States of America is a freer and safer nation."

He outlined some of Carlo Tramonti's suspected illegal activities, not only in Louisiana but throughout the South and in Florida. Mr. Tramonti listed "motel owner" on his income tax return where, according to the

A.G., it should say "crime boss." He was a part of "a vast criminal under-world" in which he had conspired to swallow up so many businesses—both legal and illegal, everything from a chain of beachwear shops in Florida to a chain of bordellos in Texas—that he was commonly known as "the Whale." Mr. Tramonti claimed to be Italian, but now it seemed that all along he was a citizen of Colombia, at least according to documents pro-cured during a lengthy Justice Department investigation. Mr. Tramonti was being returned to the documented town of his birth, a tiny mountain village called Santa Rosa. Shea looked into those cameras and, with God's perfect straight face, told the world that this deportation had been handled in strict adherence with the laws of the state of Louisiana and federal im-migration statutes as well.

"But make no mistake," he said. He paused. He seemed to be looking beyond the cameras, to some elusive paradise that only he could see. Near baggage claim, maybe. "The matters at hand are grave. There are more men out there like Mr. Tramonti, many more, evildoers who are destroy-ing liberty in cities all over America. All over the world, in fact. Mr. Tra-monti is an archenemy of our basic American freedoms, but he's not the only one. There are others, and we will not rest until they have been brought to justice."

A reporter asked the A.G. what he meant by that.

Daniel Brendan Shea was still in his thirties, but he was a born politi-cian. Ordinarily he discussed accomplishments and objectives by saying *we* did this, *we* believe that, *we* will do the other thing. He avoided the first person singular, affixing credit to others, both to individuals and to "this administration" or "our department." But he was visibly excited now, enough so to abandon any semblance of humility.

"I plan to go down in history," he said, straight into the lens of the top-rated evening news show in the world, "as the man who brought down the Mafia."

This claim provoked a brief, stunned silence. Then one of the reporters raised his hand. "So what you're telling us is, the so-called Mafia—it's real?"

There was nervous laughter, but not from Danny Shea.

"They're real," he said. "They're among us."

AT THE MEDELLÍN AIRPORT, THE MPS TOOK CARLO TRA-
monti straight to a back room where VIPs went through customs. They
were met by several uniformed Colombian officials and two other Americans. One wore a guayabera shirt and green sunglasses. Under the sunglasses was a pirate-style eye patch. The other man was weak-chinned with
thick-framed black glasses, good posture, and a cheap black suit. He was the
one who did most of the talking. He spoke Spanish and seemed to be a
previous acquaintance of the Colombian official with the most medals.

Tramonti looked dizzy. He asked if the Americans were from the em-
bassy or the INS.

"Pardon me," said the weak-chinned man, "but perhaps you'd be more
comfortable sitting down?" The man's voice dripped with Waspish old
money. It made the cheap suit seem like a costume. "Sir? Please." He
pointed to what seemed to be a row of seats from a dismantled stadium.
Tramonti sat.

Badges were shown and paperwork exchanged and eventually the men
all started laughing, all but Tramonti. The MPs handed the keys to the
handcuffs and Tramonti's bogus passport to the American with the eye
patch and then left. The Colombians and the weak-chinned man left, too,
laughing all the way.

The man in eye patch freed Tramonti's hands and feet and tossed the
chains in the trash can. Resentment came off him like a stink. He looked
like someone whose friends had gone fishing for tarpon and left him back
at camp to do woman's work.

"Are you going to tell me who you are?" Tramonti said. "What you are?
Because I think I get the picture. CIA, eh? I worked with some of your people before, you know."

"Then you know that if I was or if I wasn't," he said, "I'd say I wasn't."

He had a New Jersey accent. He took Tramonti out a side door, where a battered taxi idled at the curb. A sign in Spanish welcomed them to the Land of Eternal Spring.

They got in the back together. In Spanish, the agent told the driver to go to the Hotel Miramar and suggested a particular route.

Darkness had fallen. Tramonti seemed to be having trouble breathing. He returned the agent's silence with silence. Like many men in his tradition, he had a talent for waiting people out.

Carlo Tramonti had been one of three American bosses (Silent Sam Drago and Michael Corleone were the others) who, independently, had cooperated with the CIA to train assassins to go into Cuba and take care of some things from the top down. The bosses had compared notes and concluded that the government's plan all along had been to effect a regime change in Cuba and blame the assassination on the so-called Mafia—although rumor had it that the Corleones had gotten fancy and tried, unsuccessfully, to pin one particular botched attempt on a *caporegime* named Nick Geraci. Geraci was said to have betrayed them, though there were other versions of that story swirling around, too. Tramonti had no way of knowing that both the Yale-educated Wasp, slumming in that cheap suit, and Joe Lucadello, the man with the eye patch, had worked on that project, too—with Geraci, in fact.

The taxi came to a stop in front of the hotel.

"Get out," Lucadello said. "You have a reservation. In the restaurant here, my advice is, stick with the steak dinner."

The Hotel Miramar had a doorman, the sign of a reasonably classy joint.

"You forgot my passport," Tramonti had the presence of mind to say.

Lucadello shook his head. "Sorry."

"You're leaving me here," he said, "just like that? No money, no passport, no papers, no real knowledge of Span—"

"*Bisteca,* the word is. Beefsteak. Pronounced the same as in Italian. Roger that? Charge it to your room, whatever you need to do. But right now, sir, you need to get out of the car."

Tramonti nodded and, because he had no choice, obeyed.

He got out.

The doorman closed the door for him and did not kill him.

The bellboy did not kill him, either, or even seem to find anything remarkable in Don Tramonti's lack of luggage.

The desk clerk spoke serviceable English. The room was indeed reserved, but the hotel requested some kind of payment up front.

Tramonti frowned. "Do I look like that kind of a bum, sir? The sort of man who doesn't settle his accounts?"

He did: unshaven, stained clothes, stinking of sweat and vomit.

"No, sir," the clerk said. He extended a key as if he might jerk it back at the last second. Tramonti grabbed it. The clerk's smile oozed contempt. "Thank you," he said. "The bill, it is in our futures."

The hotel was not the sort to have a menswear shop where Tramonti could buy clothes and charge them to his room. He went up to his suite.

He sent his suit out to be cleaned and ordered fish from room service. Better to be sick than poisoned. He tried to make a phone call back to his wife and family, but the operator's English and Italian were as weak as Tramonti's Spanish. The call never had a chance. He ordered bottled beer as a way of not drinking the water. He spent a sleepless night tossing and turning in the too-soft bed and every so often going to the bathroom to vomit. The fish had not agreed with him.

In the morning, the manager knocked on the door and said it would be necessary to address the issue of payment. Tramonti came to the chained door in his boxer shorts. The manager had the police with him and Tramonti's dry-cleaned suit as well.

They waited patiently for him to perform his ablutions and get dressed. Then they took him to jail, to his own private cell, which was clean and modern and, like his office back in New Orleans, did not contain a trash can. Out the barred window was a lovely view of the mountains. He was not formally charged with anything.

His first caller was a government official who asked in impeccable English if it might be possible that Tramonti, as the most famous and indeed most prosperous person ever to come from the impoverished mountain town of Santa Rosa, would be willing to donate a hundred thousand of his American dollars to build a new elementary school. The school they had now was an unheated, rat-infested garage.

Tramonti did not look at the man. He hunched over and stared at his shoes.

The man repeated the request in Italian.

"I am not a famous man," Tramonti said in English. "Or a wealthy one."

The newspapers, the official said, are filled with speculations about Tramonti's exploits and origins. He produced a copy of one called *La Imparcial*. On the front was a picture of Carlo Tramonti in chains at the New Orleans airport and a flattering file photo of Daniel Brendan Shea.

Tramonti handed it back, stone-faced.

"Whatever small help I might be able to give you for that school," he said to the official, "will be impossible while I am in here. I am a victim of the kind of injustice men face only in nightmares. Without my lawyers or my accountants or my brother Agostino . . . " His voice trailed off, and he shrugged.

Three days later, that was where Augie Tramonti found him. Carlo's shoes had been spit-shined and a trash can had been placed right outside the bars. A bedsheet concealed the cell's sink and toilet.

The brothers embraced. The brothers wept. They could hardly breathe. Even Augie, who had been to Colombia before, had never really strayed far from the coast. They had spent their lives at sea level or, more often, below it.

Augie, whose pockets were swollen with wads of American cash, told his brother he had things under control. He had connections in this country, plus lawyers who, at that very moment, were working to get Carlo out of this hellhole and back home. As jail cells go, this was hardly a hellhole, but Carlo did not correct him. All over Colombia, Augie said, the newspapers were attacking the government for allowing a notorious gangster like Carlo

Tramonti into their country, especially under such a fraudulent pretext. The story had actually died down in America, even in New Orleans. This was partly because of Americans' indifference toward anything that happened beyond their shores and partly because of a few strategic favors Augie had engineered. Here in Colombia, though, the crusading newspapers and the political pressure they'd whipped up were a godsend.

Agostino Tramonti then lowered his voice and told his brother that two days ago, deep in a bayou south of New Orleans, the INS agent in charge of Carlo's deportation had died in a boating mishap: a fire on board that had been ruled an accident. The news item on it had been brief—a tiny story, buried in the *Picayune*, with no mention of the particular cases the agent had worked.

Carlo clenched his teeth and, in Sicilian dialect, whispered that to kill a snake, one does not cut off the tail but rather the head.

Augie nodded. He seemed to understand this cryptic rebuke immediately. They found no need to discuss it further.

The guards brought a cot, and Augie moved into the cell as if he were a hospital visitor unwilling to leave a loved one unattended.

The next day, Augie and Carlo Tramonti stuffed their shoes with cash and waited for the Colombian military detail to come and deport them to Guatemala.

There, Augie had arranged for them to be met by the Dominican Air Force. They'd be taken to Santo Domingo, where a United States senator—a second cousin of the Kingfish himself, that old friend of the Tramontis'—would then personally arrange an escort from there to Miami. From there, they could turn their attention to Michael Corleone.

Back in 1960, it had been Michael Corleone's support of the Shea family that had gotten Jimmy Shea elected president. The other members of the Commission—especially the southern Dons, Tramonti and Silent Sam Drago—had preferred the man who was now the vice president. It was Michael Corleone who had turned the Commission around. True, he had been backed by the late Louie Russo of Chicago and, to a lesser degree,

Black Tony Stracci, who was from New Jersey and was thus partial to the devil he knew. But Michael Corleone had been the ringleader, trading favors and pulling every string he had to get Jimmy Shea into the White House. The other Dons should not have been surprised. The Corleones had a weakness for the Irish. They even had an Irish *consigliere*, a fellow named Tom Hagen, who was also somehow but not really Michael's brother. A *consigliere* who was not Italian was unique in their tradition—a violation of it, in fact, at least to someone like Carlo Tramonti, whose organization was by far the oldest in America and was run more like a Sicilian clan. For years it had been autonomous from the rest of the Families, and even now, its rules were distinct from everyone else's. For example, any time Carlo Tramonti wanted to open the books and initiate a new member, he, alone among the twenty-four Dons in America, didn't need to get the Commission's approval. Any time an associate of any other organization wanted to so much as set foot in Texas, Louisiana, Alabama, Mississippi, or the Florida Panhandle, he had to go to his boss and have him get permission from Carlo Tramonti. To do otherwise, Tramonti deemed an "insult." These requests were all but unknown. He'd approved a few weddings, when some wiseguy fell for a New Orleans girl who'd moved away, but only if Carlo and some associates were invited, too, if all out-of-state guests cleared out by noon the next day, and if it was crystal clear that, in the future, the in-laws went to visit the happy couple and not vice versa. But if someone from another Family merely wanted to go to Mardi Gras, just as a tourist or what-not? He could be sure his boss would simply tell him to forget it. Don't go.

Tramonti's seat on the Commission was permanent but somewhat honorary. His attendance was optional. He rarely went. He was unaccustomed to making decisions by committee, by *voting*. Men like Michael Corleone might have gotten into this thing of theirs to transform it into a corporate board of directors. But Carlo Tramonti was another kind of man.

Nonetheless: so be it. What was past was past. The Corleones had gotten their wish, and, predictably, the gods were now punishing them for it. Yet Michael Corleone, whatever his flaws, had proven himself an honorable man, a *uomo di panza*. As such a man, he would have no choice but to act.

THE TRAMONTI BROTHERS TOOK OFF FROM MEDELLÍN IN A Ford Tri-Motor that, officially, belonged to a private subcontractor of the Colombian postal service. In fact, it was part of a fleet of such planes that helped smuggle marijuana, cocaine, and heroin from Colombia to various airstrips in the swamps of Florida and Louisiana. For a few delirious minutes, they rose into a perfect blue sky, high above the mountains and jungles of the Colombian interior, gasping not just from the thin air but at the preposterous beauty of it all, too.

When the sputtering plane suddenly began its descent, the Tramonti brothers asked if it was engine trouble.

The pilot said no. He pointed to the sleek, unmistakably American fighter jets escorting them down.

Moments later, the Tramontis were dumped at an abandoned army base, somewhere in the densely forested mountains of they didn't know where, relieved of their personal effects and all the cash that had not been in their shoes.

Speechless, they watched the planes take off.

They tucked their remaining cash in their pockets. The brothers had little choice but to trek through the jungle. The brush reduced their exquisite silk suits quickly to rags. The stones in their pathway ruined their fine, thin-soled loafers. They wheezed and cursed every step of the way, plotting their revenge as they made their way through the undergrowth, stepping around large and unfamiliar forms of vermin, never sure just which slithering, scuttling creature might be full of deadly poison.

CHAPTER 2

Tom Hagen sat in the back of the chapel of the Fontainebleau Hotel and waited for an old woman to finish her prayers. She was kneeling at the altar rail, wearing a tropical beachwear getup, parrots and pineapples. Going to church like that offended the *consigliere*'s sense of propriety. Organ recordings of droning Protestant hymns played from a pulpit-mounted loudspeaker. Not for a million bucks and a blowjob could you get Hagen to live in Florida.

The chapel was needlessly large. The Fontainebleau had been built to be a casino, but the political support fell through. A resort hotel doesn't need the kind of chapel a casino does.

Across the aisle, a man in a plain black suit paged through a white leatherette Bible. Hagen caught the man's good eye—the other was glass—and turned his palms heavenward. The man, a CIA operative named Joe Lucadello, shrugged and looked away. He used to have an eye patch and more hair.

Outside, a pounding rain all but drowned out the shouts of the crowd, herded away from the entrance of the hotel by the Secret Service. President Shea—in full view of a horde of TV cameras—was scheduled to play golf with the vice president, former Florida senator Ambrose "Bud" Payton, who had once been his biggest in-party rival (and a longtime friend of Sam Drago's in Tampa and Carlo Tramonti's, too). Tom's wife was out seeing some art-world people—her own collection of modern paintings was, quietly, among the finest in the country—but the real reason Theresa had come along on this trip was to attend a fund-raiser tonight in the Fontainebleau's ballroom. The party's convention would be here in Miami Beach, in fact, in a little more than a year—hard for Hagen to believe. It seemed like only yesterday that he'd helped put together some of the deals that got Shea elected in the first place.

Ordinarily a paragon of taste and good sense, Theresa was fascinated with the dashing young president and his doe-eyed rich-bitch wife. The Sheas were just people, Tom kept explaining, full of flaws, like everybody else. Theresa was *from* New Jersey. She knew what an unremarkable governor Shea had been. But Theresa believed what she wanted to believe. Like everybody else. Even Michael, of all people, had been drawn in, though he made a distinction between Jimmy and Danny. He thought Jimmy was an inspirational and potentially great president. There had been problems: Cuba and his own brother. But Cuba was an impossible situation, Michael believed, and so was Danny. Brothers can be that way.

Hagen looked at his watch. The crone at the rail rocked silently back and forth. Hagen considered praying, too, if only to settle his mind. He closed his eyes. He had no real regrets. In his life, there were only things that had to be done, and he did them, end of story. This left little to pray about. Hagen would be damned if he treated the Almighty like some department-store Santa, making childish requests for things a man should be able to acquire or control without need for supernatural intervention. He opened his eyes. To hell with it. No prayers.

Finally, the old woman stood. She had a big white bandage on her forehead and mascara running down her cheeks. *Eight million stories in the naked city*, Hagen thought, averting his eyes.

As she left, Lucadello nodded toward a man he'd stationed outside the door, who would tell anyone else who came by that the room had to be sealed off until the president was secured in his suite upstairs. Still toting the Bible, Lucadello went to the pulpit and turned up the organ music, then took a seat in the pew behind Hagen. "Too much is never enough."

He grew up outside Philly and had a Jersey accent, though he turned it on and off.

Hagen turned around to face him. "Say what?"

"The architect who designed this hotel. That was his favorite saying."

"Sounds about right."

"I used to want to be an architect, I ever tell you that?"

"No."

"Idealist that I was, this was the kind of building I dreamed about building. Curves galore in boxy times. Zigging where others zag. Ever hear that record, *Fontane Blue*?"

Hagen frowned and gave Lucadello a *Who do you think you're talking to?* look. In truth, Hagen had little use for music in general and Johnny Fontane in particular, but it would have been embarrassing in all kinds of ways for him to admit that.

"You know it was recorded in the ballroom here, right?" Lucadello said.

"Hence the title. You going to jabber all morning or are we going to do business?"

"What a record. Talk about zigging where others zag, huh?" Lucadello shook his head as if he were humbled to be near such a hallowed site. "You know Fontane pretty well, I guess?"

"Friend of the family is all," Hagen said.

"The family." Lucadello laughed. "I bet. Seriously, though, how's your brother?"

Lost. Michael put on a good show, but his heart clearly wasn't in his work. It wasn't anywhere else, either, that Tom Hagen could see. "He's doing great."

"Glad to hear it." Lucadello sounded both glad and skeptical. He and Michael had known each other since Mike was in the Civilian Conservation Corps, trying to piss off his father and find his way in the world. Joe and Mike had also gone off together to join the RAF. Hagen, working behind the scenes, had gotten Mike tossed out. The day after Pearl Harbor, though, Mike volunteered again, this time for the Marines. The rest was history. Mike came home a war hero. And, with little fanfare, so did Joe. That was how he lost his eye: the war. Noble. Michael was fond of him and trusted him, which should have been enough for Tom Hagen. But some guys, he thought, just rub you the wrong way.

"Look," Hagen said, "I appreciate you coming all the way down here—"

"I live ten minutes away," Lucadello said.

"—but I've got a busy day, so if it's not too much trouble . . . "

Lucadello patted him on the shoulder. "Easy, *paisan*."

Hagen didn't say anything. He'd eaten so much shit about not being Italian, what was another teaspoonful from this smug bastard?

"I got good news and bad news," Lucadello said. "What do you want first?"

Maybe he was just trying to be friendly, but Jesus. Fuck him. "The bad."

"I better start with the good."

Then why ask? "People usually start with the bad," Hagen said, "but shoot."

"We've finally got a lead on your missing package."

Nick Geraci.

The thought sent Hagen's heart racing. The traitorous *capo* was last seen boarding a ship to Palermo. Button men had been waiting on the docks when it arrived. Michael watched from a yacht in the harbor. They'd been left holding their respective dicks. Other than some information that seemed to place him, at least briefly, in Buffalo, there had been no sign of him for months—long enough that within the Corleone Family, he was becoming the unnamed suspect behind every misfortune large or small. An arrest that stuck. A fixed title fight none of the Family's bookies knew about. A heart attack a lot of people thought wasn't really a heart attack.

If a guy slipped and fell in his bathtub, men wondered if maybe Geraci had rigged it.

A protégé of the late Sally Tessio, Geraci had been the best earner the Corleones ever had. In the words of the late, great Pete Clemenza—Vito Corleone's other, more loyal *capo*—Nick Geraci could swallow a nickel and shit a stack of banded Clevelands. He was an ex-heavyweight boxer who'd almost finished a law degree, and he knew the virtues and limitations of both force and reason. He'd built the Family's narcotics operation into what Hagen, some fifteen years earlier, had tried to convince Vito Corleone it was destined to be: the most lucrative part of the business. This generation's Prohibition. Geraci was as likable as Fredo had been without being a flake, as tough as Sonny but with none of the recklessness, every bit as shrewd as Michael but with more heart. Yet even though Geraci's parents were Sicilian, he had been born and raised in Cleveland, and so—like Hagen, a Corleone and a Sicilian in all but name and blood—Geraci was the quintessential insider doomed never to get all the way in. Hagen had always liked him. Now he hoped someday to enjoy a long, remorseless piss on the man's grave.

Hagen put a finger to his throat to feel his racing pulse. His heart did that, raced. "I wasn't sure your people were actively looking for him. For *it*. The package."

"What'd you think this was about?" Lucadello said. "That immigration circus?"

Hagen shrugged. It wasn't just Carlo Tramonti's deportation to Colombia, which might be comical were it not for the things Tramonti knew. There were also the related, mounting complications posed by that self-righteous prick Danny Shea.

"So where is he?"

"It," Lucadello said.

"Excuse me?"

"It. The package."

"Jesus Christ."

Lucadello tossed the white Bible aside. "In a place of worship, you talk like that? What ring of hell you figure that'll get you sent to?"

"It's not a . . . It's just a hotel." Hagen took a deep breath. "Fine. Where'd you find *it*?"

"We didn't so much find it as figure out where it's been. Guess where."

Sicily, Hagen thought. The narcotics operation had given Geraci connections all over that island. But Hagen wasn't about to guess. In a tactic he'd learned from watching the great Vito Corleone, Hagen remained utterly still, addressing this show of disrespect with withering silence.

"All right, killjoy," Lucadello said, "but you're gonna love this. In a huge man-made cave underneath a certain Great Lake."

"Erie?"

"Positively spooky, actually."

Hagen sighed. Lucadello bobbed his head in concession.

"Anyway, if the Russians dropped the bomb," Lucadello said, "two horny kids could've gone down there and restarted the whole human race, that's how well stocked this place was. Or so I hear. It was attached through some kind of passageway to a lodge on a private island up there. I'm sure you know the one." The agent laughed. "A secret passageway. What a riot. We live in interesting times."

Vincent Forlenza, the former owner of that lodge on Rattlesnake Island and the boss of the Cleveland mob, had also been Geraci's real-life godfather. For his part in the conspiracy with Geraci and the Chicago outfit, Forlenza's body was at the bottom of Lake Erie, chained to a tugboat anchor, food for the sludgeworms.

"I figured you'd be happy about this," Lucadello said. "No doubt your brother, too."

Hagen thought he heard a note of sarcasm in the way Lucadello said *brother.* "*Happy*'s not the perfect word," Hagen said. "But you're right to think it's good news. The bad news I'm guessing is that he's not there anymore."

"*It's* not there anymore."

Hagen closed his eyes.

"I'm sorry." Lucadello laughed. "I can't keep this going. I'm just bust-ing balls. You're right—he's not there anymore, but that's not the bad news. The bad news is the way we found out about it, which was the FBI."

Hagen's heart wasn't slowing down at all. No boss or *caporegime* had ever cooperated with a government investigation, but few had ever been backed into more of a hole—literally, as it turned out. "Is he in custody?"

"We think Geraci is still at large." Lucadello pronounced it the Italian way—*Jair-AH-chee*, rather than the Americanized way—*Juh-RAY-see*—that Nick preferred.

"You *think*?" Hagen said.

"Think, yes. That's why we call this process *intelligence*, counselor. What we know for certain is that our boy was sloppy getting out of there, threat-ening the lives of two children and a retired cop who plowed snow up there. The ex-cop angle was probably what got the Bureau interested. Then they found the cave, found prints everywhere, even found the gun he used."

"He shot at kids?" It was unthinkable that anyone with Geraci's skills would threaten children, and unlikely that he'd have left a security guard alive as an eyewitness.

"Threatened. It hadn't been fired."

"But it had his prints on it?"

"We're not sure. Maybe the guard just recognized it as the same gun he'd looked down the barrel of. We're just getting our bearings here ourselves. We do have a source who in the past has cut us in on certain ongoing investigations."

"How good's this source?"

Lucadello sighed. "What, on a one-to-ten scale? It's good." He started flipping through the Bible. "As for the company I represent, you have clearance from the top"—he mouthed the name *Soffet*—"to take this to the next level."

As in CIA Director Allen Soffet, whom Hagen knew from his own stint in Washington. Michael had met the director, too, while serving on President Shea's transition team.

Lucadello found what he was looking for. He held the Bible out to Hagen and jabbed a finger at a passage in Exodus.

It concerned personal-injury law. Hagen looked up, puzzled.

Lucadello winked his glass eye.

Hagen nodded. This must be where the eye-for-an-eye thing came from, though that wasn't exactly what the passage said. He'd humor the guy. Despite his revving heartbeat, he felt a sense of calm. He sat back and pointed at the white Bible. "Always meant to read that thing."

"Good book." Lucadello said.

"Hence its informal name."

"Clever. We'll do everything we can to get you, yes, intelligence that points you in the right direction. Once your objective is achieved, we'll help in any way possible with post-event damage control. It goes without saying that the need for same should be kept to a minimum. But make no mistake. We're on the same side as you are, believe me."

Geraci—via Lucadello (who he knew as "Ike Rosen")—had been involved in certain Cuban initiatives. The thinking on the part of Michael and Tom Hagen, who had approved it, was that it was a win-win. If things worked out, they got their casinos back, and if not, Geraci was the fall guy, his ambitions forever thwarted. Things had not worked out. One of Geraci's men, a Sicilian kid named Carmine Marino, was caught down there trying to assassinate the Cuban dictator. Marino was shot trying to escape (by whom, Hagen didn't want to know). It became, briefly, an international incident. There was also the problem posed by Marino's epically vengeful relatives back in Sicily, which the public didn't know about, though Hagen thought that the CIA might. Geraci's disappearance had kept him from being the fall guy, yet. Done right, the killing of Nick Geraci could actually solve a matrix of interlocking problems.

Hagen nodded. "I've been involved in the law, in negotiations, for most of my life. One thing I've learned is to be skeptical of anybody who says *believe me*."

"You calling me a liar?" Lucadello said. He seemed more amused than offended.

"In this sacred place?" Hagen gestured toward the altar. "No. But what assurances do we have that this isn't a setup? That you won't get us to take out the trash for you and then while we're at the curb—red-handed, so to speak—stuff us in the can, too? Why don't you just take it out yourselves?"

"Nice pun there," Lucadello said. "On *can*."

Again, Hagen went blank.

"C'mon, counselor," Lucadello said. "The scope of what really went on down there and what led up to it is far from public knowledge. We have every reason to want to keep it that way. Which rules out one sort of *can*. As for the *shitcan* sense of . . . Listen to me; you're a bad influence. At any rate, why would we want to do that? You people are still in power, I'm still friends with your boss—as I've been for a *quarter century*, almost, don't forget—and we all live to fight another day, as it were. I know a little about the traditions of your *people*, all right, *paisan*? The government's no different. Example: a man's going to the electric chair, and he has a heart attack. What happens? A team of doctors and nurses swings into action and does everything it can to save him. The moment he's back on his feet, they reshave his head and march him back to the killing floor. The object isn't for the person to die; it's to kill him. *You* tell *me*: if I'd have sat down with you here and told you the job was already done on your *package*, you'd have been furious. Don't deny it. And if I'd told you that we were planning on taking care of it, you'd have tried to persuade me to let your people have the satisfaction. Don't pretend like you're talking to some *mortadell'*, all right? Our desire to avoid any kind of embarrassment and your need for revenge—it all dovetails perfectly."

Lucadello sat back in the pew.

Hagen's heart had slowed without his noticing exactly when. These episodes came and went like that. Outside, the rain wasn't slowing, but the noise of the crowd seemed to pick up.

Hagen jerked a thumb toward the crowd. "So do we have time to discuss the great man's brother?" Meaning Attorney General Daniel Brendan Shea.

"Him, I don't know what we could possibly help you with."

"Is that right? You don't think you have as much to lose in all this as we do?"

"Me personally?"

"Are you really that mercenary?"

"Aren't we all?" Lucadello said. "Wait, I forgot. With you people, it's all about family. Cute concept. I can't say as I think it's one you've really embraced. You personally."

Hagen didn't dignify that with a response.

"What's going to happen," Hagen said, "when a certain Colombian uses his get-out-of-jail-free card?"

"I told you, we don't really talk like that." Lucadello pointed to the pulpit. The music would make any attempts to record their conversation unintelligible. Plus, both his and Hagen's people had swept the room for listening devices. "The Colombian—you mean Carlo Tramonti, right? You know that guy or is he just *un amico degli amici*?"

Friend of the friends. "Very funny."

"I hear he's out of the woods down there. He threw some money around and managed to set up shop in a two-star hotel in Cartageña, right on the coast, which is hardly jail." Lucadello looked heavenward and grimaced as he pretended to do math in his head. "He can probably take care of business from there indefinitely, the way Luciano did in Sicily. But he won't need to. Tramonti is I would say three bribes and two good lawyers away from coming home and sleeping in his own bed. Forgive me, though: you're not suggesting, with your Monopoly allusion, that Tramonti might try to get off the hook by blackmailing the federal government, are you? What a joke!"

"I wouldn't call—"

"No, *literally*. Guy walks into a courtroom. Now, this fella's been to court before, seen a little jail—arson, robbery, et cetera. But now he's got the whole state of Louisiana in his pocket, see, so *he's* the one making accusations. He claims that top-secret government agents came to him in his official capacity as the head of a crime syndicate and asked him nicely if he'd let them train some of his assassins to go—what's that word? right: *whack*—to go whack the leader of Cuba. What natural partners they would make! The government's fighting the good ol' Red Menace, and the mobsters want revenge because the Commies stole their casinos. Brilliant. Naturally, the man agrees. So what they do is, they set up a camp in a nice sunny place near the beach, like they're ballplayers in spring training. They take target practice, they go marching around in government-issued tracksuits, and they sit around discussing how they might for example be able to get the maximum leader to go scuba diving and pick up this one special seashell that explodes. The assassins are more meat-and-potatoes, guns-and-knives men, but they come up with a few ideas of their own, and a good time is had by all. Unfortunately, they never get into the game, see, because—get this—it turns out the government has gone to two *other* gangsters and put together two *other* hit-man squads. Sadly, a numskull from one of those *other* squads goes to Cuba and botches it. Kills a *double*, a man hired by our Commie nemesis in anticipation of just such an eventuality. Then the idiot gets caught, but before he can come to trial, he's shot trying to escape. A lot of this is only what our guy in the courtroom has heard about. But, hey, forget that it's hearsay. The punch line is, it's all true! Every last word!"

Hagen bit his lip. That *was* the punch line.

To be precise, Carmine Marino, a Corleone soldier, hadn't been a numskull. Just a brave pawn. But everything else really happened.

Lucadello shook his head in mock awe. "But wait. The laughs keep on coming. The guy goes on to tell the judge that the only reason he came to court to share his hilarious tale is that recently some *completely different* government agents kidnapped him! They sent him to a country he'd never been to—though he does import coffee, hookers, and many profitable varieties of narcotics from there. He's also got a passport from this country, but, um, see, it's fake. What happened was, the Ivy League–educated attorney general, the president's *brother*, was too stupid to figure out how to prosecute this criminal mastermind, who, by the way, is a grammar school dropout who signs his name with an X. So instead, young Shea, a frat boy at heart, resorted to a mindless prank: he took our guy out in the woods and left him there. Har-de-har-har. Tap that keg, brother!"

"A mindless prank?"

"Explain it to me, then. Our friend the A.G. goes on TV and brags that he wants his legacy to be . . . no, that he wants to go down in *history* as the man who brought down the Mafia. Which, as you and I and the FBI director know, doesn't exist. Just an ethnic slur, et cetera, right?"

The FBI director had not, in fact, ever publicly admitted to the existence of the Mafia. Tom Hagen was in possession of photographs of the director in a hiked-up taffeta dress, enjoying fellatio from his loyal assistant, which had proven helpful in this regard.

"So what's the A.G.'s first big move against this invisible empire?" Lucadello continued. "Where does he start? With Carlo Tramonti. But not with a grandstanding trial where he and his crackerjack staff put the guy away for murder or even tax evasion. Nothing *substantial.* Just some harebrained deportation scheme. Why? Why start there? He's got no case. No due process, no anything. And he *knows* that Tramonti thinks he's got this *get-out-of-jail-free card* he can and will play."

"You think Danny Shea *wants* him to play the card, don't you?"

"Common sense decrees."

Hagen waved his hand in disgust.

What Danny Shea wanted—and, for all Hagen knew, what Joe Lucadello and his people wanted as well—was for Tramonti to realize *the card wasn't playable.* They wanted Tramonti to understand that his story, though true, wouldn't hold up in a court of law, and no good lawyer would let him tell it there. Danny Shea was trying to win the hearts and minds of the people. In the court of public opinion, it would be easy to convict a man who'd lived in this country since he was a boy but had no valid passport except a fraudulent one from a country in which he'd never set foot. It would be easy to use that to scare the people that we have another evil conspiracy on our hands, a worthy sequel to the Red Menace. It was great political theater, and the Shea brothers were politicians to their telegenic pussy-mad Irish cores.

"Common sense," Hagen said, "is for suckers."

"Come again?" Lucadello said.

"Common sense is the true opiate of the masses."

Lucadello slapped Hagen's back. "I'm beginning to like you, *paisan*. Who said that?"

"What do you mean, who said that?"

"You're quoting somebody. That sounds like a quote."

From habit, Hagen started to say he was quoting Vito Corleone, then realized Vito had never said that. Still, what could Hagen do, say that he'd come up with it himself? Unseemly.

"I heard it from Vito Corleone," he said. An honorable lie, which Tom Hagen garnished with another: "My godfather."

CHAPTER 3

What a great day." Theresa Hagen didn't sound sarcastic. More like she was trying to sell herself on the idea. They were alone in the hotel elevator, dressed for dinner, heading down. Because of the rain (and a behind-the-scenes tiff between Bud Payton and Jimmy Shea), President and Mrs. Shea had cut their visit short and were on their way back to Washington.

"I'm sorry," Tom said. His own day had been no picnic—one piece of good news, then a day's worth of going downhill from there.

"Don't be," Theresa said. "I'm serious."

"Hubba-hubba," he said, bending to kiss the nape of her sleek neck.

"Stop it."

"I can't." She had on a backless red dress. It was a dark, muted shade of red, but still: red. Her ass looked great in it. For better or worse, she'd lost most of the fleshiness she'd had when she was younger. You could squint and see her mother's dried-up bony frame, but Theresa's ass was a still an onion-shaped wonder. "I'm powerless."

She blushed. What could be more lovely than a blushing, olive-skinned woman in her forties? The blushing gave Tom a glimpse of the bookish

schoolgirl she'd once been—smart enough to see through everybody, too
nice to use what she saw as a weapon—and of all the stages in between, too:
the chain of life and circumstance that had produced this woman and
somehow, via fate or chance, brought her here, with him, still weirdly vulnerable to flattery and maybe even that great nothing and everything, love.

"Great how?" Tom said. "Your day."

They'd been together in the room for the past half hour, rushing around
getting ready, speaking in little more than the familiar grunts and two-
word sentences that sustain old, childbearing marriages. *Behind you. No
idea. Want coffee? Excuse me. Zip this.*

"Long story," she said, straightening his bow tie, smoothing the lapels
of his tux.

"Tell me," he said.

"For starters," Theresa said, "there was a monkey farm, I kid you not,
three miles wide."

The elevator dinged. "This is your stop," Tom said.

"Are we really going to do this?"

He grinned. "This is the main reason we came here, doll."

"*Doll?*"

Tom shrugged. So what? *Doll.* Common endearment. "Go on and make
your entrance."

She got out, one floor from the bottom. The door closed. Tom rode the
last floor alone.

The broad, curving stairway in the lobby of the Fontainebleau had no
other purpose than this. The ladies get off first (earlier today, when he'd
told this to his mistress, who was also staying here, she'd made an annoying and lascivious comment). Then their gentlemen ride down, take their
positions in the lobby, and watch the ladies descend.

As Theresa started to do this, Tom shot a look at the bellman, who
threaded the crowd in the lobby and, as Tom dropped to one knee, deftly
handed him a dozen roses. Perfect timing. Tom presented the bouquet to
his wife. Here he'd put together this grand, romantic gesture, and nobody

smiled or reacted, not even Theresa, who received the bouquet as nonchalantly as if it had been the afternoon paper.

"You call the mother of your children *doll*?" she said.

"Don't ruin the moment." Tom stood up and gestured toward the dining room. "C'mon and tell me about the monkeys, OK?"

"Sorry," she said, stroking the flowers. "This is thoughtful. They're really beautiful."

A billboard-size banner in the hangar-size ballroom read WELCOME PRESIDENT SHEA! The Hagens were among the first to arrive, which annoyed Tom (rigid punctuality was another lesson from Vito Corleone that now coursed through his blood) almost as much as looking around and seeing that most of the other men there were dressed in business suits, not formalwear, for a formal event. He shook his head. Florida.

Tom and Theresa's seats were all the way in the back, which was fine, especially without the Sheas for Theresa to ogle. The Hagens had gotten their fill of political glitz during Tom's brief, miserable stint filling out a term as a Nevada congressman.

As they were about to sit down, Tom, seized by a crazy impulse, put his mouth to her ear. "Let's go," he whispered.

Her eyes lit up. Impulse, yes, but not crazy. He was on the money. "Go where?"

"Anywhere but here," he said. "Somewhere nice, just you and me."

They kept walking, went out the side door, and took a taxi to Joe's Stone Crabs.

On the way, they talked about when they'd last done this: a night on the town, no kids, no rings for Tom to kiss, no important painter or museum board member for Theresa to indulge. Maybe not since they lived in New York the first time, seven years ago.

The place was packed, but Tom duked a few people, and he and Theresa were ushered straight to a dark corner booth. The waiter took their drink order and produced a vase for the roses.

"So," Theresa said, "want to hear about my day?"

"I was just about to ask," Tom said.

She rolled her eyes, but affectionately.

She'd had breakfast with some people who were talking about setting up a museum of modern art in Miami, something she'd done in Las Vegas, and they were eager to pick her brain. Flattering, obviously. Then she went to see a collector up in Palm Beach, some crackpot cash-poor heiress who sold off several great pieces to help fund the monkey farm in question. She rescued them from bankrupt zoos and then trained them to be "helper monkeys," whatever that was. Also, the government bought monkeys from her, including the ones NASA sent into space.

"Or claimed to have," Tom said.

"Who cares?" Theresa laughed and clinked wineglasses with him. "Print the legend."

"Exactly," Tom said, though he wasn't exactly sure what she meant by that.

"Then, this afternoon . . . " She took a long swig of wine. " . . . I bought a house."

"You did *what*?"

"Don't look at me like that. I bought a house. I got a great deal on it."

She told him the price and called it a steal, but his head was swimming. It was too much to process. "You bought a *house*? Without even talking to me about it? Jesus Christ, Theresa, I didn't even know you were *looking* for a house. What the hell do we need a house for?"

"I was going to talk to you about it—I was just looking as kind of a lark—but this place . . . Oh, Tom, wait'll you see it. A bungalow not far from here. Bigger inside than it looks from the street. Six blocks from the ocean, with a backyard facing a canal. It's got a pool, grapefruit trees, tile roof, arches, cypress floors, even a widow's walk. It's adorable. A classic old Florida home. As the kids start moving away, a vacation house like this can keep us all together. It'll be a place that we can all gather as a family."

Frank, their oldest, was in his first year of law school at Yale; Andrew was a divinity major at Notre Dame. "None of our kids have moved away. They're just away at school. The girls are just babies."

"The boys are gone, Tom. Face it. And it pains me to admit this, but nine and four aren't babies. It'll go fast. Look how fast it went with Frank."

That was all true, but not quite what Tom was trying to say. "How can you buy a house without me signing something?" Which wasn't exactly the point, either. "Without me even *looking* at it?"

"I have my own money. There are pieces I could sell and pay cash for this thing."

Also not the point. The point was, the more he—and Theresa—threw cash around, the more of a trail it left. The account she used to buy art was actually an offshore corporation. Bermuda. But this house? Who knows?

"Art is one thing," he said, "but a house?"

"Sure, it's another thing," she conceded. "But it's all just business, isn't it?"

He liked being married to a smart woman, but it posed certain challenges. "I don't like Florida," Tom said.

"Nonsense," Theresa said. "Everybody likes Florida."

"I wouldn't live here for a million bucks."

"Over time, we'll probably *make* a million bucks. It's a great investment."

"We have other investments."

"We have *family* here, Tom."

Suddenly, he understood.

"This was you and Sandra," he said, "wasn't it?"

"You're quick, counselor."

"I'll say this," Tom said. "This gives new meaning to *thick as thieves*." Sandra Corleone, Sonny's widow, lived in Hollywood, Florida, which was not that far away. She'd been engaged for ten years to a former New York fire marshal who, as a reward for some of the fires he ruled to be accidents, now fronted a chain of liquor stores here. Sandra and Theresa weren't blood, and they could hardly have been more different, but they were as close as any sisters Tom had seen. "How long have you two been cooking this up?"

Triumphant, Theresa clinked his glass again. "Just look at it, OK? Keep an open mind."

Tom shook his head, defeated. "I don't have to." He could put accountants on this, too. If she wanted it, she wanted it. He did see how it was good for his family. A little place in the sun. It wasn't as if he'd have to actually live there. "If you want to do this, just do it."

"I love you, Tom."

"You better."

The waiter came by and refilled their wineglasses.

"Keep 'em coming," Tom said, only half joking.

"So," she said, "how was *your* day?"

Their eyes met. In this light, anyway, she looked as if she really thought that, this time, he might answer. He held her gaze. After all these years, after all the vague answers he'd given to this question, she kept right on asking it.

He reached for his glass and took a long drink.

What, really, did she want him to say?

Gee, it was swell, dear. This gentleman who almost destroyed our whole organization turned up, only maybe the FBI's got him. The things he knows could get us all thrown in jail, which he'd never have talked about in a million years except that Michael, unbeknownst to me, tried to sabotage this guy's airplane a few years back. Mr. Geraci didn't just survive, he eventually figured the whole thing out—well before I did. Long story short, somehow we need to find this guy and kill him. Purely out of self-defense.

Then this afternoon, just as I told you, I had some routine legal matters to address. A lawyer with his briefcase can steal more than a hundred men with guns can, and I thank you again for the lovely briefcase. After that, I went for a quick meeting with the president of the United States; sorry I had to keep that from you, hon. It didn't work out anyway. The president's father was our connection, but he's dead and his sons are turning on us, which is ridiculous. Jimmy Shea would have lost the election without us, and Bud Payton has been on the payroll of some friends of ours for so long that his retirement plan should have kicked in. Then again, it's a ridiculous world. I know you agree, which is part of why you've got such a great eye for art. Anyway, Shea's golf game gets rained out, but instead of meeting with me, he and Payton zoom off to a slapped-together rally at the gym where a Cuban fighter, a defector, is training for his shot at the title—which, by the way, if you want to make back some of the money you spent on that house, bet the other guy. At any rate, some snot-nosed aide tells me the meeting will happen in the limo, after the rally. I get to the gym in time to hear liberty championed, America blessed, common ground asserted, and a better world imagined. Payton hates Shea's guts, by the way, and his smile looks like rigor mortis. All of this is staged inside a boxing ring. The fighter stands there clutching a tiny American flag. When it's all over, a Secret Service agent pulls me aside and says the meeting is a quote-unquote no-go.

Tom finished his wine and then reached out and took Theresa's other hand. He leaned slightly across the table. They stared into each other's eyes.

So I come back to the hotel. At about the same time you and Sandra are out shopping for a house behind my back, what I'm doing behind your back is worse. Unforgivable. It's where I went last night, too, when I said I couldn't sleep and needed to take a walk. That was a lie, since—unlike Mike with his insomnia and his nightmares—I sleep just fine. Which you know. Yet you didn't question it, did you? I got up from our bed and got dressed and took the stairs three flights down, and I knocked on a door to a room where I was expected.

It doesn't mean anything.

That's not exactly true, but I certainly don't love her. She's no threat to you or our family. I couldn't explain it myself if I tried, except that, as you know, men do this sort of thing. You probably already know about her. How could you not? It's been going on for years. She lives in Vegas. Where I go on business all the time. And, yes, you guessed right: she likes it when I call her doll.

When I think about how I should feel about this—which is almost never—I know it's awful. I'm not a stupid man. At every turn of my life, I understand that I should feel all kinds of things that I don't feel. A person can make himself understand a thing, but how do you make yourself feel? What's a man supposed to do about that?

If this were all out in the open, probably our family would be destroyed. I'd be devastated. But as long as you never really know these things, as long as we never talk about it, as long as I'm not found out, I have to be honest: I don't feel bad.

I don't feel anything.

That's *what I feel bad about.*

I've helped plot the deaths of many men and one whore. I've stood in rooms where the body was still warm and calmly discussed business. I've killed three men myself, Theresa. The first time, I was only a boy, eleven years old, an orphan, living on the streets. I don't like to think about it. I think about the good that came from it, which was that Sonny brought me home to live with his family. The other two happened last year, right before that Notre Dame–Syracuse game you and I saw with Andrew. On one of the men, I used the belt I'm wearing right now, which seems odd only when I stop to think about it, which I never do. The other man, the one I shot in the head, was Louie Russo, head of the Chicago crime syndicate, and a sick man, in ways I don't like to think about. The world is a better place without this individual, I can assure you. Here again: self-defense. All three times, it was kill or be killed, and I killed.

These things do not haunt me.

Nobody suspects me of anything—nobody except, I suspect, you.

As you must know, sweetheart, I'm not just Michael's lawyer and his unofficial brother. I'm also his consigliere, *and, lately, his* sotto capo *as well. His underboss.*

Which I can't be officially, because, unlike you, my love, I'm not Sicilian, not even Italian.

You know all this. You must. Right after Pearl Harbor, when your parents got thrown in detention, like a lot of Italian immigrants did, how do you think I got 'em out so fast, huh? When your cousin fell on hard times, didn't you wonder how a high school gym teacher who'd never set foot in Rhode Island made such a smooth transition into the vending-machine business there?

How many times have you wanted to buy a painting and done so with an envelope of cash I gave you that you took, no questions asked? You're a smart woman, Theresa. If—as I never will—I asked you to estimate the amount of money you've laundered, not to mention the number of art dealers whose tax fraud you've abetted, I'm certain you could tote it up in your head.

You know things. You keep asking me questions I can't answer, but, Theresa, my love, you know.

Their gaze was broken by the arrival of two plates piled high with stone crabs.

"Well?" Theresa said. A little hurt, it seemed, as she always was. "Nothing to say?"

"Ah, you know," Tom Hagen said, throwing up his hands. "Not much to tell, I guess. A day's a day."

"Wow," she said. "Look at all this food! I'll never eat all this."

Theresa had ridden out his long silences countless times before, often without the aid of candlelight and a tart white wine.

"Call Sandra," Tom said. "Bet you she'll help."

"I already did." Theresa grinned in a way she must have hoped was wicked. "When I went to the Ladies. She and Stan are on their way."

Theresa had a good heart, Tom thought. At this point, it was probably as broken as it was going to get.

CHAPTER 4

The *indios* had a name for the land of the dead. They called it Mictlan. Nick Geraci was under no illusions that he was the only one in Taxco who'd conducted business there.

He stood on his balcony in the waning desert light, draped in a bathrobe, postponing the ordeal of having to get dressed again. His fists throbbed. Behind him, on the green tile floor inside, were the clothes he'd cursed himself trying to zip and button this morning, now soaked with blood and rolled up inside a rug along with the stranger who'd come to kill him.

Centuries ago, Taxco was hacked from this steep hillside by the colonizing rear guard of the conquistadors, who enslaved the natives and marched them into dark holes to mine silver. The big shots stayed up top, basking in the thin air and idyllic weather, supervising what was destined to become a maze of tortuous cobblestone streets, shooting dice and despoiling the local women, drinking first one sort of spirits, then bracing themselves for the visits from another. On such a foundation rose this small city, still a source of silver, lovely beyond reason, filthy with jewelry shops and bars, fragrant with bougainvillea and boiled chicken, with fried cornmeal and rotting straw, a haven for outsiders and eccentrics. Around every corner were views that provoked tourists and newcomers to gasp and unholster their cameras.

Geraci's apartment was on the third floor. From its balcony, he could see the zócalo, the baroque dome of the church of Santa Prisca, and an exultation of tile-roofed colonial houses, each forced by the sheer angles of the hillside and its spurs of virgin rock to be ingeniously different from the next. From here, the city seemed aglow in white, red, and green, same as the Mexican (and Italian) flag. But Geraci had been in Taxco long enough to see past beauty.

He could pick out sad-eyed women behind counters in silver shops or seated at café tables and watch them swallow grimaces they'll never unleash on their haggling customers and oblivious lovers. He could spot isolated men muttering to themselves, walking with awkward, hurried gaits: away from something and not toward it. He noticed dogs trotting alone down side streets, their heads bobbing as if silently cursing their demons. His heart went out to those dogs.

He looked back over his shoulder at the rug. He'd bought it on the street. It was wool, brightly colored, turquoise and orange, black where it needed to be. It had a warrior on it, in noble profile. He'd liked that rug.

Even though Geraci hadn't wanted to kill the guy, and even though his now-aching hands stood to make a tough job, getting dressed, even tougher, it was wild—in every sense of that—to feel his fists throb again. He couldn't remember the last time he'd thrown a real punch. In his time of need, his body, to his surprise, had not betrayed him.

He leaned out over the railing and was able to glimpse the distant gorge, safely downwind, where four centuries of the city's garbage had been dumped, where today's trash hill often became tomorrow's sinkhole, where brown lakes of putrefied sewage formed and vanished, where children were warned never to go. Buzzards circled it all day, and wolves patrolled it all night. There were no doubt other corpses in that gorge, but this would be the first Geraci ever heaved there. It didn't bother him. He'd been to New Jersey.

Getting dressed, though: that bothered him.

The tremors bothered him, too, but they came and went.

Charlotte, his wife, was upset about his face, the way it sometimes lacked expression, but until he figured out a way to reunite with her that wouldn't get him killed, that was no problem at all. If other people can't see his expressions, what's it to Nick Geraci?

Losing track of his thoughts was disturbing, but it didn't happen often. Anyway, he was pushing fifty. Everybody forgets things. It might be a mercy. Geraci would *like* to be able to forget how miserable he felt every day when he thought about his wife and kids and how little hope he had of seeing them any time soon. He'd *like* to be able to forget the plane crash he was in and the blow to his head that he was convinced caused all his problems (he'd been a heavyweight prizefighter, but so many of his fights were fixed, he'd rarely been hit in the head much harder than he slapped himself when he forgot something). But what Nick Geraci could never, ever forget was that Michael Corleone had arranged to have the plane sabotaged. Geraci would never abandon hope of somehow settling that score, no matter how long it took. His fine motor skills were shot. Every time he went to button a shirt or fasten a goddamned pair of pants, it was like Michael Corleone was staring at him with that cold and, come to think of it, expressionless face.

Geraci steeled himself for the task at hand and turned to walk back inside.

Then he panicked.

For a moment, he'd forgotten the other task at hand. For a split second—though it had the force of much more time—Geraci even forgot who the dead man had claimed to be.

ONLY MONTHS AFTER HIS DISAPPEARANCE, NICK GERACI had begun to attain the status of myth. Even the great, gray *New York Times* weighed in, late in the game, with an editorial headlined JUDGE CRATER, AMELIA EARHART, PLEASE MEET ACE GERACI.

Only a few members of the secret society to which Geraci belonged and certain augmented elements of the CIA knew precisely who Geraci was— and even for those people he had become, seemingly overnight, larger than life. They knew about the assassin squad he led and the debacle in Cuba that came from that, though few blamed Geraci. They knew that Michael Corleone had tried to kill him, sacrificing Geraci as a pawn in the young crime boss's obsessive quest to become a legitimate businessman. They knew that Geraci had found out about this, and they knew that he'd conspired with the bosses of the Cleveland and Chicago organizations in an attempt to get revenge. And they knew that it had almost worked. This conspiracy had been directly or indirectly responsible for the deaths of dozens of notable men associated with the American Cosa Nostra, including those two bosses themselves—Luigi "Louie" Russo of Chicago (aka "Fuckface," because of his penis-shaped nose) and Vincent Forlenza of Cleveland (aka "The Jew," because he had so many Jews in top positions in his syndicate), as well as several top men in the Chicago and Cleveland organizations. Other notable casualties had included the most powerful Jewish mobster in the country (a man named Hyman Roth), the bosses of the Los Angeles and San Francisco syndicates, and an assortment of Corleone Family underbosses and *caporegimes,* including Rocco Lampone, Frank Pantangeli, and Fredo Corleone. The chaos had forced Michael Corleone to return to New York to more closely oversee his businesses there, both legal and illegal.

The people who knew these things were of course not talking—except among themselves.

As for the FBI, it had an imperfect sense of who Geraci was and what had happened. The Bureau had assigned a fairly large number of agents to the case but had not assumed jurisdiction from the NYPD, reputedly because of a difference of opinion between the Bureau's director, who believed this to be a local matter and thus in the hands of New York's finest, and the attorney general, a man half the director's age but his putative boss, who had ordered the investigation to be a top priority. These things were reported in several sleazy true-crime gazettes and girlie magazines but turned out to be true.

The NYPD's understanding of the case was more flawed than the FBI's. It had identified Geraci as the *capo di tutti capi,* the boss of all bosses, when all he'd ever been was Corleone *caporegime* acting as boss for the Family's interests in New York—and even that had been something of a setup. But the investigation had nonetheless provoked dissension within the NYPD, which the press was gleefully exploiting. A faction of the department's true believers—eyes on the promotions or federal appointments—was actually trying to find him. Another faction was occupied by efforts to pin a number of absurdly unrelated cases it wanted to close on the missing crime boss. The faction in ascendancy was pushing to close the investigation and hand it off to the FBI and/or someone in Ohio. Given that Geraci was the literal godson of Cleveland crime lord Vincent Forlenza (who, with less fanfare, was also missing and not technically dead), it was common sense that those responsible for Geraci's disappearance or demise were based in Cleveland and/or nearby Youngstown, a mob haven. It should be said that not all the police in this faction wanted this case off their desks because they were disinclined to investigate anything related to the brown paper bags of cash that had helped pay for their remodeled basements and their kid's braces.

The press, especially in New York, could not restrain its glee. For weeks, the front pages were awash with colorful nicknames and wild speculation. One "highly placed gangland source" even claimed that Geraci had disappeared once before, in 1955, that he was actually the pilot of a plane that crashed into Lake Erie and killed the bosses of the San Francisco and Los Angeles crime syndicates. The pilot had been taken to a Cleveland hospital, unconscious, but then vanished, only to be found several months later, rat-gnawed and badly decomposed. The pilot's name was supposedly Gerald O'Malley, but efforts to learn anything about him failed. At the time, two different papers opined that he might never have existed. That did not prove that Geraci and O'Malley were one and the same. But it was true that in his boxing days, Nick Geraci did use various aliases and participated in various fights of dubious resolution, so in the minds of many, these allegations seemed to fit a pattern.

The word on the street? Nick Geraci's body was encased somewhere in the fresh cement of the new baseball stadium at Flushing Meadows Park.

Instead—far-fetched as it might seem—the truth was, the most powerful nation on earth had deployed skilled intelligence and law enforcement personnel to conduct a gigantic manhunt for a powerful and resourceful leader of a secret criminal society—a tall, imposing, bearded man with a chronic, withering disease—and somehow failed to find the cave where he was hiding.

GERACI HAD FOUND REFUGE UNDERNEATH LAKE ERIE, IN A bomb shelter the size of a ballroom, complete with its own water treatment system and power supply and seemingly endless cache of canned food. Geraci had learned about the place doing some business with Don Forlenza. Most of the people who knew about it either were dead or wouldn't think to look for him here. On the train from New York, Geraci thought that at any second someone would kill him. He took it past Cleveland to Toledo, where he didn't know anybody, stole a boat, and, hugging the shore, took it to Rattlesnake Island. The lodge was empty, as it usually was when Forlenza wasn't there. Geraci disabled the alarm, climbed in a window, ransacked the liquor cabinet, and left a radio tuned to a rock-and-roll station so that it would look like kids had broken into the place. Then he made his way down to the shelter.

The genius of the setup was that it was carved into bedrock underneath a secret guest room, where Geraci had stayed a few times and so knew how to make the hidden door open, and another well-stocked shelter. It was possible that even if people searched the lodge, they'd never find the hidden door. Even if they did, they might never think to look for the other, larger shelter below.

Always at the edge of Geraci's attention was what might be waiting for him up there, outside his door, what catastrophe might seek him out, how this might end. A pack of strangers in long, dark coats. Or waves of G-men with square jaws, bad suits, and tommy guns—images he realized came from the movies, but where else? He'd never had a run-in with the Feds in his life.

Or maybe just one man. Michael Corleone's pet killer, Al Neri, smiling and alone.

Or Geraci's own protégé, Cosimo Barone—Momo the Roach. That was more Michael's way. He'd had Geraci, as a test of loyalty, kill Sally Tessio—Momo's uncle, a man who'd been like a father to Nick Geraci.

When, if ever, would Geraci know he could come out? What would force his hand?

For months, no one knew where Nick Geraci was except Nick Geraci.

One of his many difficulties, down in the hole, was that he had no way of knowing what anyone knew. There was a ham radio, but Geraci didn't know how to use it and was afraid to try, for fear it might send out signals that would tip off his location. There was a TV, hooked up to an antenna on the roof of the lodge. Much as Geraci detested television, he did watch it off and on. There was nothing on the TV news about his situation. There wasn't much on the TV news that could tell a person what anyone knew about anything. Everything else on TV was just as bad. But then the TV stopped working, too.

When that happened, Geraci braced himself for the other shoe to drop. He dragged a chair to face the heavy steel door and waited there with a shotgun across his lap. If cops of some sort came to get him, they'd announce themselves. He'd keep the gun trained on them until he saw badges, at which point he'd lay down his weapon and go peacefully. He didn't want to die. But anyone else, he'd say a little prayer and open fire.

This was if he wasn't having a bout of tremors and could fire the goddamned thing at all.

Hours passed. He fell asleep. When he woke he realized to his horror that he'd forgotten to wind his watch. He'd allowed himself to depend on television as a backup to winding the watch. He wanted to shoot the TV, but he didn't want to make any noise. Also, there was a chance it might start to work again. No matter how much you hate TV, the monster lulls you back.

But it didn't come back on.

In this hole, there was no day, no night, and now no time. It could have been anywhere from two days to two weeks before he put the chair back where it was and gave up his vigil.

He wondered why he hadn't started making tally marks on the wall, like a hard case in a prison movie, so he'd know how long he'd been down here. His clothes were starting to come apart from the harsh detergent he'd used too much of and the scrub board he'd used with too much force. That and the trouble getting dressed made him start walking around naked. He kept bathing but stopped shaving. A beard might come in handy.

Geraci was a reader. He had a night school history degree and half a law degree, too, and he prided himself on reading big new biographies and histories. Once he finished the history of Roman warfare he'd brought with him, all he had left were the books that were already there: dime novels, dog-eared pornos, and Machiavelli's *The Prince*. He couldn't bring himself to read the dime novels, and even touching another man's pornos gave him the creeps (though of course he did, in a few weak moments). He'd already read *The Prince,* but he reread it several times as a hedge against going nuts. Soon he realized that it wasn't exactly the right tool for the job.

That was about when he started messing around with the typewriter. It was hulking old black one. At first, he used it to try to write letters—the Parkinson's made longhand difficult—but the impossibility of ever sending the letters made him stop. He liked the writing, though. Banging on that old contraption was a good thing to do with his hands. And it gave him something to do with his mind. He started to fool around with what he eventually thought of as a book. His life's story. If he didn't make it, it would let his daughters know who he'd been and how he'd lived. If it was good enough to be published, maybe it could provide for them.

He pined for his wife and daughters. Every session at the typewriter, his longing for them crept in. He'd read over what he wrote and cringe. He loved them, but they were human beings, too; he was idealizing them into nothingness. He'd wad up the page, then close his eyes and try to *see* them. Moments later, all he'd be picturing is Charlotte naked and doing various things in bed, especially that cute maneuver of hers when he made love to her from behind. He'd jerk off and then spend the next however-long time hating himself. Also, she'd done that thing maybe twice. Maybe one time and then just a little bit once more.

Another problem was that he'd get carried away and write exciting, violent passages that felt true as he wrote them but had never happened. By and large, these scenes amused him. It was what people wanted, wasn't it? But then he'd think that what readers really want are books that give them the inside dope on how things are. Thus, more wadded-up paper, more time wondering just who the fuck he thought he was kidding.

The wadded-up pages far outnumbered the keepers. His supply of typing paper wasn't going to last, so he started unwadding and using the other sides and brown paper towels, too. He used fresh sheets only when retyping a page he thought was done.

Strike that. They were never done. Invariably, he'd read back over what he thought was done—a day later? a week?—and he'd hate himself all over again. Geraci was a smart man who'd always done well in classes where he'd had to write papers, but it turned out—to his surprise—that writing a book was a pain in the ass.

He loved his title, though: *Fausto's Bargain.* By Fausto Dominick Geraci, Jr. He hadn't decided whether to use Ace, his nickname. It would help people say his name in the Americanized way he preferred. He'd boxed under that name (on those occasions he hadn't pretended to be somebody else entirely), so some readers might know him for that. Also, Geraci planned to write about his adventures flying planes in the early days of his narcotics operation, which made using Ace a good idea and had, in fact, been partly why the nickname stuck. On the other hand, it might give people the wrong idea. Geraci wouldn't get on a plane now for anything. Plus, when he typed out *Ace,* it looked bad. *Look at me, I'm Ace!* Nobody would want to read that asshole's book.

And that was just the work the title page took.

Soon, he was reading the dime novels, if only for pointers. He was shocked how good many of them were. *Home Is the Sailor. I Am Legend. A Swell-Looking Babe. Cassidy's Girl. Sweet Slow Death.* So good, it was hard to stop and think about how the writers were doing what they were doing and how Geraci might steal from them. Even the worst ones—like *Sex Life of a Cop,* which turned out to be a porno—seemed better than what Geraci had been churning out, although he was aware that he might be losing his mind.

It was about then that he started hearing things.

The bedrock underneath Lake Erie was honeycombed with salt-mining tunnels. For years, there had been rumors that Forlenza had contracted to have a passageway drilled that would allow someone to walk from here to the mainland, yet even though Geraci sometimes thought he could hear drilling, he wasn't holding his breath.

He heard what he thought might be footsteps. Off and on, he heard what sounded like furniture being dragged around. Several times, he thought he heard dogs bark. Occasionally, he'd have sworn he could hear rushing water, and he'd stare at the walls, waiting for the lake to burst through and drown him like a rat. Once, Geraci thought he heard Handel's *Messiah*, which might have meant that it was Christmas but might also have meant that he was dreaming.

Soon he found himself asleep and dreaming about being asleep, awake and unsure if he might really be asleep.

He might have been down in that hole for a year. Or it might have been six weeks. One morning, he woke up and thought, fuck it, whatever's up there was better than living no life at all in this rat hole. Or maybe he dreamed it and then woke up, he wasn't sure. Still, he got out of bed with a sense of mission. He bathed. He did what he could to trim the beard. His shortcomings with the scissors convinced him that trying to cut his shaggy hair would make him look even worse, so he slicked it back with pomade—there was a case of the stuff—and hoped this would not be how he looked in his mug shot. He found a ball of twine and tied together what he had of his book, cursing at the difficulty of making a decent knot. Then he found clothes that weren't yet reduced to rags, took a deep breath, and submitted to the hell of buttoning and fastening. But he was having a good day, and it came easier than he'd feared. His clothes hung on him loosely.

The two wads of cash he'd brought with him weighed about the same as baseballs. They had the same pleasing heft. In his pants pockets, they bulged out like tumors. He tucked a pistol in his waistband.

Go.

He stood in front of the steel door for what, even by his wrecked internal clock, was a long time. He kept his hand on the handle. Even if he somehow made it out of there, where would he go? Canada was only a few miles away, but he didn't know shit about Canada. The Ohio shore was closer. He'd thought about it countless times but never settled on a plan.

Just go.

He went. Manuscript in one hand, the other on the butt of the pistol.

His shoes on the metal stairs echoed in the stairwell like thunderclaps. The upper shelter was empty. It gave Geraci that feeling he got when he came back from a vacation and everything in his house was exactly as he'd left it and yet different. The reality of how a thing was didn't square with how he'd been remembering it.

Geraci flicked on the light in the hidden guest suite, which was dusty and exactly as he'd left it, however long ago. His mind was pushing him back, but his legs carried him forward. He strode into the abandoned casino that had been down here since Prohibition. The bar was draped in a tarp. The mirror behind the bar was cracked, the bandstand water-damaged.

Broken, dust-caked gaming tables were stacked with mundane household clutter too worthless to sell or give away. All just as he'd left it.

Then he heard the sound of running feet—boots—and froze. He set his papers on the bar and slowly pulled out his gun.

"You're dead!" a shrill voice cried out. A boy's. "I killed you."

"*You're* dead!" shouted a second boy. "I got you good! I'm telling."

"If you tell, I'll kill you for real!"

"If you kill me, my dad will kill you!"

They were running down the stairs, toward Geraci.

"My dad will kill your dad!"

"You think your dad can do anything, but he's just a dad."

"My dad *can* do anything."

Geraci put the gun back in his waistband, letting his untucked shirttail fall over it.

Two dark-haired boys dressed in cowboy gear came skidding around the corner, both about eight years old, the taller one chasing the shorter one, the taller one wearing a black hat, the shorter boy a white one. They saw Geraci and stopped. The smaller boy slipped on the old ballroom floor, then scrambled to his feet. The taller boy looked like he might be related to Vincent Forlenza—a grandson? great-grandson?—but Geraci couldn't be sure.

"Are your parents home?" Geraci said. His voice sounded strange in his ears.

The boys exchanged a look, then, as one, raised their guns and pointed them at him.

"Who wants to know?" said the taller boy.

"I'm a friend of theirs," Geraci said. "Are they home?"

"Where'd you come from?" the taller boy asked.

"You're hairy," the shorter boy said.

"That's right," Geraci said. "I'm Harry, a friend of your parents." Then he realized what the boy meant. The beard.

"Give me one good reason I shouldn't just kill you now," said the taller boy.

"Everybody's over at my house," the shorter boy volunteered, and the other boy glowered at him. They kept their guns on Geraci.

"Right, *your* house," Geraci said, banging the heel of his hand against his forehead, then grabbing the manuscript and rushing past them. "That's where I was supposed to meet everybody. How could I have been so absentminded?"

He took the stairs two at a time while, behind him, the boys set off a hail of cap gun fire.

"*Got* you, mister!"

"I shot him *first*!"

"I shot him *deader*! Die, Injun, die!"

OUTSIDE, THE MIDDAY SUN SHONE ON WHAT LOOKED LIKE six inches of new-fallen snow, and Geraci, half blinded, couldn't remember when he'd seen anything more beautiful. He took a searing lungful of winter air. A sob caught in his throat. The mere thought of beauty made him think of Charlotte and the girls. He wiped tears from his face (it was the wind; unavoidable) and kept going, down the freshly plowed driveway toward the dock. There was no one in sight. He considered running back in the lodge and taking a coat, but odds were he wouldn't find anything big enough. For now, the cold felt good, like the blade of a shovel driving the life back into him.

And then he saw that trying to brave the subarctic wind in a summer-weight sport coat was the least of his problems.

The lake was frozen.

Short of walking across the ice, the only way off the island was by air. There was an airstrip at the other end of the island, private planes he could (theoretically) steal or commandeer. But stealing a plane was tough even if you knew how to fly (which probably he still did), since making sure the maintenance had been done took time he didn't have. Getting a pilot to fly the thing at gunpoint posed other problems.

Who was he kidding? Even under the best of circumstances, if given the choice between flying and the worst-case scenario, Nick Geraci would take his chances with that scenario.

He ducked into a service garage near the boathouse. He looked out a window, back up the drive. The boys hadn't followed him, at least not yet.

"Who's there?" A man in a red plaid overcoat and an earflap hat—the kind Nick's father used to wear—peered out from behind a stack of bagged rock salt. He was sitting at a metal desk, sipping coffee from a thermos cup and flipping through a girlie magazine. "You a guest?"

Startled, Geraci took a moment.

The man frowned and got up. "Can I *help* you with something, buddy?"

"Sure, *buddy*." Geraci drew his gun. "What do you use to plow the snow?"

Geraci relieved the man of his hat and coat, stuffed a clean rag in his mouth, and wrapped him to the desk chair in duct tape.

The man had pissed himself.

Leave this guy here, and he's a witness. Kill him, and move on.

Geraci squeezed the man's shoulder. "The worst," he whispered, "is over."

But then Geraci lowered his gun.

If the cops or the Feds *were* on his ass, clipping this *pisciasotto* was a sure path to becoming the highest-ranking made guy ever to hit death row.

"Cold in here." Geraci found a thermostat and turned up the heat. "My good deed for the day." He winked.

Minutes later, atop a sputtering red tractor, in the caretaker's hat and too-small coat, swaddled in horse blankets, Geraci bounced along on the rough surface of the lake, snow chains biting into the ice and drifted snow, cursing the wind and learning as he went how to use the plow. The sitting duck to end all sitting ducks.

Canada was out of the question now. Ohio was closer. Again and again, he looked back for the men who, surely, were coming after him. Slowly, Rattlesnake Island receded from view.

He was sitting on his manuscript. He'd lashed a gas can to the back of the tractor, just in case. Geraci had never even been on a riding lawn mower. He guessed he had six or seven miles in front of him. Who knew how far a tank of gas would go?

The only signs of life were off to the east—ice fishermen just off South Bass Island, with sleds and little shanties on skis that must be at least as heavy as the stolen tractor.

It occurred to him that his father was an ice fisherman, too. He'd never taken Nick. Nick always imagined the old man sitting in his homemade coffinlike shanty, stewing in cheap red wine and bitterness, head down, staring into the void—just like home, only colder.

He laughed. First he hears a kid say his dad can do anything, then he sees that earflap hat. Now this: ice fishing. While Nick Geraci was not especially superstitious—he'd walk under a ladder if it saved him a step—he chose to take all this as an omen. And why not? He certainly had no one else he could call who'd be as trustworthy as his father. Before he retired to Arizona, Fausto Geraci worked as a Teamster and did other jobs for friends of the Forlenzas. He could put Nick in touch with Cleveland guys who would help. Presuming his father was still alive.

A handful of the ice fishermen must have heard the motor and came out of their shanties. A few called to him. Geraci turned his face into the wind and headed the other way, southwest around Green Island, an uninhabited little bird sanctuary, the long way to the mainland. Then he looked back. The ice fishermen seemed to be pointing at him and laughing, but no one was following him.

No airplanes that he could see or hear.

As he passed the skeletal lighthouse on Green Island—more of a scaffolding, really—the mainland came into view. Geraci kept his eyes on that lighthouse, but there didn't seem to be anyone up there. He was waiting for the other shoe to drop, and it kept not dropping.

There were no ice fishermen that he could see anywhere near the coast-line. He pointed the tractor toward what looked like a sloping bit of shore he could pull onto.

As he drew closer to land, he had to plow through bigger drifts, a few higher than the plow blade, several that forced him to throw the tractor into reverse and make an end run around the piled-up snow. Several times, he jammed the blade into the ice too hard and nearly got stuck.

Then, finally, he did get stuck.

Just like that, he buried the tractor in snow up to the hubs of the rear wheels. He went back and forth a few times. The plow blade seemed to be stuck in a crack in the ice. The ice made dull cracking noises. The rear wheels spun and melted patches beneath them but didn't move the trac-tor at all. Wisps of acrid black smoke wafted from the engine.

Geraci climbed down into snow and immediately cursed his stupidity. The snow was wet and so, now, were his feet. He had on Italian loafers, when he could have lifted the caretaker's boots, too. He grabbed the man-uscript and sized up the task ahead: maybe half a mile to go. He regarded the stuck tractor. As if in answer to a prayer he hadn't gotten around to of-fering up, there was a dull grinding noise, like a building about to collapse.

Geraci took off running, after a fashion. In recent years he'd gotten a little lax about his roadwork. The gun fell out of his pants, but behind him there was a loud, sharp crack. He kept going. His shoes were soaked. His lungs were on fire. The cracking continued, and he kept running, and he heard what sounded like a gigantic slurp, and he kept on running.

He stopped, bent at the waist, and cocked his head to see the hole in the ice where the tractor had been.

He recovered enough to keep walking. He kept hearing the cracking, kept thinking that at any second he was going to fall through the god-damned ice. Finally, with a wet *whooshing* sound, he plunged up to his knees in filthy brown icewater. He stifled a yell. But he was only ten feet from shore, tops.

Sometimes, it's just your lucky day.

Though luck's the wrong word. Geraci had made a mint off saps who thought they were on a roll. Gambling profits by and large came from idiots who thought math class was a waste of time. Geraci believed in probability and randomness but not luck. Logical explanations you'll never hear about.

The reason there were no ice fishermen here was that a sewage pipe as big around as a railroad tunnel pumped warm, nitrogen-rich water into the lake near where the tractor sank. When Geraci finally made it ashore, he saw THIN ICE warnings all over the place. Amusing, but he had business to attend to. He had to steal a car, crank up the heat, get a county or two away from here, where he'd be safe from any local yokel John Law out to make his career-making grand-theft-tractor bust.

For the first time in ages, Geraci wasn't some crazy degenerate living in a rat hole, some fuck who spent his life looking over his shoulder. All a man can do is keep moving. Play offense, play defense, but for Christ's sake, play. For too long, Nick Geraci had failed to do even that.

He was back.

CHAPTER 5

Geraci told the barber he had a job interview coming up. The frayed clothes gave credence to the down-on-his-luck story. The barber asked what line of work he was in. Bookkeeping, Geraci said. The barber said he had a brother who was an accountant. He said it was kind of a straitlaced field, accounting. He demonstrated his point by giving Geraci a horrible haircut. The reason Geraci gave for keeping the beard was that it covered a scar. Better trim it, the barber said, and did. Geraci thanked him and asked for directions to a JC Penney's. It was the sort of neighborhood where there had to be one nearby, and there was. He was somewhere between Cleveland and Akron—nowhere, in other words.

At Penney's, he went into the dressing room and stood in front of a mirror holding up clothes. He wasn't screwing around with buttons and snaps in a public place. He bought a suitcase and enough unstylish clothes to fill it. He felt as if he were shopping for a Halloween costume.

It was late enough now for Nick to find a closed body shop where he could swap a license plate from some wrecked car with the one on his stolen Pontiac. Then he checked into a Howard Johnson's, that orange-roofed avatar of the anonymous, out by the Ohio Turnpike.

Still, no one seemed to be following him.

He would have gone back out, but he couldn't bear getting dressed again. He bought toiletries from a vending machine in the lobby and went to bed.

In the morning, he suffered through getting dressed, and, miraculously bland-looking, he went back to the shopping center, this time to Sears, where he bought a hunting knife, a Ted Williams–brand shotgun, and a box of shells. Then he stopped at an A & P. He bought necessary-looking items like milk and cat food, plus detergent, so that the rolls of dimes he'd come there for would seem laundry-related and mundane. On the way back to the motel, he threw away everything but the dimes.

Buying or renting a car was too risky, at least until he got some new fake identification. But keeping the Pontiac was an even bigger risk. He gassed it up, ran it through a car wash, and drove to the nearest high school. He wiped down the interior, rolled down the windows, and left the car running, begging to be re-stolen.

He walked back from the school, took a Howard Johnson's postcard from the desk drawer in his room, and went around to the motels, restaurants, and filling stations in and around the Turnpike exit, jotting down payphone numbers.

He was officially squared away.

Nick had phones back in Brooklyn he could call, but it would take time to figure out which of his associates he could trust. There was nothing he'd have liked more than to call Charlotte, but if anyone in his family was under surveillance, it would be her. Nick couldn't call his father, not cold. His daughter Barb, a junior at Skidmore, was excitable, a more brittle version of Charlotte: a beauty, with all the benefits and responsibilities attendant thereto. It was Bev he'd call first. She was a freshman at Berkeley. Charlotte hadn't wanted her to go so far away, but Bev had had her reasons, and she'd quietly stuck to her guns; she was Nick's daughter, all right. Barb lived off campus, but Bev lived in a dorm, where the only phones were payphones.

He walked to the Sohio station across the street and went through a lot of dimes calling various numskulls at the university to get Bev's number, nearly as many waiting for the girl who answered the phone to go summon Bev.

"Whoever this is," Bev finally said, "you're a jerk."

True, he thought. "Is that what they teach you at that school?" he said. "How to talk like that to your father?"

"Daddy? I thought you were some . . . Oh my God! Daddy! Where are—"

Then she started to cry.

He let her. He had a warm coat and plenty of dimes. He kept an eye on the cars coming in for gas and the men pumping it, but no one was giving him a second look.

He knew Bev would come around, and, when she did, she justified every bit of his faith in her. She didn't ask any questions he couldn't answer. He assured her that he was fine and that he'd be grateful to her if she passed the good word along to her mother and sister. "In the case of your mother, call what's her face. Her friend across the street."

"Mrs. Brubaker."

"Yeah, her. See if she'll go get your mom and bring her to the phone. Say you tried to call home but the phone was all screwy."

"I can handle it, Dad."

"Tell her that payphone up by the park, across from that statue thing. She'll know the one. Tell her I'll call her there tomorrow at eight."

"Eight. Got it."

"But if I don't call, don't worry. I'm just tied up with business, is all."

"Business." Her voice was faint.

He hated it that he was putting her through this. He hated Michael Corleone for being the cause of it all. He changed the subject, and for a long time they talked about how she was doing at school: well, apparently. She claimed to be OK for money, but he got her address and told her he'd send her some anyway. "Just don't tell your mother," he said.

"Do you think I tell her anything?"

This was said with a hard edge, well beyond the standard father-daughter mock conspiratorial. He should have said something, but he didn't feel like getting into it now. He needed to take care of business. "How's your grandpa?"

"Which?"

"Both, I guess."

Bev laughed. "Yeah, right." She wasn't close to Charlotte's snooty parents, either. "He's terrific, actually."

"Still in Tucson, there?"

"Why wouldn't he be in Tucson?"

Because the last Nick Geraci knew, his father was en route to Sicily, sailing into an ambush, his main protection being that he wasn't the Fausto Geraci they were looking for. "No reason. Can you do me one more little favor? Can you call him, too?"

"Call him *where*?" Didn't miss a beat, this one.

"Seeing as you're getting an A in Spanish, try a lady down there named Conchita Cruz. She doesn't speak much English, but she's a friend of your grandfather's." He started to give her the number.

"You're kidding, right?"

"You said A. I took notes." A white lie, but he did remember her saying it.

"Nonno Fausto and Miss Conchita got married."

"*Married*?"

"Married."

Geraci looked at his reflection in the phone booth glass and barely recognized himself. "Married." He jabbed his room key absently into the coin return. His father had married a Mexican. Hard to imagine his old pals back in Cleveland accepting that one. "So, what, I got a new mother now? When did that happen?"

"When he got back from his vacation in Italy. *Life is short*, he kept saying. They're so cute together."

"They can't understand a word the other one's saying."

"There's always the language of love." This cracked her up. "I'm sorry, Daddy. It's absolutely bonkers, you're right, but they're happy."

Hearing his daughter laugh at love provoked a little pang in his gut, but he let it go.

"Call your grandpa at home. Tell him to write down the number of the phone booth at that diner he goes to all the time, whaddayacallit's."

"Lester's."

"That's the one. Lester's. I'll call him at home, at noon his time tomorrow. He can give me the number of the payphone, and I'll call him back on it."

He gave her three of the phone booth numbers he'd just written down and a complicated schedule of when he'd be checking them. "If I don't answer, don't worry. I'm just tied up."

She started crying again, and he waited that out, too, before they said good-bye.

"WHERE ARE YOU?" SAID FAUSTO GERACI. "I'LL COME get you."

Nick burst out laughing. As if he were a boy who'd been picked up for shoplifting. "That's not going to work, Dad. For one thing, if there's anyone keeping an eye—"

"Anywhere in this country, I can be there in three days. I don't count Alaska or Hawaii, only the real America."

His father was still bitter that the move to make Sicily America's fortyninth state fell apart, only to have Alaska and Hawaii sneak in just ten years later.

"I need you to set me up with some people in Cleveland you really trust."

"I don't trust nobody, nothing. I'll come get you. Cleveland I can get to in two days. That's all the farther you got, Cleveland?"

"What about Mikey Z?"

"That Polack? He's so lazy, you'd be lucky to get him out of bed in two days."

Mike Zielinsky, a Teamster official, had been a friend of Fausto's since childhood. His son was a Cleveland city councilman now. Mikey Z would know the right people to call.

"Just call him for me, huh?"

"Two days. And don't give me it won't work. Who's gonna follow me I don't want following me, eh? How is that possible?"

"It's possible, Dad." But he had to admit, unless the person following him was the reigning champion at Le Mans, not likely. In certain circles, his father, Fausto the Driver, was a legend: a retired Teamster who'd driven at least two million miles professionally, many of them very fast, sometimes with passengers whose business he stayed out of, all without ever getting a ticket or in an accident (the exception being a few that weren't really accidents).

"C'mon, where you at, hotshot? Everything's gonna work out great. Geraci and son."

Jair-AH-chee, rather than *Juh-RAY-see,* another of the old man's running complaints.

"I hear congratulations are in order," Nick said.

"Yeah, well," Fausto said. "You gonna talk or you gonna tell me where you at?"

FORTY-SEVEN HOURS LATER, FAUSTO GERACI WHIPPED HIS Olds Starfire into the HoJo parking lot. It was two-toned, red and white, with leather seats and power everything. He'd had the black Rocket 88 it replaced for ten years.

"You made good time."

"Good time, nothing." Fausto waved at his son in disgust. "I'd have got here hours ago if it didn't take me longer to piss than it does to fill the gas tank."

Their embrace was firm, wordless, and long. They hadn't seen each other for months, had each thought the other might be dead. They had never been happier in one another's company, but their happiness might have been lost on anyone who didn't know them. They released each other. "Goddamn," Fausto said, stamping his feet. "I can't take this cold no more."

They went into the hotel to get Nick's things.

"Humor me, Dad, and tell me you took precautions."

"Look, me and her, we're married, and that's the end of it. Life is short. Leave it at that. I'm not getting into nothing personal, which, to begin with, ain't none of your business."

"Precautions *getting here*."

"Getting here?" Fausto chuckled. "I took precautions beautiful. Anybody watching me, they see Conchita leave in my car. She drives it from time to time, so nobody's thinkin' nothing. Who's gonna think I went out in the garage and climbed in the trunk? She parks it at her job, that cannery, opens the trunk a crack, walks off, and—butta-beepa-da-boppa-da-boop—I drive off. And get this: across the desert and not on no road. When I'm on a road, finally, it's straight as an arrow for a hundred miles." He pantomimed a pistol shot and laughed like a maniac.

Nick was taken aback. When his mother was alive, Fausto never let her drive his car.

"Nice haircut, by the way." Fausto touched his son's beard and just shook his head.

"Speaking of by the way: nice car. I mean that."

"Ain't it a beaut?" Beaming, Fausto slapped Nick on the back. "I did a job for a guy you maybe know. It paid real good. There's three hundred forty-five horses under that hood, every one a fucking Thoroughbred."

"This came from *that* money?" Meaning the cash he'd given his father for the trip to Sicily and a healthy tribute on top of that for his trouble. Nick was thrilled. He'd presumed his father wouldn't keep the change. "I don't think I ever got you a Christmas present you used or picked up a tab when you didn't make a federal case out of it."

"There's a difference between a gift you get and a job you do. C'mon, let's go."

"We didn't even talk about where we're going."

"I still got that spare room you used the last time you needed to lay low."

"I don't think that'll work this time."

"Wherever we go, make it anywhere but here. Someplace warm."

"I was thinking Mexico."

"Warm there, all right. Awful big place, though, Mexico."

"I was thinking about asking Conchita about that."

"Conchita? I don't know. She don't talk much about where she came from."

"She's got people down there, though, right? Family?"

Fausto grabbed his son's suitcase. "You want to talk to her, talk to her. I can't stop you."

"Why would you want to stop me?"

"Who said I did? Let's go."

As they were tossing Nick's meager possessions into the trunk of the Starfire, Fausto pointed at the shotgun. "Tell you what, you're gonna need that where you're going."

"What, in Canada?"

"Canada? You mean Mexico."

Nick shook his head. "Canada first."

Fausto shrugged. "That's the long way to Mexico, though. Also, very cold."

"I'm aware of that. We're not going to stay. I just need to take care of some things. What did you mean about needing the shotgun where I'm going?"

"Oh, that. In the car, is what I meant. You gonna *ride* shotgun." The old man cackled at his own joke.

"All due respect, Dad, I think I better drive. Did you sleep at all on the way here?"

"Let me tell you something. You get to be my age, sleep? Forget sleep." But he put his head down and trudged to the passenger side, mumbling all the way. "You want to drive, drive," he said. "Let's get the show on the road."

In the middle of the front seat was a satchel full of neatly folded roadmaps. He took one out, apparently at random. Iowa. Fausto read maps less for navigation than the way another man might study *The Power of Positive Thinking*, the way his own son read and reread *The Prince*. Soon, he nodded off.

About an hour later, Fausto snapped awake from what had seemed to be a dead sleep and, without missing a beat, said, "Faster."

"You want to drive," Nick said, pulling onto the shoulder, "drive."

"Attaboy." Fausto caressed the dashboard. "This baby rides real nice, though, eh?"

THEY WENT TO BUFFALO AND CROSSED INTO CANADA FROM there. Nick spent a few hours leaving behind traces of himself. Using different aliases—one he'd used so long he'd even thrown a few fights under that name—he rented an apartment, bought a cheap car, and even had his subscription to *Time* magazine forwarded there. He bought his father a parka and thick snowboots, which had no impact whatsoever on his complaints about the cold. They had dinner in Buffalo, at a steak joint Fausto knew about that he said was frequented by low-level guys connected to the Cuneo Family, so word would get back but not too fast.

Then they headed south.

Soon, America's heartland was a blur outside the windows of the two-toned Starfire, and so, for Nick Geraci, were the next few weeks. He and his father had all the time in the world to talk, really *talk*. They never did, which suited them both fine. Fausto, who used to insist on driving in silence, not only played the radio but also had somehow worked up an interest in country music. For hours at a time, he'd mutter along with Lefty Frizzell, Marty Robbins, and George Jones, slapping his son's hand whenever he tried to change the station. On open roads, he kept the speed between 90 and 100. His uncanny ability to sense speed traps failed him only once, outside Denver. Nick cursed and sunk down in his seat, and his father told him to shut up. Fausto flashed an Ohio highway patrolman's badge he'd gotten somewhere. Moments later they were on their way. Fausto was clairvoyant about when it was better to flash that badge and when it was better yet to flash it with a fifty tucked underneath. Fausto, back up over 80, said that maybe nobody's out to get him, did he ever think of that? Nick told him he didn't know the whole story, and Fausto said he'd just gotten the perfect idea for his own tombstone: HERE LIES FAUSTO THE DRIVER, WHO DIDN'T KNOW THE WHOLE STORY. When Nick asked his father if he would please just as a favor not drive so fast, Fausto told him that everyone in Italy drove like this, and nobody there ever got in wrecks. Had he ever seen a wreck there? Nick pointed out that they weren't *in* Italy. Fausto called his son a "goddamned fucking genius," and for another several hours they said fewer words to one another than they heard sung by Mr. Hank Williams. They had, without a doubt, never been closer.

They chose a nondescript, medium-size motel in Nogales that was walking distance from the border. They got the numbers of two nearby payphones. Nick would go to one at noon and the other at five and wait for Fausto or anyone else to call. This simple plan in place, the men parted without fanfare, though the old man drove away slowly, which seemed a gesture toward emotion.

In most decent-size border towns there can be found geniuses in the art of forged passports and driver's licenses. Go into the right bar, don't ask too many questions, tip well but not like you have anything to prove, and the next thing you know you've got two or three good ones from which to choose. Don't forget, as Nick Geraci did not, to compare the forgeries to the genuine articles.

Conchita's people were from Taxco, a place Nick Geraci had never heard of. "She says there's plenty of Americans there," Fausto said. "Plenty of Canadians, Europeans, coloreds, Germans, the works. You won't stick out or nothing. A lot of 'em are starving artists and such, so with that beard you'll be perfect. She's got a cousin who's got a friend who knows about an apartment a Canadian fella died in. It's got books, which I know is your speed. I set it up so they're holding it for you. Just say you're Flaco Cruz's friend, which is the cousin. You want me to get you there? There's a place I heard about where if you got a truck you can drive across the desert, over the border and back. I can get ahold of a truck."

"I'll be fine," Nick said. "I appreciate it, though."

"No you don't." Fausto said this with something like tenderness, maybe even love.

WHEN NICK GERACI FIRST ARRIVED IN TAXCO, HE'D KEPT TO himself. Spanish was enough like Italian for him to muddle through. The apartment had come with books, but all of them were in French, even the dime novels. But there was also, alphabetized and in custom-built shelves, a collection of jazz records, many fairly new. Geraci liked jazz but hadn't paid much attention to what had come along since the big bands. The first things he listened to were records he already knew, Benny Goodman and Les Halley and such. But one day he was flipping through the unfamiliar names and the blonde on the cover of Chet Baker's *Chet* was such a dead ringer for Charlotte it knocked the breath out of him. He played the record, and he was crazy about it. Char and the night and the music. He started exploring the whole collection. He'd sit in the dark all night, sipping mineral water and listening to Jimmy Smith and Wes Montgomery, John Coltrane, Miles Davis, Cannonball Adderly, and Sonny Rollins. Soon, he got a secondhand portable typewriter and plenty of paper, and he let the records repeat as he wrote.

Geraci settled in to the slow, easy rhythms of the town, and day by day he grew more optimistic that no one was pursuing him. He might have been a free man, except that no man with a family can ever be free.

He'd set up regular lines of communication to Charlotte and the girls—phone procedures and a post office box in Tucson where they could send reel-to-reel tapes to each other, which Fausto could then forward. And he began to think about which of the hundreds of men who'd been under his absolute control might be trusted to help him mount an offensive against the soulless prick who'd tried to kill him. He had no shortage of candidates. He was actually more worried about Charlotte. She seemed like she was near the end of her rope, embarrassed by how friends and neighbors looked at her, as lonely as he was but through no fault of her own. She was the rare sort of woman who didn't talk too much about her feelings, but once she'd broken down and mentioned divorce. He couldn't really blame her, but he did. He doubted she'd ever really do that, but then again, during his months in hiding, he'd come face-to-face with the cold reality of "ever."

In the zócalo there was one loud fiesta after another, and eventually it drew Geraci more often out into the streets and among the company of his fellow exiles. When he didn't volunteer much about himself, they didn't press him. Geraci had seen the same thing in parts of New York, where people shared not a nationality or a religion but a collective misfit fate. They'd fled or been kicked out of where they'd come from and had come together here, with little in common but that. There was a hairless, egg-shaped Russian composer. A retired Negro ballplayer who owned a restaurant and was married to a Mexican lady who painted huge pictures of herself naked. A Cuban widow whose husband had owned a candy factory in Cienfuegos. A Bulgarian actor who ran a fleet of Volkswagen taxis. Et cetera. Geraci initially kept his distance from two American writers, Wiley Moulton and Wiley's friend Iggy, not because they were *finocchios* but because they were from New York. But it turned out they'd been living in their own world so long, writing books about made-up things, that they couldn't tell you who the American president was, much less recognize the bearded, thinner version of the Corleone *capo* whose disappearance had once been news. To them, he was the fake name he'd given them, just some mook with a scraggly beard and the shakes who was trying to write a book and probably kidding himself, but so what? Who's it hurt?

Most afternoons, holding court in one bar or another, was the emperor of the expats, a haunted-looking Southerner and world-class talker named Spratling. He claimed to be (or have been) bosom buddies with Diego Rivera, John Wayne, Dolores del Rio, and Trotsky. For years, he shared (or claimed to have shared) an apartment in New Orleans with William Faulkner; he claimed to have written a book with "Bill" in which they made fun of the great Sherwood Anderson, a mentor to them both. Spratling had come to Taxco thirty years ago and built the jewelry business from nothing into a multimillion-dollar something, selling pieces he designed himself that people all over the world bought because they looked so traditionally Mexican. During the war, he let private investors into his company. Three years later, he'd lost everything. Now he lived on a chicken ranch south of town, along with twenty-three Great Danes and a pair of boa constrictors, living off the money he made smuggling pre-Columbian art into the hands of private collectors. Geraci liked him. Men like Spratling made men like Nick Geraci possible.

One such afternoon, Spratling launched into a story about a couple from Chicago who'd come down here and tried to teach an eagle to hunt. They bought it in Arkansas for some reason and named it Caligula. They had big plans that they could get it to bring them back iguanas, wild pigs, and small deer. Some of the other newcomers were skeptical. Geraci was not—he'd seen the grandiose thoughts and visions of vainglorious Chicagoans in action—and he made an early exit.

When he got back to the apartment, he went straight to the hi-fi. As he was bent over the record player, dropping the needle on *Mingus Ah Um,* he saw a flash of bright metal behind his horsehair sofa. His right arm shot up to block the knife faster than his brain registered that it *was* a knife. He had his hand around a muscled forearm, and he spun around to face a short, curly-haired young man, all in black, about as wide as he was tall, still clutch-

ing a butcher knife. The kid was strong but untrained. Geraci pulled him
into a clinch. The kid held on, and Geraci could feel his own muscles twitch-
ing and about to give. He pushed the kid away and a split second later
landed a clean left hook on the kid's melon. It sent his legs in the air. His
head took a second blow as it smacked hard against the tile floor.

The record skipped a groove but kept going. *Oh, yass!* an ecstatic voice
shouted. *Better get hit in yo' soul!*

The young man moaned and rocked slowly from side to side on the
floor, stunned but not out.

"Stay down," Geraci said, picking up the knife. "Whoever the fuck you
are, stay down. Who the fuck *are* you? Who sent you?"

Blood ran from the young man's right ear. He continued to moan.

"I asked you a question."

The man said something Geraci couldn't make out.

"Speak up."

"*Bocchicchio.*"

Nick Geraci let out a gallows chuckle. The first to find him wasn't the
CIA, the FBI, a Corleone assassin, or someone from another Family. No,
it was this primitive kid. "You're not really a Bocchicchio, though, right?
A Bocchicchio per se. What's your name?"

"I am the blood of Carmine Marino." He said it as if he were reading it
off crib notes.

A knife was what a man concerned about getting caught would use. A
true Bocchicchio wouldn't have cared. He would have recognized his own
weakness as a close-in fighter and gunned Geraci down, the consequences
be hanged, even if that meant the assassin was hanged, too. The Bocchicchios were the most single-mindedly vengeful clan Sicily had ever seen, and
once the most powerful. But after a century of unyielding vendettas, there
remained few true Bocchicchios. The handful of surviving cousins had had
their blood so cooled down by marrying outside the clan that they'd abandoned the family traditions.

As only the very young can, the young man abruptly scrambled to his feet, and Geraci shook his head and flattened him with a right cross. This time at least the kid landed on his ass and not his head.

The record didn't skip at all. A wailing sax solo handed off to the piano man.

"Stay down."

"You killed my cousin." His nose was bleeding now, too.

"Your cousin? Did you even *know* Carmine?"

The kid answered by not answering.

"Because he was like the son I never had. I knew the guy better than you ever did. I loved him. How does you coming for me avenge anything?"

"You sent him to his death." His accent was American through and through. Midwestern, even. This was someone who did not want to do this.

"Look, Carmine was a soldier. Carmine went into battle, and the other army took him out. Vanquished him. You want revenge, who you supposed to take it out on? The general, or do you go after the enemy, the ones who killed him?"

"Who are those people?"

That was a good question.

"Let me ask *you* a question," Geraci said. "How did you find me?"

The kid shook his head.

"Who knows you're here?" Geraci said.

He didn't answer, but when Geraci extended a hand he accepted it and, dazed, stood. Geraci backed him into a corner, then tossed the extraneous knife across the room. The nose and ear kept dripping blood onto the green tile.

"It would be easy for us to be on the same side," Geraci said. "The kind of revenge you're going after is penny-ante compared to the kind of game I'm playing, and it's a game I can cut you in on. You know? Because that's how you avenge Carmine's death. Do you understand?"

Clearly, this dumb-as-a-post kid did not.

"I didn't kill Carmine," Geraci said. "I'm not the one responsible for killing Carmine, and so your business here is all in vain. In fact, it could be entirely finished if you'd just tell me three simple things. Three simple things and you go back to Saint Louis."

"I'm not from Saint Louis."

"That's a good boy! But where you're from is unfortunately not a question that's on our final exam here. So here we go. Question number one: how'd you get here?"

"How'd I get here?"

"All right, good. You understand. Yes, how'd you get here?"

He thought about it a while. "Bus," he said. "Plane to Mexico City, then bus."

Geraci smiled. "I see an A coming. I bet your mama's gonna love it, you getting an A. Because I know she ain't the one who put you up to this. But those people, you think they'll be the slightest comfort to your mama when she's bawling her eyes out, howling like a broken animal, throwing herself on the coffin as you get lowered into the cold ground? The way Carmine's mother did at his funeral, which I noticed you did not attend, even though, as you so eloquently put it," Geraci said, patting him on his bloody cheek, "you are his *blood.*"

A flicker of self-doubt or maybe grief went across the young man's soft face. Carmine's mother had of course done no such thing.

"Question number two: who knows you're here?"

The kid wiped his face with the sleeve of his black shirt, as if the blood were snot. "I need a towel."

"Wrong answer. That's a tough one, though. We'll come back to it. Question number three: how'd you find me?"

The kid spat pink blood on Geraci's white shirt, for which Geraci administered another blunt-force head trauma. The kid crashed into a potted plant. Geraci flicked his hand quickly, as if it were wet.

"I don't know you, kid, and, I'll be honest, I don't care what happens to you, but I still . . . well, you know? Where does it end? What, really, is the point of you killing me? Or of me killing you? What's it accomplish? I know I'm asking a lot of questions. Give this a long think. Did you know

I was a professional heavyweight boxer? I was. I KO'd a guy who later on gave Joe Louis fits. Keep thinking. I'll wait right here."

The kid again popped up. He kept his feet much better this time, but another half dozen blows and he was back on the tile floor, his blood muddying the dirt from the toppled plant.

"I'll tell you," he said.

"That's a good boy," Geraci said.

The kid again rose. "When you tell *me* who killed Carmine."

Raise the dead! shouted the jazz man. The song finished.

"This is getting us nowhere," Geraci said.

Minutes later, he was rolling the boy up in the rug.

ON THE WAY BACK FROM THE VALLEY OF PUTREFYING garbage, Nick Geraci stopped for a drink. The doctor who'd treated him back in New York had said that many people with Geraci's condition develop an aversion to alcohol, even the smell of it. So far, this was a symptom Geraci had dodged. He'd never been a heavy drinker, but he did drink less now, afraid each sip might be the last.

Many of the same people who'd been gathered around Spratling when he was telling the eagle story were gathered around him still.

The cold bottled beer Geraci ordered felt good in his swollen hands.

Iggy the writer started to tell a story, but Spratling interrupted. He wasn't a man who liked to lose the floor. "Speaking of predators taken into captivity and brought against their will to the wilds of Latin America," Spratling said, provoking a laugh, even from Iggy, "when I was up in New Orleans last week I heard the most *amazing* story. There's a gangster there, a handsome but quite ruthless fellow named Carlo 'the Whale' Tramonti, who runs *everything* in Louisiana. Perhaps you've heard of a colorful political boss up there, our late and lamented Kingfish? Hmm? Well, the Kingfish was Mr. Tramonti's *errand* boy. He was the go-between in a deal between Mr. Tramonti and another gangster in New York, in which slot machines and other nonindigenous vices came down to the bayou. Mr. Tramonti got his nickname not because he's fat but because it's a creature much bigger than a kingfish. A whale is."

The other gangster, Geraci knew, had been Vito Corleone.

Geraci had always heard that Tramonti's nickname came from his organization's success at swallowing everything up. The New Orleans Family was the oldest in the U.S.; under Tramonti, it supposedly had become the richest as well.

A fresh martini arrived for Spratling. "*So,*" he said, taking it straight from the waiter's hand and downing half. "Apparently, Mr. Tramonti, an Italian-born gentleman, never quite managed to become a U.S. citizen, although he *did* have a passport from Colombia, which I doubt he could *spell* and where he certainly had never been. One day, there the Whale is, in his top-secret office out by the airport, dressed in a silk suit and, God knows, cooking up evil plans, when there's a knock on the door. Guess who it is, huh? Take a guess who's gone into the whaling business."

Nick Geraci smiled and took a long drink of his beer. He'd learned a long time ago—in a gym in Cleveland that smelled of camphor and wet wool and the stale sweat of ghosts—how to let a fight come to him.

BOOK II

CHAPTER 6

On Columbus Day, in the darkest hour of the early morning, forty floors above a dead-end cul-de-sac on the eastern lip of Manhattan, in a penthouse bedroom that overlooked the FDR Drive, the East River, and Roosevelt Island, Michael Corleone began to scream.

Moments later, there was what sounded like a struggle of some kind: thumping and banging and breaking glass, then the sound of something, or someone, falling to the floor.

At the opposite end of the penthouse suite, Al Neri—who slept in the nude when Michael's kids weren't around, which was most of the time—leaped out of bed, pressed a button he'd had installed on his nightstand, grabbed a long steel flashlight, and ran down the hall toward his boss. The screaming was new, and so was the sound of fighting, but these nighttime episodes were not unprecedented. The likely culprit was Michael's diabetes. Or maybe it was Michael and Rita Duvall, finally having that first big fight; she'd been in L.A. shooting a game show, but maybe it had wrapped early. Realistically, Neri had secured this building so well that there wasn't a Chinaman's chance that anyone had broken in. Still, when a guy's running bare-assed down a hallway toward strange noises in the dead of night, a guy thinks things. *Those fucking Bocchicchios. That cocksucker Geraci.* The bodyguard's face was as calm as that of some civilian out taking the family dog for a brisk walk.

Michael's heavy bedroom door was locked from the inside. Neri had arranged it so that it took a special key to open. The screaming had stopped. Neri pounded on the door. "Hey, boss!" No sound at all from inside. On instinct, Neri tried to kick the door open, slamming the heel of his bare foot against it. Then, cursing, he ran back to his room for the key.

ONE FLIGHT DOWN, LIGHTS BEGAN TO COME ON, FIRST IN Connie Corleone's bedroom and, soon after that, in the bedrooms of Connie's two sons, as well as in the suite at the other end of the building, where Kathy and Francesca lived, the grown twin daughters of Sonny Corleone, Michael's late brother. Francesca's six-year-old son, also called Sonny, did not stir. He was a holy terror when he was awake, but he'd always been a heavy sleeper. Everyone else gathered in the enormous kitchen that Connie had put in this spring, after Michael bought the whole building and moved most of what was left of his family into the top three floors. Theirs had always been a family that slept with the windows open.

Connie double-checked the locks. Francesca dialed a special number, and a guard in a war room off the lobby said everything was under control. "Everything's under control," Francesca said to her aunt. Connie nodded grimly and started coffee.

Francesca stared at the cradled phone. *Under control.*

Connie asked her boys if they wanted some eggs or to go back to bed— it was a Saturday, so she didn't care either way—and the boys said eggs. The boys asked what that noise was and their mother said it was the television. Francesca tried to make eye contact with Connie, but she looked away.

In the next room, Connie's boy Victor—a sullen mess, even by the standards of fourteen-year-old American boys—put James Brown's "Night Train" on the record player, full blast. Her eight-year-old, Little Mike—an angel, though he worshipped Victor—started dancing crazily around the room. Ordinarily, this would have gotten a rise out of Connie, whose hatred of such music had fanned the flames of Victor's love of it. But all Connie did was light a cigarette and sigh. Victor pretended to be a prizefighter, training, and Little Mike copied that, too.

Below, on the thirty-eighth floor, where the Hagens lived, Tom and Theresa and their two young daughters slept, far enough from the commotion to be excluded from it. Their sons' rooms were empty.

Michael's ex-wife Kay was living in Maine (yes, he *had* hit her, but only once, when she lied about her miscarriage and told him she'd had an abortion; the punch—and his consequent remorse—had gotten her the divorce he'd have never allowed otherwise, a cunning deception Michael Corleone would never uncover). Michael's two children Anthony, twelve, and Mary, ten, were living in Maine as well, attending a first-rate boarding school where Kay now taught. Michael hadn't seen them in months—such a source of pain and even shame that it was rare for anyone on these top three floors to mention them. Once a week, Connie sent Anthony and Mary letters, small presents, and various Italian sweets, but she didn't make a show of it.

Michael's parents, Vito and Carmela, were dead of natural causes, resting in peace in Woodlawn Cemetery in the Bronx, next to his brother Sonny (supposedly killed in a car wreck, though he'd actually been shot by Tattaglia gunmen at a tollbooth on the Jones Beach Causeway), and Francesca's prematurely born daughter Carmela, who'd lived only one day.

Not far away was Connie's husband Carlo (garroted on Michael's orders, revenge for Carlo's role in Sonny's murder, though the killing had been pinned on the Barzini Family).

Francesca's husband, Billy (William Brewster Van Arsdale III), was buried in his family's plot in Florida.

Michael's brother Fredo had gone fishing four years ago and was presumed drowned. The internal gases that make corpses float do not always form in water as cold as Lake Tahoe. His widow, the actress Deanna Dunn (from whom he'd been estranged), had purchased a headstone for him at a cemetery in Beverly Hills, but the ground beneath it was unturned.

Now, rising from below in the private elevator that served only the top three floors, came three armed and trusted security guards.

This forgettably ugly building did not look from the outside like the fortress it was. No passerby would have guessed that it contained a platoon of inconspicuously deployed guards and a small fortune's worth of electronic security devices, much of which came from the same people who supply the same devices to the CIA. This was not a building passersby would even notice: covered in white cladding, its balconies functional and unadorned. Anyone's eye would, in fact, have been drawn across the street to a block of lovely century-old four-story brick walk-ups. Nothing in the building's design would draw the eye up to the slightly more ornate post-Deco three-story penthouse and rooftop garden, which sat atop the building almost like a separate structure. In New York, only tourists look up, and this was hardly a neighborhood that drew tourists: Yorkville, a portion of Manhattan unserved by the subway, all but unmentioned in guidebooks, a residential neighborhood, mostly German but for years a harmonious mix of Irish, Jews, and Italians, too. Except for the sound of the traffic on the FDR and the garbage trucks on the next block, it was quiet at night, especially forty floors up.

MOST OF THE TIME.

"Boss?" Neri called, almost tenderly. He saw the three guards coming and motioned for them to position themselves and watch his back. Then he opened the door and inched inside, flashlight raised. His reflexes were so good, he was as deadly with that thing as most men were with a gun. He hadn't turned it on since he was a rookie cop, but it had been put to repeated good use. He used it to kill some Harlem pimp who had cut up a woman and was raping a twelve-year-old girl. When witnesses said Neri caved in the guy's skull after he was already knocked cold, Neri's superiors, frustrated over years of being unable to control him, had him charged with manslaughter. The Corleones heard about the case. They pulled strings, and the charges were dropped. Neri took the flashlight from the evidence room, quit the Force, and went to work for Michael Corleone, a fresh start he was grateful to get and that he repaid with unswerving loyalty. It was a decision he never regretted. Not once, not even when he was called upon to kill poor Fredo.

Neri flicked on the light switch.

The bed was empty. A heap of blankets and sheets were on the floor. Beside it was a broken juice glass.

"Mike?" Neri said.

On the other side of the bed, something moved.

Michael Corleone rose, slowly, rubbing his head.

"*Madonn'*," Neri said. "You scared me there. You OK?"

"I'm fine." Michael pointed at the flashlight. "Whatever you do, don't shine that thing in my eyes, huh?"

Neri lowered it. The Don was drenched with sweat and pale as moonlight. He sure as fuck didn't *look* fine.

"You, uh . . . alone?" Neri craned his neck, looking around for who or what must surely be here. He strode to Michael's bathroom. Nothing unusual. "It sounded like—"

"Al, I'm fine. Thank you for your concern, all right?"

If it was Rita, he wouldn't be hiding anything. Rita had been here for his spells before.

"So it was your sugar?" Neri said. The diabetes. The juice glass: it added up, to some degree. "Want me to get you some pills or fruit or something?"

"It's not that. It's nothing. Got it?"

Neri nodded. "Watch them satin sheets," he said, pointing. "Slippery as hell."

"I'll try to remember that," Michael said, and cracked a faint smile.

Neri couldn't imagine it was possible that the sounds he'd heard came from only one man, but contradicting Michael Corleone went against his nature. "Happy birthday, by the way."

"Bake me a cake if you want," Michael said, "but otherwise shut up about all that, huh?"

He sat down heavily on the bed. At least part of the reason he'd become something of a folk hero in New York was that he was thought of as movie-star handsome, but in the middle of the night and up close he was an old forty-three. His left cheek sagged unevenly, the result of plastic surgery he'd had to fix his face from when that police captain had crushed it. His hair had gone abruptly white—dashing, maybe, in the right light, but this was not the right light. He was thirsty all the time, and he urinated with excruciating slowness, like an old man. Once, Rita—Miss Marguerite Duvall, the actress Michael was seeing off and on—had let it slip to Neri that Michael had problems in the sack. Happens to everybody, Neri had told her, which he'd said out of loyalty; knock on wood, it hadn't happened to him, except when he was drunk, which he hadn't been since back when he was on the Force.

"No can do on the cake," Neri said. "You'll have to wait for whatever Connie bakes you. Want coffee?"

"What time is it?"

Neri glanced at the clock on Michael's nightstand. "Pushing five. Probably you should try to go back to sleep, I guess." Tonight, for the first time since the Godfather's return to New York more than a year ago, there would be a meeting of the Commission, La Cosa Nostra's ruling body. Preparations for the meeting had taken up most of Michael's time for weeks now.

Michael rubbed his face. "What the hell," he said, evenly and from behind his hands.

It was hard to tell how he meant that. Either: *What in the hell just happened?* Or: *What the hell, sure, go ahead and make coffee.*

Neri turned and padded down the hall. What the hell. Even if Mike went back to sleep, Neri wasn't going to. And he sure wasn't going to drink the percolated swill Connie made in the big kitchen downstairs. Neri didn't cook, but he was particular about his coffee.

Neri ushered the guards back onto the elevator, unself-conscious of his nakedness. "False alarm, boys," he said but did not believe. "Nothing to see."

CHAPTER 7

Johnny Fontane flew into New York the day before the parade. He and Lisa, his oldest daughter, went out for a quiet dinner at a tiny Italian place up in Harlem where they had a *bucatini all'amatriciana* as good as his sainted mother's, may she rest in peace, and where in order to get in you have to buy a table, the way you buy real estate—unless of course you know somebody or *are* somebody. Lisa—who'd once seemed mortified by her father's celebrity—clearly loved it: the attention, every morsel of the food, the flowers that magically showed up for her, the works. She was a sophomore at Juilliard. At first, Johnny had been against his daughter going off to New York alone, a girl her age. But Juilliard was Juilliard, and shy as Lisa was, onstage behind a piano, her hunched shoulders straightened, the long black hair she hid behind fell away from her face, and as her delicate hands danced over the keys, a kind of light came shining forth. Johnny had promised himself he'd look out for her. He saw her every time he came to New York, which he made sure was often. She'd dragged him to places he'd have never gone otherwise, like a strangely moving production of Jean Genet's *The Balcony,* where all the world's a crazy whorehouse, and he'd taken her to prizefights and jazz clubs. They were closer now that she'd moved away than the whole time since he'd split with Ginny, and they were all living more or less in L.A. Lisa was coming out of her shell, even away from the piano, which was unnerving for Johnny to watch, but it was also nice. The Lisa of a couple years ago certainly wouldn't have wanted to march alongside him in the parade.

As they were having their coffee and waiting for dessert—a *sfogliatella* they were going to split—Lisa started to say something but stopped herself. Johnny asked what it was, and she said it was nothing. If there was one thing Johnny Fontane had learned about women, it was that it was never nothing. "Aw, c'mon," he said. "You know you can tell your ol' dad anything."

Only after he said it did he realize that it was a line from an audition, a TV show that would have had him playing a folksy suburban father. He hadn't gotten the part.

Johnny persisted. Finally, Lisa put her hands on the table and closed her eyes. She stayed like that for a while. He let her. Another thing about women: let them have their silences.

"Daddy," she finally said, barely in a whisper. "Is it true? Even a little bit true?"

It broke his heart that she thought she had to ask this. At the same time, he admired the brass it took. She was his daughter, all right.

"No," he said. "It's ridiculous. I'm not a *gangster*. I'm not a *front* for gangsters."

She nodded. It looked like she was trying to make herself believe him.

"If a Jew or an Irishman or a Polack comes to this country and works hard—street jobs, the kind immigrants get—and he builds that up into a big business or a political career, that fella's an example of the American dream come true. But when it's an Italian, he's a gangster."

"Not every Italian."

"Yes," Johnny said. "Wise up. *Every* Italian. Every one of us who gets anywhere near the top, it happens. It's not pretty, but it's the truth."

"But some of those people, y'know, *are*." She didn't seem to want to say *gangsters*.

"Are they?" Johnny said. "Vito Corleone, for example, was my godfather. He stood up in church and took a sacred oath that he'd look after me, which he did, no different than your ma's uncle. The plumber, what's his face."

"Paulie."

"Right. Paulie. Same as Paulie did for you. His foundation—Vito Corleone's, I'm talking about—gives millions of dollars to poor kids, hospitals, the arts, including, come to think of it, grants to some of the professors at your school. He was never charged with any crime whatsoever. As for Michael Corleone, Vito's son, who runs their family business now—who's also never been issued so much as a parking ticket—Michael's a gentleman who attended both Columbia and Dartmouth and is also a decorated Marine Corps hero from I forget which battle. Maybe Iwo Jima. Or, no. That other one. Point being that despite what certain reporters and such want you to believe, a business that Michael Corleone has stock in—that's all, just stock, he's not the chairman of the board or anything—that business gave me a chance to invest in a resort in Lake Tahoe—"

"The Castle in the Clouds."

"Yep. It was the same as if Howard Johnson sold me a piece of his next motor lodge. The only difference is, *Johnson* doesn't end in a vowel."

"I thought you said he wasn't the chairman of the board."

"He's a big stockholder. He's how I heard about the investment. The son of my godfather pulled strings to get me in, and I got in."

"It's a casino, though, right? Not just a resort."

"It has a casino in it, but it's a big resort. They've got golf, tennis, the works. We ought to go sometime."

"I'd like that."

He felt like a shit for never taking her before. "Look, though: Nevada, you've been *there*, and it's the same all over. Slots in the airport, the filling stations. You start up a resort in Nevada with no casino, you'll go down the tubes fast."

She shook her head.

"No, trust me, you will."

"What I mean is, I've never been to Nevada."

"Really?"

"Really."

It didn't seem possible. "I'm sure I had you girls up to see me."

Again she shook her head. "I've never seen you sing outside L.A. and here."

"Huh." Johnny Fontane finished the final gulp of his wine. "Anyway, what I'm trying to tell you is that unlike some other investments of mine I could name, this particular venture has done great." Money was a bigger issue with him than he'd have wanted her or anyone to know. He'd had trouble with various accountants, not to mention three divorces, two from slutty, bloodsucking actresses. Also, in good times and bad, for better and for worse, he lived big, tipped big, and bet big. Johnny lowered his voice. "That place is puttin' you through Juilliard, with enough left over to send your sisters anywhere they want to go, too. That's how great it's done."

She nodded blankly. "It's not just . . . well, them. You know a lot of, y'know. People. Those pictures—"

"Honey, I've been in the public eye since I was your age. Do you realize how many times a day I get asked to pose for a picture with someone I barely met?"

She looked him straight in the eye.

He nodded. All right. Sure, he knew people. "I'm not going to lie to you, though. I've performed in places where I didn't want to know any more than I had to know about the people in charge. Last I checked, in America, it's still not a crime to know a person."

He took a sip of his coffee. Lisa clutched her napkin in her fist and held it over her mouth. Her brow was furrowed in what Johnny hoped was only confusion.

"C'mon, sweetheart," he said, louder now, dialing up the charm. "Think about it. I'm a nightclub singer. Who do you think owns nightclubs?"

That wasn't an original line. He'd gotten it from that *finocchio* actor, Ollie Smith-Christmas—*Sir* Oliver now, a grand old guy—who'd said it to get the reporters off Johnny's ass during the rehearsals for Jimmy Shea's Inaugural Ball. Lisa gave no indication that she'd heard it before. Johnny put up his hands in mock surrender, to indicate the pragmatics of his situation. What else could he have done? Nothing. What choice had he had? None.

She put down her napkin. With her other hand, she pulled her hair from her face. A nervous gesture, Johnny thought at first, until he saw a smile start to spread across her face.

He'd satisfied her, and it had the added benefit of being the truth.

She leaned across the table and kissed him on the cheek.

He was flooded with regret for all the moments he'd missed in the lives of his children. Lisa was a start. He had a ways to go with Angie and Trina. What Margot Ashton and Annie McGowan had done (much worse than breaking his heart or making off with his money) was drive a wedge between him and his family. He wasn't going to let it happen again.

"I love you, angel," he said.

"Shh," Lisa said, but she kept on smiling.

After dinner, Johnny dropped her off at her apartment and went out for a night on the town. He knew enough to spend it entirely in watering holes and clubs where he had friends who could be counted on to keep the public and the reporters away, who knew not to talk about his recent problems in Nevada or the collateral complaints in New York about naming him grand marshal. For a few blessed hours, he'd had a break from all that.

The night stretched out, as such nights do. He'd had various chances to strike something up with various broads. But it became clear to him that he'd be facing the challenges of the next day on no sleep, and he opted to take a pass on the pussy. A man learns things. When he found himself facing the harsh light of morning in the back of a limo, alone, heading uptown to his suite at the Plaza Hotel, he was actually proud of himself.

Johnny shaved and showered and felt neither drunk nor hungover. He

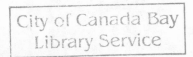

was riding high. When he was a boy, if somebody had told him that one day he'd make records and movies, that he'd make girls scream and men jealous, he wouldn't have been shocked. He was that kind of a kid: big balls, big dreams, and a mother who told him he could do anything he put his mind to. If he'd been told he'd help get a president elected and then throw the greatest Inaugural Ball in history, Johnny would have believed that, too—so long as he got the whole story, which was that after giving Jimmy Shea his blood, sweat, and tears (not to mention more than a few lady friends), the ungrateful narrowback cut Johnny off because he's Italian. Because the cunt-happy hypocrite wanted to hide the fact that his old man was a bootlegger and did what he had to do to get ahead in America. Because it wasn't enough to go to Princeton and become an All-American diver and meet and marry an heiress. He had to pretend that he'd *come* from people like that. All too predictable.

But grand marshal of the Columbus Day Parade, right up Fifth Avenue? That Johnny could have never imagined, not in a million years. It was the kind of honor that usually went to *pezzonovanti* like Fiorello La Guardia, Al Smith, or the pope. Johnny had marched in this thing while he was still in short pants, a little Italian flag in one fist, a little American one in the other. He'd played drums in his high school band and marched all the way from St. Patrick's Cathedral to Seventy-ninth Street without taking his eyes off of Annamaria DiGregorio's heart-shaped, cheerleader-skirted ass. And the year he'd had his first big hit with the Les Halley Band, he'd ridden on a float, clutching an oversize prop microphone.

Now this. Grand Marshal John Fontane.

When the hotel sent up his breakfast along with complimentary copies of the morning newspapers, though, Johnny's elation came to a rude end. The holier-than-thou *coglioni* who were planning to stage some cockamamie protest along the parade route had gotten themselves—and Johnny—on the goddamned front page.

"Slow news day," Johnny muttered. He felt like he'd taken a hard right cross to the gut.

"What's that, sir?" The waiter was finished setting up.

Sources said Fontane and a much younger woman were seen canoodling at a posh uptown eatery known to be frequented by underworld figures.

Johnny sat heavily down on the edge of his still-made bed. His ears were getting hot. "I said thanks, kid."

Fontane was overheard bragging to his date about performing in nightclubs with ties to organized crime.

Johnny tossed the papers aside and closed his eyes.

"There's also this, sir." The waiter handed him a phone message from Ginny. *Please call.*

The tip Johnny gave was lavish even by his standards. It still meant something to be Johnny Fontane. None of this garbage was going to get to him. No chance.

The foolish young punk that Johnny used to be would have called Ginny back and screamed at her for wanting to deny him the pleasure of having Lisa march beside him in the parade. (What *else* could she be calling about? She had a sixth sense for everything bad that happened to him.) Then he'd have slammed down the receiver and ripped the phone from the wall. He'd have smashed dishes against the walls, kicked in the TV. And then? He'd have started plotting revenge on those reporters. *Sources said*? *Canoodling*? Goddamn. *Nightclubs with ties to organized crime.* Goddamn, goddamn, goddamn. He'd kill them.

Believe it: Johnny still had those impulses. In motherfucking spades.

But.

Deep breath.

He was sweating from the effort of what he *wasn't* doing.

Another deep breath.

The same breathing regimen he used before recording sessions.

He *wasn't* some punk anymore. He was fifty-two jam-packed years old. His public looked to him as someone who'd fought and loved and lost and lived to tell about it, *sing* about it, on records that kept right on spinning in battered jukeboxes and lonely living rooms all around the world. Life had given him his share of raw deals, and he'd endured. Pain left a mark on him, but what could a man expect? He was just a regular joe—like you, pally, only more so.

Breathe.

Johnny could feel his rage subsiding. He looked at his omelet cooling on the plate. He poked at it with a coffee stirrer. He wasn't hungry. The early signs of a hangover were asserting themselves. He downed a small fistful of aspirin, chased it with a milky-white slug of antacid, and lit up a menthol cigarette. Both the aspirin and the antacid came from very large bottles.

It was the middle of the night in L.A., too early to call Ginny back. If he didn't talk to her before the parade, how was that *his* fault? Blame the time zones. Blame the bigness of America.

And it was still more than two hours before his appointment with Michael Corleone.

He grabbed the satchel of movie scripts he'd brought with him from California and sprawled across the suite's long red sofa.

By rights, this should have been one of the great days of his life. But instead of savoring it, Johnny Fontane was looking for redemption somewhere in a two-foot-high stack of screenplays and trying not to think too much about the day he had before him. He didn't want to think about what to say to Michael Corleone. Johnny was a performer; he'd do better if he just let a thing like that happen. It was a business meeting, but Johnny's business was show. Same for the parade, right?

He began to guzzle coffee and skim movie scripts, looking for a vehicle that would be good for his image. To his dismay (but not his surprise), most of the scripts came from people who wanted him to play a glamorous criminal—even though it was a kind of role he'd done only once, in a lighter-than-air musical. Two different pictures, in fact, were about the late Hyman Roth—one a straightforward biographical picture, the other about a character patterned on Roth. Both wanted Johnny for the lead, as if the audience would accept a mook like him as a ruthless Jew mastermind. He tossed them both into the trash.

Johnny sifted through the other scripts, making notes about good parts not intended for him but that he thought he could play. The crusading cop, for whom it's now personal. The gun for hire who wins over the school-marm by saving the town from a fellow Union cavalry veteran, a swarthy outlaw named Covelli (*J. Fontane?* someone had scrawled on page 1). The retarded gardener who rises up at the end and kills the corrupt, wife-beating senator (who is revealed to be the gardener's own brother). Johnny's agent said nobody in Hollywood would cast him in roles like that right now. Yes, he had his own production company, but he still needed help to get a pic-ture made and more help yet to get it distributed. That's leaving aside whether Mr. and Mrs. America would fork over their hard-earned cash to see it. These days, the only people who went to the movies were teenagers who needed a place to sit in the dark and feel each other up. To get a big-ger crowd than that, you had to give the people a big spectacle they couldn't see on TV or else put out pictures that were made quickly and cheaply, featuring big stars in the same kind of roles they'd played a hun-dred times before. As a wise man once said, if the crowds don't show up, there's nothing you can do to stop them.

That was the conventional wisdom, anyway.

But if Johnny Fontane had been a big believer in the conventional wis-dom, he'd probably still be back in the old neighborhood, waiting tables or selling shirts or walking a beat.

He stared at the scripts. Johnny was sure he could play a hero, given the right epic. Maybe not Jesus or King Arthur, but he could be as good as the next guy commanding an army in a just war or saving orphans from the ravages of the Great Chicago Fire—something along those lines. He could also do a great job in something classy but not too artsy, playing the little guy who's down on his luck and gets one last shot at redemption, something that could earn Johnny good notices from the critics and maybe make a buck or two.

There were ways of getting the big shots in Hollywood to think dif-ferently.

But of course resorting to those tactics, calling in those favors, was what had gotten Johnny into the mess he was in now.

Johnny did believe what he'd told Lisa, every word of it. At the same time, it was also true that he'd never asked his godfather precisely what he meant when he said he was going to make Jack Woltz an offer he couldn't refuse. Woltz, then as now the head of Woltz International Pictures, had vowed that over his dead body would Johnny get that part. There were wild rumors about why Woltz changed his mind, but Johnny dismissed them, then more or less forgot all about them. Johnny took the part, nailed the shit out of it, took his on-screen beating, and then took home the Oscar. When the Corleones bankrolled Johnny's movie production company, he didn't ask questions. When there were rumors that the Chicago outfit had a stake in his record label, Johnny's accountants asked him if he really wanted to know what there was to know about that. He'd just laughed—*laughed*—and walked out of the office.

Still, that didn't mean that any of these people were *gangsters*.

To get big things done, big people do things John Q. Public never sees. The inside dope on how the Plaza Hotel came to be would probably make your toes curl. Same with New York City itself. America? Stolen. Same with every great empire. If the thieves responsible are smart enough to build an organization around themselves and go to the trouble of sewing a flag, they go into the history books as heroes.

Johnny looked at his watch. Still too early to call. Much as he hated to give up on the idea of sharing this honor with his daughter, he was having second thoughts.

He picked up the next script from the pile. *The Discovery of America*. It was twice as long as most of the others: one of those big epics. For a few pages, he wondered if he could play Columbus, then he pitched it aside and looked for something that had a ghost of a chance. He pulled out a script called *Trimalchio Rex*. What caught Johnny's eye was the Italian name of the screenwriter, Sergio Lupo. Two pages in, through no fault of the screenplay itself, sleep fell on Johnny Fontane like a silk sheet.

He drifted off thinking Ginny was probably right, that she'd always been right, that nothing had been perfect in his life since the summer they were falling in love. His coffee cup slipped from his hand and hit the floor. It took a tiny chip out of the thing. Only at a joint like the Plaza could it qualify as broken.

CHAPTER 8

Eddie Paradise had been up since dawn. He left his waterfront house in Island Park and drove himself to a softball field not far from the docks in Red Hook, even closer to the precinct house where the police captain he was waiting for worked. Nothing on the radio sounded good until he found a station playing rock-and-roll instrumentals—Herb Alpert & the Tijuana Brass, Dick Dale & the Del-Tones, Link Wray & the Wraymen, James Brown & the Famous Flames, and his personal favorite Booker T. & the MG's, with that "Green Onions" number. *Eddie Paradise* was a good name for a leader, he thought. *Eddie Paradise & the* . . . what?

Finally, the captain showed up in a gleaming '59 Riviera, silver with a black top, and still in his bathrobe. Eddie gave him a Marlboro carton full of money—not a payoff, since the captain was on the payroll already: a gift is all it was, half now, half this time tomorrow, presuming tonight's Commission meeting reached its peaceful conclusion. Did the captain even say thank you? He did not. Did Eddie need to give him the money personally? No. That went above and beyond. Did this crooked fucknuts give a shit? Eddie shook his head as the cop drove away. No. He did not.

Eddie got back in his car and went by the restaurant on Union Street, where the meeting would be, just to check on things—how fresh the calamari was (very), whether any chairs were tippy (the two that were had been replaced), how well the black roller shade was able to cover the front window (perfectly), the dope on the chefs and all the waiters who'd be working tonight (every one of whom was a member of the owner's family, though Eddie vetoed a Neapolitan in-law he'd never seen in here before), if the neighbors had taken advantage of their all-expenses-paid getaway weekends to the Jersey shore (they had). Eddie listened to various petty requests—some cousin in jail for getting in a fight, some dishwasher who wanted a loan just until next month so he could bring his grandmother over from Racalmuto, et cetera. The usual. And, as usual, Eddie said he'd see what he could do. He wrote nothing down. He had a mind for remembering shit like this. On his way out, Eddie grabbed a broom and swept the front sidewalk himself, even though it seemed to have already been done.

Having the Commission meeting on Eddie's turf was an honor, especially for someone who'd just been promoted to *capo*. If everything went perfectly, Michael Corleone would get the credit. If anything went wrong, it'd be Eddie's ass. Which suited Eddie fine—that's how you moved up, you deny credit for anything and heap it onto your boss. But an honor? It was getting harder for Eddie to see it that way. When what's heaped on you is the level of bullshit that was heaped on Eddie Paradise, it's hard to see much past the end of your own flat and broken nose.

Eddie commended the restaurant owner on the way things were coming together, then went to his regular bakery, on President Street, where he took his morning espresso and held court. Then he headed to his social club, hoping for a civilized gentleman's nap, but no such luck. He turned the corner and saw five men from Flatbush Novelties, dressed in work shirts with their names stitched above the pockets, waiting for him in front of the red door of the Carroll Gardens Hunt Club. The fireworks guys.

Why the Roach hadn't already taken care of whatever they needed, who knows? It was always something. Somebody always wanted some goddamned thing from Eddie Paradise. At home, at the bakery, at his club, sitting down eating lunch, even out on his boat. Like they say, gotta pay the cost to be the boss, but Jesus Geronimo Christ. A whole *regime* under him now, yet nothing important got done and stayed done unless Eddie saw to it himself. If he did have a group, know what he'd call it? Eddie Paradise & the Worthless *Coglioni*. Or better yet, Just Eddie. He'd have thought that by now he'd be at a station in life where once in a while he could take the day off from anyone's needs but his own. One day. Why does Columbus need a day? Fuck Columbus. *Merdaiolo*'s been dead for centuries.

The two men walking with Eddie asked him if he knew the people in front of the club.

"I'll take care of it," Eddie said.

The day hell freezes over's got a name, and its Eddie Day.

Say this for the men in his crew, though: they were well trained—a tradition in this *regime* since Salvatore Tessio started it up. Without even needing to be told, they positioned themselves between the Flatbush Novelties panel truck and their boss.

The owner of the fireworks company, sitting on the stoop, tried to hand Eddie his morning paper. *George,* his shirt read. George Spanos.

"Anything good in there, George?"

The men behind Eddie shot one another a look.

"What do you mean?"

Unfolding his morning paper, reading it fresh, was one of Eddie's pleasures. Once it'd been around awhile—into the can and who knows where—he wouldn't touch it.

"You read my newspaper," Eddie said, "and I'm asking you what you got out of it."

Spanos started to say something and stopped himself. "Rained out the Series again yesterday. Supposed to rain again today. It's what the Giants get for moving out west."

The thing Spanos thought better of saying was probably something about Eddie or his associates. Spanos was such a lousy gambler, Eddie's little girl could have read his tells. Eddie glanced at what he could see of the headlines and didn't see anything earthshaking.

"The World Series can kiss my hairy ass," Eddie said. "All I follow is the Mets."

The fireworks people snickered.

There was a day when Eddie Paradise would have snapped right there, but watching Nick Geraci had taught him things. Even if the guy had gone bad, he'd been a good teacher.

"Laugh." Eddie shrugged. "But I got news for you, the Dodgers and Giants ain't comin' back. I live in the present, y'know? I got season tickets and everything."

Spanos stood, still proffering the newspaper. "You got season tickets for the present?"

"For the Mets, you fat Greek fuck." Eddie was also the sole provider of all cement poured for the team's new ballpark and all the construction trash hauled away from the site. "What made you think you could read my paper?"

Eddie went up a step, so he'd be eye to eye with Spanos. Eddie also had a thing about his height (he was five-one), though he prided himself on not having a short man's personality.

"I put it back in order," Spanos practically pleaded. "Perfect order."

"Keep it," Eddie said.

Spanos, like most degenerate gamblers, had a tendency to push his luck. "Really, take it," he said. "I'm done with it."

On the other hand, that tendency was what led to Eddie taking over the man's business. Eddie smiled his menacing smile. "Then shove it up your ass."

Eddie had practiced that smile in the mirror. He'd worked up a lot of different looks.

He glanced up, at the window of his office, and saw Momo the Roach looking down on him. Momo had come back from Acapulco so tanned he could have joined the Harlem Globetrotters. He'd been back awhile now, but he was using a sunlamp to make the tan linger, like some Holly-wood *finocch'*.

"Is there anything you gentlemen actually need," Eddie said, "or are you going to block my path for the rest of this beautiful fall morning?"

"They wanted to see permits," Spanos said.

"Who wanted to see permits?"

"The city."

"The whole fuckin' city wanted to see permits? Who'd you talk to?"

"We're down at the waterfront there, setting up." Spanos fished a business card from his shirt pocket and gave it to Eddie. "And this guy here told us we needed permits. We showed him what we had, and he said no, those are the wrong kind."

"It was this guy here?" Eddie said, flicking the business card with his middle finger. It belonged to a councilman. "Or somebody who works for this guy?"

"That guy there. He had a detective with him, Chesbro, and a uniformed cop, too."

Greedy double-dipping *stronzoni*. Chesbro was already on the payroll. As was the councilman, who'd apparently stopped to wet his beak on his way to the Columbus Day Parade. Eddie had just taken over as *capo*. This was part of a bigger pattern these days: men who won't *stay* bought. Happened more and more all the time. At every turn, even when all Eddie Paradise was trying to do was something nice for the good people of New York, hard-ons like this were testing him.

Let 'em. There was power in being underestimated. That was the Corleone way.

"And it took five of you to come here and tell me this?"

"What else could we do? They made us stop working."

"Did you tell 'em who you was working for?"

Spanos shook his head. "He knew, though. He mentioned you by name."

Eddie nodded to the men standing by the panel truck, took another step up, and reached down to put his hand on the taller man's shoulder. "Go back down to the pier. My associates here will follow you. When our friends show up, they'll reason with them."

On the way to get their car, one of the men whispered to Eddie that he needed money. That figured. Eddie jerked his thumb toward upstairs. Get it from the Roach. Carroll Gardens was home-field advantage, but Eddie wasn't about to stand on the street and pull out cash.

He watched them drive away. Then he met the eye of a neighborhood kid. They were always around, the way sea gulls trail tourist boats. "Newspaper," Eddie said.

"Which one?"

He waved dismissively. "All of 'em. Make sure they're today's."

The boy sprinted off. He knew not to ask Eddie for money. Whatever the kid spent, he'd get it back tenfold.

Eddie Paradise stepped over the sullied newspaper, then walked around back and entered the Carroll Gardens Hunt Club through the basement door.

He and Momo had grown up in this neighborhood, and they'd bought the place together. It was tucked on a residential street, all brownstones, on a block that was still a hundred percent Italian. It had once been a real hunt club, and it came with a built-in pistol range down in the basement. Also down here was an empty cage made with iron bars supposedly pinched during the construction of the Bronx Zoo. The guess was that the cage was originally used for dogs. It was Eddie's dream to get a lion—a real lion—and keep it down there. He'd made inquiries. It could be done.

The ground floor had a kitchen and a lounge—sofas, card tables, a pool table, and an ornately carved bar. On the walls—Eddie's personal collection—were dozens of old World War II posters. HE'S WATCHING YOU. WHO WANTS TO KNOW? IF YOU TALK TOO MUCH, THIS MAN DIES. THE ENEMY IS LISTENING/HE WANTS TO KNOW WHAT YOU KNOW. The popular favorite was a fabulous pouty-lipped dame, hunched over a table toward the camera so you could see the great dark valley of her cleavage, pointing at a red pair of dice.

PLEASE DON'T GAMBLE WITH YOUR LIFE! it read. BE CAREFUL WHAT YOU SAY. Personally, Eddie loved the one with two gunners drawn in profile, a tough Italian-looking guy with a rivet gun that looked like a *lupara* and, below him, a helmeted soldier with a tommy gun. GIVE 'EM BOTH BARRELS. Every time he looked at it, it made him smile.

On the second floor were storage rooms, crash apartments, and the business office. The desk sat on a six-inch platform (Eddie's idea), so that the person behind the desk looked down on anybody sitting across from him. The whole top floor was a banquet hall with a kitchenette and a spiral staircase to a small rooftop terrace.

He closed his office door. "Downstairs still looks like a pigpen."

"The way you are with the having to have your new soap," Momo said, "or your new socks, all that bit, those are things you can pass off as you wanting to be classy. But friend to friend? Your newspaper thing has gotten fucking *calabrese*."

Eddie didn't wear socks more than once. He also threw away bars of soap once the lettering disappeared. As if he hadn't earned some of the finer things in life.

"Yeah, well, we all got our little eccentricities," Eddie said, feinting as if he was going to muss the Roach's shellacked hair, which really was about as hard as a cockroach's exoskeleton. Momo's given name was Cosimo Barone. He'd hoped to get tabbed as *capo*, which if it had happened wouldn't have surprised Eddie or pissed him off, either. Momo was a good man who'd earned what he'd gotten. There were rumors that the Roach was considered too close to Nick Geraci to take over as *capo*, but he wasn't all the much closer to Geraci than Eddie had been. When the shake-up happened, Momo had been in the joint, sent upstate on a fluke bust at a Family-owned chop shop. He'd done his time and kept his mouth shut, which, on the one hand, was a reason to reward him but on the other made him, first, maybe too hot to tab as *capo* and, second, definitely out of the swing of things. So Eddie Paradise got promoted, and Momo the Roach got paroled and was rewarded with a month at a resort in Acapulco, all expenses paid, including women. Fair or not, that needed to be the end of it. Unless the Roach wanted to go the way of Nick Geraci or Momo's own uncle Sally, the guy needed to live in the present. Eddie prided himself on living in the present.

"It was real nice of you to leave those guys waitin', by the way," Eddie said. "I'd have hated like hell to miss out on the chance to solve even more of the world's fucking problems."

"I been on the phone."

"On the phone lining up someone to clean up this dump, I hope. Or do I have to do every goddamned thing myself?"

"The guys can do it."

"If the guys could do it, they'd have done it. The guys ain't here." It was a Saturday, Columbus Day on top of that.

Momo laughed. "You may have noticed this ain't exactly a report-to-work-early line of work."

"It's a do-what-you're-fucking-told line of work," Eddie said. "Get a cleaning lady, a service, whatever."

"Don't look at me like I ain't doin' my share," Momo said. "I been runnin' around all morning, entertaining the yats."

"The yats?"

"Our New Orleans friends." Meaning Carlo Tramonti, and some of his associates. Tramonti was in town to address the Commission tonight. The job of squiring them around had fallen to Eddie Paradise and his crew, on top of everything else. "Yats. As in *where y'at*? It's a common term down there."

"Fuck do you know that?" said Eddie.

"I get out."

"You get out? You barely get out of Brooklyn."

"What the fuck do you call Mexico?" Momo held out his tanned arms as Exhibit A.

Eddie was going to say something about the faggot sunlamp, but let it go. "I call Mexico," Eddie said, "the exception that proves the rule."

Momo shook his head.

"What?" Eddie said. "C'mon. Say it. Just say it."

Because Eddie Paradise figured that what Momo would call Mexico was the consolation prize, the vacation he got instead of the promotion he deserved. The sooner they got it out between them, the better.

"Say it," Eddie said. Because he sure as hell wasn't going to.

"Say what?" Momo said.

"Mexico," Eddie said. "Just fucking say it."

Momo held up his hands in mock surrender. "I don't have the first goddamned idea what you're talking about."

Eddie Paradise knew that in a situation like this, Michael Corleone would smoke a man out with silence. He tried counting up to his age, which was a tip Geraci had taught him. If you maintain eye contact, people will give you a second for every year you've lived.

"I don't know what you're drivin' at," Momo said (as Eddie got to thirteen). "But for your information, I was out of Brooklyn *last night*, picking up the yats at the airport."

Eddie decided to let it go.

"I was thinking, you like that nigger rock and roll so much," Momo said, "I can't believe you never heard of the word *yat*."

Eddie didn't have to ask what one thing had to do with the other. Music was an ongoing topic of affectionate bickering between them. The Roach meant only that he was incredulous on both fronts. The running joke successfully lightened the tone of things.

"So," Eddie said, "is that something you can call a man to his face? Yat?"

"Everybody calls me Roach, and I got a sense of humor about that there."

"Yeah, but you take offense at *dago*, *guinea*, *wop*, et cetera and so forth."

"That's when it comes from people who ain't like us."

"You ain't exactly like Tramonti and them," Eddie pointed out.

"Maybe not, but, no offense, I see some resemblance between you and what's his face."

"Funny," Eddie said, but again he was able to translate effortlessly. Tramonti had five younger brothers. The one Momo meant was Augie the Midget, his *consigliere*, who wasn't a true-blue midget but was even shorter than Eddie. "So where are they?"

"The yats? I got 'em a driver and a Cadillac, got 'em a charter tour of the harbor. After that, they take a late lunch at Manny Wolf's Chop House. Best table in the house, and no matter how hard they try, the tab comes to us."

Eddie nodded in approval.

"Manny's, also, is out of Brooklyn, for your information."

"I hit a nerve, eh?" Eddie grinned, the extra-large one he'd practiced so it looked like he was both joking around and not to be fucked with.

"I'm just making a point."

"You don't have to actually *go* to Manny Wolf's to make a reservation," Eddie said.

"You have to go there to know it's good."

"Every wiseguy in New York knows it's good."

"Goddamn. You know goddamned *well* I been out of Brooklyn."

The Roach was a literal-minded man, or pretended to be. All in the game. "Maybe you're right," Eddie conceded. "Come to think of it, the state pen is also out of Brooklyn."

WHEN THE KID CAME BACK WITH THE NEWSPAPERS, EDDIE finally saw what Spanos had been about to say.

Protests were expected at the parade because of Johnny Fontane's difficulties with the Nevada Gaming Commission and his *alleged ties to the oft-investigated Michael Corleone, as well as to crime syndicates in New Jersey, Chicago, and Los Angeles.* That was a low blow—*oft-investigated*—though Eddie understood that only in the courts (and then only theoretically) are you innocent until proven guilty. In the press, you're whatever they say you are.

On the bright side, they used an unquestionably flattering photo of the Don, dressed in a tux, leaving a benefit for the Metropolitan Opera with his niece Francesca, who helped run the Vito Corleone Foundation. That was a good indicator of the paper's true position. It's always possible to find an unflattering picture of anybody.

There was a long stretch of the article in which upright citizens made the self-evident point that Italian-Americans are honest, hardworking people who helped build America. Most had never even seen a so-called gangster. Toward the end, after some stupid shit about some young broad Fontane was supposedly balling, the story mentioned the fireworks display, scheduled for that night, on a pier in the Red Hook section of Brooklyn, sponsored by the Italo-American Policemen's Guild but underwritten by an anonymous donor, *which an unnamed source has confirmed to be Michael Corleone.*

Eddie tossed the newspaper to Momo and picked up another one. Again, the anonymous source was mentioned. The donation had actually come from the Vito Corleone Foundation, but that was reporters for you. Those people are like puppies: cute, fun to have around, wagging their tails at you every time you feed them. But sooner or later, they're going to chew your slippers and piss on your rug. Whether it's an accident or spite, you'll never know. They're dumb animals, and you're a sap if you ever think otherwise. Still. They're cute. Given enough time and free food, you can teach them to do some amazing tricks.

Again in this paper, the editor had chosen a glamorous-looking photo of Michael Corleone, this one with the lovely and talented Miss Marguerite Duvall on his arm. These newspaper guys had almost as much invested in building up the legend of Michael Corleone as Eddie Paradise did.

"Ten to one," Eddie said, "that the unnamed source there is that public relations company Hagen's got working for us."

A white lie. Hiring that outfit had been Eddie's doing, an initiative he was proud of. Fontane's getting tabbed as grand marshal—that was Eddie's doing as well. He had a guy on the committee. Eddie, knowing that Fontane was the late Vito Corleone's godson, figured it would please Michael Corleone to see Fontane get some positive publicity to counteract the negative shit he was facing because of those Nevada hard-ons in their ten-gallon hats. It hadn't worked out perfectly, but it stood to work out. Like they say, no publicity is bad publicity.

"You think so, eh?" The Roach was by no means a stupid man, but he was a slow reader.

· "It probably seemed like a good idea at the time, leaking it. Good for the Don's image and thus-and-such. Y'know? How could they fucking know it'd wind up in the same story with that Fontane business?"

The phone rang.

Momo answered. He listened for a few moments, told the caller to hold on, and covered the mouthpiece with his hand. "Yeah, well, *twenty* to one," the Roach said, handing Eddie the receiver, "it's why your Greek fireworks guys find themselves stuck sideways on shakedown street."

Eddie sighed.

But in the end, the way Eddie figured it was like this: there are two kinds of people in this world, the ones who break things and the ones who fix things. If you're born to be a fixer, then what are you supposed to do? Complain? No. Hell, no. What you do is, you fix. You make use of your God-given talents and go out in the world every goddamned day and you fix.

CHAPTER 9

Someone from the parade called Johnny Fontane from the lobby. "Did we wake you, sir?"

"No," he said, though they had.

"Because we called earlier," the man said.

Johnny remembered having a dream in which he answered the phone but it kept on ringing. "I had a meeting," Johnny said. But he'd slept through that, too. He'd slept most of the morning. He didn't have time to call Ginny. And it was too late, anyway. The parade people had said they'd send a car for Lisa; she must already be downtown. "I'll be right down," he said.

"That's a relief, sir."

Johnny called the number he had for Michael Corleone. A service answered.

"Could you tell Mr. Corleone I'm running late?" Johnny sat on the bed, bouncing the meat of his fist against the marble-topped nightstand. "We were supposed to have a . . . coffee together this morning and . . ." What excuse would be good enough? *Be a man,* he could hear his godfather saying. ". . . and I was exhausted from my trip and fell asleep. *Mea culpa.* Please tell him I'm sincerely sorry, and if it's in any way possible—"

"Hold, please," she said.

He *was* exhausted. It had been one of those naps that just made him more tired.

Moments later she came back on and told him that Mr. Corleone said that immediately after the parade would be fine.

Johnny splashed cold water on his face, grabbed his suit jacket—dove-gray, part of his own signature line of suits—and was about to run out when out of the corner of his eye he saw those morning newspapers. He stopped. He gathered them up, stuffed them, emphatically, in the trash, spit on the lot of them, then ran to the elevator.

A squadron of handlers rushed him out a side entrance and into a limo. They got away clean.

The head handler was a bland-looking bald man in a cheap black suit. As they headed downtown, the man barked cryptic instructions into a handheld radio, the same kind Johnny had seen the Secret Service use. Johnny's hangover was now in full eyeball-hammering bloom.

"Was there a . . ." Johnny didn't know how to ask the handler about the protestors. He didn't want to make it seem like it bothered him. "A crowd?"

"Sir?"

"That protest I read about," Johnny said.

"At the hotel?" he said. "No."

"What about where the parade is? Where it starts."

"We have things very much under control, sir."

They arrived at the staging area, a few roped-off blocks not far from Times Square. A white VIP tent was set up in the middle of Forty-fourth Street. A lone protestor with a sign turned the other way was giving a TV interview. A clutch of reporters, cordoned off behind a wooden police barrier, faced the other way, too, and didn't see Johnny until he was ducking into the tent, too late for him to make anything of their shouted questions except the words *Johnny!* and *Is it true . . . ?*

Johnny Fontane, a virtuoso at working a crowd of well-wishers and people who wanted a piece of him, worked his way past the people on his guest list—schoolteachers, nuns, high school friends—making a polite and efficient beeline for his daughter. Even his old friend Danny Shea failed to get more of Johnny's attention than a dead-eyed nod.

When Lisa saw Johnny, her face lit up. His knees nearly buckled from the joy of seeing it. "What a *hoot*!" she said, hugging him.

She was wearing a red cashmere turtleneck, and the black Italian knee-high boots he'd bought her the last time he was in New York.

"Hoot?"

"*Canoodling?* What a word!"

"Yeah? It means kissing. It—"

"I know what it means, Daddy. How funny! They thought we were a couple!"

"I know what they thought. You're not angry, or, I don't know—"

"It's hilarious."

Johnny cocked his head. "Those other things in there—"

She waved him off. "Old news, pun intended."

"*Jaaaaahn.*" The attorney general, his phony Brahmin accent dialed up all the way, clapped a hand on Johnny's shoulder. Flanking him was a man Johnny didn't know but whose very bearing screamed *cop*. Northern Italian, Johnny would guess. "Great to see you, Mr. Grand Marshal," said Danny Shea. "We were all starting to worry."

Johnny started to introduce him to Lisa.

"We met," said Danny Shea. "While we were waiting. You have a lovely daughter, Jaaahn." Lisa shrugged, embarrassed. "How's the rest of your family?"

"As people used to say in my old neighborhood, they're good as bread."

"Good as bread? I never heard that."

"Because nothing's as good as Italian bread."

"How true that is!" Shea said.

He was a man playing to a nonexistent crowd. He and Johnny had once been friends. After Jimmy got elected—due in no small part to the efforts of one Johnny Fontane—the Shea family froze him out, for no reason Johnny could see other than the simple fact that he was Italian. Even after that, when the problem with the Gaming Commission had come up, Johnny had humbled himself and asked if there was any way the administration might intercede and get those Nevada cowboys off Johnny's balls. Johnny had struggled even to get one of the Shea brothers on the phone, and when he did it was Danny, who'd politely and briefly said there was nothing he could do. Seeing Danny Shea now, pretending to be pals just like old times, made Johnny want to give this soft, pretty-boy shitweasel a hard right cross to those big shiny horse teeth.

"So," Johnny said. "How're Jeannie and the kids?"

"They're fantastic. Say, I'd like you to meet Agent Charles Bianchi of the FBI."

"I'm a big, big fan, Mr. Fontane," Bianchi said. "My wife and I have all your records."

Johnny had been recording for almost thirty years. *Nobody* had all his records. Though if everyone who'd told him they had all his records really *did* have them all, Johnny Fontane could have hired J. Paul Getty to hold the toilet paper and King Farouk to wipe his ass. "Much appreciated," Johnny said, looping an arm around Lisa. "Food in the mouths of my children."

Danny Shea and Agent Bianchi laughed louder than he'd given them reason to.

Johnny remembered reading about Bianchi in the newspapers, too; he was an assistant bureau chief out in one of those rectangular states, which made him the highest-ranking Italian-American in the FBI. Johnny was surprised there was anyone even that high up.

"Nice of you to take part in our parade, Mr. Attorney General," Johnny said. "You got some Italian blood in you we don't know about?"

"I wouldn't have missed it," Danny Shea said. "It's a great opportunity for all of us to honor the contributions of the hardworking Italian people."

"The cameras are all outside, Dan," Johnny said. Lisa laughed, but there was a flicker of anger in Danny Shea's eyes.

"Well, I think they're about to start," Shea said, though no one had signaled to him. He was walking toward the front of the parade, alongside the governor and the mayor, both already out working the crowd. "Duty calls. Anything I can ever do for you, Jaaahn, let me know, all right?"

"Thanks. I'll do that."

Johnny would grant Danny Shea this: he was the only politician who didn't steer clear of him. This parade was full of more strivers vying to become the next mayor or governor, more councilmen and Albany nobodies than Carter has liver pills, but did any of them come by and say hello to Johnny Fontane? No. Truth be told, thank God. It gave Johnny a chance to say hello to old friends and to hear compliments about Lisa from the likes of Sister Immaculata, his old music teacher, who must have been a hundred by now and who claimed she'd always known Johnny would make it big. Again and again, these well-wishers said how sorry they were about the protests, and again and again Johnny thanked them and told them it didn't bother him, it was a small price to pay for an honor such as this.

Finally, the handlers came to get them. Johnny donned his sash—white with red and green letters. "If you don't want to do this," he whispered to Lisa, "it won't hurt my feelings."

She straightened the sash. She seemed slightly deflated. "Don't you want me to do it?"

"Of course I do." Either way, Johnny was afraid he'd set her up to be hurt.

The head handler told the reporters that Mr. Fontane would hold a brief press conference at the end of the parade. After a few noisy complaints, the reporters dispersed.

Johnny and Lisa took their places behind a clown troupe riding in Sicilian carts and a marching band from a Jesuit high school.

The band started off playing "The Stars and Stripes Forever."

"Gee, I didn't know John Philip Sousa was Italian," Lisa said.

"Got any aspirin in that purse of yours?"

She gave him a bottle, and he dry-swallowed four.

He nodded toward the band and shook the bottle. "Mind if I hang on to this?"

A security detail appeared, a half dozen cops, two uniformed and four plainclothes. They all seemed to be fans. Johnny asked if this was more security than usual and was assured it was routine. "All the bigwigs get walkalongs," said the youngest plainclothes. Lisa scrunched up her face, bemused.

Soon after they turned onto Fifth Avenue, on their left were a dozen-plus people, carrying signs that looked like the same person had lettered them, sporting slogans condemning negative stereotypes of Italians. Johnny ignored them. A guy with millions of fans ought to be able to take it in stride when twenty cocksuckers hate him.

As they headed up Fifth Avenue, reporters appeared on the wrong side of the wooden police barriers, shouting questions. The cops minding the barriers were in easy-duty-overtime mode. The walkalongs seemed untroubled.

Johnny put his mouth next to Lisa's ear. "Just smile and wave," he said, jaw clenched, continuing to smile and wave. The sole virtue of the band's pounding out the same Sousa medley over and over was that it drowned out the roving vermin.

The crowd was in Johnny Fontane's corner. They screamed for him the way they had when he was a teen idol. Off and on, they'd stop chanting *Italia! Italia! Italia!* and chant his name instead. A few times, one of the reporters stumbled over someone's outstretched foot. Stray protesters were swallowed up by the ten-deep crowd, a sea of billowing Italian flags, and signs proclaiming WE LOVE YOU JOHNNY and FONTANE FOR PRESIDENT.

"My daughter!" he'd yell out from time to time, pointing at Lisa. It made her blush, but she loved it. If he didn't think she loved it, he'd have stopped.

The Sicilian clowns had some kind of elaborate puppet act. It was hard to see it from where Johnny was marching, but whatever the clowns were doing, it left the crowd in high spirits as Johnny and his daughter approached.

"Remember that place?" They were approaching FAO Schwarz.

"Every girl remembers that place," she said. "Every kid."

"See," he said, "I maybe never took you to Vegas, but I took you there."

"That you did."

"Remember that doll I got you? A Madame Alexander doll."

"Do I." The drone of the band made it hard to hear, but her voice seemed to have an edge to it. It was an expensive doll, and she'd begged for it.

"What was wrong with the doll?"

"Nothing," Lisa said. "Ma wouldn't let me play with it."

"She what?"

"She said it was too nice to play with. I used to look up at it on the mantle and cry, but then I forgot about it."

The reporters had kept pace. Johnny was fairly certain they were too far away to hear anything he and Lisa were saying.

"Your arm tired?" he asked. From the waving. "Because mine is." His face was frozen in a garish smile that, abetted by the hangover, seemed sure to leave a scar.

"It's OK," Lisa said. "I may have picked the wrong shoes, though. This is farther than I thought."

They were nearing the reviewing stand, by Central Park Zoo. "Not much farther now."

"I still love them," she said. "The boots."

"They are great boots, miss," said the young walkalong detective. "If you don't mind me saying so, you certainly have the legs for them."

Lisa looked down and thanked him. Johnny now realized Lisa had been giving the detective furtive looks the whole parade. He had an elegant Roman nose, wavy black hair, and looked young to have made detective.

In the bleachers was another thicket of protesters—maybe the same dozen-plus cocksuckers. Johnny imagined them cutting over to Madison and racing uptown, signs flailing, hoping for another chance to make their point. Which was *what*? Aside from tax penalties that weren't his fault and a few stray misunderstandings he'd landed on a few stray jaws, Johnny had never been charged with a crime. Johnny had raised millions for charity, which he'd done quietly and for its own sake, but it still ought to count for something. This Nevada situation was just a publicity stunt by some bigoted political hacks. As for the protests, Johnny shared the sentiments on most of those signs. Criminals *aren't* heroes. Most Italians never *have* met a gangster. Many *are* doctors, lawyers, industrialists, professors, and priests. There *were* great Italian-Americans who'd have been more worthy. He was excruciatingly aware of his epic shortcomings. He was an artist. He had the requisite self-loathing.

Just then, the band paused, and there was a dull, wet *pop*. Then another. Johnny might not have noticed them at all if the walkalongs hadn't reacted, craning their necks, spinning around, and collapsing toward Johnny and Lisa. Uniformed cops fanned out in front of the bleachers.

Johnny realized he was still waving. Cameras whirred, a plague of steel locusts.

As Johnny lowered his arm, an egg smacked against the young detective's shoulder and spattered flecks of egg white onto Lisa's face. Out of the corner of Johnny's eye, he saw what looked like a misshapen volleyball plummeting toward them from above, spewing a tail of water. Johnny put his arm out to protect his daughter. The wet mass exploded against the pavement in the middle of the brass section, splattering globules of toilet paper on the boys' uniformed pant legs. The band director blew his whistle, and a few strides later they resumed their blaring. The people in the reviewing stand laughed.

"Sogball," Johnny said, handing Lisa a monogrammed handkerchief.

Lisa frowned.

"You soak a roll of toilet paper in the sink or the toilet for a while, then

bombs away. I almost got kicked out of school once for dropping a sogball on a nun."

A total lie. He was trying to make light of the situation. The doll had
made her cry, the boots hurt her feet, and sogballs and eggs rained on
his parade.

"Don't worry about it, Mr. Fontane," said the young detective. "There's
a few bad eggs in every crowd. You should've seen what happened to
Joe DiMaggio."

Johnny bent his head to Lisa's ear. "You see?" he said. "Every Italian."

"Bad *eggs*?" Lisa smiled at the detective.

"Geez," he said. "I didn't mean it like that."

"What did happen to Joe DiMaggio?" Johnny said.

One of the other walkalongs cuffed the kid on the shoulder about where
the egg had hit. "Nothing, really, sir," he said. "Dodger fans."

They were well past the reviewing stand now.

Johnny kept smiling and waving and did the math in his head. If the
crowd was even *five* deep, that was, say, a thousand people per block, each
side. So two thousand—conservatively, since people watched from windows, too, including at least one sogball-hurling *mezza sega* Johnny wasn't
going to count. So: two thousand a block, thirty-five blocks up Fifth, call
the people on Seventy-ninth gravy. Seventy thousand. Versus: a dozen-plus
cocksuckers, a few turds from the press, and two or three quote-unquote
bad eggs. Double that number, to account for various isolated crackpots
in the crowd. Seventy, total—tops. Thus, *conservatively*, ninety-nine-point-
nine percent of New Yorkers have no quarrel with Johnny Fontane.

At the end of the parade route, there was another, smaller VIP tent. Images of Christopher Columbus's ships were stenciled on the sides. An
American flag and an Italian flag flanked the podium.

Johnny and Lisa went inside. Johnny wasn't much of a beer drinker, but
he took an iced Moretti to wash down four more aspirin. The Sicilian
clowns came in with the puppets slung over their shoulders and grabbed
beer, too.

"Thank you, Daddy." Lisa hugged him. "I'm so proud of you."

"You sure you're not—"

"Like Detective Vaccarello said. Bad eggs. And I learned a new word and also something about your childhood. *Sogball*. But, seriously, Daddy, seeing the way everyone looks at you, seeing you through their eyes, it was really . . ." She hugged him again. "Amazing."

She'd learned another word somehow, the kid detective's name.

"How're your feet? I can get you a taxi."

"You don't want me to stay for the press conference?" Seeing his face, she laughed. "Gotcha. I have a music history exam I need to study for, anyway. But, no, I don't need a ride. Detective Vaccarello, Steve, said he'd take me."

Steve? As if on cue, the detective introduced himself.

Disapproval throbbed on the tip of Johnny's tongue. But it *was* just a ride. Johnny settled for giving Detective Vaccarello a silent, heavy-lidded stare.

Sometimes it was useful that people thought they knew things about the friends Johnny Fontane had. He let the detective think about that for a while, then thanked him for his help and kissed Lisa good-bye.

The VIP tent was filling up with reporters. Johnny posed for pictures with nuns and old friends and chomped at the bit to get moving. Finally, the bald parade official took the podium. "Ladies and gentlemen," he said, "I present to you a man who needs no introduction, a native New Yorker and a father of three lovely girls including one who was able to join him here today; a man who is a star of stage and screen and a hit maker *extraordinaire*, including my personal favorite LP, *The Last Lonely Midnight*; a man who has won an Oscar, a Golden Globe, the West Chicago Knights of Columbus's Humanitarian of the Year Award, and other honors too numerous to mention; a man who also happens to be a third-generation Italian-American, with ancestors from Sicilia and Napoli. It's my very special honor to present, the grand marshal of the 1963 Columbus Day Parade, Mr. John Fontane."

Between the TV lights and the cacophony of the questions, Johnny felt like he was getting hit with the hot winds of a sirocco.

He waited for it to die down a little, then tapped the microphone with one finger. He cleared his throat. Miraculously, they shut up.

"America," said Johnny Fontane, smiling that wide, frozen smile one last time. "What a beee-yoo-tiful Italian word."

Then he winked, bowed, and left the podium.

CHAPTER 10

Friends and family gathered on the huge rooftop garden to wish Michael Corleone a happy birthday. It wasn't a party, per se, although Connie had baked a cake and the little Hagen girls had made decorations out of construction paper. Several of the men who'd come by for business had stuck around. A few more people stopped by on their way home from the parade.

The cake sat on a table beside a modest stack of presents. It was a chocolate fudge sheet cake shot through with espresso and Grand Marnier—a specialty of Connie's. Knowing that Michael wasn't big on birthdays, she'd written *Cent'anni!* on the cake instead, though she was a better baker than decorator. Several guests asked, in whispers, why the cake said *Cemetery!*

Francesca's little boy kept begging to be allowed to unwrap his great-uncle's presents. Michael was still upstairs, meeting with Tom Hagen and Richie Two-Guns, but Al Neri had come down to tell Connie that Michael knew they were waiting and would be down in a minute. Little Sonny kept asking if it had been a minute yet.

The garden was Connie Corleone's attempt to re-create the one their father had so lovingly tended behind the house in Long Beach. Connie—

whose use of her maiden name seemed now to have foreshadowed this even more vain attempt to reclaim her innocence—had made a pilgrimage to the original, which the new owners (civilians, not even Italians) had allowed to fall into heartbreaking disarray. She'd diagrammed what was left to see, taking countless snapshots of the sagging grape arbor, measuring the distance between the ailing fig trees, and paying the new owners an exorbitant price for the statue of the Holy Virgin, even though it was identical to ones that could be bought cheaply on any commercial street in Bay Ridge or Bensonhurst. An epic amount of time and money had gone into the new garden, including reinforcing the building so that the many tons of new dirt didn't cave in the roof and bury the Hagens. Yet the more the garden came to resemble the original, the more it became a monstrous parody of the ordered sanctuary where Connie's wedding reception had taken place, where Vito, fanning himself with a sweat-stained straw hat, had sat in the shade of the grape arbor and taught Michael the nuances of the business. The rooftop version of the arbor had been blown down last month in a thunderstorm. Repairs were ongoing. The whole *project* had the feel of something that would never be finished.

Connie rushed around rechecking details she'd checked again and again already—napkins, forks, whether her lighter worked so she could fire up the cake's big red candle, whether her sons looked presentable. She was a brassy woman a few degrees shy of attractive, with vigilantly dyed black hair and an incongruous girlish habit of flipping it away from her face. She'd changed her clothes several times today and now wore a jade-green cocktail dress more appropriate for dinner at the Stork Club than a modest cake-and-coffee get-together for her brother's odd-numbered birthday.

Amused by this display of nervous energy, the twins stood at opposite ends of the little crowd, sipping glasses of wine, Francesca's white and Kathy's red. Even as toddlers they'd refused to dress alike, and for years they'd seemed as different as identical twins could be. Kathy had been an honor student; Francesca was popular. Kathy was a chain-smoking bohemian, Francesca a good Catholic girl. Kathy had a Ph.D. in continental literature from a university in London; Francesca had dropped out of Florida State to marry a rich boy. But now that they were a little older and once again under the same roof, they'd come to realize their differences might have been more willful than real. Lately, Kathy splurged on clothes from the same designer the First Lady used, and Francesca seemed to always have her nose in a novel (recent favorites included *Emma*, *The Talented Mr. Ripley*, Sergio Lupo's *An Immigrant's Tale*, and, especially, Lampedusa's *The Leopard*). Each twin wore her hair in a stylish bob. Each was devoted to her work: Kathy taught freshman composition and continental literature in translation at City College, and Francesca was, in essence, the face of the Vito Corleone Foundation, keeping the foundation's good works quietly but persistently in the news. The twins had differences, of course, beyond their taste in wine. Kathy needed glasses; Francesca did not. Kathy was, discreetly, cutting an erotic swath through her neck of the groves of academe, while Francesca had been on only two clumsy kissless dates since her husband died. Kathy was slim and slightly dried-up-looking. Francesca, perhaps as a result of her pregnancies (Sonny and the baby who had died), had full womanly hips and a round behind. Her breasts had swollen to D cups. She'd see them in the mirror and avert her eyes. She gave Kathy all her button-up blouses.

But the twins both understood, without ever having talked about it, the source of their aunt's anxiety. Connie had known Johnny Fontane all her life, even before he was famous, yet the prospect of his coming over for a brief business meeting with her brother still reduced her to behaving like some skittish bobby-soxer. The twins hadn't met Johnny before. They were looking forward to it, but within reason. Kathy was just naturally unexcitable and difficult to impress. As for Francesca, her late husband's wealth and position in the attorney general's office had allowed her to meet all measure of the powerful and the famous. On the other hand, Francesca had been lucky enough to see Fontane perform at the Inaugural Ball. She doubted there was any woman who'd seen Johnny Fontane that night—a feral, vulnerable man in a swallowtail coat and a voice like no one else—

and been unmoved. Francesca had seen Elvis perform, and also James Brown. She'd seen Mario Lanza at Carnegie Hall, Louis Armstrong at the Copa in Miami, and Frank Sinatra at the Sands in Las Vegas, but Fontane's twenty-two-minute set was the best thing she'd ever seen on stage.

It was not necessarily the memory of that night that was giving Francesca goose bumps, though. It was cold for October—colder still up there on the roof.

SIX MEN WERE CRAMMED IN THE SMOKE-FILLED, WALNUT-paneled private study off Michael Corleone's bedroom. Michael Corleone and Tom Hagen sat at a partners' desk that nearly filled the room. Everyone else stood—Al Neri behind Michael, and, near the door, Richie "Two-Guns" Nobilio and Tommy Neri, Al's nephew. Nobilio was wrapping up his discussion of opening up the books, the pros and cons of the men proposed for initiation into the Corleone Family. The reputation of these men preceded them. The presentation was a sacrament as routine as any performed in church (where Richie, unlike the rest of them, was active and sometimes even played the organ). At tonight's Commission meeting, Michael's presentation of these same names would be brisk and even more of a formality.

Richie Two-Guns was bug-eyed, acne-scarred, and greyhound-thin, with slicked-back hair and a taste for garish clothes he must have thought made him look tough. Leather, mohair, sharkskin, guayaberas, sometimes even cowboy boots. He was proving to be one of the great talents the Corleone Family had ever developed. He'd grown up down the street from Peter Clemenza in the Bronx, and as a boy he'd buzzed around the fat man like a swift, unkillable fly, begging for the chance to do anything, anything at all. Clemenza knew how to turn an insect like that into a sleek and deadly hornet. Nobilio got his nickname from an incident in his young-buck days. He'd taken an unloaded gun to kill a man—a highway official who processed contract bids, a cog in Robert Moses's vast and crooked empire,

and one of the last pieces in the puzzle that was the greater New York cement monopoly. The man was working late in his office. A former captain
of the Harvard swimming team, he was almost twice Nobilio's size. Richie
pulled the trigger of his empty silencer-equipped Colt Woodsman twice,
realized it was empty, and without missing a beat, punched the larger man
and started rifling through his desk. By the time the guy got to his feet,
Nobilio had found a .32 Davis behind a whiskey bottle in the bottom
drawer. He emptied it into the man's broad chest and got away clean. For
a while people called him Richie Lucky and Richie Two-Guns, inter-
changeably. Two-Guns was what stuck. Nobilio laughed it off and even
started telling (an embellished, greatly self-mocking version of) the story
on himself. All the way around, his humility had served him well. When
Frankie Pantangeli was tabbed to take over for Clemenza, a different sort
of man would have harbored a grudge. Richie seemed to have thought
nothing of it. He'd kept his head down and not only continued to get his
work done but also expanded the Family's holdings in Rhode Island and
Fort Lauderdale. When Frankie did himself in, Richie Two-Guns was the
obvious choice to take over—particularly since he'd been trained by
Clemenza. Deaths, betrayals, and jail sentences had left the organization
shorthanded, and Nobilio's ability to find talent and develop it was proving to be as good if not better than the fat man's. In the years since
Clemenza's death, his legend had only grown, but the fact remained that
he'd handpicked for promotion such eventual traitors as Paulie Gatto and
Nick Geraci. On the mean streets of New York, Peter Clemenza had at-
tained gangland sainthood, but in this dark and smoky room, despite
everyone's affection for him, the fat man's legacy was that of a man who
was all too human.

"If that's all," Michael said, looking at his watch, "I need to get going."
He looked at Tommy Neri, aka Tommy Scootch, who'd just gotten back
from a long trip out of town, and back at Nobilio. "Any other news
for me?"

Richie Two-Guns made eye contact with Tommy, then grimaced and shook his head. "Not really. Scootch, you want to kind of give us an update?"

Tommy took a step toward the desk. Despite his thinning, prematurely gray hair, he looked like a nervous schoolkid called upon to give the book report he thought was due tomorrow. Organizing the hunt for Nick Geraci was the biggest job ever given to him. All things being equal, Michael thought it best to kill traitors with their closest associates, but Donnie Bags wasn't up to the job physically, Carmine Marino was dead, Momo Barone was still in prison at the time, and Eddie Paradise had his hands full getting up to speed as *capo*. Dino DiMiceli had started out by taking two good men and flying into Cleveland to look for leads there. When their rental car got precisely ten miles down the road, the bomb wired to its odometer went off; all three were killed instantly; one of DiMiceli's arms landed in a public swimming pool a quarter mile away. As for Willie Binaggio, he was a chain-smoker, so it was possible that his house really did burn down by accident, as the fire marshal had ruled. No one Willie B. worked with believed that. That's when Al asked Michael to give the job to Tommy.

Scootch took a deep breath and began. "Paradise wasn't using Donnie Bags as a driver—he was the, uh, traitor's guy—so I asked if I could have him. He's clean, I think, but if he ain't, I got him," and he pointed toward an imaginary front seat, "where I can keep my eye on him."

Michael nodded, impressed at the initiative. Donnie Serio—known as Donnie Bags because of the colostomy bag he'd needed since the time he was shot in the gut—was some kind of cousin to Geraci. That didn't make Bags a traitor, too, but it had still been smart to draw him away from his old *regime* and put him where, if the need came, Tommy could pull the trigger on him at a moment's notice. "Good," Michael said.

"The other men in that crew check out good, which for all I know is what Dino and Willie B. thought, too. But I just wanted to make sure, so I started from scratch on that."

Michael nodded.

The traces of a grin flickered on Tommy's face. "In addition," he said, "I did like you asked and had another conversation with the father, Fausto. In Arizona there. Tried to reason with him, right? But god*damn*. He's one of them silent, old-country Sicilians. *Coglioni quadrati,* y'know? I get the feeling that if we killed him for what he knows but won't say, it'd be the happiest day of his life. He's got a new Mexican wife who don't speak English, so that's a dead end, and they ain't been married long anyway. On the other hand, there's the wife and the daughters of the *disgraziato.* If I turn up the flame on them three—"

Michael shook his head. Fausto Geraci had been a *cugin'* striver in Cleveland for Vinnie Forlenza's outfit, but the other members of Nick Geraci's family were off-limits for anything but surveillance and questioning.

"Right, right, right, of course," Tommy said. "Of course, sure. Also, um, I followed through on those new tips you gave me from your source," Tommy said, looking at Hagen.

Both Michael and Hagen perked up. *This* was news.

"You went down there?" Hagen said.

"Just got back," Tommy said. "The person in question ain't in that town Taxco." He pronounced it *Tax-co* instead of *Tahs-co.* "He *was* there, or at least some of the people we talked to recognized his picture. He was down there passing himself off as a book writer. Thing is, he didn't leave in a hurry or nothin'. He had plenty of time to pack up all his things in the apartment he had, but nobody saw him leave or knew anything about it. One day he just vanished. My thinking was, somebody tipped him off. But this fella Spratling, an American businessman who knows everybody down there, he says that's just Mexico for you."

"Tipped him off?" Hagen said. "How so?"

"That, I don't know," Tommy said. "But it stands to reason that if he does have somebody tipping him off, he'll eventually risk coming back to the U.S. If he does that, we'll find him. We got an eye on his family, plus, in any city where we have friends, it's certain that our friends know the situation and how grateful we'd be for their help. The word's out—quiet, you know, but real effective. This guy can't hide in spider holes or in the mountains south of the border and such, not forever. Especially not *this* guy. He's got a medical condition he's been keeping under wraps. This Parkinson's disease, what it does is, it makes you shake, it maybe makes you forget things, and also it makes it so it's rough to get dressed—you know, 'cause of the buttons and the shakes and whatnot. Or at least that's what he was complaining about to his regular doctor, back before he, uh—not the doctor—before he disappeared."

Michael frowned. Geraci had been shaking the last couple times Michael had seen him. "You found all that out, but you didn't find him?"

"I found all that out on account of I pulled some strings and got a look at his medical files," Tommy said. "A secretary. Very nice girl. I'm turning over every stone, so to speak."

"So to speak." Michael turned over his palms and made a *Who's to say?* gesture. "But not actually." Tommy started to stay something; Michael raised a hand to stop him. "Tommy, you're doing a fine job," he said, though his affectless voice made it sound like the opposite might also be true. "I'm a patient man. What matters is that it gets done and done right. I understand that, and I'm sure you do, too."

Tommy nodded. "I'm grateful to hear it," he said, clearly unsure whether he really was. "I'll tell you what, though: I think it's safe to say he's not in FBI custody somewhere. And he's sure not dead. My theory, which I mean no offense by and you can take it or you can leave it, is that whoever it is that's feeding you information is jerking you around. Jerking *us* around, I should say. Tipping us off, as it were, and then tipping off you-know-who as well."

"Why," Tom Hagen said, "would anyone want to do that?"

"We were talking that over," Nobilio said, jumping in. Visibly grateful, Tommy Neri stepped back from the desk to the wall. "I don't know how or where you're getting the tips that you're getting," Richie said. "I don't want to know. I just think—*we* think, Tommy and me both—that whoever's tipping you off, Mike, is either out to make you look bad—that's theory number one. Theory number two is, there's someone who *your* source knows, maybe *his* boss or something, who's making sure we don't find this cocksucker."

Michael pursed his lips. He let the silence hang there, largely for effect. If the information they were getting from Joe Lucadello was tainted, so be it. Joe was a trusted old friend, but those are the most dangerous kind, perfectly positioned to betray you or be used against you. This was no longer anything that Michael found surprising. The worst part of this might be Hagen. He did not know Joe well and had always been suspicious of him. There seemed to be nothing in life that brought Tom Hagen more pleasure than earning the right to say I-told-you-so and then bathing in silent self-regard as he didn't say it.

As for Nick Geraci, Michael could afford to be patient. He had an empire to run, thousands of people depending on him, directly or indirectly, for their livelihoods if not their very lives, and he was running it well. Geraci was just one pathetic man. He had no power, no life. Even though he wasn't in the hole under Lake Erie anymore, or in Taxco, either, he was nonetheless trapped in some other rat-hole hell of his own devising. Every moment, he must feel the cold steel of the sword of justice pressing against the back of his neck. Even better, because of the surveillance on his family, Geraci had no realistic chance of seeing his wife or his children.

He did have some means of talking to them—some complicated system involving friends' phones and payphones and prearranged times to call, a system too well put together to crack. Geraci was too smart to leave any trail. While the old Sicilian code would have allowed for the intimidation of Geraci's family and, under the right circumstances, even their execution, Vito Corleone—who often admitted to being sentimental about his family—had established a different code. For him, harming a man's family was unthinkable. Michael had been trained both by his parents and the United

States Marine Corps to live his life by a code. Violating that code was not an option—especially now, with Michael's own children in Maine, protected by nothing stronger than Kay's good intentions.

Finally, by way of dismissal, Michael nodded.

"Gentlemen," Hagen said. "Let's hope that the next time we all sit down together we'll be discussing results and not theories."

AT LAST, THE GUEST OF HONOR APPEARED ON THE ROOFTOP, flanked by his *consigliere* and his most trusted *caporegime*. Richie Nobilio's shiny new motorcycle jacket made him look like an appliance salesman auditioning to be a Shark or a Jet in a community theater production of *West Side Story*. Hagen wore a blue Brooks Brothers suit. Michael Corleone's suit was black, custom-made, and from Milan. As he'd gotten older, he had the strange, oddly endearing ability to make expensive suits look off-the-rack.

The party guests broke into polite applause.

"Open your presents!" shrieked Little Sonny, which cracked everyone up.

The Don crossed the garden the way royalty would, hands clasped at the small of his back, the guests beaming in his presence. There was a tiny, preening bounce in each step, an unconscious habit. His broad smile was at odds with the dark circles under his eyes, the permanent furrow in his brow. He muttered niceties about how everyone shouldn't have.

Everyone sang "Happy Birthday," and as they finished the doors of the thirty-ninth-floor elevator parted and Johnny Fontane sprang out, arms spread, Jolson-parodic, singing, "*And many moooooore!*"

Michael Corleone closed his eyes, made a wish that would have surprised everybody there, and blew out his candle.

"*Johneee!*" squealed Connie Corleone. She ran to him and threw her arms around him, nearly knocking him off his feet. She managed to press herself against him in a way that wasn't quite brazen but did allow her to brush her thigh against Johnny's legendary *cazzo*. She'd never seen it, but ever since she'd had her first independent confirmation of its existence, when he'd danced with her at her first wedding, the thought of it had gotten her through some lonely nights.

"Hey, sweetheart," Johnny said, recovering his balance. Some of the same men who wouldn't be seen with him at the parade stood with him now on this rooftop. He winked. "I thought it was your *nephew* who was the big football star. How's he doin', anyway?"

"It's his knee," she said. Frankie, the twins' brother, had played linebacker at Notre Dame. Undersize even in college, he'd gone to play in Canada and gotten hurt in training camp. "His football days may be over. It's breaking his heart."

Connie grabbed Johnny's arm to indicate empathy for Frankie's plight, though that was just a cover. Johnny was between marriages. He was in the gossip columns all the time with different starlets, but most of those items, Connie knew, were planted by someone's publicist.

"Tough break," Johnny said. "That Frankie played with as much heart as anybody I ever saw. It ain't the size of the dog in the fight, like they say."

She nodded absently, which provoked Johnny to explain the whole cliché. Connie had heard it, though. Her first husband, Carlo, used to use a version of it in the bedroom. *It ain't the size of the dong in the fight, it's the size of the fight in the dong.* Carlo had the yapping toy poodle of pricks. Johnny's was supposedly more of an Italian wolfhound. His tailor, who made suits for Michael and Tom, too, had confided to her that Johnny's pants needed to be tailored to accommodate it. Connie shuddered. "Football's so violent," she said, thinking quickly to cover that erotic throb. "I have a hard time watching it."

Michael Corleone bent over and whispered to Little Sonny that he could open the gifts for him. The boy whooped and headed for the presents.

As the wrapping paper flew, Michael muttered his thanks, slipped out, and went back upstairs. Hagen whispered something to Richie Nobilio, and

Nobilio waved him off, like whatever Hagen wanted was amply covered. Nobilio and his men headed for the elevator. Hagen went back upstairs, too.

"What about these tough hombres, eh?" Johnny Fontane said, tousling the hair of Connie's sons. "They look like they could do some good on the ol' gridiron."

Victor and Little Mike seemed instantly to adore him.

"Let me introduce you," Connie said, "to Frankie's big sisters."

Johnny rubbed his eyes. "I'm seeing double."

Kathy laughed, as taken in as Connie. Francesca rolled her eyes—at the cheesy witticism and more so her sister's appalling reaction to it. "Believe it or not," Francesca said, "we've actually *never* heard that one before."

Johnny cocked his head.

"I'm kidding," Francesca said.

"I got it," Johnny said. It was something other than confusion she'd sparked.

Connie grasped Johnny's elbow but followed through with the introductions.

Johnny eluded Connie's possessive grip and kissed each twin's hand in turn.

Most women have had their hand kissed, but invariably the man doing the kissing is being self-conscious, mock gallant. Johnny Fontane knew how to kiss a woman's hand with the pure gentlemanly ardor of a Sicilian prince.

Kathy giggled, perhaps for the first time since grade school.

But it sent a shiver through Francesca.

The only other person Francesca had ever met who had this kind of magnetism was the president, who was also a man who knew how to take a woman's hand. Perhaps because of that experience, Francesca told herself that the shiver meant nothing. The kiss, the shiver: merely the parlor tricks of a domesticated wolf. Also, it was getting colder up here, by the minute, it seemed. But Francesca was not tempted to go get a sweater.

Johnny somehow—more tricks!—remembered that Kathy was a college professor, and he told her that nothing would have made her grandfather happier. Kathy thanked him, clearly awed that he knew who she was.

"And you," he said to Francesca, "I hear good things about your work for the foundation."

She smoothed her dress. A part of Francesca suspected that Johnny had heard nothing at all, but that wasn't the part of her that was, at present, in charge. "Thank you, Mr. Fontane," she said. She smirked. "We try."

"No, no, no, please," he said. "Call me Johnny, sweetheart."

"OK, Johnny Sweetheart," Francesca blurted. She stifled the urge to put her hand over her mouth.

"Good one," Johnny said. "You do more than try, is what I hear. I hear you get things done." He smiled. "That's what I like," he said. "I live my life around people who talk, talk, talk. I'm guilty of it, too, God knows, right? But I like people who do things."

"That's deep," Francesca said. It was the kind of caustic remark Kathy would have said. Kathy, for her part, was mooning about, seemingly struck dumb. "That's what *I* like," Francesca said. "People who are deep."

Francesca couldn't stop herself.

Connie backhanded Francesca's shoulder.

But Johnny laughed like hell.

Francesca felt herself go weak in the knees, and she hated herself for it. There was, however, no denying that in that moment Johnny Fontane didn't seem like a big movie star or a big recording star. What he seemed like—enjoying a joke at his own expense, the center of attention, filthy with charm—was her father.

Behind her, Little Sonny was asking if there were any more presents to open.

"Don't mind her, John," Connie said, widening her eyes at Francesca in disapproval. "She's been sick." She again took Johnny by the arm. "C'mon, let me get you some of my fudge cake. You had it once before. Maybe you remember?"

Johnny kept those famous eyes on Francesca. The rest of him had stopped laughing well before the eyes did. "You see right through me, don't you?"

Connie frowned. She didn't let go of Johnny's arm.

Francesca tried to do just that, to look through him.

When a person is blessed with *that thing*, whatever it is, it ordinarily does its miraculous work at a distance—from the pulpit, the stage, the screen, the ring, the podium, even the head of a long family table. At close range, the results are more unpredictable. It might not work on such an intimate scale. It might be so remarkably unlike recognizable human behavior as to provoke pity. Then again, it might be so strong as to strike fear into the hearts of the righteous.

"Eat some of Aunt Connie's cake," said Kathy, breaking the silence. "It'll make it so nobody can see through you."

"See?" Connie erupted in a piercing, mirthless chortle: a madwoman's laugh. "Despite their different figures, they really *are* twins. Everybody's a critic, right, Johnny?"

"You better believe it," Johnny said.

"Sorry," Kathy said.

"It's actually really good, the cake," Francesca said. She smoothed her dress again, unsure whether to feel like the betrayed or the betrayer.

"Rich but good," said Kathy.

Just like me, Francesca almost said, but this time, she curbed the impulse. "Excuse me," she said, and went to keep her little boy from making any more of a scene. He was now dancing around on the table, draped in a robe someone had given her uncle, shouting that he was the champion of the world.

Connie crooked her arm in Johnny's and followed.

"Hey there, champ," Johnny said to Sonny.

"*Un*defeated!" Sonny said, arms raised in victory. "And *un*tied!"

The guests were getting a kick out of all this and so, apparently, was Johnny. With her free arm, Connie Corleone started cutting the cake.

"Get down," Francesca said to Sonny. "Now."

"Yours?" Johnny said.

Francesca turned around. "I could be wrong," she said, pointing, "but I think the honor of your presence is requested."

Tom Hagen was now standing at the foot of the staircase to the top floor, his finger crooked, beckoning. He was making no effort to conceal his impatience. Johnny made eye contact with him, then broke from Connie's grasp, backing away.

"Listen," he said to Francesca. "Don't go anywhere, OK? I wasn't just . . ." He kept backing away. "All I'm trying to say is that I have an idea you can maybe help me with."

"Where would I go?" Francesca said. "I live here."

"Great," Johnny said, and jogged toward Hagen with the same gait he used when he trotted back onstage for an encore.

"I'll save you some chocolate cake, Johnny!" Connie called after him.

Francesca took her son off the table, set him down, then removed and folded up the robe. She turned around, and her eyes met Kathy's. A look passed between the twins. Ordinary people would have taken an hour to say as much.

CHAPTER 11

At the granite wet bar near his floor-to-ceiling living-room window, Michael Corleone lined up three cordial glasses and filled two of them with Strega. Michael's own glass was mostly water, with just enough of the liqueur to be vaguely yellow.

Tom ushered Johnny into the room.

"Michael!" Johnny said, his arms extended in supplication. "I'm sorry as hell if I upstaged—"

Michael set the bottle down sharply enough to cut Johnny off. "Upstaged? This is your big day, John."

He said it so flatly it would have been impossible to read anything into it and, therefore, impossible not to.

The men embraced.

Michael shook his head. "If it weren't for my family, I'd probably forget my own birthday, as any grown man would. But you? This honor? I'm the one who owes you an apology."

"Apology for what?"

Michael's self-deprecating shrug had become a spooky echo of his father's. "I wanted to go, to watch the parade, but I've been tied up in business meetings all day. On a Saturday. Terrible." He patted Johnny on the back. "No rest for the wicked, right?"

Johnny Fontane strode to the window. "Nice view." He circled the gleaming room like a man who'd never been in a penthouse.

"You'd never know from the street," Johnny said, "that there's a view up here like this."

Hagen folded his arms and watched this performance through narrowed eyes. He had a low opinion of show business people in general and Fontane in particular. Go to the opera any night of the week, and you'll hear better singers. Any night of the week, you could go see an off-Broadway play where every actor in the cast had more talent than Johnny. Dancing, telling jokes? Hagen's little girls, in his opinion, were almost as good on both counts. Johnny was a punk, an irresponsible child whose problems were solved by others—too often by Hagen himself (it was Hagen who, on Don Vito's orders, had made certain investments that got Fontane his Academy Award). Yet for reasons that escaped Tom Hagen, everybody treated Johnny Fontane as if he were an important man. Even Michael seemed to have a weak spot for the guy.

Michael handed out the glasses.

"My father would be proud of you, Johnny," Michael said. "*Cent'anni.*"

They all three clinked glasses and drank.

Michael and Johnny asked about each other's families. They were divorced fathers—common enough in Johnny's circles but practically unknown in Michael's. Divorced *Catholic* fathers. "How often do you get to see them?" Johnny said. "Anthony and Mary, right?"

"Often," Michael said automatically. "I go up there as often as I can. They come here for school holidays."

They hadn't been here since the Fourth of July. Michael had his own airplane and yet had not flown himself to Maine in a month, since he'd gone to watch Anthony sing in a middle-school production of *Flower Drum Song.* And he'd been late for that.

"That's good," Johnny said. "Because a man who doesn't spend time . . ."

He stopped himself, gave his head a quick scratch and screwed up his face at this difficult situation. "The thing I've learned—from painful experience—is that if you aren't around, you miss a lot. As you know. I'm not presuming to tell you anything, but I will say this: it gets better, if that's any consolation. My daughter's going to school in the city here and just last—"

"At Juilliard," Michael said. "So I hear. Very impressive."

"How's Rita?" Johnny said.

At the sound of her name, Michael's features softened. "She's doing well," he said. "She says hello."

"Look at this guy!" Johnny said to Tom Hagen, then turned back to Michael. "You're crazy about her, aren't you? I can tell. Don't shit a shitter, pally."

Michael, blushing slightly, raised his arms in resignation. What can a man do?

"I knew it," Johnny said. "I told you, didn't I? Those dancer's legs, and not a phony bone in her body. What a great girl she is. I'm happy for you."

Marguerite Duvall owed much of her career to Johnny Fontane. When he'd met her, she was just another dancer in a classy nude review, a wholesome, high-kicking French kid who really liked to fuck. Johnny connected her with a singing coach and some other good people to know. Soon she had her own lounge act at the Kasbah. That led to a supporting role as the French madam in the Broadway show *Cattle Call*. Critics hated it, but the burning-bordello scene was a showshopper, and, to the surprise of the New York theater snobs, she walked off with a Tony Award. Johnny had also included her in some of his movies and on the bill at the Inaugural Ball, among much bigger stars. She was not sleeping with Jimmy Shea at the time; that had come earlier. Over the years, Johnny had introduced Rita to several of his pals. Squares wouldn't understand, but in Johnny's experience, sleeping with the same woman bonded pals closer together.

Michael Corleone motioned for Johnny to have a seat on the sofa. Michael sat in a club chair beside him. Both were covered in the softest, finest Italian leather. Hagen perched on a chrome stool beside the bar.

"You really think your father would have been proud of me?" Johnny asked.

"I do," Michael said. "When I was a boy, he took me to that parade many times. He'd always point out the big shots marching by and made a point of telling me that in America you can be anything you want to be. Christopher Columbus came here and found a place big enough to stage the biggest dreams. A new world."

"Christopher Columbus never set foot here," Johnny blurted. "To be technical about it. But, uh, I see your point, which as a matter of fact I happen to agree with you about."

Hagen sighed heavily.

"My father's point," Michael said.

"No disrespect," Johnny murmured.

"So how can I help you, John? On your big day."

"I guess you saw the newspapers, huh?" Johnny said. He stared into the eyes of the son of his godfather. Michael Corleone had gone as still and cold as the marble floor beneath their feet. "It wasn't . . . what I mean to say is, *none* of it . . . that those bloodsuckers . . . y'know? You do know. Right, Mike? What they don't make up, they twist around, and . . ."

Michael did not even blink.

Johnny lowered his head. He started nodding and kept at it awhile. "I want to say," he said, "that I take full responsibility for everything. I've made mistakes, plenty of 'em, especially with money. You and your family, my godfather . . . you've been great sources of . . . you could really call it wisdom. That includes you, Tom. I've had opportunities that a guy like me . . ."

He finally looked up.

"The long and the short of it," Johnny said, "is this. I need to sell my share in your . . . in the casino out in Tahoe before I'm forced to do it. That may not come to pass, and, to be honest with you, I could use the dough this investment generates every month, but I'll make some quick cash by selling. What I'm trying to say is, after all is said and done, I think it's best for all parties involved if . . . if it looks like it's my decision. To sell."

Michael rubbed his index and middle fingers back and forth across his lips. To Fontane, it might as well have been the report of a pistol.

"I'm confused," Michael said. "You're asking *my* permission to sell your share of the Castle in the Clouds?"

Fontane shrugged.

"It's an investment, John, just like any of your others. It's just business, I assure you."

"Because if you want, out of loyalty to you and your family, I'll fight those cowboy bastards on the Gaming—"

"That's entirely up to you, John."

Johnny hadn't expected this response. He was the kind of man who worked things out by talking and doing, and he was facing down a man who was his polar opposite. Johnny scooted forward on the sofa and kept talking.

"I'll be honest with you. I tried to see if Jimmy Shea would pull some strings for me there. With the Gaming Commission, but—"

"You went to them first?"

"I didn't go to them at all, Mike. Those ungrateful Irish fucks—no offense, Tom—but damn their eyes, y'know?"

Hagen held up his hands to indicate no offense had been taken.

"After all the hard work I did for them," Johnny said, "this is the first and only thing I asked for."

"So I'm Plan B. Coming to me."

"No. God, no." Fontane could feel himself redden. "Plan A was to keep my share, any way I could. It didn't make a whole lot of sense to go to you when the Gaming Commission has an issue with me being associated with you in the first place. If I handled it in a way that was less than perfect, Mike, from my heart, I'm sorry. I wanted to talk to you about it, but you weren't available, which Tom can vouch for. I had commitments, too. This was the first time it was possible for us to talk face-to-face."

Michael shrugged in concession—again that spooky echo of Vito.

"My fear," Johnny said, "is that if I *don't* sell, they'll drag this out just to see their names in the papers. These guys are politicians. They think that if they repeat a lie loud enough and often enough the public will believe it. And the newspapers, they print the accusations on page one, but the day it turns out it's all a bunch of nothing, just watch: they'll run a little mention next to the funny pages. The problem, as I see it, is that if I *do* sell, it puts an end to the investigation but it also looks like I'm telling the bastards that the lies they're spreading are true. I have to think everyone will forget about it once it's out of the headlines. But there's the risk that because it looks like I admitted to something, they'll keep on investigating and—"

Michael closed his eyes and held up his hand to halt. Johnny did. Some things were better left unsaid.

"Forgive me," Michael said, "but there's something I don't understand." Most people, when discussing something they don't understand, will look at the ceiling or off in the distance. Michael stared right at Johnny. "Money's an issue with you? How is that possible?"

Johnny frowned. "How's it possible? I got overhead like you can't believe. My last concert tour, we had to take a forty-piece orchestra on the road, which means not just meals and hotels but also trucks, crew, a traveling secretary, even—get this, Tom—a lawyer. Just what we paid every night for the Teamsters who stood around watching *other* Teamsters work—it'd blow your mind. Blow it. The shows drew great, and—knock wood—my records keep selling, but a lot of people wet their beaks on the way from each concert ticket or record album I sell to any sort of check that comes my way. Then there's taxes. Uncle Sugar'd be half as sweet if it wasn't for yours truly. Out of what's *left*, I've got to pay the expenses on the house in Palm Springs plus the one in Vegas. I've got all the various bills for my kids—a college education ain't cheap, by the way—which I can afford, but affording it is expensive. Then there's being in the public eye. Fame doesn't just bring money in. Fame needs to be fed, which means managers, publicists, security, a valet, clothes, cars, gifts, what have you, not to mention the way you're a target for every supposedly good cause under the sun. Then toss in an accountant who disappeared on me. On top of which, imagine taking everything that's a challenge with one ex-wife like you got, huh? And multiply it times three. Still, I'm not complaining. Believe me, I'm blessed. In the scheme of things, things are so jake they're Jacob. But you asked."

Michael and Tom exchanged a look. "Disappeared?" Michael said.

"That guy? Somewhere in the tropics sipping mai tais, I bet, and—"

"You *bet*?" Hagen said.

Johnny turned around. "Excuse me? Was I talking to you?"

Tom lit a fresh cigarette. "How much would you say your gambling debts were last year, Johnny?"

"Because I wasn't *aware* that I was talking to you."

Johnny turned back to face Michael, whose face had once again gone cold.

"I see your point, counselor," Johnny said. "But I'm way ahead of you. I've cut back on all that. For a while there, everything I touched was charmed, including my efforts on behalf of our friend the president, but also the records and pictures I was making, my investments, so on and so forth. When a fella's on a roll like that, it stands to reason he'd want to try his luck at the track or playing hunches on various ballgames and fights. When my luck started going south, I cut back on risks like that. Not that it's any of your business, but you asked."

Michael offered Johnny a cigarette. Johnny quit a year earlier on the advice of his doctor. The pipes. He took one anyway.

"The *reason* Tom and I were curious about your financial situation," Michael said, lighting up, "was that if you're expecting to sell your portion of the Tahoe property, it might not provide the return you're looking for. In fact, you're not going to recoup your initial investment or anything close to it."

"You're joking, right? That joint's a goddamned gold mine. A mint."

"John, this can't be the first time you've noticed that the value of a privately held business sometimes has little to do with the company's revenue stream." Michael flicked his ash in a floor ashtray and gave his father's *powerless to do anything* shrug. "With publicly traded stocks, it's even worse." He laughed. "Now, *there's* a racket, don't you think? There's not a trader on Wall Street who could survive the kind of investigation you're under in Nevada, John."

Fontane looked tortured by everything he wasn't saying. He couldn't remember ever smoking a cigarette any faster. "Not anything close to my initial investment?" Johnny finally managed to say. "It's hard for me to believe that—"

"It's a fairly new venture," Michael said. "New ventures have various expenses older ones don't. Then there's also the bad publicity, the lawyers' fees. So no." He looked at Hagen. "Nothing close."

Johnny nodded, resigned. His whole body seemed to shrink.

Tom Hagen stifled a laugh.

Johnny reached into his coat pocket for the aspirin bottle he'd taken from his daughter, refused Michael's offer of a glass of water, shook out four pills, and dry-swallowed them. "I would," he said, "take another cigarette, though. If you have one."

Michael tossed Johnny the pack. "With my compliments," he said. "But before you go, there's something else I need you to understand," Michael said. "Your share in the Castle in the Clouds is, as I've said, your business. But our share in your movie company? That," Michael said, "is mine."

He did not need to mention that it was—in fact if not entirely on paper—a majority share.

Johnny frowned. "I don't know why you'd be unhappy about that. Nearly every picture we've put out the last few years—well, they aren't going to win any awards. But they do all right by the standards of today. Last year was the worst year for Hollywood productions in fifty years. With television and everything, I don't know if you're ever again going to see a motion picture business like what you saw back in the glory days."

Michael and Hagen exchanged a look.

"I'm not talking about profit, John." Michael smiled. This smile matched the look in his eyes perfectly. Both belonged to a man about to say *checkmate.* "I'm talking about control."

CHAPTER 12

I'll bite," Johnny Fontane finally said. "Control of what?"

At first, Michael Corleone didn't answer. He was tempted to say *dreams*. Didn't people sometimes call the movie studios dream factories? Other people's dreams. Talking about dreams wasn't something he was up to. *Control of everything,* a younger version of himself might have said. But life had long ago humbled him too much for that.

"Let me ask you this," Michael said. "When was the last time you had a meeting with Jack Woltz?"

"Oh, Jesus," Johnny said. "Him?" He sized up Michael's face and then looked over at Tom Hagen, then sighed, resigned. "Woltz," Johnny said. "Well, Hollywood's a small town. I see him at events, but it's been a long time since I did anything with his studio. If there was a project we helped produce, it wasn't one I, personally, had anything to do with."

"We've done some research," Hagen said. "There are two kinds of pictures that seem be making money now. One is the sort that your company, to your credit, has been doing—star vehicles with responsible budgets. The other kind, though, are the big spectacles. With the, uh, anamorphic . . . the—"

"CinemaScope," Johnny said.

"Right. CinemaScope. The thinking here is—correct me if I'm wrong—that these are event movies. People will turn off the TV and go see them."

Fontane nodded. "That's the thinking. But it's Hollywood, so don't be surprised when what everybody's thinking today is what nobody remembers tomorrow."

"Be that as it may," Tom said. "You're in a position to make both kinds of pictures, John, but you don't. All we see are those small ones."

"Right, because you need much more involvement from a studio to make epics like that," Johnny said. "Money's only part of it. It's more because of all the people involved, the locations, the sets—everything. The kind of control you're talking about? That's exactly what you have to give up to put together something on such a big scale. Don't forget, too, by the way, that spectacles can make you a king's ransom, but they can lose just as much. The kind of projects we've been doing are just better bets."

"Exactly," Michael said. "Bets. In all your unlucky trips to the racetrack, did you ever see anyone get ahead who played nothing but the favorites?"

"No, you're right," Johnny said. "You're speaking my language here. To be honest with you, I always thought of you gentlemen as different. Everything you have a business interest in—or your father before you, may he rest in peace—seems like a sure thing."

"There's a world of difference," Michael said, "between a favorite and a sure thing."

"I'll give you that," Johnny said. "You know, your timing's perfect on this. I was just reading some scripts this morning and thinking along these same lines. For example, there was a great one I read about a Roman slave. Big story. Huge. Or Columbus. There's never really been a great movie done about Columbus. But here's what I need help understanding. Even if it was possible to develop a project like that with my company, our company, whichever, why would you, would we, want to work with Jack Woltz? The man's almost eighty years old and *oobatz*. He brags at screenings that he's got a magic bladder, that he can tell how much money a movie's going to make by how often he's got to get up and go piss. The less, the better, obviously, but this is the last guy in the industry I'd want to be making a big, long, expensive movie with. Not to mention that Woltz International ain't exactly the hottest studio in town." Johnny turned to face Tom. "In your *research*, Tom, you probably came across that."

"We have a relationship with Mr. Woltz," Michael said. "Whenever possible, I prefer doing business with people I've done business with before. The trust is already established."

Hagen nodded, slowly, in corroboration.

Also, Woltz had a relationship with the Sheas and could probably still get in to see them on Michael's behalf. And he could get the Corleones at the table with the Russian Jews who were the secret power behind everything in California. Even the Los Angeles and San Francisco Families essentially answered to them. Woltz's lawyer, a man named Ben Tamarkin, was, for the Jewish syndicate there, a more powerful version of what Tom was for the Corleone Family.

"The kind of business venture I'm interested in building here," Michael said, "is more complicated than just getting one picture made. Increasingly, movies are being filmed out of the country, and we can help with that. People we know in Italy, for example, who can keep the cost of shooting on location to a minimum. Also, the studios had to sell off their distribution companies, but we can help with that, too. The big, downtown movie theaters are struggling because of the crime in the inner cities, but we have interests in shopping malls in the suburbs, and nearly all of them have movie theaters in them."

"With all due respect," Johnny said. "That's a problem. Nobody wants to see a spectacle on one of those little screens out in East Jesus."

"They do if they already live in East Jesus," Michael said. "If the reason they moved to East Jesus in the first place was to get away from the problems of the modern city. The screen may be a little smaller, but it's new, it's clean, it's safe, there's plenty of free parking, and on the way in or out you can duck into a store and buy shoes. It's a vertically integrated business, or rather several businesses, completely separate from one another, working out of mutual interest. You're not going to have any of the problems you had with the casino, because first of all Hollywood, as you know, is hardly regulated at all, at least in comparison with something like legalized gambling. And, second, because we're going to help you. Tom will work with you. When the time is right—and I expect that will be very soon—he'll go with you to meet with Mr. Woltz."

Johnny looked over at Tom.

Tom shrugged. "The trust is already established."

MICHAEL CORLEONE STOOD BY HIS KITCHEN WINDOW, PEELing an orange and looking down at Johnny Fontane as he crossed the courtyard.

"You all right?" Tom Hagen asked.

Michael kept peeling the orange. Down in the courtyard, Connie rushed after Johnny like a common *puttana*. "With Johnny? Frankly, it doesn't matter all that much if—"

"I don't mean about Johnny. Or, for that matter, our Hollywood interests." Hagen said *Hollywood interests* with a tinge of contempt so faint it would have registered only on a family member.

"What *do* you mean?" Michael asked.

"I mean, are you all right? I've known you since you were seven years old, for Christ's sake. Something's bothering you. Something's *been* bothering you. And I don't mean Tommy Scootch's problems down Mexico way, either."

That was Tom to a T: he got the dig in and didn't even mention Joe Lucadello.

Michael shook his head. "It's nothing."

"Rough night last night, I hear."

"Al told you that?"

Hagen smiled. "No," he lied. "You just did."

"Touché, counselor." He finished peeling the orange and began to eat it.

"So you just couldn't sleep or what?"

Michael turned to face him. For a moment, he thought about telling Tom about the series of dreams he'd been having. *I have dreams about Fredo. A series of dreams. They feel real. In the most recent one, we had a fistfight. In all of them, he is bleeding. In all of them, he mentions a warning but won't tell me what it is.* But no. Michael Corleone was a man of reason, of logic. There were logical explanations: the diabetes, the medicine for that, stress. Maybe the dreams had to do with Rita. She never appeared in the dreams and was rarely mentioned, but she was always a presence in them somehow—just as Fredo was a presence in Michael and Rita's waking moments, even though they never talked about him. (Why should they? She'd been with Fredo only once.) The dreams had begun after Michael had a sugar imbalance; now they were happening when he slept. It was ridiculous for Michael to think he'd seen Fredo's ghost. Crazy. It was just a dream. What, among men, was less worthy of discussion than dreams?

"Forget it," Michael said, turning back to the window. "It was a night, OK?"

"Fine."

"Fine."

"I keep telling you," Tom said, "when that happens, the insomnia, you can't just stay in bed. You need to get up and go do something, maybe take a walk."

Michael smirked, then paused for effect. He knew about Tom Hagen's mistress, and Tom clearly knew he knew, though they'd rarely spoken about her, and never by name. She'd been a blackjack dealer in Vegas, a renowned beauty, married to a man who used to beat her, a situation Tom helped remedy. She also had a grown son in some kind of hospital, the cost of which Tom paid for entirely. She and Tom had been together for longer than Michael and Kay's marriage had lasted. The whole matter struck Michael as the most characteristic thing Tom had ever done. He wasn't Sicilian but was always trying to be, so leave it to him to have not just a *comare* but a steady one. Better yet, he found one he could feel noble about. He'd helped her, stayed loyal to her: it was perfect. He even used her as one of the Family's fronts (real estate holdings, parking lots, movie theaters) and as a courier, delivering money to various people throughout the country. She lived in Las Vegas most of the time, but she was in New York now, too, staying in the apartment Tom kept for her here, a walk-up over a flower shop.

"A walk, huh?" Michael said.

"I mean a real walk." Hagen said. "It'd do you good."

Michael gave him a look. If there was ever a perfect way for a boss to ensure his own demise, it was to become such an insomniac that he got in the habit of taking walks at three a.m.

Michael watched Johnny Fontane, downstairs, waiting for the elevator. Connie was hanging on his arm. Francesca, arms folded, was watching them, shaking her head in obvious and—to Michael's eye—overcompensating disapproval.

"Think she'll ever get him to take her out?" Tom asked.

"Who, Francesca?"

"*Francesca?*" Tom frowned. Fontane was the same age as he was. "Jesus. No. Connie."

"Never," Michael said. "Didn't you hear? Johnny's distancing himself from our family."

"Sure," Tom said. With his index and middle fingers, he gently jabbed Michael in the chest. "But with the human heart, who the hell knows?"

Michael and Hagen discussed a few petty logistical matters and agreed to meet at the elevator in two hours for the car ride out to the Carroll Gardens Hunt Club.

"Plenty of time for a walk," Michael said. Tom ignored him.

ONCE TOM LEFT, MICHAEL WENT OUT ONTO A SMALL BALcony facing the river, where he kept the telescope his children had given him for Christmas. Mary had made a bittersweet joke about using it to watch over them up in Maine.

Now, in the twilight—*magic hour,* Hollywood people apparently called it, a term he'd learned from Fredo—Michael sat on a stool and looked through the telescope in that same general direction. His eye came to rest on what he could see of Randall's Island, where Robert Moses lived and did business in a mansion there, hidden in plain sight beneath a tollbooth complex. A castle, practically. Michael knew more than a few things about Moses, that supposedly visionary builder of roads and parks, the de facto designer of the modern New York City, and practically a sainted figure in political circles and in the press. A native Clevelander, just like Nick Geraci, Moses had never been elected to any office, yet he was the most powerful politician in New York—city and state, both. He was also the most extravagantly corrupt. This would have surprised most people, but not anyone in Michael Corleone's world. The dimmest *cugin'* sitting on the stoop outside his social club could have told you that Robert Moses's enormous power had an inevitable chicken/egg relationship to the epic scale of his sleaze and greed.

Somewhere on that island was a man who had thrown half a million New Yorkers out of their homes, most of them Negroes and poor immigrants, many of then Italian. *Half a million people.* More than the population of Kansas City. Moses tore their homes down and built buildings the evicted could never afford or—more often, more diabolically—housing projects that, even new, were more grim than the worst slums. All built with taxpayer money. Robert Moses built roads that cut the heart out of neighborhoods, creating crime-ridden ghost streets where families had once thrived, all to make life easy for the rich people from the suburbs, all to make Moses himself rich beyond Michael Corleone's wildest imaginings. Moses had three yachts, each fully staffed, ready day and night. He had a hundred waiters and a dozen chefs on call around the clock as well. As gifts, he gave his friends skyscrapers and stadiums. Moses's island was its own nation—a secret nation, one the American public did not know existed and yet paid for. And kept paying for it. Anyone who wanted to pass over the bridges their taxes had already funded had to pay a silver tribute to the Don, Robert Moses. He had his own seal, his own license plates, his own intelligence agency, his own military force, his own constitution and laws, even his own flag. Once, the mayor of New York took Michael aside and, friend to friend, whispered this warning: "Never let Bob Moses do you a favor. If you do, rest assured that one day he'll use it to destroy you."

Yet despite all this, there Moses was, out on his island, presumably cooking up new schemes to ruin the greatest city on earth and line his own pockets in the bargain, while in the eyes of the public and the eyes of the law, he was a pillar of the community.

A hero.

Robert Moses was not under constant threat of indictment or assassination. He wasn't even under *occasional* threat of indictment or assassination.

His association with various crimes and atrocities had not caused him to lose two brothers to violent death.

It had not caused his children to come home from school crying because of what the other kids said about him. It had not caused his children to be fired upon with machine guns.

Robert Moses's accomplishments were studied in university classes in political science and urban planning. Not criminology or criminal law. Robert Moses was a behind-the-scenes character known to everyone, and everything most people knew about him was good.

And most of it was bullshit.

Michael pushed himself away from the telescope.

Robert Moses probably possessed enough pure evil that he could sleep well. He probably woke up every morning refreshed and without the slightest anxiety about who might try to defame him today, who might try to throw him in jail, who might try to blow up his car or put a bullet in his heart. Robert Moses was probably never once tempted to go to the window of his mansion at dusk and stare through a telescope at the top of this building, wondering why he'd been so lucky, wondering, just for a moment, what it was like to be a man like Michael Corleone.

CHAPTER 13

Ever since the raid on the farmhouse in upstate New York—a meeting of all the Families, bigger than a Commission meeting, and an event that made many Americans aware for the first time of the word "Mafia"—the Commission had met as rarely as possible. Tonight's meeting would be the first since Michael Corleone returned to New York.

Like the meetings in any large organization, its success depended on settling everything of any importance long before anyone took a seat at the table. Michael served on the boards of several corporations and charitable organizations and was always amused to hear otherwise sensible people champion open debate—a fine notion, for fools more concerned with being self-righteous than effective. The only unresolved matter Michael could foresee concerned Carlo Tramonti. Tramonti's deportation had not held up in court, although his ongoing citizenship woes were making a battalion of lawyers rich. He had refused to discuss his grievance in any other forum but before the Commission. But no matter what Tramonti proposed, Michael had enough votes in this pocket—Altobello, Zaluchi, Cuneo, Stracci, probably Greco—to block anything. And Tramonti had, via intermediaries, agreed not to say nothing about the Cuban assassination plot.

The security precautions for the Commission meeting were intricate—though, for the first time in decades it did not involve the Bocchicchio clan. Cesare Indelicato, the Sicilian *capo di tutti capi* and Carmine Marino's godfather, had put a stop to it. There were too few of them left.

The restaurant chosen for the meeting was tucked in a corner of Carroll Gardens that had been cut off from the rest of the neighborhood by the construction of the BQE, the Brooklyn-Queens Expressway, a walled concrete canyon that whined with constant traffic.

The buildings closest to the restaurant were empty, save for the apartments loaned to appreciative friends of the Corleone Family, who were using them for both lodging and security. The nearby street fair and upcoming fireworks display in Red Hook would draw most people in the area down by the East River for the evening.

Down the block from the restaurant, an open fire hydrant spewed water into the darkening street. A nicely compensated crew from the water department cheerfully pretended to be fixing a water-main break. As promised, the precinct sergeant had dispatched uniformed cops to close off the street and keep the curious at bay. The cops at the scene had no idea what was going on inside the restaurant. They were clock-punchers—men handpicked for their purposeful lack of curiosity.

At seven sharp, five men gathered at the back door of the restaurant, five more at the front, so each door had a trusted soldier from each of New York's Families: the Barzinis, the Tattaglias, the Straccis, the Cuneos, and the Corleones, whose turn it was to provide the security detail—a job that Eddie Paradise had overseen. Men grunted hellos to each other but otherwise milled around and smoked and did not talk. Paradise came by and shook hands and thanked everybody for their efforts, then hovered around the periphery.

The arrivals of the Dons were staggered between seven-thirty and eight. Michael Corleone and Tom Hagen were already inside.

First to arrive was Carlo Tramonti. His seat on the Commission was a complicated formality. He did not always attend, but when he did, he was allowed to take his seat first, one of several courtesies granted to him because of the nature of his organization, by far the nation's oldest. Behind him trailed a bodyguard and his little brother Agostino. Augie the Midget's promotion to *consigliere* was recent; this would be his first Commission meeting.

The embrace that Carlo Tramonti and Michael Corleone shared betrayed nothing of the differences these men had had over the years. The men exchanged pleasantries about their families. A casual observer would have mistaken them for friends.

Tom Hagen, whose shoes were new and squeaking, showed the Tramontis to their seats at one of the two long, facing tables in the back banquet room. Each was covered with a white tablecloth, bottles of red wine, baskets of bread, and plates of antipasti. Hagen plucked an olive from one of the plates. He used to feel like a sideshow attraction at these meetings; when Vito first tabbed him as *consigliere,* Tom was the youngest man in the room and the only one who wasn't Italian. Now, almost twenty years later, Hagen felt entirely in his element.

"The shoes, they start doing that there," said Augie the Midget, pointing as he sat, "squeak like that, got to throw 'em out, eh? And start over." Only with his strange accent—a cross between Brooklynese and Southern Negro—it sounded like, *De shoes dey start doin dat dere, squeak like dat, gotta trow 'em out, eh? And start ovah.*

Hagen smiled and nodded and told them to make themselves at home.

"What shoes?" asked Carlo, who was a little hard of hearing.

"Forget it," Augie said. "Just shoes, all right?"

BY NOW, TWO OF THE OLD LIONS HAD ARRIVED, ANTHONY Stracci from New Jersey and Joe Zaluchi of Detroit. As was customary, each brought his *consigliere* and a preapproved bodyguard. Zaluchi and Stracci were the Corleones' oldest friends and strongest allies. Zaluchi was a moon-faced, grandfatherly man in his seventies. He'd married one daugh-

ter off to the scion of an automobile company and another to Ray
Clemenza, son of the late Corleone *capo* Pete Clemenza. Joe Z had taken
over in Detroit after the chaos of the Purple Gang and built up an empire
known for being one of the most peaceful in the country. Lately, though,
there were rumblings that the Negroes were taking over in Detroit, and that
the auto unions were getting their marching orders from the Chicago outfit. Many of the Dons believed Zaluchi was going senile. When he greeted
Michael by calling him "Vito," Michael chose not to correct him.

Black Tony Stracci, also in his seventies, doggedly maintained that he
did not dye his thinning ink-black hair, which seemed to get blacker every
year. He'd always been so loyal to the Corleones that some outsiders
wrongly believed the Stracci Family was merely a Corleone *regime*. The
Corleones' narcotics operation used Stracci-controlled docks and warehouses (an alliance cemented by Nick Geraci, but not a part of Geraci's
conspiracy). Black Tony had also—in one of the most bitter arguments the
Commission had ever known—joined with Michael Corleone to overcome
the opposition of several other Dons (particularly Tramonti and Silent
Sam Drago) to secure the backing of the Commission for New Jersey governor James K. Shea's bid for the presidency. The Straccis had dealings in
New York, but their power base was in New Jersey, which was less presti-
gious and lucrative, thus relegating them to their perpetual status as the
least of the New York Families.

Next to arrive were the two newest members, both in flashy suits and
loud ties: Frank Greco from Philadelphia, who'd replaced the late Vincent
Forlenza (leaving Cleveland without a seat at the table), and John Villone,
who'd returned from Vegas to take over in Chicago from the late Louie
"Fuckface" Russo. When Michael greeted Frank the Greek by saying he
looked good, Greco scoffed. "When I was a young man, I looked like a
Greek god. Now I just look like a goddamned Greek." Michael smiled. He'd
heard Greco make this joke before. In fact, at fifty, Greco still *was* a young
man, compared to most of the Dons. Philadelphia was another outfit that
was losing ground to the Negroes, but Frank the Greek remained strong in

South Jersey, which had given him connections to several men in the Shea administration.

John Villone had overseen the Chicago outfit's interests in Nevada, which was how Michael first met him. He was a "man with a belly" from the old Sicilian tradition, connoting both power and courage as well as literal corpulence. Unlike such men, however, he wore shiny, clownish clothes, tailored, oddly, to make himself look even fatter. Still, Villone was the kind of man everybody liked and wanted to be around, and Michael envied him for it. John Villone had been close to Louie Russo and remained so even after Russo froze him out of important Family business over some dispute concerning a woman. Villone walked to his seat in the back room with his meaty arm around Tom Hagen, unaware that Hagen had used the very belt he now wore to strangle the fat man's dear friend Louie Russo.

The deeply tanned boss of the Tampa syndicate, Salvatore "Silent Sam" Drago, was next to come though the door. On his shoulder he bore a webbed bag of oranges, as was his custom. Smiling, without a word, he deposited them on the bar. He and Michael embraced. Al Neri checked the oranges for anything concealed there. Drago must have expected this and took no offense. Despite their differences, Michael and Sam Drago had much in common. Drago, like Michael, was the youngest son of a boss, and, like Michael, he'd set out in life hoping to avoid the family business. Drago's father was the late Sicilian boss Vittorio Drago, a close friend and ally of Lucky Luciano's. When Mussolini seized power and threw Vittorio and all the other bosses in prison on the island of Ustica, young Sammy Drago—who was in Florence, studying to become a painter—fled to America and settled in Florida. He'd tried to make a go of it as a commercial fisherman, but he lost everything. He was in danger of being deported. Back in Sicily, his mother got Lucky Luciano himself to pull a few strings, though Sam Drago did not know this until he was already beholden to the exiled American. He told himself he was helping run some of Luciano's interests in Florida only to provide support for his sainted mother while his father was in prison. But soon the War started, and the years dragged on, and Sam Drago, who'd been a promising painter, seemed to find his true calling as a racketeer and leader of men.

Al Neri shook his head. Nothing in the bag except oranges. He began to peel one. Hagen showed Drago and his men to the back room.

The last to arrive were the three remaining New York Dons—Ottilio Cuneo, Paul Fortunato, and Osvaldo Altobello.

Altobello held the door for the other two Dons and their men. He'd been on the Commission for a year, but it had not met in that time. This gesture of humility drew approving nods from the wheezing Fortunato and the jolly-looking Cuneo.

Sweating and breathless from the strain of the ten-foot walk from the curb to the restaurant door, Fat Paulie Fortunato, Don of the Barzini Family, sat heavily on a chair just inside the door and exchanged embraces with Michael and Tom Hagen from there. Fortunato looked fat enough to have eaten John Villone for breakfast. His eyes were slits in his doughy face, and his leonine head was perpetually bowed, as if his neck muscles couldn't hold it up. Fortunato was the closest thing the Corleones had to an enemy among the Five Families. He'd been a devoted *capo* to Emilio Barzini, whose murder had never been pinned on the Corleones (or on Al Neri, who'd donned his old cop uniform to do the shooting), and he'd been close to Vince Forlenza in Cleveland, who—to be technical—had disappeared and was only presumed dead. Fortunato's personal power base was the Garment District. He'd also been one of the Barzini men pushing to expand into narcotics, which, on Fat Paulie's watch, the Family had done. He resented what he called the hypocrisy of the Corleones, who'd withheld their political support for the drug business while Vito was still running things, and then, under Michael's reign, created a covert *regime* that seized a piece of the action. Despite these differences, Fortunato was not, by nature, a man who took offense or took the offensive. He'd been boss for eight peaceful years, ruling Staten Island the way the Barzinis had for decades.

There might have been no greater testament to Michael Corleone's power than Ozzie Altobello's elevation to Don of what was still known as the Tattaglia Family. Once the Corleones' bitter rivals, the Tattaglias were now headed by Connie Corleone's literal godfather, a loyal friend of Vito Corleone's since Prohibition. The Tattaglias—less diverse than most Families—specialized in prostitution, strip clubs, and pornography. This empire was built by Philip Tattaglia, who enjoyed its fruits with epic gluttony. After he was killed in 1955, his brother Rico came out of retirement to succeed him. The organization started falling apart. It was undercapitalized and increasingly vulnerable to police raids and the crusades of the self-righteous. When Rico died last year of natural causes, most expected the new Don to be one of the Family's glorified pimps or, failing that, one of its young warriors. Instead, the courtly Altobello, a born *consigliere*, found himself thrust into the role of Don. Most saw him as a human olive branch extended toward the Corleones.

Leo "the Milkman" Cuneo was a small old man who somehow had the presence of a large one, the way a skilled but tiny actor might. He wore a plain, sensible suit. He'd been given the honor of arriving last not in deference to his power but as a gesture of respect, now that, with Forlenza's disappearance, Cuneo had become the senior member of the Commission.

Michael Corleone, briefly, took Cuneo's hat and coat himself, until a horrified waiter swooped in and relieved Michael of that imagined indignity. "On the contrary, it was my honor," Michael said in Italian, "to touch the hem of Don Cuneo's garment."

Michael forced a smile so that Cuneo would not think he was being sarcastic.

Cuneo mumbled a few bars of a Sicilian song Michael didn't know and didn't understand. "Am I right?" he said in English, patting Michael on the cheek.

"As rain," Michael said, showing Cuneo toward the banquet room.

The Cuneo Family had some business in New York City, mostly in Manhattan and the Bronx, but it ran upstate New York (and owned the biggest milk company in the region, too, which was how Ottilio Cuneo became Leo the Milkman). Leo Cuneo had played a key role in negotiating peace after the Five Families War, but his tenure as a statesman of the underworld had been short-lived. It had been his associate's white farmhouse where the infamous raid had occurred. Half the mob bosses in America were caught as they tried to run away through the woods. How was it possible that no one from the Cuneo Family heard about the raid in advance or noticed the cars approaching? Michael had no idea; it passed beyond all human understanding. *He'd* noticed men in the bushes as he drove up, and he'd kept going. It was supposed to have been the meeting at which he negotiated his own retirement from all this, a goal that was not abandoned but was no longer even on the horizon, which Michael tried not to think about.

Nobody spent more than a few hours in jail. Lawyers pointed out that the United States Constitution guaranteed the right to free assembly. These points, however, came later in the story and were not featured on the cover of anything. They were also too complicated to be admissible in the court of public opinion.

The fallout from the raid was still falling. Without all the publicity and public outrage, the FBI would have almost certainly continued to keep its distance. If not for the raid, the public—perfectly willing to ignore that its government killed innocent people all over the world, every day of the year—would have never felt so threatened by men like those on the Commission. What, after all, posed more of a threat to the average American: the business discussed at a meeting such as this one? Or—to cite only one current example—the CIA-sponsored efforts under way in the obscure nation of Vietnam? So why the public scrutiny of Michael's business and the indifference to the larger-scale dangers carried out in the name of the American people? Simple. Look what made the most money in Hollywood, that whorehouse of the American dream: morally uncomplicated comic-book depictions of heroes and villains, simple stories for uncurious people. That raid had given the people what they wanted. Now, largely as a consequence of the hysteria the raid touched off, flawed and complicated men of goodwill like Michael Corleone and James K. Shea had been reduced in the public eye to the stuff of comic books. Never mind that both were sons of men who'd emigrated to this country as boys, men who'd been in business together, making their fortunes selling something that was no longer a crime. Michael Corleone and James K. Shea were both decorated war heroes. They both attended Ivy League schools and married a woman they met during those years (never mind that Michael, who had been resolutely faithful, was a Bad Man, or that Jimmy Shea, a cunt-drunk philanderer, was Prince Charming). They both had two young children, a boy and a girl. They were both Catholics who went to church only when appearances decreed. Their families had each suffered a series of operatic tragedies. Together, in Chicago and West Virginia and Florida, they stole the American presidency. Each man's love for his country was deep and sincere.

Never mind all that. All the public wanted was black hat/white hat.

On one side, the public faced the threat of a vast, thrilling, and terrifying criminal conspiracy, conducted by the members of a secret society: nefarious super-fiends, swarthy men with foreign-sounding names. On the other side, protecting the public from evildoers everywhere, stood the fair-skinned and handsome Jimmy Shea, a square-jawed superhero from central casting, and his sidekick Danny, the toothy boy wonder.

All of which came about only because Leo Cuneo bungled the security detail.

Vito Corleone had taught his sons that great triumphs and great mistakes were rarely representative incidents in a man's life, but only a child would think it unfair to judge a man by such things. The issue was not fairness. The issue was what it meant to be a man.

In fairness, though, Leo Cuneo had taken responsibility for the security lapse. As he entered the banquet room, his fellow Dons greeted him with genuine warmth. But the blunder had cost him, in ways he had no doubt noticed and others he would never know about. Leo Cuneo had been a good friend to the Corleone Family. He had voted with Vito and then Michael on every important issue that came before the Commission. His people had even located the killer of Michael's first wife, Apollonia, a man named Fabrizzio, who'd been working under an assumed name at a pizzeria in Buffalo. Cuneo himself had made the arrangements to send Fabrizzio Michael Corleone's regards, along with three shots from a 9mm pistol, two to the chest and one point-blank into his skull. Such loyalties had kept Leo the Milkman alive.

ANOTHER HALF HOUR OF GREETINGS AND DRINKS WENT BY. The preliminaries might have gone on even longer if not for Michael Corleone's blood sugar. He'd eaten some olives and cheese and cappacolla off the antipasti plates, but that wasn't going to cut it. He needed to really eat. He took his place at the table and gulped down some water. Tom Hagen slipped into the seat beside Michael, signaling Neri to corral the other bodyguards and go wait in the main dining room. The other Dons saw that Michael had taken his seat and quickly followed suit.

As Neri stood in the doorway and watched, the waiters brought out steaming bowls of macaroni and scrambled around refilling the drinks and replenishing the bread. When the last waiter left, Al Neri gave Michael a nod and pulled the door closed.

The Commission had not met in two years and thus had a backlog of relatively routine matters to decide. "If no one objects," Michael said, "I'd like to work while we eat, so we can maybe go see the fireworks or, at least, get home by dawn."

This inspired no objections. For all the lurid images people have of men like this—the beatings, extortion, and murder—this was in fact the kind of business where almost everything truly important got decided over a meal. Same as in real estate or publishing or out in Hollywood. But for these men it wasn't just business. Some of them did practically everything while they ate. Paulie Fortunato, for example, regularly fucked two women at a time while eating beef-spleen sandwiches, the puzzling choreography of which Fredo Corleone—who'd claimed to have seen it with his own eyes—had once explained to Michael in foul and loving detail.

The first order of business was the approval of the promotion of the new bosses, Greco and Villone, and also the new man out in Los Angeles, where Jackie "Ping-Pong" Pignatelli had stepped down for health reasons. Unanimous, no discussion, warm calls of welcome all around.

Then came the approval of men who'd been put forth for membership by various Families. Families not represented here had to get permission to open their books in the first place and by how many. Then they had to find a Commission member to present the names. Families with seats at the table not only had a better chance of being allowed to open their books but also could speak up if anyone had a problem with one of their nominees. By and large, though, once names got this close to the table, the men in question had been vetted and the process was something of a formality—despite which, Michael thought, it took *forever*.

As a courtesy to the new Dons, they were allowed to go first. Villone graciously deferred to Greco.

"OK, so," Greco said, "Vinnie Golamari. Some of you may know his family maybe, I don't know. Good man. Good, good man."

"I know a *Vicente* Colamari," said Black Tony Stracci, squinting and cocking his head as if at that angle some distant memory might emerge. "No disrespect, but if it's the guy I'm thinking of, you gotta be kiddin' me."

"It's *Go*lamari," Greco said.

"Because if it's the same Vinnie Colamari I'm thinking of, he must be, forget about it. Old. Eighty, if he's a day. Help me, Elio." He turned to his *consigliere,* who shrugged.

"You're thinking of another gentleman, I'm afraid," Greco said.

Carlo Tramonti, frowning, drummed both hands on the table. He bent toward his brother's ear and whispered something.

"I may be wrong about this Vinnie," the New Jersey Don admitted, "because who can be sure about everything, especially at my age? But isn't he the fella they caught with the broad in the monkey house? Remember that? Young kid, the girl was, something like thirteen. Terrible."

"Different guy altogether. I know the guy you're talking about and—"

"Enough," said Sam Drago. He pointed a breadstick at Stracci.

"Wait," Stracci said to Greco. "Golamari's the one who did that job in the Pine Barrens with what's-his-face, Publio something."

"Right!" Greco said, visibly relieved. "Yes. Publio Santini."

"Santini I can vouch for personally," Ozzie Altobello said.

Greco tapped the table with his index finger, as if at an invisible sheet of paper. "He's the next guy on my list here."

There was no written list. Nothing was ever written down.

Tony Stracci bobbed his head and pursed his lips in concession. "Those are good men, Vinnie and Publio. I hear good things."

Carlo Tramonti threw back his head and heaved a sigh.

Several other men gave him a look. Augie Tramonti put a hand on his brother's shoulder.

Carlo looked like he was about to say something but didn't.

Things kept going like this: names tossed out, briefly discussed, and approved—one Family at a time. All the while, Carlo Tramonti did not disguise his impatience. His brother, a known hothead, kept trying to calm Carlo down. At one point Augie even cleared the dirty dishes in front of his brother and cleaned up the crumbs, too, like a busboy.

Carlo Tramonti, of course, would not be proposing any names. He, alone, didn't need such approval from the Commission.

Leo Cuneo peppered Ozzie Altobello with questions about the Tattaglia nominees—even though at a benefit last week for a crippled children's fund, he'd told Michael that everything he knew about everyone proposed for membership by the other New York Families was good.

Carlo Tramonti put his face in his hands.

Michael Corleone was sympathetic. He might have tried to streamline the process, too, except that people already spoke behind his back about him being a college boy, too American, a modernizer who just pretended to embrace tradition, somebody who never wanted to be here in the first place, who wanted out from the moment he was in. The one time he'd even brought up his desire to make the process more professional, it was to Tom Hagen. Tom told him to let it go. These men were friends, Tom had pointed out, who don't get to see each other so much. They want to talk, let 'em talk. The tide of Tom's disappointment had drowned out anything else Michael might have said or done.

AFTER THE PASTA COURSE CAME A STANDING RIB ROAST. Over exclamations about how tender it was, the men settled various disputes—conflicts that couldn't be settled simply with a sitdown with the right two or three men. As Michael's father had explained it, the Commission existed for two things only: opening the books and making peace. On Michael's watch, it had branched out into the realm of politics, but even if the problems with the Shea administration had become the elephant in this particular room, Michael still tried to stick to the fundamentals.

Tramonti gave Michael a look. Michael shook his head. Not yet.

The conflict that had provoked this particular meeting in the first place was not the Danny Shea situation or even the need to initiate new members and confirm the new Dons. The conflict was about pushcarts.

It had started as an argument between two hot-dog vendors over a street corner on the Upper West Side, one vendor who was under the protection of the Barzinis, another whose cart was sharecropped from a man who reported to Eddie Paradise. The corner had been worthless, but then two new office buildings opened, and now it was a gold mine. Each man claimed to have been the first to stake his claim. After a few days, the vendor who worked for Eddie's soldier threw boiling hot-dog water on the other vendor, who nearly died from the burns.

In retaliation, the Barzinis sent someone to break the first vendor's arm. Then they parked a brand-new cart a few feet away from a different cart, one they thought belonged to the Corleones, undercutting the prices for everything, but in fact that cart belonged to the Cuneos, and the soldier who watched over it retaliated by having two of his men blow up the encroaching Barzini pushcart (with the advent of propane tanks, the carts were rolling bombs). But the Cuneo men got their wires crossed—literally—and blew themselves sky high instead, along with a pushcart that was under the protection of the Tattaglias.

One thing led to another.

By the time any of the Dons caught wind of these squabbles, they were no longer petty. The newspapers weren't covering this yet—other than the one mysterious explosion—but that wasn't going to last much longer. All five Families had pushcarts jockeying for position, and the ad hoc decisions that had been made about who got what corner were proving inadequate. They were also being ignored. There was no systematic way in place about how to divide up the turf, and the Commission had been charged with developing one. This was not an uncomplicated matter, but they'd come to the table with a basic plan, hatched in various small conversations over the last few months. All the Commission needed to do was approve it.

As the plan was explained, Carlo Tramonti, red-faced, gathered enough composure to excuse himself in a level voice to go use the john, though he practically leaped from his chair. Michael knew Neri could be counted on to keep an eye on the guy.

The other out-of-town Dons patiently listened, perhaps counting their blessings that each had a city all to himself, even if that meant it was a second-rate place, less lucrative than what a fifth of New York was.

But it was unlikely that anyone there thought that pushcarts were, in and of themselves, a trivial or even tedious matter. This humble business was a gangster cash cow everywhere. The carts were pricey enough—several grand, the last Michael heard—so that average citizens had a hard time affording them. Instead, they'd sharecrop the carts from someone else. Everybody made out. Some hardworking immigrant got a small business to run, and his benefactor got two-thirds of everything and didn't have to pay out one dime in salary. Permits the immigrants would have otherwise struggled to get from the city magically appeared. Other Family businesses supplied the pushcarts with food, beverages, condiments, paper napkins, butane, umbrellas, tires—the works. A good pushcart, bottom line, could be as profitable as a restaurant but with none of the risk. No taxes to speak of, no utilities, nothing much in the way of maintenance, none of the headaches that go along with having a payroll, and none of the paper trails that go along with owning or leasing real estate (or getting a front to own or lease it). Plus, if a neighborhood goes bad, a restaurant goes bad with it. But a pushcart just moves on. Pushcarts made money: every cart, year in and year out. The only thing that could mess up a good thing like that would be if the men bankrolling the system started fighting among themselves.

Which, by a unanimous vote, they agreed not to do.

CHAPTER 14

As dessert was served—plates of simple cookies, plus a pear and grappa pound cake that was a specialty of the chef's own mother, not to mention coffee and amaretto—and the waiters left once again, Carlo Tramonti was finally called upon to say his piece.

"I come a long way," said Carlo Tramonti, "to give a short speech. Some of you are good talkers"—he shot a glance at Michael, then Altobello—"but I come from a humble background where it's nothing I ever got good at, even in front of such good friends. Most of you know about my recent difficulties. I don't want to tell that story no more to nobody. Some of the rest of you's got stories to tell that are like it, I don't gotta be told that, eh?"

This provoked murmurs of approval.

"So if I may, I'll tell you a different story. Forgive me if you heard it. My organization's got a few rules different from some others for the simple reason that we're older. A hundred years ago, when the niggers got set free, the plantation owners got Italians to do such work. They made some of us into what might as well have been slaves, one of which was my grandfather. He worked hard, like a lot of 'em. Before long Italians was comin' up in the world, not just as tinkers and cobblers but in the fruit trades and also great in the fishing and the oysters."

Tramonti left his place behind the table and started pacing, like a trial lawyer delivering his closing arguments to the jury. Carlo Tramonti had been in court plenty of times himself.

"What happened next," Tramonti said, "was the Anglos, they killed this chief of police they had, who was popular with a lot of people but crooked as a cypress root. And they blamed it on us, the Italians. Our most successful Italian businessman, fella had a big tomato cannery, biggest one in the state, he got stabbed in the eye by an assassin. Honest Italians was rounded up, put in jail. They accuse *us* of being Mafia, a word I never heard used the way they use it. But the official leaders, elected and all that, *they* act like Mafia, or at least the cartoon they got in their head about Mafia. They make a vendetta against a whole class of people, one of which was my own grandfather. When a lynch mob got formed, the police led innocent men out into the prison yard, handed 'em right over. The men huddled in a corner, trapped. The Anglos—shopkeepers, lawyers, even a Baptist preacher— what they do is, they line up ten feet away and open fire. Rifle shots, shotguns, everything. My grandfather, he's still alive, it's a miracle. Then someone says, wait, this one's not dead. Someone with a shotgun comes up, steps on his chest, blows his head off completely. The killers, they *laugh*, they *cheer*. This is reported in all the papers. President Theodore Roosevelt himself hears about it and right away he gives his approval. I got those newspapers hung up on the walls of my office, so I don't never forget what the people who run this country think of us. I don't never forget it, never."

Hagen leaned toward Michael's ear. "Anybody," Hagen whispered, "who says he's going to make a short speech is just about to deliver a stemwinder."

"Most of you," Tramonti said, turning to glance over his shoulder at Hagen, "are Sicilian. You understand in your guts how the rulers of nations have treated our people for a thousand years. We can't be surprised to find ourselves in the position we are with regard to those Sheas. Eh? I don't fault you, Don Corleone, for putting forth your friend Mr. Shea for president, because I understand that your family and his go way back and all that there."

Michael cleared his throat.

Tramonti smiled. "I agree, Don Corleone. This is no time to play Who Shot John."

"James," Leo Cuneo blurted. "Jimmy Shea. Not John."

Tramonti spun to face him. "I know the fucking president's *name*. It's a figure of speech, for Christ's sake."

Leo Cuneo's *consigliere* leaned forward and said something to him. Don Cuneo looked confused. "Then who the fuck is *John*?"

"I said it was a figure of speech," Tramonti said. "I'm only trying to say that there's no point wasting our time working out who's to blame. The thing is done, he's in the White House, end of story. *Whoever* would have wound up in that White House, he wasn't going to be no friend to the Italians, in the end, which is how it is. We all know that."

They all also knew that Tramonti had given a million laundered dollars to the campaign of Shea's opponent, in defiance of the Commission's decision to support Shea—hardly the act of a man who thought all non-Italian candidates would be equally hostile toward Italians.

"The thing we got to talk about here," Tramonti said, "is what we're going to do about it, how we're going to get that little prick Danny Shea off our balls. Eh? Or at the very bare minimum, make it so he don't do no damage while he's on 'em. Which, see, is the reason I told you that story. The moral of which is this. Most of you's city boys, but down in the bayous, we learn early that if you want to kill a snake, you don't chop off the tail. Like with the chief of police I was tellin' you about. Or." He paused for effect, finger in the air. "Or, like what would happen if anything happened to Danny Shea, see. All that kind of thing does is make the snake mad. If Danny Shea becomes a martyr, take it from me, that's the end of us. His brother'll call out the National Guard. You want to do away with the snake, how do you do it?" He strode to the table in front of Michael

Corleone, paused, and held out his hand in an imitation of a meat cleaver. "You got to chop it off at the head." Tramonti slammed it down on the table, spilling water from both Michael and Hagen's water glasses.

Neither Michael nor Hagen even blinked.

"'If history teaches us anything,' eh?" Hagen whispered to Michael.

In a moment that seemed to last much longer, Michael saw Fredo in that unluckiest of lucky fishing hats, sitting on the dock, teaching Anthony how to fish, something Michael had somehow always been too busy to do. A few feet away in Michael's office, Tom had said that getting to Roth would be impossible, like trying to kill the president. Michael had glanced at Fredo, then mocked Tom. *If history teaches us anything*, he'd said, *it's that you can kill anybody.*

Michael felt dizzy and downed what was left of his water.

"Jimmy Shea," Tramonti said, "if he gets taken care of, then what? Then nothing. It's the end of all our biggest problems. Payton's the president, and he hates that Danny Shea just about as much as we do. Sam Drago can vouch for me on that."

Drago, in fact, nodded to indicate that he could.

"Bud Payton's not going to have us over to the White House to help him hide Easter eggs or nothin', but he ain't gonna keep Danny Shea on his payroll, neither. And the FBI, forget the FBI, the director hates Danny Shea more than we do. He ain't gonna want to keep coming after us, since Danny, he'll get the credit, whether he stays on or not. Danny, he'll *take* the credit. *Everybody* knows what Danny Shea wants to go down in history as. The FBI, the fellas we see, regular agents, they'd like to help him. But their *boss*? Forget about it. He don't want that no more than we do. So, like I say," Tramonti said.

He reached into his jacket pocket, as if for a gun.

Some of the younger men with faster reflexes began to dive for cover, but before anyone embarrassed himself there was a flash of steel: a meat cleaver, smallish and new-looking. Tramonti faced his own place at the table and raised the blade over his head and let out a grunt and brought it down hard and it stuck there, about a quarter inch deep.

Then he held out his hands to the other men to indicate that there was nothing to it, a regular guy killing everyday vermin, and returned to his seat.

Agostino Tramonti patted his brother heartily on the shoulder, more like a cornerman than a *consigliere.*

There was a stunned silence in the room.

How had he gotten that thing in here? Why had he seen the need to pull a theatrical stunt like that? Of more concern, though: could it be that the Don of the least violent Family in America was suggesting something so purely crazy?

Neri opened the door a crack.

Michael shook his head.

Neri nodded and closed it.

The Dons exchanged looks with one another and back at that meat cleaver. Gradually all eyes drifted toward Michael Corleone.

Michael stood. He willed himself to stop thinking of Fredo. He tried to keep his eyes off the meat cleaver as well. He nodded toward his empty water glass. Tom obediently filled it.

Like his father, Michael was in the habit of waiting a long time between the time he rose to speak and the time he spoke. This time, however, Michael—though his face was an expressionless mask—was scrambling for the right thing to say. Michael reached down and took a sip from his water glass and shook his head in theatrical disappointment.

"Don Tramonti," he began. "My dear friend. With full respect for you and your organization, I believe I speak for everyone in this room when I say that what you are suggesting is an outrage. I understand that you are angry, you're frustrated, and so, in this matter, are we all. But surely you must understand that what you're suggesting would ruin us. I don't need to remind you, or anyone else, either, that it's strictly forbidden even to kill a common police officer without first getting permission from this body. These are crimes the authorities don't rest until they solve. We can't protect those responsible. Yet what *you*—"

"Bullshit." Tramonti stood. The cleaver quivered. "I say *that* with full respect, too, my friend. You *yourself* killed a common police officer without getting no permission—"

"Sit down," Paulie Fortunato said, raising his enormous head. "You don't know what you're talking about."

The last person in the room Michael would have expected to defend him was the boss of the Barzini Family—a good indication of how far over the line Carlo Tramonti had stepped.

"If I may, Don Corleone?"

Michael extended his arm toward Don Fortunato, yielding the floor. Tramonti, too, sat.

Fortunato remained in his chair, no doubt because the effort to stand up would have left him out of breath. "Back then," he said, speaking more than loud enough for Tramonti to hear, "which was almost twenty years ago, Mike was a civilian, all right? Not involved in no way with this thing of ours. He was a simple college boy, up at Harvard or some such."

Dartmouth, but there was no need to correct him.

Fortunato wiped his chin with a napkin. "What you're referring to, Don Tramonti, is an event another man confessed to, all right? Even if it happened the way you said, it would've been done to atone for a hit that was put on his father, which is the kind of thing that is also never supposed to happen—a hit on the boss of *any* Family—unless first it gets approved by this body. In the situation you're talking about? Nothing like that was approved, believe me."

Everyone did, since it had been the Barzinis who'd ordered the hit.

"What happened back then, *if* it happened like you say, was that two men who were trying to kill Vito Corleone were, some say, killed by his son. One of them happened to be a crooked police captain, the other was a scumbag dope smuggler. Now, if this incident *did* happen, it's both understandable and, more important, *personal*. It means it don't concern us."

Fortunato smiled. The devil himself would have struggled to flash such malevolence. "So my advice, friend, is maybe you should watch your tongue. OK? I thank you."

Fortunato balled up the napkin and tossed it aside.

Carlo Tramonti turned to his brother. They whispered counsel to each other. Carlo did most of the talking. He waited a long time before addressing the rest of the Commission.

When he did, he merely faced them, bowed his head, and nodded.

A split second after this apparent concession, there came from outside what sounded like distant gunfire.

"The fireworks," Michael said, jerking his thumb vaguely toward Red Hook. He bowed his head. "My apologies."

"Fireworks?" Carlo Tramonti looked disoriented.

"The fireworks, yes," Don Altobello said. "Outside."

"There's a fireworks display over the East River," Michael explained. "To celebrate Columbus Day."

Tramonti muttered what sounded like a curse toward the mercenary nature of Genoans. Then he thanked the Commission for this opportunity and for their patience.

But the matter was on the table now, as unavoidable as the meat cleaver. And, absent Carlo Tramonti's fanatical and unreasonable solution, there was much to discuss.

As the fireworks continued, the Dons learned that everyone there was being audited by the IRS. All over the country, the length of the prison sentences imposed upon convicted associates had increased dramatically. Carlo Tramonti's deportation had been followed by several others that had been more meticulously executed; nearly every Family had lost a man or two this way. There were other issues. All the men agreed that, if nothing was done, the worst was surely yet to come.

Michael Corleone and Tom Hagen listened patiently. They certainly shared most of these concerns. The Corleones' support of the Sheas had come somewhat out of loyalty, given the business relationship their father

had enjoyed with Mickey Shea, but, more so, out of the desire for access—
and, in Michael's case, legitimacy. There had been other reasons, too. For
example, Jimmy Shea was more hawkish on Cuba than anyone else running. Michael continued to believe that, in the long run, his interests were
best served by keeping the Sheas in power and figuring out a way to combat Danny's excesses.

The assassination efforts in Cuba were still unknown to most of the men
in this room. A rumor, perhaps, but no more. As an ace in the hole,
Michael and Tom Hagen had long since written it off as unplayable. But
they had a better ace in a more literal hole. The Shea brothers were both
cunt-happy. Johnny Fontane, in the not-too-distant past, had practically
served as their pimp. Providing the Sheas with women, particularly starlets,
had a certain value, and the Corleones were, in fact, quietly but dramatically expanding their holdings in Hollywood. The Shea brothers could
distance themselves from certain people all they wanted, but they were permanently attached to their own disloyal pricks.

Yet, as the discussion went on, Michael realized that Tramonti's crazed
desire to kill the president put the Corleones in an impossible position.

The Commission would not, of course, approve Tramonti's proposal,
but if Tramonti carried through on it or even attempted to do so, everyone here was now an accessory.

It was possible that Tramonti could be dissuaded or appeased. But knowing the habits of mind of those closest to the old Sicilian ways, Michael
wasn't optimistic. Even if the Commission rebuked Tramonti, so what?
Michael certainly did not have the resources to monitor the Tramontis, to
make sure they didn't merely have someone else do the job and cover
their tracks.

Killing Tramonti was forbidden and would start more fires than it extinguished.

Warning the Sheas wasn't an option, either. It was unthinkable to betray the confidence of another Don, especially about anything said at a
meeting of the Commission.

The only true solution would be to figure out how to get the Sheas to call off the dogs, to call a halt to the persecution of the men in Michael Corleone's tradition. The dirt the Corleones had on the Shea brothers might have been the right ammo for the job, but how could Michael fire it? Leaking it to the press wasn't the right play. The job had to be done via the *possibility* of leaking the information. The government played it the same way. No one wants nuclear war, but a nation unable to create the *possibility* of it may as well be armed with rocks and sharpened sticks. Michael didn't want scandal. He wanted the fruits that came from the fear of scandal.

To do this, he'd need to find an emissary, someone the president trusted and would see. If that wasn't a tall enough order, it also had to be someone who would then (faithfully, subtly) let the president know what the Corleones knew and what they were prepared to do with that knowledge. Who could do that?

A few possibilities sprang to mind, none of them ideal.

But there would be someone. There was always someone.

Michael needed time to think.

He wouldn't have to figure this out today. But he'd have to figure it out, and soon. Tramonti's proclamation meant that this might not be able to wait until next year's election. Nonetheless, Michael decided to go ahead and deliver a slightly modified version of the speech he'd rehearsed.

As he rose to give it, the grand finale of the fireworks got under way. Light strobed through the grid of drawn blinds. This inspired good-natured chuckling from several of the men and a shrug from Michael to indicate he couldn't have known to time it like that.

"The president and his brother," Michael began, practically shouting, "are men with a gift for inspiring the masses. They are leaders. They may even be good leaders, if, admittedly, not as good for us as we might like. But they're also politicians, and so let's not be naïve. Like all politicians, they want one thing most of all."

"Pussy," Hagen muttered, too softly for anyone else to hear.

"To be reelected," Michael said. "The Sheas need to be reelected next year. They're doing this to us now in order to *get* reelected, and to do so without the need for our support. The Sheas aren't stupid men. They know that they're biting the hands that fed them. They've undoubtedly reached the conclusion that once they bite our hands *off*, millions of other hands will applaud. Millions of hands will reach for their wallets. And then millions of hands will reach for the lever that reelects the president."

Carlo Tramonti stared toward the meat cleaver, frowning.

"The attorney general of the United States has declared war on our way of life," Michael said. "In the past, we have declared war on one another as well, yet we manage to come to rooms like this one and, through the efforts of this very body, achieve peace. Our differences then become things of the past. Former enemies sit at these tables now as friends. If the president and his brother, who were once friends to some of us, now wish to declare war on us, so be it. But let us not abandon reason. Let us not abandon the ways of our tradition. War, unfortunately, has become part of that tradition, something we all understand too well."

He shot a quick glance at Carlo Tramonti, who'd been tested neither by actual war, as Michael had, nor by the siege wars most of the other Dons had fought and survived. The New Orleans Don had a hand cupped over his ear but did not look up.

"We are men skilled in the art of war," Michael said, "and as a wise man once said, achieving a hundred victories in a hundred battles takes less skill than subduing your opponent *without* battle. We certainly possess such skill. Whether Don Tramonti's proposal would work or whether it would ruin us is a matter of debate, but we are men who prefer action to debate. So let's act. But let's do so in a way that doesn't threaten us with a counterattack. Let's use the system against itself. It's not our system, but we control enough of it to get this job done. We have friends within the president's own party, people who could cause him trouble in the primaries. We have friends in the other party as well, men who could be troublesome opponents and yet friends to us. The presidential election isn't a national election, remember. It's won state by state. There's not a man in this room who doesn't have dozens of important state officials who could be called upon for favors. There's not a man here who doesn't have an interest in a newspaper, a radio station, a TV station, even if it's only somebody there who's a degenerate gambler or on the hook to one of your shys. What easier way to subdue an opponent without battle than to forgive a debt here and there? And there is one more thing, the most powerful force we can unleash."

Purposefully, he had not mentioned the possibility of blackmail. A man showing his cards still hangs on to the one up his sleeve.

Michael smiled. "Our labor unions. Millions of Americans, who every year vote for the man their union endorses. Without these votes, Jimmy Shea would have lost the last election, and, without those endorsements, he'll lose this one, too. The point isn't to defeat him, of course, but to withhold those endorsements until we get what we want. Our power comes from the *possibility* that—"

There came a booming knock on the door. It opened before anyone had time to say anything.

It was Al Neri, flanked by the other bodyguards.

Outside, car doors slammed.

"OK, three things," Neri said. "First, stay calm, cool, and collected, all right?" He strode to Tramonti's place at the table and removed the cleaver and handed it to Carlo the Whale. "This ain't what it looks like, believe me, nothing to fear, so whatever you do, just stay put." Neri hurried back toward the door. "Second, excuse me for interrupting. Third, um, Tom? Can you give me a hand out here?"

Behind Al Neri now were several uniformed cops and a pair of detectives in the kind of cheap suits that must have come free with the badge.

The strobing lights were actually coming from their police cars. The fireworks were out of synch with those lights, of course, and too far away to see. It's not the eye that sees, it's the mind.

Most of the Dons were able to make eye contact with their respective bodyguards in the hall, and none of the bodyguards seemed anxious or even concerned. Several tried to convey in gesture that, appearances be damned, everything was fine.

To everyone's surprise, the man the police had come for was Tom Hagen.

"Are you Thomas Feargal Hagen?"

The detective pronounced Hagen's middle name correctly. He even looked Irish.

"What's this about?" Hagen said.

"You need to come with us, sir," said the second detective.

"I need to see my lawyer," Tom said.

He didn't have a lawyer, as far as Michael knew. Tom *was* the lawyer. He got *other* people out of situations like this.

"We got a telephone at the precinct house," said the second detective. "It's new. Works like a charm. We even give you the dime."

The men at the tables were hunched over, obscuring their faces, even though it really did seem that the cops didn't know what was going on here— or didn't want to know. Michael wondered if Neri had engineered this, if it was some kind of professional courtesy extended Neri's way. As Michael had seen on various occasions, there was no such thing as an ex-cop.

"What's this about?" Hagen said.

"Do you know a woman named Judy Buchanan?" the first detective said.

Hagen went white.

"Who?" he said.

Pretending not to know his mistress's name, Michael thought, wouldn't change a thing.

"We need you to come with us, sir," the detective said. "We need to ask you a few questions in connection with the murder of Judith Epstein Buchanan."

BOOK III

CHAPTER 15

Two investigators—an ex-cop named Dantzler and the brother-in-law he'd reluctantly agreed to employ—had been following Judy Buchanan for about two months. They didn't know precisely who had hired them. The job had come in via a detective friend who was still on the force, a man more bent than do-it-yourself plumbing. The detective, Dantzler knew, was nothing but the guy who was working for the guy who was working for the guy. Whoever the top man was, the detective probably didn't even know.

The brother-in-law, who hadn't held a steady job since he came home from Korea, didn't even know that much. As far as Bob Dantzler could tell, he was a shell-shocked mooncow mooch who barely knew enough to tie his own shoes.

Bob Dantzler understood the contours of the situation he had taken on, and he was comfortable with it. A different sort of man would have gotten spooked once he figured out that the guy who'd set Judy Buchanan up as a kept woman was much more than just the attorney to the Corleone Family. A different sort of man would have been unwilling to take pictures of Tom Hagen's fishbelly-white buttocks while he screwed his mistress and then hand them over to who the hell knew, to do God knows what with them. A different sort of man, realizing just who Hagen was and what he controlled, would have given back every dime of the money he'd already been paid, along with a sizable gift of some sort. A different sort of ex-cop would have remembered Al Neri from their days together on the force— Neri had been one of those maverick free-styling time bombs you either knew or knew *about*—and understood what kind of threat the Corleones posed, having apparently domesticated such a man as that. He might even have remembered that Neri and the detective who sent Dantzler the job had a history—that the detective had testified against Neri in the manslaughter trial that had gotten Neri kicked off the force and sentenced to one to ten years in the state penitentiary (a sentence mysteriously suspended only days before Neri was to be sent upstate). But Dantzler didn't want to know things he didn't need to know. He talked a lot about destiny and letting the chips fall where they may. He investigated the things he was paid to investigate. Anything more would have been hazardous to his financial health—and thus, by extension, to the health of his marriage to the acquisitive and much younger Mrs. Bob Dantzler.

Planting the bug in that Buchanan woman's apartment, however, had been Dantzler's brother-in-law's idea. He had recently taken a two-day class in electronic surveillance at a Holiday Inn in Paramus, New Jersey. Afterward, he bought so much spy gear—both electronics and clever weaponry—that he needed help carrying it all out to his car. He purchased it on time, presuming that Dantzler would foot the bill, which, grudgingly, Dantzler had. As it turned out, the Judy Buchanan case had been the first chance they'd had to use the new bugs. It had been an unnecessary and frankly illegal step to take. They already had plenty of information to embarrass and perhaps even blackmail Tom Hagen. Maybe even send him to jail, if the client knew the right people. Photos galore, duplicate receipts of all kinds of things that Hagen had bought for her or paid for on her behalf, including years upon years of the nursing-home bills he footed for her

severely retarded son. The yellow Buick she drove in Las Vegas was still registered to a dealership there, which Dantzler could all but prove that the
Corleones secretly owned. She had been married to a Las Vegas auto mechanic, an abusive man (the police had responded several times to do-
mestic disturbances) who was crushed by a limousine when a lift
malfunctioned. She invested the proceeds from his life-insurance policy in
two holding companies. The money had grown at an eye-popping rate and
was, at least on paper, her only source of income.

One of those holding companies developed shopping centers in the
Midwest, Arizona, and Florida. It was headed by a man named Ray
Clemenza—the son of the late Peter Clemenza, believed to have been a
caporegime in the Corleone Family, and the son-in-law of Giuseppe "Joe Z"
Zaluchi, rumored to be the most powerful gangster in Detroit. Ray
Clemenza checked out as a completely legitimate businessman, but by
Dantzler's stars, there was enough smoke here that the fire he couldn't find
could kiss his ass. The other holding company, which was not doing as well,
seemed primarily concerned with buying up movie theaters.

Judy Buchanan spent most of her time in Las Vegas, although she did
take frequent day trips to small, unglamorous cities in the American heartland, always with no luggage but a satchel. She paid cash for everything,
stayed only a few hours, and returned carrying nothing but her purse and
a mystery novel. Dantzler couldn't prove anything that would hold up in
court, but common sense decreed that she was a courier for the Corleone
crime syndicate.

The way Dantzler figured it, the Buchanan job was already done. He and
his brother-in-law broke into Judy Buchanan's apartment that day for no
better reason than to pass the cost of the new gizmos on to a client.

Whenever Judy Buchanan came to New York to be with Hagen, she
spent most of her time in the apartment he kept for her—a walk-up over a
flower shop. Any time she and Hagen were going out on the town, Hagen
sent a car for her. Otherwise, she walked or took a taxi. The car she got into

that night was one familiar to the investigators, so they presumed, reasonably enough, that she'd be gone for at *least* an hour or so.

JUDY BUCHANAN WAS A HARD WOMAN, IN EVERY SENSE OF that, but she was flirting with paranoia. The accidents attributed to the missing *capo* Nick Geraci—poisoned dogs, faulty brakes, overdoses by people who weren't known to be drug users, fires, explosions, drownings—more often than not had absolutely nothing to do with him. A great many were, in fact, accidents. Still, she was afraid. Her doctor gave her a prescription to help with the fear, but all it did was help her sleep. Awake, things just got worse. Eventually, her fear of what might happen grew larger than her fear of guns. And guns terrified her.

It was a fear she'd always had, one that had amused her late husband. Marvin Buchanan had grown up on a ranch, guns everywhere, and he'd been in the service, too. But she'd refused to have one in the house, and he'd gone along with it, even keeping his hunting rifles at a friend's house, which may have saved his life for a while, during the years he was beating her. (Judy had had the good sense never to ask Tom Hagen if he knew what really happened when that limousine fell on Marvin. In truth, it hadn't bothered her.) But the circumstances and the times had changed. There were things she knew now that she hadn't known then.

And so it was that, on the day of Judy Buchanan's death, Richie Two-Guns came to get her, bearing three guns he thought she might like. The guns had all been purchased over the counter at a sporting-goods store in the Bronx, which seemed fine, given the way they'd be used (not at all, Nobilio had to assume). Nobilio had volunteered to handle this personally as a favor to Tom Hagen, not because the job needed to be done by a man at his level. Also because Richie Nobilio, after the incident that gave him his nickname, had become a gun buff. In Nobilio's world, this was an exotic, even eccentric passion—there were men who'd killed a dozen other men, never thinking about the manufacturers of the guns they'd used. Nobilio's love of guns had less to do with function than with the way it made him feel to touch them and hold them and admire them and caress and even—when no one was looking—taste them.

All three guns Nobilio showed Judy Buchanan were smallish—a .32 Ladysmith and two .22s. All were suitable nightstand pieces for novices who would probably never use them. She and Nobilio drove around the neighborhood while she looked the pistols over. Nobilio's recommendation was that she go with the .32. It was a simple snub-nosed revolver, small enough to fit in a purse, more able to knock a man down. She was intimidated by the way it looked, although what she said was that she hated the name of it.

"Ladysmith?" Nobilio said. "All it is, is short for Lady Smith & Wesson."

"Even so," she said. "I want that one."

She chose the .22 caliber Ruger: a rimfire five-and-a-half-inch bull-barrel Mark I Target model, with a micro-adjustable rear sight and a walnut stock instead of the standard black hard rubber. It was a humble but elegant-looking weapon.

Richie Nobilio called it "a good first gun." He said that he knew a place out in Brooklyn, the Carroll Gardens Hunt Club, which was owned by some friends of his. He offered to take her and show her how to shoot it. Right now, if she wanted. "No time like the present," he said, winking and then pointing at her with both index fingers, a gesture that had to do with his love of his own nickname but which struck her as what a salesman would do.

A wave of panic came over her.

She didn't know Richie Nobilio from the man in the moon. Even if he *was* a friend of Tom's, who's to say that Tom didn't want to kill her? She didn't want to think this, which made her think about it every day. She was the other woman, an inconvenient woman, someone who *did* things, bad things, both in the bedroom and on errands she knew too much about. She tried like hell not to know, but that didn't mean they wouldn't kill her for what they thought she knew, or might have known. She wasn't thinking straight. She knew that. She was short of breath. She was alone in the back of a car with a gangster. The driver was no doubt a gangster, too. A bug-eyed man in slicked-back hair and a shiny suit was trying to sell her on going to Brooklyn. To a *hunt club,* which suddenly struck her as an obvious lie. A *hunt club*, in Brooklyn? She didn't really know Brooklyn, but that made her think of that line, some famous writer's line: *Only the dead know Brooklyn*. She to started to shake.

They were going to kill her.

Nobilio picked up the Ruger.

"Tom loves me!" she blurted.

Love was a lie that she and Tom whispered to each other in the dark. They were both too sensible to say it out of bed or believe it. But she didn't know what else to say to save herself.

"You know that," she said, "right?"

Richie Two-Guns stuck out his lower lip, wagged his head, and turned up the palm of the hand that wasn't holding the .22. Who knew anything about such things?

"I really must *insist*," she said, "that we turn around. I want to go home right this instant. Immediately. Back to the apartment, I mean."

To her shock, he shrugged and told the driver to do just that.

As the driver obeyed and turned around, Nobilio loaded the clip for her. "If you ever need to use this," he said calmly, "try and aim for the gut or the, uh, whaddaya. The groin region. Whatever you do, stay away from the ribs. The head is good if you're real, real close, but you need to know what you're doing for that."

She kept waiting for him to shoot her.

This had not been the first time she thought she was about to be killed, and, like every other time (obviously enough), she'd been wrong.

As they pulled up in front of her building, Nobilio handed her the papers for the gun. "You change you mind, or you don't like it or whatever else, you call me—or if you want, you can take it right back to this place here. Ask for Rodney, mention my name, and, butta-beepa-da-boppa-da-boop, you can swap it out for anything you want." Nobilio handed her the gun and showed her again how to use the safety.

"The groin region, huh?" she said, biting her lip, trying to breathe normally, hoping to regain some small measure of composure.

"Yes, ma'am."

"Betcha *that* knocks a man down. Shooting his nuts off."

Nobilio blushed. He clearly did not like hearing a woman talk like that.

"Yes, ma'am," he said. "It's been known to happen."

She laughed mirthlessly, slipped the gun into her purse—she'd brought a big summer bag, just in case—and got out. The old man who owned the flower shop underneath her apartment was just locking up. "Thomas Wolfe," she muttered.

"Ma'am?"

"*Only the dead know Brooklyn,*" she said. "That was him, right? Who wrote that? Or was it Hart Crane?"

Nobilio looked confused.

"Never mind," she said.

The car idled at the curb until she was safely inside.

"You think you're better than me?" murmured Nobilio, still watching the door.

"What's that?" the driver said.

"Women," Nobilio said. "Am I right?"

"I could tell you stories," the driver said.

"Don't," Nobilio said. "You eat?"

JUDY BUCHANAN HAD BEEN GONE FOR LESS THAN FIFTEEN minutes: fifteen anomalous minutes, at least from the two investigators' perspective.

They'd been inside her apartment for maybe five of those minutes when there was the sound of her key in the lock. A moment later she was inside.

She grabbed the gun and cast off the purse.

The brother-in-law, in the middle of putting a floor lamp back together, stood, cocked his head, and looked at the gun she'd drawn on him as if he didn't know what such a thing was for. It was aimed at his crotch.

Judy regarded him as if she wasn't quite sure he was real, as if she were afraid he was a ghost brought to life by her darkest, most irrational fears.

Dantzler had been in her bedroom, where he'd gone to attach a bug to the underside of a dresser drawer. He'd removed the drawer but had taken time to enjoy smelling her clothes. It was the one thing he'd yearned to know about her that surveillance hadn't yielded. He heard the door open and came running. He wasn't sure how he was going to talk his way out of this, only that he could.

At the sight of a second man, Judy screamed, fired, then spun toward Dantzler and fired twice more.

Dantzler, unscathed, dove toward her. As he tackled her, there was an explosion.

She was dead before she hit the ground.

Dantzler rolled off her, saw the pulpy mess that had just been what Judy Buchanan thought of as her good side, then turned away. A wave of nausea hit him, every bit as hard as he'd just slammed into her.

Dantzler fought it off and sat up and looked at his brother-in-law. Blood streamed from a gash in his cheek. His right arm hung limply at his side. The smoking barrel of his odd gun looked big enough around for a deer slug. "Fuck's that?" Dantzler said, meaning the gun. "Russian?"

"Shit," the brother-in-law said.

"You could have *killed* me."

"Shit," the brother-in-law said again.

"Are you OK?" Dantzler said. "Your face is—"

"I'm fine." The brother-in-law touched his cheek where the bullet had grazed him and studied the blood on his fingers.

Dantzler looked again at the dead woman. Tom Hagen might be a rat bastard who'd just used her, but there were other people out there who loved this woman. Dantzler had learned who they were. Judy's mother,

Ruth, a retired nurse living next to a canal in Florida, in a nice house trailer, its walls lined with pictures of Judy at all ages. Or Judy's retarded son, Philip, who lit up with joy every time his mother visited him at that institution. Maybe even Dantzler himself. He had sympathized with her plight so deeply, seen her naked so often, yet only now, nauseated by the coppery smell of her blood and the flecks of pink brain that he tried not to look at, did he realize that he'd come to feel like her protector. He could not accept that it had been Judy Buchanan's time.

"Shit is *right*," Dantzler said.

He wasn't thinking clearly. He needed to think clearly. They should take the body. Bodies found outdoors lead to convictions half as often as those found indoors. "We'll carry her down the back stairs," he said.

"Fuck you, Bob." He raised the gun.

"Oh, perfect," Dantzler said. "Shoot *me*. That's goddamned perfect. Drop the gun, numbnuts, before you hurt yourself."

The brother-in-law didn't move. He'd killed people before, dozens of them, men and even—also accidentally—a few women. But not since Korea. He wished that Korea would go away, though he doubted that it ever would. Now *this*. The gun aimed at Bob Danztler had been taken off a dead man near Pusan. In the chamber there was one more of those supposedly untraceable shrapnel bullets he'd bought at the Holiday Inn in Paramus, New Jersey.

"Drop it, you faggot," Dantzler said.

All that horseshit about destiny Dantzler always talked about? What if it was true? It wasn't just Dantzler the brother-in-law was sick and tired of. He was sick and tired of pretty much everything. "I could kill you," he said.

Dantzler laughed at him. "A lot of things *could* happen, y'know? But it ain't *gonna* happen," he said, "now, is it?"

The brother-in-law dropped his gun to the floor and began to cry.

Family.

Dantzler grabbed the big gun and snatched the bug from the lamp. They were wearing gloves already, so prints weren't a problem. He briefly considered throwing the poor sap over his shoulder, fireman-style. But then there was the matter of the body.

"Get up," he said to the brother-in-law. "I ain't carrying you."

The brother-in-law wouldn't move.

Blood pounded in Dantzler's ears. He still wasn't thinking clearly. They were running out of time. There was no time for the body. They had to get out of there. He pushed his brother-in-law into a chair and shoved the gun in the poor sap's mouth. The brother-in-law offered no real resistance.

"It'll look like you killed her and then yourself," Dantzler said. "*Or*, you can get up and haul ass."

The brother-in-law had stopped crying. "Aul aa," he said, his mouth full of gun barrel.

"Attaboy," Dantzler said.

Several blocks uptown, as soon as he was sure they hadn't been followed, Dantzler pulled his car up to a phone booth. The brother-in-law stayed in the car and started crying again, this time without making any noise. It was spooky to see. Dantzler tried not to look.

Her prints were on the gun. There was that. There was the brother-in-law's blood, but with any luck he didn't have one of the rare types. Otherwise, they hadn't left behind anything that could be pinned on them. Dantzler was all but sure no one had seen them leave. They definitely weren't followed out of the building, and his car had been parked far enough away that nobody who hadn't followed them would have had any reason to write down the plates. It would be fine. Bob Dantzler took a deep breath and dialed.

CHAPTER 16

Get out of town," the detective barked into the phone. "And never come back."

"Just like that? It's bad," Dantzler said, "but it's not—"

"Look, it's your funeral," the detective said. "Do what you want. I got to go fix your mess, fucko."

The detective hung up, ran outside to the phone on the corner, and called a number that, according to phone company records, belonged to the rectory of a Catholic church in Brooklyn that didn't exist.

It actually rang upstairs in the Carroll Gardens Hunt Club.

Momo the Roach answered it himself. They went through the security precautions he'd worked out with the detective, though there was no need. Momo was the only one around. Eddie Paradise had told him to stay there during the Commission meeting and quote-unquote watch the fort. Crazy little shitbird. Eddie had been awfully quick to fall this much in love with being in charge.

"This *something* that happened," Momo said, "she did it to herself, right?"

"That's not an explanation I'd use."

"We talking about a permanent condition?"

"So I'm told."

"So you're told," Momo said. "You know how to pick 'em, don't you? I told you: top men, price was no object. And you give me *this*? I'm disappointed in you. Very disappointed."

"It was an accident, all right?"

"Accidents don't happen to people who take accidents as a personal insult," the Roach said. It was part of the code a made guy in the Corleone Family was expected to live by. The code the Roach had been taught by his uncle Sally.

"Well, these ain't those kind of people," the detective said.

"They the kind that does a job when you give it to 'em?"

"Meaning what?"

"Meaning, do the geniuses you hired have photos or some such? Evidence. Understand? The job they were paid to do."

"Sure," the detective said, though he couldn't have known this for a fact. "Of course."

"They still got 'em, or they give 'em to you yet?"

"Still got 'em," the detective said, "but I can get 'em."

"Witnesses?" Momo asked.

"They weren't sure," said the detective. "We'll have to see."

Momo stared at the phone. "OK. Get down there as fast as you can, and call me back from a payphone the split second you do."

Because he wasn't doing this on his own.

Then he took a deep breath and called Nick Geraci.

Making the call from there was a risk, but Momo was the one who took care of the phones, so it wasn't much of one.

IT WAS MIDDAY OUT IN ACAPULCO.

Geraci's speech sounded a little funny, though maybe that was just the connection. Even if the guy was punch-drunk—or whatever it was that his condition was called—Nick Geraci's mind, the Roach marveled, was as sharp as ever. Momo didn't have to repeat a thing, and Geraci, with no hesitation, figured out things his loyal soldier hadn't, not fully. In fact, the first thing Geraci asked was if that Commission meeting was under way by now.

"Yeah," Momo said. "It started about an hour ago."

"We do have things that can tie him to her, right? Photographs, receipts, and so on?"

"We do," Momo said, hoping it was true.

"No disrespect to that poor woman," Geraci said, "but this has all the markers of a happy accident."

Momo wondered why Nick was worried about the respect due some scumbag's filthy whore, but he kept it to himself. "Happy how?"

"Even if nothing sticks to our lawyer friend," Geraci said, "this still ought to do plenty of damage, both to him and to his, uh, his little brother. If it's handled right, it might not even hurt the organization. At first, yes," Geraci said. "But not in the end."

The Roach smiled. He knew immediately what Geraci meant. It was Nick's path back. They'd weaken Michael, so that those close to him questioned his ability to be the boss, until—for the good of the Family—the time came to push him aside. Or to push him aside very, very hard.

THEY'D FIRST DISCUSSED IT THIS SUMMER, WHEN MOMO was stewing in resentment during his booby-prize trip to Acapulco, and Nick Geraci had materialized one night—as miraculously as any ghost, it must have seemed—on the terrace of the Roach's private cliffside *casita*.

Geraci had to wait there for more than an hour. The Roach had gone out to dinner with a high-class American whore he'd been provided. From the sound of things when they came back, she was talented, too. Ordinarily, Geraci didn't lie down with whores the way a lot of guys did, just because they could, but he'd been away from Char a long time now. It would have been tough to listen to Momo going at it if Nick hadn't taken care of business a few times. Better with a whore, he'd reasoned, than with somebody he cared about. Plus, it would have aroused suspicion back at his hotel if he hadn't accepted the hotel manager's offer to send a girl to his room. He was an American, a little off the beaten track, staying alone. Three times now, another American had met him there, a man with a glass eye— once at the poolside bar and twice in his room. Bad enough to be in bed with a federal agency without it looking like he was literally in bed with a federal agent, too. So when the manager offered, Nick had accepted. The girl was heavy in the hips and thighs. She'd been clean, efficient, and professional, and now she came by once a week. It wasn't hurting anyone. It was like taking a garaged sports car for a spin to keep the engine in good shape.

When the Roach finally finished, he sent the woman on her way, pulled on a baggy pair of graying underpants, reslicked his hair, and went outside for a smoke.

Geraci was sitting at a tile table. He had a .38 in the waistband of his gabardine slacks.

Plainly startled, Momo Barone tried to play it cool. "Grew a beard, huh?" he said, touching his own face.

Geraci poured more mineral water into a glass and took a sip.

"Friend to friend," Momo said, "it looks like shit."

"How are you, Roach?"

"*Madonn'*. People think you're dead, you know?"

"People?"

"Yeah, *people*," Momo said. "The word is that either you're dead or you're doomed."

"What do people think about Dino DiMiceli?" Geraci said, expressionless. "What's the word on Willie Binaggio?"

The Roach took a long drag off his cigarette. "You really rig both of them jobs?"

Geraci took another sip of water. Adrenaline reliably kept even his small tremors at bay.

"Forget I asked," Momo said. "Let me ask you this, though. How'd you know I'd be here? What makes you so sure I won't kill you? What kind of place is this anyway, lets somebody like you into my room, just like you was I don't know what? Huh?"

Geraci smiled. "Clearly, you have a lot of questions, Roach. Have a seat. We'll talk."

Momo tossed the mostly unsmoked cigarette off the balcony and remained standing. "What makes you so sure I won't serve up your head on a silver platter? Y'know, to get ahead in the world?"

"I'll tell you why," Geraci said. Because if Momo had surprised *Nick*, that would have meant that Michael had sent him there to prove his loyalty. But the Roach had been in Acapulco for three days and hadn't made the first move toward Nick Geraci. The Roach was a man of action. Geraci had set up shop, not in Acapulco proper—an open city but a stronghold for what was left of the Hyman Roth syndicate, a place that on any given day might be crawling with people who'd recognize him—but rather up the coast a few miles, in Pie de la Cuesta. If the Roach had known that, he certainly wouldn't have waited three days to make a move. "Because we're friends."

"Har-de-fuckin'-har-har. Friends? Fuck friends."

Meaning Eddie, Geraci rightly presumed. Geraci had known Momo since he was a boy. He'd always been this easy to read. It was a fine quality in a *leccaculo*.

"So you here to kill me, Nick? Huh? Is that it?"

"Sit down, all right?" Geraci fished two bottles of Tecate from a steel tub. He'd ordered the beer from room service while the Roach was out. "I think you'll like what I have to say. I'm coming back, and you're going to help me. I've got a few other guys in mind I think we can trust. Once everything plays out, you'll be my *consigliere*."

"*Consigliere*?"

"*Consigliere*."

"Don't fuck with me, all right?"

"Roach." Geraci was, in fact, sincere. He held out his arms in a *What more can I say?* gesture. The Roach seemed to accept this. He broke into a smile. And just like that, Cosimo Barone was so deep in Nick Geraci's pocket he was munching the lint.

"Can I go get a robe or something?" the Roach asked. "I'm freezin' my nuts off out here."

Geraci stood and patted him on his hairy back. "After you," he said, and followed Momo inside. The Roach put on the terry-cloth job the hotel provided. He raised his eyebrows to indicate that Nick could check the pockets if he wanted. Geraci shrugged and did so. The Roach shrugged to indicate that he'd have expected nothing less.

As with most miracles, Geraci's apparition on that terrace seemed miraculous only if a person didn't think it through. Geraci had known, of course, that Michael would see to it that Momo got shipped off to Las Brisas when he got out of jail, because *everybody* who pulled a stretch and kept his mouth shut got a trip there as a token of the Family's appreciation. It had been Fredo's idea—he loved the famous people who stayed at Las Brisas and also the pink Jeeps that took you down to the beach. Nobody in the Family talked about Fredo, but the things he'd set up that worked had become traditions, utterly cast in stone. When he first came here from Taxco, Geraci had merely gone into Acapulco at eight in the morning (when no self-respecting wiseguy would be up and around), given the bell captain at Las Brisas Cosimo Barone's name, a description, and fifty dollars for his trouble. Then he went back to his hotel in Pie de la Cuesta and waited for the inevitable phone call. After it came, he waited two days for Momo to come kill him. When that didn't happen, he'd gotten up early again and spent a nerve-fraying day following Momo around to see if anybody else they knew was with him or keeping an eye on him. They didn't seem to be. When Momo had left with that whore to go get dinner, all Geraci had to do to get into the room was duke the bell captain another fifty.

Guessing that Michael would elevate that loyal *coglione* Eddie Paradise to *capo* while Momo was upstate wasn't a giant intuitive leap, either.

Back out on the balcony the Roach opened the beer bottles. They clinked them together and drank.

Nonchalantly, Geraci pulled out his gun and set it on the table in front of him and out of Momo's reach. It was a snub-nose, the kind issued to cops.

The Roach did not react.

The men exchanged what news each could impart, though most of it had to do with goings-on in New York. It went without saying that Nick wasn't going to explain the ins and outs of how he'd stayed alive the last year, and Momo didn't press him on anything.

Nick's wife and kids, according to the Roach, were doing great. The girls were off at school, getting good grades and all. Momo and his wife had gone to see Charlotte a few days ago, and she seemed to be keeping her head about her.

Geraci didn't put too much stock in this—he had other sources for staying in contact with his family and knowing how they were doing. Charlotte was getting close to her breaking point; if he wanted to save his marriage, Nick needed to get back to her soon. His older daughter, Barb, didn't want to talk to him, and his younger daughter, Bev, was a wreck. Still, it would be good to have the Roach there to keep an eye on them, as best he could.

Momo seemed to be working hard not to look at the gun, but he continued to be more or less successful.

"It's Tommy Scootch they put in charge of finding you," Momo said. "Believe that?"

This was news to him.

"*Tommy* Neri? Not Al?"

"Tommy."

Geraci shook his head and considered this. Tommy Scootch had grown up as Tommy Palumbo. Neri was the maiden name of his mother, Al's older sister. Tommy had taken his uncle's name to get ahead (though also, to be fair, to distance himself from a series of pickpocket arrests and other petty-theft convictions, which is where the nickname had came from: *scucire*—to unstitch, to steal). He left Sing Sing as Tommy Palumbo (Al had personally contacted Geraci, who'd pulled some strings himself to get the boy out early) and got on an airplane to Nevada as Tommy Neri. In no time flat, he became a top muscle guy, working directly under Rocco Lampone, who was then a *capo* out there, and Fredo Corleone, the nominal underboss (and thus, by Nick Geraci's stars, the epitome of nepotism run amok). "Dino and Willie B., I can see, but, honestly, how can Michael really be serious about finding me until he puts someone like you on the job?"

Momo's chest puffed out slightly before he had time to stifle it; the flattery had hit its mark.

"You, it means he's serious," Geraci continued, ticking off choices on his fingers. "Richie Two-Guns, serious. Even one of the Rosatos, or one of those zips we used on the thing with what's his face and the union problems: serious, serious, serious. And, of course, *Al* Neri—that'd tell you it's critical."

"That's probably *why* Don Corleone didn't give it to Al to do, though, don't you think? He don't want to look desperate."

"Maybe," Geraci said. He paused so that Momo would think he'd given him pause. Geraci had missed Momo. He loved the guy, plain and simple, and not just because anyone this easy to lead by the nose was fun to have around. The Roach was barely sneaking so much as a glance at the .38 now. "But this is fucking *oobatz*," Geraci said. "*Tommy Scootch*? He's still wet behind the ears. You know I'm right, Roach. No offense, my friend, but mark my words: nepotism's going to be the death of our whole goddamned way of life."

For a second, Geraci was afraid Momo would take offense, not at the concept of nepotism but at the big word. It turned out, though, that the Roach had heard it before, probably more than once on the barbed end of an insult. He gave a little snarl, like a dog. "I earned everything I got, all right?"

"I know. That's true. I said no offense."

"How's it any different than what the big shots do? Executives, senators, what have you. Even presidents. Half of 'em got where they got only because of who their people are."

"More than half, believe me," Geraci said. "There's nothing wrong with any of that, in and of itself. It stands to reason, a racehorse sired by a champion has a good shot of becoming a champion, too. Nothing against Tommy, either, who I hear is a good man. My point is just that Michael put Tommy on the job, I guarantee you, because Al was pushing for the kid to have a shot. In the same situation, Roach, when your uncle was watching over you as you were coming up? I can tell you: Michael never took any kind of interest. And Eddie Paradise: just because you were in the joint didn't mean Michael had to pick him. Every Family I know of has once in a while had a *caporegime* in Lewisburg or Atlanta or even Sing Sing. Eddie got picked because he was Rocco Lampone's brother-in-law, and you *didn't* get picked because as long as he lives, Michael's going to hold a grudge against your uncle Sally."

Momo nodded, deep in thought now.

Geraci paused for a few moments to admire the evenly spaced grill marks of further resentment he'd administered. "Getting back to Tommy, though," Geraci continued, "if Michael could see past the favoritism, he'd send someone after me who'd worked in my own crew, somebody who knew how I thought and could use it against me."

"You still think I'm here to settle things with you, don't you?"

Geraci regarded him and didn't answer.

Momo sighed and opened two more beers. "A man works hard to prove what he is, but proving what he ain't? Forget about it, y'know?"

Geraci smiled. He'd heard Momo's uncle espouse the same homely truth. "I know."

The Roach unnecessarily smoothed his helmet of shellacked-looking hair. "So how're you coming back? How're we gonna work this?"

The nervous gesture was a good sign, too. It meant he realized the risk but was with Nick. Anybody who just wanted out of there so he could go back and line up with Michael would overplay it, trying to look calm. Momo wasn't doing that. Such a person's eyes would betray him, too, darting glances at that gun, wondering if Nick was going to use it or if he should lunge for it: his chance to be the big hero and take Geraci out. But Momo seemed to have forgotten the gun was there.

Geraci finished his beer. "The only way I can ever come out of hiding," he began, "the only way I can step back into my life and get it back to something like normal is if I come back not as *capo*, which isn't an option, but as boss of the whole thing."

Geraci had, he continued, lined up some other useful allies during the time he'd been underground. He didn't say exactly who—this was not the time for Nick to go into the details of his negotiations with the Tramontis—but he said things to leave Momo with the (accurate) understanding that it was at least one of the other Families that had been involved with the Cuban fiasco. Momo had helped get that operation rolling—he'd met the man in the eye patch who'd called himself Ike Rosen—but he'd been in the joint for all the marching, the target practice, and the skull sessions on that fenced-off farm in New Jersey. The details about the outside help he was trying to get could all wait. But right now, he said, what he needed was to get more allies inside the Corleone Family. This would be a tough job, but it was possible.

The Roach nodded vigorously, like a man asked if he would agree to accept a fortune. The ordinary soldiers and associates had always liked Geraci better than Michael Corleone. Geraci had started on the streets and moved up. He'd earned every dime, every break he got, every promotion. Plus, he was one of the guys. He'd take a drink with you or go to a prizefight or a nightclub. Michael, for the most part, kept to himself and his little inner circle. Now they were in a goddamned white tower, which was perfect. Geraci had spent his adult life in social clubs and the back-room gambling joints. Michael had barely ever set one of his dainty pedicured feet in such a place. Michael was a college dropout, whereas Geraci had a degree and half a law degree, too, yet it was Michael and Hagen, with their superior attitudes, who were distrusted on the street for being quote-unquote college boys. Geraci's night-school law classes were seen as just another weapon he had at his disposal. His idea of using bankruptcy laws (rather than arson) as the Family's preferred method of busting out a legitimate business, for example, seemed to the men in the street like a scam refined, and it was this kind of cunning that helped earn Geraci such widespread respect. Yet Tom Hagen, an actual lawyer, struck a lot of men as a garden-variety German-Irish hard-on with a briefcase. All these things afforded Geraci certain advantages, but it was also true that the men had sworn loyalty to the Corleone Family, of which Michael was the Godfather, and most of them had been indoctrinated to believe, for their own good, that this was a fact of life, upon which life depended.

The members and associates of the Corleone Family, to a person, understood that it was more important to be feared and respected than to be loved. Michael Corleone had not come up through the ranks, but he'd amply earned the respect of his men. Geraci had killed men with his bare hands and managed to escape his own death sentence not once but twice (so far), yet it was Michael who inspired more fear within the organization. No one doubted the rumors that he'd had Fredo, his own (lovable) brother, killed for some minor, inscrutable disloyalty. Michael and Hagen had supposedly rigged the last American presidential election, too, the enormity of which had stirred something in the hearts of men who'd considered themselves too cynical to feel awe. Less universally believed were the rumors of the brutality that he'd done to Japs in the war, or the jobs he'd done on various powerful Sicilian *Mafiosi* during his exile there. Still, the stories got told. With each retelling, the legend grew.

"Even if Michael Corleone the man dies," Geraci explained to Momo Barone, "there's the risk that Michael Corleone the legend—a spook, a ghost, something that doesn't even exist—will live on."

The Roach was hanging on every word. A man whose interest was remotely insincere would have not forgotten so completely about the presence of that .38.

"I probably have the right friends in place now," Geraci said, "to see to it there's a change at the top." Meaning the killing of Michael Corleone and Tom Hagen. "But for it to work so that the change lets me come home, I need more people on the inside—just a few, not so many that things get out of control. What's going on with that crew of zips we set up in Bushwick?"

"The Don's got 'em reporting to Nobilio now."

Geraci nodded. His business dealings in Sicily had allowed him to branch out from the narcotics trade and start importing Sicilians, too. Most of them were civilians. Geraci had removed the stones in their pathway to citizenship and kept the hellhounds off their trail. For many of them, he'd used his connections in Cleveland and Chicago to set them up with jobs in restaurants in cities and towns all over the Great Lakes states: never for a fee, always as a favor. Often the jobs even came with an apartment, rent-free for the first few months, just until they got on their feet. But for a few of the Sicilians who'd been involved in the life over there, Geraci had shown them the ropes on how things were done in New York. They'd been fast learners. It might actually be better that they were no longer in the same *regime* as Momo. "Are they still using that smoke shop on Knickerbocker as an office?" Geraci asked.

"Last I heard. I don't see those guys too much."

"That's about to change," Nick said. "There's a couple men there I think we can use."

"That guy Renzo what's his face," Momo said, clearly excited to have thought of it.

"Interesting," Geraci said. "How do you figure?"

Momo's defense of his choice was animated—and also beside the point. Renzo Sacripante was cut from the same cloth as Geraci: he was good with his fists, had worked his way up, and was a great earner; men below him loved him, men above him feared him, and he'd survived various petty beefs with Michael Corleone—differences that, in fact, seemed to have increased his stature. What was important right now wasn't the choice, though, but that Momo clearly wanted to be an active participant in making it.

"All good points," Geraci told the Roach. "So maybe him and a few others. At any rate, the key thing here, the job for the inside men, is going to be to weaken and disgrace Michael and Tom Hagen. Otherwise, even if a few things happened and we did take over, we'd have no real power." Momo was eating it up each time Geraci said *we*. "I'd be a weak boss," Geraci said, "watching my back all the time for the men who miss Saint Michael. Believe me, the other New York Families would smell blood in the water and take advantage."

"Weaken and disgrace 'em how?" Momo did not so much as glance at the gun.

Geraci explained that this process was already nicely under way. His own ability to elude capture had been a step in the right direction. The petty mayhem he'd been able to orchestrate while in exile had been another (this was by and large a fabrication, but Geraci had heard the rumors, via his father and via his new contacts in New Orleans). The Nevada Gaming Commission's very public pursuit of Johnny Fontane, repeatedly causing Michael Corleone to be called an "alleged organized-crime figure," had been a stroke of dumb luck, but what the hell: Geraci would take it.

What had been done already, though, was only a beginning, Geraci said. There were other things. And so he and his loyal soldier had sat on that balcony and discussed various ways, large and small, they might dismantle the legend of Michael Corleone. Scandals and apparent screwups that might encourage the Corleone loyalists to lose enough faith in Michael to accept the truth: that it was Michael who had betrayed Nick. In addition, the bosses of the other Families, particularly the New York Families, needed to see that Nick Geraci would be better to deal with than (weakened, blundering) Michael Corleone, both now and in the future. Then and only then would it be possible to take the next step.

"Revenge," Momo said.

Machiavelli wrote that a prince must make himself feared in such a manner that he will avoid hatred, even if he does not acquire love.

"Maybe," Geraci said. He finally reached for the .38 and put it back in his pants. Momo didn't react. There was nothing more the gun could prove, for now. "But from where I sit," Geraci said, "I'm inclined to call it *justice.*"

IN THE WEEKS SINCE COSIMO BARONE HAD RETURNED TO Brooklyn, he'd helped set a few small things in motion—including a nerve-frying meeting with two of the zips from Bushwick—but the death of Judy Buchanan and how it could be used was bigger. The opportunity knocking now was loud enough to hear two thousand miles away.

"You need to take care of some things, my friend," Geraci said, "and fast."

The Roach, as he had so faithfully done for so many years, listened to Nick Geraci's instructions, eyes closed in concentration, ready to follow instructions to the letter. It felt good to be back taking orders from Geraci. It felt to the Roach like being where he was supposed to be, a little bit like the way he felt after he'd been with other women and then went to bed with his own sweet wife.

Moments after Momo hung up, the detective called again. He was outside the murdered woman's building now. "We got cops on the scene here," he said.

"Detectives?"

"Doesn't look like it. Not yet."

"Figure out how to make this your show," Momo said. "I don't care how. I don't need to say where the clues are gonna point to, do I? You don't need to put lover boy at the scene or nothin' like that. Just make it look like a contract job, and don't leave nothin' to chance, all right?"

"A contract job? You're not serious."

This, too, was something Geraci had thought of immediately that Momo might not have come up with given all the time in the world. Even if there were witnesses who saw the two private investigators run off, the killing could still be linked to Hagen. If the case against Hagen stood up in court, fine. If not, that was fine, too. It would hurt him to have been charged in the court of public opinion with the crime of hiring killers to whack his inconvenient mistress.

"Serious as a judge," Momo said.

"Look," the detective said. "I been thinking. I can tell you from experience that any time a gal dies, anybody she's been sleeping with is *automatically* a suspect. I guarantee you that this mess here is going to take the course you want it to take *without* me. All I'm trying to say is, I don't want to get caught in the middle of a thing that's none of my business."

This hadn't apparently troubled him when he'd taken that lunch sack full of cash in appreciation of his passing the job on to a suitable investigator.

"I don't give a shit what you want." The Roach had enough dirt on the detective to bury him twice, and they both knew it. "Go in there, now. When you find what you need to find, which I'm confident will happen in no time flat, let me give you the address of where at the present time you'll be able to find the suspect in question. Anytime in the next hour or so, you'll be fine. My advice is also to send over a whole fleet of cars, lights on and all that good stuff, loud as shit, OK? Just in the interest of what-tayacallit. Safety. Everybody's safety."

The Roach hung up and went downstairs to get a glass of water. He drank, closed his eyes, and tried to picture the look on Eddie Paradise's face when the cops pulled up. Eddie's big chance to show off in front of all the *pezzonovanti*–ruined. Embarrassed. Weakened. It'd go through the self-important little prick like God's perfect stiletto.

Momo opened his eyes.

He was standing right in front of one of Eddie's World War II posters, the one with the woman with the nice tits, pointing at those red dice. PLEASE DON'T GAMBLE WITH YOUR LIFE! BE CAREFUL WHAT YOU SAY. For the first time, the poster struck him as a big joke. The broad with the tits was in on it, too. Just look at her. Snake eyes on the dice, bedroom eyes on the broad. The Roach put a finger up to her flat, pouty lips. Against her small, porcelain-pale face, his suntanned skin looked almost black. He winked at her. "Shh," said the Roach.

Then he laughed and went up on the roof to enjoy what was left of the fireworks.

CHAPTER 17

The killing of Judy Buchanan played in Peoria. It became one of those murder cases that—arbitrarily, it would seem—takes on a circus-logic life of its own. It did have all four basic ingredients of such cases. It was frosted with lurid extramarital sex. It had ambitious politicians who used it as a stage. It had a sociopath who was widely presumed to be guilty but who somehow remained free. Most crucial of all, the victim was a strikingly beautiful blonde (that it was dyed was irrelevant), one unknowable enough to be a blank slate upon whom the masses could project their own prejudices, hypocrisies, and fears.

The sidewalk outside the building where Judy Buchanan's supposed contract murder took place was nearly always crowded and strewn with flowers. (*Location, location, location,* the old florist on the ground floor muttered each night, counting his money.) Periodically, earnest Protestant ministers in shirtsleeves came there to bellow sweet nothings about the wages of sin. But most of the people on the sidewalk had come to embrace each other and cry crocodile tears suitable for any newscast's B-roll. Often, these people waved cheaply printed posters of Judy Buchanan's now-famous head shot (for sale at souvenir stands throughout New York). It was ten

years old and was something she'd had taken during her brief, fruitless stab
at acting. Any appreciation of the irony of this—blowing up a head shot
of a woman whose lovely head had been nearly blown off—seemed lost on
most Americans, perhaps like irony in general. Increasingly, the mourners
and gawkers waved one of the surveillance photos that had been sent,
anonymously, to the NYPD, the FBI, the Justice Department, and a host
of newspapers, tabloid and otherwise. The shot of Judy Buchanan in an exquisitely tailored pantsuit, on the train platform in Milwaukee—alone and,
in the opinion of many, looking trapped—became an especially popular
choice. Once in a while someone would even deploy photos of her mentally retarded son, Philip, who, despite his afflictions and the violent deaths
of his parents, seemed always to have a smile for the camera.

Outside the building where Tom Hagen lived, Al Neri stationed uniformed private security officers—off-duty or retired cops all. Despite this,
the cul-de-sac was often clogged with curious civilians, both from the press
and the public. Miles of TV footage was shot, nearly all of it featuring dark
cars with tinted windows emerging from the building's underground garage
and driving uneventfully away. Even early in the morning, when Neri went
out to get his roadwork in, there was always some clown looking up toward
the building's top floors and pointing.

The case dragged on for months, spewing money, minting new minor-
key celebrities, selling newspapers and magazines, garnering book deals
and reliable TV ratings, and inspiring debates in barber shops and beauty
shops from sea to shining sea. All this for a case that was yet to yield a single arrest.

WHEN HE WAS INITIALLY BROUGHT IN FOR QUESTIONING,
Tom Hagen had, of course, said nothing until his attorney showed up. The
attorney he hired was Sid Klein, famous for his role as a congressional
counsel during the anti-Communism investigations. Hagen had admired
his work for years and had put him on retainer for a rainy day. There was

no one, anywhere, who was more vicious, more zealous, more comfortable in the glare of a high-profile case. Defending those alleged to be connected with the so-called Mafia had actually become one of Sid Klein's specialties. Both the Barzini Family and the Tattaglia Family—following Hagen's lead—had Klein on retainer as well.

It looked like the police didn't have much. They seemed to want to make something of the .22 caliber pistol, a Ruger, that they'd found on the scene. It had recently been fired three times, and someone had wiped it clean. "We have evidence that shows the gun belongs to an ex-convict named Richard Antony Nobilio, Jr.," one of the detectives said. Richie had done a stretch in Lewisburg for conspiring to violate federal narcotics laws.

"Was it the murder weapon?" Klein said.

"At this point, we're not sure."

Meaning *no,* Klein and Hagen immediately understood.

"Mr. Nobilio is an associate of yours, though, right?"

Hagen and Sid Klein exchanged whispers, and Klein let him answer.

"Yes. I do some legal work for Mr. Nobilio—who has, by the way, paid his debt to society and plays the organ at his church. I am an associate of his in a few investments. As for the pistol, I think I can save you some time. Mrs. Buchanan wanted to get a pistol for her protection—she travels frequently in connection with her job as a courier for some businesses I work for as well. I don't know a thing about guns myself, so when she asked me what to get, I referred her to my dear friend Richard Nobilio, who's something of a buff on the subject of firearms. He was supposed to drop by this afternoon and help her out. I'm not sure if the gun you found is the gun he got for her, but I do know that he thought she should get something smaller, easy to handle for a lady. A .22 is a gun like that, right?"

"No man who took his woman's safety seriously would set her up with just a .22."

Right, Hagen thought. *Exactly.* He started to answer, but Klein shut him down.

"Questions, detective," Klein said. "Not statements."

"All right, *question*." He sneered. "Would Mr. Nobilio have had any reason to harm Mrs. Buchanan?"

"None," said Hagen.

Sid Klein laughed. "I don't mean to tell you gents how to do your job—for which I thank you. I mean that. My father was actually a cop, as you may know, one of the few Jews on the force in those days, but maybe you knew that, too. At any rate, if the gun really is Mr. Nobilio's, doesn't that tell you something? Who'd leave a gun at a crime scene if it could be easily traced? That gun being there, don't you think it rules Mr. Nobilio *out* as a suspect? And by extension, his associate Mr. Hagen as well? I think we can safely say that what you have there is either a plant or tampered evidence or both."

"Tampered *evidence*?" one of the detectives said. "Sweet Jesus Christ. This early in the game, you're pulling out your cheap lawyer tricks."

"*Cheap*?" Klein said. An elongated beat later, he raised an eyebrow. It looked vaguely motorized. "I doubt that when Mr. Hagen gets my bill, he'll agree that I'm cheap," Klein said. "And I certainly don't have to tell you that the laws of the land are not *lawyer tricks*."

Klein had struck a nerve, the way for which had been paved by preying on the detective's anti-Semitism. Even under the circumstances, it was a pleasure for Hagen to watch Sid Klein work.

Another detective started talking, but Klein interrupted him and turned to the first one.

"That was her gun, probably, right? How could she have been in any position to wipe her prints off of it? Why would the killer have bothered?"

"I don't know," the detective said, clearly working to put on a front. "You tell me."

Klein raised his palms. "I can't! All I'm trying to say, those are some interesting questions. Food for thought, I guess would be the expression."

When the interview was over, the police let Hagen go, though he was asked to remain within the five boroughs of New York until further notice. He looked at Klein, and Klein closed his eyes and very slightly shook his head. Fighting that could wait.

A pool of reporters were waiting for them. "Mr. Hagen!" one shouted. "Why would an innocent man need to hire Sid Klein?"

Hagen started to answer, but Klein—almost like a third baseman cutting off a waiting shortstop—strode forward to field the question. "It is a sad fact," Klein said, "that in this cruel and fallen world, only small children are innocent. There is no such thing as an innocent adult. It's an oxymoron. However, not-guilty people hire me all the time for various matters, and I'm happy to announce that Congressman Hagen is among them." Hagen had been Nevada's lone congressman for less than six months, appointed to fill out the term of a man whose ranch was downwind of the nuclear testing ranges and died of cancer. Sid Klein's use of the title was calculated. Every breath he took seemed calculated. His pregnant pauses, his gestures, even his eye blinks made him seem like a remarkably lifelike robot. "Congressman Hagen is merely here to be of service to the authorities," Klein continued. "It is certainly our hope that those responsible for this reprehensible act are brought swiftly to justice. As you may know, Mrs. Buchanan was a valued employee of a company in which Congressman Hagen is a member of the board of directors, and she will be missed. Our sympathies and indeed our hearts go out to her family." Klein took an unnecessarily deep bow. "Gentlemen."

Al Neri—who hadn't been around this many cops since he was one himself—squared his shoulders like a football lineman and led the way to a waiting car. It sped away.

Hagen showed no remorse.

Why should he? He *hadn't* had anything to do with the murder. And what could he do about it now? Nothing. Nothing, that is, except to swing into what he'd spent half his adult life doing: damage control (the other half had been spent on negotiation). Hagen did *have* some remorse, at some level, about various things—he was not a heartless man; quite the opposite, he believed—but it was nobody's business but his own.

Nobody said anything. When the car pulled up outside Klein's building, Klein patted Hagen on the knee and got out. Hagen nodded his appreciation.

Neri got in back with Hagen, and Hagen raised the partition so that the driver couldn't hear. The car was not a limo, but Neri had had it tricked out with limousine details. It was also armored, of course. What used to be one of Momo Barone's chop shops, over on Bergen Street, now did exclusively legal custom work, specializing in jobs like this.

"How bad was it," Hagen asked, "after I left?"

Neri stuck out his lower lip. "Not so bad."

Meaning *very*, Tom understood. "The cops didn't . . ."

"Nah. They left when you did. Mike tried to conduct more business and wrap things up, but from what I understand, the other fellas, they was all excited and this and that, so there was various concerns raised about the security, and everybody pretty much left after that. You didn't miss nothin', believe me. Unless you was of a mind to see the boss take Eddie Paradise aside and quietly rip him a variety of new assholes."

Hagen nodded.

They rode the rest of the way home in silence.

She was dead. It didn't seem possible. Gone. Just that afternoon, she'd been susceptible to the little death, at least twice, and thereby seemed breathtakingly alive. Tom couldn't think about that. About *her*. About Judy Buchanan, who was dead. Murdered.

He closed his eyes, took a deep breath, and tried to focus.

Tom Hagen's biggest fear now wasn't that he'd get pinned with the murder itself. He had too much on his side, too many strings he could pull or have pulled, to get taken down by a crime he did not commit. His biggest fear was that the killing had had something to do with Theresa. That she'd somehow arranged it.

In any event, some ugly things were bound to come to light. What and how and how much? That was still up in the air and might remain that way for a while. Obviously, Tom needed to have a long and difficult talk with his wife. He obviously needed to talk to Michael as well.

When he got home and he and Al got into the elevator, Tom did not hesitate.

"Penthouse," he said.

Al nodded.

This thing of ours must come before your wife, your children, even your mother. Tom Hagen would never take the vows, but he knew them. No man was ever more faithful to them.

"We have any idea who tipped off the cops?" Tom asked on the way up. "How they knew where I was?"

Neri shook his head. "Unless somebody shows us his hand, I doubt we ever will."

"How you figure?" Tom said.

"Too many possibilities," Al said. "My first thought was that it was a cop. There are plenty of men on the force who'll look the other way at a lot of the things we do but not when it comes to a murder, especially of a white woman. If it *is* a cop, we'll probably never know who, and we'll never be able to retaliate. But then I started considering all the people on the scene— almost forty, by my count. Who knows who *they* told about where they were going to be tonight? How many top men in various Families knew when and where the meeting was going to be? How many of those people might have some kind of axe to grind against you or Michael or our whole organization, who'd like to see us taken down a notch the way I guess it happened with the Cuneos? I'm not ruling out that it's one of our people, either. And, yeah, it could be the *disgraziato*, too," meaning Nick Geraci, "although, you ask me, that cocksucker gets credit for too much already."

"But if you had to bet?" Tom asked.

"Cop," the ex-cop said, shrugging. "And we'll never know who."

The elevator doors opened.

It was almost three in the morning, but the lights in Michael's study still burned.

WHAT TOM TOLD THERESA WAS THAT THERE WERE PEOPLE who wanted to hurt the family, and that, rest assured, they would not succeed.

They were in their bedroom, behind a locked door.

She dissolved before his very eyes, wailing and sobbing. Theresa was a tough woman, and this, what he'd reduced her to, was hard for him to watch.

When he lifted her up, she spit in his face and called him a filthy name. She was on the edge of hyperventilating.

The look in her eyes was not Theresa. It was barely human. It was the look of a wounded and dangerous animal.

Tom forced himself not to react. He greeted her passions by turning his to stone.

He was, in fact, relieved.

There was nothing at all in the way she was handling this to suggest she'd had anything to do with it. She could have never been so purely angry if at the same time she'd been worried about her involvement in a murder.

Tom told Theresa the accusations were lies, each and every one of them.

Hope flickered across her face. But then she slapped him, then told him to leave her alone. He did, optimistic that she'd come around, that everything would be fine.

The accusations were not all lies, of course. Just the criminal ones. It was an overstatement he soon came to regret. He'd been paying more attention to her reaction than to his presentation.

Hagen's fingerprints turned up all over both the apartment where Judy Buchanan had been killed and her apartment in Las Vegas as well. This

looked bad, but it meant nothing to the case. In the court of public opinion a person could be found guilty of adultery and thus convicted of murder, but in actual court, that was a tough one. In court, going up against
Sid Klein, forget it.

But it wasn't just the public who found the fingerprints meaningful.
Theresa took their two daughters and their dog—a collie named Elvis—and
went to stay with her parents in New Jersey. She'd done that before, though
never over another woman.

Tom wasn't crazy about the idea, but he understood and supported
her decision.

Soon after that, a "police spokesman" cited a "vast cache" of evidence
they had come upon that corroborated the illicit nature of Mr. Hagen and
Mrs. Buchanan's relationship.

An incriminating photograph had also been mailed, anonymously, to
one of the New York tabloids and had been reprinted in newspapers and
magazines across the country.

Not long after that, Theresa had taken nearly all her things and all the
girls' things, too, and moved to the house she'd bought in Florida. She en-
rolled the girls in school there. She begged Tom not to be in contact with
her, told him she hoped he rotted in hell.

"I'm sure I will," he said.

She laughed at him and hung up.

It made him think of the girl he had married, that laugh. That girl didn't
have it in her to laugh like that. Tom had to face up to it: the bitterness in
that laugh, the anger and the cynicism, the loss of innocence, had been
his doing.

He'd work this out, he told himself. He was sure of it.

His heart started revving, but as these episodes went, it was a mild one.
He stayed at his kitchen table, staring at the phone, alone in his huge white
apartment, sipping Crown Royal on the rocks from a misshapen coffee mug
little Gianna had made for him. He got up to get more ice, then picked up
the phone and called his son Frank in New Haven. He let it ring for a long

time, but there was no answer. He called his younger son, Andrew, at Notre Dame, but when he heard the boy's voice he couldn't think of what to say.

"Dad?" Andrew said.

"How did you know it was me?"

"Nobody else calls me and doesn't talk."

"When else did I ever do that?"

"How are you, Dad?"

"Have you talked to your mother?"

"Yeah," he said. Every day. He was Theresa's secret favorite, which probably only Theresa thought of as a secret. "Mom said you'd call. Have you been drinking?"

How was it possible at that age to be such a prig? "What are you, my father?"

"No," he said. "Your father died from drinking too much."

"God willing, you'll live long enough to see that things aren't so black and white as how I think you see the world."

"God, huh?"

"How's school?"

Andrew humored him and talked about it for a while.

"You know that what's going on here," Tom said, "it's a crock, all right? It's just harassment."

"I believe you, Dad."

He said it in a way that sounded reassuring, like absolution. When Andrew first said he was considering the priesthood, Tom was afraid it was because he was such a mama's boy and worried that she'd loved him so much it had turned him into a fairy, the way Carmela had done to poor Fredo. Now Tom was thinking it was something else. That Andrew thought he needed to atone for the proverbial sins of the father.

"This is all going to blow over," Tom said. "This is all going to work out, believe me. Things aren't what they seem."

"'There are more things in heaven and earth than are dreamt of in your philosophy.'"

"Is that right?"

"It's from *Hamlet,* Dad."

"That's the problem with education. You learn something new and you forget that other people sat at that same desk before you got there."

"I love you, Dad."

"Good luck with those exams," Tom said.

He hung up. He rubbed his face, then poured the last of the bottle into the mug. Tom missed them, Theresa and the girls, and his sons, too. It was clouding his judgment, making him sentimental.

Tom realized now that he'd been mistaken. What had happened to Theresa—that hardness that he'd heard in her laugh—was something that happened to everybody. It was the goddamned human condition. Sid Klein was right. There are no innocent adults.

THE FIRST BIG BREAK IN THE CASE SEEMED TO COME WHEN, canvassing the neighborhood for witnesses, the homicide detective who'd first taken the reins of the case found a woman who'd seen the killers leave. She would have come forward sooner, but she'd heard that the killers were "Mafia hit men" and she was afraid. On the night of the murder, she said, she'd been out walking her dog and had seen two men run out of Judy Buchanan's building, one carrying a big gun. The woman hid behind a parked car. The men got into a late-model Plymouth and drove away. As they did, the woman got a look at their license number, which she had committed to memory. The woman was a musician and good at memorizing things, which were the only clues the public had about her identity. There were various rumors about the woman and how the detective knew her. There also seemed to be some holes in her story. Until such time as a trial, though, her identity was being protected. Even the breed of her dog was confidential.

The cops ran that license-plate number, and it led them to a Mrs. Robert Dantzler, in a modest house in the outer reaches of Queens. The Plymouth was in the driveway, with a new Corvette parked behind it. They asked the young woman who answered the door if they could speak to her mother, but that *was* Mrs. Dantzler: a plain-faced twenty-year-old in clingy pajamas at noon. She was unfazed by the insult. Her husband (a retired beat cop and licensed private investigator) and her big brother (Vernon K. Rougatis, who was "between jobs") had gone away suddenly on what they'd called a business trip. They'd packed in a hurry and taken a cab. She didn't know if *business trip* was code for something else. All *she* knew, she said, was that she was getting tired of her husband's "bullcrap" ("Mr. Dantzler's [non-sense]," according to the newspaper of record). The house was crammed with things: new appliances, new furniture, and one whole room full of ex-pensive china dolls. Later, there would be feature stories about how these dolls had been a comfort to her. Mrs. Dantzler stayed on the periphery of this story for a while, unsuccessfully suing to get her husband's surveillance photos back and to get paid by anyone and everyone who had published them. Even after that, she was a regular guest on *The Joe Franklin Show*.

The sheer amount of material goods—her Corvette had only eighty-three miles on it—seemed beyond Bob Dantzler's means, but apparently the only sinister element lurking behind all that was a mountain of con-sumer debt. The finished basement was Bob Dantzler's part of the house, she said, but police didn't find anything there that was of much use. Mrs. Dantzler said that in addition to a suitcase, her husband had taken a "re-ally big" satchel with him on his trip. He did have a sizable arsenal down there—sixty-one guns, rifles, and shotguns, as well as hundreds of boxes of ammo, which led to many people's assumption that he'd been a contract killer for the Mafia, and not merely a man enjoying the bejesus out of his constitutional right to keep and bear arms.

Dantzler's personnel file—he'd spent twenty-five years on the Force—revealed no ties or noteworthy run-ins with elements of the Mafia. Neither did the interviews with the men who'd worked with him. He'd been re-garded as a capable, unambitious cop, remarkable only because he got di-vorced and remarried every few years, the way movie stars do.

Days after the search of her house, the plain young woman in the pajamas, the fifth Mrs. Bob Dantzler, found out that she was the last of the line.

Responding to an anonymous tip, police found Bob Dantzler and his brother-in-law on a garbage barge in New Jersey, docked but as yet unloaded. Each man had been shot twice in the back of the head and wrapped in a bedspread. The bullets came from a .45, more gun than was usually used for such assassinations. Their wallets were still in their pants pockets. No acid or quicklime had been used to accelerate decomposition. Their heads, hands, and feet were still attached. Whoever killed them obviously wanted them to be found.

The brother-in-law had A-negative blood, which occurs in only six percent of the American people, the fourth-rarest type. Judy Buchanan's blood was O-positive. The other blood type found at the scene, which must have come from the shooter, was A-negative. There seemed to be a strong circumstantial case that these were the killers and that the investigation should focus on who had hired them.

"It's just simple common sense," Sid Klein pointed out to a group of reporters assembled outside his law office, "that these deaths have nothing to do with my client. What, after all, did Mr. Hagen have to gain from killing the killers? Nothing. No tie between him and these men has been or will be found. What did the people who hired the killers have to gain? Everything. Is it time to look beyond my client and try to find the person or persons behind these heinous crimes? It is. It is past time."

Nonetheless, the garbage had been loaded at a city sanitation facility only a block from where Tom Hagen lived. That, of course, meant nothing—garbage came there from all over the East Side—but it certainly didn't look good.

What about the allegation that the police had evidence that showed that Judy Buchanan had been a kept woman for almost ten years, that Hagen had even paid for the bills incurred by her mother and her son?

"It's a misunderstanding," Klein said. "Minor accounting blunders, is all that is. The payments in question were perfectly legal fringe benefits she had been given. These payments should have been funded by a company for which Mr. Hagen was a signatory, not by Mr. Hagen personally. It was an honest mistake, and the accountant who made these mistakes has been fired. He accepts full responsibility for these errors, however, and he's prepared to admit to them, under oath, in a court of law."

MANY OF THE EFFORTS TO BUILD A CASE WERE VISIBLE TO the naked eye, and it seemed safe to assume that any number of behind-the-scenes things were happening, too. An arrest seemed to be getting closer every day.

And kept not happening.

As the investigation dragged on, it started to seem to some observers that the law-enforcement officials in charge—and it was challenging, from the outside looking in, to discern just who *was* in charge—seemed more interested in keeping the drama before the public than they were in solving the actual murder.

Exhibit A: the hapless NYPD detective initially on the case might never have been replaced at all if not for a newspaper column that revealed corruption galore in his past. Federal prosecutors threatened the columnist with jail if he did not reveal the "underworld kingpin" who'd been his anonymous source, which he refused to do. Years later, however, in the deeply moving and often hilarious memoir *Hard-Bitten,* he claimed he'd been contacted by an expensive public relations firm in lower Manhattan, which had then coordinated his interview with Eddie Paradise, who had committed to memory the intricate details of the many payoffs the detective had accepted—from the Corleones as well as several other New York Families. They'd all checked out.

According to the book, at the time of the murder, Paradise had no idea that the detective was under his friend Momo Barone's thumb. He also had no idea that the Roach, his best friend, was conspiring against him. That—

and the famous lion—all came out later. At the time, the way Eddie Paradise saw things was that he'd found a progressive and bloodless means of hurting the detective, someone he believed to be a threat to the Corleone Family, and the little guy was intemperately proud of himself for his own cleverness. The chapter begins this way: "Little Eddie Paradise was the first mobster to ever hire his own P.R. flak. He would not be the last." Later in the chapter, *Hard-Bitten* chronicles the troubles that fateful column unleashed: "It was all just theater. I was acting tough, but that's all it was—an act. And the sabers the Feds were rattling came straight from the prop department. Fool that I was, though, it all seemed real to me. I was a young man with three kids to feed and a long-suffering wife, so from where I stood the blades on those sabers looked pretty sharp. I had to look inside myself, but back then all there was to see was booze and fear. So I just played my part, like the enterprising red-blooded, true-blue American fake that I was. I put on a brave face, spent a few nights in jail, and when it all blew over, I was a hero. A poster boy for the First Amendment. A couple years later, I won a Pulitzer Prize. Anyone who says this isn't a great country can kiss my saggy white ass."

The men the NYPD next assigned to the case were skilled and respected straight arrows well known to anyone on the New York crime beat: Detective John Siriani, one of the most decorated Italian-Americans on the force, and Detective Gary Evans, a brush-cut telegenic blond of no discernible ethnicity. From the beginning, though, there was something peculiar in the set of their jaws, some oddly glazed look about them, as if they were two proud star ballplayers stuck on a team that's given up on the season. They were not men given to self-pity. If they ever asked *why me*, there is no record of it. They would have known full well that there were any number of reasons two homicide detectives with astronomically high clearance rates might get assigned to a case that, among other things, was preordained to bring that rate down.

It became possible, though, for even casual observers to see some of what was behind the deadened look in the detectives' eyes. Every few days, some public official called some kind of press conference or made some statement about the case that was clearly calculated to make news; each time it happened, it must have driven home to the detectives what pawns they were. The coroner came to work every day with TV makeup on. The mayor and several members of the NYPD's top brass—including Chief Phillips—were unshy about discussing the case and, more so, what it represented. The district attorney's office installed a new bank of telephones for their friends in the press. The increasingly reclusive director of the FBI reversed field and discussed the case as part of an hour-long interview with the dean of the network-TV anchormen.

Attorney General Daniel Brendan Shea, of course, was engaged in his quest to go down in history as the man who brought down the Mafia, to destroy the sorts of men who'd made his family filthy rich, who'd helped fund his Ivy League education, and without whom his meteoric ascent to becoming the youngest attorney general in American history would never have been possible. It was therefore natural that in the speeches he made at college graduation ceremonies and in the proximity of the petty arrests his people were racking up, he might at least in passing mention this high-profile case with its supposed Mafia ties. He also spoke not once, not twice, but *three times* at fund-raising events for a lowly New York State Senate candidate—a man who just happened to be the prosecutor assigned to the case. On all three occasions, Danny Shea mentioned "the scourge of organized crime" in general and "the tragic events surrounding the death of Mrs. Buchanan" in particular. In the third, he actually used the term "hit men."

MICHAEL CORLEONE MET WITH SID KLEIN OVER LUNCH IN the upstairs back room at Patsy's, an old-school red-sauce Italian place on Fifty-sixth Street. Michael's office was almost certainly free of wiretaps, by dint of Al Neri's love of gadgetry, and Michael often cooked lunch himself for meetings there, but Rita Duvall was there with two nuns visiting from France. (She'd been raised in a convent after her mother shot her father and then herself.) The law prohibited wiretaps in lawyer's offices, but Michael was wary of relying on that, as was Sid Klein—who, amazingly, had no office. He got by with a photographic memory and a file clerk who worked in a converted bank vault in Chinatown. Klein never took notes and rarely carried a briefcase.

They arrived separately, came in through the kitchen, and took the back stairs to their table. Patsy's knew how to make things easy for important people who didn't want their meals interrupted by the intrusion of the public.

Al Neri sat alone at the next table.

"He could join us," Klein said.

"He's fine," Michael said.

"I should get a man like him," Klein said. "A person can't be too careful these days."

"'These days'?" Michael said. "When was it ever different?"

"Ah, a philosopher," Klein said. "A history buff. I like you. Where'd you find him, anyway? Not through a service, I bet."

Michael suspected Klein already knew the answer. "He was a cop," Michael said.

"I thought people in your line of work hated the cops."

Neri chuckled softly.

"What line of work would that be?" Michael said.

"You tell me," Klein said. He held up his hands. "Or better yet, don't. "

"You're on retainer," Michael said.

"That's true," Klein said. "But I only want to know what I want to know, and when I want to know it, I ask. Keeps my life simple."

Michael lit a cigarette. What people never seemed to understand about him—even people who knew enough to know better—was how little of his time was taken up with things that might be considered criminal. A typical day in the life of Michael Corleone was indistinguishable from that of any other successful private investor and real estate developer. He was, in fact, a little bit of a history buff, though. He understood that while a man's life is made up of typical days, it is only the atypical days that history can use.

Sid Klein opened his menu. Michael didn't and wouldn't. It was something he'd learned from his brother Sonny. Any fine restaurant will try to make you whatever you ask for. Just ask.

"This is what's beautiful about the Italian people," Klein said, jabbing a finger at the menu for emphasis. "At all your important discussions, you sit down, break bread. I shouldn't say just *bread*. Great food and plenty of it."

Michael ignored this.

"Enlighten me, counselor," Michael said. "Isn't there a rule of law that requires the police, the prosecutors, either one, to turn over evidence to you?"

"And who am I?"

Michael frowned.

"I'm nobody," Klein said. "That's who I am. I'm Tom Hagen's lawyer, but he's not charged with anything, he's not indicted, nothing. So until there's a real trial on the horizon somewhere—which I'm sure you don't want that, a trial—but until that point in time they don't have to give anybody anything. If you ask me, they're playing this out the way they are because they *don't* have anything."

Which is one of the many points Sid Klein was making in the many interviews he was granting to what seemed like anyone who asked.

"So is that why you're conducting so much of your business—which in this regard is often *my* business—on the front pages of the newspapers?"

"Ah, all right. I see. *That's* why you asked me here. Though I have to wonder why you didn't just ask Tom, or why you didn't ask him to ask me."

Michael Corleone's smile was disconnected from anything happy or amusing. "I asked you here, as I thought I told you, because I got a call from the chef himself that said the veal would be good today."

"I'm getting the gnocchi, extra sauce." He pronounced it *ga-no-chee*. "I love that stuff, can't get it at home. I've had it here before, actually."

Michael corrected his pronunciation.

"Are you sure?"

"How could I not be sure about a thing like that?"

"Let's ask the waiter."

"I only corrected you because you said you loved the stuff. I didn't want you to embarrass yourself."

"You're aware of what I do for a living, right?" Klein said. "You think I'm real worried about embarrassing myself? Let's ask the waiter."

But when it came time to order, he neither asked the waiter nor mispronounced it.

"Is there anything I'm saying," Klein said when they were alone again, "when those notebooks and microphones are in my face that isn't positive for Tom and by extension you and your business? I hardly think so. They're playing this whole thing out in the press, and if there's never a trial, who's going to be in a position to rebut all those false allegations? Nobody. As Tom's lawyer, I'd have to forbid him from doing it, and if he did so, I'd have to resign. You can't do it, either. Commenting at all would look like an admission of guilt. I'll tell you what, the thing I'd really like to say is that this isn't what a contract killing looks like. This isn't how it works in the . . . in the line of work they're talking about. Those men who killed her would have been Italian, for one thing, and—"

"What are you talking about?"

"Don't worry, I'd never say things like that in public. But it's true that the public has very little idea about how all this works, the mechanics of it. Even the cops don't understand it, but if I could just—"

"You don't know what you're talking about. So maybe you shouldn't talk about it."

Klein rubbed his chin. He looked over at Al Neri. Neri smiled, in the manner of a patient cat who knows it will eventually get its shot at the mouse. "All right," Klein said to Michael. "You're right. I was out of line."

Michael lit another cigarette and took his time doing it.

"How sure are you," Michael said, "that they aren't going to charge Tom with this?"

"A good lawyer is careful to never be overly sure of anything," Klein said. "As for *how* sure I am, I'm bad with odds-making, which I'm sure you've heard from some of your associates."

Michael had, of course. Klein was a lousy gambler who bet often and fairly small and thus never had any trouble covering his losses. That the betting didn't escalate, that he didn't dig himself deeper by trying to make up everything he lost Saturday on Sunday's games, did show unusual discipline, which Michael admired. Still, few habitual gamblers manage to maintain such discipline over time.

Michael excused himself to go wash his hands and to give Klein a chance to grow anxious over not really answering the question. Silence was a fine tool for working over a big talker. Al caught his eye as he passed. He'd seen the tactic before.

"Please don't misunderstand, young man," Klein said when Michael returned to the table. "I'm not being coy with you or . . . what's the term? Busting your balls? I'm confident that there's not a good case here, but they're going to make sure it gets played for everything it's worth and then some."

"Curious: who's *they*?"

"C'mon. Who do you think?"

"I want to hear your perspective. I've paid for it."

"If they charge Tom Hagen with this horrible crime," Klein said, going into an impression of James K. Shea's phony Brahmin accent, "they shall suffer an ignominious defeat on the field of battle." He sounded more like Morrie Streator, the Vegas comedian who'd popularized the impression, than he did a Shea brother. Klein shook his head in self-deprecation. "I'll stop. But, see, if charges are never filed, they get to use this thing until they get bored with it. Sooner or later they'll drop it—probably after the November election—but they'll do it quietly, and therefore they'll never look like they've suffered any sort of defeat—"

"Because the public's memory is as short as a senile dog's."

Klein smiled. "Tom told me that little saying of yours. Catchy. Can't say as I disagree."

"So what right do the authorities have in telling Tom he can't leave the area?"

"The five boroughs of New York?" Klein clarified. "No right whatsoever."

"But if I sent him on an out-of-town business trip—"

"A business trip where?"

To meet with Jack Woltz in Los Angeles, for one thing. Michael had had to trust Johnny and some of his people out there to get the ball rolling, but it was a project that needed Tom's touch. Or to meet with Pat Geary, the Nevada senator and their old friend, who was running against Jimmy Shea in the primaries, a glorified favorite-son candidate who appealed to voters in the South and the mountain West and other, more conservative elements in the party—a campaign that presumably was aimed less at winning than at being enough of a pain in the ass that he could make a speech at the convention and garner other, more substantial favors. "Why does it matter where?"

"I suppose it doesn't. Go ahead. Feel free. Nothing will happen."

"Nothing?"

"Nothing legal," Klein said. "But I'd think he'd be followed. Given the interest the Justice Department has shown in the case, I'd wager that those doing the following will be FBI."

"Though, as you say, you have no talent with the odds," Michael said.

"Sure, it's true," Klein said. "But in a wager like this, think of me as the house."

"I have my own airplane," Michael said. "I fly it myself, as kind of a hobby. If Tom and I took a business trip together, and I flew us—"

"What are you saying, that you're going to take airborne evasive action against the FBI?"

"You watch too many war movies," Michael said.

"You still have to file flight plans with someone, though, right?"

"If I fly from private airstrip to private airstrip in a private plane—me, a hired pilot, either way—who knows who the passengers are? What can the FBI do, take an airplane up, follow me in the air, and land right behind me—or my employees—on a privately owned airstrip? Is that legal?"

"What do you think?"

"I think I'm getting tired of you asking me questions when I want answers."

Klein shrugged. "My apologies. You want opinions, ask a cabbie or a judge. I do two things for a living. I ask questions and I argue. I get my answers from other people."

"I thought maybe you were going to say the two things you do are suck blood and kiss ass," Michael said.

Klein laughed. "Those, too."

"That's four things."

"They're all related."

"So what's your point?"

Their food came.

"Don't be naïve, is my point," said Sid Klein when they were alone again. "The Feds don't want to take you to court for any of this, they want to ruin you. Under those circumstances, they're much less concerned with what's legal than you are." He beckoned toward his plate. "Ga-no-chee?"

CHAPTER 18

On one of the first warm days of spring, Francesca Corleone Van Arsdale—shrouded with dread, as she was almost all the time now—was cooking dinner with her aunt, just the two of them. It was one of the nights Kathy taught class. The kitchen windows were open. Francesca could see and hear Connie's boys, Victor and Little Mike, out in the courtyard, tossing a football with her little boy, Sonny, who'd just turned six. Victor had a radio out there, too—he took one with him almost everywhere. The station was playing that new Beatles record, "She Loves You." The Hagen girls, Christina and Gianna, would have ordinarily been out there, too, until they were called upon to set the table, but they were in Florida with Theresa. The men were all upstairs.

In their treehouse. That's what Kathy called it, behind the men's backs. She joked to Francesca that she was going to give them a NO GIRLS ALLOWED sign for Christmas. This was disrespectful and, of course, not even strictly accurate, especially since Rita Duvall seemed to be spending more time with Michael lately—but Francesca saw the truth in it. The whole setup here was the realization of a boy's grand fantasy—a prince who grew up to be king, who moved to an island and built a fortress atop a high building, complete

with a garden that was a replica of the one so beloved by his father, the
dead king. True, the garden had been Aunt Connie's project. But all she
was doing was re-creating something her father had created inside something her brother had created. Boys have the luxury of yearning for the past
while living in their dreams of the future. Women might wish to do the
same, but they spent their days enslaved to the present. And what sort of
present was it? The Great Age of the American Boy, featuring a boyish,
cocksure president who still played boys' games (touch football, little boats)
and inspired his citizens by espousing a boy's dream of flying to the moon
(and, subliminally, of becoming the first to urinate on its surface when no
women were watching). The styling of new radios, record players, cars,
speedboats, fighter jets, and reconnaissance planes came straight out of
boys' comic books. Tall, phallic TV towers shot millions of tiny particles
of light into space, where they would swim toward infinity. The most popular TV show in this world, *Bonanza*, was a boy's story about four "men"
living alone on a ranch (the manly oldest-brother character was dropped):
Ben, the grandfatherly patriarch; Hoss, the giant boy-man middle child; Little Joe, the headstrong, baby-faced teenager and certified ladykiller; and
Hop Sing, the infantilized Chinese cook (thus obviating the need for any
mothers or wives). The most popular musical act in the world, the Beatles,
featured four mop-topped British lads dressed in cute matching suits and
Cuban-heeled boots, singing in the style of such American-boy originals
as Larry Williams—whose biggest hit, "Bad Boy," the Beatles played in all
their concert performances—and Little Richard, the greatest Peter Pan figure American culture had yet produced. And it all played out against the
chilling backdrop of the Cold War, that secret-gadget nirvana, the most dangerous boys' game of all time. All the world was now at the mercy of
double-dog dares and lines drawn in the dirt. As the world's very existence
hung in the balance, the most important question of the day was who had
the biggest concealed missile and at whom it might be pointed.

Or so went the thesis of a scholarly book Kathy was writing.

Francesca handed her aunt the ricotta filling for the manicotti and got started on the salad. Connie started assembling the shells. Connie and Francesca were talking about nothing, as usual—the status of various homework assignments, cleaning the place up because the cleaning people were coming, whether certain items of clothing had or had not been picked up at the cleaners. Nothing, in other words. Nothing, Francesca thought, when, as usual, there was so much to talk about. It was as if everybody in their family had a list of all possible topics of conversation, long-term and short-term both, and honored an unspoken agreement to introduce none of the fifty most important topics—except in the heat of the moment. Then, of course, passions reigned, and it was no-holds-barred (Little Sonny loved to watch wrestling on TV and the terms bled into Francesca's subconscious). Whoever got hurt probably had it coming, and if not, what were you going to do? Nothing. Sometimes it went the other way; it was the flames of *your* passions that blistered someone else. So in the end it all evened out. Pain came at you out of nowhere, and every person's story was destined to end the same way. What was that cowboy song Uncle Fredo used to sing? *No matter how I struggle and strive, I'll never get out of this world alive.* It used to make all the nieces and nephews laugh. He'd sing it in a funny voice with little yodeling hiccups. It had seemed so funny then, and it seemed like such a nightmare now. No one talked about that, either. About Fredo. Far, far too high on the list.

The long chef's knife was crushing the tomatoes instead of slicing them, and Francesca pulled out the whetstone to give it a quick sharpening. Connie was prattling on now about how disappointed she'd been in the movie they saw together last night, which Francesca had liked, if only for the jazzy score and the way Johnny Fontane looked in tights. He was a kind of man-boy, too, but with Johnny it was different, at least for Francesca. She understood that he was the epitome of a certain sort of manly cool, a public bearer of the code. But his youthful, playful streak—the sophomoric, wise-cracking practical joking; the nightcrawling and carousing that revealed the little boy inside him who didn't want to go to bed for fear of missing any grown-up fun—kept Johnny from seeming impossibly too old for her.

Francesca and Johnny had now met twice, quietly, to talk business—once at lunch and once over drinks in a booth with red curtains at Hal Mitchell's on Fifty-fourth Street, to talk about starting up a fund that would honor the memory of his best friend, the singer and actor Nino Valenti. The meetings weren't a secret, but she hadn't told anyone in her family about them, especially not Connie. What was there to tell? That he'd asked her to come to California to meet with him a third time, and she'd said yes? It wasn't as if they'd even kissed, unless her hand and her cheeks counted.

Francesca slid the knife over the stone.

Connie, with heartbreaking earnestness, was analyzing the surprise ending of last night's movie. How—she argued—could the J. J. White, Jr., character be the rightful king of England?

Please open your hymnals to topic number fifty-one. Now keep paging.

"He's the only colored man in the entire movie," Connie said, "and we're supposed to believe he's the king? The King of Merry Old England. King Mulignan the First. To be honest with you, even in a comedy, I can't see it."

"Hmm," Francesca said. Dread wrapped around her more tightly. "Yeah."

"Speaking of Johnny," Connie said, "Michael told me that the rumors are true."

The dread closed its hands around Francesca's throat.

"What rumors?" Francesca said. She could feel herself reddening. She didn't dare look at her aunt.

"You didn't read about it?" Connie said. "He's working on a deal to play Christopher Columbus. *The Discovery of America*. He's producing it, too. Apparently he's talking to studios now. Lots of big stars, CinemaScope, everything. Sergio Leone might direct and either Morricone or Nino Rota is going to do the score, although there's also talk of Mancini or Cy Milner. There was an article in *Screen Tattler* that said they want to film on location in Italy and build exact replicas of all three boats."

"All three, huh?" Francesca said. She drew the knife one last time across the whetstone, wiped it off, and went back to chopping the vegetables.

IN HER HEART, IN THE PIT OF HER STOMACH, FRANCESCA knew where all the troubles in her family were leading: to her. She hadn't talked about it to anyone, but she couldn't stop thinking about it, either. She'd killed her husband. She'd lost her temper, that famous family temper, her father's legacy, and she'd killed her husband with his own decadent sports car. She wanted desperately to go to confession and be absolved from this mortal sin, but it wouldn't work: she didn't exactly regret what she'd done. Billy had betrayed her. He was going to hurt her family, and he'd *already* been hurting her, sleeping with that woman he'd had on the side since law school (and lying about it). So what if that whore had been blamed for killing him? There was justice in that, too. It had actually felt *good* to do what she'd done, even in the face of his broken and bloodied body. Especially that, she hated to admit. The adrenaline it had unleashed, the relief she'd felt: it would be dishonest to forget about that. On the other hand, she was not a monster. She couldn't help but be torn about what she'd done. She'd killed her husband, and she'd be rotting in jail right now if her family hadn't taken care of things for her. Her little boy, Sonny, the light of her life, would be without her. She'd be without him. That was unthinkable. But now, as this mess raged on with Tom Hagen, it seemed more and more clear to her that what she had done was going to catch up to her sooner or later—and probably sooner.

Thank God she was a twin, so at least she could feel like Kathy understood some of this without it needing to be said. She felt sorry for the members of her family who weren't twins. Which was all of them, actually, except for Aunt Connie, whose twin brother died in the womb. Poor Connie had been surrounded by death even before she was born. How must that make Connie feel? Who knew? In fairness, it wasn't just Connie. Nobody talked about it. In fact, Francesca had learned about the dead twin a few months ago, at Christmas, when Connie's godfather, Ozzie Altobello, had come over and stayed too long and drunk too much wine and sat in a corner, weeping, and telling the story to Kathy and Francesca, who'd been aghast. When they'd asked Connie about it the next day, she'd abruptly changed the subject. When they'd asked their uncle about it, Michael confirmed that it was true but changed the subject almost as swiftly. Forty-one years later, it was still too high on the topics list. No one ever talked about Francesca's dead child, either: Carmela, born prematurely, who'd lived for only one day.

Outside, Little Sonny exploded with laughter, and over and over yelled, "Touchdown!"

"You know, if you put a kitchen match between your teeth," Connie said, pointing toward the box of them over the stove, "the onions won't cause all those tears."

Francesca stood back from the counter and turned her head, wiping her cheek with the back of her hand.

"It's the sulfur in the match head that does the trick," Connie said.

Connie had told her this countless times. Francesca went back to the chopping board.

"Suit yourself," Connie said. "No sense suffering, *carissima,* when you don't got to."

Francesca sighed.

"What?" Connie said.

"Can't a person just sigh?"

"If what you did was *just* sigh, sure. That didn't sound like just a sigh to me."

And then there was this. Nobody in her family talked about anything, but they pressed you on everything.

So, fine. She'd try.

"I was just thinking," she said. "I mean, never in a million years . . . " Her voice trailed off.

Connie had all the manicotti tubes assembled now in the dish and was spooning the marinara sauce over the top. She gazed expectantly at Francesca.

Francesca looked up at the ceiling as if what she was trying to say was up there on a cue card. "I wouldn't want anyone, especially Uncle Mike, to think I didn't love working for the foundation," Francesca said, meaning the Vito Corleone Foundation, "because I do."

"You should."

Connie had been openly jealous when she'd heard that Francesca was flying to Los Angeles in a few weeks to meet with some of Johnny Fontane's people about plans for Johnny's own foundation. Not even Johnny: just his people.

"I do," Francesca said. "It's very rewarding, honestly. But by the same token, it's also the kind of thing I always thought of as something that old . . . that *older* women do. Charities and such. This isn't coming out right."

Connie put the pan in the oven and closed the door. She didn't set the timer, which drove Francesca nuts. Everyone was just supposed to remember. It's how mistakes got made, that kind of overconfidence.

"What I'm trying to say," Francesca said, "is that, when I was growing up, if somebody would have told me that when I was in my *twenties* I'd be a widow, with no prospects and only one child, doing—"

"Who tells *anybody* things like that? Snap out of it. You can what-if yourself right into the laughing academy. This is your life, not some movie where, I don't know, some *oobatz* ghost visits you from the future with news of how you turned out. You want my advice? You think too fucking much."

Francesca's eyes widened.

Connie blushed. She threw a dish towel at Francesca and turned her back on her.

Francesca had never heard her aunt—or any woman in their family—use that word. Any number of Italian swear words, sure, and a few of the milder American ones, but not *that one*.

This wasn't about Johnny Fontane, Francesca thought. This was about Billy. Francesca's blood jumped. Her aunt, too, knew what had really happened with Billy.

Connie chugged what was left of her coffee.

Francesca did the same with her wine.

Outside, the perpetually sulking Victor Rizzi had taken a seat and was wheeling through the radio dial. Sonny and Little Mike kept tossing the football. Victor was a runt for a teenager, and the two younger boys weren't all that much smaller. Little Mike Rizzi, who was nine, looked exactly like his Northern Italian father: he had Carlo's blond hair and pale blue eyes, even the same broad chest and bulging forearms. Sonny, likewise, was a near duplicate of Francesca's father—big for his age, a mop of bushy, curly hair, the same dimpled cleft chin. He'd somehow affixed balled-up socks to the inside of his school uniform shirt in a vain attempt to make it look as if he were wearing real shoulder pads. Victor found what he'd been seeking on the radio: the Beatles, yet again. He sang along, and the little boys joined in.

The women's eyes met. It was clear to both of them now that each was waiting the other out.

"You're right," Francesca finally said. "OK? I know you're right. It's just that, when I think about it, about how things turned out for me, it's . . . strange."

"Don't think about it." It was a reproach, not a suggestion.

"Did you know that's actually impossible?" Francesca said. "I learned it in school, in psychology. There's a term for it. The way the mind works, if you tell it not to think of something, it automatically thinks of it." She held up the chef's knife. "Don't think about a knife."

"School," Connie scoffed. "They didn't teach you nothing about Sicilians in school, I can tell you that." She turned and faced the oven. "I'm thinking about whether I made enough of the manicott'," she said. "There. See that? It's easy. I'm not thinking about nothing else now. And anyway, what makes you think you're special, huh? What makes you think you're different from anybody else?"

Francesca tried not to take the bait. Women in her family had probably been saying this to their daughters and nieces for centuries. Francesca had heard it countless times from her own mother. She'd heard Grandma Carmela say it to Connie several times, too. "Maybe because everybody's different from anybody else."

"Wrong," Connie said. "Dead wrong. That's what everybody wants to believe. But it's just a technicality. I suppose *maybe* it's true if you're a man, but for women—"

"Oh, Connie."

"Look, who do *you* think has got the sort of life they expect? Huh? Not even men, really. You think Mike or . . ." Connie stopped herself. She picked up the towel from the floor. "No. Nobody's got that."

"That's not what I see," Francesca countered. "Maybe not *exactly* what they thought, but more or less. From what I can see, *most* people are like that."

"Like who?"

"Like my mother. Just for example."

"Your mother? Your mother is a widow, too. Widowed young—same as you. You think she expected that? Did *you* expect that?"

Francesca made a gesture of concession with the knife. "All right, fine, but other than that, she ended up having the kind of life her parents raised her to have, more or less what she would have expected, really. Same as you, too, in that regard."

"Same as *me*?" Connie laughed. "Oh, sure. Do you think I *expected* to have my first husband go out for cigarettes and never come back? Do you—"

Francesca cocked her head skeptically.

Connie closed her eyes and waved Francesca off.

"I see your point," Francesca said. Carlo's disappearance remained the official story, though Francesca presumed that every adult member of the

Corleone family knew the truth. His murder wouldn't have been something Connie expected, either. "Go ahead. I'm sorry."

"Do you think I expected to grow up and get *divorced*?"

"No, Aunt Connie, I don't, but—"

"Divorced!" She muttered something in Latin. "I can hardly believe it myself, and, oh, that poor, sweet man. Ed! Oh, my God." She paused and swallowed hard, as if she might cry, though she did this every time her second husband came up, and she never cried.

Ed Federici was from the neighborhood, an accountant, the man her father thought she should marry, whom she *did* marry, not long after Grandpa Vito died and right after the annulment of her marriage to Carlo came through. Ed was a kind man who made an honest living and never laid a hand on her in anger, but he'd bored her. Get a couple glasses of wine in Connie back then, and she'd go around talking about how Ed's *cazzo* was the size of her thumb and to make matters worse, anytime she started to feel something down there, he'd go soft. Now, though, Ed Federici (happily remarried to a younger, heavyset woman and living in Providence, Rhode Island) was a saint her wickedness had helped martyr.

Connie regained her composure.

"I'm making it sound like it's all bad, the surprises a person has in store, but obviously it's not. Just look around. Every life has got problems, *carissima*, but we've been blessed. When I was a little girl growing up on Arthur Avenue, you think I *expected* to live in a penthouse in Manhattan? Do you think I expected to shop in the finest stores and eat in the finest restaurants and have drivers who squire me around and the best shoes on my feet, months before they even show up on the runways, like I was a princess in a fairy tale? Who could expect that?"

"No, but I bet you expected to take care of your family, and you do. That's a blessing, too, but it's one you had to have expected. You're, I don't know, what Grandma was. A real matriarch."

"A *matriarch*? Is that how you see me? Like your *grandmother*? I'm only thirty-seven years old!"

She was actually forty-one, Francesca knew. "Thirty-seven's not young."

"Thirty-seven's not old."

"If thirty-seven's not old enough to be a matriarch, how old do you need to be?"

"Older than thirty-seven. I know that much."

Maybe forty-one, then? But Francesca didn't say it. "Well, Michael thinks of you as the matriarch."

"You don't know what Michael thinks. It's a bad idea for you to pretend like you do."

Francesca grabbed the tongs and tossed the salad. "Call it whatever you want to call it, but the way things are now, especially if Theresa doesn't come back, it's you that's holding our family together, kind of the same way your mother did during some of the bad times in those days. Which is good. I mean it as a compliment."

Connie pulled out a stack of plates.

"Michael thinks of me as his *sister*, all right?" Connie said. "Not his mother or some matriarch. And believe me, Theresa will come back. Tom didn't do that nasty business, and we all know it."

Francesca started to say something, then caught a look from her aunt and stopped herself.

She finished the salad, got the drinks, and helped finish setting the table. Eight places. The table could sit three times that many, but they'd taken some of the leaves out. The room looked cavernous.

For a long time, Francesca and Connie careened from room to room with no noise but the clanging of plates and bowls and silverware, the banging of hip-checked drawers, getting everything to the table without ever for a split second getting in each other's way, as if their moves had been choreographed and not merely practiced thousands of times.

"Be honest," Francesca finally said. "You know in your heart of hearts that Tom was with that woman for years. That's *also* nasty business. And he did that. You know he did."

Connie looked around as if someone might be listening and then lowered her voice. "We don't know what he did or didn't do," she said, pointing a wooden spoon at Francesca as if in accusation. "All right? But I'll tell you something right now. If Tom says that the photos are doctored, that it's all a big frame-up, then I believe him."

"No, you don't. I don't believe that for a minute."

"I'm not having this conversation."

"You don't believe him, Connie. I know you don't."

"Tom's a man, all right? We should just leave it at that."

"Being a man? That's an excuse?"

"It's nothing, but you're the one who thinks people have the lives they expect to have."

"I was only saying that some people do."

"Right, and I'm only saying that Tom and Theresa, both of them, are exactly the kind of people you're talking about."

"I thought you said nobody has the kind of life he expects to have."

Connie ignored her. "Mark my words: Tom and Theresa will figure things out. That's what people like them do. Theresa's left Tom before, you know. Off and on, usually not for long. Did you know that? She has. She's a college girl, and, no offense, a lot of times that's what college girls do. They run."

"Wait, you're saying this is *Theresa's* fault? Her husband spoke vows before God and then he broke them. He cheated on her. Not only that, he humiliated her. His betrayal was written up in all the newspapers, on *television*. You know as well as I do that the men in this family, if they betray each other or their business associates, it's, let's just say, bad."

"Stop it. Don't talk about things you don't understand."

"*Those* vows count, I guess, but if they break their vows to God and their wives, that's OK? That's nothing, right? Right. Because we're nothing."

"It's not OK, all right? But I hate to break it to you. It *is* expected."

"I thought you were arguing the other side of that point."

"I'm not arguing nothing. I'm making dinner for my family, is all I'm doing. All right?" She glanced at the oven clock and took out the manicotti. It looked a little overcooked but not bad. "All I can say is this," Connie said. "You're a young girl, *carissima*. So, fine, you think life don't go where you expect, eh? But it goes where it goes, and what's beautiful? What's beautiful is that in the end, everybody winds up where they're supposed to be."

Francesca grabbed the chef's knife from out of the sink and raised it as if she were that madman in the shower scene from that movie. "Don't think about a knife," she said, and in frustration she drove it into the cutting board.

"What's wrong with you?" Connie said. "That's hard on the point."

"That's *hardly* the point," Francesca said.

She strode from the kitchen, shaking her head, to go tell the men and the children that it was time for dinner.

As she came into the courtyard, her little boy saw her and his laugh was euphoric.

"Mommy!" he shouted, patting his heartbreaking attempt at shoulder pads. "I'm Frankie the Hit Man!" It was her brother Frankie's nickname when he played linebacker at Notre Dame. "And I'm gonna tackle you!"

He came running.

"Don't you dare, buster," she said, grinning.

The tackle he applied was a bear hug around her waist.

"I like your shoulder pads," she said, which cracked him up again.

She staggered a step and sat down in a tulip-backed metal chair. Dread rolled over her in what seemed like a literal wave. If Francesca was *ever* away from this boy, from that laugh, if for any reason she was separated from him, she couldn't bear it.

But no.

She couldn't think about that.

"Go wash your hands," she said. "That goes for you two, too," she said to Little Mike and Victor. "Go."

She stood, went to the wall phone just inside the door, and pressed the intercom button.

"Dinner," she said.

"Be right down," said Michael Corleone. "Hey, Francie? What are we having?"

She watched Sonny run down the hall, away from her, following his cousins.

"Manicott'," Francesca said. She tried to think about whether they'd made enough.

WHEN KATHY GOT HOME THAT NIGHT — LATE, WHICH HAD become the norm—Francesca was still awake, on the couch in the living room of their suite. The TV stations had signed off the air, and she was reading *Pylon,* by William Faulkner.

"What are you doing up?" Kathy said.

By way of an answer, Francesca held up the book.

"Oh," Kathy said. "Well. G'night." She'd been drinking, and she smelled like an ashtray.

"You have a minute? A few minutes?" She hadn't stayed up to read. She didn't know why she'd held up the book to answer that question.

"What is it? Because if it's more bad news, I'm not sure if I can—"

"No," Francesca said. "It's not. Not really. There's just some things I'm worried about. Ongoing situations, you know?"

Kathy nodded. "Do I."

She wasn't weaving, wasn't drunk. She came over and kissed Francesca on the forehead. Francesca could smell the sex on her.

"We'll talk tomorrow, OK?" Kathy said. "I still need to read the last hundred pages of a novel I'm teaching at ten in the morning."

So when exactly would they talk? But Francesca let that go, too.

"What novel?" Francesca said. Topic number fifty-one plus.

"It's actually a friend's. I'm not teaching it, that's not what I meant, I'm just reading it, giving him my two cents' worth. I'm not thinking straight. It's been a long day." She turned and walked away. "It's been a long everything."

Why she was reading some man's stupid unpublished book when she should be writing her own—that was a top-fifty topic.

"So guess what?" Francesca said as Kathy was turning the corner toward her room.

"Really, Francie. I'm on fumes. Tomorrow, I'll guess."

"Aunt Connie said . . . a certain word."

"She did what?"

Francesca mouthed *fuck*.

"Who made her do that?"

"Me."

"Is that what you wanted to talk about?"

"Not really."

"OK, I'll bite," Kathy said. "What in the hell did you do to make Connie say *that*?"

"I'll tell you tomorrow," Francesca said.

"Touché," Kathy said, and then bowed. "And good night."

AN HOUR LATER, FRANCESCA CHECKED ON SONNY AGAIN. He was still sound asleep, clutching the GI Joe doll her brother sent him for his birthday. Behind the closed door to Kathy's bedroom, the light was still on. Francesca called to her that she'd be right back.

"Right back?" Kathy said, her voice groggy. "Where you going?"

"For a walk," Francesca said. "I can't sleep."

"Be careful," Kathy said. "Go walk in the courtyard, maybe."

This from a woman who's going to bed with God knows who, God knows where, and toward God knows what end. "OK," Francesca said. "See you."

Going up, it was impossible to bypass security, but going down, there were several ways. Francesca took the elevator a few floors down and then got out, walked to the other end of the hall, and took the back stairs. They didn't go all the way to the top, and the security guards didn't monitor them. She went out through the parking garage, down a narrow alley to the next street over, then headed west toward York Avenue. It would have been the path Tom Hagen took, too. It must have been a perfect setup, until whatever went wrong went wrong.

One thing that Francesca had learned during the time she'd lived in Washington was that once the federal government got involved for any reason in an essentially local criminal investigation, the investigation could go haywire. One day it's about apples, and the next it's about oranges—probably a whole grove's worth. In this particular case, Francesca was certain, the reason Danny Shea wouldn't let things drop was that he was avenging the death of his own staffer, Billy Van Arsdale, who had, in fact, been feeding him information about Francesca's family—a file Francesca had found, stolen, and destroyed. Billy had even told her himself that he was afraid his own political ambitions could never survive being related by marriage to the so-called Mafia.

At some point, he'd apparently decided to address the situation. At another point, distraught and betrayed, in the heat of emotion, Francesca had retaliated.

The simple fact was that Francesca had been backed into a corner and she'd done what strong people backed into corners do. She'd bulled her way out. She'd acted. She'd survived. And she would continue to survive and to live with it. She was a member of the Corleone family. That was her blood. Then, when she had called upon Tom and Michael to protect her, she had become something else. In some small way she was one of them now, and for the rest of her life she'd be beholden to them, and that was that.

She'd come to Judy Buchanan's apartment.

It was on the other side of the street from where she'd pictured it. At this hour, no one seemed to be around, other than an occupied squad car at the curb. The sidewalk was strewn with flowers and trash.

From the outside, the place looked like nothing—a turn-of-the-century brick three-story like thousands of others in the city. She tried to transform this in her mind's eye into the images she'd seen on TV and really couldn't do it.

She tried to conjure up the murder scene upstairs, and that, for her, was a little easier.

She crossed the street.

As she was looking at some of the discarded placards, a gray-haired Chinese man in a tuxedo seemed to materialize from thin air with a tin bucket half full of wilting yellow roses.

"How much?" she asked.

He told her. It was a reasonable price for dead flowers.

The cop rolled down his window. "What'd I tell you, huh, Hop Sing?"

The Chinese man muttered something she couldn't understand, then handed her the rest of the flowers. "No charge," he said in obvious disgust. "You enjoy." He dumped the water from his bucket and started walking downtown.

She waggled the flowers in her hand. Dozens of petals fell.

"Your lucky night, I guess," the cop said, chuckling. "You come here often?"

She shook her head.

He was about her age but had gone soft. He looked like the sort of man who still wore his letterman's sweater sometimes, even though it didn't button over his gut. Who did it hurt, that man selling flowers? He was a man out to make an honest living, and the cop was flexing his cop muscles just because he could.

"Sad situation," the cop said. "Inside this place, I mean. Not the flowers. The flowers were just something that worked out for you. Fell in your lap, as it were."

"You want these?" she said, extended them toward him.

"What would I do with flowers?" the cop said. "They're for you people."

"What do you mean, *you people*?"

"The I don't know what you'd call it. The mourners."

"Give 'em to somebody. Your wife, your girlfriend, your mother, anybody."

"My ma's in Florida," he said. "The other two things I'm still looking for. You should keep 'em."

"Fine," she said. She walked to the corner and put the roses in a trash can. "I was just out for a walk," Francesca said to the cop on her way back. "I'm not a *mourner*. I don't want anything to do with that dead whore."

"Yes, ma'am," the cop said. "I do understand. Are you going to be all right?"

"Am I *going* to be?" she said. "Who can predict the future? Not me, I'll tell you that. I'm trying not to think too much."

"I know some people you should meet," he said. "Some of 'em barely think at all."

She gave him what she hoped was a withering stare and started home, whistling past the garbage trucks, which had materialized as suddenly as the Chinaman with the yellow roses, and were out in force now, down every street. She was whistling just to whistle. Her mind was elsewhere. She'd gone through the tune who knew how many times before it clicked that she was whistling a real song, one she'd obviously heard before but couldn't place. Even if someone had identified the tune for her ("Ridin' High," by Cole Porter), it might not have clicked how or where she'd heard it before. Wherever it had come from, the song's melody had wormed its way into Francesca's brain and taken root there, unnoticed. It was a standard; it could have come from anyplace, the radio or one of Kathy's records, and not necessarily the second of the three songs Johnny Fontane had performed in a striped tux at President Shea's inaugural ball.

CHAPTER 19

The weekend before the California presidential primary, Memorial Day weekend, Tom and Theresa Hagen flew separately to the West Coast and met at the Los Angeles airport. The limousine had actually met Tom at the airstrip on Senator Pat Geary's ranch, just outside Las Vegas, and, after a quick meeting with the senator, driven him the rest of the way. Theresa left their daughters with her sister-in-law and went Pan Am.

She came out of the terminal and did not, at first, see his limo among the many. She wore what Tom was fairly sure was a new green dress, high-necked and snug in the right places but classy. Her hair was cut short—much shorter than Tom liked or even than he'd thought fashionable—and was darker, too.

The driver got out and held up the sign with her maiden name on it, just to be perfectly safe about not attracting attention.

Theresa looked like she'd lost some weight. She looked pale. She'd come from Florida and she looked pale.

The driver opened the door for her. "You look great," Tom said.

"You like it?" Theresa said, touching the back of her hairdo.

"I do," he said.

"Liar," she said. "Don't give me that look. I always know. Always have, always will."

He couldn't say anything to that. This was how it was going to have to be for a while. For a while, he'd just have to brace himself and take it like a man.

The car pulled away. Tom finally reached over to embrace her, and she pulled back a little. Then she sighed, exasperated, and they embraced.

Exasperated at *herself,* Tom realized. For being here, he supposed. For caving in and making peace for the good of the children, sure. But also because—the event that triggered it—she wanted to see Jack Woltz's art collection.

Tom had begged her and begged her to come back to New York or at least see him, yet when she'd finally relented and invited him to Florida for Memorial Day weekend, it turned out that was a bad time. He had to go away that weekend on business. She'd asked him what kind of business he had on a holiday weekend, and instead of the usual long silence he gave her when yet again she asked him to talk about his business, he'd answered her. He was going to meet with Jack Woltz, he said. He wouldn't have needed to name that name, and he was honestly unaware at the time that he had any motive more ulterior than to be more honest with her from now on, at least to the degree circumstances allowed. But he was also aware, looking back, that he'd baited the hook and cast the line and Theresa had bitten. *Jack Woltz the movie producer?* she'd said, and he'd said, *Is there another Jack Woltz?* and she said that she was asking because she knew someone who knew his curator. *Curator for what?* Tom said. *For his art,* she said. *He's got one on retainer. He's supposedly got pieces in his country house that haven't been seen in public in fifty years or more.* She asked Tom if he could get her in to see it, the house. Tom said he didn't know if that was something he could swing. He said he'd already set it up to meet Woltz at his office on the studio lot. He didn't tell her that Woltz had also said that he and his new wife were having several friends out to his house in Palm Springs for the weekend and had invited Tom to come and bring the family, too, if he wanted, which at the time Hagen had taken as a wisecrack. He also didn't relish the thought of spending the night—much less two or three nights—under the same roof as degenerates like Jack Woltz and the dope-fiend surfers he imagined Woltz's new wife's friends to be. But Theresa had him over a barrel. *You don't know if you can swing it?* she'd scoffed. She said that she knew him. She didn't have her head in the sand, she'd said. *You can set up anything you want to set up. Don't pretend you can't.* He'd told her she was overestimating him, and she said there was little chance of that.

And now here they were. Heading to goddamned Jack Woltz's house for the *weekend.*

There are times a man wants to cut off his own prick.

Not really.

Tom gave his wife a kiss.

"Take it slow," she said to Tom.

The driver, just merging onto the freeway, slowed down.

"Not you," Theresa said to him. Tom toggled the partition closed.

THEY STOPPED FOR A QUICK ROMANTIC DINNER ON THE way—a French bistro Tom had heard about from Fontane, who, to give the devil his due, knew how to impress a lady. Despite the precautions, the FBI caught up to them there. They were following him most of the time now. When Theresa went to the ladies' room, he sent a waiter out to their car to see if the agents wanted anything to eat, on him.

He and Theresa arrived in Palm Springs at twilight.

In the almost twenty years between Tom Hagen's visits to Jack Woltz's estate in Palm Springs, it had been transformed. When Tom had been there to discuss casting Fontane in that war picture, the place had looked like a movie-set replica of a British country manor—so studied in its detail that every bloom in the garden, every newly acquired painting by an old master, every graceful curve of the bridle paths, exaggerated the fakery. Now it had become a fortified monstrosity. Woltz had bought the houses on either side of him and had them bulldozed. The security guards had been replaced by black-clad machine-gun-bearing veterans of the Israeli army. Around the perimeter of the property now was an iron-bar fence about twenty feet high and spiked at the top, fabricated to Woltz's specifications by an ironworks whose principal clients were prisons. Closed-circuit televisions were everywhere.

"Those bars," Theresa Hagen said. "Are they to keep people out or in?"

Though Woltz's reputation as a cocksman was public knowledge, his taste for young girls was not. Theresa knew about it only through Tom.

"Maybe this wasn't such a good idea," Tom said.

Theresa bowed her head slightly and looked up at him with her eyebrows arched in an exaggerated way, as a teacher might regard a student who couldn't possibly be as stupid as the answer he'd just blurted out.

The FBI agents had pulled their car to the side of the road, about two hundred yards away. Guards waved the Hagens' limo through the gate. It glided shut behind them.

"Fine," Tom said. "But don't tell me this doesn't bother you."

Theresa shrugged him off, so worn down by other bothersome things, apparently, that a hulking jail-door fence and machine-gun-bearing commandos were merely today's fresh hell.

As the limo came around a bend in the driveway, Tom stared out the window in stunned silence. He'd heard about the changes from Johnny, but seeing them for himself was still a shock. Gone were the estate's tennis courts and topiary. Gone were the long rows of stables with their Victorian façades and their gleaming modern interiors. The golf-green pastures where Thoroughbreds once frolicked and the movie mogul chomped his cigars and bragged about them to guests had been replaced by long, featureless lawns and a bunkerlike structure with a marquee salvaged from an old movie palace incongruously appended to the front. On it were the names of the motion pictures that Woltz's studio had in current release.

The mansion itself had been remodeled so drastically by Woltz, in collaboration with his new wife, that if Tom hadn't known better, he'd have presumed the old one had been torn down altogether. They'd stripped away the curlicues and cupolas, sheathed the gray stonework in something beige and smooth, supplanted the contrived Old World grandeur with long glass walls, harsh right angles, and frank, cement-loving modernity.

Next to the mansion, and blocking it slightly from view, the spring-fed swimming pool remained. The statues surrounding it—and in it, too, on pedestals and in fountains—had multiplied: there were at least two hundred of them now. Most were earnest neoclassical life-size metal casts of political leaders in swallowtail frocks or military heroes on horseback. But he also had a few incongruous marble nudes—the usual chubby women swooning against one another in twos and threes—and several gaunt contemporary pieces as well. The statues were crammed close together, with no discernible pattern.

Theresa was agog, speculating about different pieces, throwing out names Hagen didn't recognize: Thorvaldsen, Carpeaux, Crocetti, Lehmbruck, Count Troubetsky, Lord Leighton. Tom loved that about her: how much she knew and how jazzed she got about it. Hagen wasn't sure he could have named a sculptor other than Michelangelo. But he appreciated culture, and he loved being married to a woman who knew things like that. Even more, he loved being married to a woman who (unlike most of the women he'd known growing up) had daily creative passions that extended well beyond the laundry and the Sunday gravy. Theresa knew what great art fetched at auction, yet somehow her first reaction to any piece wasn't what it cost or how it would appreciate but rather how beautiful it was, what the artist had accomplished, how it made Theresa feel. Which Tom loved.

"Were they always arranged like that?" she asked him.

"No," he said. "There were fewer pieces. The . . . I don't know. The flow was better."

"Who would do that?" Theresa said. "How could a person take so much beauty and make it look like a garage sale? Why would a person do that?"

"His new wife doesn't like sculpture," Tom said. "She's in a religious group that thinks a sculptured likeness of a human being is a graven idol or robs a person's soul." He shrugged. "It's California. Kooky ideas are written on the wind. All I know is, right after she moved in, she had every statue in the mansion carted out here. Her religion is one of those free-spirit ones, but somehow it also has a rule against men and women using the same swimming pools, so since Woltz takes a half-mile swim every morning, the pool's just a place she doesn't go. Actually, I heard he built another one for her someplace."

Theresa seemed as if she had other questions about the wife's peculiarities, but when they came around the final bend in the road, she burst out laughing.

"Get it out of your system now," Tom said.

"I'm sorry," she said. "*Madonn'*. Oh, my God, I need my camera."

In the middle of the oval drive in front of the mansion, a crew of workers swarmed around a cast of Rodin's *The Thinker*. They were in the process of moving it. On the far side of the house, on a flatbed truck parked in a stone lot, next to what must have been cars belonging to the other guests (convertibles, foreign jobs) was the newest addition to the collection—a commissioned bronze cast of Jack Woltz himself on the occasion of his fiftieth year in show business, conspicuously larger than life, arms outstretched, the thumb and index finger of each hand making a right angle: a movie frame.

"It's a miracle he didn't have it done in a Roman toga," Tom said.

"Or nude," Theresa said, regaining her composure. "The way Napoleon did."

"There are nude statues of Napoleon?"

"There's Canova's *Marte Pacificatore*. The original's in London somewhere, but I saw a bronze cast of it in Milan last year."

"You were in Milan last year?"

"We were all in Milan last year," she said. "You don't remember? The whole family, except you. You had whatever it was that came up at the last minute."

"I remember. I thought you went to the Riviera. France."

"We did go to the Riviera," she said. "We flew into Milan, and took a train. I showed you the pictures."

"Thaaaaat's right," he said. "Now I remember."

"You see? You're such a good liar with everyone else and such a bad one with me."

She was wrong. He was a horrendous liar, period. He operated in a world in which everything he said was not less than factual, where deception lurked only in what was not said. *Michael wants to see you* isn't a lie when, for example, it's shorthand for *Michael wants to see you killed.* Or *Michael wants to see you get in this fucking car and never come back, you fucking cocksucker, you goddamned traitor.* Typically, the only person Tom Hagen lied to was Theresa. In a perverse way, it was a compliment. Confessing this, though, seemed like an unpromising way back into her heart. "I'm a bad liar with you," Tom said, "because I don't feel about everyone else the way I feel about you."

"That," she said, "isn't so much a lie as a sentence full of loopholes." The limo driver opened the door now. Members of the household staff had rushed to get the suitcases. One of the former Israeli commandos stood ready to escort the Hagens to the front door.

Theresa patted him on the knee. "C'mon," she said. "Let's go have some fun."

THE MEN WITH THE MACHINE GUNS ON EITHER SIDE OF the front door did not acknowledge the arrival or even the presence of the Hagens. They had apparently been given the order to stand as still and be as imperturbable as the guards at Buckingham Palace.

Tom Hagen had never been this close to real machine guns, and it seemed to be bothering him more than it did Theresa. She went up the last few stairs ahead of him and rang the bell with no visible anxiety.

A uniformed butler opened the door and a blast of air-conditioning—another new addition—nearly knocked them over. The butler was British—

or sounded convincing enough—and young for the job, maybe thirty-five, with the long, sloping nose typical of both royals and their senior staff. His haircut was a perfect re-creation of President Shea's.

From somewhere in the house came the sound of distant laughter and the kind of guitar-slinger rock-and-roll music often associated with surfers and dopers, although Tom was familiar with it only because Connie's oldest, Vic, played it all the time, too.

The butler showed them through the dark and echo-filled main hallway. They seemed to be going away from the music. The furnishings, incongruously, seemed about the same as they'd been before the remodeling: thick rugs, hand-carved tables and chairs with mythical creatures carved into the legs and backs, lushly upholstered chairs and settees that seemed to have been designed primarily as good places for a corseted Victorian lady to faint. The mansion's thick velvet curtains were drawn, and it was hard to get a great look at the artwork, but that didn't seem so different, either. Every wall in every room still had at least one piece on it that had no doubt cost a bundle. Theresa was keeping her excitement to herself, though it was obvious to Tom that she wanted to stop in front of every painting and study it.

Contemporary art was her specialty—it was also what the Hagens could afford—but Theresa got a thrill from any good private collection. In a museum, she'd explained to him years earlier, you feel like the art belongs to the world, but in a private collection, you're aware of ownership. It's what makes good private collections so exciting. Ninety percent of the thrill is the work itself, but that last ten percent made Theresa's world go around. Some *person* owns this, she'd think, and the more she'd think about it—while face to face with genius and beauty—the tougher time she'd have accepting that that person wasn't her.

Woltz was waiting for them in the same glass-paneled sun porch where he'd received Hagen the first time. Johnny Fontane and Francesca Corleone sat together on the buttercream leather loveseat next to him. Francesca was brandishing a martini, Johnny his usual whiskey and water. They looked dressed for a board meeting, and they were soaked in sweat. The room was an oven. Seeing the Hagens, they all rose.

Seeing Johnny and Francesca together, Theresa did a double take. Francesca looked just a little bit afraid. Tom took it all in stride and squeezed Theresa's arm. He'd explain later. She seemed to understand.

"Congressman Hagen!" said Woltz.

"Just Tom," he said. When people greeted him that way, it always sounded to Tom like a joke at his expense.

"Sorry to hear about your legal problems," Woltz said. "I know, first-hand, there's no bigger nightmare than being falsely accused."

Now it was Theresa's turn to squeeze Tom's arm, though it was more of a vicious pinch.

"Thank you," Tom said.

The old man wasn't sweating at all. Like most men who had once been tall and strong, the ravages of age seemed to have exasperated him. Woltz was completely bald now. His upper lip sagged on one side from a mild stroke he'd suffered the year before. He still dressed the same way: Italian loafers as expensive as a good used car, freshly pressed tan linen slacks, blue silk shirt, open at the throat, a sprout of thick white chest hair asserting it-self like an unafraid fur-bearing creature.

"You haven't changed a bit," Woltz said. "How long has it been?"

"Almost twenty years," Tom said.

"Brings back memories," Woltz said. Bitterness dripped from his voice. "You know everybody, right? Some familiar faces, obviously. Obviously." He pointed at Francesca but looked at Tom. "You know about the Nino Valenti Fund, right? The Nino Valenti Fund. I'm just hearing about it. Promising idea. Old actors, singers, sick ones, caring for them. Your trip go OK? Been to your room yet? Where are my manners! This must be Mrs. Congressman Hagen."

"It must be," Theresa said.

"You'll have to forgive him," Johnny said. "Back in the nickelodeon days, right after Jack earned his first million, his first wife made him take speech and etiquette lessons, to cover up the fact of where he came from, only it looks like over the years they've worn off."

Woltz ignored him. "So I hear you're quite the art maven, Mrs. Hagen."

Theresa was studying the painting on the wall behind Woltz, a massive oil painting of nude young girls bathing in a lake and a cloven-hoofed satyr laughing on the muddy banks.

"She helped found the Museum of Modern Art in Las Vegas," Tom said. "She's on the board there and at a few other museums, too. She's really more of an expert than a maven."

"I can answer for myself," she said, but she betrayed herself by blushing. And by not being able to take her eyes off that disturbing painting. She was sweating like mad.

He always found that sexy. It's not the heat, Tom thought. It's the cupidity.

She asked him if that painting was by who she thought it was by. Her tongue might as well have been hanging out.

It was.

"That painting, I thought . . ." Theresa said. "I could be wrong," which she said only when she was certain she was right, "but hasn't that painting been missing since the Nazis seized it during the war?"

"I can't say," Woltz said. "I don't know. You'd have to ask my curator about that." He smiled, unashamed. "I just know what I like," Woltz said. "You want a tour? I'll get you a tour. Back when I had horses," he said, shooting Tom a quick, malevolent glance, "I could give that tour myself, the one of the stables, I mean. But with the art, I need a hand. You want to go on the tour, Tom? John and Jessica already had theirs."

"Francesca," Francesca said.

"I'd love to," Tom said, looping an arm around his wife.

Woltz called for the butler.

All those years ago, when Luca Brasi paid off someone in the household staff to slip something into Woltz's nightly brandy, Tom Hagen had been on the plane back to New York. Luca—Vito Corleone's Al Neri—had then chopped off the head of Woltz's prize racehorse and shoved it between the old man's satin sheets. Tom hadn't seen any of this, of course; he had only his imagination to contend with. That poor horse—Khartoum; he could still remember the name. In truth, he rarely thought of it. But when he did, it disturbed him. It provoked genuine regret.

FRANCESCA AND JOHNNY STOOD JUST OUTSIDE THE SUN-room, dabbing at themselves with white hand towels. "My mother's parents are like that," she said. "Hot when everyone's cold, cold when everyone's hot. I guess a lot of old people are like that."

She was twenty-seven, half his age. She was older than Lisa, his daughter. So there was that.

"I think we did some good in there, though." Johnny didn't want to think about how old he was. He focused instead on her wet hair and her damp summer dress. He had a thing for women when they were wet. Right out of the shower, out of the ocean, the pool. Caught in a rainstorm. Sweating. All of it did something to him. Not that he was crazy enough to get involved with her. But there was no denying she was a lovely creature, toweling off, running her fingers through her long black hair in a happily doomed effort to tame it. "He's a tightwad, but with the involvement of the Corleone Foundation behind the scenes in setting this all up—it's the proverbial offer he can't refuse."

Francesca frowned. "What's that supposed to mean?"

"Nothing, sweetheart," he said. "It's just a saying."

"A saying," she repeated.

"Just a saying." He was about to add *no need to make a federal case of it*, but he caught himself. Danny Shea was in California doing some last-minute campaigning and was in fact staying only a few miles from here, at the house of an Old Hollywood crooner turned TV game-show producer, at the other end of the golf course from Johnny's compound.

"So," Francesca said. "Do you want to go see where that music's coming from?"

"Music? I don't hear any music."

Francesca pointed in the general direction of its source.

It was a current, infamous hit, featuring a flailing drummer, an electric bass player who couldn't handle the song's three-chord progression, a guitarist who kept turning his amplifier on and off, and a drunken man with a sore throat, screaming supposedly dirty lyrics in the general direction of a microphone suspended far above his head. Other than "Louie Louie," Johnny couldn't make out a word.

"I hear noise," Johnny said, "but nothing I'd call music."

"Oh, come on," she said, taking him by the sleeve and starting down the hall. "Don't you ever have fun?"

"Fun?" Johnny said, allowing himself to be pulled along. "Why do you think they call me Johnny *Fun*-tane?"

"You mean like the way they call Mr. Sinatra Frank *Sin*-atra?"

"Nobody calls him that that I ever heard," he said.

"I'm just . . . teasing you."

For a bizarre moment he'd thought she was going to say *busting your balls*. She smiled. "I never heard anyone call you *Fun*-tane, either."

They walked down a dark hallway toward a wooden door big enough to drive a Buick through. It opened onto an indoor pool, enveloped in a noxious cloud of cigarette and reefer smoke and chlorine. There were thirty or so guests, mostly people who worked with the new Mrs. Woltz—Vickie Adair. Men in tennis clothes and women in terry-cloth robes, most of them closer to Francesca's age than Johnny's, sat on metal chaise lounges. The men all had beards and shaggy hair. Between the noise and the smoke, it took a moment for it to sink in that the people in the pool were all women and that they were all naked, too. Along the back wall was a bar and what looked like an exit, and Johnny steered Francesca toward both. No one seemed to recognize Johnny, but presumably they were just trying to play it cool.

He got them drinks, and while they were waiting, Vickie Adair got out of the pool, stark naked, and padded over to them. Someone tossed her a towel, but she didn't use it to cover up. She was a washed-up starlet, a bottle blonde who'd crammed eighty-some years of living into the forty-some years she'd lived, and it showed. If she hadn't been wet and naked, Johnny wouldn't have given her a second look. She'd shaved her bush, the sick motives for which Johnny didn't want to think about. He maintained eye contact, with her and with Francesca, as best he could. Francesca seemed nonplussed. They shouted their introductions. Vickie said that she and Johnny went way back and asked him if he remembered when. Johnny hated when people pulled this shit. He met a thousand times more people than the average Joe. How the fuck was he supposed to remember? He wanted to get out of here. Francesca remained poised and serene. Vickie said that she'd been in *Bang-Up Job* with him. He didn't recall that, either, which didn't mean anything. He barely remembered the picture. He leaned toward her ear, so Francesca wouldn't hear. "Now I remember," he said. "Back then you were doing something different with your hair."

He darted a glance at her absent bush. She gave him a mocking, *very funny* smile and then said something in Francesca's ear. Vickie told them to make themselves at home, turned her saggy, depleted ass toward them, and padded back to the pool.

Johnny and Francesca took their drinks and went outside. It was dark now. The temperature must have dropped twenty degrees. There were about the same number of people out here as inside, milling around on the lawn, but this was by and large where the older crowd had settled. A familiar ripple of recognition went through them at his presence there. Johnny, on instinct, maneuvered himself away from them. He and Francesca wandered out on the lawn together, far enough to talk but not so far that they were alone, exactly. There was what looked like a tombstone and a stone bench not far away, and they walked toward it.

"I'm sorry about that scene back there," Johnny said.

"Don't be. It was my idea. Did you think I'd be shocked?"

"No," Johnny lied. He touched his throat. "Bad for the voice—all that smoke, that chlorine in the air. To be honest with you, I couldn't hear myself think. If you want to go back, though—"

"This is nice," she said. "Out here. I've seen naked women before. I imagine you have, too."

"Those back there were my first," Johnny said. "Rough introduction."

"I've smoked a reefer or two in my time, too." She laughed at his surprise. "C'mon, John. The foundation I work for has a lot to do with artists and entertainers. My sister's a college professor, a real Bohemian, almost. I've been to college, I live in New York." She ticked these apparent virtues off on her fingers. "Just how sheltered do you think I am?"

Johnny shook his head. "Sorry. I didn't mean to offend you by assuming you weren't a drug addict," he joked. "So what'd she tell you?"

"Vickie? That the rumors about . . . uh, you." She blushed. "That the rumors about you aren't true."

"What rumors?" he said, but he knew.

Francesca shook her head. "What about you?" she asked. "What'd you tell *her*?"

"Vickie?" he said. "I thanked her for her hospitality."

The black marble tombstone featured a bas-relief depiction of a horse.

"Khartoum," Francesca said, reading the name off the stone. "Is this for real?"

"I think so. Yes. The horse was real, at any rate. It was a racehorse."

"Huh," Francesca said, staring at the grave for a long time. "He must have really loved that horse."

"Must have," Johnny said.

"So," Francesca said. "Mr. and Mrs. Woltz, huh?" she said. "Explain that."

"Who knows? There's a rumor that he had some kind of scandal that was going to break, something that getting married helped make go away." Which was that he liked to have sex with twelve-year-old girls and had been doing so for years. "Why she married him, I can't imagine."

Francesca rubbed her fingers together.

"I don't think so," Johnny said. "I heard she comes from a little money of her own. Her granddad supposedly invented the agitator for the washing machine. Though I guess you can never have too much."

"Maybe she's got daddy issues," Francesca said, staring straight into Johnny's eyes. Johnny found her expression unreadable.

"Is love out of the question?" Johnny said.

"Love," Francesca said, without any particular inflection. "I never thought of that."

Their faces drew almost imperceptibly closer.

"*There* you are," said Theresa Hagen, startling them halfway off the bench. She was done with her tour. "Sorry," she said.

"Somebody ought to put a bell on you," Johnny said. Though what he felt was relief. He wondered if he could hire this broad to swoop in on an as-needed basis and save him from himself. Long hours, though.

"How was the tour?" Francesca said, smoothing her dress.

"Hard to put into words," Theresa said. "They're looking for you, Mr. Fontane," she said, looking back and forth from Johnny to Francesca, clearly trying to figure out what she'd broken up.

"Call me Johnny."

"Tom and Mr. Woltz and apparently some other people you're meeting with . . . Johnny." She looked at Francesca and rolled her eyes. "You know. Business."

Johnny gave Francesca a kiss on the hand and did the same for Theresa Hagen.

Who, despite the way she was looking at him, hadn't exactly broken up anything that was wrong or unseemly—anything but a conversation really.

He hurried around to the front of the mansion, so that he wouldn't have to pass through that nightmare again.

You had to hand it to Vickie Adair, Johnny thought. That was a genius taunt. The rumor that he had a large penis was indeed true, but what the hell was he going to do about setting the record straight? Nothing. Johnny was a gentleman. He wasn't about to tell Francesca Van Arsdale anything about his cock. And he certainly wasn't going to show her. He knew that it was juvenile that he *wanted* to show her now, strictly in the interest of science, and he knew he'd never do it. He knew it shouldn't bother him in the slightest that Francesca thought maybe he might have a small dick. In every sense, Johnny Fontane had nothing to prove.

He was not going to get involved with this woman. Period.

All that was going on was that he was getting her help on setting up this charity. It seemed like a good way to help repair his frayed connections with the Corleones, to work together on charitable causes and not just when they need favors from each other. This one made sense: Vito Corleone had been fond of Johnny's friend Nino, who'd been a big success as a singer and an actor until the booze and the pills caught up with him. He'd have approved of a fund that honored the man's memory and helped out people in the industry who, like Nino, had fallen on hard times and could use some help getting back on their feet. Francie was a sweet kid, but he wasn't interested in her like that, and no doubt, without a couple martinis in her, neither was she. What was he, nuts? Michael Corleone's niece? Sonny Corleone's *daughter*? Whose family curse had already killed off her first husband? Never in a million years.

PRODUCTION ON *THE DISCOVERY OF AMERICA* WAS SET TO begin the following week, on location in and around Genoa, and Woltz's attorney—the legendary Ben Tamarkin, whom Tom had never met but to whom he had often been compared—joined the men in Woltz's little theater to talk about a variety of related details. Tamarkin, a foppish silver-haired man with hair-tonic-green eyes and a red cravat, sat in silence throughout, taking it all in. There are few things on earth that are ultimately more dangerous than a good lawyer who can really listen.

Hagen disliked both Woltz and Fontane. They disliked each other as well. Tom had expected to be amused, watching these overindulged, self-important boy-men pretend to be magnanimous, watching their long-standing and childish grievances fall away as they spoke with genuine excitement over the movie itself, its financial prospects, and some of the consequent doors those profits might open. But, to Tom's surprise, it was actually sad. The poor bastards really seemed to have no idea what was about to befall them.

Tom had been a little wary that he was pushing it too hard, that they'd see what was coming. Every day, the trades seemed to announce yet another big star who'd signed on for a supporting role or cameo. A cover story about the construction of the life-size replicas of the *Niña*, the *Pinta*, and the *Santa Maria* was coming out next month in *Life* magazine. Hagen, for his part, had used some connections—including the public relations firm Eddie Paradise controlled—to plant stories in other magazines and big newspapers, overhyping the movie to the extent possible. Many of those same reporters were already on the hook to write stories about how troubled the production was. The hilarious thing about entertainment writers was that they didn't even need to be bribed in the conventional way. They'd write what you told them to for the low, low price of junkets and swag, garnished with a fresh sprig of access to the stars.

The lavish production didn't stop with the three ships (four, really, since there was a spare *Santa Maria* in case the first one sank, which it was destined to do). They'd reconstructed fifteenth-century Madrid in the countryside outside Genoa, transforming a monastery there into the palace of Queen Isabella (Deanna Dunn) and King Ferdinand (Sir Oliver Smith-Christmas). The sets alone cost more than most entire movies, though, of course, sometimes that was how it went with movies like this. You had to spend money to make it. The amount of spending on this movie seemed justifiable to Woltz and Fontane for several reasons, which Hagen recapped now. First and foremost was that the movie theaters the Corleones owned or could influence seemed to ensure that the distribution costs would be a fraction of the usual, and the number of screens on which it would play was guaranteed to be especially high. Another factor was that the dollar was strong relative to the hopelessly devalued lira. Also, Hagen had helped secure highly advantageous deals with the unions here and in Italy. And Michael had gotten "a friend of ours in Italy" (they wouldn't have known who Cesare Indelicato was, anyway) to agree to have his men watch over the production, so that no one would dare steal from them or overcharge them for so much as a nail.

"And there's a final piece of good news for you, gentlemen," Hagen said. "The Italian government has agreed to help underwrite the production with an economic-development grant of one million dollars."

"Not bad," Tamarkin said, the first time he had reacted to anything.

"See, Jack?" Johnny said. "What'd I tell you about my friends here, huh? How better to make money in business than to be in business with people who never lose money in business?"

Woltz seemed pleased as well, but there was a sourness to his smile that revealed a man who knew what he was hearing was too good to be true and just couldn't figure out why. Woltz had made a mint off the last picture he made with Johnny and with the Corleones' backing. There was little reason to imagine that this wouldn't turn out even better. His bean counters—who were under Tamarkin's supervision—liked the idea largely because of all the free publicity, huge discounts, and distribution advantages.

According to Tom's research, Woltz was leveraged to the hilt. He hadn't gotten into TV when some of the other studios had, and he was getting by now by quietly selling off parcels of land, including some of the outer reaches of the studio lot (a trend the Corleones hoped to accelerate soon). He'd married Vickie Adair not just to quell the rumors of his pedophilia but for her money—which she'd promptly squandered on the renovations, believing that Woltz was so rich that her money wasn't needed. Woltz had been too proud to tell her the truth. He'd also kept thinking his studio was just one blockbuster away from turning the tide.

As for Johnny, his old accountant had turned up recently in the Bahamas—where, coincidentally, some of the movie's nautical scenes were to be filmed as well as a few of the beach scenes with the Indians. The accountant was found on the beach as well, shot in the back of the head. Most of Johnny's money had been recovered, and it was all the capital that his new accountant—handpicked by Tom Hagen—had allowed Johnny's company to invest in this movie. Johnny was going to lose every penny, but he'd lost it once before, so, in essence, it was like playing with the house's money. Johnny's career was going to take one on the chin here, too, when the movie bombed, but his career had gotten up off the canvas a time or two already, as a fighter with great will and great cornermen will do.

CHAPTER 20

Johnny left and the other three men were able to turn their attention to the matter of Danny and Jimmy Shea. To Tom's surprise, this began with Woltz calling for the lights.

"Don't worry," Woltz stage-whispered. "The projectionist isn't right in the head. He doesn't talk, he doesn't understand what he sees, he just knows how to run the projector."

"Sounds like quite a find," Hagen said.

Tamarkin chuckled. "If only you could have found a girl like that, huh, Jack? Doesn't talk, doesn't understand what she sees. Just someone who knows how to take it up her tight young ass."

Woltz, to Hagen's astonishment, didn't say a word.

Hagen had supplied this copy of the film to Woltz, but he hadn't seen it before, and he could have done without seeing it now. Pornography made him squeamish, and this was worse: a nauseating reminder of what had happened to Judy Buchanan and what had come from it.

The film started, grainy black-and-white stock, single camera, fixed position, no sound, poor lighting. A large-breasted, dark-haired woman—no one noteworthy, it seemed, just an idle conquest—was sprawled on a huge bed in a dark-colored scoop-necked dress, looking over at the camera, vamping it up. She pulled the dress down and flashed a naked breast and laughed.

A moment later, into the frame came the current president of the United States, naked only below the waist. He said something and the woman cracked up. He laughed, too. Instead of getting in bed, instead of taking off any more clothes, Jimmy Shea crossed the room and took a seat in a big armless chair, almost a throne. The camera was perfectly positioned to capture him in profile. He had a slight paunch that the cut of his suits hid. He seemed fully erect and normally endowed.

The woman came over to him, still in her dress. She sank to her knees and got right to business. It was a remarkably energetic blowjob—clearly playing to the camera, Tom thought.

Hagen started to object. Woltz shushed him. Hagen sighed, but let it play out. This reel was only a few minutes long. There were a couple hours of it in all. It had been Rita Duvall, Michael's lady friend, who'd mentioned that the Shea brothers were fond of filming their bedroom escapades. She swore she'd never done so herself, during her brief fling with Jimmy Shea— that it was actually his desire to film it that brought an end to things. After a little digging, Tom Hagen had found that Johnny Fontane's Negro valet had made a copy of some footage shot at Johnny's house in Beverly Hills, back when the Sheas and Johnny were still close.

Onscreen now, the woman, still on her knees, leaned back away from then-Governor Shea. He got to his feet and started jacking off right over her mostly covered breasts.

"Enough," Tamarkin said.

"Lights," Woltz said.

The men sat in silence for a long time.

"Where is that?" Tamarkin said. "Where was it filmed?"

Hagen said he didn't know.

"So how did you happen to come into possession of an art film such as this?"

"Attorney-client privilege," Hagen said. Which was true. Though he'd paid Fontane's valet for the films, he'd also had him give back a dollar, as a retainer.

"I need to make a phone call," Tamarkin said.

"There's a payphone in the lobby," Woltz said. "Long story."

"Two minutes," Tamarkin said, and left.

"So it's true?" Hagen asked Woltz. "About the single phone call?"

Jack Woltz put his head in his hands and didn't answer.

Some people called Tamarkin the Phantom. He was the ultimate fixer. He reported to a group of vastly wealthy men almost no one knew, and he himself, though more of a public figure, was rarely seen in public. He'd helped bring countless miracles to Southern California, including the Brooklyn Dodgers and a nearly limitless supply of water. It was often said that Ben Tamarkin could save the damned with a single phone call.

Hagen had also turned up some evidence that Tamarkin's power was derived from playing a dangerous game: feeding the FBI just enough information to keep himself out of trouble, but not enough to bring down the powerful men he served and protected. Hagen couldn't get proof, but, to be on the safe side, he was proceeding on the presumption that it was all true.

Exactly two minutes after he left, Tamarkin strode down the center aisle and returned to his seat.

"My apologies," he said. "Continue."

Hagen stood to face the other two men. "As I've told Mr. Woltz, there is quite a bit more of this unsavory material," he said. "Some of it involves the president's brother as well, who, I'm told, indulges in a much wider variety of activities. The reel we had copied for Mr. Woltz is apparently a representative sample. I'd rather not know any more than I already do. I'd rather no one know. I'm confident few people have seen these, and it's certainly our hope that this situation continues."

Tamarkin looked up at him, impassive. Even though Woltz was scheduled to introduce the president at a fund-raiser tomorrow night, Hagen realized that any meaningful change had to go through Tamarkin.

"Gentlemen," Tom said, "we are all three men who came from humble beginnings. All three of us were, for at least a little while, earning our keep while we were still boys. It's easier for us to see certain things that someone who's always been rich, like Danny Shea, cannot. For example, he fails to understand that the two union leaders he's trying to prosecute have inarguably made things better for the dues-paying, blue-collar men they serve. Union politics can be a dirty business, and a man who's able to get things done probably isn't going to be a candidate for sainthood."

Woltz still had his head in his hands, but Hagen looked: he was still breathing. Tamarkin, in contrast, was focused on Hagen with laser-beam intensity.

"By the same token," Hagen continued, "many of the men with whom Michael Corleone does business are staunch opponents of this administration. It may simply be easier for Mr. Corleone, whose background is so similar to the president's, to appreciate certain matters as well, things that those men, who can't see past their differences with some of the administration's policies, cannot. The strong economy, employment rate, the space program, the inspirational leadership, the ability to stare down the Communists: it's a long list, as I think we all agree."

Tamarkin folded his arms now.

"Michael Corleone," said Hagen, "is not the demon that Danny Shea is making him and people like him out to be. He was involved in the president's campaign in the last election and may have been instrumental in the outcome. He'd like to have that chance again—and would, gladly and aggressively, if this administration stopped treating him like an adversary."

Finally Woltz raised his large, bald head. "Let me get this straight," Woltz said. "You want us to help you blackmail the president of the United States?"

Tamarkin gave the old man a look of heavy-lidded contempt.

"Absolutely not," Hagen said. "How would we do that? What newspaper would print it? What TV station would broadcast it? Unless I'm missing something, which I suppose is possible," he said, and let the pause linger, "this material is of no political value. On the other hand," he said, pointing at the screen, "an honorable man keeps the secrets of his friends. What incentive is there to harbor the ruinous secrets of an enemy? It seems so . . . unnecessary, that the president would want us as adversaries when he can have us as friends—*did* have us as friends, until the recent unpleasantness his little brother provoked. Mr. Woltz, Mr. Tamarkin, we know that you're on a friendly basis with the president and several of the men in his inner circle. We wouldn't ask you to in any way compromise those friendships. I'm not asking you to be Mr. Corleone's messenger. I'm not asking you anything at all, really, but to consider the situation, to consider it fully, and to do what you think is right." He walked over and put his hand on Tamarkin's shoulder, then bent down and faced Woltz. "All I'm suggesting is this," Hagen said. "Let your conscience be your guide."

TOM DIDN'T RELISH THE IDEA OF STAYING OVERNIGHT IN this ghastly house under the same roof with these loud and ghastly people, but it was one more price he had to pay to atone for the hundreds of enjoyable times he'd had putting his mind and body at ease alone with Judy Buchanan. Monogamy had to have been a woman's invention, pious and unrealistic, an absurdity—like the need they think they have for all those expensive, cheaply made shoes. Monogamy, thought Tom Hagen, was the imposition of the way things ought to be onto the way they really were.

The room they'd been given had twin beds and was, aside from the Degas sketches over those beds, plainly furnished. Tom and Theresa Hagen, in their bathrobes, pulled up a couple of chairs and sat by the window, sharing a bottle of red wine that had been waiting for them and looking out at the view of the spotlighted statue of Jack Woltz.

"Woltz is a Jew, right?" Theresa asked.

"Through and through. So what?"

"So he's got I would say twenty pieces of art in this place that were stolen from the Jews during the war and unaccounted for since. I'd have to have a closer look to be sure, but if I were a betting women, I'd bet the over on twenty."

"How do you know a thing like that?"

"What the over/under bet is?"

"No," Tom said. "The other."

"I joined a group down in Miami—Miami Beach, actually—mostly Jews themselves. They work to find significant works of art that are missing, be it from World War II or otherwise, but they specialize in World War II. There's more of it than you'd think."

"What happens when they find something?" Tom asked.

"They track down the rightful owner or his heirs and the courts do their magic after that. Or, I should say, the fear of the courts. The fear of getting publicly unmasked as a receiver of stolen goods from the Nazis is enough to get people to listen to the better angels of their nature. Even if the new owner doesn't know provenance from Providence, Rhode Island, if all of his crimes are inadvertent, being an inadvertent Nazi collaborator is hardly something a person wants to have to answer for in court. People see the evidence, talk to their lawyers, and relent."

She poured him some more wine.

"You're not thinking about me," she said, "my involvement in this group, anything interesting about the project. You're just thinking about how you can use this information against Woltz."

She had always seemed to be able to read his mind, though it was something she rarely did anymore. "I was thinking about why it makes any difference that he's a Jew. Just because he's a Jew, he's supposed to be a crusader to help all the other Jews? Start thinking like that, and where does it end?"

"You're an intelligent man, Tom Hagen, but when it comes to looking at the world through anyone else's perspective, you can only do it when you want something. You're all but incapable of empathy."

She wasn't talking about Woltz, he realized.

"It just kills me," Theresa said, "and this is just one example, but it just kills me that you might think of me as the kind of wife who's so naïve she doesn't know what men do."

"I don't understand," he lied. "What do you mean?"

"I know, all right?" she said. "I'm around artists all the time. Artists are outlaws. They live outside the law; they think that rules are for other people. You think that the conditions in your world are so *secretive*. You think they're unique, which is a laugh. I can't stand it that you might think of me as some poor Italian peasant girl who's just going to accept that the *signore* is going to have his *comare*. Or that it would be a burden lifted off of me, a chore I don't want to do, like hiring someone to come in and help with the cleaning."

"Theresa, that's not—"

"How can you possibly not understand that I'd like to do what you did. I *like* sex, in case you didn't notice, and every reason you'd have for going and getting some strange *pussy*, I'd have for wanting to go get some strange hard *cock*. But I don't do it. I would never do it. You know what bothers me the most?"

Hagen's hands were thrust into his robe pockets and balled into fists. "No."

"You'll never figure it out."

"I imagine I won't. You already said I can't see the world through other people's eyes."

"Don't mock me."

"I'm not mocking you."

They sat in silence for a while. Then Theresa poured herself more wine.

"What bothers me the most," she said, "is that you keep saying that it didn't mean anything. That you didn't love her, but my God, Tom, listen to yourself. Why did you rip your family apart over something that doesn't mean anything? Why did you leave yourself vulnerable to whoever was behind the murder of that whore? If you had loved her, I could understand it. I'd have better understood why you'd run a risk like that. But more importantly, if you'd loved her, it would have shown me some passion in you."

Tom willed himself to relax, to open his fists and extend his fingers and take a deep breath. Most of the men he knew would have hit their wives by now. Tom had never laid a hand on her—her or any person—in anger. Like anyone else, he'd had the impulse. But even as a boy, Tom had the impulse control of an ascetic country priest.

"That's ridiculous," Tom said. "I can promise you that you wouldn't have thought any of this was any better if I'd loved her. Which, again, I didn't."

"You have a tremendous life, Tom. You've done well for yourself. I've heard you say so yourself countless times, and I agree. Yet you're incapable of taking pleasure in it. I feel sorry for you. Any warmth you have toward other people, any passion, any love, it's all just an act."

"An act. You think I'm putting on an act?"

"I'm not saying you're aware of it," Theresa said. "I don't think you are. I certainly hope you aren't. Maybe the act—and I'm sure there's a better word for it than *act*, I'm not a psychologist—but maybe it's mostly something you put on for your own benefit. But any emotions you display are more acted out than experienced."

What he felt, suddenly, was a pang of indigestion. He tried to think of what he'd eaten that hadn't agreed with him. It had been a long day. The pang increased, and he tried to even it out by taking a deep breath, which seemed to work. "Hold that thought," he said, patting her hand and getting up to go chug some Pepto-Bismol. *This was ulcer pain,* he thought. *They were coming back.*

He thought she might be sore at him for getting up like that, in the middle of a conversation, but as he walked back across the room to the window, carrying a glass of water for her, too, just in case, the look on her face was that of a grown woman, concerned and perversely smitten.

"Are you all right?"

"It's the ulcers, I think. I'm fine, but I think they're back."

If he hadn't known better, he'd have taken her reaction to this as a cynical attempt to show him what empathy was. But she was surpassingly sincere, as she was in everything. What he felt for her now was love. He felt almost certain of it. He didn't need a woman like her, he needed *her*. Theresa. Who told him the truth. "I know it's the wrong answer here, Theresa, but I love you."

"Listen to yourself. *I know it's the wrong answer, but.* It's . . . " She shook her head. "I love you, too, Tom. All right? May God have mercy on my soul, but I do. I love your mind, your charm, your wit. I love being married to a man who's not threatened by a woman who has a career—of sorts, anyway. Interests outside the home, as it were. I love how handsome you are. I love what we've built together, our family, the shared mission we've had as man and wife. But in the end, I can't really explain it, why I love you. All those things explain it, and yet none of them do."

Tom nodded. He couldn't talk. There was a pressure on his chest and a tingling feeling, and he had the crazy thought that maybe this was what people talked about when they talked about love.

"What do you have a passion for, Tom? Name one thing."

"You," he said. "The kids. Our family."

"Those are the right answers," she said. "You answer questions that way, with what you think the other person thinks is the right answer. Not with anything you really feel. Because you don't really feel *anything*."

"You're wrong," he said.

She turned to face him. She leaned over and gave him a chaste but tender kiss on his sloping forehead. "I hope so. I so very badly hope so."

About an hour later, in bed together with his wife, asleep, he was awakened by what he'd earlier thought of as love. This time, it hurt: a heavier feeling bearing down on Tom Hagen and some more tingling, too.

Woltz's private physician rode along with Hagen to the hospital in Palm Springs, did some tests there, and congratulated him. "It's hard to say for certain, but I think it's safe to say you had a little heart attack," he said.

"Lucky for you, your warning heart attack was just a cute little nothing. But, trust me, if you don't watch yourself, these will get worse."

"Never," Tom whispered, "trust anyone who says *trust me*." A whisper was all he could manage.

The doctor took it lightly, as a joke. "Get some rest," he said.

Theresa was standing beside the bed, her face sallow with wiped-off tears and no sleep. The doctor gave her a reassuring pat on the shoulder and then left them alone.

She held Tom's hand and took a deep breath and began. "All right," she said. "Condition number one is we stay in Florida. This is nonnegotiable. The girls, you, me. The boys when they visit. Keep the place in New York if you have to for business reasons, but I'm not coming back there. I'm keeping our distance from all that. I'll visit"—she sniffed—"for art's sake only. But our home is in Florida."

Tom nodded, woozy. He imagined that his heart might have soared if it were up to such things. "Agreed."

A FEW MILES AWAY AND AT ABOUT THE SAME TIME, FRAN-cesca Corleone, gasping for breath and drunk for the first time in years, caught sight of her own naked body in the mirror over Johnny Fontane's king-size bed, and somehow she couldn't take her eyes away. She would have liked to. What she was doing could not be called *making love*. The bedding was wadded up and ravaged, and there was nothing to see but this animalistic act, committed on sweat-stained satin sheets, accompanied by bossa nova music and lit by recessed mood lighting Francesca should have thought to ask Johnny to turn off.

Ordinarily, even when she was alone, Francesca did not take long looks at herself in the mirror when she was naked. Her mother had told her that only sluts looked in the mirror when they were naked—that what did she think, she was pretty? She wasn't pretty. She was just another girl, and the sooner she figured that out, the happier life she might lead. The cruel things a mother tells a daughter live until the daughter's dying breath. They often *are* a daughter's dying breath. Yet even if her mother hadn't said those rotten things, Francesca still couldn't have imagined that she'd want to watch herself do *this*. She'd had the chance before, when she and Billy were on vacation in Cuba. She'd either looked away or gotten on top or on her knees. Or flat on her stomach. She liked it that way. But this was different. This was *Johnny*.

What was weird about it was how weird it wasn't—how natural it felt. It had been a long time for her, and Johnny had taken his time.

His head. Between her legs. Longer than Billy ever had.

She tried to look up at *him*, at Johnny, that face, those eyes, but she could not.

She managed to look at his reflection. At his buttocks, bobbing up and down, small and tight, ridiculous and adorable. And at the back of his head, the little bald spot that bothered him but did not bother her. Watching him like this made the whole thing seem funny and sad and even less real. What a strange thing it is, to be fucked. Because when you *see* it, like this, it's not making love. It's fucking. She hated that word, but that was all she could think of. It was the right word for what she was watching.

"Fuck me, Johnny," she heard herself say.

He replied by slamming into her, hard. The rumors *were* true: he was huge, the biggest she'd ever had. It hurt, but he was tender, too. It hurt in a good way that was entirely new to her. He filled her so much, there was room for nothing else; with each thrust, he plowed her own juices right out of her.

"Like that," she blurted, loud and breathless. She couldn't have said if she meant *I like that* or *do it like that*.

He didn't seem to need to know. He was good at this.

It made her feel sophisticated and tough that she didn't care about all he'd done to get that way.

She could have looked in his eyes, *should* have, but did not. Could not. Wanted to, but no.

The only eyes Francesca could bear to look into were her own, up there, staring down at her, studying the glimpses she got of her own flopping and defiantly asymmetrical breasts. The woman up there looked more scared than happy. She was bathed in sweat. On the wall behind the bed, above the calf-leather headboard, the huge take-up reel of the hi-fi's tape player moved grimly round and round.

The bossa nova music gave way to applause. An announcer's voice introduced Johnny Fontane. It was the live LP, *Fontane Blue.* Johnny was fucking her to the sound of his own sweet music. This was not unlike the way Francesca had pictured it. Thousands, maybe millions of people every day enjoyed themselves in the bedroom while Johnny's music played.

"Yes," Francesca said, her voice strange in her own ears. *I love you*, she thought but had enough sense not to say. Or even to mean. She hated herself for even thinking it. Francesca wanted to be through with that kind of love. "Fuck me."

She finally managed to glance up at him. His eyes were closed, his face contorted into a grimace.

Shaking now, she dug her fingers into Johnny's shiny, hairless back and pulled him close, blocking her view of what was happening. The last thing on earth she'd expected to happen.

Life don't go where you expect, eh?

Just as she'd imagined, the dream she was having in real life smelled like sweat, manly soap, fine leather, and the bouquet of her own fragrant cunt.

Another word she hated but was all that she could think of now.

Cunt.

She felt a spasm there, as if it had a mind of its own. She shivered. Surprisingly, inevitably, she was about to come.

BOOK IV

CHAPTER 21

It had been nearly three years since Nick Geraci had disappeared. All things being equal, three years was not a remarkably long time to have to wait to exact revenge. Anyone engaged in Geraci's line of work could without hesitation list several situations that lasted much longer. To cite only one famous example, Don Vito Corleone waited a quarter century to plunge a dagger into the gut of the Sicilian Mafioso responsible for the deaths of his father, his brother Paolo, and, before Vito's very eyes, his sainted mother. Vito drove the blade into the man's navel and thrust it upward, sawing through skin and intestine, up to the base of his rib cage and bursting the man's full stomach with a muted, wet pop: five seconds of grim, bloody, foul-smelling pleasure that a quarter century's wait must have made only sweeter.

But other problems the Corleones were having made closing the books on the Geraci problem a priority—even if it was one quite concealed from public view.

Three years had been enough time to allow Nick Geraci to disappear from the pages of the newspapers as well. He had successfully become old news. Inside certain newsrooms, ascribing fresh mayhem to Nick Geraci had become house slang for saying that there were no suspects, like joking that the boogeyman did it. The general public had long since moved on, seeking new ways to feed its bottomless appetite for bread and circuses. The Judy Buchanan murder had served nicely, but there were so many other delicacies, too, served fresh daily. Egad, Fireball Roberts died in a crash! Cheer up: the World's Fair is opening! Only . . . my God, look what's going on down South with the Negroes! Dogs! Fire hoses! Murder! Young corpses buried in earthen dams! But, wait, kids, look over here: everybody say *yeah, yeah, yeah*—it's Beatlemania!

Take, eat.

Officially, Nick Geraci was presumed dead. His wife had filed paperwork to make that presumption legal. The only suspense that remained was when, if ever, the body would be found. One theory—that his remains had been encased in a cement pylon at Shea Stadium—had evolved into the popular notion that he was buried under home plate. Announcers sometimes made jokes about this on the air. The bad news is, the Mets were held scoreless again tonight. The good? Nick Geraci can rest in peace. Et cetera.

For most of the men associated with Geraci's tradition, however, the thinking was a little different. Here again, disappearing for three years was hardly unknown. Many had pulled off more impressive feats. In Sicily, one Mafia Don vanished for almost twenty years before he turned up, comfortable and perfectly healthy, having never even left the island or relinquished control of his empire.

Had Geraci been dead, those in the know would have expected someone to take credit for the job, given how much gratitude the feat would have inspired from the Corleones. Had the Corleones themselves done the job, there would surely have been a body.

There was an additional concern.

Even three years after Geraci's disappearance, mishaps within the Corleone organization were often blamed on him—and with none of the whimsicality used to address the New York Mets' lousy hitting. It was known that Geraci had embedded various Sicilians in pizza parlors all over the Midwest, all of whom were living honest, decent lives, far from places where they might one day be called upon to do a service. No one knew where all of these people were, except Geraci, who supposedly had it all in his head.

Some of them, though, other people did remember. In fact, those with any sort of criminal experience back in Sicily were offered opportunities in New York with Sacripante or Nobilio. But there were many more out there nobody knew about, and every time a supposedly common truck driver gunned down the men who'd come to hijack his cargo, or a courier taking the Corleones' share of the Las Vegas skim was garroted and robbed, there was a suspicion that the job had been done by, say, some friendly mook who'd already reentered his quiet life as a pizza chef in some Indiana white-bread noplace.

Once Geraci was found, there would be no need to torture him to get that list of embedded Sicilians he had in his head. Once that head had three rounds from a .22 ricocheting through it, scrambling his brains to mush, it wouldn't matter. The men, wherever they were, could live out their lives in peace, free to become pillars of the community, threats to nobody. Which, in fact, was precisely what most of them were destined to do.

Even if, dear reader, one such man had been your own father, you would never have known. His surname—*yours,* now—was probably not his father's. His given name was probably not the one his mother gave him. As many did, he might have moved on from that first restaurant job to bigger and better things, might have known enough of another language to pass himself off as a Greek, a Spaniard, an Arab, or merely someone who, like so many Americans, doesn't like to dwell on the past. The past was past, and none of it mattered now because he was an American. His children were Americans. He had escaped the inescapable pull of history merely by pledging allegiance to the flag and to the local sports teams, making money, driving a clean car, keeping a nice lawn, and paying taxes in the name of this person he invented.

The CIA had a similar program, which it called Most Special Fellows. In the CIA's case, the men usually came not from Sicily but Yale or one of the service academies. They were rarely used as assassins but rather for darker purposes. They were put in charge of companies kept afloat by the government, made rich despite their lack of dedication or business acumen, and positioned to run for public office or do business in foreign countries when the wise men said it was time. None disappeared. Many, though, did reinvent themselves—children of privilege in the heartland, playing the role of the common man. Millions of voters bought the act. Often, so did the men themselves. At least one and possibly three American presidents have come out of this program.

In the version of *Fausto's Bargain* that was eventually published, there is a scene in which Nick Geraci compares notes on his program and the CIA's with a one-eyed field agent named Ike Rosen, whose existence the House Select Subcommittee on Assassinations and Regime Changes would later doubt. At that time, a spokesman for the CIA testified that there was no such covert program and denounced Geraci's memoir as "a mere fiction novel." Recently, newly declassified documents have proved that the program did exist, though to this day no proof has come to light that there was ever an Ike Rosen.

In the book, Rosen helps Geraci stay at least one step ahead of his vengeful pursuers. Rosen is actually trying to keep Michael Corleone from getting set up for conspiracy to commit murder—Nick's murder.

Even those who stubbornly cling to Geraci's story concede that if Rosen did exist, he was probably a composite.

BECAUSE MICHAEL CORLEONE HAD FOR YEARS TAKEN A greater interest in the legitimate businesses, and now because those were the only businesses to which Tom Hagen could minister, those companies were thriving, even in the wake of the Corleones' other problems. Leaving aside the 1964 World's Fair, that huge and sacred cash cow, money flowed in from parking lots, funeral homes, pushcarts, bars, restaurants, vending machines, hotels and casinos, construction, and, best of all, commercial real estate—especially that new gold mine, suburban shopping malls. For this, Michael had two partners to thank, both of whom had ties to the Vito Corleone years. Ray Clemenza, Pete's kid, developed shopping malls all over the country. Roger Cole (born Ruggero Colombo) was one of the most successful real estate developers and investors in New York. His company, King Properties, was named after the beloved dog Roger had as a little boy, which might have been the cause of the Colombos' eviction, had Vito Corleone not reasoned with their landlord. Not only did Michael have large shares in each man's business, he hired accountants to monitor their accountants, to make sure nothing remotely illegal came anywhere near these companies' books or tax returns.

But the businesses that Nick Geraci had most closely operated were struggling. The Family's share of the narcotics trade had shrunk dramatically; the operation Geraci had secretly assembled, using the remnants of Sonny Corleone's *regime* and in concert with the Sicilian *capo di tutti capi*, Cesare Indelicato, had now become a partnership with Indelicato and the Stracci Family in New Jersey, which controlled the docks where all the drugs were unloaded. The Straccis took sixty percent of the profits on the U.S. end, where once they'd had only ten, entirely because the *capo* who ran those docks was a more capable and seasoned leader than anyone the Corleones could have pressed into service.

The unions under the Corleones' control did remain so, but several of the union leaders had started to act more like the ones giving the orders rather than taking them. The most visible of the many problems this had triggered was that the Justice Department was now coming after the union bosses, too. This was itself a form of justice, but not one in which the Corleones could take satisfaction.

The Corleone Family's greatest asset had always been the network of people it kept on its payroll—meat eaters, they were often called—and it was thus the setbacks on that front that seemed most ominous. Geraci had overseen those payments without serious incident for the seven years before he disappeared. In the years since, as the responsibility for the payments was overseen by Tom Hagen together with the Family's *capo*s, the structure of the network was intact but damaged. And now Hagen was off that job indefinitely, and it was just the *capo*s—Nobilio and Paradise. Although the problems were greater in scope than could be blamed on one inexperienced *capo*, Eddie Paradise's *regime* was having a particularly hard time getting its portion of the job done right.

Increasingly, police and public officials who were supposedly bought and paid for didn't stay that way. They were finding resourceful new ways to take money and ask for more, to double-dip from both the Corleones and a rival, to claim to have done everything they could to perform a favor that didn't quite work out as planned.

The money pouring in from the World's Fair covered a multitude of sins, one of which was the severity of what some had started to call the Meat Eaters' Rebellion. Like the onset of termite devastation, it was audible but only barely so, visible but only if a person knew where to look, yet unless the situation was addressed soon, the whole structure was destined to become a big pile of sawdust and bug shit.

EDDIE PARADISE WENT ON ABOUT HIS BUSINESS, BUT HE knew what people thought. They thought he was a journeyman, a fat little man who got where he was for lack of better options. A comical figure, who was in way over his head. They called them "the Turtle" sometimes, as in *Slow and steady wins the race.* It was starting to show up in the newspapers, even in stories by writers who were supposedly on the payroll. Apparently, people had been calling him Eddie the Turtle for a while now behind his back, as if it was an insult. Eddie didn't like to get caught up in things like this, reacting violently to every insult real and imagined, throwing his weight around and settling scores, on top of which: how was that an insult? The turtle wins the goddamned race. Like the man says, you can look it up. Somewhere along the line, while Eddie wasn't looking, America had become the sort of place that rooted for the goddamned rabbit.

Which: fine. What's one man going to do, change things? Realistically, no. What could one man do, for example, about the problems with the docks in Red Hook? Once the cargo ships all went to containers, they could dock anywhere, even at nonunion docks, and truck the goods to wherever. It was just a punch Eddie had to roll with. For better and for worse, America itself was changing. It wasn't just Eddie who thought that. It was in the air, the freedom-scented American air. One example: Eddie had a piece of a nightclub down in Greenwich Village, and recently, when he'd gone down there to meet someone in a back room to iron out something else entirely, he overheard two folk singers talking in the dressing room. One had hit it big and was just visiting. The other, who was performing that night, was an old friend. "America is changing," the famous one said. "There's a feeling of destiny, and I'm riding the changes."

It stuck in Eddie's head. In spite of his troubles and the troubles of those around him, despite *himself,* Eddie Paradise had a feeling of destiny, too. Eddie Paradise's destiny *was* to ride the changes.

He was not in over his head, no matter what anyone said. Turtles swim, don't they?

People thought Momo Barone would have been better at the job and that the only reason Michael didn't replace Eddie with Momo now was that it would look indecisive. People thought Michael had ordered Eddie to give Momo more responsibility and authority, enough that in the eyes of a lot of people, the Roach was jointly in charge of their *regime.* People were full of shit. Momo Barone was Eddie's oldest friend. They were like *brothers.* Momo was a miserable, grumpy prick, but Eddie could see through all that. He *knew* the guy. If the shoe had been on the other foot, Momo would have done the same thing. So what did people want from Eddie Paradise: that he'd screw over his oldest friend because people, some people, might see it as a sign of weakness? This made Eddie nuts. No weak man would *do* that. A weak man *clips* a strong lieutenant. Only a strong man makes his second-in-command stronger.

Nonetheless, it was true—there were witnesses—that Michael Corleone, furious right after the raid on that Commission meeting, had told Eddie that if he needed help taking care of business he should ask for it. This was the starting point for a lot of those whispers. Eddie didn't appreciate getting chewed out like that in front of others, but he'd handled it the way a loyal *capo* should, especially a new one, who had to expect a little ball-busting to go with the territory, especially after a *giambott'* like that. Which was: Eddie stood there and took his medicine like a man.

What was he going to do later on, have Michael whacked for it? No. For one thing, who the fuck would take over? The Corleones were *already* weak at the top. If someone took Michael out, there was no Plan B. Plan B was oblivion.

Even if there *had* been a Plan B, going in that direction went against Eddie's reasonable, loyal nature.

Thus: what he did was, he met with the Don in private, once tempers had cooled. Michael even left his tower and ventured out to Brooklyn, to meet with Eddie at the Carroll Gardens Hunt Club. That this happened on Eddie's turf was in and of itself an important, unspoken apology (the only kind Eddie could hope for, since bosses don't and shouldn't apologize). Michael and Eddie went up to the roof, to work things out man to man. It was a cold night, but the rooftop was Michael's idea and Eddie wasn't about to get picky about what part of his social club they should use for their sit-down. Momo came along. People made a big, fat, hairy deal out of that later, but at the time it had seemed only natural. Michael probably would have brought some kind of a second, as well—a *consigliere*, an underboss—if the cupboard hadn't been more or less bare. It wasn't just the defection of Geraci and the troubles Tom Hagen was having. For example, the late Rocco Lampone—who'd been married to one of Eddie's cousins—would have come in pretty handy at times like this, except that for who knows what reason Michael had used him to take out Hyman Roth. Who sends a *capo* to do a hit like that? Not to mention a suicide mission. Nobody Eddie Paradise ever heard of.

But that was the past.

Here in the present, Eddie Paradise took full responsibility for everything that had gone wrong. He wanted Michael Corleone to be clear on that.

"By the same token," Eddie told him, "those cops were from Homicide, and not my captain. My captain couldn't have seen that coming, not a chance. The cops we had on sentry weren't really there to keep out other cops. Or at least not other detectives, officers, cars coming in there with their sirens blaring and all that. That don't mean the buck don't stop here. It stops. Period. I want to you understand that. My only point is that it's also possible once in a while to do everything right and still have things go wrong."

"Life is one disappointing cocksucker," sighed Momo Barone, shrugging at the hopelessness of it all.

Michael considered this and then glared at Eddie.

Cold as it was up here, no one was shivering. Eddie felt as if he were cooking in the boiling oil of his boss's disapproval.

"You can do this job, Eddie," Michael said. "You're new, and I've been patient with you while you learned the ropes. But I have to tell you, the time for improvement is now. I'm not happy about what happened at that meeting, with the cops barging in and hauling Tom away in handcuffs. But I'm also not interested in going back over what went wrong. I'm interested in making sure that everything goes right from here on out."

Eddie nodded. This was why Michael needed him. The *coglioni* around them lived in the past. Michael, on the other hand, was a planner, concerned with *from here on out*. Eddie took what was right here and did with it what he could. "Thank you," he said.

"I'm not going to tell you how to do the nuts and bolts of your job, Ed," Michael said. "If I thought you needed help like that, you wouldn't *have* your job. I'd have never promoted you."

Also, Eddie thought, because everything he knew about the nuts and bolts of being a *capo* he'd learned from his father or Tom Hagen, neither of whom had ever been one.

"You got to admit, though, we're earning pretty good," Eddie said. "We got all these pressures on us, as you know, closin' in on us from the Feds right on down, and yet the numbers you're seeing from us, in most areas of our business, are as good as they've ever been, considering."

"Considering," Michael repeated flatly.

Eddie took it as a criticism, but maybe a fair one.

"To me," Michael said, "that's symptomatic of another problem. That's symptomatic of what we need to talk about."

Eddie and Momo exchanged a look. *Symptomatic.* Fucking college boy. "What other problem?" Eddie said.

"This fascination with money," Michael said. "The poisonous flowers of greed. I understand that this is how other Families work, but please understand, Eddie: it's not what my father built. This isn't our tradition, Ed, and it's not what I'm interested in seeing this Family become. My father believed that America was a land of opportunity, but he also brilliantly saw the hypocrisy and the cynicism that bloomed in darkness, right underneath such patriotic slogans. You're a pragmatic man, Eddie. A realistic man. My father would have appreciated that in you. He would have liked you."

Eddie realized that he was smiling only when he glanced at Momo and saw the Roach roll his eyes.

"What my father tried to build," Michael continued, "what he *succeeded* at building, was a realistic organization based on mutual interests, one that provided services people wanted and profited from the goodwill that came from that. Money is a *by-product* of a business like that, not an end in itself. Nobody forces anyone to come to a bookie or a shylock. They go out of free will, and they're grateful for the service. That's paramount. That's everything. The profits are incidental. The profits are a by-product of good relationships, a good reputation that spreads by word of mouth and causes other people to come to us, seeking our services. The same principle applies to people in positions of power. Nobody forces any of those people to come to us and ask for our assistance in getting into those positions. Or in staying in those positions. Or in thriving in those positions. We help people do all of this, but it's their choice. Do you understand what I'm telling you?"

Eddie folded his arms. "I understand what you're telling me, but I'm maybe a bit shaky about why."

Michael stood. He was considerably taller than Eddie but not really a tall man, per se. Yet the boss had a way of standing up during a conversation that made him seem like a giant. He commanded a room. Up here on the roof, he practically commanded the dark night sky.

"Money," Michael said, "cheapens everything. As soon as you reduce the business of our tradition to mere money, you're reducing us all to common criminals. This you cannot do. Money is a by-product of doing business the right way, and, once earned, it's the means to other ends, be that expansion of the scope of our businesses or even just creature comforts for you and your wife and your children—like your wife's new ermine stole or the new boat you have moored out in Sheepshead Bay."

A throb of fear shot through Eddie, though a split second later he was over it. It was a boss's job to know things like this, or be able to know them, and Eddie knew he had to learn to get to that point, and that Michael Corleone was an ideal teacher.

"People who want our protection can pay us for that protection—which is fine, cash for services rendered—but the danger is that if your first impulse is the money you're getting, you may miss out on other things we can get that are worth more than money, or that can lead to more money. There are times when providing protection for free can lead to more profits than anything else. It's a balance, of course, and it takes time to learn it. It doesn't come to anyone naturally."

Eddie nodded. Momo rubbed a hand across his mouth. Eddie and Momo had been soldiers coming up, as Nick Geraci had been where Eddie was now. Eddie doubted that Vito or Michael Corleone had ever sat Nick Geraci down for a talk like this. And he knew Momo was thinking the same thing.

"You're also," Michael said, "leaving us vulnerable in other ways. When either you," he said, looking at Eddie, "or the men that you supervise," he said, patting Momo lightly on his hardened, slicked-back hair, from which the Roach flinched, "when *anyone* in your *regime* goes to speak with men on our payroll, to take care of those obligations, you must understand that what you're doing may *seem* to be about money, but it's not. *Nobody* involved in this aspect of our business should be unclear on this. As soon as any of these relationships come to be about money, as soon as what you're handing out is a bribe instead of a tribute, what you'll find is that people you thought you could trust instead believe that they can sell themselves or their services to the highest bidder."

"Which if they do that," Eddie said, "we can take care of it, I promise you."

"You see?" Michael said. "You're missing the point. I don't want you to have to *take care of it*. I don't want it to come to that. When it comes to that, you've painted yourself into a corner. You have to act, but every one of those acts, again, leaves us vulnerable. Eddie, you, a practical man, must understand that there's no future in leaving behind a messy trail of pistol-whipped union leaders and kneecapped politicians."

Again with the future, Eddie thought.

"I understand," Eddie said. "We'll get it done."

They discussed a few other more specific matters—including, as they were wrapping up, the way Eddie had been using the public relations firm in which he'd become a silent partner. Eddie had been afraid for a while to say anything about this, but increasingly afraid that he'd kept Michael in the dark, too. To Eddie's relief, Michael approved. They discussed a few other ideas on how to make use of this.

When Michael left, as far as Eddie Paradise could tell, he and the boss had never been on better terms.

WHAT EDDIE WOULD HAVE LIKED TO USE HIS P.R. PEOPLE for was to get the word out about the significance of where that meeting had been held. Twenty or so of Eddie's own men and everybody in Michael's inner circle knew what was happening, but afterward, nobody seemed to be talking about it. All that really seemed to be on the grapevine was a lot of tongue-wagging about why Eddie had brought Momo with him, the implication being that he was too weak to meet with the boss himself. There was no way for Eddie to set the record straight without looking defensive about the Roach and like he was tooting his own horn about Michael coming to see him. It bugged him, but Eddie had to let it rest.

He decided that the time was right to do something really bold, something everyone would understand as a symbol of pride and strength. He started putting out feelers, making it quietly known that he was in the market for a lion. He got books out of the library to help with the feeding and caring issues, when the time came. He even got a maintenance man over from the Bronx Zoo to look at the cage in the basement.

A literal meat eater, in the basement of his social club. A lion. *Corleone*: lion-hearted. Eddie had a good feeling about how all that would play out. He'd be a legend.

He got to work rebuilding the relationships with the metaphorical meat eaters under his supervision, taking care of as many of them as he could. So many little things were going wrong, he was starting to get the feeling that there might be a rat somewhere around him. On the other hand, he was afraid he was getting paranoid. The need for the fresh newspapers, the fresh socks, the fresh soap: he knew what people said, and he wasn't going to give them more to say. Still, paranoid or not, it seemed like a smart play for him to employ the personal touch in retraining all of the men in his *regime* that he trusted to go make payments.

Michael had bolstered Eddie's confidence enough that he felt comfortable putting the boss's message in his own words.

"Let me explain something to you, all right?" he said to a young guy Momo had helped develop, a big, strapping Sicilian kid who maybe, come to think of it, had never had anyone sit him down and explain the American ways of doing things. "This thing of ours," Eddie said, "it looks like it's got to do with money. You do jobs, you kick a cut to the guy above you, who kicks a cut to the next guy, et cetera and so forth, and the guys at the very top take care of things with the cops and keep the arrests and the jail time and the other complications to a minimum. Simple, right? And on some level it is. Everybody talks all the time about money, so you'd be forgiven if you thought that was the point. But it ain't the point. It's about favors. It's like that joke, maybe you heard it. A little boy and a little girl are sittin' in the bathtub takin' a bath. The girl looks at the boy's prick and asks if she can touch it. Hell, no, the boy says. Look what happened to yours! Oh yeah? says the girl, pointin' to her pussy. Well, my ma told me that with one of *these*, I can get as many of those little things as I want. See, in our world, money's just a prick. But favors—givin' favors out, callin' 'em in, everything—favors are *pussy*."

INITIALLY, THE INFORMATION THAT PLACED NICK GERACI in Taormina had looked especially good—as so many of the other tips had. Initially.

Charlotte Geraci was seen boarding the train that went from New York to Montreal. She was seen getting off the train at Saratoga Springs. She was seen checking into the Adelphi Hotel, seen taking a cab from there to the Skidmore College campus to watch her daughter Barb's graduation. After the ceremony, she was seen entering a restaurant on Caroline Street, carrying two big gift-wrapped boxes (one, it would turn out, containing a brunette wig and a change of clothes), and she was seen going into a private party room. Barb Geraci and Charlotte's parents and several of Barb's friends were in there already.

Two men sat by the window in the bar across the street and saw no sign of Barb Geraci's father. They were locals, highly recommended, associated with the racetrack and a Corleone-operated casino there that had once been Hyman Roth's.

When the party finished, there was no sign of Charlotte, either. The men had lost her. They asked around as best they could but didn't find the first useful clue. She hadn't checked out of her room at the Adelphi, but she'd left the key in the room and had paid in advance. Wherever she'd gone, it hadn't been by train; they had friends at the Saratoga station with an eye cocked. The younger and more handsome of the men approached Barb Geraci in a bar, celebrating with friends, and, without setting off any alarms, figured out that she sincerely thought her mother had gone home. But there was no sign of Charlotte Geraci there, either.

A week later, Tommy Neri received an anonymous letter at his social club. It was postmarked Taormina. Inside was a typed note in Italian that said Charlotte had checked into a hotel there, on the east coast of Sicily. The hotel was one known for its security and discretion. Enclosed were three snapshots: Charlotte at a table at Café Wunderbar, one of her at the ruins of the Greek theater there, standing over a pit once used to house lions, and a grainy one of Nick and her, clearly taken with a telephoto lens, walking into the hotel. Nick Geraci had a full beard—something he'd grown only after he'd gone into hiding. A police detective Tommy had in his pocket dusted the photos for prints but found nothing.

Soon, a simply coded classified ad in the *Daily News* also indicated that Geraci was in Taormina. Tommy Scootch didn't know Joe Lucadello from the man in the moon except as "our source," which was what his *capo* Richie Nobilio called him. But based on previous information Lucadello had provided, the Corleones had sent Tommy or men he supervised to Taxco, Mexico City, Veracruz, Guatemala, and Panama. Every time, they'd found evidence that Geraci had been in these places, but never Geraci himself. Tommy was getting blamed for this, that somehow he wasn't taking the right precautions, that someone around him was tipping Geraci off. Tommy had actually been more excited about the Taormina information before the anonymous letter was corroborated.

As per his uncle Al's advice (which he imagined to be Michael Corleone's orders, since they'd come via Al and not Richie), the men Tommy Scootch sent to Taormina were unaffiliated with Cesare Indelicato, who was a friend of Michael's but perhaps (no one seemed sure of this) even more of a friend to Geraci. Following a suggestion by one of Nobilio's zips, Tommy had hired two freelancers from Calabria. The men sent word to Tommy that there was no one by Geraci's name at that hotel, which was no surprise, since no one expected him to be using his own name. But a hotel bartender said he'd definitely seen the bearded American and the blonde woman in those photos. A chambermaid said they'd stayed on the third floor but checked out. Several merchants and baristas in town remembered seeing the American with the beard and the shakes. He'd been looking to buy or rent a villa in the countryside, the more secluded, the better. He hadn't been seen in town for a while now, so maybe he'd found one.

That was the last anyone heard from the Calabrians.

By the time Tommy himself made it to Sicily, the men had disappeared. A few days later, their rented Fiat was discovered in an untended lemon grove outside Savoca. There was blood in the backseat and the trunk but no sign of the men. When Tommy Scootch returned home—empty-handed, once again—a small crate was waiting for him at his social club. It had been shipped from Messina, just up the coast from Savoca, although the return address—someone's idea of a joke—was that of Michael Corleone's penthouse apartment. Wrapped in plastic and packed in dry ice were the men's severed, badly beaten heads. Also inside were their hands and feet and a postcard of Mount Etna. On the back—using a fairly new portable Olivetti typewriter, the same brand as had been used to write the letter, with similar ribbon wear—someone had typed, in English, "Had a good time. Wish you were here."

Maybe some misfortune had befallen Charlotte Geraci. But it seemed more likely she'd joined her husband, wherever he was. Their daughters seemed not to know, but they also didn't seem as upset about the situation as a person might have imagined.

Clearly, someone was tipping Geraci off.

He was getting enough warning that he seemed to be toying with

Tommy Scootch now instead of killing him. If Indelicato had sided with Geraci, Michael Corleone realized, the worst of this problem was yet to come. But the best guess was that the rat was someone watching Tommy or getting information about his travel plans. Yet the reservations were made by secretaries in various Corleone-controlled companies, calling various travel agencies and (unbeknownst to them) using a different assumed name each time. To be safe, it was necessary to consider everyone in Tommy's orbit, particularly the other men in Nobilio's *regime,* as a potential rat, but nothing had been found. That kind of scrutiny made men edgy, which made the urgency to find Geraci greater than it had been already.

Only Michael and Tom Hagen had had any direct contact with Lucadello. It was theoretically possible that Joe was toying with them, too, which Tom believed but Michael didn't. Or that the rat was one of Joe's people or Joe himself.

Michael did not believe the rat was Joe.

CHAPTER 22

The 1964 New York World's Fair—which commemorated the three-hundredth anniversary of the Duke of York's muscling in and taking over the city from the Dutch, who'd scammed it from the Algonquin tribe in exchange for some *fugazi* jewels and the smallpox-laden blankets that killed them—proved to be a windfall for the Five Families of New York. It was perhaps the government's public onslaught against them that motivated all involved to split the profits equitably and with a minimum of observable conflict. The fair included well over one hundred new pavilions, mostly for corporations but also for various state governments and foreign countries, all built on the same site as the 1939 fair, a paved-over landfill in Flushing Meadows. Robert Moses was making a hundred grand to run the Fair Corporation (the mayor's salary was $40,000), on the condition that he resign from all his other posts, which he hadn't exactly done; he also had deals where he shared in the proceeds of various attractions and was actually guaranteed a salary of at least a million bucks. This was all legal, somehow, which boggled Michael Corleone's mind. As on most of Moses's grand projects, his own public idealism and private greed set the tone for the entire operation. Demolition and construction work abounded, including no-show and no-work union jobs that couldn't have come along at a better time for men in need of something wholesome to put in the "occupation" box on their income-tax returns. When the construction wound down, new no-shows and no-works sprang up, mostly as landscapers, maintenance workers, and security guards (these jobs were especially prized, for the badges). Contracts seemed to fall from the sky: to haul away the debris and garbage; to supply the food and beverages, the cigarettes and the souvenirs; to build parking lots and then repave them when the companies that built them in the first place did a poor job and then went into receivership, their offshore papers of incorporation beyond the reach of the long arm of American law. Nearby strip clubs and whorehouses thrived—thanks in part to Moses's square ideas about entertainment. Popular 1939 shows like the Little Egypt nudie act had been superseded by the insufferable, money-flushing likes of Dick Button's Ice-Stravaganza and the It's a Small World ride Walt Disney was paid handsomely to design for the Pepsi pavilion (another scam worthy of a mobster but conducted by an American legend and somehow legal: have other people pay you to design a ride for your own amusement park, and all you have to do is let them use it for two years, during which time you get a percentage of the take). The fair might have been a nod to the city's past, but it celebrated the Space Age, and the opportunities it presented for men like Michael Corleone seemed to be, to swipe a name from an exhibit at one of the corporate pavilions, "As Infinite as Imagination."

One of Michael's fronts—an old Marine Corps buddy—was actually on the board of directors of that corporation. Last year, one of its divisions received no-bid contracts from the Department of Defense to do classified jobs in Vietnam and Iran; the profits generated over there made what the Five Families were getting out of the World's Fair seem like the loose change under the sofa cushions. The secretary of defense was the company's former CEO; his stock, for now, was in a blind trust. And it was all legal. To glimpse things like this, Michael thought, was to be reassured that his dream of becoming a legitimate businessman was no delusion.

The fair provided a more subtle opportunity as well. Rarely had there been a better place to hide in plain sight, to be just a face in the crowd, and to conduct business without fear of being tape-recorded or hit. Other traditional sites for this remained in use—the big museums, the Brooklyn Botanic Garden, the lobby outside any opera, parts of Central Park, the aisles of big department stores, and so on. The fair had the novelty appeal that a suddenly fashionable new restaurant might have had, but it also seemed safer. The fairgrounds provided almost seven hundred acres where men could tell their stories walking. It was rich with background noise— abetted nicely by the roar from La Guardia Airport and the whine from the Bob Moses superhighways that surrounded the fairgrounds on all sides. Trusted men had jobs as security cops. Best of all, everyone had friends of theirs who were pulling money out of the place. It would have been sui- cide to shit where every made guy in New York was eating.

And so it was that Michael Corleone chose to meet Joe Lucadello at the fair. Michael had come with Francesca and Connie and their kids, as well as Rita Duvall, wearing a head scarf and enormous sunglasses. (Her celebrity was only of the *aren't you what's her face* variety; even when she *was* recog- nized, in New York, no one ever really bothered her.) Erring on the side of caution, Michael had two men positioned far enough behind them that no one would notice. Tom Hagen was still too hot to bring along, and the se- curity risk at the fair was low enough that Al Neri would have been overkill. But the rumors that Nick Geraci might be behind various unsolved acts of mayhem were enough to make Michael bring men along for protection, even to the World's Fair.

Michael met Joe, as suggested, at the Louisiana pavilion. Joe's sense of humor hadn't changed much over the years.

Joe himself, in contrast, looked different. The last time Michael had seen him was more than three years ago in Las Vegas, when they were put- ting together the Cuba project. It wasn't just that Joe was no longer wear- ing his eye patch or that he was wearing a wig or that, in his red

Munsingwear tennis shirt, cheap navy blazer, and crepe-soled shoes, he looked like a member of an unfashionable yacht club. It was the stiff, uncharacteristic way he was standing. Joe was a brainy, confident wiseass, with the slouchy body language that such men have. Now, here he was, in the middle of a replica of Bourbon Street, near the intersection of Grand Central Parkway and the Long Island Expressway, standing almost at attention. A miniature Mardi Gras parade was in progress, complete with a brass band of marching Negroes and strange zombie creatures with enormous papier-mâché heads. Joe was flanked by artists making charcoal caricatures of paying tourists and absent famous people, including Jimmy Shea, of course, and also Louis Armstrong and the Beatles.

Joe and Michael pretended they were old war buddies (a near truth) who just happened to have run into each other. Their embrace gave Michael a chance to dispense with his concern, however remote, that his old friend's odd posture had anything to do with carrying a gun or wearing a listening device. Joe introduced himself to Rita and Michael's family under an even longer Italian name than Lucadello.

"You are in what line of work now, Joe?" Rita asked.

She'd heard an Italian name, Michael thought, and drawn certain conclusions. Michael let it pass. She seemed to have meant it playfully, though the dark glasses made it hard to know for sure.

"I'm in sales," Joe said. "And you?"

"Ah," she said in mock disgust. "That is a good question." Her game show had been canceled. Even if Joe had meant it as a dig, she was taking it well. "I am thinking, maybe, I don't know, I will become a famous recluse."

"Nice work if you can get it," Joe said.

Michael put an arm around her.

"Your eye looks funny, Mr. Joe," said Sonny, Francesca's six-year-old.

"Sonny!" Francesca said. "That's not nice."

"It's all right," Joe said. "It's made out of glass, hand-blown, from

Germany," he said to the boy, and he bent down toward him and tapped on it.

"What happened to your real one?" Sonny said. "Did a Nazi shoot it out?"

Francesca gave the boy a look.

"It's all right," Joe said. "It was during the war, not in it. I was at a pub in London when a bomb landed, not all that close but close enough to break the window I was standing beside."

"Can you take it out?" Sonny said.

"Sonny!" said Francesca.

"Hey, does it have a camera in it?" said Victor, Connie's oldest. "I saw that once in a comic book."

"Boy, I wish," Joe said. "For a long time I wore an eye patch. The eyes they make in America are plastic, like everything else these days, but in Germany you can still find craftsmen whose families—"

"An eye patch like a *pirate*?" Sonny said, excited, and his mother again admonished him. The other two boys laughed.

"Yep," Joe said. "Mr. Joe, the *Paisan'* Pirate."

"See!" Sonny said. "What about a parrot, Mr. Joe?"

Rita, beaming, gave Michael a kiss on the cheek. She took ever more blatant delight in children. She was a damaged girl, Rita, and something about that drew Michael to her.

"I wanted a parrot," Joe said, "but my mom wouldn't let me. She was right, though. A friend of mine got one, and not only did it smell bad, it bit his pinkie finger off."

"Mr. Joe and I want to go catch up on old times," Michael said. "Over a coffee. Boring old war stories, that kind of thing." He handed cash to his sister and made arrangements to meet up with everyone later at the Vatican City pavilion, to see Michelangelo's *Pietà*, which had never before left the Vatican. Now, thanks to the exchange of certain favors, it was drawing the longest lines of any exhibit at the fair.

"Beautiful family," Joe said. "You should take 'em to see the Underground House."

"Funny," Michael said. They took a seat at an outdoor café and had coffee.

"In all seriousness, it's a real house," Joe said. "Built underground, good with utilities, a godsend if, when, the Russians drop the bomb."

"I know," Michael said. Some of his men had theoretically helped build it, an irony Joe would have appreciated. "Speaking of living underground—"

"Didn't you tell me you were going to bring *your* kids here, too?" Joe said. "I was looking forward to seeing them."

"Anthony got involved in baseball, and Mary had something, too. They had to cancel." A lie: at the last minute, Anthony had refused to come. Kay wouldn't send Mary on the train alone, and Michael hadn't had time to fly up himself and get her.

"They doin' all right, though?"

"They're great," Michael said. Michael had a feeling there was something in Joe that was broken, that he was standing tall for show. He asked about Joe's family, too, but there was nothing in the response to indicate that this was the source of his pain.

"And Rita?" Joe said. "That's going well?"

Michael smiled, despite himself. "I'm a lucky man," he said.

"That you are," Joe said. "Droopy kid like you, growing up to have a girl like that."

"What's in this?" Michael said, pushing the coffee away.

"Chicory."

"The same chicory you put in salads?"

"It's good," Joe said.

"Take it with you, then. Let's go." Michael stood and started down the fake Bourbon Street.

Joe rushed to catch up. "True story about that parrot, by the way," he said. "One day he's plain old Silvio Passonno. The next, he's got to go through the rest of his life as Silly Nine-Fingers."

"Silly Nine-Fingers?" Michael laughed, again despite himself. "It sounds like an Indian chief. Big Chief Silly Nine-Fingers. How can that be a true story?"

Joe's furtive smile, the pleasure he took in amusing a friend even when something was obviously eating at him, evoked no one so much as Fredo. Though he still wasn't loosening up entirely. "That's how it is with true stories," Joe said. "They're stupid. It'd be a better story if my eye was shot out by a Nazi, too, or when I crash-landed my plane behind enemy lines, instead of when I was drunk on warm beer, standing too close to a window during an air raid, kissing a pale, unremarkable woman whose name I never knew in a bar whose name I've forgotten. Call her Ishmaela. In my next life, I'm going to lie about everything, from the cradle to the grave."

They passed a shop selling pralines and headed back past the New York State pavilion, toward the Unisphere.

"Tell me another true story," Michael said.

"About which? New Orleans, or those skinflicks or your missing package?"

"Any order."

"Well, I know everybody's a critic these days, but judging from the reel you sent me, the movies are badly lit and weak on plot. Though I guess maybe that's where I'm supposed to come in, eh? To thicken that plot."

"So thicken it," Michael said.

"No can do. I'm a fan of the ends, but the means can't be justified."

"That *was* a friend of yours I read about a few weeks back, right?"

He was referring to the Shea administration's most recent debacle in Cuba, for which a CIA official had been made the scapegoat.

"I can't tell whether we were, or are, friends," Joe said. "However you mean that word. I can tell you that he was, that he is, a good man. The only part of what went public about him, the negative info, was that he did call Danny Shea a liar. That was on TV. That was right there in plain view. That was wrong, wrong to have done, but it wasn't inaccurate. The A.G. accused him of going off the reservation by planning that submarine attack. But what are we, the navy? We *have* no submarines. Obviously, no plan to deploy dozens of them all at once is going to get too far without the proper authority. This was not the sort of man who'd ever go off the reservation period, but in the case of what happened, it wouldn't have even been *possible*. Yet Danny Boy makes him fall on his sword, and the papers swallow it whole."

"And yet."

"Right. And yet, we have to pass. I'd like to see them out of office al-together, but we can't see any good way, any emissary I can send their way who can advance your agenda. Never say never, but for a while now, I've had to be Mr. By-the-Book. I can't touch anything irregular. The people getting forced into retirement or fates worse than that, you can't believe. Men my age, our age, men who fought in the war, got our start that way, there are a lot of us—too many of us, the way some people see it. The best field agent I ever saw, you know where the wise men stuck *him*? He's an as-sistant dean at a music college. He's supposed to be recruiting, I don't know, bassoonists with the potential to be agents. I'd die at a desk, I can tell you that, and I'm not about to wreck the slim chance I have of not winding up at one. So I have to think you have better men for this job than me anyway. Your friends in the union brass, other politicians. I don't know. I shouldn't tell you how to do your job. My apologies."

Michael glanced over his shoulder.

"They're still there," Joe said.

"Excuse me?"

"They're yours, those men. Skinny and the fatso. I can tell. Although for all you know they're mine, too."

"I'd know."

"Sure," Joe said. "I'm joking with you."

"All right," Michael said. "New Orleans and the package?"

"New Orleans, sweet mother of God," Joe said, letting out a deep breath. "New Orleans. New Orleans is complicated."

"Enlighten me."

Joe thought about this for a while.

So far, the Tramontis seemed to be abiding by the Commission's ruling, but Michael Corleone didn't want to leave anything to chance. He hadn't, of course, told Lucadello anything about Carlo Tramonti's proposal, but knowing that the Tramontis, too, had worked with the CIA on the assassination project, Michael had asked Joe to look into whether the Tramontis had any ongoing relationship with anyone Joe worked with.

"New Orleans is not America," Joe finally said. "Same way New York isn't. A place like Philly, that's America." Joe had grown up in South Philly, but it was a bigger part of his persona than when he'd first left—a reaction, Michael supposed, to working around all those Yale men at the agency. "Cleveland, Detroit, Chicago, even L.A. and Las Vegas. *Especially* those places, y'know? Hot, artificial, and so shiny that whoever you are, you can see your reflection in it. This right here," Joe said, gesturing expansively toward the World's Fair, its futuristic architecture on the site of a paved-over dump, epic vainglory surrounded by highways and cloverleafs, admission not free, "is sure as hell America. But the rest of New York is New York. It's its own thing. And New Orleans is New Orleans, and Miami's well on its way to being just Miami."

Joe lived in Miami. To the best of Michael's understanding, he was the agent in charge there.

Michael shook his head. "*New York is its own thing?* Joe, please."

Any number of tourists taking snapshots of the Unisphere with their Brownies and their Instamatics were now capturing Michael Corleone and a bushy-haired man in the corner of the frame. Michael would have been unsurprised to learn that among the tourists was an FBI photographer in short pants, flanked by nonunion actors hired to pretend to be his family.

"I didn't mean it like that," Joe said. "I mean that New York's a case apart. You people think of the rest of the world as your goddamned farm club. New Orleans isn't on an island, and it doesn't have the superior attitude, but it's also a place where—"

"I've known you more than half my life, Joe," Michael said. "You're a dear friend, and I put up with things from you I'm not sure I'd put up with from family. These wiseass routines in search of a straight man are just who you are, but cut it out. I'm in no mood."

Joe gave Michael a look. Michael stared him down and then, reluctantly, nodded in concession. It was Joe who was doing him the favor.

"Maybe this is a better way to get at it," Joe said. "Remember when your nephew was playing college ball, and you'd see all these men in the stands with clipboards and stopwatches, and you knew that some of them were scouting for bookies, some for pro teams, some for another school coming up on the schedule, and plenty of them were bullshit artists. Some, God knows, just liked the sound of hearing their lives tick away. A few were crazies who'd convinced themselves they had ties to some pro team. They'd mail these detailed reports faithfully every week to someone at the Eagles or Giants or whichever, who never took the time to call them up and tell them to cut it out. Even if you dug into who these men all were, a few would be simple to verify, but you'd never figure it perfectly. There'd be legit pro scouts who also worked for bookies, for example. There'd be skilled liars and liars who didn't know they were lying. You understand me, Mike? That's what I'm trying to tell you about New Orleans."

"Neither you nor anyone else in your company is working with my friends down there. Is that right?"

"Jesus Christ, are you hearing me? New Orleans is a colorful place, but it's all gray."

Michael clasped his hands behind his back as he walked. He had an uncanny ability to tell when even seasoned liars were lying, and he felt sure Joe was telling him the truth: that because of the nature of the place and of the intelligence business at present, Joe was shut off from figuring out what was going on.

"At a certain point in life," Joe said, "a man has to accept that ability and experience are disposable. Sometimes all that matters is that they're them and you're you and that's it. I don't have to tell you. You went to school with Ivy League fucks," which he said a little too loudly and several passersby glared at him, including a Puerto Rican woman who actually clamped her hands over her daughter's ears.

It was the kind of thing that got people noticed.

Michael tapped Joe's elbow and steered him down the road toward the Kodak exhibit, which looked like a four-hundred-foot-long oval of undulating dough, made of cement and yet somehow levitating a few feet off the ground. Atop it was a rotating pentagon, each side of which featured a photograph about four stories high: the five largest color photos in the world. The one facing them seemed to be of a Japanese warrior.

"Things have changed," Joe said. "I'm not in this line of work for the chance to file fifty-six-page operational plans with the appropriate wise men every time I need a drainage ditch blown up. Or to get second-guessed before the literal dust settles. That plan we worked on together, your people and mine, it came from the wise men. That's how they think. They labor under the *great man* theory, because that's what they learned at Yale, and that's how they see themselves. Each one: a big, indispensable man."

"The plan had its merits," Michael said, which wasn't exactly a lie. The plan itself was crazy. Michael had expected it to fail. From the ashes of that failure, he'd expected something good to pin on Geraci. And cash. If, against the odds, it had worked, the silver lining would have been that the Corleones would get their casinos back. Win-win. "After all," Michael said, "there's that old saying, if you want to kill a snake, chop off the head, not the tail."

"Never heard it. I'm a city boy like you. I know jack shit about killing snakes, but it seems like chopping off the bottom half would do the trick, too. But why focus on just one snake, is my point. There's always another snake. Why not drain the swamp? Kill the habitat."

"Other creatures use the same habitat, though, right?"

A huge sad clown stared down at them from the tower.

They took the escalator to the roof.

As they rose, Joe stood close to Michael's ear. "All we needed to do," he said, just above a whisper, "was mount a guerrilla war, island-wide. If we involved your men, it should have been for their proven skills with fire and explosives. Burn the cane fields, the tobacco fields, blow up the copper mines, then smuggle out TV footage of the fires and angry *gusanos* playing to the cameras. The world wouldn't have stood for it. They'd have thought the insurgency was bigger than it was because it looked big on TV. And, bim, bam, boom, it's over. You gents are back in business, and I'm off to the next adventure. Everybody's happy. Instead, we have now."

The surface was a hodgepodge of fountains, sloping sidewalks, rooftop gardens, and clearly marked backdrops for snapshots. PICTURE SPOT, the signs read. The tower was on one end; on the other were smooth, white twenty-foot-tall cement stalagmites meant to evoke the surface of the moon. They headed toward the moonscape.

"What's all this have to do with New Orleans, Joe?"

"New Orleans?" he said, frowning. "Nothing. Everything. Everything's connected, Mike. Goddamn."

Joe stopped to light a cigarette and offered Michael one, which he declined.

"All right," Michael said. "And so what about the missing package?"

Joe put his smokes and lighter away, and they kept walking. "I already answered that."

"Say again? If you did, I missed it."

He took a deep drag of the cigarette. "I don't know what to tell you," Lucadello said, teeth clenched and growing red in the face, "that I haven't said already."

Michael put his arm around his old friend and they started through the moonscape.

"I'll be blunt," Michael finally said. "The wild-goose chase needs to stop."

"I'm being blunt, too. You're not listening. You're missing my point. I'm not sure I can say it any more directly than I have."

"Try," Michael said.

From where Michael now stood he could see the Garden of Meditation below and, just beyond it, the Van Wyck Expressway. His bodyguards were positioned on opposite ends of the rooftop.

"This simple answer is we don't know. The simple answer is that I have not, nor to my knowledge have any other agents, seen your boy since those first few days he was in Sicily. These are the facts. What this could mean is that he's dead—by his own hand, natural causes, or what have you. In my personal opinion, it's more likely that he's found a good place to hide on that island, in which case your guess as to where he is will be better than mine. Your resources and your connections there are better than mine, not to mention your better understanding of the culture, even the terrain. Historically speaking, men have found Sicily a magnificent place to hide. Is his wife there with him? We don't know. There is some evidence to suggest yes. We don't know where she is exactly, either. Is this what you're looking for when you ask me to be direct?"

Which was when it finally hit Michael that Joe Lucadello, a man who knew things for a living, probably knew nothing for certain except that he'd been used by his superiors, by his *country*, as a pawn.

"Do you have any idea," Michael said, "any idea whatsoever, where the leaks are coming from?"

"I was sorry to hear about those kids from Calabria. The . . . " Joe stopped himself and bowed and shook his head. "I don't know," he said, "but even if I did, you know I'd have to say I didn't. I can tell you this: if there *is* a leak, the smart money says it's in your house and not mine. Common sense decrees, as the saying goes. But I'm also saying that things are complicated right now."

"Meaning the end of the line."

"The end of the line *segment*," Joe said. "Lines don't end. That's the main thing that makes them lines."

"But line segments end."

"They do," Joe said. "Goddamned right they do."

The expression, no doubt, came from railroad lines, but Michael had no reason to point this out. He thanked Joe, and the men embraced.

"Look at all this," Joe said, backing away, then turning slowly around in a circle. "What a bill of goods the future is. What are all these saps going to do when the future gets here, and they still don't beat the traffic by flying to work in a jetpack, and they still don't have free electricity in their houses from their own personal nuclear-fusion device, and America still hasn't set foot on the goddamned moon? There has never in human history been a culture where optimism and cynicism existed side by side on such a scale as this, not even ancient Rome."

"Do you mean New York?" Michael said. "Or America?"

"Touché." Joe winked his glass eye. His face lacked any trace of playfulness.

"Tell me the truth," Michael said, pointing. "*Is* there a camera in there?"

"Even if there was, I'd have to say there wasn't." This time the smile that came over him seemed real. But a moment later it faded. "I'll be goddamned," he said. "You're not joking."

Michael had been, he thought. But before he could say anything, Joe bent slightly and took the eye out. It made a sucking sound, and in one smooth motion he jammed it into the pocket of Michael's shirt.

"See for yourself."

Joe made no attempt to close his empty eye socket. It was pink and vaguely, grotesquely sexual. Michael didn't flinch and couldn't stop looking into it. As Joe reached inside his jacket, the bodyguards broke into a run. But all Joe pulled out was a pair of dark green sunglasses. The bodyguards stopped. Their running had attracted stares from the other visitors on the roof.

"Let me know if you find anything, my friend," Joe said. He patted Michael on the cheek and then, harder, on the pocket where the eye was. "Maybe send me a snapshot." He turned and headed alone toward the escalator, the exaggerated stiffness in his posture gone now, replaced with a carriage not unlike the exhausted hero at the end of a good Western. Michael wondered if that, too, was some kind of pose.

Michael ignored the stares of the bystanders and waited for his old friend to disappear—his oldest friend, it occurred to him. He did not pull out the eye, but he could feel it in his pocket, more dense, much heavier than he'd have guessed. Michael's ears were burning. Handing over that eye had been such a strange gesture that it only now registered as a terrible act of disrespect. Worse: a wiseass's version of the evil eye. He closed his fist around the eye, hard. He should shove this thing down Joe Lucadello's throat, or up his ass.

He motioned to the bodyguards. They said nothing about the eye. Protocol was for men this lowly not to speak to a boss unless spoken to.

They stopped at a men's room on the way to the Vatican City pavilion. Michael told one of the men to stand at the door and say the john was out of order and he took the other inside and asked for his gun. Again, simple protocol.

Michael stood before the sink. With his handkerchief, he took the eye out of his pocket. It was not gruesome. The detail was amazing. That someone could make something like this by hand seemed like a miracle. It was shaped more like an egg than a ball.

He wrapped the handkerchief around the eye and set it on the counter, then pulled out the gun and checked the safety. With his left hand he held the edge of the handkerchief. With his right, he gripped the gun by the barrel, raised it above his head, and with all his strength brought the butt of it down on the eye. The guard at the door stuck his head in. Michael hammered the eye with the gun again and again and everything became a blur, and when he stopped he was sweating and out of breath.

He opened the handkerchief. No camera, of course. It still looked a little like an eye, tiny particles and thin broken glass rods and a dozen or so glass chips, thicker and more rounded than Michael would have thought.

On impulse he pocketed the biggest piece.

He left the rest on the counter and washed his face and combed his hair.

His white hair, which always made the man in the mirror seem unfamiliar. He looked down at the mess and only then realized that the initials on the handkerchief weren't his. They were Fredo's.

MINUTES LATER, ALONG WITH HUNDREDS OF STRANGERS, A sliver of his diminished family, and a woman he was starting to think it might be possible to love, Michael Corleone boarded one of the three motorized platforms in the *Pietà* exhibit and trolled slowly past the spotlighted crucified Christ in the white marble arms of his mother. To bring such beauty to life, as Michelangelo had, was beyond all human understanding. To bring it to America was something much more modest, but it had nonetheless involved months of delicate negotiations and a tremendous number of exchanged favors and cash tributes. It was, Michael Corleone told himself, in and of itself the accomplishment of a lifetime.

During the fair's run, this year and next, Michael Corleone would rarely set foot in the other parts of the pavilion—the chapel on the mezzanine, the exhibit explaining the Catholic sacraments, the replica of the excavation made underneath St. Peter's Basilica (underneath this replica, Michael knew, was garbage). But Michael would return to see the *Pietà* countless times, before and after its normal business hours, alone and with others, on the platforms and strolling at his own pace on the crowded walkway. Anytime he'd see so much as a pull tab or a straw wrapper—anything at all to mar the site—he'd pick it up himself and throw it away. Above the statue were eighty-two spotlights arranged in a halo, and he would sometimes marvel to strangers that there seemed to be light coming from within that white stone, too: a piece of rock, dug from the humble soil of Italy, transformed by Italian hands into this vision of unspeakable beauty. Michael no longer prayed. He had not been to confession in fifteen years, and he doubted he would ever go again, but the *Pietà* would never lose the power to move him.

Often, as now, Michael Corleone wept.

CHAPTER 23

Charlotte Geraci dropped off the rental car at the airport and took a cab down Highway 61 into the city of New Orleans. It was mid-morning. She'd been driving nearly nonstop for two days. She was road-haggard and still wearing the wig, still looking behind her every few seconds, as she had the entire way from Saratoga. The cabbie asked if she was OK, if he could get her a glass of water or an aspirin. "I'm fine," she lied. "I'm just tired." When the cabbie asked if it was her first trip to New Orleans, she lied and said no. It seemed like the answer most likely to shut him up.

Nick was waiting for her in a slightly faded grand hotel on Poydras Street. She was getting there exhausted and famished—she'd been too frightened to stop for anything but gas and a few crummy snacks and Pepsi-Cola. She also had no luggage, which, along with the wig, made her feel like a whore. She went in the ladies' room off the lobby and brushed her teeth, washed her face, and dabbed at her underarms.

She took the elevator to the room.

"I'm sorry, little lady," Nick said, doing a corny John Wayne imitation. "You're an awfully darned purty *brunette*, but my *blonde* wife is a-ridin' into town on the next stage."

It was a regular room, not a suite.

"I'm looking for my husband, actually," Charlotte said. "Maybe you've seen him. He's a man with no beard." She tugged on it. He'd had it for nearly three years, yet she'd never seen it. He'd sent her those reel-to-reel tapes—dozens of them—but he'd never once in the time he was gone sent her a photo.

They stood in the doorway. Despite the jokes about her wig and his beard, they were sincerely flummoxed by the reality of standing there, together, after so long.

"You're real, right?" She poked him as if he might be a ghost her finger would pass through.

That did the trick. They fell into an embrace, spinning around and kicking the door closed.

Their shoes and clothes flew and moments later they were in bed. It did not go well. She was exhausted and could have used a shower and they were both fumbling and shaking. They'd done it because the situation had seemed to call for it. It was so clumsy and bad that afterward Nick threw a glass against the wall in frustration and Charlotte went into a fetal ball with the sheets pulled tight around her.

Things looked up from there. There was pink champagne on ice. It was still morning, but they drank about half of it. He gave her a painted wooden box full of Mexican jewelry, which she loved, and a gift-wrapped copy of Chet Baker's *Chet*, which confused her—she'd heard the name Chet Baker, she said, but didn't know the music. "You'll love it," he said, "it's a thing of beauty, like you. Not to mention, look at the cover." It was a picture of Baker in a beige sweater, gorgeous and haunted and looking right at the camera, and a blonde woman in a black sweater behind him, eyes closed, face nuzzled against the back of his neck, oozing unspeakable sadness, as if she knows she'll never be able to help tame the handsome man's demons. She'll never even know what his demons are.

"It's you," he said.

She was wiped out from the drive and the fear and the bad sex, and the champagne was going to her head. It took her a moment to register that he meant that the woman *looked* like her.

"Oh, sweetheart," she said. "She doesn't look anything like me."

"Because you're better-looking," he said.

"Sure," she said, shaking her head. "That's the difference."

Charlotte had a long nap and got up to take a shower.

While she was in the bathroom, Nick looked at the size of her clothes and called the place Augie Tramonti had recommended. Nick described her to the person on the phone—"Forty-four years old but youthful, elegant, classy, not too flashy but only more beautiful because of it, sort of like a cross between Audrey Hepburn and the First Lady, only blonde."

"Who were you talking to?" Charlotte said. The rooms didn't come with robes, but she was wearing his.

"Nobody," he said.

"Your girlfriend?"

"Don't even joke about a thing like that."

She shrugged.

Within twenty minutes, a woman from the store arrived and wheeled in a cart with all kinds of clothes in Charlotte's size. Charlotte had come to New Orleans with only what she could fit in a large summer purse. She melted. She picked out a few things—surprisingly nice things, so far from New York, which Nick thought sounded snobbish but which didn't visibly offend the woman. Charlotte asked if they could really afford this, and Nick told her not to worry about it. (Augie had already taken care of the damages, which Nick did not say.) They got dressed up and went for a long walk in the French Quarter. She asked him how he could just walk around in the open like this in a major American city. He told her that it was a long story, but the short version was that nobody Nick was concerned with, nobody connected with anybody other than certain powers that be here in New Orleans, could even set foot in the state of Louisiana without getting permission from a friend of Nick's.

He didn't mention Carlo Tramonti by name. And Charlotte didn't ask for more details. It was something he loved about her.

They had a magnificent meal at Galatoire's and came back to their hotel with a bottle of red wine. Nick shaved his beard for her, unbidden. She seemed to appreciate the gesture. They talked deep into the night, catching up on the two years they could never really recover and easing back into bed together twice more, with demonstrably better results.

The next morning, Charlotte Geraci sat up in bed, doing a crossword puzzle. Though a gap in the hotel curtains, a sliver of morning light cut across the bed. Beside her, in a white undershirt and blue silk pajama bottoms, Nick slept. Charlotte was naked and on top of the covers. Nick had clothes on and was under them. She was tanned, even though she was a natural blonde and until a few days ago had been in New York—where, true, it had been a nice spring and she'd spent a lot of time sunning herself beside her heated pool. She was forty-four years old; her tan lines came from a bikini, in which she did not look at all foolish. Though Nick was Sicilian on both sides, he'd always been fair-haired enough to pass for Irish or English, and he was paler now than when Charlotte had last seen him, despite having spent the last two years in the tropics. The bottom part of his face was whiter yet. Without the beard he looked more like himself, though in truth only slightly so. The muscles of his face were slack from the Parkinson's. He did not look only three years older than his wife.

Nick woke. He reached over and softly traced the curve of his wife's breast. It was a sight that, not unreasonably, he'd feared he would never see again. Her breast. But come to think of it, the crossword puzzles, too. She did them only when something was bothering her. It was one of the subtle delights of marriage, knowing a person this well, enduring long enough that quirks and strange habits go from intriguing to maddening and finally to oddly comforting. Nick could feel the heat of that shaft of sunlight through the sheets.

"I hated you," Charlotte said, not looking at him.

"Good morning to you, too," he said, pulling her to him.

It was their first morning together in almost three years.

"I understand that I should blame the people who did this to you," she said. "And I do. But it's hard. I don't know the whole story. It's hard not to just blame you for what this has done to our family."

"We've been over this," Nick said. "Our family's fine. The girls are strong. You've done a great job with those girls. We'll all come out OK. I'll make it up to you. To you, to them. I really am inching my way back, honey. You've got to believe this."

She tossed the crossword puzzle book aside and shrugged off his grasp. "Twice now, Nick. You disappeared on us *twice* now. You think some few-and-far-between phone calls and one long night on the town covers it? Some *tapes* of you talking on and on about jazz and world events and the books you're reading? We *haven't* been over it, Nick. We haven't been over the half of it. The one-hundredth of it. I love you, I do, but I hated you, too. Listen to me. Understand this. I really don't think—don't look at me like that. I really don't think you *realize* what it's been like for me."

Whatever sort of disapproving look she thought he'd been giving her was probably a result of the Parkinson's. He'd actually been studying her breasts, the tan line, thinking what a lucky guy he was, how good it would be when this all blew over. He was, on the other hand, concerned that she'd been wearing a bathing suit like that, that there might be another man. But he didn't believe that. She wouldn't dare, probably wouldn't even want to. He held out his hand, conceding the floor. "I'm listening," he said. "I'm all ears."

"I'm scared, and I'm alone, and I feel like I can't control my own life," she said. "I'm just a prop in this big production, Nick's Wild Ride. I have to do everything, your jobs around the house and mine, too. You think the girls are fine, but they're not fine. They need their father. Barb is angry, which I know you know. I know you think you'll be coming back soon, that we'll be coming back soon, but I hate to think of her alone in our house, waiting for me to come back, waiting for you, and just steaming in it. And Bev. Bev worships you—never a bad word, always defending you like her life depends on it. Bev's the one I'm really worried about. Maybe you've been gone too long to know about the kind of things that go on in California these days, especially on the college campuses out there, but it's terrifying to think about how she might be falling into some of those things. She's staying with your dad for the summer, thank God, but after that she'll be right back with the beatniks and the freethinkers and dope smokers and whatever else is there for her in Berkeley. I'm trying not to blame you for anything, but how could it not be a good thing for her, at her age, to have her father around, in her life more?"

"Give me a minute here," Nick said, and went to go take a leak and brush his teeth.

This was not like Charlotte. She kept things in. Last night, they'd talked at dinner and late into the night, too, in between making love again. But what they'd been talking about was mostly news, catching up on things, including all the details of Charlotte's trip. She'd driven, by herself. She'd walked out the back door of the restaurant in a dark wig and walked across town to pick up her rental car, afraid to look over her shoulder the whole way. Once she'd gotten in the car, she kept looking in her rearview, scared out of her wits, for well over a thousand miles. She'd been afraid to stop, and her fear had kept her from needing to, other than for gas and Pepsi-Cola. But the way Charlotte was talking now was different. By Nick's stars, it was fine. She was entitled. He had it coming. But it wasn't like her. Nick's mother had been a big talker, all the time yammering her complaints about Fausto and other emotional matters, talking to Nick like he was an adult, a confidante instead of just a boy. Nick was devoted to his mother until the end, but he thought she was a handful, too. He'd seen how his mother's candor in public had hurt his father's prospects with the Forlenza organization back in Cleveland. She'd turned Fausto's own son against him, in his own house. She hadn't meant to, Nick knew that. She had a good heart. She and Fausto had a terrific marriage, as such things go. Still, Nick had been determined to marry a woman as good-hearted as his mother and as smart, but with more control over what she said and where. He'd succeeded, too. Charlotte was just sore. More than that, she was scared, and she had every right to be. They were both struggling to act like themselves—they had been ever since she'd arrived. It would take time.

"You're right about the girls," he said when he came back. "I know that. But, you know, I do talk to Bev, maybe more than you think. She's the only one of you who still sends me those tapes. I still send 'em to her, too. If you're on dope, it comes through in your voice. She's not on dope, she's doing well with her studies, and so forth. She's been raised right, Char, and that's because of you, too. A strong person doesn't automatically become what she's surrounded by. Castles are surrounded by moats, too, but it doesn't mean the princess is drowning."

Charlotte considered this a moment and then laughed.

Nick laughed, too. "OK, well, all I'm trying to say is that I'm not as in the dark as you seem to think."

"Maybe. I don't know." Charlotte folded her arms across her chest. "The fact remains that Bev needs more of you than she's getting. I'm never going to be able to get through to her the way you do, and that's just how it is. The fact remains that over the past three years every time she and I went at it like cats and dogs, I hated you for it. I admit it. I hate myself for feeling like that, but who can I talk to? Not even Father DiTrilio in confession, since I'm supposed to be in mourning for you. I could confess *that* to him, too, I know, but I can't. I wouldn't. I'm supposed to be behaving to the whole world like you're dead. I've had to do everything. Everything. I need a spider killed, no Nick. It's me. Barb and Bev bring their boyfriends over, and I have to pull them aside and figure out their intentions, because there's no Nick. My father dies, and I go to the funeral alone, because that's the way I do everything. Not to mention the bills. Money's very, very tight. Do you know that I'm cutting the grass myself now? I am. Don't *look* at me like that, I said."

Again, he had been studying her tan lines, particularly the ones the bottom had left. Also the curve of her hips, the way her bush was much more sparse than he'd remembered. He shook his head.

She apparently misinterpreted this as his dismay over her complaints about money. "I *know* what you're thinking," she said.

"I'm not thinking anything," he said. Because what could he say, that he was wondering if her bush was going bald? Did that happen to women? It occurred to him that she was the oldest woman he'd ever seen naked. "I'm listening. My undivided attention."

Charlotte sat up now, leaning toward him on the bed. "I know that you think I'm fixated on material things, that money's what I think about all the time, but it's not. I've been here almost twenty-four hours, and this is the first time I've mentioned money, OK? Think about it. All the times when we talked on the phone, when did I ask you about money if you didn't bring it up first? Never. Not once. But I've got news for you. We're broke, Nick. Our savings are gone. I've had to borrow money from my dad. I understand that people are watching me, that sending someone to the house with a big envelope every week isn't—"

"I don't have anyone I can send," Nick said. "Much less anything to put in those theoretical envelopes. I really thought it would work with the life insurance," by which he meant getting him declared dead and collecting and then repaying it if he ever surfaced: it had seemed like the greatest interest-free-loan scam this side of the Teamsters' pension fund. "But there are other things I can work out for us. There's some stocks you can sell, or the girls can. I can get word to them how to do it. Plus, my dad can wire money to the girls, too."

"You're going to throw this back in my face." She grabbed the sheets and pulled them up to her throat, covering herself. "I can tell by the way you're looking at me."

"When did I ever say that all you care about is money?"

"Countless times."

"Honestly, I can't think of a single time," Nick said.

"Please."

"Maybe a few times," he said, "but not countless. But look. Get it straight. I didn't *disappear*. Both times I was gone, you knew where I was, and if you didn't know *exactly* where, it was for your own protection. I'm sorry for what was hard about this for you, I've told you that a million times, but none of this is a surprise to you, Char. There's nothing about my life you didn't know about long before we got married. I'm never going to become one of these hypocrites who think that instead of what they do they're going to pretend they're really J. Paul Getty or a black-sheep Rockefeller or something. You're married to a soldier, end of discussion. I know you, Char. I know you'd *rather* be married to a soldier than some pencil-necked empty suit. And you know as well as I do that there are times a soldier's going to be gone."

"You call what you've been through gone? It's been beyond gone. You're legally dead, or you would be, if people on Michael Corleone's payroll hadn't gummed up the process."

Nick asked if that was what her lawyer had said, if he had any specifics.

"Not that he can pin on anyone. But he's sure, and so am I. As you say, there's nothing about your life I haven't known for a long time."

Nick got up and ordered them room service. He ordered eggs Benedict for her without asking. It was what she'd ordered the first morning of their honeymoon. At a level just below conscious thought, he presumed this would all register with her—his taking charge, his remembering. It became conscious only when he hung up and she stood up and kissed him.

"Whatever happened to retire?" she said, her voice thick with yearning. "That you'd retire? Key West, we talked about. Maybe Miami Beach. New Orleans, I don't know about. But soldiers do retire, right?"

"I'm forty-seven years old," he said. "You want me to retire and do what? Mope around the house? Your father worked until he was what, ninety?"

"Seventy-one. He was a master carpenter, Nick. A lot of them never really retire at all."

"Same in my line of work. Question: you don't know about New Orleans why? What makes you so quick to judge New Orleans? You been here less than a day, Char. Keep an open mind. You'll love it, believe me. The place grows on you."

"What, like mold? It's damp here, everywhere. You're not honestly thinking of staying here, are you? Permanently?"

"It's the damp season. Key West is damp, too, you know. I like this place better than Key West, I can tell you that."

"Key West is a different kind of damp than this. New Orleans seems like the proverbial great place to visit."

He laughed. "As opposed to home, right?"

Charlotte used to joke that East Islip was a great place to live but you wouldn't want to visit there. "Exactly," she said. "As opposed to home."

"Get dressed," he said. He'd had her meet him here, but he was staying at a house Carlo Tramonti was letting him borrow and maybe even buy. "I got something I want to show you."

She brightened. "Really?" she said. "Can I read it?"

"Read what?"

"Your book."

"My what?"

"Your book."

His mind had been on the house and whether she'd like it, and so at first he really hadn't known what she was talking about. But it came back to him now. In a moment of weakness last night, under the cover of darkness and alcohol, he'd confessed to her that he was writing a book. He couldn't recall what had prompted this. Probably it was because, when they first started dating, she'd been a secretary for a publishing company. Nick had gotten to know her indirectly, via her boss, who was having some financial problems. Charlotte had actually moved to New York from western Pennsylvania to become a writer herself, which was ironic because, unlike him, she barely read books anymore. Still, it was probably natural that when a man and a woman reunite or are having trouble or both, they hearken back to the time they fell in love.

Maybe Nick had been trying to win her back, even though she was already here.

More and more, it became apparent to him that he should stop drinking. "Well?" she said.

"You can read it when it's finished," Nick said. "Which will be soon."

ONLY A FEW WEEKS EARLIER, NICK HAD SAILED TO SICILY, but he hadn't stayed long. Charlotte had been to Sicily, too, but not recently. Nick had made sure that Lucadello knew where he was, so that, as per his orders from his superiors, he'd feel duty-bound to feed this information to the Corleones. In due time.

The two snapshots of Charlotte had been taken during a family vacation three years ago. Over the course of Nick's fugitive years, they'd become holy objects to him. He'd kept them pristine, and he'd have sacrificed them for little else but to help reunite him with her. The third photo was recent. The woman in the photo was wearing a blonde wig to look like Charlotte. Her name was Gabriella. She'd met Nick at a café in Taormina, and they'd walked to the hotel together. The photographer was waiting for them. She tilted her face away from the camera. He made them walk to the door three times just to make sure he had what he needed. The photographer was a distant cousin on Nick's father's side, a wing of the family that Fausto had looked up when he'd last visited the island, the maneuver that sent Nick into hiding in the first place. Gabriella was his wife. No one else seemed to be watching them. She hurried into her brother's car and shed the wig. She and her husband, whose name was Sebastiano D'Andrea, were staying in a hotel across town.

Nick checked in and paid in advance for the room: a week, cash. He overtipped the bellman who carried his suitcase to his room. For a couple days, Nick made a point of being seen around town, chatting up barmen and shopkeepers. He said he was an American businessman looking to buy a secluded vacation hideaway, and he went to see a few properties to make this look good.

Sebastiano developed the photos himself, in the bathtub. Nick picked the one he liked best. Gabriella helped him with the note, to make sure it sounded like a native speaker. Sebastiano made some connections at Nick's hotel with the bartender and the head chambermaid, then they all drove back to Palermo together. The next day, Nick sailed for America.

Later, when Nick gave the word, Sebastiano had mailed the note. In short order, both the bartender and the chambermaid gave Sebastiano a description of the men who'd come around asking about a bearded American and his blonde wife, flashing the same photo of Nick and Gabriella entering the hotel that Sebastiano had already shown them. The Calabrians were not guests there. The bartender and the maid owed them nothing.

The Calabrians had been recommended for the job by a zip in Nobilio's crew. What Tommy Neri hadn't known was that, a few years earlier, these same Calabrians had killed the zip's uncle. According to Momo Barone, the zip's chance at revenge had been more important to him than any loyalty he owed to Michael Corleone.

The zip's father—the brother of the dead uncle—had the grim pleasure of overseeing the ambush and shipping pieces of them to America.

WHAT NICK TOOK CHARLOTTE TO SEE WAS THEIR HOUSE, which also seemed to him the kind of place newlyweds would live: a modest shotgun affair on Dauphine Street, freshly painted and with a new screened-in porch and window air conditioners, a few blocks east of the French Quarter. "I have to admit," Charlotte said, enchanted despite herself, it seemed, "that this seems like the very definition of a quiet little place away from it all. Or at least, away from *all that*."

In a remarkably short time, she settled in.

In no time, she and Nick again became something like themselves.

The Tramontis owned the whole block, and the one next to it as well, and everyone in every house had some connection to them. Charlotte

didn't know this at first, and by the time she made friends with some of
the other wives in the neighborhood, by the time she'd have been able to
put two and two together, she was back to her old self. She knew what she
knew, and she didn't talk about it. She kept the house spotless. She took
perverse pleasure in the Sisyphean task of beating back the tide of unfamiliar vermin: little green frogs and lizards; swarms of flies, bees, wasps,
and mosquitoes, too many for the frogs and lizards to repel; the unavoidable, euphemistically named palmetto bugs; pamphlet-wielding evangeli-
cals in ties and short-sleeved white shirts. It was a way of keeping her mind
off other worries.

She and Nick bickered about nothing serious all the time and never got
truly angry about anything. She encouraged Nick with his writing and told
him how it made the house a home to hear the clacking of that typewriter,
however infrequent it was. He kept the pages and his notes and carbons
locked in a steel Confederate States of America footlocker he'd bought in
an antiques store on Canal Street. He brought her home a color television
set with teakwood cabinetry and a nineteen-inch screen—the biggest there
was. She told him that, knowing how much he hated TV, it was a gesture
that meant a lot. She bought him books about how to write books. In her
spare time—which she pretended was not all the time—she took out his little reel-to-reel tape recorder and sat on the sofa with an electric fan trained
on her. She closed her eyes and sipped sweet tea and bravely talked to her
daughters about nothing at all until the end of the tape started flapping
from the take-up reel. Then she mailed the tapes to strangers, who forwarded them to her girls, her babies.

NICK GERACI'S JOURNEY TO NEW ORLEANS HAD BEEN
brokered initially by Spratling, the former Mexican jewelry tycoon, who'd
merely put out some feelers, and to a greater extent by the one-eyed man
he'd once known as Ike Rosen.

The CIA agent had shown up in Taxco. Geraci was having lunch alone, enchiladas suizas and a cold beer, in a rooftop café overlooking the cathedral, reading the *New York Times.* "Ever try the iguana?" said the agent. "I hear it's supposed to be an aphrodisiac."

Geraci set down the paper. It took a moment to recognize him without the eye patch. The last time they'd spoken had been outside Geraci's house in East Islip, the meeting that had sent Nick into hiding in the first place. "Tastes like chicken," Geraci said. "Take a load off, why don't you?"

"The beard's a nice touch."

"So's the eye," Nick said. "What do you want from me?"

"Did you really think no one was watching you?" Lucadello said. "Do you really think that you could have gotten anywhere if we didn't want to let you go?"

Geraci certainly did. He'd seen enough of these vainglorious bumblers to think the *I* in CIA was a big joke. Then again, Lucadello had found him here, somehow.

When the waiter came, Lucadello, in fluent Spanish, discussed the way the iguana was prepared and cooked and what all went into the sauce and then ordered it.

"I asked you," Geraci said. "What do you want?"

"You had electricity down in your cave," Lucadello said. "Even a TV for a while. There was an antenna. There were electrical bills. I really hate to burst your balloon about your *daring escape*, because, swear to God, it was just so cute, but"—he winked the glass eye—"we had an eye on you the whole way. You hid underneath a house your godfather owned. When you came out, you went straight to the town where you grew up, you called your father, and he drove you to Mexico. Understandably, this threw some of your associates for a loop, but please understand: I do this for a *living*."

"Congratulations," Geraci said. "Your mother must be very proud. So what next?"

"My supervisors think you're going to kill yourself, can you believe that? That's why I'm here. You fit the profile. The odds are off the charts."

"The profile?"

"Don't take offense. I fit it, too. Men who live by a code who are trapped, who perceive that there is no chance of escape or of resuming their regular lives, have a seventy-one percent chance of attempting suicide. Those who try have a truly amazing eighty-seven percent chance of success. But I told him, them—my supervisors, that is—that you won't do it. Like me, you're in that other twenty-nine percent. You're too egotistical. You're the kind of man who keeps looking at a problem, even an insoluble one, thinking he can fix it. My supervisors disagreed. They sent me here to give you a ray of hope, to make you think you really might be able to see your family again, resume your life, et cetera. So, here I am. To help you."

"You're from the federal government, and you're here to help me. Funny guy."

"I considered killing you," Lucadello said, "and opted for this instead, if that's any consolation."

"It was you who sent that kid to find me," Geraci said.

"What kid?" Lucadello said. "The one in the rug?"

So now we've each killed a Bocchicchio, Nick thought. The CIA hit Carmine in Cuba so Carmine wouldn't talk, Nick was sure of it. Carmine would never have talked. "What rug?" Geraci said.

"Let me be completely straight with you," Lucadello said. "My supervisors want you dead. But it's no good to them if you do it yourself. Also, as you probably know, your . . . I don't know what you'd call him . . . *your* supervisor wants you dead, too. He wants revenge. He'll take it as a slap in the face if anyone else does the job for him. The solution here's pretty elegant, from where we stand. Mr. Corleone has you killed, and then we pin it on him. That way, you're gone, and Mr. Corleone is served up to our friends at the FBI—a gift, a peace offering, a make-good for any bad feelings about those camps you and I helped put together, call it what you will. For personal reasons I'm not going to get into, I'd prefer that this didn't happen. Which is neither here nor there. I'm also a man who follows orders. In this regard, too, maybe you're like me. My orders are to find you. I've found you. Here you are. My orders are to then tell Mr. Corleone exactly where you are. This I will do as well. Forgive me if I think out loud. I suppose I could get into Mexico City sometime tomorrow. Then a day to figure out what flight I want to take, another day to get it approved—government red tape, right? You have no idea. Then there's another day to travel, say maybe a day or two to get in to see such a busy man as Mr. Corleone. At the point that I talk to him, one hundred percent of what I tell him will be true. To the best of my knowledge, you are in this lovely place. Taxco. After that, I imagine it will take another two or three days for the job to get assigned and for the person or persons assigned to do it to travel all the way here. That's what, a week? A week plus? I'm not telling you anything you couldn't figure out yourself. I'm not telling you anything specific. Five to ten days or who knows, maybe more. I don't know how such things work—hits, vendettas, how fast they happen. I'm just thinking aloud, as I said. Oh. Also. As per my orders, I'm pleased to be able to tell you that we're working on it so that you can see your family again. This is the ray of hope we're providing you so that you don't blow your brains out. Blowing your brains out has the highest success rate of any kind of suicide, which I mention apropos of nothing."

"You're a wealth of interesting information," Geraci said. He tapped the folded-up *New York Times* on the table. "If you and I ate lunch together more often, I could cancel my subscription to the paper."

"I think that's in the cards," Lucadello said. "A few more lunches like this."

His iguana came, and he liked the sauce but quickly lost patience with all the little bones.

"Furthermore," Lucadello said, pushing the half-eaten entrée aside, "if for no particular reason you happen to leave here and go somewhere else, we'll know about that, too, and here again, I will follow orders. I will personally confirm where you are, although it's possible that a colleague of mine may contact you to achieve said confirmation, and then as soon as is practical, your new location will be conveyed by some means to Mr. Corleone."

"What you're saying is that you don't want Michael Corleone to kill me."

"I'm saying that I'm following orders."

"And that you're not going to kill me, either, or have me killed."

"Who can predict the future?"

"You're going to keep me running, and you're going to keep them running after me. That's what you're saying, right? How long can that last?"

"Piece of advice." Now Lucadello tapped the folded-up paper. "If you're so fixated on the future, maybe you should buy a different newspaper. One that runs horoscopes. I could ask you the same sort of things, you know? I could ask you how long you intend to sit around all day listening to records and picking on kids half your age. I could ask you how long it's going to take you to work out a scheme to fix your unfixable situation. I could ask you to guess how high a priority this matter will be for my supervisors once the next big world crisis arises, which it will, just a matter of time. I could ask you to guess how long the average field operative stays in the field before the wise men make it clear that there's a desk in his immediate future. But I don't ask you these things, because I'm not here to discuss the future. This," and he reached up and rapped on his glass eye with his index finger, "is not a crystal ball."

Geraci pointed to the iguana with his fork and arched his eyebrows. "You're not going to finish that?"

Lucadello slid it to him.

"I've got two more questions," Geraci said, pulling iguana vertebrae from his mouth. His hands shook, just a little. "Neither of them require you to use, as you've said, a crystal ball. Question number one is why you don't get rid of me and make it look like a suicide, or just send someone to do the job and then vanish. I'd be surprised if you lacked the expertise. And question number two is—"

"—why am I telling you all this? Right?"

Nick shrugged and reached for a tortilla.

"I need you to trust me," Lucadello said, sitting back in his chair. "And

I know you don't. You'd be a fool if you did. We worked together well when we were training those men in New Jersey, but you don't even know my name. You don't know if maybe I've gone off the reservation on this. You don't know if maybe I'm not even with the company anymore. For all you know, I'm a crazy one-eyed freelance mercenary with sociopathic tendencies. I'm not, of course. The eye notwithstanding. I'm being this candid with you because candor and truth accelerate the creation of trust, not for any other reason. If I can, in fact, build a little trust, my thinking is, it snowballs. You take the information I give you, and you see that it's the truth, and you act accordingly. The more you can take what I say at face value, the more predictable your reaction will be. That's what I want. In addition, I don't have any good reason not to be this candid with you. In the eyes of a lot of important people, you're a dead man, or destined to be one soon, by your own hand or someone else's. Nothing in your profile suggests that you're remotely likely to cooperate with the FBI or go making wild accusations to these folks," he said, again tapping the newspaper.

Geraci spit out a few more iguana bones into his napkin and signaled for the waiter to bring him another beer.

"It's your other question that really interests me," Lucadello said. "What a fascinating glimpse into the way you think. Because this is where we're so different, you and me. We each have this code, but mine is written down. Mine is the law of the land. I'm not going to have a *job* done on you for the simple reason that I have no legal means of doing so. It's against the law. I'm not a lawbreaker, period. It's amazing to me that you don't understand that, Nick. Don't you see? I'm one of the good guys. The white hats. We shave, we love God, we sleep well at night, and in the end, we get the girl." He laughed. "Which is fortunate, I guess, in case that lizard really is an aphrodisiac."

"Good luck to you," Geraci said. "Lot of pretty girls in town. Whether they'll be eager to fuck a one-eyed good guy in a cheap suit, time will tell."

Lucadello tossed money on the table—regulations prevented Geraci from picking up his tab—and he stood and bent over toward Geraci's ear.

"Don't get fancy," Lucadello said. "Fool me once, shame on you. Fool me twice, *vaffanculo*. Up your ass."

Geraci nodded. "I know what it means, *paisan'*."

NOT LONG AFTER NICK ARRIVED IN NEW ORLEANS, HE MET with Carlo "the Whale" Tramonti for the one and only time, at the Don's vast hunting preserve he had in the bayous west of New Orleans. Augie the Midget, who would be Nick's contact here, drove him, in a yellow Cadillac with the brake and gas pedals modified so that he could reach them.

Augie and Nick sat outside a decaying antebellum mansion on tulip-backed metal chairs, as a wild peccary Carlo Tramonti himself had shot with a machine gun rotated on a spit. He'd shot the thing up enough that he'd needed baling wire to keep the carcass from falling apart. The mansion itself had been part of a sugar and timber plantation and had been unoccupied for years until Carlo bought it for what he vaguely called "tax reasons." Carlo was in charge of the grilling of the pig, too. Augie did most of the talking. Their brother Joe had an easel set up and was painting the scene—pig in the foreground, mansion behind it, no people, and, unlike today, a raging black storm bearing down. Carlo was constantly getting up and down to baste the pig or inject it with gigantic hypodermic needles, marinades and spices he said were family secrets.

In the distance there was almost constant shooting. "Target practice," Augie said.

"Isn't that rifle fire?" Geraci said.

"We got a firing range. It's all farther away than you think. Don't worry nothin' about it. Coffee?"

"Is it the kind with chicory in it?"

Carlo chuckled.

"It's got family secrets in it, too," Augie explained, pouring them each a mug. "Our own blend. We're importers. It's roasted in a warehouse not far from the place you're stayin' at."

"For which you have my deep and sincere gratitude." Nick raised the mug in a toast. "The house and this delicious coffee both."

"We thank you, too," Joe said, looking up from his canvas.

Nick had recently overseen a simple problem for him, vending machines and jukeboxes from some distant source cropping up in several businesses out by the interstate. "Glad to be of service," Geraci said.

The men all lit up cigars. Joe and Carlo stopped what they'd been doing, and they all sat down together.

"We just want to be clear on some things," Augie said, "so there ain't misunderstandings later. First and foremost is sanctuary. That's what you got with us now, the term we use for it. We don't grant this too often—in fact, I can't remember the last time. We can promise you that in your time here we won't grant it to nobody else, either, meaning no friends of yours from New York or nowhere else will be showing up unannounced. Or showing up at all, if they're showing us the proper respect. As for the issue of your couriers or contacts, what have you, my brothers and I talked it over, and we can grant you that, too."

"Thank you," Geraci said. Momo Barone and Renzo Sacripante had found men they trusted to do this.

"What you should do," Augie said, "is give us three days' notice. Either me or Joe here'll assign someone to escort 'em around while they're here, meaning never out of their sight, meaning *never*. They need to piss, they got company doin' it. You got secrets, unfortunately these men'll hear 'em. They'll be trustworthy, don't worry about that there. This might not be what you see as an ideal situation, but it's how it's got to be. Speak now if you got problems."

Nick shook his head.

Carlo Tramonti reached over and put a hand on Nick's shoulder, squeezing it the way a grandfather marvels at his grandson's muscles. "You seem like a nice fella," he said. "Maybe we'll get to be friends. Right now, we ain't friends yet. Right now, we're men with common interests. We need to take care of the disrespect Michael Corleone has shown us. The situation I had with the government, it would have never happened if old Bud Payton was president, the way nature intended, which is water over the bridge and under the dam, OK? We accept that. What our beef is with Mr. Corleone is none of your concern. We won't ask nothing from you in connection with it. My advice to you is, the less curious you are about it, the better. We want you to know this, however: I did business with Vito Corleone, I worked with him in certain things, and I see you, Mr. Nick, as someone more in that vein. Someone we'd be happy to work with. We pledge our support for you to take over as boss of that Family—if, God forbid, anything happened to Mr. Corleone. If anything did happen, who else even *could* take over? We looked into it some, the answer is nobody. You'd ride through the streets of Brooklyn like a hero to the rescue. We've got two conditions. One is that you never say a word about anything you see in Louisiana outside Louisiana. Two is that you do some work for us while you're here. Simple things, things that pay the bills, more or less along the lines of how you helped out my brother. Shouldn't be nothin' for a man of your talents."

Nick agreed to everything.

He and the three Tramonti brothers embraced. To celebrate, they hacked off a few chunks of the pig above its shoulder and started eating while bloody juice crackled on the coals below, the bulk of the pig still turning on the spit.

Afterward, Augie and Nick boarded one of those boats with the enormous fans in the back: swampers, they're called. The men were a ridiculous pair: side by side on a swamper, dressed in suits, representing the two extremes of how tall a normal Italian-American might be expected to grow.

Nick, on the run for so long, had a bad feeling about this—as he had often, about nearly everything. He was on guard, afraid that he was about to be shot in the head and kicked overboard into the bayou, to be eaten by crocodiles or alligators or whatever it was they had down here. The Creature from the Black Lagoon, maybe. Which is how all this looked, like in that movie: live oaks and dense gnarled pines and groves of cypress trees;

Spanish moss and green lily pads and spiky green shoots from something in the palm family and brown-green grasses and plains of dimpled black mud that looked like the sludge at the bottom of a crankcase. And to think guys in New York thought they had it good with Idlewild Airport or those big landfill projects out on Staten Island. The Tramontis had *this*. Learn these swamps well enough, and a man would never need to use a shovel or have a second thought about the disposal of inconvenient items.

Nick put his arm around Augie and smiled.

Augie clapped a hand on his knee.

The roar of the boat made it hard to talk. Nick couldn't hear the gunfire anymore, either.

Nick had crapped turds about Augie's size, he thought. But it was the little angry guys you had to watch out for. How better to get Michael Corleone to lay down and let the Tramontis do whatever the hell they want to do than to deliver Nick Geraci to him?

Instead, though, what happened to Geraci was that, as Augie had promised, he got a tour of the aquatic portions of the property and some of the surrounding area. Oil derricks. Tank farms filled with every variety of petrochemical. A trailer-park brothel. A casino built on a barge, anchored in what looked like the primordial ooze, but in fact only two miles off Highway 61, down a well-maintained and patrolled cement road, built on pylons and paid for by a grant from the federal government.

Seeing all this, coupled with being away from home so long, had rekindled in Nick what he'd believed when he first moved to New York, that New Yorkers lacked imagination about the rest of the world. Most of it seemed to them either beneath contempt or ominous. Moe Green had to get out of New York to think up what was possible in Vegas. Cuba had made people more creative for a while there. Mexico, Geraci thought, had the potential to be the greatest mob haven of all time. Why get all weepy over losing out in Cuba, a little island nothing a hundred miles from Florida, when there was a perfectly good country right across the border, one that already ran on bribes, one that had only scratched the surface of its potential as a source of dope, one that offered up thousands of square miles where anyone who needed to lay low could do so with ease and in a grand style. Hyman Roth and the Kosher Nostra, the California Russian Jews, had run the Mexican national lottery for years. Geraci couldn't see what was stopping enterprising men like himself from moving in and sewing up the whole country. Maybe it was a Sicilian thing. Cuba was an island just like Sicily, vulnerable and corruptible at the foot of a great, powerful continent. New York was basically a bunch of islands, too. Mexico was something else. Mexico could be a bigger version of Louisiana.

The swamps also reminded Nick of that idea Fredo Corleone had had— to change the zoning so it would be illegal to bury people in the five boroughs of New York and then make millions off the Jersey swampland where the dead would need to be buried after that. Why not? It had never struck Nick as so crazy. The scam had already been pulled once before, by the boys out in San Francisco, which had been where Fredo had thought of it. Nick had helped Fredo with the project for a while—purchasing options on swampland; making inquiries into the stonecutter business—until Michael had whistled the play dead. Reconsidered from the passenger seat of Augie Tramonti's swamper on an idyllic spring day in Louisiana, more than a thousand miles from New York, Geraci couldn't remember what Michael and Tom Hagen had thought was wrong with the idea—other than that Fredo had thought of it first.

If Geraci ever got back in power, he vowed, he would make Fredo's plan work.

He and Augie came fishtailing around a bend. Augie pointed to a dock, reaching into the bayou from a hillock of ground. At the top of it stood a tar-paper church with no glass in its windows. Filthy white children in overalls milled around near the base of a rough-hewn cross. "Leak," Augie shouted. "Cocktail."

He gunned the boat. Two Negro men dressed in red doormen's suits rushed to meet them, and Augie blew past the dock and skidded up onto shore, cackling like a joyriding schoolkid. Nick could hear the gunfire again. The firing range was behind the church.

As they climbed to the crest of the hill they saw about a dozen men on the range and at least that many milling around. Here, in the middle of a vast, miserable swamp, the firing range was a facility so impeccably maintained, it could have hosted an Olympic event. Yet most of the shooters were aiming away from the formal targets toward targets of their own: cans of tomato sauce balanced on fence posts, rotting fruit—things that spewed.

Augie ducked into a gleaming white outhouse. It was the only one in sight; black letters stenciled on the door read WHITES ONLY.

Nick waited.

"Want to shoot?" Augie said when he finished. "We got marksmen you can get lessons from or go up against, if you're up for a friendly wager of some kind. You want a cocktail, I'll get you one. There's a full bar up in that church."

"I'm fine," Nick said. "Who are these men? Friends of yours?" Meaning members of the Tramonti Family.

"A few of 'em," he said. "But we also got navy, we got retired FBI, believe it or not. There's cops from here and someplace in Florida, some Cuban fellas who don't talk much, a former airline pilot—we even got a coon-ass country boy who can shoot a mosquito off a frog's ass a hundred yards away. It's unbelievable. Unbelievable. You've got to see it."

Nick had never spent much time in the South before—although people kept telling him New Orleans wasn't the South, it was New Orleans—and he rarely went more than a few hours without, as now, being startled by something he saw. It wasn't just the heat and the languid speech and manner, or the extreme segregation or clothes that were fashionable two years before, if ever. The South had somehow bred cockroaches as big as his fist— *flying* cockroaches as big as his fist. The South had bred a numbers runner who took a chicken with him everywhere, along with little cards on which the bird pecked out suggested plays. The South had bred this, too: misfits in the swamp, shooting cans of tomato sauce and arguing in thick accents and a few foreign voices about the government.

"Our thing here has gotten beaucoup bigger," Augie said. "We hear that you disbanded yours."

"My what?" Geraci said.

"Your assassin squad, the men you was trainin' up there in your swamp, in New Jersey, with our friends from the government."

"How do you know about that?"

"Probably what choice did you have after your boy in Cuba screwed the pooch?"

"How do you know about that?"

Augie slapped him on the back. "Aw, c'mon, brother! We're in the knowing-things business."

NICK COULDN'T HAVE BEEN HAPPIER, BACK OUT ON THE streets again. He wasn't known in New Orleans. He didn't look Italian, didn't have a New York accent, he shuffled a little bit when he walked, and sometimes his hands shook. He was constantly misread and underestimated, and, despite everything, he couldn't remember when he'd had more fun. Even if New Orleans hadn't already been known as the Big Easy, he'd have thought of it that way.

At first, most of the jobs they fed him were small—collections and payments, the nuts and bolts of what made any business thrive. As he had back when he was coming up, he always paid himself a smaller cut than he had coming. Cheating yourself in the short run on behalf of people in authority was always a good move in the long run. It built trust, kept him safe, and sped him along toward bigger jobs and thus more money. Sure enough, in no time the Tramontis asked him to do some freelance troubleshooting. He negotiated the forgiveness of a gambling debt in exchange for an FM radio station and that almost-new nineteen-inch color TV. He fixed a problem with the skim from the state's third-busiest toll bridge. He outlined the mutual benefits of a new profit-sharing plan to a smart young drug dealer in a Negro neighborhood and was kind enough to drop him off afterward at Charity Hospital. He blew up a Corvette in Gretna Parish—nobody hurt, just as a warning to a stranger. Even though Nick had help on the job, he wired the charge himself. Only later, euphoric, did it click that usually his hands shook too much to do anything like that.

What Nick had learned was that nothing helped his symptoms more than physical exertion or, sometimes even more so, the prospect of it. Although when he quit boxing, he'd promised himself (and, more to the point, Charlotte) that he'd never set foot in the ring again, he found a small gym on North Robertson Street and went three times a week. Back in Cleveland, when Nick was a kid, the boxing gyms were full of Italians and Irish and a few Jews, but here it was nearly all Negroes, a few tattooed country white boys, and a cadre of Cuban kids, recently arrived and wizards on the speed bag. Geraci knew more than enough Spanish to get by, but their accents were strange, and they pretended not to understand him. Once he'd been coming to the gym for a while, he started sparring. He could still hurt a man who didn't know what was coming, but in the ring the kids he fought took it easy on him, and he let them. It was just sport. He never told Charlotte about any of it. She noticed that he'd lost weight and that the muscles in his arms and legs were starting to thicken, and he told her it was from all the walking he was doing. When she looked skeptical, he said it was also from all the great sex, too.

Geraci remembered enough details about how the Corleone Family had operated that he could coordinate his insurgency from a distance, still mostly via Momo Barone. The Roach said that Eddie Paradise was watching him too closely for him to be seen calling from payphones all the time, and so the Roach set up a secure line at his mother's house in Bay Ridge. Since he'd always visited her once a day, that raised no suspicions. The most satisfying offensive so far—one that bankrolled several others—took place in the same cemetery where Vito Corleone was buried. In a mausoleum nearby (DANTE read the carved name over the door), the vaults were filled with cash. It was Michael Corleone's personal piggybank. Two zips—one of whom, under a fake name, was the night watchman—knocked down one wall of the building with the cemetery's own backhoe and got away with most of the money. The watchman went back to Agrigento to work in the family winery. The other could easily have returned to his job making pizza in Cleveland Heights, but he flashed too much of his new money around, which, to Geraci's mind, was a form of suicide, nothing he needed to give a second thought.

FOR YEARS, BACK IN EAST ISLIP, CHARLOTTE HAD MADE little effort to share her husband's interest in jazz, but they were in New Orleans now, and she'd always said she was a big believer in *When in Rome*. Now they went to shows together two or three times a week, and it was fun for Nick to see the thrill she got from the way the waiters talked to them, the tables they got, and the free drinks that ominous-looking strangers sent over without a word. This, too, reawakened memories of when they'd first started dating. She was probably overcompensating, Nick thought, for the anxiety she had about "abandoning" their daughters (her word), but still: it was fun. The girls were safe. And they'd be on their own soon anyway.

One day, after Nick and Charlotte had been together in New Orleans a few weeks, they went out onto Lake Pontchartrain on a borrowed boat. The boat had the same name as a famous album by a jazz pianist with a heroin problem. It now belonged to one of Carlo Tramonti's cousins. Charlotte stripped down to her bikini and was sunbathing on the front deck with the strap in the back unfastened when Nick finally got around to asking her if, that whole time he'd been gone, she'd been true to him.

"I have." She answered him as if it weren't a serious question. He wasn't sure he believed her, but he hadn't the slightest evidence to the contrary. It took her at least another mile of lake before she finally raised herself up on her elbows, so that he could get a glimpse of her tits, and asked him the same question. Had he been faithful?

He told her he had been.

It was essentially true. Not factual, but true. Nick wondered what drove him, her, and any other otherwise sane people to ask questions like this, when no matter what the answer really was, the only answer anybody in their right mind would give would be *yes*.

People used to mock Geraci for not going to whores or having a *comare*, but who gets ahead in life being like everybody else? That's what he'd always say to the boys. He loved his wife was more like it. Look at her: she was a knockout. A dream. She really was enough for him. Most of the time, it hadn't been a hardship, fidelity. Friends accused him of being wired differently than other men, and that might have been true. How the fuck would he know? Nobody gets the chance to be other men. A man was stuck being his doomed fucking self.

"Never?" she said.

He anchored the boat, and he told her he loved her.

"Come below deck," he said.

"I'll do my best," she said, grabbing him by his stiffening cock and leading him there.

Our thing here has gotten beaucoup bigger, he thought.

CHAPTER 24

The twin-engine plane carrying Al Neri and his nephew landed early in the morning at a private airstrip in the Arizona desert. The airstrip was the one that movie people used when they were coming to Old Tucson to film Westerns. The plane was a charter from Las Vegas, and the pilot seemed to think they were in the movie business. They had done nothing to encourage or discourage this assumption. They were dressed, per Al's instructions, in snap-brim tams, windbreakers, sport shirts, and loafers, like golfers whose spikes and clubs were waiting for them somewhere. Tommy's loose, untucked shirt—he'd lost a lot of weight lately—hung over his gun. All the way from Las Vegas, the pilot had gone on and on about all the stars he'd had in his plane, and Al and Tommy had just let him talk. "Break a leg," he said as they climbed out. "Or is that just for the theater?"

"Thank you," Al said. "It was a nice flight."

"In my neighborhood," Tommy said, "we said *in culo alla balena.*"

Al gave him a look.

"I never heard that," the pilot said. "What's it mean?"

"Up the whale's ass." Tommy caught Al's eye. "It just means break a leg," Tommy said. "More or less."

"What language is that?" the pilot said.

"We'll see you at six," Al said, guiding Tommy away.

They started down the blacktopped sidewalk from the airstrip to the car-rental lot a couple hundred yards away. "Talk a little, people forget you," Al muttered. "Too silent, people remember. Teach people colorful slang, you might as well hand 'em your mug shot and rap sheet as keepsakes."

"My rap sheet?" Tommy said. "I'm not sure you could call what I got a *rap sheet*. The only thing that ever stuck to me was that thing with the skim in Reno, which got reduced to time served."

"That's not really my point," Al said.

Tommy had his good qualities—loyalty, doggedness, a great singing voice, devotion to his mother, good in the kitchen in his own right—but intelligence probably wasn't one of them.

The Mexican at the car-rental lot asked which production they were with and named two as guesses. The Neris didn't answer him. The Mexican assured them he didn't sell news to the tabloids. "Seems like good business to me," said Al Neri.

"I seen you in that one movie, didn't I?" the Mexican said. "With that guy who always plays the sheriff? It had that actress in it, too, what's her face; the one with the hair and the big tits. It's on the tip of my tongue."

Al handed the man cash. "You're thinking of that other guy," he said.

Tommy drove. He cranked up the air-conditioning and turned onto a road that would take them into Tucson proper. On the right, as far as the eye could see, were hundreds of derelict airplanes, most of them World War II combat planes.

"Look at this shit, huh?" Tommy said, rubbing his eyes.

"You all right to drive?" Al said.

"Why wouldn't I be?"

"The rubbing your eyes, sweating," Al said. "I wanted to make sure you were all right."

"I'm fine." Tommy reached to turn up the already full-blast a/c. "We're in the fucking desert, Uncle Al. It's been known to make people fucking sweat. I got some allergies to the plants out here, too. If you recall, when we was living in Nevada, up in Tahoe I'd be fine but down in Vegas I'd start sneezing, my nose would run, itchy eyes, all that."

It wasn't just the sweating and the eyes. There was the weight he'd lost, the eternity Tommy spent on the can first thing in the morning. Al knew the signs. "Allergies, huh?" Al said. "Not a taste for smack?"

"Get the fuck out of here."

"Look me in the eye and tell me you ain't using dope."

"I ain't using dope," Tommy said. "I swear to God."

"Fuck God," Al said. "Swear to me."

"I swear to you, Uncle Al. I'm not going to lie to you. I've used it here and there. But *using* it, no, no fucking way. Not in the ongoing sense of that, and *definitely* not in the am-I-on-it-now sense. Call Ma, if you don't believe me about the allergies."

In the airplane boneyard, there were now rows and rows of B-29 Superfortress bombers, their engines and windows covered with tarps.

Al folded his arms and studied his nephew. There was nothing whatsoever in Tommy's driving or his manner to suggest he was on dope right now. There was no need to overreact here. All the younger guys seemed to have used it *here and there*. Al himself, no choirboy, had tried the stuff. "Don't bullshit me, kid," Al said. "All I want to know is the last time you used."

Tommy took a deep breath. "Two days ago."

"You hadn't fucking better be lying."

"Two days ago," Tommy reasserted, more forcefully this time. "And before that it'd been months. Maybe almost a year."

"Maybe, huh?" Al said. *"Maybe almost?"*

"You want to take someone else in to do this job, you want to do it yourself, whatever you want, y'know? Anything you want me to do to prove I'm not high on junk, tell me, and I'll do it."

Al didn't say anything for a while. Maybe he was reading too much into things. Al really didn't want to do this job, and maybe that was clouding his judgment. "Just drive," he said.

Tommy turned on the radio. *Who's gonna jump*, Buck Owens sang, *when you say frog?* Tommy improvised a credible harmony line.

"Turn that peckerwood shit off," Al said.

Tommy snickered, but he did it.

"What's so funny?" Al said.

"Nothing," Tommy said.

"I asked you a question. What's so funny?"

"The guy in the song sings *who's gonna jump, when you say frog*, and then you tell me to turn off the radio."

"What the fuck does that have to do with saying *frog*?"

"Nothing."

"You want to listen to the radio, listen." Al said. "Sing along if you want. Just not that peckerwood shit."

"Forget it." Tommy stared out at the dusty road ahead. "Out here, what else you think there is?"

This would be Tommy Neri's third trip to Tucson to speak with Fausto Geraci.

"You're telling me you like that shit?" Al said.

"I was just turning on the radio to turn it on," Tommy said. Absently, he touched the gun at his hip. It was probably unconscious, Al knew. A lot of guys did that. There were cops who touched their piece every thirty seconds for thirty years. Al himself had not brought a gun. His heavy steel cop-issue flashlight was tucked inside his small suitcase.

Again, Tommy touched the pistol. It was a newish 9mm Walther: a beauty, Al thought. A weapon that no right-minded individual would want to use once and then dump. If it was Al, he'd have brought some cheap *strunz* good only for close-in work, but Al tried his best to keep from second-guessing his nephew's every move. It was what Al's own father had done to him—beaten him almost to death, in fact, more than a few times, for not doing things by the old man's arbitrary, contradictory code of conduct. With Al's big sister, Tommy's mother, his father had been even more ruthless about telling her everything she did that was wrong and then punctuating it with his fists. So fuck it. All that really mattered was that Tommy's gun was clean and untraceable, and it was. If today's job went at all well, Tommy wouldn't need to fire the thing anyway and thus wouldn't need to shitcan it. If he *did*, so be it. It was just a goddamned gun. The good Germans at Walther would make more.

The ghost planes they were passing now were nearly all decorated with fading paintings of busty women in stockings or bathing suits or both.

"You sure you know where you're going?" Al asked.

"Relax."

"Let's swing by the airport real quick on the way."

"We just came from it."

"Not the air*strip*. The airport. It's—"

"I know where the airport is."

"Right," Al said. He pulled a map from his jacket pocket and followed along anyway.

AS HE APPARENTLY DID EVERY MORNING, FAUSTO GERACI returned home from driving his wife, Conchita, to her job at the cannery on the other side of town, which he did dressed in a ratty old bathrobe and an undershirt, and took a seat in a webbed lawn chair on his back patio, smoking Chesterfield Kings and staring out at his swimming pool.

"Why don't he just get her a car?" Al said. "She don't drive?"

He and Tommy were parked the next street over, situated so they could see a judicious sliver of Fausto's backyard.

"She drives," Tommy said. "But he likes to drive her. Like I told you, he likes to drive, period."

Every Sunday, Fausto Geraci took his car out in the middle of nowhere and opened it up, well past 100. It was one of the things Al planned to ask him about.

"The Mexican wife," Al said. "Why don't she quit that job, then? She's married now. All of our money this old fuck's probably sittin' on, I can't imagine she needs it."

"Maybe she likes to work. How the fuck should I know? She's a Mexican. Who knows what they think?"

Al took out his binoculars.

"What'd I tell you, huh?" said Tommy. "Have you ever in your whole life seen a *stronzo vecchio* who looked more like he was just waitin' to die?"

"To be honest with you, he looks like he's been that way awhile," Al said. "Like that's just who he is." Appearances could be deceiving. The man was, after all, practically a newlywed. He was by all accounts enjoying the attention his son's disappearance had brought his way. "I thought you said he kept it empty, the pool."

"He does. He did."

"Full now." That ruled out one of the ideas Al had come up with, which was to handcuff Fausto Geraci to the bottom and turn on the water. He'd seen it work before. He had a pair of cuffs in the pocket of his windbreaker. Al probably wouldn't have done it that way anyway. Too many neighbors around to hear the old man if he started yelling—and getting the old man yelling was key, Al figured, to getting the information they wanted. But the way Al liked to do jobs—hits or muscle, either one—was to come in with a few options swirling around in his head and then size up the situation quickly and go with what felt right. Like a basketball guard bringing the ball down the court, or a jazz horn player soloing off a simple melody everybody already knew, or a gunslinger riding into a town where men were waiting for him.

"Maybe it suddenly occurred to the old bastard that it's hotter out here than the devil's morning piss," Tommy said. "Figured it'd be nice to be able to take a dip now and then."

"Could be," Al said, raising the binoculars again.

"Or maybe it was the Mexican's idea."

"Possible," Al said, though Fausto had married Conchita a little more than a year ago.

The story on the pool—which Nick Geraci himself had often told—was that Fausto and his first wife had moved down here from Cleveland after she was diagnosed with the Big C. Her people were from Milazzo, fishermen and sponge divers, and she herself swam in meets as a girl. Loved the water, never had a pool, always wanted one, finally got it, used it all the time. She was in that pool when her weakened heart gave out. Fausto found her there, pulled her out himself. Before she was even in the ground, he drained the pool and never refilled it. Maybe out of grief, maybe because he was a cheap son of a bitch—who knew? Nick would refill it whenever he visited, but the old man would drain it the minute he left. At least that was the story.

Suddenly, a metal screen door slammed. Fausto Geraci sat up straight in his lawn chair, beaming. "More likely," Al said, handing Tommy the binoculars, "doting grandpop that he is, our man here did it for her. Filled the pool."

There was the sound of a splash and then the distant laughter of a young woman.

The information they'd gotten was good. Bev Geraci, Nick's younger daughter, had finished her sophomore year of college at Berkeley and had come to spend the summer with her grandfather. The poor kid took after her father. Even from the sound of the splash, Al Neri would have guessed, correctly, that she was a big hulk of a girl.

AL AND TOMMY NERI DROVE AROUND THE BLOCK AND PULLED their rental car into the driveway of Fausto Geraci's stucco-clad ranch style, coasting in with the engine already killed, blocking the red-and-white Olds Starfire in the garage. The old man was supposedly a fancy driver and

prided himself on it. There wasn't much chance of his getting to the car—
or of his granddaughter getting that far, either—but Al wanted it blocked
anyway. When he was a kid and certainly when he was on the force, he'd
expected to die young and in a blaze of glory, like a mysterious hero in one
of the Westerns he loved so much. He even courted it, that stupid boy's
stupid dream. Things had changed. He still loved Westerns (movies, TV,
even books), and he still thought of himself as a young man (he'd turn forty
next year but could pass as the brother of his gray-haired, balding nephew).
But the older he got, the more attached he became to the idea of getting
even older yet. And getting older—as any fan of Westerns could tell you—
meant paying attention to all the little things that could go wrong.

They put on gloves, got out, and pressed the car doors shut. The garage,
a converted carport, was open. They hurried inside, but not so fast that a
neighbor or a person driving by would think anything of it. The garage
smelled of machine oil and pine cleaner. Its floor was painted. Hoses,
cords, and well-maintained tools hung on pegboards, silhouetted by black
Magic Marker. Al took a roll of duct tape and a coil of clothesline rope.
They crouched on either side of the door to the backyard.

Even through the pebbled glass, Al could see that the girl was still
swimming, and Fausto was still smoking and watching her. The sound of
a whiny-voiced man with a guitar came from what must have been the
girl's tinny radio. Beatnik music, Al thought. Some guy singing about a
clown crying in the alley. Al chuckled. Grow up, kid. Look around. Good
luck finding an alley without some goddamned clown in it, crying
about something.

Al jerked a thumb toward the interior of the house to indicate that
they'd be taking Fausto and the girl inside to talk to them, and Tommy nodded. Al set the rope and the duct tape down, held up his index fingers side
by side, then moved them apart: put them in separate parts of the house.
Tommy nodded again.

Tommy stuffed his hat in his pocket and drew his gun. The look on his
face was one of almost carnal relief.

Al hit him in the shoulder and shook his head. Not unless or until they needed it. This was an old man and a girl. Al had left his flashlight in the car. Overkill. He didn't regret bringing it, though. For him, the flashlight was as much a good-luck charm as a weapon.

What'll you do now, my blue-eyed son? What'll you do now, my darling young one?

Al motioned with both palms out for Tommy to slow down, take it easy. Tommy put the gun away. Al picked up the rope and the tape, counted to three, and they strode through the door.

"Gentlemen," Fausto said, as if he'd been expecting them. Though he did not stand up. "Can I get yuz coffee and a bun or some such? Cigarettes, I'm running low on. Food, coffee, we got. Kind of warm out for them gloves, don't you think?"

"We need to talk," Tommy said.

Bev was swimming laps, her head in a white rubber bathing cap with rubber flowers on the side.

"I bet you that's right," Fausto said. "Like I always say, life is short. Important men like you, come all this way just to see me, what you want to waste your time with the simple courtesies for, am I right?" He jerked a thumb at Al. "Who's your ugly friend in the funny hat?" he asked Tommy. "He looks like a cop in a costume."

"Get up," Al said, resisting the temptation both to knock the old guy's teeth out and to take off the tam. "I said, get up."

"Fausto Geraci," he said, finally and slowly standing. *Jair-AH-chee*, not *Juh-RAY-see*. He did not extend his hand. Fausto pointed at the rope and the tape. "Hey, y'know, in my garage there, I got some rope just like that, new roll of tape just like that, too. With all we got in common, we ought to be able to figure out how to be friends."

Bev must have caught sight of something. She stopped in the middle of the deep end of the pool and, treading water, called to her grandfather. She was squinting. Her cat-eye glasses were upside down on the table beside her grandfather.

"It's all right, *nipotina*."

"We're just friends of your grandpa, all right?" said Tommy Neri, walking toward her on the deck of the pool.

For a moment, the girl's eyes widened, then she spun around in the water and sprinted for the opposite side of the pool. Her kicking feet made that thumping sound only good swimmers can make.

Tommy ran to the other side of the pool. He was not a speedy man.

Fausto thrust his hand into the pocket of his bathrobe.

As he did, the heel of Al Neri's right hand slammed into Fausto's breastbone.

The old man's gun went flying, and he fell down into his lawn chair so hard it toppled over backward. His slippers sailed a good fifteen feet in the air.

Bev got to the side but saw Tommy coming. Before he could grab her, she pushed off the side and started sprinting the other way. Tommy, already winded, cursed and starting running back around to where he'd started.

"She don't know nothing," Fausto muttered, then lapsed into what Al presumed was Sicilian dialect. All Al knew in that was how to ask for a kiss and how to cuss. Al hurried over and fished the gun out of the oleander bush where it landed. It was a Smith & Wesson .38, an old one but in good shape. The safety was still on. He tucked it in his jacket pocket. The old man was gasping for air a little but not moaning. Al had felt the soggy give of the old man's chest, and he knew there were a few broken ribs. Broken ribs were good. They hurt like hell, but they weren't usually serious. A person would suffer from pain like that but probably not pass out or die.

Bev Geraci dove underwater and turned around again and went a different direction.

"I may need your help here," Tommy said.

"I'm busy." Al heaved Fausto into a nearby undamaged lawn chair. "Dive in and get her."

"I can't swim."

"You what?"

Al picked up the tape, started it with his teeth so he wouldn't have to take off the gloves, and ripped off a long strip. Fausto flinched. The terrible ripping noise duct tape made was always good for jobs like this, too.

"I can swim a little," Tommy said, "but not like this here. Fucking Aquagirl or something—what's her face, with those water movies." He circled the pool yet again with his hand on his gun. "I should have brought the silencer."

At this, Fausto perked up.

Al Neri slapped the tape on his face and bound it tightly around his head. The old man's hands rose to fend him off, but Al was already done. He pushed the old man against the back of the house, his knee in the small of Fausto's back, and grabbed his hands and lashed them together at the wrists with clothesline rope.

"Get her inside before you use the piece," Al called, but bluffing. The last thing in the world he was going to OK was shooting that girl.

Al considered tying or duct-taping Fausto to the chair as well, but the questioning needed to be done inside, and he didn't want to have to carry him. If Al marched him inside now and tied him up or taped him to something in there, he'd have to trust Tommy not to shoot the girl and also to keep the girl from eluding him and running away. Tommy was red-faced from the exertion of trotting around the pool. If she did get out now and wasn't totally gassed herself, she could probably outrun him. Tommy would shoot her then for sure.

"C'mere," Al said. "Hurry up. Watch this one, see to it he don't move."

Relieved, Tommy did as he was told. Al ran over and grabbed the leaf skimmer. The pole was about eight feet long. He pulled it back, the way a person would a sledgehammer. He hit her in the head with it, hard.

Harder than he'd meant to. He'd misjudged it, maybe because she was swimming so fast. He'd only been trying to make a point.

She went under.

Al Neri cursed and flung the skimmer aside. Fucking Scootch. Al had managed to go this long without ever hitting a woman, not even a whore.

Even when he'd been ordered to kill one, at one of the legal cathouses Fredo used to have, out in the desert near Vegas, he'd given the job to a younger associate.

She was at the bottom of the pool and didn't seem to be moving. If he killed her, he reasoned, she'd float. He waited her out.

Sure enough, the girl suddenly shot to the surface, dead-bang in the middle of the pool, bleeding from her temple but apparently all right otherwise. She stared at him, treading water and terrified, then she put her bleeding head down and again started sprinting to the farthest corner of the pool.

"Maybe you should dive in and get her," Tommy said.

Al ran to the other side. He ran three miles almost every day, so, unlike Tommy, he wasn't going to wear down before the poor girl did. He would deal later with his nephew's show of disrespect. Tommy Neri was a made guy, which meant that even his uncle couldn't lay a hand on him, but there were always other things that could be done.

On her next trip across the pool, Bev Geraci got to the wall and pulled herself out of the pool in one smooth motion. She made a run toward the back of the yard, wailing in what could only be called hysterics. There was a fence. Al Neri grabbed her as she was almost over it.

She was awfully strong for a girl. He managed to hold on to her, wrapping his arms around her in a bear hug, dragging her back across the deck of the pool, past her madly grunting grandfather, and into the house through the patio door. In the first bedroom he found, the master, he threw her down on the bed.

All the roadwork, all the time he spent at the weight bench he had at home: people made jokes about it, but in a line of work that sometimes got physical, what sense did it make to let yourself go?

One of the straps on Bev Geraci's bathing suit had broken. Al caught a glimpse of her breast and averted his eyes, looking for a towel for her. On the wall there was a three-foot-wide jigsaw puzzle of *The Last Supper*, assembled, glued down, framed, and hung over the bed. The bathroom door was across the room and he didn't want to leave her even for a moment. He was soaked himself, he realized. And his shirt was smeared with her blood. He grabbed a pink bathrobe from a hook on the back of the bedroom door and wiped himself with it.

She sat up, tugging at the strap, sobbing quietly now, blood and tears streaming down her already wet face.

"We don't want to hurt you," Al said, tossing her the robe. "I swear on my mother's grave, all we want is information."

Bev flung the robe to the floor. She pulled off her swimming cap and let her matted hair fall. She looked up at him, squinting, then balled the cap up and held it in front of her face.

Al thought of her glasses, upside down on the patio table. It broke his heart. He didn't want to be here. He wanted to go get her glasses and tell her this was all a big mistake. Al had an image of those two girls in Harlem that pimp Wax Baines had cut up with a razor, right before Al had caved in Baines's skull with the flashlight, which had gotten him kicked off the Force. He thought again of that hooker in Fredo's cathouse, blue and tangled up in cheap blood-soaked sheets, as Senator Geary sat on the edge of the bed, blubbering and bewildered, just as this poor girl was now. Baines, Geary: fair fucks to 'em. But never again, Al promised himself, was he going to come anywhere near a job where he'd have to watch an innocent girl bleed.

"I'm sorry," Al said, "about the . . . the pole. I didn't want to hurt you. You didn't do what I said, though, and you got hurt. Listen to me, sweetheart. Just do what we tell you, and you'll be fine." He tossed her his handkerchief for the blood. "You understand me?"

Still blubbering, she looked up at him, squinting again, and nodded.

"Your grandfather," Al said, "I unfortunately can't make promises about."

She dabbed at her head and kept crying. The blood was everywhere now, but the cut didn't look too bad. With head wounds, you couldn't go by how much blood you saw.

"He's just an old man," Bev said to him. "Please."

"He's done bad things," Al said. "Which is unfortunate."

Bev Geraci wailed.

"My associate is an animal," Al said, though this was just for show. "He's not as patient as I am, and I'm not always all that patient, as you've just unfortunately seen."

"I don't know anything you can use," she said. "I get calls from pay-phones. I never know where they're from. I just—"

"Time out," Al said. "Tell your story to my friend, all right?"

"I will," she said. "I want you to know, I'd never go to the police unless I had to."

Al closed the bedroom windows, though she had stopped screaming. He smiled. "I know that, sweetheart," he said.

Because what was she going to do? Give up information about her father, then give it up again to police? No. Lie to them, and then lie to the police about what she'd told him and Tommy? Maybe, but that caused her as many problems as it solved for her. The likeliest path was that she'd hear her grandfather's screams and say what she knew to save him, then—if she did talk to the police, leave out the details about her father, to save him. Whether she went to the police or not wouldn't matter anyway. Nothing she could tell the police could prove that he and Tommy had ever been here.

"OK, Sport!" Al called to his nephew. "You're all set. Bring me the old man."

He did, gun drawn, naturally, marching Fausto into his own house at the point of a pistol.

As Al left Tommy with the girl, he bent toward his nephew and put his mouth flush against his ear. "Touch her and I'll kill you," Al whispered.

Tommy Neri smirked. Al had, after all, just brained the young woman with a pool skimmer, but he still didn't have to accept an attitude like this.

Tommy handed his uncle the tam he'd left in the backyard.

———

EVEN WHEN A PERSON HAS DUCT TAPE WRAPPED SNUGLY around his head, when he says *fuck you*, over and over, it's surprisingly easy to understand.

Al pushed Fausto Geraci down into an orange chair in the guest bedroom and lashed him to it with the duct tape. He used the rest of the roll. Fausto's arms were pinned to his sides now. He was fighting back tears, possibly tears of rage, possibly from the broken ribs. The bedroom walls were covered with pictures of Bev and Barb Geraci and various Mexicans who were presumably the wife's people. There were none of Nick, Nick's wife, or Nick's sister, a dyke gym teacher who lived in Phoenix now. Another jigsaw puzzle hung over the bed, this one of Jesus on a straining donkey. Palm Sunday.

The girl's sobs were audible from across the hall.

The doors to each of the bedrooms were closed. The idea here was to make them each hear the other one screaming and weeping, so that their love for each other would make them give up what they knew. The girl, being a girl, should be easy enough to scare so that she'd scream and cry without harming. Fausto Geraci was fair game.

Al took out a switchblade, which had actually been a Christmas gift from Tommy last year. He held it in front of the old man's face long enough to inspire more cursing, then he pulled the tape away from Fausto's cheek and sliced through the tape with the knife, just grazing the old man's unshaven gray skin. Then Al grabbed one end of the tape and in one motion ripped the tape from Fausto's head, hard and counterclockwise, taking a hank of bloodied hair from the back of his head and inspiring a scream so loud and piercing Al's ears rang.

Bev Geraci's scream followed a moment later, calling out to her grandfather.

Fausto clenched his eyes tightly shut for a few moments, fighting back pain.

"I'm all right," he called to her.

Knowing she could hear him apparently put an end to his cursing. He began to beg and beg on his granddaughter's behalf, claiming she knew nothing.

"What about you?" Al said. "You tell us where your boy is, and we leave you alone. We know you talk to him."

"I don't talk to him never, nothing. He don't call, he don't write. It's the usual thing boys do to their old man once the mother is dead. He don't like it that I got remarried. It's hard for the kids when that happens. What can I do?"

Al punched Fausto in the face—a hard right to the uncut cheek—and followed it with a little left jab to the already broken ribs. Fausto sent out a wail made even more anguished by the tough old bird's determination not to show any pain at all.

On cue, Bev Geraci called out to him once more.

He did not call back that he was all right. Pain-sweat flowed freely. He was as drenched now as if he'd been in the pool, too.

She was crying again. Al hadn't heard anything that made him think Tommy had hit her.

"He's an animal," Al said. "Which I'm sorry about, but there you have it. He's what I got stuck with. The thing is this. Your son unfortunately is doomed either way. Sooner or later, we'll find him. Like the man said, if history teaches you anything, it's that we'll find him. But, her, she's innocent. Her, you can spare. You can give us some information, and we'll go. Five minutes from now, this could be all over, *capisce*? We'll walk away, and that'll be that."

He shook his head. "Ah, *va fa Napoli*. Eh? We're dead already." The ribs were making it hard for him to get the breath to speak. "You'll think. We can identify you."

"Actually, you can't," Al said. "We're not here. There's no record of it. We're ghosts, is what we are. The real him and me, we're nowhere near here. And the people we're with right now will swear to it. Honest, hardworking people, strangers with no reason to lie, will remember seeing us. I tell you all this so you can rest easy. So that we can get this done and go on about our lives. Cigarette?"

Fausto nodded his bloodied head.

Al went out onto the patio to get them. He came back and tortured Fausto by smoking one in front of him.

It was sad, Al thought, the attitudes men have about how they'll stand up to pain. Done right, pain gets everybody. The holy trinity of pain—broken ribs, burns, hard blows to the balls—can bring any man to a crossroads. Resolve to give up and die. Or the main road, which is to talk. The problem is that the ones who talk almost always lie first. But between what Fausto said and what the girl said, he and Tommy ought to be able to walk out of there with something.

"I don't take no pleasure in none of this," Al said. "You're just an old man. So do us all a favor, huh? Where is he?"

"I got no idea. You probably know. Twice as much. As me. I admit I helped him. Get over there to Mexico. After that. All I know is. What he tells me. He don't tell me sh— . . . Diddly-whatnot. Don't hit me again. No jokin'. That's how boys are. With their fathers. You got boys?"

Al put a cigarette between Fausto's lips and lit it. Fausto inhaled and worked it to the corner of his mouth. He closed his eyes, savoring the drag. Al admired Fausto for not wanting to curse within earshot of his granddaughter, but *diddly-whatnot*? Fucking Cleveland *cafone*. Al lit another cigarette for himself.

"Again: where is he?"

"We arrange calls to payphones, you're right, but what do I know about where he's calling from, huh? It's impossible. How you supposed to know a thing like that?"

Al took the lit cigarette and screwed it into Fausto's forearm. The old man's screams brought on uncontrollable sobs from his granddaughter.

Al relit it and did it again on the palm of Fausto's hand.

Fausto Geraci's spirit was as visibly broken as his body. He summoned up his strength and called to her that he was going to tell them everything. Al picked up Fausto's cigarette from the floor and replaced it between his lips. Fausto then gave Al Neri a list of places: someplace outside Cleveland, Taxco, some little town near Acapulco, then Mexico City, Veracruz, then someplace in Guatemala, then Panama City. Whether it was the one in Panama or the one in Florida, he didn't know. It was the same list of places in the same order that the Corleones had received from Joe Lucadello, other than the inclusion of the town near Acapulco, which was news, and the possibility, however confused, that Nick Geraci might be hiding out in the wilds of the Florida Panhandle. If he really had been to all these places, it was an impressive itinerary for a man who wouldn't fly.

Fausto's broken ribs made it hard for him to talk, but he seemed determined to get the information out, a good sign that he might be telling the truth. He claimed honestly not to know where Nick was now, but that if they wanted to go to the payphone outside the Painted Pony Lounge tomorrow at noon, they could wait until the fifth ring and then ask him themselves.

This could be a lie, Al knew, a trap, but there were ways of puzzling out what to do. It was something, anyway.

"Also," Fausto said. His breathing had become a sickening wheeze. "I got a birthday card. From him. On top of the TV. Stack of papers. Open, but. Still in the envelope."

As if Nick Geraci would show his tracks that brazenly. Al went to get it anyway.

He found what seemed to be the envelope. It was typed. The return address on the birthday card read *Wm. Shakespeare, London, England.* Inside, there was a note in some kind of foreign language or code, also typed, maybe four or five sentences long. The only thing that wasn't typed was a block-printed *N* at the bottom. The postmark was New York, New York. Al slipped it in his pocket.

In the next room, the gun went off. Bev Geraci shrieked. Fausto called her name. The gun went off twice more.

Al came running.

When he got there, Tommy was frowning at him. Bev was sitting on the bed. She'd washed her face and head and, while she was still obviously terrified, she was in better shape than Al had left her in.

"What the hell?" Al said.

"What the hell nothing," Tommy said. "It's under control, *Sport.*"

He was pushing his luck, this kid.

"What are you shooting at?"

"Nothing," Tommy said. "Jesus."

He wagged his eyebrows. Al realized Tommy had just been firing the pistol to scare the girl and Fausto, too.

"Not Jesus," Al said, as calmly as possible, pointing to the new bullet hole in the jigsaw puzzle. "I think that might be Judas, which would be what you call it."

"Ironical," Tommy said.

"Apropos," Al said, which was the word he was trying to remember. "Stay put," Al said to Bev Geraci. "C'mere," he said to Tommy. "Let me show you something." He led Tommy into the hall and closed the door, leaving the girl there. Then he slapped his nephew on the back of the head and pointed to the door that led to the garage. Al held a finger to his lips, and, as quietly as they'd come, they walked out.

Al didn't want to seem to be in a hurry, but they needed to haul ass out of there. This was precisely the sort of neighborhood where some nosy old bat would hear those shots and summon Tucson's finest.

"So what do you think?" Tommy said, pulling out of the driveway.

"Go," Al said. "Don't speed, but go." He was twisted around in his seat, looking for anyone watching them, listening for the cops. He was glad now they'd taken the time to swing by the airport and boost the license plates off a car in the long-term lot. "You get a ticket, I'll kill you."

Tommy turned the corner.

"Go toward where the motels are," Al said. "Semi-nice. Howard Johnson, Holiday Inn, shit like that." Wholesome nowheres, perfect for their current situation. Tommy would have to go in to register for the room, though. Al had the blood of Nick Geraci's father and daughter all over him. He silently cursed himself for not bringing the flashlight. How can something bring you good luck if you leave it in the goddamned rental car?

"So what do you think?" Tommy repeated.

"Think about *what*?" Al snapped at him.

"You think we did any good back there?"

Al looked at him. He might not be a dope fiend, but he was without a doubt a fucking dope. Al slapped him again on the back of the head.

"Drive," he said.

THE MEXICAN AT THE CAR RENTAL LOT MUST HAVE BEEN done with his shift. Behind the counter was a leather-skinned white man in a white shirt with metal snaps instead of buttons. He looked Al and Tommy Neri over, then looked at the paperwork with their fake names on it.

"Short trip," he noted.

"Best kind," Al said.

"Amen, brother," the man said.

He'd most likely forgotten them before they got out the door.

They walked back down the blacktopped sidewalk to the airstrip.

Al Neri had changed clothes back at the motel, but he still had on the tam. The clean clothes were similar to the ones he'd shit-canned, though he hadn't brought a second windbreaker. He'd scrubbed all the blood off his skin with a bar of pumice soap that he carried in his travel bag for times like this. Experience had also taught him, during his years in Nevada, that most trailer parks had their own incinerators, and most boondocks towns had trailer parks galore. In the first incinerator they found, he dumped a pillowcase containing the bloody gloves and clothes and the license plates. In the second, Tommy tossed in the Walther. They drove around a while and didn't see a third, so Al just went into a men's room at a gas station.

The trash can was predictably full. He wiped Fausto Geraci's .38 clean, wrapped it in paper towels, shoved it halfway down, washed his hands, and left. Back at the motel, Al and Tommy sat around comparing notes about what they'd learned, taking a futile stab at breaking the code on the birthday card and trying to figure out someone they could call who either would go to the Painted Pony tomorrow at noon and answer the phone or at the very least park nearby and see who did. They'd come up with nothing. Too risky, all the way around.

Later, they would learn that, in this regard at least, they'd made the right decision. Fausto Geraci didn't show up for the call. Bev Geraci did, though, her head bandaged, and she took it on the fifth ring. The Arizona State Police had driven her there. The FBI listened in.

Fausto Geraci had passed out in the guest bedroom. When Bev Geraci got to him, he was still alive. She called an ambulance. A few hours later, in the hospital, with Bev and Conchita at his side, his heart gave out, at just about the time Al and Tommy Neri boarded their plane.

Their pilot was ready for them, engine running. "So how was it?" he asked, grinning as he closed the door.

Tommy looked at Al. Al shrugged. Too late now. "How was what?"

The pilot belted himself in. "How was it up the whale's ass?"

"Same as usual," Al answered. "Thank you."

BOOK V

CHAPTER 25

The heat was almost unbearable. August in South Florida. Dressed in a perfectly tailored summer-weight suit, Tom Hagen stood in the shade of a magnolia tree in the backyard of his house in Florida, smoking a cigar, watching an alligator sun itself on the banks of the canal, no more then forty feet away. His daughter Christina, who was eleven, sat under an umbrella beside the fenced-in pool, reading *Gone with the Wind*. Gianna, who was six, was inside with Theresa and her aunt Sandra, helping to get dinner together. The air-conditioning had conked out, and all the windows were open. Tom could hear the drone of the televised convention coverage all the way out here. Over it, he could hear Gianna singing a song she'd learned that helped her set the table correctly. Their old collie, Elvis, barked on cue each time she finished a place setting. Tom smiled. He was a lucky man. He was, in his way, happy.

He looked at his watch. Almost six; the president's plane would be landing about now.

Frankie Corleone was grilling sausages while his new girlfriend sat in a lawn chair in a short summer dress and watched, almost worshipful. Frankie had his own place—he'd been set up with a beer distributorship, a joint venture with Sandra's perpetual fiancé Stan Kogut—but he still ate nearly every meal at his mother's house or here, though he, unlike Stan (who no doubt was on the couch watching TV), often helped cook. "You get used to it," Frankie said.

"Used to what?" Tom said, squinting into the late afternoon sun.

"Gators. Guarantee you that little fella's more scared of you than you are of him."

"That's true," said the girlfriend. She was a lithe brunette whose name Tom had learned moments before and forgotten. All he recalled was that she'd competed in the Miss Florida pageant. "Alligators have primitive fight/flight impulses. When they're afraid, they freeze."

"That one's little?" Tom said. "He must be twenty feet long."

Frankie raised his head and shoulders for a split second in what looked like surprise before he burst into laughter, precisely as his father always had. "Wait'll you see a big one."

He was a dead ringer for Sonny Corleone at the same age, so much so that Hagen sometimes felt as if he were seeing a ghost. Though if anything, the boy did even better with the ladies.

Just then a mosquito bit him and he slapped himself. "Florida," he said, disgusted.

"Paradise by the sea," the brunette said. She didn't sound sarcastic.

"My uncle's still adjusting," Frankie explained. He'd been a baby when his father was killed, and Sandra took the kids and moved down here. He thought of himself as a Floridian. "Wait'll your first winter," he called to Tom. "At least you don't have to shovel the heat, right?"

"You sure about that?" Tom plucked his sweat-damp shirt away from his chest. "It sure feels like it."

But Tom was smiling as he said it. Nothing was going to bring him down today, not even his disdain for the place he now nominally called home. He put out the butt of the cigar against the trunk of the tree and crossed the thick carpet of centipede grass to tell Theresa he was going.

From inside the house, there came a tinny roar and, over it, the shrill, white-bread patter of an excited reporter. The crowd at the airport had gotten its first glimpse of President Shea. There had been calls to move the convention to a city that didn't so vividly underscore the failures of Jimmy Shea's Cuban policy, and that, as a corollary, didn't pose such a security risk. But Miami was also Vice President Payton's hometown (Coral Gables, actually), and Florida was a state that could go either way in what figured to be a close general election. So the convention stayed in Miami. Judging from the noise on the television and the earlier reports of the thousands of cheering people, baking in the sun alongside the route from the airport to the Fontainebleau, it had been a popular choice. The right choice, Tom believed.

"Wish I could stay for those," Tom said as he passed the grilling sausages.

"You're missing out," Frankie said. He winked at the girlfriend. "Nothing like my big sausages."

The boy had inherited Sonny's sophisticated wit, too. Tom glanced back at Christina, but she seemed too engrossed in her book for the vulgar comment to have registered.

"Where you going?" the woman asked Tom.

"He's going to meet the president," Frankie joked. "Ain't that right?"

"I already met him," Tom said, also joking, although he had, years ago.

"Are you *serious*?" the brunette said. "President *Shea*?"

"What are you, stupid?" Frankie said. "No, he's not serious."

"Nothing so glamorous as that, I'm afraid," Tom said. "Just business."

"You know I'm not stupid," the brunette said to Frankie.

"Then don't say stupid things."

"Stupid things?" she said, folding her arms. "Listen to *you*."

"Remind you of anyone?" Theresa said, stepping out onto the patio, pointing at the young couple with a wagging wooden spoon. She was smirking playfully. Her hair was pinned up but falling away. She had on Bermuda shorts and an orange sweated-through Hawaiian-print blouse.

Tom gave her a hug and a kiss. He kept his arm around her. She smelled like a million bucks: her own raw scent lurking underneath sweet basil, sautéed onions, and Chanel No. 5.

"Your aunt's right," Tom called to Frankie. "If I've learned one thing in life," he said, sneaking a chaste, furtive squeeze of Theresa's hip, "it's that there's no better quality a woman can have than standing up for herself and telling you when you've said something stupid."

"Oh, yeah?" Frankie said. "I thought all women did that."

"He should know better," the brunette said, turning to Tom and Theresa. "Football players get the same thing that pageant contestants get, which is that people automatically think they're stupid. I was a straight-A student at Florida State."

Frankie dismissed her with a wave of his tongs. "A really smart person wouldn't have to say that all the time."

Theresa and the brunette exchanged a look. Frankie's prospects with this girl were irradiated to subatomic dust.

"I have to go," Tom said. "Keep the girls away from that alligator." He pointed at it. It hadn't moved an inch.

"Who, Luca?"

"You named it?"

"Remember that man who used to work for Vito? The tough guy? Luca Brasi?"

"I remember."

"Doesn't he look like him? Same brow, same dead look in his eyes."

"All alligators do," Tom said. "Just keep the girls away. Sorry I can't stay for dinner."

From the blaring television came the news that the president's motorcade was under way. He was going straight from the airport to the Fontainebleau. Several roads had been closed off for security, none of them likely to cause Tom any inconvenience. The airport was due west of the hotel, and Tom was coming from the north.

He and Theresa kissed again. He started toward his car, a new and sensible blue Buick.

"I'll have a plate waiting for you in the fridge when you get home," she called after him.

"I'm not sure when that will be," Tom said.

"Whenever it is," she said, brushing a wet strand of hair from her face, "it'll be there."

"Bye, Daddy!" Christina called, looking up from her book.

It was hard to tell at this distance if his daughter's face was streaked with sweat or tears. If it was tears, Tom decided, it was probably that book.

"Bye, sweetpea," he called, and kept going.

WHEN TOM SAW THE BLACK CHEVY BISCAYNE IN HIS REAR-view mirror, he pulled over and got out. The Chevy stopped about a hundred yards back. Although the tails were becoming erratic and halfhearted, FBI agents still followed Tom Hagen fairly often. He'd learned the names of the regular agents, and he was unfailingly polite to them. He was especially pleased to see one today. Having an FBI agent on your ass was better than having a bodyguard. Tom waved for the car to come closer, and when it didn't, he started walking toward it.

"Agent Bianchi," Tom said.

"Mr. Hagen."

"I'm going to the Deauville Hotel," he said.

"Isn't that where the Beatles played?" the agent said. "My kids went to that. That's where the Napoleon Ballroom is, right?"

"No idea."

"So what's at the Deauville?"

"I just wanted you to know I'm not going to the Fontainebleau," Tom said. "The Deauville's a little bit north of it, I understand. I don't know a better way to go than the way we're heading, which is the route to the Fontainebleau, too. Is there a better way?"

"You want directions," Bianchi said, "you're going to have to wait'll it's Agent Rand McNally's turn to babysit."

"That's fine," Tom said. "I was just afraid that, as we got closer to the Fontainebleau, you'd be back here wondering if you should pull me over, call ahead to whoever your contact might be with the Secret Service, et cetera. I'm sure it's a mess down there already. This is a president people turn out to see. I'd hate to be responsible for making it even a little bit worse. Do what you think is best, of course. But have I ever steered you wrong?"

The agent sighed. "Just get back in the car," he said, "and do what you need to do."

"Certainly," Hagen said. "I'll need gas on the way. But otherwise," he said, patting the roof like a stock car mechanic signaling that the pit stop was finished, "straight to the Deauville."

True to his word, Tom stopped at a filling station, not far from the Seventy-ninth Street Causeway. He used the phone booth to call Michael Corleone. Michael had flown himself and Rita up to Maine, to visit his children and for a getaway. He'd been waiting by a payphone in the lobby of the inn where they were staying.

"It looks like seven," Michael said, meaning the number of made guys in the Family who, in the time since Geraci's disappearance, finished a prison sentence and took their thank-you trip to Acapulco. The thinking now was that Geraci had made contact with someone there. The Family had sent a few others, too, but only a made guy would have had enough clout to be Geraci's inside man.

"Any names on that list jump out at you?"

"To be honest," Michael said, "no." Naturally, he did not list them on the phone. "Five of the seven were reasonably close associates of the person in question. But Nobilio isn't ready to rule out any of them, even the other two."

"What does Al think?"

"Same as Richie."

He'd put them both on this, his two most trusted men. Nobilio, as a *capo*, would take the lead, of course, which pleased Hagen. He liked Al and trusted him, but he was a man of action, not a strategist.

"What about you?" Tom said. "What do you think?"

"To be perfectly honest," Michael said, "they weren't names I knew very well."

Which was a barometer, Tom now realized, of how far Michael had removed himself from the men on the streets. That removal, until recently, had been the name of the game.

"No go on the other place?" Tom said, meaning Panama City, Florida, the only other place Fausto Geraci had mentioned that had come as news to Al Neri and Tommy Scootch. Tommy had been there a week, looking for leads.

"Nothing," Michael said. "You know, despite everything, this matter isn't my biggest concern right now."

"If you mean down here, everything's so jake it's Jacob."

Tom heard himself blurt this pet saying of Johnny Fontane's and shook his head. He didn't know how Ben Tamarkin did it, working around those Hollywood people all the time without the phoniness rubbing off on him.

"Call me when it's finished. This phone is fine. The innkeeper will come get me."

"It's finished now," Tom said. "It's all set up. But, yeah, I'll call. How are Kay and the kids?"

"Rita and I just got in. A couple hours ago," Michael said. "We pick up Anthony and Mary first thing tomorrow."

"Well, send them my love." Tom hated to think about how long it had been since Michael had seen them. More than a few visits had been canceled at the last minute, sometimes on Michael's end, just as often by Kay or the kids. Rita had never even met Anthony and Mary. It was a big step, but if she and Michael really were getting serious about each other, it had to happen. "How's Rita? Nervous?"

"She did great. A couple of pills for the motion sickness, and she was fine."

He wasn't asking how Rita was on the flight up but how she *was*. Tom let it go. "Look, I'll call somewhere I can get a drink. We'll raise a glass in each other's general direction."

"You know, Tom, Pop would have—"

"Save it." As much as Tom himself had worshipped Vito, Michael's increasingly frequent mentions of the old man were starting to get on his nerves. "I'll call."

On his way back to the car, Tom bought two bottles of Pepsi-Cola from a machine and walked one over to Agent Bianchi.

TOM PULLED UP IN FRONT OF THE DEAUVILLE AND HANDED the valet his keys and a hundred dollars. The valet gave a nod and just like that, three other cars pulled in and blocked Bianchi's way.

It was something Tom did as a precaution and because he could, more than because it was necessary. Tom wasn't doing anything illegal. Bianchi was almost certainly the only agent assigned to watch him. And anything he managed to figure out would be thwarted at the top.

Inside the lobby, Tom didn't recognize anyone as an agent, but just to be on the safe side he made a beeline for the stairs. He was almost to the third floor before he heard anyone else in the stairwell. Hagen couldn't see who it was, but it sounded like a shuffling old man, a person in no hurry. Gassed, Tom opened the door to the third floor and went down the gilded hallway to the other end of the building. No one was following him. His heart was racing. He tried to take long, even breaths. He needed to get back to playing tennis. It was so goddamned hot, but maybe he and Theresa could join a club with an indoor court somewhere and play together. They used to play together all the time . . . when? A lifetime ago. When they were first married.

He should cut back on the cigars, but he knew he never would.

He took the stairs one more flight up and, confident no one was watching, rode the elevator the rest of the way to the suite.

Tom rapped on the door. Pat Geary opened it, as if he were Ben Tamarkin's butler and not, at least for now, the ranking member of the Senate Judiciary Committee. The light from the suite was so bright it almost knocked Tom over. The suite itself was awash in glass, white leather, and blond wood. Along one mirrored wall was an upholstered bar. The sound of a television—convention coverage—wafted in from another room. Tamarkin, dressed in a black guayabera and white linen pants, had positioned himself in a thronelike leather chair in the far corner.

"Always a pleasure," Geary said, showing Tom in. For a man who'd once clumsily tried to shake them down for a bribe and then told Tom and Michael never to contact him again, Geary had certainly seen a lot of them over the years. That the relationship had become a pleasant one was all Fredo. Fredo and Geary had gotten along well, and it had helped the Corleones get innumerable things from Geary with a minimum of fuss. People liked Fredo, and Tom and everyone around him hadn't appreciated the value of that until he was gone.

"I gather you and Mr. Tamarkin know each other?"

Tamarkin stood, and they shook hands. Tamarkin did not take off the dark glasses.

"Good work," Tom said.

"Knock wood," Tamarkin said, making a fist and tapping his skull with it.

"Everything's still set?"

"He'll be here," Tamarkin said, meaning the president's campaign chairman, a former lobbyist for Walt Disney Studios, through whom Tamarkin had negotiated their deal. Hagen hadn't met the man before. He sat back down. "He's coming from the Fontainebleau. You and I have other things to talk about, but it can wait."

"Other things?" But he knew. *The Discovery of America* was now hemorrhaging money. The first *Santa Maria* had sunk. The actress playing Queen Isabella was back on heroin. The grant from the Italian government had been rescinded. And that was just for starters.

"It can wait," Tamarkin said. He wasn't in on the plan, at least not yet.

Tom nodded and turned to Geary. "Listen, before I forget, Senator," Tom said, "tremendous speech last night. I liked what you had to say, sincerely."

"Why, thank you," Geary said. He ducked behind the bar to make them drinks. "I thought it went well."

"It was a triumph," Tom said. "Scotch, rocks."

"I remember," Geary said.

"I'll have a mojito," Tamarkin said.

"A mosquito?" Geary frowned. He seemed legitimately confused.

"Forget it, Festus," Tamarkin said. "I was just banging your cymbals. I don't drink."

Geary stared him down for a second, but he knew what side his bread was buttered on and turned back to Hagen. "*Triumph* may be laying on the bullshit a little thick, Tom. But it was rewarding, getting a chance to speak out for people who otherwise wouldn't have been heard."

Ben Tamarkin folded his arms, apparently set off slightly by the word *rewarding*. Geary was a notorious anti-Semite, and Tamarkin couldn't have relished doing the man any favors.

"On several of your issues," Tom said, "I'm one of those people." Like many men in his position, he took a hard line against street crime. The crimes with which he himself was associated, he considered either victimless (gambling, moneylending, drugs) or perpetrated against people who opted to be involved, who agreed to certain rules and then broke them. "Your common thief," he said, "your mugger, your wife beater, your rapist, and your child molester and the like—we need to keep people like that off the streets."

"Hear, hear," Geary said, and handed Tom his drink. "As I say, we need to reclaim the streets of our cities for decent Americans."

"Looks like you're going to have your chance soon enough," Tom said. "Here's to the right man for the job," he said, and they clinked glasses.

Pat Geary was the right man for the job only in that he was infinitely preferable to the noisy debacle that had been Danny Shea's tenure as attorney general. But Pat Geary didn't know *the streets of our cities* from his flat Protestant ass cheeks. Geary was the son of a wealthy rancher. He'd never *lived* on the streets, the way Tom had. He'd never had to fight for his life every day, or fight just to have something to eat. As a *child,* although Tom hadn't felt like it at the time. He'd been a grotesque creature, he now realized: an eleven-year-old man. Scabbed and filthy and not even mourning his dead parents or thinking about them and the life he'd had, such as it had been. He was overmatched against the regular bullies and the people who'd steal a penny and crust of bread from an orphaned eleven-year-old man, and the predatory boy-fucking freaks—and yet Tom Hagen had survived it. He'd *escaped* it.

Tom excused himself and went out to the balcony and looked out over the ocean while he waited. It was twilight. The view was spectacular but about what he'd have thought: an expanse of white sand and the vast blue-green Atlantic, oil tankers gliding near the horizon, Coast Guard boats closer to shore. Glimpses of the art deco buildings to the north, crisp modern hotels to the south. From here he couldn't see the Fontainebleau, and he certainly couldn't see the Miami Beach Convention Center, where the vice president would soon be giving his speech. He couldn't see Cuba but it seemed to him that he could feel it. He couldn't hear anything wafting his way up here from ground level, but he could feel that, too. Tom Hagen wasn't one to go in for crap like *excitement in the air,* but he had to admit: what he was feeling was about more than the view, more than himself.

Salut', he thought, raising his glass toward the darkening sky, toasting whatever it was.

"WHAT ASSURANCES DO WE HAVE," SAID THE CAMPAIGN chairman, "that even if we do agree to all this, these films won't surface somewhere else when we least expect it?" He was a bald and florid man with pale, nearly invisible eyebrows and the gray pallor insomniacs get. His body seemed to be all curves and no angles.

"If I may?" Tom said.

Tamarkin shrugged. "Be my guest."

"It's impossible," Tom said, "to prove that someone doesn't have a thing, only that he does. Furthermore, who knows how *many* of these films there are out there, somewhere? I'm sure you've discussed this with the president and his brother. I'm sure they have some sense of how often the camera was rolling. What point would there be in us giving every frame of film we have? You probably won't believe us. And there's probably more of this material out there. Unfortunately, sir, we can give you no assurances at all," Tom said, "beyond our word—which I'm sure you've checked out enough to know is a better bet than the sun coming up tomorrow."

"Dick," Geary said, "I can personally vouch for you that this is true."

"If you don't mind," the bald man said. "I'll take the sun and give the points."

"Gambling man, are you?" said Ben Tamarkin.

"As little as possible," the man said.

"What you're really saying," Tom said, "is *why trust us*? What's in it for you? This is where this all makes such good sense. The films are just what got your attention, what got us to the table. I don't see who'd ever print anything like that and show it to the public, and, while it would be a shame if they came into the possession of either the First Lady or the current A.G.'s lovely wife, for all we know, those women have made their peace a long time ago with their husbands' proclivities."

Tom glanced at Geary. The senator immediately leaned back and looked at the ceiling.

"So forget the films. There's *still* more in this for the Sheas than anyone. You saw the response that Senator Geary got last night. If he runs as an independent—which I can assure you we can raise the funds for him to do—he's not going to win, but he's going to siphon off votes from the president. There are voters whose bigotry against Catholics, Jews, and colored people could make them vote for the other guy in November. Senator Geary can either work for you, a voice of moderation that would bring those votes back into the fold, or he can take them with him."

"You're prepared to do that, Pat? To betray the party that's been your home for your whole life?"

"Cut the bullshit, Dick," Geary said. "If it comes to that, it'll be the party that's betrayed me."

"But," Tom said, "if you appoint our friend here as your attorney general, everyone wins. *Everybody.* Senator Geary gets a platform to express and implement his passions."

Geary nodded in assent.

"You get the ranking member of the Senate Judiciary Committee as your attorney general and all the experience and clout that goes with that. As a replacement for—if you'll forgive me—that boy Danny Shea, whose main qualification for the job is that he's the president's brother. He has next to nothing to show for all his reckless, grandstanding initiatives. His so-called war against the so-called Mafia—just to cite one example—has resulted in how many convictions?"

"Ninety-one."

Tamarkin and Geary both chuckled.

"I'm not talking about bookies and pimps," Hagen said. "I mean the kind of big-time gangsters you see in the movies. How many of those people has Danny Shea sent to prison?"

The answer, as they all knew, was zero.

"I get your point."

"Daniel Brendan Shea is in over his head," Tom said, "and I'm sure you and the president agree with us on this count, delicate as that might be to express. But if he steps down now and announces that he's going to run for the Senate in 1966, everyone would understand."

"Because it looks like he's parlaying his success into something else," the bald man said. "I understand."

"*Parlaying*?" Tamarkin said, his thick eyebrows arched impressively. "I don't care what you say, you're a gambler."

"Naturally," Hagen said, "we can't give you any *assurances* that Danny Shea will win, but we do pledge to you that we won't work against him. He'll have a fair and square shot, which is all anyone can ask for, right?"

"Now maybe *you* should cut the bullshit, Mr. Hagen."

"Call me Tom."

"If it's all the same to you," said the bald man, "I'd rather not."

He had the kind of face it was impossible not to imagine punching.

Hagen took a deep breath, and it triggered a coughing fit. Geary shot to his feet and brought Tom a glass of water.

"Sorry," Tom said. "I should switch brands of smokes, I guess."

The bald man shook his head, slowly. "I've got you pegged as the sort of gent who'd rather fight than switch."

It was an allusion to some advertisement. Hagen didn't dignify it with a response.

"As for *this* November," Tom said, "The union vote is very much up in the air, but we've shown that we can deliver that, and overwhelmingly so. There's no third-party candidate to worry about, no scheming little brother looking over the president's shoulder. What's shaping up right now as a close election in November could very well become a landslide—a real mandate for the president. He'll be the biggest, most literal winner in all this." Tom smiled. "All in all," he said, "it's an offer you can't refuse."

The bald man rocked gently back and forth. Denial and anger must have happened before he arrived; he was keening his miserable way through bargaining and depression and toward acceptance.

Ben Tamarkin took out a briefcase. It was full of banded packs of thousand-dollar bills and a list of names and addresses of real people to whom its donation could be severally ascribed, should the campaign wish to go to the trouble.

"Whattaya say, Dick?" Tamarkin popped open the latches. "Friends?"

GEARY AND THE CAMPAIGN MANAGER HURRIED TO THE convention center to go watch Vice President Payton's speech, and Tamarkin joined Tom Hagen on the balcony for a celebratory Cuban cigar. Like his father, Michael Corleone insisted on hearing bad news right away. But good news, like a full-bodied red wine, needed to breathe for a while to be fully savored.

He'd done it.

He imagined that this was how a person must feel right after he realizes he's been elected president but before he emerges from private to share this with the world.

Tamarkin, who'd been paid handsomely for the services he'd just rendered, made them two more drinks and proposed a toast.

It was dark now, but it still must have been ninety degrees outside.

"Here's to the mercenaries," he said. "To every soldier of fortune, every gun for hire, and every goddamned American lawyer who ever drew a breath."

Tamarkin didn't understand. Hagen was not a mercenary. It was too complicated to explain, though. But as he started to raise his glass, exhaustion hit him like a wave, like a wall of water, and he all but collapsed into a chair.

"You going to be all right?" Tamarkin said.

Tom shook his head. "I'm fine."

Tamarkin cocked his head, dubious. "I should maybe call a doctor?"

"It's not my heart, OK? Nothing like that. I'm fine. I'm just . . ." Happy? He ran his fingers through his thinning hair. "I've just been burning the candle on both ends, that's all."

More than a year after he'd met with Joe Lucadello in the chapel of the Fontainebleau, here Tom Hagen was, just up the road. He'd made it through tough times before, but nothing like this. With Michael falling apart, with the government of the most powerful nation in the history of the world on his balls, Tom had come out the other side, a little the worse for wear but in every important way unscathed. Nothing that just happened was a surprise to Tom—that was how he liked it, always, and he busted his ass so that things went like that—but there was a difference between anticipating a happy ending and experiencing it.

"You need to get your rest," Tamarkin said. "Take a vacation, for Christ's sake. The cemeteries are full of people who thought they were too busy to take a vacation."

"I'm really OK." And he was. He stood. He was steady on his feet now. His second scotch sat sweating on the table, untouched. His cigar had gone out. The cocktail of elation and fatigue surging through him was all he could handle. He'd call Michael from home. Tom wanted to be home, with his family. "But I think I'm going to shove off."

Tamarkin patted him on the back. "Do that," he said. "Call me tomorrow, though, about our emerging fiasco back in the old country."

Hagen had forgotten. The Corleones' takeover of Woltz International Pictures was, like everything all of a sudden, going just the way it was supposed to go. "Will do."

He took the elevator down. He stared into the mirror, at the face of the gloriously happy fool grinning back at him.

CHAPTER 26

A few blocks away from the hotel, Hagen felt a cold gun barrel press against the back of his neck and nearly jumped out of his skin. There, in the rearview mirror, was Nick Geraci.

"That was a nice trick," Geraci said, "duking that parking guy a hundred bucks." He laughed. "Take a wild guess what two hundred bucks can do."

Tom started to pull the car over.

"Ah-ah-ah," Nick said. "Keep driving."

The other man in the stairwell, Tom thought. The shuffling footsteps. It had been Geraci.

"So how long have you been following me?" Tom asked.

"Turn left up here," Geraci said. Wherever he'd been all this time, he'd come back with a nice tan and bulging muscles.

"You're making a huge mistake, Nick," Tom said. "For a number of reasons."

"Please don't say *You'll never get away with this.*"

"You do know I've got the FBI tailing me wherever I go, right?"

Hagen looked again in the rearview and tried to see around Nick's big, square head, but there was no immediate sign of Agent Bianchi's black Chevy.

"Gee, that's funny," Nick said. "I don't see him, either. This is just a guess, but it might have something to do with one of those parking jockeys back at the hotel. You've seen the way they whip those cars around. I wouldn't be surprised if every once in a while they hit something." Geraci gave Hagen's shoulder a squeeze, the way a pal would. "You want to take a guess at what a *thousand* bucks can buy, you cheap Irish prick?"

Tom couldn't believe this was happening to him. He touched his neck. The pulse, oddly, didn't seem much out of the ordinary. He took it as a good sign. "German-Irish," he said.

"My apologies," Geraci said. "You German-Irish prick."

"I'm pulling over," Tom said, but didn't, yet.

He glanced in the mirror again. There was a bread truck right behind them. Maybe Nick was bluffing. Maybe Bianchi was behind that truck.

"Maybe you should drive," Tom said.

"You're doing fine."

"I'm not going to do you the service of driving us to wherever you've decided to do this."

"Decided to do what?" Geraci said.

"You were always a wiseass," Hagen said. "But I was never amused. Cut the crap, huh?"

Tom kept driving. There was some way out of this mess, he thought. If he could figure out how to get the Justice Department off his ass, he could surely come up with something that would throw off a punch-drunk mook from Cleveland. He'll still get to take a remorseless piss on Geraci's grave. Maybe sooner rather than later.

"Hmm, let's see," Geraci said, mocking him. "You're thinking maybe you could go for the gun, right? But then you remember what a pussy you are compared to me, so that's out."

Tom stared straight ahead. They were going though a neighborhood of nurseries, trailer parks, and tawdry little motels.

"Then you're thinking," Geraci said, "I'll just convince this dumb *cafone* that we can bury the hatchet, and not in each other's skulls. Where's it all end, this cycle of revenge? Nick, we need you. Everyone but you and me and Mike: they're morons. Let's all make the music of beautiful business together. Sadly, that's such a load of shit, even a lying bastard like you couldn't keep a straight face."

"You're good," Tom said, as dryly as he could. "It's amazing."

"Yeah," Geraci said. "I've been on the lam with a traveling carnival, working as a mind reader. Turns out, I have a gift."

Tom unconsciously started to shake his head at Geraci's pathetic sense of humor. A split second later, when it provoked Nick to dig the gun barrel harder against the base of Tom's neck, it became conscious.

"Bear right," Nick said. "Right here."

Tom obeyed. The bread truck turned right as well. It let Tom see what was behind it: a yellow convertible, top down, a girl in a bikini behind the wheel and a shirtless boy beside her. Definitely not FBI.

"By now," Geraci said, "your mind is racing. Because, hey, you're Tom Hagen! Let's see . . . you could say you have to take a leak, and if I don't tell you just to piss yourself, you can try something to or from the john. Or maybe we'll pass a police station and you can just duck in there. Maybe that'll work. You want me to be on the lookout for a police station?"

No. He'd keep it simple. He'd stop in a well-lit place, with as many people around as possible. That's all it would take.

"I guess this is why we never found you. Because you're such a mind reader."

"No," Geraci said. "You never found me because that fucking CIA shitbird you and Mike went into business with was playing us all for fools. You never found me because he was protecting you. Kill me, and the FBI would have nailed you guys for murder. He was ordered to tell you where I was, and he followed those orders. It's just that he took it on his own initiative to tip me off right before he told you. Not for my benefit, but for yours. This is your federal tax dollars at work, Tom. These are the people who think they're the good guys."

There had to be a bargain he could strike with Geraci. But Hagen was drawing a blank.

"Pull over, if you want," Geraci said. "Ideally, someplace brightly lit and with a lot of people. We're going to pass a dog track pretty soon. That'd be just the ticket, huh?"

Tom had to fight off any feelings of anxiety—any feelings at all.

Geraci pulled the gun very slightly back, then started tapping it against Tom's head, no harder than someone might tap a person's shoulder to get his attention.

"You think you've got this all figured out," Geraci said, "don't you?"

Hagen made eye contact in the mirror. Both *yes* and *no* seemed like the wrong thing so say. Nick's face was slack and unreadable, unnaturally so, a symptom of his Parkinson's that was exaggerated by the pale glow from the streetlights. "Why isn't your hand shaking?" Tom said. "Isn't that part of what's wrong with you?"

"Thank you for your concern," Geraci said. "Those things come and go. I have a theory that it helps to be active. I go to a gym a little bit, and, you know, even when I'm on my way there, thinking about hitting the speed bag or some ugly sonofabitch such as yourself? The tremors—*poof.* They're just gone. Magic. Hey, where's my manners? How are *you*? Take a left up there, by the way. At the light."

The street they were on had become brighter and more commercial, flanked on both sides by retail stores and storefront offices, all of them closed. It was a little after ten. Fucking Florida.

"Your manners?" Tom said.

"I heard about your heart attack. How are you doing with that?"

"How did you hear about that?"

"You're an important man," Geraci said. "People talk about important men."

As Tom got in the left lane, the light turned red. From the sheer force of habit, he stopped. It didn't matter. Even if he'd gunned it, there were no cops around to pull him over.

"Nobody outside my family knows about that," Tom said. "The doctor actually said he didn't know for sure that it even *was* a heart attack."

"That's great," Geraci said. "That's good news. But I've been watching you awhile now. A person should really take better care of himself. Eat better, maybe cut down on the smoking and such."

"Thank you, Dr. Geraci."

"Scoff if you want," Nick said, "but you know, my father died of a heart attack."

Geraci pulled the gun away, and Hagen glanced up at the mirror in time to see the bread truck behind them and the butt of the gun coming down toward him.

Then everything exploded into white light.

WHEN TOM CAME TO, HIS HEAD WAS POUNDING, PAIN SO blinding he could hardly bear to open his eyes. He was tied up. There was something wrong with his hearing, too, as if he were in a cave under a waterfall.

But he was still in his Buick, he realized, still in the front seat, tied to it, upright. He could barely see. There was a yellow haze from his headlights but no other light he could see. He tried to shake the wooziness out of his head. It hurt so bad that it was almost like getting hit again. It was the pain and the wooziness that kept him from immediately feeling the water or hearing the splashing.

He wasn't under a waterfall. He was *in* water, fetid and brown, rushing into the car. He was *under*water. All four windows were open. He couldn't have been here long. And he wouldn't have long. He wasn't tied up with rope. It was duct tape. He was encased in it from his waist to his shoulders. His ankles and knees were taped together, too.

Tom felt the tires of his car sinking into the muck. The water was warmer than his blood.

He began to shout and to thrash against the tape, which made the pain in his head even more agonizing. The water was above the seats now. Above his navel. Above his heart.

He would still get out of this. The water would make the duct tape lose its adhesive. He kept struggling. He thought he felt some give in the tape that was around his ankles.

The Buick's electrical system sizzled. Just as the headlights flickered out, a big black snake swam by on the other side of the windshield, but Tom Hagen's heart withstood that, too.

"If you want to kill a snake, you don't chop off the tail," he said out loud. It gave Tom a perverse feeling of satisfaction that Geraci had come for him first and not Michael.

He kept struggling. He definitely felt give in the tape now, everywhere. The water was up to his chin.

He tilted his head toward the roof of the car and got ready to take a deep breath. He could do this. It was a matter of will. Who had more will than he did?

His ankles were free now and so, almost, were his knees. There was all kinds of give around his right arm. Any second now, his arm would be free.

The back of his head was in the water. It was time to take the breath. *Now.*

He started slowly, evenly, drawing air into his lungs.

Suddenly there was a tickle in this throat and a catch in his chest, and his head snapped forward, and he was having a coughing fit.

Gasping for air, except that there was no air to breathe. What he'd already breathed in was swamp water, and any air there was to breathe was now above his head, somewhere.

He'd heard that drowning was the most peaceful way to die.

There was nothing in Tom Hagen's convulsing body that suggested peace.

He tried to stop coughing and tried to stop taking in water, but his body betrayed him.

His mind, he thought, would not betray him.

He would concentrate.

He would think his way out of this.

No. He couldn't. He had to accept that.

He willed himself to let go, because there was no other way to think about what he wanted to think about. In his mind, he drew his family to him, and for one horrible, lovely moment, he looked into the imagined faces of Theresa, of his boys, Frank the lawyer and Andrew, who would be a priest, and his girls, Christina, who would be a beauty, and Gianna, who would be a beauty, too.

And then he lost any control that he had of anything, and, just as the Buick's electrical system had shorted out moments ago, Tom Hagen's life started flickering out, and what he thought about was not his whole life but Sonny.

Sonny Corleone, who was dead. Shot to pieces.

But what he saw was Sonny, as a boy, in that alley.

Tom hadn't been *friends* with Sonny Corleone, at least not at first. That was a lie he and Sonny made up, one they told even to each other, even to themselves. All they'd ever said, even to one another, about what led up to Sonny's decision to bring Tom home to live with his family, was that it had been a cold day in Hell's Kitchen. But what had really happened was that Sonny and two older boys had wandered into an alley in an Irish part of the neighborhood, a bad place, but one where Tom knew how to hide and where to sleep and stay warm and even what nearby garbage cans had the best food. Snow fell. It was a big snowstorm. A man on the corner was selling switchblades. He was really a pimp, and he wasn't right in the eyes, and the boys asked how much for a stick, and the man said he didn't sell to boys. They weren't boys, they argued, and he laughed in a way that was almost a scream and said that *proved* it: only a boy would say he wasn't a boy. Tom Hagen would have said he wasn't a boy, too, but he didn't want to take any hope whatsoever from the pimp who wasn't right in the eyes. Also, he was hiding and didn't want to say anything. The pimp told the boys that he also refused to sell to dagos, and when they started to get tough about the slur, he pulled one of his knives and grabbed Sonny by the throat, and the two older boys took off running. The man selling switchblades who was really a pimp was also something else, and Tom knew about it. Tom had seen the man cut his girls, but the man didn't

seem to want to be with his girls. The man with the switchblades who wasn't
right in the eyes found kids in trouble who'd suck his cock for half a sandwich, except that usually he pulled a knife on them and didn't bother with
the sandwich. Tom Hagen had stayed clear of this man, and he'd never sucked
anybody's cock for a sandwich or anything else for that matter, though there
had been times when he'd been so delirious with hunger pain that he knew
he'd have done it, and he thought that maybe he'd just been lucky about how
he'd felt on the days when he'd seen this man, this pimp, who also sold
switchblades. But now the man was dragging Sonny down the alley, and Tom
didn't think about anything, he just acted. Like the grotesque creature that
he was, he came up howling from out of the ground, out of the space under
a stoop where he was getting too big to hide, and he grabbed a splintered board
and hit the man in the back of the head. It was everyone's good dumb luck—
Sonny's, to be sure, but Hagen's more so, and even humanity's—that the
board had a nail in it and the nail impaled the man who sold women and
switchblades in the side of his neck and a gout of blood spewed out onto the
falling snow like red sleet. It was that man's good luck, too, because his life
was violent and miserable and now it was almost over. Tom's life was almost
over, too, now. Why wasn't his whole life flashing before his eyes? Why was
it this he was seeing? What he was seeing was this: he and Sonny were pum-
meling the man with the eyes that weren't right, and when he fell they kicked
him, too, and when they realized he wasn't moving, which might have been
a fraction of a second or it might have been forever—the way this felt, Tom
thought, underwater, his head lolling to the side—then Tom and Sonny
stopped, gasping for breath. They looked around and saw that there were witnesses, adults, men and women—fathers and mothers, probably—wrapped in
cloth overcoats. No one was going to miss this man with the eyes that weren't
right, and, one by one, the adults turned their backs on him and walked away
muttering things. Tom and Sonny looked at each other, and they could have
done a lot of things more likely than what they did do, which was to laugh,
to let go of everything that had just happened to them and laugh, hard. And
the laughing hurt because the air was so cold and they were doing it so hard.

They were a cunt's hair shy of crying, but they didn't. Tom had cried when his mother died, when his father died, but he did not cry now, and he would never cry again, not once, the rest of his life—which was flickering out now, somewhere in the Everglades. Sonny didn't cry then, either, but was a big-hearted, sentimental lug who wept fat, unashamed tears at weddings and funerals and sad movies and especially, epically, when he stood in the hospital hallway and got his first glimpse of his beautiful twin girls, Francesca and Katherine, and then his boys, too. Tom was there with him, all three times. Mike and Fredo were there for the twins. Tom was happy to have seen this now, and he almost wept with joy when he saw his own children behind that big hospital window, too, but then a thunderbolt of pain hit him now, too, which wasn't supposed to happen—was it? When you're dying? Tom would have given anything to feel his wife's fingertips brush his skin—anything, *anything*—but instead he was back with Sonny, who was also dead, standing in the snow over that dead pimp. Tom looked the bigger boy squarely in the eyes and told him—the way an adult would, the way a father would—that there are things that have to be done and you do them and you never talk about them. You don't try to justify them, because they can't be justified. You just do them. Then you forget it. *My name is Santino Corleone,* Sonny said, his arm outstretched. Steam rose from the wound in the dead pimp's neck. *Tom Hagen,* Tom said, and they shook hands.

They walked away, together. Sonny looped an arm around Tom, and Tom did the same to Sonny. Sonny asked where Tom lived, and Tom just shook his head. Sonny asked Tom what was wrong with his eye, and Tom said it was some kind of infection, he didn't know. His mother had had the same thing, and then she died. Sonny asked about Tom's father, and Tom couldn't even bring himself to say it, that his father had been torn up with grief over his mother's death, and a few months later he'd successfully drunk himself to death. *Well, all right then,* Sonny said. *You and me. We're brothers now.* Tom Hagen's final living thought was of that huge blue bowl of spaghetti Mama Corleone, who was dead now, too, put before him that day: the aroma of her oily, rich tomato sauce, the sound of her voice, ordering him to eat.

CHAPTER 27

"Come to bed." Rita Duvall, in a nightgown and with a sleep mask pushed up in her mussed red hair, came padding into the darkened lobby of the inn. Michael was slumped in a wing chair he'd dragged over by the payphone. "Tomorrow's . . . well, it's three in the morning, so I suppose that today is tomorrow. All the more reason you should come to bed, darling. Get some sleep."

"I don't think I could sleep," Michael said.

"Come to bed, anyway," she said.

"I don't think I could do that, either."

"I'm not suggesting you do anything," she said, "except rest. C'mon. Let me just take care of you. I can do that, you know."

"I just can't."

"I gather there's no word."

Michael shook his head.

"Did you call Theresa back?"

"I didn't," he said. It was so unlike Tom not to call when he said he would that when Michael called his home in Florida, he'd let it slip to Theresa that he'd been expecting to hear from Tom about an hour earlier. Given Tom and Theresa's recent troubles, she'd jumped to the conclusion that this all had something to do with another woman. Michael had told her he hoped like hell that another woman was all they had to worry about. That sent Theresa on a screaming tirade. He'd had to hang up on her. "I'm giving it until at least dawn, I think."

Better yet, he'd have Al Neri call her. He was on his way up here, driving.

"Sunrise is nearly an hour later down there, remember."

"Yeah? How do you know that?"

"I am French," she said.

"What does being French have to do with it?"

Her hands danced, making some kind a kind of voilà gesture. "We are passionate about the sun and the sunrise. The promise of a new day, yes? And more to enjoy."

"Yes."

"Speaking of a new day, did you check your sugar? Because you're not going to be any good to anyone tomorrow if—"

"It's fine," Michael said. He'd gotten better about keeping tabs on his diabetes. It had been a long time since he'd had any sort of incident.

"You don't think we should go back to New York?" There was a heart-breaking mixture of fear and hopefulness in Rita's voice. "Do you?"

Yes, he thought. "No," he said. "Of course we're not going back." He couldn't.

She brightened.

Rita was pushing to get engaged, which Michael wasn't even going to consider until she and his kids had a good relationship. More important, Michael had canceled so many other visits with Mary and Anthony at the last minute that he couldn't bear the thought of coming all the way here to see them and then not seeing them. Also, he had presents to deliver, deliveries he was supposed to coordinate. So he had to see this through.

"There's probably a logical explanation for why Tom didn't call," Michael said. "I may be overreacting. This is all probably nothing."

"If it's probably nothing," she said, "then you should definitely come to bed."

Michael looked at the telephone, as if he might be able to will it to ring.

Moments later, he lay in bed, staring up at the frilly canopy. For maybe two minutes, Rita rubbed her hand over his chest in consolation, then dropped off to sleep.

Michael lay still and awake until the sun came up, then got out of bed, showered, got dressed, and went to sit by the payphone.

"SO WHAT DOES YOUR GUT TELL YOU?" MICHAEL SAID.

"Three eggs over easy with sausage," Al Neri told the waitress. Michael hadn't noticed her. He wasn't hungry, but he ordered the same thing and would force himself to eat it.

They were having coffee in a diner down the street from the inn. Rita was back in the room getting ready. Al looked reasonably rested. He'd had someone drive him up here, and he'd slept in the car. Michael had bags under his eyes and his white hair was disheveled. He could have passed for sixty.

"My gut," Neri said, "says he's in custody."

"Wouldn't we have heard from Sid Klein by now?"

"Did you call Sid Klein?"

"I did. He hasn't talked to Tom in weeks."

"I'm not necessarily saying they have him for that thing that blew over," Al said. Meaning Judy Buchanan. "I've got a bad feeling that maybe the Feds have some dirt on him. Tom mentioned he had his FBI tail when he talked to you, right? So that seems to rule out anyone making a move on Tom *except* them. Plus, we know that the FBI is getting some kind of information from that girl out in Arizona." Meaning, Bev Geraci. "So that's my feeling."

"Just your feeling?"

"Maybe a little more than that. Tom goes to strike that deal and then, *poof,* he's gone. Whether it's bribery they got him on or whether it's something unrelated, I don't know. What I'm doing is answering your question.

You asked me my gut, I'm telling you my gut." Neri shrugged. "To tell the truth," he whispered, "I'd be kind of relieved if it *wasn't* custody."

"Relieved?" Michael said. "Relieved how?"

"Look, Tom's almost as much a brother to me as to you," Al said, "but the fact remains he's not Sicilian, not Italian even. I know of Irish gangsters who sold out their friends, but never one of us."

"Tom is one of us."

"I'm not saying he's not, in that sense," Al said. "But if it ever comes to pass that he's looking at a long prison sentence of some kind, I, personally, would be nervous. Tom's got loyalty in spades but no conscience. You know this better than anybody. Nothing he's ever done has been for anything but the greater good of Tom Hagen. Loyalty to you and your family has been good for him, but if the time ever came that things changed . . ." Al blew on his coffee. "Let's just hope we never get to that moment."

Michael tapped his knife against the chipped Formica tabletop.

"Tom is my brother," Michael said. "I'm going to try to forget you ever told me this."

"Right," Al said. "You're right. If I overstepped, I'm sorry. Thank you."

Their food came, and Michael gave it a try. Al's was nearly gone before Michael had made it through his first rubbery egg.

"So," Michael said. "We're one hundred percent certain Tom got the deal done?"

"I talked to Geary and Tamarkin directly, and they both say yes," Al said. "Ben Tamarkin swears Tom left the hotel at about nine. So that all checks out."

"And the contributions were delivered?"

"They were," Neri said. "I'm convinced that the deal was done. I even talked to some people we know in New Jersey." He waggled his black sunglasses case to underscore that he was talking about Black Tony Stracci. "The ball's rolling. The senate thing in '66, all that."

"Forget about New Jersey. Who are you talking to down in Miami? Which of our people?"

Neri shrugged hopelessly.

"What's that supposed to mean?"

"Other than Tom, what do we got who does business down there? Richie Nobilio's up to his eyeballs with business in New York, and the men he's got running his Fort Lauderdale things are just low-level guys," Al said. "Which is about all we got down there period. Nobody of consequence."

"Are you sure?" Michael said. "Nobody?"

It took Al a few tortured moments to realize that Michael was referring to Nick Geraci. Or maybe Al was just preoccupied with the last few bites of his final sausage.

"I don't think so," Al finally said. "We can't rule it out entirely, but even if he's in the area, I don't see how he'd get to Tom. Seems like that FBI tail rules it out."

"And we can't find out anything from the FBI?"

"This is your lack of sleep talking," Al said. "How would we do that?"

Michael sighed. "It would be difficult," he said, "but not impossible."

"Well, if you want to send me out on that, give me the details. In the meantime, I got calls in to some friends of friends down in Miami," Al said, signaling the waitress to bring more coffee. "Real subtle ones, so don't worry about nobody figuring nothing out. Also, as a kind of just-in-case, Tommy's driving down from Panama City as we speak. Tommy can be our man on the scene in Miami, if unfortunately there ends up being a scene."

"Tommy," Michael said. "You sent Tommy?"

"He was already in Florida."

"Do you have any idea what a big state Florida is? That's probably a ten-, twelve-hour drive. Anyone we flew down from New York would get there faster."

"You want me to send someone else down, boss, say the word. And no offense if it's because you don't have enough faith in Tommy."

"I don't have *any* faith in Tommy. For all I know, Tommy's our traitor. It would explain why the rat he's chased all this time has never bitten him."

"Tommy's not the traitor," Al said, "and if he is, I'd be the first to take care of him."

"You say that as if you'd have any choice in the matter."

"I wouldn't *want* a choice in the matter. If it came to that."

Michael nodded. Good old Al. For better or for worse, they'd be together forever.

"Tommy's fine," Michael said. "For now anyway."

He pushed his plate away. He'd eaten maybe half his food.

"Tell me this, though," Michael said. "Geary is a known commodity, but tell me why we should trust Ben Tamarkin?"

"Don't take this wrong," Al said, "but I'm starting to worry about you. What would it benefit Ben Tamarkin to do anything to Tom?"

Michael took a long pull from his coffee. "I don't know," he said. "But, right now, we can't take anything for granted."

"When would I ever do that?" Al said.

Michael reached across the booth and gave his old friend a pat on the shoulder.

IN LIGHT OF THE SITUATION WITH HAGEN, AL AND HIS driver—Donnie Bags, who'd proven himself loyal in the months he'd been reporting to Tommy—opted to stay in Maine as long as Michael did. When it came time to go pick up the kids, they took Al's car—a black Coupe de Ville—since it was bigger. Donnie Bags stayed behind at the inn. Al drove. Rita prattled on, sweetly vulnerable, about not knowing how to behave around kids. He'd told her before that all she needed to know came from having been a kid herself, but now he just let her talk. The trick with women is knowing when to just let them talk.

Soon they were coming up the winding, tree-lined road to the Trask Academy. Not far behind were a delivery van and two pickup trucks, one towing a boat, the other a trailer. Kay taught in the middle school here, and she and the kids lived on a lake, in one of the old stone houses supplied to faculty. Every time he visited this place, Michael Corleone couldn't shake the feeling that he was coming home. Kay and his children were having exactly the life Michael had planned for them, except that Michael found himself standing outside it. He could trace the events that had made this happen. Explaining it was another matter.

Back when he was in college, he'd hoped to someday teach mathematics, either at a university or at a prep school like this. When Michael had been in the Civilian Conservation Corps—and, later, when he'd lived in the Sicilian countryside outside the town of Corleone—he'd vowed that he'd raise his children in the fresh air, away from the literal and the metaphoric filth of the cities. Kay was from New Hampshire, and after an initial period of excitement over living in New York, she'd gotten her fill of it and had come to share this dream with him. And they'd tried. The house on Lake Tahoe had come close. There were times at Lake Tahoe he'd looked around and thought that—despite the difficulties—he was living his dream. And maybe, for a time, he really was.

But there were other times. The worst times of all. The machine guns that opened fire on him and his family. What Fredo allowed to happen to himself. The bloody and intricate nightmares that lay behind those things.

This place, though, was the genuine article. Ordinarily, Michael hated himself for second-guessing any of his decisions, business or personal. In his world, that was a defect that could get a man killed. But the Trask Academy was—to paraphrase a line from a short story often taught here—a summons to all his foolish blood: perched on a wide, sloping hill, surrounded by a lush Maine woods and yet only an hour away from the beach, featuring such other attractive qualities as finely coached athletic teams and the opportunity to grow up alongside boys and girls from America's ruling-class families.

Now he was coming here as a guest, to try to get reacquainted with his children and to introduce them to the woman he was dating, who'd gotten it in her head that maybe someday he'd consider marrying her. Despite her background in the entertainment business, Rita was a lovely person in every sense of the word. He was very fond of her. He was accustomed to her. She was easy to be with. It was possible that he loved her.

But at the first glimpse of Kay on the white porch of her stone house, Michael knew that he could never be married to anyone else.

Like most intelligent women, Kay was getting better-looking as she grew older. Her hair was drawn back, pleasantly askew in the summer breeze off the lake. Her arms were bare, and she had a deep tan a half-shade lighter than her blouse. Her cream-colored slacks had a 1940s-style drape that couldn't help but remind him of when they'd first met, but there was so much more to her now: fuller-hipped, her arms toned from swimming and playing tennis, her girlishness conquered and replaced by what looked like serenity.

Best of all, she was flanked by her children, with her arms around them, but not possessively: it looked, in fact, more like she was gently pushing them toward their father. Mary, on the left, was all coltish exuberance, an eleven-year-old girl in a summer dress, her dark hair meticulously styled, barely able to contain herself. Anthony was on the right, gawky from a recent growth spurt, sulky and insolent-looking from being a thirteen-year-old boy. Although his game wasn't for a few hours, he was already wearing his baseball uniform—*Wolves* written in red chenille script across his son's newly broadened chest.

For a giddy moment, Michael wondered what it would take, how it might be possible, to get Kay back, to reassemble his broken family.

"Penny for your thoughts," Rita said, grabbing him by the knee, startling him. He'd almost forgotten she was there.

"They're not worth it," Michael said. "Keep your money. You ready?"

She nodded.

Rita, by comparison with Kay, seemed starved-looking and uselessly pretty. A flamingo to Kay's lioness.

"You'll do great," Michael said.

They got out of the car. Mary sprinted across the lawn to embrace him. Anthony, carrying their suitcases, dutifully walked over and followed suit.

Michael made the introductions. This was no surprise to any of them. They'd all heard about one another and seen pictures. Everything was cordial. Kay stayed back but Michael drew her in, too. What disturbed him, though, was the look of alarm in Kay's eyes when she sized him up. "You're looking good, Michael," she said, without a trace of sarcasm. "Have you lost weight?"

"Kay," he said, "this is Marguerite Duvall."

"It's an honor," Kay said. "I saw you on Broadway in *Cattle Call*."

"Call me Rita."

From his perspective, the women's handshake did not seem unduly awkward.

"Yeah," Anthony said. "It was really great. I loved the burning bordello scene and that one song, the one about Dallas. We talked about doing it in drama club."

Rita thanked him.

Michael plucked at Anthony's uniform. The boy flinched, but only slightly. "I thought we were all going out to lunch before the game," Michael said.

"I get too nervous," Anthony said. "I can't eat until after."

"That's fine," Michael said. "We can just get hot dogs or something."

"You don't have to go to the game, Dad," Anthony said.

"Are you kidding?" he said. "I wouldn't miss it for the world."

Anthony looked skeptical.

"It's fine if you and Mary and Miss Duvall all go and do something else. I may not even play today."

Michael glanced at Kay, and she gave him a look that let him know he was on his own. "Are you saying you don't want me there?"

"No, sir."

Michael had to admire that *sir*. It was both respectful and got its dig in at the same time. It was the sort of thing he'd prided himself on doing at that age, before he grew up and came to understand his father's greatness.

Just then, the delivery van and the two pickups rolled up. They parked behind the Coupe de Ville, and Al Neri got out of the car to help them. A tractor sputtered toward them as well.

"Oh, my God," Kay said. "This is a joke, right? You brought Al here?"

Abashed, Al gave her a little wave and went to talk to the man on the tractor.

Anthony seemed to shrink back behind his mother. Suddenly, he looked more like a boy than a man. There was something akin to terror in his eyes.

"Michael," Kay said, "if you thought you needed Al Neri's *protection*, then explain to me what you're doing here? What you're doing anywhere *near* my children."

Anthony, his eyes still on Al, took another step back, toward the house.

"Our children, Kay. And it's not what you think. He came up here to give me a message."

"He couldn't have called you?"

"He also came up to help me with this," Michael said. A lie, but a white one. He was helping now, wasn't he?

"What's *this*?" Kay said.

But then the back doors of the trailer opened.

"A *pony*!" Mary shrieked. "Oh, Daddy!"

She threw her arms around him and then ran to the horse.

"Connie had one," Michael said to Kay.

"Wait," Kay said, "you just show up here for a visit, and you bring—"

"I called the headmaster," Michael said. "He said it would be fine to stable it here."

"You called the headmaster and not me?"

"The fishing boat is for you, Anthony," Michael said. The man with the tractor was hooking up to the boat trailer now.

Anthony scowled as only a teenage boy can. "I don't *fish*."

"You'll love it," Rita said. "It is so relaxing, to fish. When I was a girl, my father . . ."

Rita caught the looks from Kay and Anthony and her voice trailed away.

"You're giving him a *boat*? Michael, I . . ." Kay seemed almost to be sputtering for breath.

"Of course you fish," Michael said to Anthony. "You used to fish with . . ." He stopped himself. "We can go fishing together, this week, just you and me."

"You need a license," Anthony said. "It's the law."

"We'll get the license."

"If you don't have a license, it's poaching."

"What did I just *say*?" Michael said, and Anthony took another small step back.

Red-faced, Kay pointed at the delivery van.

"Please tell me that whatever it is that's behind Door Number Three," she said, "it's not for me."

" 'Door Number Three'?" Michael said, confused.

"It comes from a television game show," said Rita, who, until recently, had a game show herself, though not that one.

"Thank you for your *help*," Kay said.

The women stared each other down. "You're very welcome," Rita said.

Mary was still gamboling around the horse, ecstatic, accompanying it as the groom led it to the stable. Nearly every other girl on campus—other faculty brats, since classes didn't start for another two weeks—had come wandering out to see it, too. But only girls. It was as if the receipt of a gift pony sent out a high-pitched whistle only girls could hear. Rita took it as an excuse to tag along.

"It's a pool table," Michael said to Kay. "It's a donation to the school, although I was hoping that the kids and I could break it in while we're here. Do you play, Anthony?"

"Not really."

"I'll teach you," Michael said.

"I guess," Anthony said, and went to put the suitcases in the car.

"I called the headmaster on this one, too," Michael told Kay. "He said that the school was already redoing the rec room."

"News to me."

"It was his suggestion, Kay. I asked him to mention a few needs, and pool table was on the list. It sort of spoke to me. When I was your age, Anthony," Michael called to him, "your uncle Fredo and I used to go into the city all the time and play pool. We both got to be pretty good. Made a little money, too."

Michael caught Kay's look.

"Give it a rest, Kay. When did you become such a . . ." Words failed him. It was contagious. "He's thirteen," Michael said. "He's a man."

Anthony slammed the trunk shut and looked at his father as if he were grateful for the recognition, which had been the effect Michael was hoping for.

"He is a man," Kay agreed, "but he's never going to be a man who—"

"Let's not get into all this, Kay," Michael said. "All right? If you and I need to talk alone, that's fine. But otherwise, let's not."

Kay took a deep breath. "Forget it," she said. "Just . . . forget it."

"I'll try," he said.

She gave him a list of typed instructions—a lesson plan, she joked, but she wasn't joking. It spelled out all the activities the kids had this week and detailed directions about everything, as if he'd never taken care of his own kids before. She told him she had a carbon copy of the list in case he lost it.

What he was trying not to lose was his cool. Around everyone but his wife and his kids he was unflappable. His ex-wife, rather. It was pathetic how she could get to him, so fast, with so little apparent effort or volition.

How long had it been that he'd wondered about getting back with her? How goddamned crazy was that impulse?

Kay's hypocrisy about him using his money and influence to help the school, and help make this visit a nice one—it was a little much, he thought. Kay didn't need to teach, of course, but she'd been determined to do so. Michael had no quarrel with that. She found it rewarding and so God bless. Trask had, in fact, been her dream job, a place she'd talked about teaching, back in college, when they were still dating. As far as Michael knew, Kay believed she'd gotten this job on her own, and not because of an anonymous donation from the Vito Corleone Foundation. She must have had her suspicions. Her previous experience—she'd taught briefly, right out of college, at a school in her hometown in New Hampshire, and then not at all for twelve years—hardly made her an irresistible candidate for a position at perhaps the best coeducational prep school in the country.

AS THEY WERE MAKING THEIR WAY TO THEIR SEATS, Michael thought he was aware of furtive whispers from the other parents, but no one had the nerve to come up and introduce himself. Al Neri stayed in his Cadillac, listening to the Yankee/Red Sox game on the car radio. The car was parked beside a payphone. They sat in the bleachers behind home plate, right next to the concession stand. Michael went to go get the hot dogs and sodas himself.

"I saw *Cattle Call*, too," Mary said to Rita. "Mom said to be sure to remember that no matter how good you were in that play, it doesn't mean you're really a prostitute. Isn't that hilarious?"

"Mmm," Rita said. "Yes, that's hilarious."

"Like I haven't seen my own brother in plays. Like I haven't been in them myself. Like I'm a *little kid* who doesn't know the difference between real and make-believe."

"Sometimes it's hard," Michael said, "for mothers to see their babies grow up."

Mary didn't react to this. "Do you like baseball?" she asked Rita.

"I don't understand it," Rita said.

"I don't understand why people like it," Mary said. "I like to watch my brother play, though. Sometimes. He's a pretty good player."

Anthony actually did seem like a pretty good player. Not great, but pretty good. He played third base and—to Michael's surprise when his son stepped up to the plate the first time—batted left-handed. He was right-handed and, like all third basemen, threw right, too.

He asked Mary if Anthony had always batted left-handed. She said she had no idea.

"Is he a switch-hitter?" Michael asked. "Because the pitcher is a righty."

"I'm not sure," Mary said.

Some of the other parents within earshot craned their necks to fish-eye him for this, passing silent judgment, no doubt, on a father who didn't know how his son batted and everything that implied.

Mary cheered politely for the Wolves, but she had a faraway look in her eye.

"You want to be with that horse," Rita said, "don't you?"

"This is OK," Mary said. "This is fine."

She leaned over to Michael and gave him a kiss on the cheek.

"You didn't have to do that, Daddy," she said. "But thank you."

Michael was too overcome with emotion to talk, and so just returned the kiss and gave her a wink.

The game wasn't even close. The other team, the Senators, had nicer uniforms and newer equipment, but Anthony's team, the Wolves, owned them. The Wolves had a couple great players—the shortstop and the catcher—and a solid supporting cast that didn't make many mistakes and in short order they were ahead by more than ten runs. It was the sort of game anybody would have left early, except that nearly everyone there was somebody's ride home.

In the last inning, the coach brought Anthony in to pitch. Michael, Rita, and Mary all stood up to applaud, and for no reason Michael could comprehend, several other people in the stands gave them dirty looks. Anthony looked over, too. Michael waved, and—despite himself, no doubt—the boy grinned and gave a barely perceptible little wave back. Michael sat. "That's my boy," he said to no one in particular. He didn't shout it. It was a simple, proud declaration.

Anthony sailed three of his warm-up pitches to the backstop, but he did throw hard.

Another buzz began to sweep over the parents in the bleachers, this one much more pronounced than the one Michael had perceived upon arrival. This one was unambiguously not a figment of his imagination. Almost as a reflex, he looked around and, sure enough, Al Neri had gotten out of the car and was walking toward them. Al stopped and crooked a finger toward Michael. Michael shook his head. He couldn't leave now, not with Anthony about to pitch. Al frowned and continued toward them.

"What's going on?" Mary asked.

Michael had no idea. This had nothing to do with Al—no one else was looking that way. Al's news, Michael presumed, had something to do with Tom Hagen, which of course was of no concern to anyone else there. It had to be about Anthony, but that, too, was puzzling. How could a wild pitcher in the final ending of a lopsided game provoke anything like this, no matter who his father was? There was shock on some of the faces, what seemed like anger on others. One of the coaches pulled the umpire aside.

The umpire was just a kid, probably a college boy home for the summer. Michael heard him ask the coach if he was sure, and the coach nodded.

The umpire's face was ashen. He strode toward the plate, then turned to face the bleachers. Behind him, Anthony stood on the mound with his glove on his hip and scowled.

Rita and Michael exchanged a glance, but he shook his head. He didn't know what was going on.

"Ladies and gentlemen," the umpire said, "may I have your attention. There's just been . . . we're suspending the . . ." And then he hung his head and started sobbing and did not move from the spot where he stood. Anthony came off the mound toward him.

Al Neri, beside Michael now, bent and cupped his hand around his boss's ear, as if what he was about to say could stay a secret, as if he himself hadn't just heard about it on the radio.

"Somebody shot the president," Al said. "They shot him. He's dead."

CHAPTER 28

For the rest of her life, Francesca would always remember exactly where she was and what she was doing when she heard the news about President James Kavanaugh Shea, who had once kissed her hand in a receiving line.

She'd spent the better part of the night waiting for Johnny in his dressing room, a trailer near the beach, not far from the custom-made temporary pier where the camera boats and the replica ships were moored. She wasn't wearing a watch. Johnny often joked that it was bad luck to have a clock in his dressing room because "movies should be timeless." But it was safe to say that when she left the trailer, it was well after midnight.

For the past few weeks, she and Johnny and their children and Johnny's ex-wife, Ginny, and a few actors close to Johnny had all been living together in a huge rented villa in the countryside, not far from the monastery that had been turned into the Madrid set. Francesca and Johnny were openly a couple now, but in that situation, they were not of course staying in the same bedroom, any more than were Lisa Fontane and her fiancé, a New York City police detective named Steve Vaccarello, who were here together just for a week, on vacation. Francesca had been more than a little wary of this arrangement, but she was falling hard for Johnny, and he'd assured her that Ginny and his daughters would love her and Little Sonny, too, and to her surprise everything was working out.

But if Francesca and Johnny wanted any time alone, any intimate time, it had to be in his dressing room or at least somewhere away from the villa. Once, they'd even snuck into the monastery and made love on the throne built for King Ferdinand.

She'd been waiting for at least two hours, maybe three, and she was running out of patience and wine. She came outside to see if Johnny was close to being done for the day.

She was a little drunk.

A few hundred meters out into the blue-black Mediterranean, the *Santa Maria* and two modern boats were sailing in circles. Even this far away, she could hear the new director screaming. The movie had been shooting for a month, and this was the third director. According to Johnny, they were on their seventh screenwriter and they still didn't really have a shootable script.

She crossed the beach and saw Johnny in costume, striding across the deck. The director yelled cut, and said something to Johnny. Johnny wadded up his hat in what looked like anger and threw it overboard. Someone from one of the camera boats dove in to retrieve it.

It struck Francesca as funny.

On the ship, they'd gotten the news, but Francesca would learn that only later. Johnny had reacted by throwing that hat and was now sitting on the deck of the ship, stunned silent.

Francesca sat down on the sand.

She was actually much more than a little drunk.

When she saw Lisa Fontane and her fiancé holding hands and walking on the beach not far away, she thought it was maybe a hallucination, but Lisa greeted her—cheerfully—and they walked over to where Francesca sat.

"Steve has an early flight home," Lisa said.

Apparently that was supposed to explain what they were doing here. "All right," Francesca said.

"Mind if we join you?" Lisa said.

Francesca shook her head. "You're staying, though?" she said.

"For another week," Lisa said. "Until classes start."

They sat together in uncomfortable silence, staring at the ship. The shouting had stopped. The motors were cut, and all three vessels were drifting.

Lisa and Steve exchanged a look, and Lisa took a deep breath. "My father and you," Lisa said, "make a great couple."

"Thanks."

He'd obviously put her up to it, but it was still sweet. Lisa had actually been reasonably nice to her already.

"At first," Lisa said, "I had the same reaction you would have if your father was dating somebody who was just a little more than seven years older than you."

That didn't seem so strange. Her age plus seven equaled thirty-four. Her father had been thirty-seven when he died. Actually, her *mother* had been thirty-four when her father had died. But then Francesca realized she was doing the math wrong. She was very, very drunk.

"Of course," Francesca said.

"At any rate, it's not for me to say," Lisa said, "but I hope it works out for you guys. I'm glad to see him happy. He and Mom were more like brother and sister even when they were married, but you guys . . ." She blushed and looked again at Steve. "Well, I know what love is."

Francesca nodded. "I'm happy for you, too."

Just then, in full Queen Isabella regalia, Deanna Dunn—the Oscar-winning actress who had briefly been married to Fredo Corleone and therefore had briefly been Francesca's aunt—came careening out onto the beach, hysterical, kicking up sand, and, it would seem, also spectacularly drunk. She was a pill freak, too, so it was hard to tell. Steve and Lisa and Francesca stood up. At first, Miss Dunn seemed to be speaking in tongues, but as she drew closer Francesca made out what she was saying.

"The goddamned Cubans killed the president!"

THAT WASN'T EXACTLY TRUE.

There was, incontrovertibly, one Cuban involved. But Cubans plural? The Cuban government? Cuban expatriates frustrated by the president's betrayal of their efforts to regain power? All seemed possible, none certain.

Details were initially sketchy.

Here was what came clear in short order.

At the Fontainebleau Hotel, only a few hours before he was to accept, once again, his party's nomination for the presidency of the United States, Jimmy Shea—surrounded by Secret Servicemen—came out to the pool for his daily vigorous one-mile swim and a few recreational dives. The pool at the White House had neither a three-meter springboard (Jimmy's event at Princeton) nor a ten-meter platform (which he was known to enjoy for the thrill of it), but the Fontainebleau's had both, on a tower flanked by two one-meter boards. The chance to take a few dives had helped make the Fontainebleau his regular hotel in Miami.

A row of luxury cabanas separated the pool from the beach. These had been secured. There were men on the roof of the cabanas as well, and on several of the balconies of the hotel. Everyone coming into the hotel for a week had been thoroughly searched. No other guests were allowed in the pool area while the president used it. The closest that the public could get to Shea was a small gap between the cabanas—through which, ordinarily, guests passed from the pool to the beach. This was packed with placard-bearing well-wishers, kept safely behind a patrolled barricade. The Secret Service had screened the crowd, ridding it of anyone who was or looked Cuban, with no evidence whatsoever that those turned away were anything but law-abiding citizens. The agents, however, missed Juan Carlos Santiago—a light-skinned man who spoke perfect English and carried a

Florida driver's license that identified him as Belford Williams. He carried his real driver's license, too, but the agents had been satisfied seeing just one.

A photographer from *Life* magazine—a woman—waited by the pool. This was an exclusive. The White House would get the chance to approve the shot, and it was guaranteed to run on the cover next week. The regular members of the press—including any and all television cameras—were already at the Miami Beach Convention Center.

The president came out in a navy blue terry-cloth robe with the presidential seal on the breast, and he smiled and waved to the crowd and made a joke about the heat and dropped the robe. People gasped. He had been working out with dumbbells and had recently lost about twenty pounds, explicitly for this moment. The photographer from *Life* captured it, and— with cheaper cameras and poorer angles and light—so did several people in the crowd and in the hotel.

President Shea wore stretchy, modestly cut jade-green trunks that came about a third of the way down his thigh. It was the same style he'd worn in college and only one size bigger.

He swam his laps first. Whether he went his whole, usual mile would become among that afternoon's more petty matters of debate.

The president got out of the pool and took two practice dives on the one-meter springboard and then told the photographer he was ready and then mounted the steps to the three.

The photographer stayed on the deck and used a telephoto lens. She had promised her editor she would come back with the hero shot to end all hero shots—America's youthful president, hurtling through the air like a sculpted god, with nothing in the background but blue sky.

After about a dozen dives off the springboard, culminating in a very clean one-and-a-half, he comically exaggerated his reluctance to continue and then climbed the stairs to the ten. The crowd laughed. People loved this. People loved him.

He hadn't dove from a ten-meter platform in years, and he didn't try anything difficult. The first time, in fact, he paused up there and looked down and pretended to be afraid. This, too, was a hit with the crowd.

The first dive—like the two that would follow—was a simple swan dive, the president's back nicely arched, his entry unimpressive but clean enough to cause no pain. Each time he got out of the pool, he acted humble and relieved not to have screwed up. After the third dive, the photographer gave him a thumbs-up, and an aide rushed over to the president and draped his robe on him the way a cornerman would, then handed him a pair of aviator sunglasses.

Which the president handed back.

He looked directly into the eyes of the people. His supporters, his countrymen, who'd been wildly cheering his newly svelte torso and his airborne trip down memory lane. He put his arms through the robe and tied the sash and ran his fingers through his hair. It fell strangely, perfectly into place. His was a great head of hair, exquisitely cut.

And he headed toward the crowd. The Secret Service agents' headsets buzzed. New positions were taken, the detail remobilizing on the fly.

The agents famously hate these spontaneous shows of common-man populism. Every president is asked, warned, begged, all but ordered not to do this. And every president does it, anyway, some more often than others, but none more often than Jimmy Shea, who liked to touch people, who waded into crowds the way hopeless drunks stagger into bars, the way degenerate gamblers finish off a day at the track by betting on the serial number of their last dollar bill. Jimmy Shea walked the length of his first Inaugural Parade, and he presumably had every intention of doing so again.

Great men, like children, often regard death as a thing that happens to other people.

Santiago, a slender man with thinning hair and a shy smile, was wedged behind two much larger men. No one seemed to have noticed him draw his gun, a 9mm Beretta.

As the president drew near, Santiago squirmed his way between the men with no apparent difficulty, almost as if they let him through, darting into the president's view like a sprinting child coming out into the street from between parked cars.

He bared his teeth, shoved the barrel of the gun against the presidential seal, and fired.

Jimmy Shea's arms flew backward, above his head.

In a grim parody of triumph, some would say.

Like an evangelical minister, flung backward by the Holy Spirit, said others.

Like surrender.

A split second after the first, Santiago's second shot grazed President Shea's neck. The president careened farther backward, his eyes were wide. Disbelief, fear, pain. Blood spurted from his neck.

Sprayed, some would argue.

In an arc, others said. A ribbon. Spewing, several feet.

Two teams of Secret Service agents scrambled into action—those whose job it was to throw themselves on the target, and those ordered to ignore the target and eliminate the attacker with extreme prejudice.

Screaming, stampeding civilians were suddenly everywhere.

An agent dove between Santiago and the president, but the third shot missed him and hit Shea in the shoulder and spun him around, away from a second agent who was about to catch him.

The president of the United States fell dead into the pool.

Three other agents jumped in after him.

Two agents drew their weapons—semiautomatic Colt .45s—and opened fire on the assassin.

This was protocol. There was no reasonable chance of hitting an accidental target. These were some of the finest handgun marksmen in the world. The bullets they fired further ensured the safety of bystanders. They had X's notched in the tips: mushroom rounds that explode against the target mass with no chance of a through-and-through.

The agents each shot twice.

Oddly, Santiago fell momentarily forward, as if hit in the back, and then four rounds exploded in his chest, and he sailed backward and hit his head on a post.

The carnage, it seemed, was all over.

CONNIE CORLEONE SPENT THE MOMENTS RIGHT BEFORE she heard the news on her hands and knees, pulling weeds from the rooftop replica of her father's garden. A table radio was tuned to a Top 40 station, where someone else had left it, and she hadn't bothered to find something more to her liking. This was fine, just something to keep her company. It was the summer everything grew. The beefsteak tomatoes were bigger and better than anything she'd managed up here before, and the peppers seemed to go from blossom to skillet overnight, but the weeds were thicker than anything she'd ever seen. When she'd been planning this garden, she'd thought—irrationally, she now realized—that weeds wouldn't find their way up here. Her boys—who were at the movies—had grown like mad that summer, too.

Johnny Fontane's new single came on the radio and, in disgust, she leapt up to change the station. It had been Louis Armstrong's recording of "Hello, Dolly" that stopped the Beatles run at the top of the charts, and now it looked like Johnny Fontane was headed that way, too. *The revenge of the geezers*, Connie thought. Johnny's song—a version of "Let's Do It (Let's Fall in Love)," with several new, vulgar examples of what sort of creatures do it—seemed like a tarted-up caricature of his great records of only a few years ago.

She turned the dial.

The first station she came to interrupted its regularly scheduled programming to bring its listeners a special announcement.

When Connie heard what it was, she pulled up a tulip-backed metal chair and sat down. She hated herself for wondering if her brother might have had anything to do with this.

Then again, she thought, like most people worth knowing, she was filled with self-loathing already.

NICK GERACI NEEDED A GOOD NIGHT'S SLEEP AND A HOT shower, and he was going crazy from the mosquito bites, and his shoes were probably ruined. But as he headed up I-95, a little south of Jacksonville, driving a ten-year-old bread truck with a broken radio and an engine that shimmied when he tried to take it past 60, he was still a happy man: just days away from being reunited with his whole family and maybe a month or so from having this ordeal draw to a close.

As planned, he stopped into Lou Zook's jewelry store in downtown Jacksonville, to get another car, presents for his wife and daughters, and to thank Lou for everything.

Lou—who'd long since eluded the burdens of his given name, Luigi Zucchini—had grown up in Cleveland's Little Italy, between Mayfield Road and Lakeview Cemetery, ten years older than Nick Geraci and a few blocks north. They'd been friends, though—chiefly from playing basketball against each other at Alta House: they were about the same size and usually guarded each other. Lou went on to build a nice business for himself in Cleveland, as a fence and small-scale shylock. When Nick took over the remnants of Sonny Corleone's *regime,* his first big responsibility had been to set up the Family's narcotics operation, but he was shorthanded, and so he'd pulled in a few old friends from Cleveland. Lou had been instrumental in creating a literal and figurative beachhead in Jacksonville. He solved problems at the docks and helped oversee the acquisition of the cars and trucks and drivers necessary to ship the goods where they needed to go. He was also an all-purpose source for moving the other interesting items that are prone to show up in the course of doing a vibrant import/export business. Over the past year—because, other than Momo Barone, the men in New York didn't know Lou Zook from an actual zucchini—he'd been among Geraci's more useful and reliable allies as he maneuvered his way back into power. Even the literal and figurative Philadelphia lawyer who'd reviewed Nick's legal situation and judged that nobody had anything on him that could stick, any legal charges: that gentleman had been a Lou Zook find as well.

Zook's place didn't look like much from the outside, just a metal-clad storefront in a neighborhood that was neither black nor white. The brands of watches for which Lou was an authorized dealer were listed in decals on the plate-glass window, many of them peeling.

"A bread truck?" Lou said, looking up from behind the counter as Nick entered. He pointed at Nick's temporary vehicle and chuckled.

Nick crossed the store, and the men exchanged a warm embrace.

"You know, my old man drove one of those when we were kids."

"I was sorry to hear. I sent flowers to the widow."

"Thank you, my friend." He hadn't been able to go himself, which inspired a fury he doubted would ever subside.

"So, you picked that thing up for sentimental reasons or what?"

"Something like that. Actually, I figured you'd thank me," Nick said. "National brand of bread, good-size cargo area. Somebody ought to be able to take it just about anywhere, packed with just about anything. Stack a few flats of bread at the end just in case."

"Oh, is that how we do things?" Zook said, bemused. A big part of his job was making sure the people above him, Nick in particular, didn't know exactly how he did things.

"Wiseguy," Nick said. "Forget I said anything."

"Did you say something? I don't hear so good no more."

"So what do you got for me?"

"See for yourself." He pointed toward his parking lot in back. Nick looked out the door.

"That Dodge a '59?"

"It fit your description," Lou said. Which was to say: a used car, bland-looking, good title, well maintained, no customizing except for bulletproof glass.

He showed Nick the three diamond-encrusted Cartier watches, symbolizing the time he wanted to make up for with Charlotte, Barb, and Bev, each engraved on the back.

"Perfect," Nick said. "Wrap 'em. What do I owe you?"

"Nothin'."

"Listen, all you done for me, I ought to be buyin' you a gift, too. How much do I owe you?"

"I'm telling you, Nick, we're square. I'm pushing sixty years old, and I got a house out at the beach and enough saved up, even my worthless kids don't need to work. Without you, I'm an old broken man freezing my balls off in Cleveland and dealing with dumb fucks trying to fence Avon bottles and Tupperware."

Nick didn't know what those things were, but he got the picture.

He patted Lou on the shoulder. "Without you—"

"Forget it," Lou said, waving him off. "Where does it end, eh? Listen, I don't want to pry," Lou said, "but ain't there a bakery owner somewhere wants his truck back?"

Nick shook his head. The New Orleans distributorship of that bread had been swallowed up by Carlo the Whale. The truck had been depreciated off the books. Its serial number was gone. The Florida plates had come from a room full of them—various states, passenger and commercial, even dealer—next to the counting room in a casino outside Bossier City. "A friend of mine gave it to me," Nick said.

Just then the barber from the shop next door burst in. "It goddamned sure wasn't me," the barber said.

"What wasn't you, Harlan?" Zook said.

"It wasn't me what shot the president."

"Who said you did?"

"Nobody said I did, but somebody done *went* and did."

"Somebody shot him?" Geraci asked.

"Down in Miami, they did, yessir. It's up on the TV, even."

"You're fucking kidding me," Zook said.

"All the times I said I wanted that nigger-lover shot and now someone shot him and there ain't no pleasure in it, which is for damn sure. I been right next door all the time. I got witnesses."

"Don't even joke about shit like that, Harlan," Zook said. "Is he dead?"

"How would I know? I wasn't there, and I don't know what happened to the guy what did it."

"Not that guy," Zook said. "The president."

"Him, it seems like maybe yes."

"Who shot him?" Geraci asked.

"I will swear on a stack of Bibles, mister, I don't know and couldn't guess," and he slammed the door behind him.

"Crazy Nazi fuckstick," Zook muttered. He had an old tube radio on the counter crackling to life now.

Geraci didn't see a picture of Juan Carlos Santiago until the next day, when the paper he bought ran the mug shot taken after Santiago's 1961 arrest in a bar altercation. Geraci recognized him right away as one of the people he'd met at the Tramontis' rifle range.

IT WOULD SWIFTLY BECOME AN INDELIBLE IMAGE IN American history, that, when Daniel Brendan Shea heard, he was holed up in a tiny, borrowed office at the Miami Convention Center, stripped down to his undershirt and white boxer shorts, laboring over the introduction to his brother's speech that night. The room was filled with wadded-up paper and crumpled coffee cups. Earlier that day, the A.G. had told those close to him that he had decided to run for the United States Senate in 1966 and thus would not be a part of his brother's second term. He had done this, by all accounts, with real tears in his eyes. It might have been true that his Senate career was to be launched from the podium, on national television, via this speech. But Danny Shea would not mention this in the speech. He made it clear to those who mattered that he was honored to have this chance to tell the world—directly, candidly, and specifically—what a great man his brother was.

Although Jimmy Shea had been a skilled orator, most of the things he was supposed to have written (including both his books and his senior thesis) were penned by seasoned professional writers. Danny, on the other hand, was a gifted writer and, more important, someone willing to work at it. He had professional speechwriters at his disposal, of course, including two accomplished American novelists. But even the things they worked on, he rewrote and rewrote until he got them the way he wanted them; remarkably, those writers usually thought Danny Shea had improved the speech.

Danny, like many good writers, believed that he wrote better while stripped down to his underwear.

When the knock came at the door, he said he thought he was almost finished—though he'd been saying this for hours.

"No, sir." It was his brother's chief of staff. "It's not that. May I come in, please?"

The attorney general got up and unlocked the door.

The chief of staff was not fazed by Danny Shea's standing before him in an undershirt and boxer shorts.

Danny, in contrast, seemed devastated just by the look on the chief of staff's face.

"It's your brother," the man said.

Danny Shea froze. Then, as he listened to the details about what happened, he started to take short breaths—not so much hyperventilation as an effort to keep a lid on his emotions.

Suddenly, he began frantically to get dressed, as if getting out of that small room and going to his brother's side would make any difference now.

"I'm a fool," he said.

"Sir?" said the chief of staff.

"This is all my fault," said Danny Shea.

"I'm not following you," said the chief of staff.

WHEN EDDIE PARADISE HEARD, HE WAS ABOUT TO GO DOWN-stairs at his Hunt Club and show Richie Nobilio the lion, which Richie Two-Guns had been good enough to help him acquire from a down-on-its-luck circus that was about to cash in its chips.

Richie had met him for a late lunch at a place on Court Street, bearing gifts: a box of twenty-four pairs of socks—the right brand, too—and a poster in a tube. It was another World War II poster for the collection. In it, a lone man sank into a blue-black sea, his arm extended, his hand huge in the fore-ground, pointing right at the viewer. The caption was SOMEONE TALKED!

Eddie thanked him profusely for two such thoughtful gifts. "How you been?" Eddie asked. "You been all right?"

"Can't complain, but I still do." He bugged out his eyes comically. "Yourself?"

"Not exactly number one on the hit parade," Eddie said, "although who is?"

"One guy, I guess, is," Richie said. "By definition."

"Yeah, but it don't last long. There's always that next song rising with a bullet."

They ordered.

"Listen," Eddie said when the waiter left. "How did you mean this here? Because I think maybe you're trying to say something about me not wear-ing socks more than once and also maybe being the traitor. Or if not me, one of the men under me. *Someone talked.* Eh? Real cute. Admit it."

Richie poker-faced him and milked it. "You know you're nuts, right?"

Eddie stared him down and then gave up and laughed.

"You're right." Eddie rapped his knuckles on the box full of socks. "Very thoughtful. Again, I thank you. It's just, with everything going on . . ."

"Trying times," Richie said, nodding in commiseration.

"Exactly."

Richie Two-Guns raised his glass. "*Salut'.*"

They drank.

They discussed the rumor about Acapulco, that Geraci's whole counteroffensive had been launched via someone he'd contacted down there. They each had a top guy they were hoping pretty passionately it wasn't. They talked about the timing of when they—and others—were down there, and it was inconclusive.

"So, how do we ever figure it out?"

"We keep a close eye, I guess," Eddie said. "We keep on doing what we're doing. Sooner or later, it all comes to a head. Like the turtle says, huh? Slow and steady wins the race."

"That's *tortoise*, Ed. The tortoise and the hare."

"Same difference."

"Not to a tortoise." Richie smiled. "But the principle still holds, I guess. Obviously, you're right. If we act too fast, if we act like we're concerned, the men under us get nervous, which we don't want. But if we act too slow, Geraci's our boss again, and, to use your analogy, we're knocked right off the pop charts."

Eddie flinched slightly when Nobilio said *Geraci*. No one said his name aloud.

"What I say," Nobilio said, "is we use a little more psychology, watching our men. I'm a smart guy, you keep long hours. Between us, we can figure it out."

Eddie chose to take the ballbusting in the lighthearted spirit in which he hoped it was intended.

"Psychology, huh?" Eddie said. "I'm a graduate of the Brooklyn Streetcorner School of Economics. Most of the courses we got, that's what they boil down to—psychology."

They ate and talked about this and several other items of business. They agreed to keep the lines of communication open between them. If the Corleone Family was going to survive, it would be men like Eddie Paradise and Richie Nobilio who'd take it there.

"Who's to say that when the dust settles from this thing with Michael and my old captain," Eddie said, meaning Geraci, "that one of us might not wind up as boss. Though, God forbid, not any time soon."

"In this Family? Never happen. Your name's got to be Corleone."

"They're out of Corleones," Eddie said.

"Maybe," Richie said. "But Sonny had a couple boys, didn't he? Michael's got a son, Connie's got two of 'em."

"I don't see any of them getting into this thing."

"At one point people said the same about Michael, if you remember. Oh, and Fredo's got at least one that I know of."

"Fredo? Fredo never had any kids."

"Fredo knocked up half the showgirls in Las Vegas. You really think every one of those got taken care of?"

"So, you know of one? How do you know about it?"

"I shouldn't have said nothin'."

"Mike knows about this, right?"

"Let's change the subject, all right?" Richie said. They got ready to leave. "So, you really got the lion, huh?"

"Beautiful animal," Eddie said.

"Amazing that's working out for you," Richie said.

He realized Richie was fishing for either another thank-you or an invitation to come see the lion. The thank-you was out of the question. Eddie already sent a thank-you in the form of four Mets tickets, right behind home plate, which was plenty of thanks for just giving Eddie the tip about the circus and how to contact the debt-ridden schmuck who owned it. That hadn't been the half of things. There was finding a way to transport it, modifications to that old jail cell downstairs so it was a comfortable cage for it, getting training on what to feed it and how to get in and clean the cage, then getting one of the worthless *coglioni* to go down there and actually do it. Half the time, Eddie did it himself. He didn't mind, necessarily, because Ronald really was a beautiful animal that seemed to have genuine affection for Eddie. Despite which, lion shit is lion shit.

So Richie could shove any more of a thank-you up his skinny ass. But he could certainly come see Ronald, if he wanted.

"You want to go see it? We can walk. It's just over and down, the club."

"I know where it is," Richie said.

"So, come. You should come. Let's go."

They went.

Eddie carried the socks under his arm and, with the other, brandished the cardboard poster tube almost like a scepter.

"Very humbling, standing right next to a big, powerful jungle cat like Ronald," Eddie said on the walk over. They were trying to walk side by side, which was awkward in places where the sidewalk narrowed, but Eddie kept a straight, unswerving line and made the whippetlike Nobilio dodge the trees and hydrants. They each had men behind them, following at a polite distance.

"Ronald?" Nobilio said. "You named it?"

"The lion's got a name, yes. Ronald."

"Why Ronald?"

"You see? There you go again, busting my balls. Why the fuck do I know, why Ronald? Ronald was the name it had when I got it."

"Why not call it something you want to call it?"

"Because I want to call it by the name it's used to," Eddie said. "Common sense. Common courtesy."

"You're extending common courtesy to a lion?"

"Go ahead and be rude to it," Eddie said. "See where that gets you."

"A lion in fucking Brooklyn," Richie said. "I admire you, my friend. It'd scare me to death, having a lion in my social club."

"It's like anybody else," Eddie said. "Treat it with respect, you got nothing to be afraid of."

Eddie looked over at Richie.

"What I'd be afraid of," Richie said, "would be that people would say that a lion's a house cat for a man with a small dick."

Fuck people. Fuck what they say.

"Well, maybe," Eddie said, "we ain't all got the same kind of anxieties as you have in that department."

"Bullshit," Richie said, but not with any apparent anger. "Unless— speaking of circuses—you're a circus freak down there, you got anxieties. It's just some men aren't as comfortable admitting it as me."

They climbed the stoop. Inside, the worthless *coglioni* had the TV on.

"You bust a lot of balls, Rich," Eddie said.

"To know me is to love me, baby." He slapped Eddie on the back. Eddie didn't like to be touched unless he knew it was coming, but he let that go, too.

They walked inside just as the TV reporter said that the killer had been identified not as Belford Williams, as initial reports had said, but rather as Juan Carlos Santiago.

"What killer?" Eddie said, and his own men shushed him and did not rise. Momo Barone was right in the middle of them. It should have been the Roach's job to speak up and tell the others that that was out of line.

Juan Carlos Santiago, the reporter said, is believed to be the younger half brother of a high-ranking official in the Batista government, a man believed to have been killed by rebels during the revolution. Santiago also participated in the failed invasion of the island a year earlier. Some who knew him have described him as "kind of a loner" and "a troubled young man." He had apparently been in and out of mental hospitals since childhood, both here and in Cuba.

Richie Two-Guns pulled up a chair.

"Who got fucking killed?" Eddie asked.

KATHY CORLEONE WOULD ALWAYS REMEMBER THE PIE-faced man. She was seated at a carrel in the New York Public Library, working on her book. She had never seen the man before, but he seemed like the sort of man half her male colleagues were: pudgy, pasty, bearded, obsessive on three or four narrow subjects, dominated by his mother, either a virgin or a deviant or a sad, sour-smelling combination of both.

When he told her the horrible news, he did so in a hushed voice and with what seemed to be real emotional turmoil, but he betrayed himself with a smile. She knew this didn't mean he was happy about what had happened in Miami. He was happy because he'd been the first to tell her, as if doing so allowed him to ride back to his village with her scalp.

In no time, librarians were wheeling out television sets.

The library patrons got up as if summoned and hurried to the screens.

The broadcasts featured exhausted-looking white men wearing thick eyeglasses they rarely wore on the air. No one seemed to have footage of what happened.

The pie-faced man came back. He came up behind Kathy.

"I know who you are," he said.

She shushed him.

"You're that gangster's niece," he said, far too loudly for a library, "who's making the beast with two backs with Johnny Fontane."

People glanced her way, but they had other things on their minds.

Kathy would have voted virgin.

"Yeah, sure," she said. "And you're that annoying man who's making me nuts."

She went home to get her sister's phone call. She just knew. It was ringing when she walked in the door.

VICE PRESIDENT AMBROSE "BUD" PAYTON WAS AT HIS HOME in Coral Gables, asleep. He'd expected this to be a long night, and he was a man ever vigilant about when to wrest magic from his good friend, the catnap. Which, whenever he could, he took with one or more of his cats. He and Mrs. Payton had twenty cats in Coral Gables and fourteen at their residence in D.C. For this nap, he had his favorite with him, a fat old tom named Osceola.

His wife had told the Secret Service she would deliver the news. Trembling, she awoke him by calling him *Mr. President.*

Bud Payton sat up, and without missing a beat, asked if the Russians were behind it.

She didn't seem to know how to answer that. She told him that their yard was filling up with government-issue sedans and then had trouble saying any more. She had a stuttering problem that got worse in tough situations. They had been married a long time, and he was not in the habit of pushing her.

He kissed her and got up and inhaled deeply and softly started humming "I Am a Pilgrim," a hymn his late mother had sung to him when he was a boy, growing up on a sun-blasted truck farm outside Plant City. He stood tall and walked down the hallway, toward the full explanation of what the world had come to.

THERESA HAGEN WAS SITTING AT HER KITCHEN TABLE WITH the telephone in front of her, fearing the worst.

The phone rang. It was a friend of hers, an art gallery owner in South Beach, his voice shaking with the bad news he was about to deliver.

Strangely, she felt relieved when she heard what it was.

It was bad news, but it wasn't about her husband. It was horrible, but it wasn't, yet, the end of the world.

TOMMY NERI SHOULD HAVE BEEN IN MIAMI BY THEN, BUT he was still in Panama City. It had to do with a woman. Nothing special, just a lot of laughs for both parties involved, and hard for Tommy to walk away from. He could do without all the stress he'd been under. He'd been doing heroin, but never this much in such a short time. It was a day after the president was killed that he realized she'd told him about it yesterday. Fucking yesterday.

EARLIER THAT AFTERNOON, CARLO TRAMONTI HAD, AS expected, been cleared of all charges in the tax-evasion case against him, an even more flimsy legal assault the federal government mounted against his empire. No one, not even the prosecution—whose heart was visibly not in the case—expected any other verdict. Still, it had cost the Whale time and the money he shelled out to his handsomely paid lawyer. So a person still might have expected Tramonti to leave the courtroom with something other than a broad and unforced smile on his face.

"This is vindication," he told the assembled reporters.

At the time of the shooting, he was celebrating this vindication at a private party at Nicastro's, the restaurant near his offices, along with his brothers, several prominent state officials, and Paul Drago, the younger brother of Tampa crime boss Salvatore "Silent Sam" Drago. There was no radio or television in the main dining room, and, supposedly, no one there learned about what happened in Miami until the party stopped.

AL NERI WOULD ALWAYS REMEMBER THAT THE YANKEES were losing. He would remember the way the dial of his car radio looked, like something from a spaceship. The Coupe de Ville was his first Cadillac, and nothing he had ever bought or would ever buy would give him such satisfaction. It still had the new smell. He would remember staring at the wide dial as if it were a television. He would remember looking up from the dashboard and seeing a woman in a battered panel truck drive by. She was maybe thirty, with her hair tied in a scarf, and the windows down and her radio turned up full-blast. *"I'm all through ever trusting anyone,"* she sang along, happily enough. *"The only thing I can count on now is my fingers."*

Al held up his own fingers and looked at them.

She turned the corner. He couldn't hear the music anymore, but she got only two more blocks and pulled over. Her radio station must have interrupted its regular programming now, too.

Al rarely thought about how desperately lonely he was, but he thought about it then. The violent, childless path he'd chosen. He wanted to go to her, the woman with the scarf around her head. To see if she was all right.

Instead, he snapped out of it. He got out of his car and went to give Michael the news.

CHAPTER 29

Michael Corleone did stay for a whole week in Maine, as planned, but it had hardly been a vacation. Al Neri and Donnie Bags set up shop at the inn, working the phones on the Tom Hagen situation and trying to figure out how to confirm Michael's suspicions about Carlo Tramonti. Al worked out a deal with the innkeeper and soon all eight rooms were either vacant or occupied by Michael and his family or the men in his employ.

The television in the lobby was on almost constantly, usually with the sound off, flickering images of Jimmy Shea's presidency and of the encomia he'd received at the now-postponed convention. There were also countless exterior shots of the Fontainebleau, and the swearing-in of President Payton—*that* would take some getting used to, *President* Ambrose "Bud" Payton—seemed to come up again and again, as if this were all a film loop.

For the most part, Rita, too, stayed at the inn, glued to the TV, although she did go out for meals and a few game attempts to get closer to Anthony and Mary. Generally, these attempts seemed to have been debacles, most memorably including the time she was thrown from a horse and the time she went out on the fishing boat and got seasick and Michael and Anthony had an argument about cleaning up the vomit.

The billiard table was set up in the rec room at Trask, and, in no time, Michael's ability to see the angles on the table as if in a vision came back to him. He tried to teach this to his children, but the game came too naturally to him. He struggled to articulate its yielded secrets even to the two people on earth he loved most. They soon lost patience with one another.

Somehow, the New York newspapers got wind of the fact that Tom Hagen was missing and ran stories about it, all sources anonymous. The stories were buried deep in the Metro section. He was yesterday's news, particularly relative to the news about Jimmy Shea.

A sleazy tabloid newspaper reported the rumor that Tom Hagen was in the custody of the FBI. Al Neri, in telling Michael about it, told him not to worry, which only engendered more worry.

The day of the president's funeral it rained, and they all stayed in and watched it together. Kay came over, too. The day was too sad for anyone to argue. The Shea children, a boy and a girl, were slightly younger than Michael's children. This seemed to get to everyone. The mourning children on TV were in fact the ages of Tom Hagen's daughters. There seemed to be nothing that could come out of anyone's mouth that didn't just make everything worse.

As the graveside ceremonies began, Kay hugged her children and as she was leaving whispered to Michael to call if there was any news about Tom.

That night, Michael and Rita and the kids went out for lobster, which Mary wouldn't eat because of the live ones in the tanks in the waiting area, and Anthony wouldn't eat because he claimed to be allergic. Then they all went to see a Marlon Brando movie that had been filmed on the Riviera. Brando and David Niven are trying to trick a woman into bed. It was supposed to be funny. Michael found it tasteless and in the middle of a bit where Brando's character is pretending to be a mentally retarded man with a Napoleon complex, he got up and started to herd Rita and the kids out of the theater.

Rita said she thought it was funny and wanted to stay.

"Can I stay, too?" Anthony said. "I think it's funny, too."

"No," Michael said to him, but he was glaring at Rita.

"I'm staying," Rita said.

"Suit yourself," Michael told her. And he took the kids and left.

Rita came back to the inn four hours later, drunk. From then on, Rita slept in a different room.

And Michael barely slept at all.

The last few nights in Maine, Michael had Donnie Bags drive him out to the school. The security guard let Michael into the rec room. While Bags napped behind the wheel of Al Neri's idling Cadillac, Michael played rotation, alone, running the table well after midnight.

Upon his return to New York, Michael Corleone was greeted with a tidal wave of unmet responsibilities and a mountain of unopened mail.

Michael went to his office and got to work on the responsibilities, and Al Neri went to the kitchen table for more coffee and to open and sort the mail. The kitchen was at the opposite end of the penthouse, and when Al shouted out, it sounded like he'd been stung by a wasp or stubbed his toe— something startling but insignificant. Michael went to see what was happening, just in case.

As Michael entered the kitchen, he smelled something rotten. Al Neri stood over an opened box, holding up a suit jacket wrapped around a bundle of newspapers.

Miami newspapers.

Inside was a dead baby alligator.

To the surprise of neither man, inside one of the pockets of the suit jacket was Tom Hagen's wallet.

WITH JAMES K. SHEA BURIED AND A NATION STILL NUMB with grief and confusion, the delegates reconvened. With a minimum of pomp and circumstance, preceded by a brief, emotional nominating speech by Senator Patrick Geary of Nevada, they made President Payton their nominee for the fall election.

Life magazine never ran those diving photos, believing that doing so would have been in bad taste. For years, the photographer fought to have them returned to her. Years later, she prevailed. She made millions, not only from the exhibit of those shots but also the companion coffee-table book (with essays by a dozen members of the American literary elite) and other licensed material (T-shirts, calendars, and so forth).

Instead of the photo spread, the magazine published both the introduction Daniel Brendan Shea never gave for his brother and the speech accepting the nomination that James Kavanaugh Shea never delivered (which Danny Shea personally rewrote, it would later be revealed). These ran with no illustrations at all. The cover was plain white. Centered, moderately sized bold type read JAMES KAVANAUGH SHEA/1919-1964. It was the best-selling issue in the magazine's history.

Who, in the end, was Juan Carlos Santiago?

There was no evidence that he was in any way connected with the current Cuban government. In fact, he was its sworn enemy. He was a skilled fisherman, who, since he'd fled his homeland and in between bouts of manic behavior, had been a valued member of crews both in South Florida and, more recently, in New Orleans. He was, it seemed, simply the bad seed from a good family. A confused and delusional man who wanted to be a patriot, who tried to avenge the death of his brother by participating in the botched invasion and then tried to avenge the humiliation he'd suffered during that debacle by killing the president.

Case closed.

To appease the worried masses, President Ambrose Payton launched an investigation. He offered the chairmanship of the investigation first to Danny Shea, who understandably declined (and, perhaps less understandably to most people, seemed to have little interest in getting to the bottom of what had happened; those closest to him said it was as if he already knew). Payton's second choice accepted: a retired Speaker of the House of

Representatives, a wholesome Iowan and a beloved American statesman. Those picked to assist him would be similarly august names.

The public appreciated the thoroughness of this, and for all but a few—a fringe element, it seemed, in a fringe-loathing nation—the earnestness of the endeavor allowed them to get on with their lives—shaken by this act of random gun violence but secure that the Star-Spangled Banner yet waved, that the Union was preserved, and understanding that the right of the people to keep and bear arms shall not be infringed.

Nonetheless, the investigation would solemnly pursue every confusing or mysterious element of the case—a rapidly lengthening list, according to some among the fringe element.

There were *no* television cameras? *No* home movies that showed anything of note?

And what about the two large men Santiago squirmed past? The ones who, some felt, seemed to screen him from view until the last second. They were dressed about the same, built about the same. They appeared in countless grainy, blurry photographs, taken by tourists and the *Life* photographer alike, but all attempts to find or identify them had proved fruitless.

Santiago's fake driver's license was not a forgery. Neither was it issued in Miami, where Santiago lived, or anywhere in South Florida, but rather in Pensacola. The birth certificate used to get the license was a legal copy, though the real Belford Williams had died in a flood in Louisiana when he was three years old. No one in Pensacola remembered having ever seen Juan Carlos Santiago. The woman who processed the paperwork for it and supposedly took the photo admitted that she believed it to be a scientific fact that your darker-skinned people all look alike to members of the white race.

Santiago was apparently shot five times, but the Secret Service agents advancing on him, from the front, apparently fired only four shots. There were accounts of a shot coming from behind him, although nothing had been conclusively proven. There were conflicting accounts about whether or not Santiago spun around as he was shot; if he did, that would explain the shot in his back (which was just a rumor, since his autopsy had been rendered classified).

Ballistics would prove nothing. Dum-dum rounds break up into pieces that are nearly impossible to trace to a specific gun. All that could be said for certain was what had already been released to the public: all the bullets that killed Juan Carlos Santiago had been fired at about the same time, all from the same *kind* of gun.

Even citizens with less conspiratorial frames of mind had to wonder how a lone gunman—a crazy, a nothing—got that close to a president of the United States with a loaded handgun.

Dumb luck?

Why not?

It would happen at least three more times in the twentieth century, after all, each time by someone even less formidable than Santiago. Each time the event seemed a little less plausible, but nonetheless, there it was: a thing that happened.

Call it luck, call it probability, call it what you will, but if each was a one-in-a-million longshot, wasn't that explanation enough? Billions of people walked the earth in that time. Millions have, at least fleetingly, wished the president dead. Three (that we know of) came close.

The statistically unlikely fact may be that only one succeeded.

BOOK VI

CHAPTER 30

Metropolitan Heating & Cooling was an almost perfectly cubical two-story gray cinder-block building in Kenilworth, New Jersey. Black Tony Stracci kept his office upstairs. Nick Geraci arrived in the middle of a downpour. He was characteristically early. He parked in back. Stracci, his old friend, was seated at the window and saw Nick and waved him up.

The Shea assassination had thrown off Nick Geraci's timetable. His wife was back at home in East Islip, and his daughters were back in school (Barb was getting a master's in education at Johns Hopkins). But Nick needed a Commission meeting to happen before he could surface, and the one that had been scheduled in late August had been pushed back. Maybe it had been needless. Danny Shea was rumored to be stepping down as A.G.— the unconditional surrender in his "War on the Mafia." There had been a fear that the investigation that the former speaker of the house was leading would wash up on the shores of the underworld, but it apparently hadn't done so. The only accusations Carlo Tramonti faced had been discreet, leveled in whispers. But, necessary or not, the Commission meeting *had* been moved back, and the rumor that Tramonti had had something to do with the president's killing—the *presumption* he had, which Nick shared—made it risky for Geraci to rely on him to get the Commission votes he'd promised he could deliver, the votes Nick would need to take over as boss. At this point, Carlo Tramonti could deliver Tampa's Silent Sam Drago, and that was about it. Nick needed three more.

The meeting was back on now—in Staten Island as originally planned, the heart of the Barzini Family's empire and the home of Fat Paulie Fortunato, the Barzinis' new boss. It was only a week away. Now was the time for Geraci to reason with Black Tony, to do whatever was necessary to get his make-or-break support.

The old man rose to greet him. "Nick Geraci! Let me look at you!"

Stracci's remaining strands of hair were blacker than ever. The office was as impersonal and meticulously neat as a surgical theater and yet smelled of anisette and mildew.

Their embrace was warm and lengthy. They'd made a lot of money for each other over the years, with barely a whimper of discontent. Stracci and Sally Tessio had been friends, and Nick thought of Black Tony as a dear uncle he didn't see as often as he'd have liked.

Stracci's *consigliere,* Elio Nunziato, ducked in the door, bearing a big white bag of pastries. He apologized for being late (even though he was early). He turned on an old air-conditioning unit that they'd rebuilt just to make noise, enough to thwart anyone's attempt to record their conversation.

Other than the fact that he didn't dye his gray hair, Nunziato looked remarkably like Stracci had twenty years ago. Some said Black Tony was really Elio's father. But Nick subscribed to the notion that two people who work that closely together do sometimes start to look alike, the way people start to look like their dogs.

"Fausto Dominick Geraci, Jr," Black Tony marveled. "Back from the fucking dead." He motioned for Nick to take a seat across the desk from him. "Look at you. This is a pleasure I thought we seen the last of."

Nick thanked him. He said he'd sometimes had his doubts in that regard himself.

They asked after each other's families. Elio passed the pastries around and got coffee for the other two men from a pot balanced on an old typing table.

"And business?" Nick asked.

"Business is good," Black Tony said. "All in all."

"It's nice to see some things don't change," Nick said, indicating Stracci's office.

"What the hell, y' know? It's not like a lot of men do, bosses and captains with their offices, I mean. This ain't a place I took over. This place, it's a place of business I started up myself. Me and my brother Mario, may he rest in peace. I still go out on the occasional service calls, you know."

"Still?"

"Still," Elio confirmed. He puffed up with touching, vicarious pride. "Last night, matter of fact."

"Ah, last night, nothing," Stracci said. "Last night was for family. The thought of my grandson having to sleep in heat like that, I did what anybody in my position would have done. This rain is a nice break from all that Indian summer."

"We need the rain," Elio said.

"But, in general," Stracci said, "these days I just go on calls for my own petty entertainment. I get a little exercise, fresh air, meet some nice people or see old friends, use my hands, get dirty. I get satisfaction out of fixing things. I enjoy it."

It also allowed Stracci to keep the common touch and to maintain, however ludicrously, the illusion that this company was where his money was coming from.

"I feel the same way," Nick said. "A lot of my jobs give me the same opportunities."

"Nick fucking Geraci," he marveled again. "I have to say, if you wasn't right here before my very eyes I wouldn't have believed it."

Nunziato nodded in agreement.

"You don't mind me askin' where you been," Stracci said, "do you?"

"It's a long story."

"Because maybe give me the *Reader's Digest* version."

Nick tried to.

Stracci seemed content to follow the gist of it.

"It's a sad story in a lot of ways from where I sit," Stracci said. "I'm sure you been in a similar position from time to time. Friends you got which for mysterious reasons can't work things out with other friends you got. It breaks your heart, you know? But, as I get older—as a matter of fact, maybe one good reason I *did* make it to this old—is that I make it my business to stay out of everything I can that's not my business."

"Don't you think it is your business, though?" Geraci asked. "Our import operation we worked out, that was us, Don Stracci. You and me."

Stracci shrugged. He had a bigger part of the business now, in Nick's absence, than when Nick had been there to run his side of things. "It was Michael who was over you," he said. "It's Michael I'm still in business with, when it comes right down to it."

"But I have your word you haven't talked to him about—"

"On my honor," Stracci said. He folded his arms.

"Forgive me for even asking," Geraci said.

"You have a question you want to ask, ask," Stracci said. "This right here, it's just friends talking."

He kept his arms folded. Nick had no choice but to continue.

"All right," he said, "I understand your perspective. I respect anybody smart enough to take the long way around someone else's crossfire. But I really think it *is* your business, Don Stracci. Don't you think it's your business that Michael Corleone—however good he is at handling outside situations—always seems to be having internal problems? Always some kind of problems in his *borgata*? That kind of instability—we both know in the long run, that's bad for everyone. Plus, you've got him in the news all the time for his various mishandling of things I don't need to go into now, but it's a long list."

"Ah, Nicky. Wait'll you're a boss," Stracci said. "If you ever are. Because if and when that happens, you'll see we're, all of us, always fighting with that."

"With all due respect," Geraci said, "the things I'm talking about aren't your everyday situations that anyone running any business has to contend with when his employees fuck up. Michael is a bright, capable, ruthless businessman, without a doubt. But he never wanted to be involved with this thing of ours in the first place. From the very *beginning* up to the very moment, he's constantly been flying in the face of the rules that everybody else has to live by. He's constantly shown *contempt* for those rules."

"Contempt?" Stracci said. He unfolded his arms. He had a sip of his coffee.

"Contempt, yes. The thing that took him from college boy to eventual bane of my existence was that he shot a police captain, executed him, completely against the rules and with nobody's sanction. Was Mike ever a *capo* or *consigliere* on the way up? Or did he ever even run so much as a sports book and kick upstairs? No. Those ways of doing things don't apply to him, either. Mike never proved himself as an earner at all, he didn't come up through the ranks the way I know all three of us here did, and yet the next thing *you* know—and this must be particularly hard to take, out here in New Jersey—he's not just the boss of our Family but just because he's in New York, he winds up as I guess what you'd call first among equals of *all* the bosses. Something like being *your* boss."

Stracci looked slightly stung. "It's more complicated than that," he said. "But, uh . . . whattayacallit. Go on."

Geraci had him on the hook now, he was sure of it. Now he just had to reel him in.

"Michael moves his base of operations to Nevada for a while there, when Las Vegas and Tahoe are supposed to be open cities for everybody, which I know for a fact he never ran by the Commission. *And* he's divorced, which just goes to show you what taking sacred vows means to him. *And* he tries to kill me, Don Stracci: me, your friend and business partner, his best *capo*, he *sacrifices* me so that other people he gave the orders on—

without the approval of the Commission in that case as well, if I'm not mistaken—so that it doesn't look like he's behind what happened to those men."

"*Tried* to sacrifice you," Elio pointed out.

"Right," Geraci said. "Lucky me. And then when he's trying to find me, he has his goons torture civilian members of my family, did you know that?"

From his reaction and the look he and Elio exchanged, it was clear that he did not.

"Torture?"

"He had my daughter tortured and my father *killed,* did you know that?"

"I asked about your family," Stracci said. "You didn't say nothin' about that."

"It's hard to talk about in a how's-your-family context. And my daughter's doing fine," he lied, "which is not the point. The point is that was a vile act, a horrible betrayal of our code."

"Really? Your father wasn't in this thing?" asked Elio Nunziato. "I thought he was."

"My father was just an around-town guy, back in Cleveland. He'd been retired from even that for a long time, down in Arizona, which is where they killed him."

"Come to think of it," Elio said, "I heard about this at the time, only I heard it was a heart attack."

"That was no heart attack," Geraci said.

He dug in the bag and took out a jelly doughnut. One bite and he set it down on a napkin. Presti's, back in Cleveland, a block from the house where he grew up, was such a magical place that it ruined a man for the rest of life's doughnuts.

"Then there's the matter of his *consigliere,* Tom Hagen, remember him? What I heard is, his big scandal last year just about got the whole Commission run in for questioning. If that's true, that's surely your business, Don Stracci. On top of that, now he's been missing for almost two months.

I know the prevailing wisdom is that he skipped the country because he's afraid he's going to finally get prosecuted for killing his whore. But—maybe you heard this, I don't know—there's a rumor going around he's in FBI custody and going to rat us all out."

Stracci looked at Elio, and Elio nodded in confirmation. This had found its way into the tabloids. It would be a tough rumor for Michael to stamp out, especially with no body. Nick had done his homework: the sinkhole in the Everglades where Hagen and his Buick now rested was so deep no one had yet found the bottom. There were more of these than people would think.

"Rumors," Stracci said, waving his hand in dismissal. "Whattaya gonna do, am I right?"

"You may be right," Geraci said. "But on the other hand, Hagen, he's not Italian, and so not a made guy, of course. He never took vows or anything like that, never swore to *omertà*, and yet he was Mike's *consigliere*. He even had him as acting *boss* for a while, which I don't know if you knew. Tom Hagen was at Michael's side for things nobody but a Sicilian should ever see or hear about, certainly nobody but an Italian, and if he does sing like the narrowback canary I'm afraid he is . . . Well, to cite an old New Jersey saying, we're all in Trouble River, six feet high and rising."

"That's *if*," Stracci said.

But Geraci felt like he had him. "My sources tell me that Sid Klein—you know him, right?"

"Know of him."

"Klein's been given all the lawyer jobs Tom Hagen used to handle, back when Michael still limited Hagen to just those specific areas of the Family business. As to who Michael's going to bring to the Commission meeting as his *consigliere*, it's anybody's guess, but I'm picking Sid Klein and giving the points."

Stracci shook his head.

"You have to admit, though," Geraci said. "Stranger things have happened."

Stracci finished his coffee and handed his empty cup to his *consigliere,* who dutifully got up to refill it.

"I understand your frustration, Nicky," the old man said. "But what I think you're asking me to do, I cannot do."

"This is the beautiful part," Geraci said. "All I'm asking you to do is give Michael Corleone what he always wanted."

Stracci fish-eyed him. "Go on."

"Michael didn't want to be in this thing of ours," Geraci said, "so fine. He wants out, we let him out. He wants to be a legitimate businessman— how many times you heard that, huh? Enough to make you sick of hearing it, I bet. Here again, we give him what he wants. We let him be just that—and nothing more."

"Meaning specifically what?" Stracci said.

"We retire him."

He paused to let that sink in.

"Or, rather," Geraci said, "the Commission does it. I take over as boss, which I can assure you I've already laid the groundwork to do. You've worked with me for twenty years: you know that the men in the street believe in me. In taking over, I give certain assurances. I pledge to the Commission that Michael Corleone will walk away from our thing a rich man, with full control over a few perfectly legal businesses, enough to provide for his family for decades if he can run them without the advantages of enforcement and connections he was handed on his silver platter by his father, may he rest in peace."

Stracci raised his pastry heavenward in acknowledgment.

"If Michael Corleone agrees to this and goes peacefully, there will be no reprisals whatsoever from me or from the men who work for me. This I can guarantee."

"And you want me to make this proposal on your behalf?"

Geraci nodded.

Stracci seemed to be pretending to think this over, but Geraci was certain he had him, and he let the barbs of the plan sink in.

"And what if I *do* make this proposal? What if others don't agree?"

"If you do it, Don Stracci," Geraci said, "others *will* agree. Enough others. Not counting Michael, of course, there are nine voting members. So the proposal needs five votes and—to be safe—one strong advocate. If you are that advocate, Don Stracci, it's certain this would get six votes."

Geraci broke it down. Three—and only three—Dons were blindly loyal to Michael: Ozzie Altobello and Leo Cuneo here, plus Joe Zaluchi from Detroit. Nick could promise the support of Tramonti and Drago, plus John Villone from Chicago, who Geraci knew from his Cleveland days and had met with personally. Villone, new on the Commission, saw the wisdom in the plan, but he understandably didn't want to lead a charge like this. He'd pledged to keep as quiet as possible and vote to retire Michael so long as it looked like that was the side that was going to win. He and Nick had agreed that Don Stracci was the pivotal vote. Not only did he make a fourth vote for Geraci, his support delivered Frank Greco, too. Greco was new on the Commission and, though he had little stake in what happened in New York, as the boss of the Philly/South Jersey outfit, he had dealings with the Straccis every day. Frank the Greek had every incentive in the world to go along with the wishes of his older, wiser associate to the north.

"That makes it five to three," Nick said. "Without even *considering* the Barzinis."

Geraci enjoyed watching Nunziato and Stracci's faces and seeing the gears turn.

For as long as anyone could remember, the peace between the Barzinis and the Corleones had been uneasy and fragile, with at least three outbreaks of what could be called outright war. While Fat Paulie Fortunato, the Don of the Barzinis now, was known to be a man disinclined to take the offensive, it was difficult to imagine what objection he would raise to the retirement of the last Corleone left in the Corleone Family. He'd be able to do so without initiating the idea himself *and* do so on his home turf in Staten Island *and* be the vote that would make Michael's three loyalists see the handwriting on the wall and therefore, most likely, accede to the inevitable.

Geraci could practically see the lightbulb go on over Black Tony Stracci's grotesque head.

"It could be unanimous," Stracci said, a faint note of awe in his voice.

"That's right," Geraci said. "It most certainly could be."

"And what do I tell my friend Michael as he sits there and we discuss all this? That it's only business?"

Geraci smiled. "He understands that."

Stracci nodded, seeming to warm even further to the idea. Nunziato came to his side and Stracci whispered something to him, and the *consigliere* nodded and whispered something in return.

"I'll speak with Frank Greco personally," said Stracci. "You'll have your answer within forty-eight hours."

Black Tony Stracci stood. The men embraced again. As Nunziato showed Nick to the door, he offered him a doughnut for the road and Nick took it so as not to be rude.

"If you can content yourself with this resolution," Stracci said, and Nick paused in the doorway and turned around, "I can only conclude two things. One, you, the new generation, are not as caught up in revenge as we have been, for which I congratulate you. And, two, that you must have had something to do with what happened to Tom Hagen."

Geraci frowned. "What did happen to Tom Hagen? Was there news?"

"Very quick, young man," Stracci said, wagging his bony finger. "I'll be in touch."

"Forty-eight hours," Nick said. "Take as much of it as you need. And, from my heart, thank you, Don Stracci."

"*Prego.*"

"By the way," Nick said, backing away, "next time we talk, remind me to tell you about an investment opportunity in the cemetery business. Large-scale."

"Welcome home, Nicky."

CHAPTER 31

The answer, delivered the next day via intermediaries, was yes.
Stracci sent word, however, that Frank Greco, since he and
Geraci had never met, wanted to get together for a drink, right beforehand. Geraci sent word that he looked forward to it. The drinks were
on him.

NICK HAD BEEN LIVING ON MOMO BARONE'S BOAT, WHICH
the Roach bought from Eddie Paradise when Eddie got a new one. It was
tied up at a small marina on Nicoll Bay—so close and yet so far away from
his house in East Islip—rather than Sheepshead Bay or Canarsie, where
most of the wiseguys Nick knew who had boats kept theirs. It had proven
to be a perfect short-term hideout: close enough to the city that he could
go meet with people he needed to meet with (including a few carefully
arranged meetings with Charlotte), yet far enough out that it seemed pretty
unlikely he'd run into any connected guys. For most of the people he was
trying to avoid, New York City extended no farther east than the airports.
The cabin downstairs was perfectly comfortable. He'd even set up his type-

writer on a poker table below deck and managed to finish his book—all but the last chapter, which he felt like he needed to live before he could write about it. He had some notes, though.

"So how's it going to work?" Momo asked him. It was the night before the meeting. They were out on the water, pretending to fish. "Michael's going to this meeting without knowing what the agenda for it is?"

Geraci shook his head. "He's going to it, thinking it's something else. They've got the usual series of bullshit conflicts to hammer out, and the word from a couple of the other Dons is, Michael's going to ask the Commission to sanction a hit on the yats."

Momo brightened. "The New Orleans guys. What's that going to accomplish?"

"He just wants a scapegoat," Nick said, "in case the government's investigation into the assassination of Jimmy Shea starts sniffing around, making trouble for friends of ours. Look, Roach, it's academic. It's moot. It doesn't matter. Michael's going to walk in there, he's going to hear the sensible reasons he ought to retire, and with any luck at all, that'll be that."

"What about afterward?"

"Don't get ahead of yourself," Nick said.

"So you're just going to go to this meeting and, *poof,* magically you'll take over?"

"Something like that. What is it you're worried about?"

"Jesus Christ, Nick. How long you known me? I'm worried about everything."

Geraci laughed. It was all he could do not to muss the Roach's cemented-down hair, or try to. "Why do you do that? I always meant to ask."

"Do what?"

"With your hair."

"What's wrong with my hair?"

"Nothing."

"C'mon. What's wrong with my hair?"

"Nothing's wrong with your hair. Forget about it."

"OK, well, take the present moment, just for one example," the Roach said. "Out on the water with the wind and such, but do I have a worry in the world about if I'm going to look like a bum when we're done here?" He pointed to his hair with both hands. "No, I do not. It's all in place. Shipshape, if you will. Just one example of why I do it. But, you know, when it comes to fashion-type choices, who knows? Why do some guys want their tailors to show a lot of cuff and some guys not so much?"

"You've given this a lot of thought," Nick said.

"What the fuck, you know?" Momo said. "To be honest with you, it's a trademark at this point, is all it is."

"To answer your original question," Nick said. "Retiring a guy this big, against his will, hasn't been done since Charlie Lucky got put out to pasture, which was years ago, so there's not exactly much of a playbook for us to follow. The night of the meeting, you go to your social club, stick close to there so I know where to find you afterward, but I really don't think there's going to be trouble. To use Michael's way of looking at things, it'll be no different from when the board of directors of a company fires the company president."

"Maybe," the Roach said. "Only, up to now, his family has *been* the company. So, it'd be more like the board at Getty Oil shitcanning J. Paul Getty."

Geraci arched his eyebrows.

"What?" Momo said. "You know, just because I'm not allowed to touch fucking Crazy Eddie's newspapers before he does don't mean I don't read 'em at some point. If I'm going to be a good *consigliere,* I—"

"No need to be defensive," Nick said, making a *Halt!* sign with his hands. "You've already got the job, OK?"

The Roach nodded. "OK."

"Who's our representative for the security detail?"

"Not sure. Richie Two-Guns took care of that."

"And still no word on who, if anybody, Michael's going to have sit in as *consigliere*?"

"None."

"It almost has to be Richie or Eddie, which means that they'll be in the room when the other Dons hand down the order. Neither one of those men strikes me as an unrealistic man. On the contrary, Richie is a opportunist, which I mean as a compliment, and Eddie—"

"Lives in the present. I know. You got no idea how many times I've had to listen to him go on and on about what he don't like about the past and the future."

"Even if Michael wasn't going to be blindsided by this—which from what you're telling me, and from what I'm hearing elsewhere, is still the case—"

"It is."

"—but even if he wasn't, even worst-case scenario, how does Michael assemble a core of vigilantes numerous enough and powerful enough to go against the Commission's orders? It's impossible. If he tries that, it's suicide."

The Roach considered this and seemed to agree.

"If I was a betting man," the Roach said, "I'd bet you that as soon as people hear about the decision that gets handed down at the meeting, the only people Michael's going to have in his corner real strong are Al and maybe Tommy Neri."

"An ex-cop hooked on pornography," Geraci said, "and his nephew, Skippy the Dope Fiend. This we can take care of."

He drew out a pause, using it to suss out the other sense of *take care of*.

"Pornography?" Momo asked.

"Remember that place downtown I had for a while? Neri was one of the regulars. Next time you see him, look him in the eyes and tell me that's not the haggard masturbator of the century. And anyway," Nick said, "unless you've found a miracle cure for your own vices, you *are* a betting man."

"I've cut way back," he said. "Not that I ever had a real problem with it or nothin'."

"I'm not saying that you did," Nick said. "Don't be so sensitive."

The Roach nodded in concession.

"All right," Geraci said. "Much as I'd like to stay out here all day with my unbaited hook and watch the pretty sailboats go by, I've got business in the city I need to take care of. So, real quick, two things and then we need to head in. First, I wanted to make sure you haven't told anybody else about this."

"About you coming back? Yeah, I—"

"No. About using the Commission to retire that cocksucker."

"Oh. No. Not a soul. Not Renzo, none of the zips, not my cousin Luddy, nobody."

"Are you sure? Think about it a minute."

Geraci wasn't fishing for anything—he just wanted to be thorough. The Roach, bless his heart, was the sort of man who took orders seriously. Most people would interpret *a minute* as *a few moments*, but Momo gave it pretty much the full sixty ticks.

"Nobody," he said. "I'm positive."

"All right," Geraci said. "So that's how we're doing this. Obviously, anybody with half a brain's going to wonder if I initiated this, but keep 'em guessing. I don't want anybody, beyond the people that I personally had to talk to, to be able to prove that this was anything other than an idea one of the other Dons came up with."

"You're going in there with no bodyguard?"

"I'm not even really going in there. It's more like I'm waiting in the wings."

Momo cleared his throat. "You want me to go along, either as your, uh . . . in my official capacity, or if you just want to bring along a man you know has got your back, it'd be my honor."

Nick tried not to smile, for fear Momo would find it condescending, but it really was endearing how devoted the Roach had become.

"I appreciate it," Nick said. "But we still have to keep you away from any hot situation until after Michael is sent packing. The second they figure out what you quarterbacked from the inside out, you're a dead man."

Momo's shoulders sagged just a little, and he nodded. "Well, just take a bodyguard then. Because you never know."

Nick thought about this.

In the shipping channel, there came a black-and-brown cargo ship, flying the Liberian flag, essentially similar to thousands of vessels Nick used to ship drugs and other profitable goods to America. For all he knew, this was one of them, steaming to a Stracci-controlled dock.

"Send a Sicilian," Nick finally said. "The more just-off-the-boat, the better. Tell him nothing until the last minute. Have him meet me across the street from the restaurant. Give him the bare minimum information and, uh . . . give him a Beretta M12 as well. Anything goes wrong, that'll even the odds a little."

The M12 was a handsome machine pistol that shot ten rounds a second and was accurate to more than two hundred yards.

"Count on it," Momo said. "And the second thing?"

"Oh, right. This Frank the Greek character. What do we know about him?"

"He's a good man," Momo said, "from what I was able to learn. Heavy on the flashy jewelry and the cologne, but when it comes to anything important, everybody speaks highly. And you was right about him and Black Tony. Everything they been involved in together, Greco's followed the old man's lead. He's still too new on the Commission to pull anything clever, is my thinking. Plus, nobody's going to plan nothing within a mile of whatchacallit, Jerry's Chop House. Which I heard is good, as a quick off to the side. The food. But anyhow, I think why he wants to meet you is, he don't want people to start thinking he's Black Tony's *leccaculo*."

Momo, Geraci's own *leccaculo*, said this with no apparent irony.

"Thank you, my friend," Geraci said, "for a job well done."

They packed the rods, and Momo revved the engine and started for shore. "One more question, though," he shouted. "Michael Corleone killed your father, tried to kill you, on and on, and you're not going to get satisfaction? You're going to let him walk?"

Geraci put his arm around Momo Barone.

"What I promised," Geraci said, "was *if* he goes in peace, I won't whack him and neither will my men."

"Right," the Roach said. "Like I said."

Geraci shook his head. "Big *if*," he said. "And that's just for starters."

The Roach understood. "There are a lot of men in the world," he said, "who don't work for you."

"And just from a purely statistical standpoint," Geraci pointed out, "some of those men are surely going to be your accident-prone individuals—dangerous to themselves and others."

Momo erupted in a high-pitched and almost girlish laugh that Nick had never heard before.

"This time tomorrow, eh?" the Roach said.

"Don't worry," Geraci said.

A QUARTER CENTURY AS A NEW YORKER AND YET NICK Geraci had never set foot on Staten Island. He was too impatient to ride that goddamned peasant-hauling, cheap-date-carting ferry if he didn't have to, but the only other way was to cross over to New Jersey and drive down and then back over. A new double-decked bridge—the largest suspension bridge in the world—connected Bay Ridge in Brooklyn to Staten Island; it looked done, but it wasn't scheduled to open until next month. So Nick took the liberty of taking Momo Barone's boat. Also, if anything went wrong, it seemed like a much better way to get the hell out of there than a roadblock-able bridge to Jersey or that slow-moving, easily searched ferry.

It was harder to navigate his way there than he'd thought—in the water, the perspectives of New York are so profoundly different from the ones a person sees walking or driving around every day. But he hugged the shore and kept looking where the sun was and kept picturing a map of New York in his head, and soon he saw the towers of that suspension bridge, and he headed toward it. Before long he was sailing under it—the Verrazano-Narrows Bridge, it was originally going to be called, after the Italian explorer, the first white man to sail through here and view New York Harbor (following a big petition drive and the backing of the mayor, it was apparently going to be named after the slain president instead). Now, Nick Geraci became the most recent Italian explorer to view the harbor. He gasped at its beauty—including a dead-ahead view of Lady Liberty, just as his own mother and father must have seen it when they sailed through here on their way to Ellis Island—and in no time he was tying up at a pier near what turned out to be Stapleton.

It was getting dark. The restaurant was supposedly somewhere not far from the northeastern shore. He stopped a slim, almost-pretty woman, light brown hair but clearly Italian, probably about thirty, and asked for directions.

"Where *you* from?" she said, as if she expected the answer to involve some other planet.

"Cleveland," he heard himself say. Why, he couldn't have said.

"What are you doing here, Cleveland?" She had abnormally small eyes. Staten Island was already giving him the creeps. There was supposedly a dump someplace out here that was visible from space, just like the Great Wall of China. The Great Dump of Staten Island.

"It's Open-Borders Week, right here in the USA," Nick said. "It was in all the papers, lady."

"Really?" she said.

"No," he said. "You know where this joint is or not?"

"What difference does it make? They're closed on Mondays, Cleveland. Hey, you got something wrong with your hand or what?"

He hadn't noticed the tremors.

"Look," he said, "I'm supposed to meet my wife outside this place." A lie, but he figured the mention of a wife would shut down any part of this that the woman thought was flirtation. "She gave me directions, I lost 'em, and now I'm asking you nice and gentlemanly for your help, but—"

"Touchy, Cleveland," she said.

He thought she might have meant *touché.*

But she gave him the directions and—to his surprise, given the source— they got him there. Even by his standards, he was early: about an hour.

The door to Jerry's Chop House was locked. But then again, it was Monday, he was early, and he wasn't from here.

Spooked a little by what was striking him as this insular island world, Geraci did not want to call attention to himself, either by walking around and around the block or, worse, loitering outside the door of the restaurant—this seemed like precisely the sort of place they'd run you off to jail and charge you with mopery. There was a bar across the street, but its front was brick and glass blocks, and he wouldn't have been able to see out, to know when either Frank Greco or the Sicilian bodyguard showed. There was a little bookstore, but he lost track of time and sometimes space in bookstores.

He headed down the block to find a phone booth and burn off some of the time that way. He'd been away from his family so punishingly long, it was second nature to travel with plenty of change, which he carried in a hand-tooled leather pouch he'd bought back in Taxco.

He went through the complicated ring pattern, and Charlotte picked up when she was supposed to.

"I'm sorry," he said.

"What's wrong?"

"I'm sorry about all this," he said. "About what happened. About what it's done to our family."

"Is there anything wrong?"

The television was on in the background. It sounded like news or maybe bowling. He had not set foot in this, his house, since . . . He didn't want to think about it. He didn't want to think about how soon he might be there again, either.

"No," he said. "Nothing's wrong." He was afraid to say anything that was optimistic. He'd never been quite this close to it all being over before. He leaned his forehead against the glass and closed his eyes. "It's fine."

"I'm proud of you," she said. "I love you."

"I'm not fishing for a compliment," he said, "but *proud*?"

There was a long pause, and tinny music from the TV. A cigarette ad.

"It's not about the adjectives," Charlotte finally said.

She'd also said this when he'd finally let her read the first draft of *Fausto's Bargain,* and she'd been right.

"Don't be sorry, OK?" Charlotte said. "Do your work and come home, and the things that are messed up, we'll fix. I'm fine. The girls are fine. We're all in this together. We've had our setbacks, but in for a dime, in for a dollar. Isn't that what people say?"

"It's what they say," Nick said, "but in most of life's tough situations, it's not what people generally do."

"Well, your family isn't quote-unquote people," she said. "We're just us."

"Justice," he whispered.

"What's that?" she asked.

"I love you, too," he said. "I gotta go, but warm up my side of the bed, will you?"

He hung up and stared at the phone. He wasn't up to any more calls. What he'd have liked to do was find a gym and pummel someone, some fast, cocky kid, maybe one who started out laughing at the shaky old man. Or better yet, one who reminded Nick of himself at that age.

Nick did not want to think about his father, dead, and how he died, and the funeral he hadn't dared to attend. But he could not afford to forget it, either.

He found a Woolworth's and he walked around the aisles and every few minutes he popped outside and looked down the street and when he didn't see them, he went back inside, and every few times outside he'd walk back down and check the door at Jerry's Chop House, which remained locked.

The street was just commercial enough that nobody seemed to be noticing him.

First to arrive was the bodyguard. He and Nick exchanged subtle, prearranged hand signs to confirm to one another who they were. Then Nick signaled him to stay back, just a little, for now. The bodyguard, like Nick, was a light-skinned, light-haired Sicilian. He wore a trendy-looking suit and Cuban-heeled boots and, even though it was dark now, gold-rimmed aviator sunglasses. The outline of a shoulder-holstered machine pistol was barely visible through the bodyguard's sport coat. Nick would have bet the kid was aping the style of some movie star, but he couldn't have said which one. He hadn't been to a movie in years.

Frank Greco arrived moments later, just as Nick was yet again tugging on the door at Jerry's Chop House.

"The door's locked," Greco said. He had his *consigliere* and a bodyguard with him.

"Amazing powers of observation you've been blessed with, friend."

They introduced each other. The Roach had been right about Greco's cologne.

"It's supposed to be open," Greco said. "You did call and check," he asked his *consigliere*, "right?"

"You want to be a boss?" Greco muttered to Nick. "Welcome to the glamorous world of it." Greco folded his arms and took a deep breath and nodded toward the bar across the street, the one with the glass-block front, and they all followed his lead.

Inside, the place was narrower than it looked. An ancient-looking carved oak bar ran almost the length of one wall. The only other seating was two round, cheap laminated four-tops toward the front, next to a jukebox, which was playing Marvin Gaye's "Can I Get a Witness?" The bartender, a fat man wearing a Yankees cap, had been the only person in the joint.

The bodyguards stopped right inside the doorway.

"You got a back room or something?" asked Frank the Greek.

The bartender gestured expansively toward all the unoccupied tables and chairs. "It's fucking Monday," he said. "Sit wherever."

"Watch your mouth, asshole," said the bodyguard with Greco.

Geraci's mod Sicilian looked over the top of his sunglasses, and Geraci shook his head. No need to overreact. Or react at all. It's just a bartender, some hapless civilian.

The *consigliere* said he'd go make some calls about the situation across the street and left.

"No back room at all?" Greco asked.

"We got a john," the bartender said, shrugging.

"We'll just have a cocktail, how about?" Geraci said to Greco. "Then soon as they open Jerry's, we'll zip over there."

"*Jerry's?*" the bartender said. "Where you from? Jerry's ain't open on Mondays."

"Shut the fuck up," Geraci said. "I wasn't talking to you."

Greco looked slightly alarmed and ordered a scotch and soda.

Geraci got a red wine and took a seat over by the jukebox. Greco joined him.

Sam Cooke's "Havin' a Party" came on. It wasn't either man's favorite kind of music, but they had their minds on weightier matters. And it did provide some cover from eavesdroppers, electronic or otherwise.

Greco raised his glass. "*Salut*," he said.

"*Salut*," Geraci said.

"Nick Geraci," Greco said. "The man, the myth. At *my* table."

The bodyguards had taken seats now, too, and seemed relaxed. Momo had been smart to push Nick to bring a man with him. And that M12 gave them the chance to shoot their way out of anything.

"Me, on the other hand . . ." Greco said, shaking his head. He pointed at his own reflection in a mirror on the wall. "Look at that old man," he said. "When I was young I looked like a Greek god." He took a sip of his drink. "Now I just look like a goddamned Greek."

Geraci laughed politely. He and Frank Greco were about the same age.

"All the times I been to New York," Greco said, "I've never been to Staten Island."

"Nobody's ever been here."

"They will once that suspension bridge opens, though, right?" Greco said. He pointed vaguely in its direction. The towers would have been visible from here if the front had been plate glass instead of glass blocks.

"I wouldn't hold my breath," Geraci said.

Next on the jukebox was Rufus Thomas's "Walkin' the Dog."

"Eh," Greco shrugged. "You never know. Tell you what, lot of history for us here, the Italians. Meucci invented the telephone here. In school, they teach you it was Alexander Graham Bell, but—"

"I know the story," Nick said.

Greco looked surprised. "What are you, a reader?"

Nick took a deep breath, trying not to lose his patience. "I just know the story."

Greco nodded. "Well, did you know Meucci and Garibaldi lived together? Not like faggots or nothing. Meucci was married, and Garibaldi apparently really liked going to the whores when he was here. But Garibaldi was between revolutions, or something, and came here for some reason. Because of his friend, I suppose."

"Amazing," Geraci said, his voice flat enough to cover the sarcasm. He'd read everything he could get his hands on about those two great, sad men, but they were hardly the topic of the day. "Look, let me cut to the last reel here. You wanted to see me about Don Stracci's proposal?"

"I did," he said. "I do." He winced, as if from a stab of pain.

"You all right?" Nick said.

Frank the Greek rose and grabbed his crotch. "I have to take a leak," he said, and headed toward the dark hallway in the back.

Nick glanced over and saw that at some point the bartender had slipped out.

Things started happening so fast, they started happening more slowly.

Geraci's mod Sicilian stood up.

As if following his lead, the other bodyguard stood, too.

The needle dropped on "Night Train," by James Brown and the Famous Flames.

Nick heard Greco's cackling laughter. There was a glint of light down that dark hallway, and Nick got a glimpse of Greco heading not into the men's room but outside into an alley.

Miami, Florida, screamed James Brown.

A split second later, over the honking saxophones, Geraci heard the front door opening. He leaped to his feet, and as he was spinning around he saw that his Sicilian, who should have been guarding that door, who maybe even should have locked it, had pulled out the M12. The other bodyguard had a plain old .38 special drawn. Nick found himself looking down the silencers screwed onto both weapons. It was the man he'd brought as his own bodyguard who shouted at Nick Geraci to freeze.

And he did.

Dear God, don't let me die in Staten Island, Nick thought. *Dear God, don't let me wind up in the goddamned biggest fucking landfill in this, our fallen world.*

Through the door staggered Momo Barone, with a gun shoved in his back, and behind the gun was Al Neri.

Behind Neri was Eddie Paradise, who locked the front door behind them.

Footsteps came from the dark hallway in the back. Michael Corleone emerged into the light, his hands clasped behind him. He looked like a disappointed officer reviewing his troops.

Philadelphia! screamed James Brown. *New York City, take me home!*

"Hello, Fausto," Michael said. He was the only man alive who called Nick by his given name.

"Hello, Don Corleone."

And don't forget New Orleans, the home of the blues.

Michael walked over to the jukebox and unplugged it.

Then he turned toward Nick and smiled. "Sit down, Fausto."

Nick Geraci glanced at the M12 and the resolute body language of the young man training it on him. That, alone, pretty much ruled out making a run for it. Geraci's mind raced for a solution. Under no circumstances would he beg or show weakness.

Nick heaved a sigh and sat.

Eddie Paradise took his place against the wall, between the bodyguards and the bar. He folded his arms, exasperated-looking, like a man dragged along while his wife shopped for clothes.

Michael clasped his hands behind his back again and walked very slowly over to Geraci's table. The Don had been hit in the face all those years ago by that police captain, and in certain half-light the plastic surgery he'd had to repair his cheek and jaw seemed to be sagging, almost falling away.

Geraci was nearly a foot taller than Michael. Seated, he wasn't all that much shorter. Nick could grab him. Dive at him, tackle him. The bodyguards couldn't open fire. They couldn't be sure they'd hit Nick and not Michael.

"You were close, Fausto," Michael said, his voice barely above a whisper. "I mean, you really almost did it. Years in caves and hovels, on the run, and yet against all goddamned odds, my former friend, you almost did it. I bet you could almost taste it."

He paced back and forth past Geraci, but Nick ruled out grabbing him. What would that accomplish, in the end? He could punch the guy a couple times, but eventually they'd get separated, and that would be the end of things. Like most touchy situations, there was no way to get out of this with physical violence.

Michael stopped pacing and faced him now. "I can only imagine how painful this must be for you, Fausto. It's tragic, to come this close to regaining everything you've lost and in the same maneuver gaining everything you ever wanted. And have it all come down to this."

Momo still wouldn't look up. He'd been brought here to prove his loyalty by killing Nick—just as Nick had had to kill Tessio. But the Roach couldn't have looked more like a guilty man. He was already blowing any chance he had of proving himself.

Neri was breathing hard and looked eager to see the killing start.

Eddie looked at his watch.

The bodyguards looked willing.

"For all our differences, Don Michael," Nick said, "I had a higher opinion of you than this. You're acting with your emotions and not your intellect. What I negotiated for you with our friends on the Commission gives you exactly what you've always said you wanted, to the letter, and it comes with a pledge from me to the other Dons that no harm will come to you or your family. It made me sick to give up on having my revenge against you, but I did so, because it's the best thing for everybody. Nobody loses, nobody dies, nobody's dealing with messy murder cases that might be surprisingly easy to pin on you. Or friends of yours. I'm not some bloodthirsty feudal lord, Michael, and neither are you. We're modern men, modern businessmen. You'll walk away from this thing a millionaire, Michael, a perfectly legitimate American millionaire. And when the dust settles, I will personally put a million dollars of my own money into the charity that bears your father's name."

Michael remained standing before Nick Geraci, silent and still, regarding the most talented man he'd ever had in his employ—the most talented, it would turn out, that he'd ever have.

"If you kill me," Nick said, "everything you've ever wanted is a lie. You'll be choosing revenge over what you've yearned for. Kill me, and you'll never get out of this thing of ours. Even as you stand here, you know I'm right. If you don't take this way out, the path I made for you, then from this day forward, every time you think you're out, you'll hear my voice in your head, telling you that you blew it. Kill me, and at your very core, you're a liar and a hypocrite. And it doesn't matter if anyone outside this room ever knows that, because you'll know. In just a single puff of gunsmoke, your whole life will be reduced to one big fucking lie."

Michael shook his head in what seemed like wonder. "You don't understand," he said.

Geraci waited out a long pause. "All right," he said. "Enlighten me."

"Your friend in New Orleans," Michael said, "is in the process of setting you up as the fall guy in the plot to assassinate President Shea. There are pictures of you with Juan Carlos Santiago in New Orleans, evidence placing you both in Louisiana and in Miami at incriminating times and in incriminating places. I don't know all the details, but I do know one thing: the government's whole case is leading to you."

This was, Geraci was all but certain, a bluff. "That's going to be pretty easy to get out of," Geraci said. "Since none of it is true."

"I had a higher opinion of *you*," Michael said, "than this. You've got half a law degree. The truth, as you must know, bows down before what the government can prove in court."

Momo Barone lurched off his barstool, and Al Neri punched him in the face, and the Roach sat back down.

Eddie looked over as if what happened was a mother giving a misbehaving brat a flat-palmed swat to the bottom.

The bodyguards shifted from foot to foot but kept their guns pointed directly at Nick Geraci's heart.

"Believe what you want," Geraci said. "You're just saying what you're saying so that if what happens here gets out, you'll sound noble. You'll sound like you didn't have any choice." Nick forced a smile. "And that's fine. Because in your heart you'll always know otherwise."

Michael closed his eyes and let out a long breath and looked like he was about to speak but did not. Instead, he looked over at Neri.

Neri handed the pistol to Momo the Roach, butt first, then pulled out that old steel flashlight and used it to shove the Roach up to the table. Momo, blood oozing from the corner of his mouth, aimed the gun—a .44—at Nick's head.

"Good-bye, Fausto," Michael said. "By the way, would you like to hazard a guess," he asked, "what his last name is?"

"Whose?" Nick said.

Michael headed for the door and pointed toward the mod Sicilian with the M12.

"This loyal man in my employ," Michael said, "who was sent here at your request." He glanced back at Momo. "You and a friend of yours."

"I don't know what you're talking about," Nick said.

Michael unlocked the door, shook his head, and then extended an arm, cuing the young Sicilian.

"My name," he said, "it is Italo Bocchicchio."

Geraci told himself that the shiver that went through him was just a tremor, and he regained his composure as swiftly as he'd lost it.

"Pleased to meet you," Geraci said. "Call me Nick. Everyone does." He smiled. "Everyone except the brother-murdering cocksucker you've chosen to work for."

Michael slammed the door behind him.

The other bodyguard—presumably, not Greco's man but rather a part of the Corleone Family as well—again clicked the deadbolt.

"In the face," said Al Neri.

Sweat was pouring from Momo's helmet of hair. His eyes shone with fear and self-pity, and his hands were shaking.

In this same situation, Sally Tessio had dropped to his knees and called Nick a pussy—a kindness, trying to make it easier for him to shoot. But the Roach had already screwed up. He had already shown weakness, and he thus was already believed to be the traitor. For all Nick knew, he'd already confessed. With utter clarity, Nick saw his way out of this.

"On your knees," Neri said.

Nick obeyed.

The Roach pressed the gun unsteadily against Geraci's forehead.

Why bring this Bocchicchio into this at all unless the presumption was that Momo wouldn't have the nerve to do it? Unless he'd been promised he could do the job when the Roach failed?

Nick looked up from the gun barrel between his eyes and at Momo Barone's bleeding face. "Roach," he whispered. "Give me the gun, Roach."

Momo was almost imperceptibly taken aback, but enough so that Nick was able to throw a quick left jab to the gut. The Roach gasped and doubled over, and Nick grabbed the .44 away with his right hand and fumbled with it and started firing, blindly in the general direction of the two bodyguards, and the air was filled with the sound of silenced bullets, and there was a burning in Nick's leg and throat, and he could feel the warmth of his own hot blood on his skin.

He managed to stand.

As Al Neri was winding up to swing the flashlight, Geraci fired the .44 into Neri's chest, and the ex-cop flew backward as if he'd been shot from a cannon.

Nick turned toward the bodyguards. The one with the .38 was hit in the hip, not dead but down. The Sicilian was shot but getting up now, swiveling the gun in Nick's direction. The Sicilian let fly a few seconds of fire, but the .44 caught him in the throat and he was dead.

Nick Geraci crumpled to the floor, disoriented and in agonizing pain, aware of his vision blurring, the cold tile floor, willing himself to fight off unconsciousness, to fight off the darkness, and he tried to push up with his right leg, but there was nothing there, he had no right leg, it had been shot off, and the shard of thighbone buckled as he tried to plant it against something and white pain hit him like boiling water everywhere.

"Why me?" he heard Eddie Paradise say. "Why does this fucking shit always happen to me?"

Someone—it must have been Eddie—walked out from what must have been behind the bar, and Nick heard the Roach crying and Eddie sigh. "Ah, shit," Eddie said, and fired.

There was no more crying.

Geraci took a deep breath and gritted his teeth and tried to see past the white light and the dizziness and managed to prop himself up very slightly on one arm. His eyes couldn't focus on anything.

"Nothing personal, pally," Eddie said.

"They'll never," Nick said, "give you. An even break."

"Ain't that what they say not to give a sucker?" Eddie said.

The pain was too much, but Nick clenched his eyes closed and took a breath and held it. And he could feel the darkness and the cold coming over him now, like a soft hood.

"That's my point, Ed," Nick said, collapsing backward, to the floor. "To them. You'll always just be—"

"Aw, shut up," Eddie said, and fired.

CODA

CHAPTER 32

When that suspension bridge was dedicated the next month, it would, after all, be named after Giovanni da Verrazano.

Thirteen years earlier, while the project was still on the drawing board, the Italian Historical Society of America approached the Triborough Bridge and Tunnel Authority with the idea of honoring this explorer—not only because he was the first to sail these waters but also because the bridge connected two Italian-American enclaves, Bay Ridge and Staten Island. It would be a dignified way of combating those who had already begun to refer to the proposed bridge as the "guinea gangplank." Robert Moses, Triborough's emperor, fought the Verrazano name at every turn. He'd never heard of Verrazano, he repeatedly said. The name was too long, too foreign. Even after the new governor of New York had been convinced to champion and sign a law that named the bridge after the explorer, Moses kept fighting it. Most recently, he'd backed the petition drive to name the bridge after James K. Shea and then cited the importance of honoring the "will of the people" to anyone with a notebook or a microphone.

The Commission members in general and Paulie Fortunato in particular were pleased when Michael Corleone informed everyone that tomorrow, prior to Daniel Brendan Shea's resignation, the outgoing attorney general would also release a statement citing his admiration for the accomplishments of that great Italian explorer and Danny's wish that the bridge, as planned, be named not after his brother but after Verrazano. Michael thanked Don Stracci and Don Greco for their support as well. The offer of a New Jersey senate seat in 1966 had been one Danny Shea couldn't refuse.

Not only that, Michael announced, Moses himself was finished. The New York governor was thrilled at the prospect of being the man who'd get credit for forcing the despot out.

In the context of a long and difficult series of issues, the Commission members enjoyed this bit of comic relief. They held their sides in laughter at the knowledge that they would remain in power after the supposedly most powerful man in New York fell, his final public works project graced by the name of an Italian hero.

NICK GERACI'S BULLET-RIDDLED CORPSE WAS FOUND ON A boat cast adrift in New York Harbor, his shot-off leg wrapped in newspapers and tossed on board as an apparent afterthought. Authorities soon learned that the boat belonged to former Corleone *soldato* Cosimo "Momo the Roach" Barone, who was missing (and whose body, as it turned out, would never be found). This sensational news almost immediately shifted away from the Corleone Family, though. The special bipartisan investigation into the death of President Shea had already learned that Geraci was in Miami at the time of the assassination, and it had placed his name on the list of witnesses it wished to call. It had also learned that Geraci had spent the months leading up to the assassination in New Orleans, in the employ of underworld kingpin Carlo "the Whale" Tramonti—another name on the investigation's list. In addition, photographs and eyewitness testimony showed Momo Barone meeting with Carlo Tramonti and his brother Agostino during a visit to New York the previous year. In both the media and in various court documents, Geraci and Barone were portrayed as defectors to the Tramonti syndicate—often, even members of it. If there *had* been a conspiracy to kill the president, common sense seemed to decree that Nick Geraci was at the center of it.

(And most people didn't even know about Geraci's involvement in the Carmine Marino affair, the still-classified attempts to kill the leader of Cuba.)

The bipartisan investigation would drag on for months. Its final report was more than four thousand pages long and ruled that Juan Carlos Santiago acted alone.

Still, many continued to believe that the assassin was sent to the Fountainebleau by the CIA. Or the FBI. Or the vice president. Or the Cuban government. Or the Mafia (if there was a Mafia). Or some combination of the above. Or all of the above.

The century would be buried long before this, its greatest mystery.

No hard evidence would ever come to light that the bipartisan investigation was a cover-up or less than scrupulously executed. No conclusive proof of any sort of conspiracy surfaced—either to kill the president or to cover up the truth behind the killing. Nonetheless, suspicion remained that the public had not learned—and might not ever learn—the whole story. This possibly paranoid notion—fostered over the years by a library-wing's worth of books—was, from the outset, fed by the bizarre chain of coincidence that claimed the lives of so many of those who were allegedly involved, either directly or tangentially, with that great national tragedy. Even more suspiciously, many of these people died days, sometimes even hours, before testifying about what they knew.

For example, former CIA agent Joseph P. Lucadello died in a hotel room in Arlington, Virginia, two days before his scheduled closed-door meeting with the bipartisan investigation. The death was ruled a suicide, but many found it hard to believe that a one-eyed man would choose to kill himself by ramming an ice pick through his remaining eye.

The most famous example was Carlo Tramonti. A week after he was subpoenaed and a week before he was scheduled to fly to Washington,

Carlo the Whale turned up dead in the middle of Highway 61 in New Orleans, thrown from a moving car right outside the Pelican Motor Lodge. The cause of death was two shots to the back of the head, a classic gangland hit, and not the meat cleaver that had been rammed into his heart, which came after the shooting but which the authorities could never explain.

A less commonly known example was Carlo's brother Agostino—Augie the Midget, who took over from his late brother. He was not called to testify before that first investigation, but a few years later, a maverick U.S. attorney in New Orleans sought to reopen the case. The night before Augie Tramonti was supposed to appear in court, he died in his country home— a newly renovated antebellum mansion, once part of a sugar and timber plantation west of New Orleans. The coroner attributed the death to "natural causes" and was no more specific than that. The police report, however, mentioned a suicide note. It did not say what the note said. The note, along with several other pieces of evidence related to the case, disappeared from the evidence room. It might have been stolen. It might have merely been misplaced. Either way, it was gone.

A FEW MONTHS AFTER SHE BURIED HER HUSBAND, CHARLOTTE Geraci boxed up the carbon copy of Nick's manuscript and went into Manhattan to meet with her old boss, at the publishing house where she'd worked before she and Nick got married. How much of it she wrote or rewrote herself is debatable. Her claim would always be that Nick had given it to her to retype the day before he was killed. She did at least that much. Her daughters came home to help her. Charlotte claimed to have put the original in a safe-deposit box and the pages Nick gave her in a different one. To this day, Charlotte and her daughters (Barbara Kennedy, now a Maryland attorney, and Moonflower®, now a San Francisco performance artist) have never released more than a Xeroxed copy of a brief excerpt of Nick Geraci's original.

The publisher, initially skeptical, agreed to read it. He was amazed by the manuscript's raw power, dismayed by its crude craftsmanship. But that, he thought, could be fixed.

He called up a struggling novelist he'd published and invited him to lunch. Sergio Lupo was then best known for *An Immigrant's Tale*, based on the life of his mother, which had been a *New York Times* Notable Book. It had also sold about a thousand copies. Lupo's next novel, the autobiographical *Trimalchio Rex*, had done even worse. Since then, he'd been trying to make a go of it in Hollywood, with little success. He was back in New York, visiting his family. He was not in a position to turn down a free lunch.

Neither was he in a position to turn down the rewriting of *Fausto's Bargain*.

At first, though, he did. Lucrative as the offer was, it seemed like work that was beneath him. "It's a sellout," he said.

"I say this as a friend," the publisher said, "but don't you think maybe it's time to grow up?"

"Fuck off," Lupo said. He was forty-one years old.

"It's only a sellout," the publisher said, "if you write it that way."

Lupo thought about this for a few moments and then shrugged.

"Do me two favors," the publisher said. "One—read the thing." He slid the manuscript across the table. "Two—let me read you this."

He pulled out a copy of *Trimalchio Rex* and flipped to the last page.

"'I would love to be evil,'" the publisher read, "'to rob banks, commit murder and mayhem, have everyone fear me because I'm a tough guy. I'd love to be unfaithful to my wife, shoot kangaroos, the works. But I can't. And you know why? Because I'm timid. I'm shy. I'm afraid I'd hurt somebody's feelings.'"

"That's a goddamned novel," Lupo said. "That's a fictional character talking."

"Sure it is," the publisher said. He rapped his knuckles on the manuscript. "Just read it, OK?"

Two years later, Lupo's reworking of the book was finished. *Fausto's Bar-*

gain hit the bestseller list the first week out and stayed there for three years. It would go on to sell more than twenty million copies worldwide. The three films it inspired neither used the word "Mafia" nor mentioned any real member of the Corleone Family by name (other than Nick Geraci). The first one earned Johnny Fontane his second Academy Award. The first two—often credited with putting Woltz International Pictures back in the black for the first time since *The Discovery of America* debacle—are considered classics.

THE WEDDING OF JOHNNY FONTANE AND FRANCESCA COR-leone Van Arsdale was a quiet affair, right on the beach in the Bahamas, under a makeshift arch of palm fronds. *The Discovery of America* had wrapped a week earlier, and they'd stayed on Grand Bahama Island, making plans for the festivities, executing an elaborate (and ultimately successful) ruse to keep the press away, and waiting for their closest family members to arrive.

Johnny wore a white tux. Francesca wore a pink, batik dress made right on the island. The weather was idyllic: a cloudless blue sky and a breeze.

As Michael Corleone walked his niece down the boardwalk that functioned as an aisle, he was unashamed to find himself in tears.

He and Johnny made eye contact.

Johnny winked.

Michael tried to smile. He truly was happy for them both.

After the ceremony, Michael Corleone and his sister Connie went for a walk on the beach.

Connie reached out her hand to him, and he took it. They had not walked this way since they were little kids, since he was walking her to school.

"What a great couple," Connie said. The breeze whipped her hair away from her face. She looked like a woman in a heroic painting. "You wouldn't think so, but look at what a success the Nino Valenti Fund is already, so obviously they work together well. That's important. And look how happy they look. Their kids get along. Everything looks . . ." Connie shook her head. "What a great couple," she repeated, more softly this time.

"I know this must be difficult for you," Michael said.

"Difficult?" she said. "Why would this be difficult?"

Michael just squeezed her hand, and they kept walking.

Finally Connie gave a dry little laugh. "Believe me," she said. "I'm over it. I had a crush on him, sure, but so did a million girls. I'm a grown woman. I know what love is worth. I'm happy for them."

Michael nodded.

"Speaking of love," she said, "I was sorry to hear about you and Rita."

"Don't be," Michael said. "I'm over that, too."

They walked for a long time in silence. At the next hotel up the beach, they stopped at the bar for a drink. Connie got a piña colada, and Michael got ice water. They took their drinks and sat under an umbrella beside the pool. The only people swimming were children.

"So," Connie said. "Did she ever tell you?"

"Did who ever tell me what?"

"Did Rita ever tell you she had a baby?" Connie said. "A son. It was Fredo's. She was still a dancer out in Las Vegas then, and she went away to have the baby, to a convent out in California. Fredo paid for everything. Usually, the girls he got in trouble had it . . . taken care of. But Rita . . . well, of course, Rita wasn't like that. She couldn't do that. She had it put up for adoption. I've tried everything I can imagine to find out who the boy is, where he is, but it's the Church I'm up against, and I'm pretty sure it's hopeless. I thought she might have told you. I'm sorry."

"She told *you* all that?"

Connie shook her head. "Fredo did."

"When?"

"At the time," Connie said. "You know, I can keep secrets as well as any of the men in this family." She turned to face him. "Are you OK? Maybe you should get something to eat."

"I'm fine," he said.

"You look like you . . . " she said. "I don't know. You look pale."

"I'm fine," Michael said again. His sugar was fine, he was sure. He went back to the bar and got something stronger to drink.

He sat back down beside his sister.

They looked out at the swimming children and, beyond them, the white sand and the ocean.

Connie reached over and put an arm around him. "He'd be eight years old," she said. "He's out there, somewhere. Think of it as a comfort."

IT WAS PROBABLY THANKS TO MICHAEL CORLEONE THAT Carlo Tramonti did not—as Michael had once asserted to the other members of the Commission—ruin them all. President Payton discontinued the so-called War on the Mafia. The director of the FBI reassigned most of the agents who'd been on that detail. After his election to the Senate in 1966, Daniel Brendan Shea pursued other weighty matters.

In the long run, though, tremendous damage had been done. Younger FBI agents who'd been on the case didn't forget what they'd learned. Younger U.S. attorneys reassigned to other matters or elected to office themselves didn't forget what they'd learned, either. President Shea himself had proven much easier to kill than the public's suspicion that "the Mafia" had the president "whacked." All of these sentiments paved the way for the passage of the RICO statutes, which gave prosecutors powerful new ways to send gangsters to jail. It would be another ten years, however, before these complicated laws sent a Mafia boss to prison. But the threat loomed, and nothing would ever be the same. By the 1980s, both Michael Corleone and the Corleone Family often seemed like they'd been reduced to parodies of their former selves.

Yet the years that immediately followed the deaths of Tom Hagen, Jimmy Shea, and Nick Geraci might have been the most peaceful that Michael Corleone and the Corleone Family had ever known: one of the rare stretches of his life in which Michael would have considered himself almost happy.

During those years, he would often think back to that night in Staten Island, savoring the memory of the drive back home.

Michael and Richie Nobilio came out the front of Jerry's Chop House into a pouring rainstorm. The bodyguard they'd brought handed them an umbrella, and they hurried into the back of a waiting black Lincoln. The bodyguard got in the front. Michael nodded to the driver, Donnie Bags, and they sped away.

By now, the mess across the street had been cleaned up. Fat Paulie Fortunato owned the bar and, for all intents and purposes, the neighborhood and the police that patrolled it, and, in exchange for other favors from Michael Corleone, he'd offered it up as a safe place to conduct that sad and ultimately grim showdown. Al Neri and Cato Tomaselli, the Corleone associate who'd posed as Greco's bodyguard, were now under the care of a first-rate surgeon on Staten Island, a man Don Fortunato had actually moved here to address inconvenient situations such as this. Tomaselli's wounds were minor. As for Neri, the bullet had gone through him cleanly, grazing and puncturing a lung but nothing worse than that. His recovery was expected to be lengthy but full.

Eddie Paradise had supervised the removal of the dead. Geraci's body was on the boat Eddie had sold Momo. The earthly remains of Cosimo Barone and Italo Bocchiccio had been hauled off to the Fresh Kills Landfill, Robert Moses's presumably unintentional gift to both kinds of Staten Island wiseguys. The slightly higher big hill next to it, where Fortunato and the top Barzini men had homes, was called Todt Hill; *todt* being the Dutch word for *death*. Staten Island gave Michael Corleone the creeps.

Michael Corleone and his men drove a few miles down dark, leafy residential streets until Donnie turned left, toward the waterfront. They pulled into a filling station, closed now, beside a panel truck with FLATBUSH NOVELTIES painted on the side. Through the rain, the towers of the new bridge loomed in the distance. The bodyguard got out of the front seat of the Lincoln. Eddie Paradise got out of the panel truck. The portly little man's suit was torn and filthy. Eddie walked though the rain, unhurried and with no umbrella. He took the bodyguard's place in the front seat and closed the car door.

"How was dinner?" Eddie said, running a hand through his wet hair. "I heard it's good, Jerry's Chop House. The chops, especially."

The bitterness in his voice was unmistakable, understandable, and forgivable. Tonight would have been tough on anybody. Barone was Eddie's best friend, and Geraci had shown him the ropes, yet Eddie had handled the whole business like a champ.

Michael patted the weary *caporegime* on his damp, tattered shoulder.

"You've rewarded my confidence in you, Ed. You have my gratitude."

Eddie Paradise mumbled his thanks. Michael signaled to Donnie Bags to go. The Lincoln and the panel truck pulled out of the filling station in different directions.

Richie Two-Guns shook his head. "I take my hat off to you, Eddie," he said. That same night, the man he'd started to groom as his own lieutenant, Renzo Sacripante—who, from all outward appearances, had done a fine job running the zip-laden Knickerbocker Avenue crew—had been garroted in a men's room on Mott Street and was now a part of a different garbage heap, on a barge at the refuse station in Yorkville, courtesy of a city sanitation official for whom the day had come when it was necessary for him to perform a service for Michael Corleone.

"Not that you got a hat to take off," Eddie said.

"On account of it's already off to you," Nobilio said, patting Eddie's shoulder now, too.

Michael had heard that Eddie was also put out that—as the Corleones settled all Family business—two traitors from his crew had been fed to his beloved lion in the basement of the Carroll Gardens Hunt Club. Eddie said he'd heard that once lions got a taste for human flesh, they'll never again be happy eating four-footed mammals. Al Neri had assured him that was a myth, but what the fuck did Al Neri know about lions? Still, Al had reported to Michael, Eddie had gone along with it with a minimum of complaint.

Now Eddie let out a deep breath, then turned on the radio, to a rock-and-roll station, and slumped down in his seat, clearly exhausted. Out of respect, no one asked him to change it.

The men were all talked out.

Donnie Bags—another of Geraci's men who'd proven himself loyal to the Family—was a terrifically skilled driver, weaving through traffic, hitting lights perfectly, negotiating the wet roads without ever fishtailing or hydroplaning, all without calling attention to the many laws he bent to his own will. In no time they were crossing the Bayonne Bridge into New Jersey. Nobilio fell asleep. Eddie tapped a pinkie ring lightly against the glass, perfectly in rhythm with the beat of the song.

For too long, Michael Corleone had taken for granted the skills of men like Donnie Bags, Richie Two-Guns, and Eddie Paradise.

It had been after Michael's sit-down with Eddie, the lecture about the traditions at the core of the organization Michael's father had built, that the nightmares—or whatever they'd been—had stopped. Michael's doctor attributed it—and the corresponding lack of any significant diabetic episodes—to better diet and less stress. But to Michael's mind, it was because he'd figured out Fredo's warning: to connect with the old ways, the old traditions, to remember that the source of their father's greatness had been the relationships he built with people, relationships in which money and power were but by-products of fear and love.

The car carrying Michael Corleone now sped into the darkness of the Holland Tunnel. The radio went to static. It startled Nobilio awake.

"Don't worry," said Eddie Paradise. "We're just underground."

ACKNOWLEDGMENTS

For support in the writing of this book,
the author would like to thank
the Corporation of Yaddo,
Florida State University,
Dan Conaway, Neil Olson, and Amy Williams,
and the incomparable Tom Bligh.